Andrew A. Bonar

Letters of Samuel Rutherford

With biographical sketches of his correspondents. With a sketch of his life. Part 1

Andrew A. Bonar

Letters of Samuel Rutherford
With biographical sketches of his correspondents. With a sketch of his life. Part 1

ISBN/EAN: 9783337042370

Printed in Europe, USA, Canada, Australia, Japan

Cover: Foto ©Raphael Reischuk / pixelio.de

More available books at **www.hansebooks.com**

LETTERS

OF

SAMUEL RUTHERFORD.

PRINTED BY MURRAY AND GIBB,

FOR

W. P. KENNEDY, AND JOHN MACLAREN.

| LONDON: | . | . | HAMILTON, ADAMS, & CO. |
| GLASGOW: | . | . | DAVID BRYCE & CO. |

LETTERS

OF

SAMUEL RUTHERFORD.

WITH

Biographical Sketches of His Correspondents.

EDITED BY

THE REV. ANDREW A. BONAR,
GLASGOW.

WITH SKETCH OF HIS LIFE.

VOL. I.

EDINBURGH:
WILLIAM P. KENNEDY, 79 GEORGE STREET;
JOHN MACLAREN, 138 PRINCES STREET.

———

1863.

" He would fend me as a fpy into this wildernefs of fuffering, to fee the land, and to try the ford ; and I cannot make a lie of Chrift's crofs ; I can report nothing but good both of Him and it."—[LET. 118.]

PREFACE.

Most juftly does the old Preface to the earlier Editions begin by telling the Reader that "Thefe Letters have no need of any man's epiftle commendatory, the great Mafter having given them one, written by His own hand on the hearts of all who favour the things of God." Every one who knows thefe "Letters" at all, is aware of their moft peculiar charaéteriftic, namely, the difcovery they prefent of the marvellous intercourfe carried on between the writer's foul and his God.

This Edition will be found to be the moft complete that has hitherto appeared. Attending carefully to the chronological arrangement, the Editor has fought, by biographical, topographical, and hiftorical notices, to put the Reader in poffeffion of all that was needed to enable him to enter into the circumftances in which each Letter was written, fo far as that could be done. The Explanatory Notes, the appended Gloffary of Scottifh words and expreffions (many of them in reality old Englifh), the Index of Places and Perfons, the Index of Special Subjeéts, and the prefixed Contents of each Letter, will, it is confidently believed, be found both interefting and ufeful. The Sketch of Rutherford's Life may be thought too brief; but the limits within which such a Sketch muft

neceffarily be confined, when occupying the place of a mere Introduction, rendered brevity inevitable.

Every Letter hitherto publifhed is to be found in this Edition.
The ten additional Letters of the Edition 1848, along with two
more, added fince that time, are all inferted in their chronological
place. The publifhers have taken great pains with the typography.

A. A. B.

GLASGOW, *27th November* 1862.

CONTENTS OF VOL. I.

Page

Page

SKETCH

OF

SAMUEL RUTHERFORD.

———◆———

"WHEREVER the palm-tree is, there is water," fays the Eaftern proverb; and fo, wherever the godly flourifh, there, we are fure, muft the Word of God be found. In the hiftory of the Reformation we read of Brother Martin, a poor monk at Bafle, whofe hope of falvation refted folely on the Lord Jefus, long before Luther founded the filver trumpet that fummoned fin-convinced fouls to the One Sacrifice. Having written out his confeffion of faith, his ftatement of reliance on the righteoufnefs of Chrift alone, the monk placed the parchment in a wooden box, and fhut up the wooden box in a hole of the wall of his cell. It was not till laft century that this box, with its interefting contents, was difcovered: it was brought to light only when the old wall of the monaftery was taken down. The palm-tree fpeaks of the exiftence of water at its root; the pure Word of God taught this man his fimple faith. And herein we learn how it was that Bafle fo early became a peculiar centre of light in that region: the prayer and the faith of that hidden one, and others like-minded, and the Word on which they fed, may explain it all.

There is a fact not unlike the above in the history of the district where Samuel Rutherford laboured so lovingly. The people of that shire tell that there was found, some generations ago, in the wall of the old castle of Earlston, in the Stewartry of Kirkcudbright, a copy of *Wickliffe's Bible*. It seems to have been deposited in that receptacle in order to be hid from the view of enemies; but from time to time it was the lamp of light to a few souls, who, perhaps in the silence of night, found opportunity to draw it out of its ark, and peruse its pages. It seems that the Lollards of Kyle (the adjoining district) had brought it to Earlston. We know that there were friends and members of the family of Earlston who embraced the Gospel even in those days. In the sixteenth century, some of the ancestors of Viscount Kenmure are found holding the doctrines of Wickliffe, which had been handed down to them. May we not believe that the Gordons of Earlston, in after days, were not a little indebted to the faith and prayers of these ancient witnesses who hid the sacred treasure in the castle wall? As in the case of the monk of Basle, their faith and patience were acknowledged in after days by the blessing sent down on that quarter, when the Lord, in remembrance of His hidden ones, both raised up the Gordons of Earlston, with many others of a like spirit, and also sent thither His servant Samuel Rutherford, to sound forth the word of life, and make the lamp of truth blaze, like a torch, over all that region.

SAMUEL RUTHERFORD was born about the year 1600. His father is understood to have been a respectable farmer. He had two brothers, James and George. But the place of his birth was not near the scene of his after labours. It is almost certain that Nisbet, a village of Roxburghshire, close to the Teviot, in the parish of Crailing, was his birth-place; and not long ago, there were some old people in that parish who remembered the gable-end of the house in which he was born, and which, from respect to his memory, was permitted to stand as long as it could keep together. Some one may yet light upon the well where, when very young, Samuel nearly lost his life. He had been amusing himself with some companions, when he fell in, and was left there till they ran and procured affiftance; but on returning to the fpot, they found him feated on a knoll, cold and dripping, yet uninjured. He told them that " A bonnie white man came and drew him out of the well!" Whether or not he really fancied that an angel had delivered him, we cannot tell; but it is plain that, at all events, his boyifh thoughts were already wandering in the region of the fky.

He owed little to his native place. There was not fo much of Chrift known in that parifh then as there is now; for in after days he writes, " My foul's defire is, that the place to which I owe my firft birth;—in which, I fear, Chrift was fcarcely named, as touching any reality of the power of godlinefs;—may bloffom as the rofe." * We have no account of his revifiting thefe fcenes of his early life, though he thus wrote to his friend, Mr Scott, minifter of the adjoining parifh of Oxnam. Like Donald Cargill, born in Perthfhire, yet never known to preach there even once, Rutherford had his labours in other parts of the land, diftant from his native place. In this arrangement we fee the Mafter's fovereignty. The fphere is evidently one of God's choofing for the man, inftead of being the refult of the man's gratifying his natural predilections. It accords, too, with the Mafter's own example; He having never returned to Bethlehem, where He was born, to do any of His works.

Jedburgh is a town three or four miles diftant from Nifbet, and thither Samuel went for his education; either walking to it and returning home at evening,—as a fchool-boy would fcarcely grudge to do,—or refiding in the town for a feafon. The fchool at that time met in a part of the ancient abbey, called, from this circumftance, the Latiners' Alley. In the year 1617 we find him farther from home,—removed to Edinburgh, which, forty years before, had become the feat of a College, though not as yet a Univerfity. There he obtained, in 1621, the degree of Mafter of Arts. Soon after, he was appointed Regent, or Profeffor, of Humanity, though there were three other competitors; for his talents had attracted the notice of many. But, on occafion of a rumour that

---

* Let. 334.

charged him with fome irregularity,—whether with or without foundation, it is now difficult to afcertain,—he demitted his office in 1625, and led a private life, attending preleftions on theology, and devoting himfelf to that ftudy.

That there could not have been anything very ferious in the rumour, may be inferred from the faft that no church court took any notice of the matter, though thefe were days when the reins of difcipline were not held with a flack hand. But it is not unlikely that this may have been the time of which he fays in a letter, "I knew a man who wondered to fee any in this life laugh or sport."* It may have been then that he was led by the Spirit to know the things that are freely given us of God.† We have no proof that he was converted at an earlier period, but rather the oppofite. He writes, "Like a fool as I was, I fuffered my fun to be high in the heaven, and near afternoon, before ever I took the gate by the end."‡ And again, "I had ftood fure, if in my youth I had bor-rowed Chrift for my bottom."§ The clouds returned after the rain ; family trials, and other fimilar dealings of Providence, combined to form his charafter as a man of God and as a paftor.

In 1627 he was fettled at Anwoth,‖ a parifh fituated in the Stew-artry of Kirkcudbright, on the river Fleet, near the Solway. The church ftood in a wide hollow, or valley, at the foot of the Boreland Hill. Embofomed in wood, with neither the fmoke nor the noife of a village near, it muft always have been a romantic fpot, the very ideal of a country church, fet down to cherifh rural godlinefs. Though at this period Epifcopacy had been obtruded upon Scot-land, and many faithful minifters were fuffering on account of their refiftance to its ceremonies and fervices, yet he appears to have been allowed to enter on his charge without any compliance being de-manded, and "without giving any engagement to the bifhop." He began his miniftry with the text, John ix. 39. The fame Lord

---

* Let. 224.   † 1 Cor. ii. 12.   ‡ Let. 177.   § Let. 241.
‖ See notice of the topography at Let. 199. It is a mile and a half from the modern Gatehoufe of Fleet, a clean, Englifh-looking village.

that would not let Paul and Timothy preach in Afia,* nor in Bithynia, and yet fent to the one region the beloved John,† and to the other the fcarcely lefs beloved Peter,‡ in this inftance prevented John Livingftone going to Anwoth, which the patron had defigned, and fent Rutherford inftead. This was the more remarkable, becaufe Livingftone was fent to Ancrum, the parifh that borders on Nifbet, while he who was by birth related to that place was defpatched to another fpot. This is the Lord's doing. Minifters must not choofe according to the flefh.

During the firft years of his labours here, the sore illnefs of his wife was a bitter grief to him. Her diftrefs was very fevere. He writes of it : "She is fore tormented night and day.—My life is bitter unto me.—She fleeps none, and cries as a woman travailing in birth; my life was never fo wearifome."§ She continued in this ftate for no lefs than a year and a month, ere fhe died. Befides all this, his two children had been taken from him. Such was the difcipline by which he was trained for the duties of a paftor, and by which a fhepherd's heart of true fympathy was imparted to him.

The parifh of Anwoth had no large village near the church. The people were fcattered over a hilly diftrict, and were quite a rural flock. But their fhepherd knew that the Chief Shepherd counted them worth caring for; he was not one who thought that his learning and talents would be ill fpent if laid out in feeking to fave fouls, obfcure and unknown. See him fetting out to vifit! He has juft laid afide one of his learned folios, to go forth among his flock. See him paffing along yonder field, and climbing that hill on his way to fome cottage, his "quick eyes" occafionally glancing on the objects around, but his "face upward" for the moft part, as if he were gazing into heaven. He has time to vifit, for he rifes at three in the morning; and at that early hour meets his God in prayer and meditation, and has fpace for ftudy befides. He takes occafional days for catechifing. He never fails to be

---

* Acts xvi. 6, 7.   † Rev. i. 11.   ‡ 1 Pet. i. 1.   § Let. 18.

found at the fick-beds of his people. Men faid of him, "He is *always* praying, *always* preaching, *always* vifiting the fick, *always* catechifing, *always* writing and ftudying." He was known to fall afleep at night talking of Chrift, and even to fpeak of Him during his fleep. Indeed, himfelf fpeaks of his dreams being of Chrift.*

His preaching could not but arreft attention. Though his elocution was not good, and his voice rather fhrill, he was, neverthelefs, "one of the moft moving and affectionate preachers in his time, or perhaps in any age of the Church."† Efpecially when he came to dwell upon the fubject he fo delighted in, Jefus Chrift, his manner grew fo animated that it feemed as if he would have flown out of the pulpit. An Englifh merchant faid of him, even in days when controverfy had forely vexed him and diftracted his fpirit, "I went to St Andrews, where I heard a fweet, majefticlooking man (R. Blair), and he fhowed me the majefty of God. After him I heard a little, fair man (Rutherford), and he fhowed me *the lovelinefs of Chrift*."‡

Anwoth was dear to him rather as the fphere appointed him by his Mafter, than becaufe of the fruit he faw of his labours. Two years after being fettled there, he writes, "I fee exceedingly fmall fruit of my miniftry. I would be glad of one foul, to be a crown of joy and rejoicing in the day of Chrift." His people were "like hot iron, which cooleth when out of the fire." Still he laboured in hope, and laboured often almoft beyond his ftrength. Once he fays, "I have a grieved heart daily in my calling." He fpeaks of his pained breaft, at another time, on the evening of the Lord's day, when his work was done.§ But he had feafons of refrefhing to his own foul at leaft; efpecially when the Lord's Supper was difpenfed. Of thefe feafons he frequently fpeaks. He afks his friend, Marion M'Naught, to help with her prayers on fuch an occafion, "that being one of the days wherein Chrift was

---

* Let. 286.   † Wodrow's Church Hift. i. 205.
‡ M'Crie's Sketches.   § Let. 185.

wont to make merry with His friends."* It was then that with ſpecial earneſtneſs he beſought the Father to diſtribute "the great Loaf, Chriſt, to the children of His family."

Anwoth church was filled, but not altogether by pariſhioners.† Many came from great diſtances ; among others, ſeveral that were converted, ſeventeen years before, under John Welſh, at Ayr. Theſe all helped him by their prayers, as did alſo a goodly number of godly people in the pariſh itſelf, who were the fruit of the miniſtry of his predeceſſor. Yet over the unſaved he yearned moſt tenderly. At one time we hear him ſay, "I would lay my deareſt joys in the gap between you and eternal deſtruction."‡ At another, "My witneſs is in heaven, your heaven would be two heavens to me, and your ſalvation two ſalvations." He could appeal to his people, "My day-thoughts and my night-thoughts are of you ;" and he could appeal to God, "O my Lord, judge if my miniſtry be not dear to me ; but not ſo dear by many degrees as Chriſt my Lord."§

All claſſes of people of Anwoth were objeĉts of his care. He maintained a friendly intercourſe with people of high rank, and very many of his Letters are addreſſed to such perſons. He ſeems to have been remarkably bleſſed to the gentry in the neighbour-hood—more far than to the common people. There was at that time ſome friend of Chriſt to be found in almoſt every gentleman's ſeat many miles round Anwoth.

---

* Let. 14.

† The oak pulpit out of which he preached was preſerved till a few years ago. The old church (60 feet by 18) is in the ſhape of a barn, and could hold only 250 ſitters. The years 1631 and 1633 are carved on ſome of the ſeats,—perhaps the ſeats of the Gordons, or other heritors. We may add, while ſpeaking of this old edifice, where "the ſwallows building their neſt," ſeemed to the exiled paſtor "bleſſed birds," that the ruſty key of that kirk-door is now depoſited in the New College, Edinburgh, ſent to the muſeum there as a precious relic ſeveral years ago by a friend, through Dr Welſh. The church is now roofleſs, its walls overgrown with ivy, in which the ſparrows build their neſts at will.

‡ Let. 217.   § Let. 217.

But the *herd boys* were not beneath his fpecial attention. He writes of them when at Aberdeen, and exclaims, " Oh if I might but fpeak to thee, or your herd boys, of my worthy Mafter." * He had a heart for *the young* of all claffes, fo that he would fay of two children of one of his friends, " I pray for them by name ;"† and could thus take time to notice one, " Your daughter defires a Bible and a gown. I hope fhe fhall ufe the Bible well, which, if fhe do, the gown is the better beftowed." He lamented over the few that cry " Hofanna " in their youth. " Chrift is an *unknown* Chrift to young ones ; and therefore they feek Him not, becaufe they know Him not."

He dealt with *individual parifhioners* fo clofely and fo perfonally as to be able to appeal to them regarding his faithfulnefs in this matter. He addreffes one of them, Jean M'Millan : " I did what I could to put you within grips of Chrift ; I told you Chrift's teftament and latter-will plainly."‡ He fo carried them on his heart (like the prieft with the twelve tribes on his breaftplate), that he could declare to Gordon of Cardonefs, " Thoughts of your foul depart not from me in my fleep." § " My foul was taken up when others were fleeping, how to have Chrift betrothed with a bride in that part of the land," viz. Anwoth. ‖ He fo prayed over them and for them, that he fears not to fay, " *There* I wreftled with the angel and prevailed. Woods, trees, meadows, and hills, are my witneffes that I drew on a fair match betwixt Chrift and Anwoth." ¶ It is related that, on firft coming to the parifh, there was a piece of ground on Moffrobin farm, in the hollow of a hill, where on Sabbath afternoon the people ufed to play at foot-ball. On one occafion he repaired to that fpot, and pointed out their fin, folemnly calling on the objects round to be witneffes againft them, efpecially three large ftones ** jutting out from the face of the hill, two of which ftill remain, and are called " *Rutherford's Witneffes*," though the third was wantonly diflodged fome years ago. This is the fpot

---

* Let. 163.   † Let. 14.   ‡ Let. 132.   § Let. 180.
‖ Let 186.   ¶ Let. 277.   ** Jofh. xxiv. 27.

which is specially taken notice of by Dr Chalmers, in recording a visit to Anwoth and its neighbourhood (Life, vol. iii. 130) :—

"*Wednesday, August* 23, 1826.—Started at five o'clock; ordered the gig forward on the public road, to meet us after a scramble of about two miles among the hills, in the line of *Rutherford's Memorials.* Went first to his church; the identical fabric he preached in, and which is still preached in.[*] The floor is a causeway. There are dates of 1628[†] and 1633 on some old carved seats. The pulpit is the same, and I sat in it. It is smaller than Kilmany, and very rude and simple. The church-bell is said to have been given him by Lady Kenmure, one of his correspondents in his Letters. It is singularly small for a church, having been the Kenmure house-bell. We then passed to the new church that is building; but I am happy to say the old fabric and Rutherford's pulpit are to be spared. It is a cruel circumstance that they pulled down (and that only three weeks ago) his dwelling-house, his old manse; which has not been used as a manse for a long time, but was recently occupied. It should have been spared. Some of the masons who were ordered to pull it down refused it, as they would an act of sacrilege, and have been dismissed from their employment. We went and mourned over the rubbish of the foundation. Then ascended a bank, still known by the name of *Rutherford's Walk*.[‡] Then went farther among the hills, to *Rutherford's Witnesses*,—so many stones which he called to witness against some of his parishioners who were amusing themselves at the place with some game on the Sunday, and whom he meant to reprove. The whole scene of our morning's walk was wild, and primitive, and interesting."

Once, while in Anwoth, his labours were interrupted by a tertian fever which laid him aside for thirteen weeks. Even when well recovered, he could for a long time only preach on the Sabbaths : visiting and catechising were at a stand. This was just before his wife's death in 1630, and he writes in the midst of it, "Welcome, welcome, cross of Christ, if Christ be with it." "An afflicted life looks very like the way that leads to the kingdom." And some years thereafter, when his mother (who came from Nisbet, and resided with him six years after his first wife's death) was in a dangerous illness, he touchingly informs one of his correspondents, to whom he writes from Anwoth, "*My mother* is weak, and I

---

[*] It has not been preached in since the year 1827.

[†] A mistake for 1631.

[‡] It was a walk among trees, close to the manse.

think fhall leave me alone; but I am not alone, becaufe *Chriſt's Father* is with me."*

And what was his recreation? The manfe of Anwoth had many vifits of kind friends, who, in Rutherford's fellowſhip, felt that faying verified, "They that dwell under his ſhadow ſhall return; they ſhall revive as the corn."† The righteous compaſſed him about, becaufe the Lord had dealt bountifully with him. His Letters would be enough of themſelves to ſhow that his friendſhip and counſel were fought by the godly on all ſides. One of his vifitors was his own brother, George, at Kirkcudbright. This good man was a teacher in that town, who often repaired to Anwoth to take fweet counfel with Samuel; and then together, they talked of and prayed for their only other brother James, an officer in the Dutch fervice, who had fympathy with their views, and, in after days, conveyed to Samuel the invitation to become Profeſſor at Utrecht. Vifits of thofe friends who refided near were not unfre-quent, fuch as the Gordons, Vifcount Kenmure and his lady, and Marion M'Naught. But at times Anwoth manfe was lighted up by the glad vifit of unexpected guefts. There is a tradition that Archbifhop Ufher, paffing through Galloway, turned afide on a Saturday to enjoy the congenial fociety of Rutherford. He came, however, in difguife; and being welcomed as a gueft, took his place with the reft of the family when they were catechifed, as was ufual, that evening. The ftranger was afked, "How many com-mandments are there?" His reply was "*Eleven.*" The paftor corrected him; but the ftranger maintained his pofition, quoting our Lord's words, "*A* NEW COMMANDMENT *I give unto you, that ye love one another.*" They retired to reft, all interefted in the ftranger. Sabbath morning dawned. Rutherford arofe, and repaired, as was his cuftom, for meditation to a walk that bordered on a thicket,‡ but was ftartled by hearing the voice of prayer,—prayer too from

---

* Let. 49.   † Hos. xiv. 7.

‡ The place is ftill pointed out by tradition, as "Rutherford's Walk." It was clofe to the old manfe, which was pulled down many years ago. It

the heart, and in behalf of the fouls of the people that day to affemble. It was no other than the holy Archbifhop Ufher; and foon they came to an explanation, for Rutherford had begun to fufpect he had "entertained angels unawares." With great mutual love they converfed together; and at the requeft of Rutherford, the Archbifhop went up to the pulpit, conducted the ufual fervice of the Prefbyterian paftor, and preached on "the New Commandment."

Scarcely lefs interefting is the record of another unlooked-for meeting. Rutherford had one day left home to go to the neighbouring town of Kirkcudbright, the next day being a day of humiliation in that place. Having no doubt fpent fome time with his like-minded brother, he turned his fteps to the houfe of another friend, Provoft Fullerton, whofe wife was Marion M'Naught. While fitting with them in friendly converfe, a knock at the door was heard, and then a ftep on the threfhold. It was worthy Mr Blair, who, on his way from London to Port Patrick, had fought out fome of his godly friends, that with them he might be refrefhed ere he returned to Ireland. He told them, when feated, that " he had a defire to vifit both Mr Rutherford at Anwoth, and Marion M'Naught at Kirkcudbright; but not knowing how to accomplifh both, had prayed for direction at the parting of the road, and laid the bridle on the horfe's neck. The horfe took the way to Kirkcudbright, and there he found both the friends he fo longed to fee." It was a joyful and refrefhing meeting on all fides. Wodrow tells* another incident that, in part, bears fome refemblance to this. Rutherford had been reafoning at Stirling with the Marquis of Argyle, and had fet out homeward. But his horfe was very troublefome, and he was feeling in his mind that he fhould have been more urgent and plain! He returned, and dealt freely this time. And now his horfe went on pleafantly all the way.

---

ftood about a quarter of a mile from the church, and bore the name, " *Bufhy Bield*," or *Bufh o' Bield*, *i.e.*, the bufh of fhelter. A fketch of it, as it was, is given in *Murray's Life of Rutherford.*

* *Analecta*, vol. ii., p. 161.

In 1634 he attended the remarkable death-bed of Lord Kenmure, a narrative of which he publifhed fifteen years after, in " The Last and Heavenly Speeches and Glorious Departure of John Vifcount Kenmure." The inroads of Epifcopacy were at this time threatening to difquiet Anwoth. His own domeftic afflictions were ftill affecting him ; for he writes that fame year, in referring to his wife's death many years before, " which wound is not yet fully healed and cured." About that time, too, there was a propofal (never carried into effect) to call him to Cramond, near Edinburgh,* and another to get him settled at Kirkcudbright.

Meanwhile he perfevered in ftudy as well as in labours, and with no common fuccefs. He had a metaphyfical turn, as well as great readinefs in ufing the accumulated learning of other days. It might be inftructive to inquire why it is that wherever godlinefs is healthy and progreffive, we almoft invariably find learning in the Church of Chrift attendant on it ; while, on the other hand, neglect of ftudy is attended fooner or later by decay of vital godlinefs. Not that all are learned in fuch times ; but there is always an element of the kind in the circle of thofe whom the Lord is ufing. The energy called forth by the knowledge of God in the foul leads on to the ftudy of whatever is likely to be ufeful in the defence or propagation of the truth ; whereas, on the other hand, when decay is at work and lifeleffnefs prevailing, floth and eafe creep in, and theological learning is flighted as uninterefting and dry. With Samuel Rutherford and his contemporaries we find learning fide by fide with vital, and fingularly deep, godlinefs. Gillefpie, Henderfon, Blair, Dickfon, and others, are well-known examples. Nor lefs diftinguifhed was Rutherford, who was led by circumftances in 1636 to publifh his elaborate defence of grace againft the Arminians, in Latin. Its title is, " Exercitationes de Gratia." So highly was it efteemed at Amfterdam, where it was publifhed, that a fecond edition was printed that very year ; and repeated invitations

---

* Let. 43.   His friend and neighbour Mr Dalgleifh, minifter of Kirkdale and Kirkmabreck, was tranflated to Cramond in 1639.

were addreffed foon after to the author to come to Holland, and
occupy one or other of their Divinity chairs. Soon after, the con-
teft for *Chrift's kingly office* became increafingly earneft and keen.
To Rutherford it appeared no fmall matter. "I could wifh many
pounds added to my crofs to know that by my fuffering Chrift was
fet forward in His *kingly office* in this land."* July 27, 1636, was
a day that put his principles to the teft. He was called before the
High Commiffion Court, becaufe of non-conformity to the acts of
Epifcopacy, and becaufe of his work againft the Arminians. The
Court was prefided over by Sydferff, Bifhop of Galloway, and was
held at Wigton, about ten miles from Anwoth, acrofs the Bay. He
appeared in perfon there, and defended himfelf. The iffue could
not be doubtful, though Lord Lorn made every exertion in his behalf. He was deprived of his minifterial office, which he had
exercifed at Anwoth for a period of nine years, and banifhed to
Aberdeen. The next day (writing at evening on the fubject), he
tells of his fentence, and calls it, "The honour that I have prayed
for thefe fixteen years." He made up his mind to leave Anwoth
at once, obferving, with a submiffivenefs which we might wonder
at in the author of Lex Rex, "I purpofe to obey the king, who
has power over my body." His only alarm was left this feparation
from his flock might be a chaftifement on him from the Lord, "becaufe I have not been fo faithful in the end as I was in the two
firft years of my miniftry, when fleep departed from mine eyes
through care for Chrift's lambs."†

On leaving Anwoth he directed his fteps by Irvine, fpending a
night there with his beloved friend David Dickfon. What a night
that muft have been ! To hear thefe two in folemn converfe ! The
one could not perhaps handle the harp fo well as the other ; for
David Dickfon could exprefs his foul's weary longings and its con-
foling hopes in fuch ftrains as that which has made his name
familiar in Scotland, "O *mother dear Jerufalem* ;" but Rutherford,
neverthelefs, had fo much of poetry and fublime enthufiafm in his

---

* Let. 115. See alfo Let. 54.   † Let. 109.

foul, that any poet could fympathife with him to the full. Many of his letters " from *Chrift's palace* in Aberdeen" are really ftrains of true poetry. What elfe is fuch an effufion as this, when, rifing on eagles' wings, he exclaims, " A land that has more than four fummers in the year ! What a finging life is there ! There is not a dumb bird in all that large field, but all fing and breathe out heaven, joy, glory, dominion, to the High Prince of that new-found land. And verily the land is fweeter that He is the glory of that land."*
" O how fweet to be wholly Chrift's, and wholly in Chrift; to dwell in Immanuel's high and bleffed land, and live in that fweeteft air, where no wind bloweth but the breathings of the Holy Ghoft, no fea nor floods flow but the pure water of life that floweth from under the throne and from the Lamb, no planting, but the tree of life that yieldeth twelve manner of fruits every month ! What do we here but fin and fuffer ? O when fhall the night be gone, the fhadows flee away, and the morning of the long, long day, without cloud or night, dawn ? The Spirit and the bride fay, ' Come !' O when fhall the Lamb's wife be ready, and the Bride-groom fay, Come ?"† Whoever compares fuch breathings with David Dickfon's hymn, will fee how congenial were their feelings and their hopes, and even their mode of expreffing what they felt and hoped, though the one ufed profe and the other tried more memorable verfe.

We follow Rutherford to Aberdeen, the capital of the North, whither he was accompanied by a deputation of his affectionate pa-rifhioners from Anwoth, in whofe company he would forget the length and tedioufnefs of the way. He arrived here in September 1636. This town was at that time the ftronghold of Epifcopacy and Arminianifm, and in it the ftate of religion was very low. " It confifted of Papifts, and men of Gallio's naughty faith."‡ The

---

* Let. 323.   † Let. 334.

‡ Let. 76. Dr James Sibbald, faid to have been a man of great learning, was minifter in one of the churches of New Aberdeen. Rutherford attended his preaching, and finding that he taught Arminianifm, teftified againft him.

clergy and doctors took the opportunity of Rutherford's arrival to commence a feries of attacks on the fpecial doctrines of grace which he held. But in difputation he foiled them ; and when many began to feel drawn to him in confequence of his earneft dealings and private exhortations, there was a propofal made to remove him from the town. "So cold," writes he, "is northern love! But (added he) *Chrift and I will bear it;"* deeply feeling his union to Him who faid to Saul, "Why perfecuteft thou *Me?*" Often, on the ftreets,† he was pointed out as "the *Banifhed Minifter;"* and hearing of this, he remarked, "I am not afhamed of my garland." He had vifitors from Orkney, and from Caithnefs, to the great annoyance of his perfecutors.‡ Some blamed him for not being "*prudent enough,*" as we have feen men ready to do in fimilar cafes in our own day ; but he replies, "*It is ordinary that that fhould be part of the crofs of thofe who fuffer for Him.*" Still he enjoyed, in his folitude, occafional intercourfe with fome of the godly ones, among whom were Lady Pitfligo, Lady Burnet of Largs, Andrew Cant, and James Martin. His deepeft affliction was feparation from his flock at Anwoth. Nothing can exceed his tender forrow over this flock. §

It was a faying of his own, "Gold may be gold, and bear the king's ftamp upon it, when it is trampled upon by men." And this was true of himfelf. But he came out of his trial not only unfcorched, but, as his many letters from Aberdeen fhow, greatly advanced in every grace. The Latin lines prefixed to the early editions of thefe Letters fcarcely exaggerate when they fing,—

> " Quod Chebar et Patmos divinis vatibus olim ;
> Huic fuerant fancto clauftra Abredæa viro."

He was, during part of two years, clofely confined to that town, though not in prifon ; but in 1638 public events had taken

---

* Let. 117.

† The impreffion of fome readers might be that he was *in prifon.* But he never was fo. He was *in exile ;* but the whole town was his prifon. He was, in this refpect, like Shimei confined to Jerufalem.

‡ Let. 161.   § Let. 181.

another turn. The Lord had ſtirred up the ſpirit of the people of Scotland, and the Covenant was again triumphant in the land. Rutherford haſtened back to Anwoth. During his abſence, "For ſix quarters of a year," ſay his pariſhioners, "no ſound of the Word of God was heard in our kirk." The ſwallows had made their neſts there undiſturbed for two ſummers.

His Letters do not refer to the proceedings of the Glaſgow Aſſembly of 1638. It is well known, however, that he was no mere indifferent ſpectator to what then took place, but was preſent, and was member of ſeveral committees which at that time ſat on the affairs of the Church. Preſbytery being fully reſtored by that Aſſembly, it was thought right that one ſo gifted ſhould be removed to a more important ſphere. He was ſent by the Church to ſeveral diſtricts to promote the cauſe of Reformation and the Covenant : and at length, in ſpite of his reluctance, ariſing chiefly from love to his flock,—his rural flock at Anwoth,—he was conſtrained to yield to the united opinion of his brethren, and removed to the Profeſſor's Chair in St Andrews in 1639, and made Principal of the New College. He bargained to be allowed to preach regularly every Sabbath in his new ſphere; for he could not endure ſilence when he might ſpeak a word for his Lord. He ſeems to have preached alſo, as occaſion offered, in the pariſhes around, eſpecially at Scoonie, in which the village of Leven ſtands.*

His hands were neceſſarily filled with work in his new ſphere;

---

* "1651, July 13.—The comm. was given at Scoonie. Mr Alex. Moncrieff, m. there, did preach the Preparation Sermon, and on Monday morning Mr Sa. Rutherford did preach; his text at both occaſions was Luke vii. 36 till 39 v. At this time was preſent, beſides Mr Sa. Rutherford, Mr Ja. Guthrie, and Mr David Bennet, Mr Ephraim Melvin, and Mr William Oliphant, m. in Dumfermlin. Thither did reſort many ſtrangers, ſo that the throng was great. Mr Ephraim, and Mr D. Bennet, both did ſit within the pulpit while the miniſter had his ſermon." "1654, Jan. 4.—Being Saturday, there was a Preparation Sermon for a Thankſgiving preached at Scoonie in Fyfe, for the continuance of the Goſpel in the land, and for the ſpreading of it in ſome places of the Highlands in Scotland, where in ſome families two, and

yet ftill he relaxed nothing of his diligence in ftudy. Nor did he
lack anything of former blefling. It was here the Englifh merchant
heard him preach fo affectingly on the lovelinefs of Chrift ; while
fuch was his fuccefs as a Profeffor, that "the Univerfity became a
Lebanon out of which were taken cedars for building the houfe of
God throughout the land."

In the year 1640, he married his fecond wife, Jean M'Math,
"a woman," fays one, "of fuch worth, that I never knew any
among men exceed him, nor any among women exceed her. He
who heard either of them pray or fpeak, might have learnt to
bemoan his own ignorance. Oh how many times I have been convinced, by obferving them, of the evil of unferioufnefs unto God,
and unfavourinefs in difcourfe." They had feven children ; but
only one furvived the father, a little daughter, Agnes, who does not
feem to have been a comfort to her godly mother.

In July 1643, the Weftminfter Affembly began to fit ; and to it
he was fent up as one of the Commiffioners from the Church of
Scotland. A fketch of a "*Shorter Catechifm*" exifts in MS., in the
library of the Edinburgh Univerfity, *in Rutherford's handwriting*,
very much refembling the Catechifm as it now ftands, from which
it has been inferred that he had the principal hand in drawing it up
for the Affembly. He continued four years attending the fittings
of this famous fynod, and was of much ufe in their delibera-
tions. So prominent a part did he take, that the great Milton has
fingled him out for attack in his lines, "On the new forcers of

---

in fome families one, began to call on God by prayer. Mr Samuel Rutherford, m. in St Andrews, preached on Saturday ; his text, Ifai. xlix. 9, 10, 11,
12. On the Sabbath, Mr Alex. Moncrieff, m., then preached ; his lecture,
1 Thefs. i. ch. ; his text, Colofs. i. 27. In the afternoon of the Sabbath, Mr
Samuel preached again upon his forementioned text. On Monday morning,
Mr Samuel had a Lecture on Pfal. lxxxviii. He did read the whole Pfalm
Obferve, that on Saturday Mr Samuel had this expreffion in his prayer after
fermon, defiring that the Lord would rebuke Prefbyteries and others that had
taken the keys and the power in their hands, and keeped out, and would fuffer none to enter (meaning in the miniftry) but fuch as faid as they faid."—
Lamont's Diary.

conscience, under the Long Parliament." Milton knew him only as an opponent of his sectarian and Independent principles, and so could scorn measures proposed by " Mere A. S. and Rutherford." But had he known the soul of the man, would not even Milton have found a sublimity of thought and feeling in his adversary, that at times approached his own lofty poesy? How interesting, in any point of view, to find the devoted pastor of Anwoth, on the streets of London, crossing the path of England's greatest poet.

During his residence in London he was tried with many afflictions. Several of his family died; and his own health began to give way, so that he and his brother minister, Mr G. Gillespie, visited Epsom to drink the waters. Yet such was the amazing spirit of the man, under a sense of duty, that amid the trials and bustle of that time he wrote " *The Due Right of Presbyteries*," " *Lex Rex*," i.e. *The Law, the King*, and " *Trial and Triumph of Faith*." Nor was he soured by controversy. In the preface to one of his controversial works, he discovers his large-hearted charity and manly impartiality in regard to what he saw in these parts. He writes : " I judge that in England the Lord hath many names, and a fair company, that shall stand at the side of Christ when He shall render up the kingdom to the Father ; and that in that renowned nation there be men of all ranks, wise, valorous, generous, noble, heroic, faithful, religious, gracious, learned."*

Returning home to St Andrews, he resumed his labours both in the college and in the pulpit with all his former zeal. He declined two invitations to the professorship in Holland ; one from Harderwyck in 1648, the other from Utrecht in 1651 ; though the former offered the chair both of Divinity and of Hebrew. He joined the Protesters in determinedly opposing the proceedings of the Commission of Assembly, who had censured such as protested against the admission to power of persons in the class of malignants. His friend David Dickson keenly opposed him, and Mr Blair also,

---

* Preface to Survey of the Spiritual Antichrist.

though lefs violently.* It was this controverfy that made John Livingftone fay, in a letter to Blair, " Your and Mr D. Dickfon's acceffion to thefe refolutions is the faddeft thing I have feen in my time. My wife and I have had more bitternefs in this refpect, thefe feveral months, than ever we had fince we knew what bitternefs meant." Rutherford wrote too violently on this matter. Some fay he was naturally hot and fiery; but at this time all parties were greatly excited. Still he did not lofe his brotherly love,—the fame brotherly love that led him fo fervently to embrace Archbifhop Ufher as a fellow-believer. We may get a leffon for our times from his remarks on occafion of thefe bitter controverfies. " It is hard when faints rejoice in the fufferings of faints, and redeemed ones hurt, and go nigh to hate, redeemed ones. For contempt of the communion of faints, we have need of new-born croffes, fcarce ever heard of before.—Our ftar-light hideth us from ourfelves, and hideth us from one another, and Chrift from us all." And then he fubjoins (and is he not borne out by the words of the Lord in John xvii. 22?): " A doubt it is if we fhall have fully one heart till we fhall enjoy one heaven." The ftate of things lay heavy on his mind : " I am broken and wafted by the wrath that is upon this land."

It was in 1651 that he publifhed his work " *De Divinâ Providentiâ*," a work in which he affailed Jefuits, Socinians, and Arminians. Richard Baxter (tinged as he was with the Arminian theology), in referring to this treatife, remarked (fays Wodrow), that " His *Letters* were the beft piece, and this work the worft, he had ever read." Of courfe, this was the language of controverfy, for the book is one of great ability. It was this work, indeed, that drew forth feveral invitations from foreign Univerfities. The ten years that followed were times of much diftraction, being the times of Cromwell and the Commonwealth, as well as of the Protefters and Refolutioners.

---

* When the Lord's Supper was to be difpenfed, Blair in vain ufed every argument to induce Rutherford to take part with himfelf and Mr Wood in ferving tables; and being forced to do it alone, began thus: " We muft have water in our wine while here. O to be above, where there will be no miftakes!" —(Wodrow's *Anal.*)

One incident, however, in 1651, is worthy of notice. " In that year the Scottiſh nation reſolved to crown Charles II., as lawful king, at Scone ; and when the young king was at St Andrews, in proſpect of that event, he viſited the colleges. It fell to Rutherford to deliver, on that occaſion, an oration in Latin before His Majeſty, on a ſub-ject which he could handle well, both as a patriot and a Chriſtian, " *The Duty of Kings.*"

Milton ſings,—

> —————" God doth not need
> Either man's work, or His own gifts; His ſtate
> Is kingly ; thouſands at His bidding ſpeed,
> And poſt o'er land and ocean without reſt :
> *They alſo ſerve who only ſtand and wait.*"

The days were evil, and Rutherford was longing now for ſuch quiet ſervice. He ſometimes refers to this deſire ; he wiſhes for a harbour in his latter days ; only (adds he), " failing is ſerving "— and he did delight in ſerving his Lord to the laſt. His friend M'Ward, in an advertiſement prefixed to the earlier editions of the " Letters," bitterly laments the loſs of a Commentary on Iſaiah, on which " this true Zechariah, who had underſtanding in the viſions of God,"* employed his leiſure time during the cloſing years of his life.† " His heart travailed more," ſays he, " in birth of this piece than ever I knew him of any ; neither was there ever any-thing he put his hand to that would have ſo powerfully perſuaded this panter after the enjoyment of his Maſter's company, to have had his heaven and the immediate fruition of God ſuſpended for a ſeaſon, as the eager deſire he had to finiſh this work before he finiſhed his courſe." But all theſe papers were carried off, and never re-covered. So true is it, that of the ſeed we ſow, we " know not whether ſhall proſper, either this or that " (Eccles. xi. 6).

When Charles II. was fully reſtored, and had begun to adopt arbitrary meaſures, Rutherford's work, " Lex Rex," was taken

---

* 2 Chron. xxvi. 5.

† He planned a Commentary on Hoſea in 1637, but the deſign was not executed. Reference is made to this in Let. 110.

notice of by the Government; for, reasonable as are its principles in defence of the liberty of subjects, its spirit of freedom was intolerable to rulers, who were, step by step, advancing to acts of cruelty and death. Indeed, it was so hateful to them, that they burnt it, in 1661, first at Edinburgh, by the hands of the hangman; and then, some days after, by the hands of the infamous Sharpe, under the windows of its author's College in St Andrews. He was next deposed from all his offices; and, last of all, was summoned to answer at next Parliament a charge of high treason. But the citation came too late. He was already on his death-bed, and on hearing of it, calmly remarked, that he had got another summons before a superior Judge and judicatory, and sent the message, "I behove to answer my first summons; and ere your day arrive, I will be where few kings and great folks come."

We have no account of the nature of his last sickness, except that it was a disease that left him lingering some time. All that is told us of his death-bed is characteristic of the man. At one time he spoke much of the white stone and the new name. Some days before his death, after a fainting fit, he said, "Now I feel, I believe, I enjoy, I rejoice." And turning to Mr Blair, "I feed on manna: I have angels' food. My eyes shall see my Redeemer. I know that He shall stand on earth at the latter day, and I shall be caught up in the clouds to meet Him in the air."* When asked, "What think ye now of Christ?" he replied, "I shall live and adore Him. Glory, glory to my Creator and Redeemer for ever. Glory shineth in Immanuel's land." The same afternoon he said, "I shall sleep in Christ; and when I awake, I shall be satisfied with His likeness. O for arms to embrace Him!" Then he cried aloud, "O for a well-tuned harp!" This last expression he used more than once, as if already stretching out his hand to get his golden harp, and join the redeemed in their new song. He also said on another occasion, "I hear Him saying to me, 'Come up hither.'" His little daughter Agnes, only eleven years of age, stood by his bed-side;

---

* See Fleming's *Fulfilling of the Scripture.*

he looked on her, and faid, "I have left her upon the Lord." Well might the man fay fo, who could fo fully teftify of his portion in the Lord, as a goodly heritage. To four of his brethren, who came to fee him, he faid, "My Lord and Mafter is chief of ten thoufands of thoufands. None is comparable to Him, in heaven or in earth. Dear brethren, do all for *Him*. Pray *for Chrift*. Preach *for Chrift*. Do all for *Chrift*; beware of men-pleafing. The Chief Shepherd will fhortly appear." He fpoke as if he knew the hour of his departure; not perhaps as Paul (2 Tim. iv. 6) or Peter (2 Peter i. 14), yet ftill in a manner that feems to indicate that the Lord draws very near His fervants in that hour, and gives glimpfes of what He is doing. On the laft day of his life, in the afternoon, he faid, "This night will clofe the door, and faften my anchor within the veil, and I fhall go away in a fleep by five o'clock in the morning." And fo it was. He entered Immanuel's land at that very hour, and is now (as himfelf would have faid) " fleeping in the bofom of the Almighty," till the Lord come.

We may add his lateft words. "There is nothing now between me and the Refurrection but 'This day thou fhalt be with Me in pa-radife.'" He interrupted one fpeaking in praife of his painfulnefs in the miniftry, "I difclaim all. The port I would be in at is redemption and forgivenefs of fin through His blood." Two of his biographers record that his laft words were, "Glory, glory dwelleth in Im-manuel's land!" as if he had caught a glimpfe of its mountain-tops.

It was at St Andrews he died, on 20th March 1661, and there he was buried. Had he lived a few weeks, his might have been the cruel death endured by his friend James Guthrie, whom he had en-couraged, by his letters, in ftedfaftnefs to the end. The fentence which the Parliament paffed, when told that he was dying, did him no dis-honour. When they had voted that he fhould not die in the College, Lord Burleigh rofe and faid, "Ye cannot vote him out of heaven."

His death was lamented throughout the land; and to this day few names are fo well known and honoured. So great was the reverence which fome of the godly had for this man of God, that they requefted to be buried where his body was laid. This was

Thomas Halyburton's dying requeſt. An old man in the pariſh of Crailing (in which Niſbet, his birth-place, is ſituated) remembers the veneration entertained for him by the great-grandfather of the preſent Marquis of Lothian. This good Marquis uſed to lift his hat, as often as he paſſed the ſpot where ſtood the cottage in which Samuel Rutherford was born.

If ever there was any portrait of him, it is not now known. We are moſt familiar with the likeneſs of his ſoul. There is one expresſive line in the epitaph on his tombſtone, in the churchyard of the Chapel of St Regulus :—

> " What tongue, what pen, or ſkill of men,
> Can famous Rutherford commend !
> His learning juſtly raiſed his fame,
> True greatneſs did adorn his name.
> He did converſe with things above,
> *Acquainted with Immanuel's love.*"

A monument to his memory was erected in 1842, by ſubſcription, on the Boreland Hill, in the pariſh of Anwoth. It is 60 feet in height, and thus, ſeen all around, it ſeems to remind the inhabitants of that region how God once viſited His people there.

His " LETTERS " have long been famous among the godly. The preſent edition of them has ſeveral things to recommend it. 1. The letters are chronologically arranged. 2. They have biographical notices prefixed to a large number of them. Moſt of theſe are from the pen of the Rev. James Anderſon. The preſent editor has added, here and there, topographical notes that ſeemed to have ſome intereſt, moſt of them gleaned on the ſpot. The explanatory notes in the edition by the Rev. C. Thomſon, 1836, have often been conſulted, with much advantage. 3. There are contents prefixed to each letter, deſcribing generally what are the main ſubjects of each. 4. *There are ſome new letters inſerted in this collection ; and there is a fac-ſimile of an unpubliſhed letter directed to the Provoſt of Edinburgh*, at the time when there was an attempt made to call Rutherford to that city. The letter, which is preſerved in the

Records of the Edinburgh Town Council, entreats them to drop the matter. It is written in a very fmall hand, as was ufual with him; and the feal on it has the armorial bearing of the Rutherford family.

If it be afked how it came about that thefe letters fhould have been at firft printed in an order entirely unchronological, the explanation is fimple : The firft edition appeared in 1664, and in it there were only two hundred and eighty-four of his letters gathered and publifhed; but many being edified thereby, an edition foon appeared with fixty-eight more letters appended. All thefe feem to have been printed very much in the order in which they came to hand, and the additional fixty-eight, more efpecially, difturbed all arrangement. The collector was Mr M'Ward, who, as a ftudent, being much beloved by Rutherford, went to the Weftminfter Affembly with him as his amanuenfis or fecretary. He was afterwards fucceffor to Andrew Gray in Glafgow, and finally minifter in Rotterdam. He gave them to the public with an enthufiaftic recommendation, under the title; " *Jofhua Redivivus;* publifhed for the ufe of all the people of God, but more particularly for thofe who are now, or afterwards may be, put to fuffering for Chrift and His caufe; by a well-wifher to the work and people of God. John xvi. 2 ; 2 Theffal. i. 6." The edition was in duodecimo, and was printed at *Rotterdam.* And we may here notice, that the Letters were not only firft publifhed in Holland, but alfo, in 1674, they appeared in a Dutch tranflation at Flufhing.

It will be noticed, in reading the letters as they ftand chronologically, that at times the pen of the ready writer ran on with amazing rapidity. He has written many in one day, when his heart was overflowing. It was eafy to write when the Lord was pouring on him the unction that teacheth all things. He would have written ftill more, but he had heard that people looked up to him and overpraifed his letters. During his confinement at Aberdeen, he wrote about 220 of thefe letters.

There are a few diftafteful expreffions in thefe epiftolary effufions, the fparks of a fancy that fought to appropriate everything to fpiritual purpofes; but as to extravagance in the thoughts conveyed, there is none. Dr Love fays, "The haughty contempt of that book which is in the heart of many, will be ground for condemnation when the Lord cometh to make inquifition after fuch things" (Let. xiv.). The extravagance in fentiment alleged againft them by fome, is juft that of Paul, when he fpoke of knowing "the height and depth, length and breadth," of the love of Chrift ; or that of Solomon, when the Holy Ghoft infpired him to write "The Song of Songs." Rather would we fay of thefe letters, what Livingftone in a letter fays of John Welfh's dying words, "O for a fweet fill of this fanatic humour!" In modern days, Richard Cecil has faid of Rutherford, "He is one of my claffics ; he is a real original ;" and in older times, Richard Baxter, fome of whofe theological leanings might have prejudiced him, if anything could, faid of his letters, "Hold off the Bible, fuch a book the world never faw." They were long ago tranflated into Dutch, and of late years they have been trans-lated into German. Both in thefe, and in his other writings, we fee fufficient proof that had he cultivated literature as a purfuit, he might have ftood high in the admiration of men.*

His correfpondents were chiefly perfons refiding either in *Galloway*, where Anwoth was, or in *Ayrfhire ;* for thefe two counties at that time were rich in godly men of fome ftanding.

His pen fuggefts often, by a few ftrokes, very much that is profound and impreffive. There is fomething not eafily for-gotten in the words ufed to exprefs the Church's indeftructiblenefs when he fays, "The bufh has been burning thefe five thoufand years, and *no man yet faw the afhes of that fire.*" How much

---

* Even in his controverfial works, fparks of the fame poetic fire fly out when opportunity occurs. In his Treatife, "De Divina Providentia," the following paragraph occurs, extolling the glory of Godhead wifdom. "Comparentur cum illa increata fapientia Dei Patris umbratiles fcintillulæ creatæ gloriolæ quotquot nominis celebritate inclaruerunt. Delirat *Plato.* Mentitur *Ariftoteles. Cicero* balbutit, hæfitat, nefcit Latine loqui. *Demofthenes* mutus et elinguis obftupefcit ; virtutis viam ignorat *Seneca ;* nihil canit *Homerus :* male canit *Virgilius !* Accedant ad Chriftum qui virtutis gloria fulgent ! *Ariftides* virtutem mentitur. *Fabius* cefpitat, a via juftitiæ deviat. *Socrates* ne hoc quidem fcit, fe nihil fcire. *Cato* levis et futilis eft : *Solon* eft mundi et vo-

truth is conveyed in that saying, "Losses for Christ are but goods given out in bank in Christ's hand." There is an ingenious use of Scripture that often delights the reader; as when he speaks of "The corn on the house-tops that never got the husbandman's prayer," or of "Him that counteth the basons and knives of His house (Ezra i. 9, 10), and bringeth them back safe to His second temple." But the more general topics of his letters are worthy of attentive consideration.

These Letters will ever be precious to—

1. *All who are sensible of their own, and the Church's, decay and corruptions.* The wound and the cure are therein so fully opened out : self is exposed, even *spiritual self.* He will tell you, "There is as much need to watch over grace, as to watch over sin." He will show you God in Christ, to fill up the place usurped by self. The subtleties of sin, idols, snares, temptations, self-deceptions, are dragged into view from time to time. And what is better still, the cords of Christ are twined round the roots of these bitter plants, that they may be plucked up.

Nor is it otherwise in regard to corruption in public, and in the Church. We do not mean merely the open corruption of error, but also the secret "grey hairs" of decay. Hear him cry, "*There is universal deadness on all that fear God. O where are the sometime quickening breathings and influences from heaven that have refreshed His hidden ones!*" And then he laments, in the name of the saints, "We are

luptatum servus et mancipium, non legislator. *Pythagoras* nec sophos, nec philosophus est. *Bias* nec mundi nec inanis gloriæ contemptor. *Alexander Macedo* ignavus est," &c. Another work bears this title: "*Exercitationes Apologeticæ pro Divinâ Gratiâ,*" *studio et industria Samuelis Rhætorfortis, Anwetensis, in Gallovidiâ, Scotiæ provinciâ, Pastoris.*" The preface, or dedication, to *Gordon of Kenmure,* is very characteristic, ending thus: "Non enim ignoras in hac valle miseriarum minime sistendum, neque tentorium figendum; ad æternitatem ipsam (quod vere magnum nomen est & ineffabile) te vocari; crescere iter, decrescere diem, omnia alia aliena, tempus tantum nostrum esse, si modo nostrum est." In this preface he calls himself "*Pastor Anwetensis,*" the old spelling of Anwoth being *Anweth.*

half-satisfied with our witherednefs; nor have we as much of his ſtrain who doth eight times breathe out that ſuit (Pſa. cxix.), Quicken me!" " We live far from the well, and complain but dryly of our drynefs."

2. *All who delight in the Surety's imputed righteoufnefs.* If thoroughly aware of the body of ſin in ourſelves, we cannot but feel that we need a *perſon* in our ſtead,—the perſon of the God-man in the room of our guilty perſon. " To us a Son is given ;" not ſalvation only, but a Saviour. " He gave *Himfelf* for *us.*"

Theſe Letters are ever leading us to the Surety and His right-eoufnefs. The eye never gets time to reſt long on anything apart from Him and His righteoufnefs. We are ſhown the deluge-waters undried up, in order to lead us into the ark again : " I had fainted, had not want and penury chaſed me to the ſtorehouſe of all."

3. *All who rejoice in the Gofpel of free grace.* Lord Kenmure having ſaid to him, " Sin cauſeth me to be jealous of His love to ſuch a man as I have been ;" he replied, " Be jealous of yourſelf, my lord, but not of Jeſus Chriſt." In his " Trial and Triumph of Faith," he remarks, " As holy walking is a duty coming from us, it is no ground of true peace. Believers often ſeek in themſelves what they ſhould ſeek in Chriſt." It is to the like effeɕt he ſays in one of his letters, " Your heart is not the compaſs that Chriſt ſaileth by,"—turning away his friend from looking inward, to look upon the heart of Jeſus. And this is his meaning, when he thus lays the whole burden of ſalvation on the Lord, and leaves nothing for us but acceptance ; " Take eaſe to thyſelf, and let Him bear all."* Then, pointing us to the riſen Saviour as our pledge of complete redemption, " Faith may dance, becauſe Chriſt ſingeth ;"† " Faith *apprehendeth pardon*, but never payeth a penny for it."‡ On his death-bed he ſaid to his friends, " I diſclaim all that ever God made me will or do, and I look upon it as defiled and imperfeɕt." And ſo in his letters he will admit of no addition, or intermixture

---

* Let. 182. † Let. 183. ‡ Let. 182.

of other things; "The Gofpel is like a fmall hair that hath no breadth, and will not cleave in two."* He exhorts to affurance as being the way to be humbled very low before God : "Complaining is but a humble backbiting and traducing of Chrift's new work in the foul." "Make meikle of affurance, for it keepeth your anchor fixed."† He warns us, in his "Trial and Triumph of Faith," "not to be too defirous of keen awakenings to chafe us to Chrift. Let Chrift tutor me as He thinketh good. He has feven eyes : I have but one, and that too dim." In a fimilar ftrain he writes :— "The law fhall never be my doomfter, by Chrift's grace; I fhall find a fure enough doom in the Gofpel to humble and caft me down. *There cannot be a more humble foul than a believer. It is no pride in a drowning man to catch hold of a rock.*"‡ How much truth there is here! Naaman never was humble in any degree, until he felt himfelf *completely healed* of his fcaly leprofy; but truly he was humbled and humble then. And what one word is there that fuggefts fo many humbling thoughts as that word "*grace?*"

4. *All who feek to grow in holinefs.* The Holy Ghoft delights to fhow us the glorious Godhead, in the face of Jefus. And this is a very frequent theme in thefe letters. "Take Chrift for fanctification, as well as juftification," is often his theme. And in him we fee a man who feems to have fought for *holinefs* as unceafingly and as eagerly as other men feek for *pardon and peace.* In him "Holinefs to the Lord" feems written on every affection of the heart, and on every frefh-fpringing thought.

Fellowfhip with the living God is a diftinguifhing feature in the holinefs given by the Holy Ghoft; we get "accefs by one Spirit to the Father through Him."§ Rutherford could fometimes fay, "I have been fo near Him that I have faid, 'I take inftruments that this is the Lord.'"‖ And he could from experience declare, "I dare avouch, the faints know not the length and largenefs of the fweet Earneft, and of the fweet green fheaves before the harveft,

---

that might be had on this fide of the water, *if we would take more pains.*" *   "I am every way in your cafe, as hard-hearted and dead as any man, but yet I fpeak to Chrift through my fleep."† All this is from the pen of a man who was a metaphyfician, a controverfialift, a leader in the Church, and learned in ancient and fcholaftic lore. Why are there not fuch gracious, as well as great men now ?

5. *All afflicted perfons.* Here he had the very "tongue of the learned, to fpeak a word in feafon to him that was weary." And with what tender fympathy does he fpeak, leading the mourner fo gently to the heart of Jefus! He knew the heart of a ftranger, for he had been a ftranger. "Let no man after me flander Chrift for his crofs."‡ Yes, fays he, His moft loved are often His moft tried: "The lintel-ftone and pillars of His New Jerufalem fuffer more knocks of God's hammer and tools than the common fide-wall ftones." § Even as to reproach and calumny, he declares, "I love Chrift's worft reproaches."

It was to Hugh M'Kail, uncle of the youthful martyr, that he penned the words, "Some have written me that I am poffibly too joyful of the crofs ; but my joy overleapeth the crofs,—it is bounded and terminated on Chrift." § And there it was he found a well of comfort never dry.

6. *All who love the Perfon of Chrift.* We have too often been fatisfied with fpeculative truth and abftract doctrine. On the one hand, the orthodox have too often refted in the ftatements of our Catechifms and Confeffions ; and, on the other, the "election-doubters" (as Bunyan would have called them) have preffed their favourite dogma, that Chrift died for all men, as if mere affent to a propofition could fave the foul. Rutherford places the truth before us in a more accurate, and alfo more favoury way, full of life and warmth. The Perfon of Him who gave Himfelf for His Church is held up in all its attractivenefs. With him, it is ever the Perfon as

---

much as the work done; or rather, never the one apart from the other.   Like Paul, he would fain know *Him*, as well as the power of His refurrection.*

Once, when Lord Kenmure afked him, "What will Chrift be like when He cometh?" his reply was, "*All lovely*."   And this is everywhere the favourite theme with him.   At times he tells of His love.   "His love furroundeth and furchargeth me."†   "If His love was not in heaven, I fhould be unwilling to go thither."‡   Often he checks his pen to tell of *Chrift Himfelf:* "Welcome, welcome, fweet, fweet crofs of Chrift;"—then correcting his language,— "Welcome, fair, lovely, *royal King, with Thine own crofs*."§   "Oh if I could doat as much upon *Himfelf* as I do upon His love." ‖   "I fear I make more of His love than of *Himfelf*." ¶   How ftartling, yet how true, is this remark, "I fee that in communion with Chrift we may make more gods tham one," **—meaning, that we may be tempted to make the enjoyment itfelf our god.   It was his habitual aim to pafs through privileges, joys, even fellowfhip, to God Him-felf: "I have caften this work upon Chrift, to get me *Himfelf*." ††   "I would be farther in upon Chrift than at His joys; in, where love and mercy lodgeth; befide His heart." ‡‡   "He who fitteth on the throne is His lone a fufficient heaven."§§   "Sure I am He is the far beft half of heaven." ‖‖

In a word, fuch was his foul's view of the living Perfon, that he writes, "Holinefs is not *Chrift*, nor the bloffoms and flowers of the tree of life, nor the tree itfelf." ¶¶   He had found out the true fountain-head, and would direct all Zion's travellers thither.   And let a man try this;—let the Holy Spirit lead a man to this *Perfon;*—and furely his experience will be, "None ever came up dry from David's well."

7. *All who love that bleffed hope, and the glorious appearing of the great God our Saviour.*   The more we love the Perfon of Chrift, the

---

* Phil. iii. 10.   † Let. 104.   ‡ Let. 104.   § Let. 61.
‖ Let. 160.   ¶ Let. 179.   ** Let. 168.   †† Let. 187.
‡‡ Let. 286.   §§ Let. 352.   ‖‖ Let. 279.   ¶¶ Let. 336.

more ought we to love His appearing; and the more we cherish both feelings, the holier shall we become. Rutherford abounds in aspirations for that day; he is one who "looks for and hastens unto the coming of the Day of God!" While in exile at Aberdeen in 1637, he writes, "O when will we meet! O how long is it to the dawning of the marriage day! O sweet Jesus, take wide steps! O my Lord, come over mountains at one stride! O my Beloved, flee as a roe or young hart upon the mountains of separation." Now and then he utters the expression of an intense desire for the restoration of Israel to their Lord, and the fulness of the Gentiles; but far oftener his desires go forth to his Lord Himself. "O fairest among the sons of men, why stayest Thou so long away? O heavens, move fast! O time, run, run, and hasten the marriage day!" To Lady Kenmure his words are, "The Lord hath told you what you should be doing till He come. 'Wait and hasten,' saith Peter, 'for the coming of the Lord.' Sigh and long for the dawning of that morning, and the breaking of that day, of the coming of the Son of Man, when the shadows shall flee away. Wait with the wearied night-watch for the breaking of the eastern sky." Those saints who feel most keenly the world's enmity, and the Church's imperfection, are those who will most fervently love their Lord's appearing. It was thus with Daniel on the banks of Ulai, and with John in Patmos; and Samuel Rutherford's most intense aspirations for that day are breathed out in Aberdeen.

His description of himself on one occasion is,—"A man often borne down and hungry, and waiting for the marriage supper of the Lamb."* He is now gone to the "mountain of myrrh and the hill of frankincense;" and there he no doubt still wonders at the still unopened, unsearchable treasures of Christ. But O for his insatiable desires Christward! O for ten such men in Scotland to stand in the gap!—men who all day long find nothing but Christ to rest in, whose very sleep is a pursuing after Christ in dreams, and who intensely desire to "awake with His likeness."

---

* Let. 63.

LIST OF HIS WORKS.

————◆————

1. *Exercitationes Apologeticæ pro Divina Gratia.* Amftelodami, 12mo, 1636· Franckeræ, 1651.

2. *A Peaceable and Temperate Plea for Paul's Prefbytery in Scotland.* London, 4to, 1642.

3. *A Sermon before the Houfe of Commons,* on Daniel vi. 26. London, 4to, 1644.

4. *A Sermon before the Houfe of Lords,* on Luke vii. 22 ; Mark iv. 38 ; Matt. viii. 26. London, 4to, 1645.

5. "*Lex Rex :*" *The Law and the Prince.* London, 4to, 1644·

6. *The Due Right of Prefbyteries.* London, 4to, 1644·

7. *The Trial and Triumph of Faith.* London, 4to, 1645.

8. *The Divine Right of Church Government and Excommunication.* London, 4to, 1646. Appended to this is *A Difpute touching Scandal and Chriftian Liberty.*

9. *Chrift Dying and Drawing Sinners to Himfelf.* London, 4to, 1647·

10. *A Survey of the Spiritual Antichrift.* London, 1648. To which is appended, *A Modeft Survey of the Secrets of Antinomianifm.*

11. *A Free Difputation againft Pretended Liberty of Confcience.* London, 4to, 1649·

12. *The Laft and Heavenly Speeches of John Gordon, Vifcount Kenmure.* Edinburgh, 4to, 1649.

13. *Difputatio Scholaftica de Divina Providentia.* Edinburgh, 4to, 1651.

14. *The Covenant of Life Opened.* Edinburgh, 4to, 1655.

15. *A Survey of Mr Hooker's Church Difcipline ; or, A Survey of the Survey of that Summe of Difcipline penned by Mr Thomas Hooker.* London, 4to, 1658.

16. *Influences of the Life of Grace.* The laft work publifhed in his lifetime. London, 4to, 1659. The original title page adds :—"A Practical Treatife concerning the way, manner, and means of having and improving fpiritual difpofitions and quickening influences from Chrift, the Refurrection and the Life."

POSTHUMOUS.

17. *Joshua Redivivus;* or, *Mr Rutherford's Letters.* First Edition, 12mo, 1664. No printer's name and no place mentioned.

18. *Examen Arminianismi.* Ultrajecti (Utrecht), 12mo, 1668.

19. *A Testimony left by Mr S. Rutherford to the Work of Reformation in Great Britain and Ireland before his death.* Date uncertain.

20. *Sacramental Sermons:* taken by a hearer. This includes " Christ's Napkin; Christ and the Dove's heavenly Salutation," &c. These have internal evidence in their favour, viz., the language and general strain of thought.

21. *The Cruel Watchman. The Door of Salvation Opened,* 1735. *Exhortation at a Communion to a Scots Congregation in London,* 1730. (These three are doubtful; at all events, very imperfect.)

There is a separate *Treatise on Prayer* ascribed to him in Watts' Bibliotheca and Thomson's edition of the Letters.

An old *Catalogue of the most Vendible Books,* in 1658, gives as one of his works, *A Rationale on the Book of Common Prayer,* 8vo.

LETTERS.

I.—*For* MARION M'NAUGHT, *on the return home of her daughter.*

[In the early editions the date ftands " 1624," by a miftake for " 1627;" for Rutherford was not fettled in Anwoth in 1624.

For a full notice of *Marion M'Naught*, fee what is prefixed to Letter VI.]

(CHILDREN TO BE DEDICATED TO GOD.)

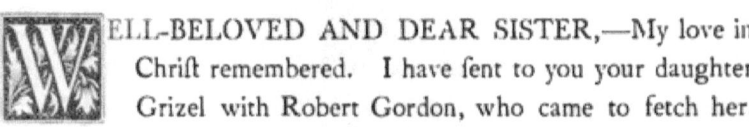ELL-BELOVED AND DEAR SISTER,—My love in Chrift remembered. I have fent to you your daughter Grizel with Robert Gordon, who came to fetch her. I am in good hopes that the feed of God is in her, as in one born of God; and God's feed will come to God's harveft. I have her promife fhe fhall be Chrift's. For I have told her fhe may promife much in His worthy name; for He becomes caution* to His Father for all fuch as refolve and promife to ferve Him. I will remember her to God. I truft you will acquaint her with good company, and be diligent to know with whom fhe loveth to haunt. Remember Zion, and our neceffities. I blefs your daughter from our Lord, and pray the Lord to give you joy and comfort of her. Remember my love to your hufband, to William and Samuel your fons. The Lord Jefus Chrift be with your fpirit.

Yours at all power† in the Lord Jefus,

S. R.

ANWOTH, *June* 6, 1627.

---

* Security.   † To the utmoft of my power.

II.—*To a Chriſtian Gentlewoman on the death of her daughter.*

(*CHRIST'S SYMPATHY WITH, AND PROPERTY IN US—REASONS FOR RESIGNATION.*)

ISTRESS,—My love in Chriſt remembered to you. I was indeed ſorrowful at my departure from you, eſpecially ſince ye were in ſuch heavineſs after your daughter's death. Yet I do perſuade myſelf, ye know that the weightieſt end of the croſs of Chriſt that is laid upon you lieth upon your ſtrong Saviour ; for Iſaiah ſaith,* "In all your afflictions He is afflicted." O bleſſed Second† who ſuffereth with you ! and glad may your ſoul be even to walk in the fiery furnace with one like unto the Son of Man, who is alſo the Son of God. Courage ! up your heart ! When ye do tire, He will bear both you and your burden.‡ Yet a little while and ye ſhall ſee the ſalvation of God. Remember of what age your daughter was, and that juſt ſo long was your leaſe of her. If ſhe was eighteen, nineteen, or twenty years old, I know not ; but ſure I am, ſeeing her term was come, and your leaſe run out, ye can no more juſtly quarrel your great Superior for taking His own at His juſt term day, than a poor farmer can complain that his maſter taketh a portion of his own land to himſelf when his leaſe is expired. Good miſtreſs, if ye would not be content that Chriſt would hold from you the heavenly inheritance which is made yours by His death, ſhall not that ſame Chriſt think hardly of you if ye refuſe to give Him your daughter willingly, who is a part of His inheritance and conqueſt ?§ I pray the Lord to give you all your own, and to grace you with patience to give God His alſo. He is an ill debtor who payeth that which he hath borrowed, with a grudge. Indeed, that long

---

* Iſa. lxiii. 9. † Supporter. ‡ Pſalm lv. 22.

§ Acquired by purchaſe and pains, not *inherited*. "The young heir knows not how hard the *conqueſt* was to his poor father" (Sermon at Anwoth, 1634, on Zech. xi. 9).

loan of such a good daughter, an heir of grace, a member of Christ (as I believe), deserveth more thanks at your Creditor's hand, than that ye should gloom* and murmur when He craveth but His own. I believe you would judge them to be but thankless neighbours who would pay you a sum of money after this manner. But what? Do you think her lost, when she is but sleeping in the bosom of the Almighty? Think her not absent who is in such a Friend's house. Is she lost to you who is found to Christ? If she were with a dear friend, although you should never see her again, your care for her would be but small. Oh, now, is she not with a dear Friend? and gone higher, upon a certain hope that ye shall, in the resurrection, see her again, when (be ye sure) she shall neither be hectic nor consumed in body? You would be sorry either to be, or to be esteemed, an atheist; and yet, not I, but the Apostle, thinketh those to be hopeless atheists† who mourn excessively for the dead. But this is not a challenge‡ on my part. I do speak this only fearing your weakness; for your daughter was a part of yourself; and, therefore, nature in you being as it were cut and halved, will indeed be grieved. But ye have to rejoice, that when a part of you is on earth, a great part of you is glorified in heaven. Follow her, but envy her not; for indeed it is self-love in us that maketh us mourn for them that die in the Lord. Why? Because for them we cannot mourn, since they are never happy till they be dead; therefore we mourn for our own private respect. Take heed, then, that in showing your affection in mourning for your daughter, ye be not, out of self-affection, mourning for yourself. Consider what the Lord is doing in it. Your daughter is plucked out of the fire, and she resteth from her labours; and your Lord, in that, is trying you, and casting you in the fire. Go through all fires to your rest; and now remember that the eye of God is upon the bush burning and not consumed; and He is gladly content that such a weak woman as you should send Satan away,

---

* Put on a sullen look.   † 1 Thess. iv. 13 and Eph. ii. 12.
‡ A rebuke, or upbraiding accusation.

fruftrate of his defign. Now honour God, and fhame the ftrong
roaring lion, when ye feem weakeft. Should fuch an one as ye
faint in the day of adverfity? Call to mind the days of old. The
Lord yet liveth. Truft in Him, although He fhould flay you.
Faith is exceeding charitable, and believeth no evil of God. Now
is the Lord laying, in the one fcale of the balance, your making confcience of fubmiffion to His gracious will, and in the other, your
affeftion and love to your daughter. Which of the two will ye
then choofe to fatisfy? Be wife, then ; and as I truft ye love Chrift
better than a finful woman, pafs by your daughter, and kifs the
Lord's rod. Men do lop the branches off their trees round about,
to the end they may grow up high and tall. The Lord hath this
way lopped your branch in taking from you many children, to the
end you fhould grow upward, like one of the Lord's cedars, fetting
your heart above, where Chrift is, at the right hand of the Father.
What is next, but that your Lord cut down the ftock after He hath
cut the branches? Prepare yourfelf; you are nearer your daughter,
this day than you were yefterday. While ye prodigally fpend time
in mourning for her, ye are fpeedily pofting after her. Run your
race with patience. Let God have His own ; and afk of Him,
inftead of your daughter which He hath taken from you, the
daughter of faith, which is patience ; and in patience poffefs your
foul. Lift up your head : ye do not know how near your redemption doth draw. Thus recommending you to the Lord, who
is able to eftablifh you, I reft, your loving and affeftionate friend in
the Lord Jefus,   S. R.

A NWOTH, *April* 23, 1628.

III.—*To the* VISCOUNTESS OF KENMURE, *on occafion of illnefs and fpiritual depreffion.*

[LADY JANE CAMPBELL, Vifcountefs of Kenmure, was the third daughter of Archibald Campbell, feventh Earl of Argyle, and fifter to the Marquis of Argyle who was beheaded in 1661. She was a woman diftinguifhed, in her day, for the depth of her piety, and her warm attachment to the Prefbyterian intereft in Scotland. Nor was fhe lefs diftinguifhed for generofity and munificence, than for piety. Her bounty was in a particular manner extended to thofe whom fuffering for confcience' fake had reduced to poverty or exile. In the year 1628, fhe was married to Sir John Gordon of Lochinvar, afterwards Vifcount Kenmure and Lord Gordon of Lochinvar. This union did not laft many years. In 1634, fhe became a widow, his Lordfhip having died at Kenmure Caftle, on the 12th of September that year, in the 35th year of his age. But her forrow on this occafion was alleviated by the Chriftian refignation and faith, which he was enabled to exercife under his laft illnefs. To this nobleman fhe had two daughters, who died in infancy, one about the beginning of the year 1629, and the other in 1634, as may be gathered from allufions to thefe bereavements, contained in two confolatory letters written to her by Rutherford in thefe years. She had alfo, by the fame marriage, a fon, John, fecond Vifcount of Kenmure, who, however, died under age and unmarried, in Auguft 1649. This event forms the fubject of a letter written to her by Rutherford the 1ft of October that year. She married for her fecond hufband, on the 21ft of September 1640, the Hon. Sir Henry Montgomery of Giffen, fecond fon of Alexander, fixth Earl of Eglinton; but this marriage was without iffue. Sir Henry's religious views were congenial to her own; and he is defcribed as an " active and faithful friend of the Lord's kirk." She was foon left a widow a fecond time, in which ftate fhe lived till a very venerable age, having furvived the Reftoration a number of years, as appears from the fact that Livingftone, at the time of his death (which took place at Rotterdam in 1672), fpeaks of her as the oldeft acquaintance he then had alive in Scotland. She was a regular correfpondent of Rutherford, the laft of whofe letters to her is dated July the 24th, 1661, after the execution of her brother, above mentioned. Nor after Mr Rutherford's death was fhe unmindful of his widow. " Madam," fays Mr M'Ward, in a letter to her, " Mrs Rutherford gives me often an account of the fingular teftimony which fhe met with of your Ladyfhip's affection to her and her daughter."

Kenmure Caftle is well feen from the road that leads along the banks of the Ken. The loch, the river, and the old baronial houfe, combine to attract notice. It is built on an infulated knoll, well wooded all around.]

*(ACQUIESCENCE IN GOD'S PURPOSE—FAITH IN EXERCISE—
    ENCOURAGEMENT IN VIEW OF SICKNESS AND DEATH—
    PUBLIC AFFAIRS.)*

MADAM,—All dutiful obedience in the Lord remembered. I have heard of your Ladyſhip's infirmity and ſickneſs with grief; yet I truſt ye have learned to ſay, "It is the Lord, let Him do whatſoever ſeemeth good in His eyes." It is now many years ſince the apoſtate angels made a queſtion, whether their will or the will of their Creator ſhould be done; and ſince that time, froward mankind hath always in that ſame ſuit of law compeared* to plead with them againſt God, in daily repining againſt His will. But the Lord being both party and judge, hath obtained a decreet,† and ſaith, " My counſel ſhall ſtand, and I will do all my pleaſure."‡ It is then beſt for us, in the obedience of faith, and in an holy ſubmiſſion, to give that to God which the law of His almighty and juſt power will have of us. Therefore, Madam, your Lord willeth you, in all ſtates of life, to ſay, " Thy will be done in earth, as it is in heaven :" and herein ſhall ye have comfort, that He, who ſeeth perfectly through all your evils, and knoweth the frame and conſtitution of your nature, and what is moſt healthful for your ſoul, holdeth every cup of affliction to your head, with His own gracious hand. Never believe that your tender-hearted Saviour, who knoweth the ſtrength of your ſtomach, will mix that cup with one drachm-weight of poiſon. Drink then with the patience of the ſaints, and the God of patience bleſs your phyſic.

I have heard your Ladyſhip complain of deadneſs, and want of the beſtirring power of the life of God. But, courage! He who walked in the garden, and made a noiſe that made Adam hear His voice, will alſo at ſome times walk in your ſoul, and make you hear a more ſweet word. Yet, ye will not always hear the noiſe and the din of His feet, when He walketh. Ye are, at ſuch a time, like Jacob mourning at the ſuppoſed death of Joſeph, when Joſeph was

---

* Appeared.   † Judicial ſentence.   ‡ Iſa. xlvi. 10.

living. The new creature, the image of the second Adam, is living in you; and yet ye are mourning at the suppofed death of the life of Chrift in you. Ephraim is bemoaning and mourning,* when he thinketh God is far off and heareth not; and yet God is like the bridegroom,† ftanding only behind a thin wall, and laying to His ear; for He faith Himfelf, "I have furely heard Ephraim bemoaning Himfelf."‡ I have good confidence, Madam, that Chrift Jefus, whom your foul through forefts and mountains is feeking, is within you. And yet I fpeak not this to lay a pillow under your head, or to diffuade you from a holy fear of the lofs of your Chrift, or of provoking and "ftirring up the Beloved before He pleafe," by fin. I know, in fpiritual confidence, the devil will come in, as in all other good works, and cry "Half mine;" and fo endeavour to bring you under a fearful fleep, till He whom your foul loveth be departed from the door, and have left off knocking. And, therefore, here the Spirit of God muft hold your foul's feet in the golden mid-line, betwixt confident refting in the arms of Chrift, and prefumptuous and drowfy fleeping in the bed of flefhly fecurity. Therefore, worthy lady, fo count little of yourfelf, becaufe of your own wretchednefs and finful drowfinefs, that ye count not alfo little of God, in the courfe of His unchangeable mercy. For there be many Chriftians moft like unto young failors, who think the fhore and the whole land doth move, when the fhip and they themfelves are moved; juft fo, not a few do imagine that God moveth and faileth§ and changeth places, becaufe their giddy fouls are under fail, and fubject to alteration, to ebbing and flowing. But "the foundation of the Lord abideth fure." God knoweth that ye are His own. Wreftle, fight, go forward, watch, fear, believe, pray; and then ye have all the infallible fymptoms of one of the elect of Chrift within you.

Ye have now, Madam, a ficknefs before you; and alfo after that a death. Gather then now food for the journey. God give you eyes to fee through ficknefs and death, and to fee fomething

---

* Jer. xxxi. 18.   † Cant. ii. 9.   ‡ Jer. xxxi. 18.
§ So it is in the earlier editions; not "faileth."

beyond death. I doubt not but that, if hell were betwixt you and Chrift, as a river which ye behoved to crofs ere you could come at Him, but ye would willingly put in your foot, and make through to be at Him, upon hope that He would come in Himfelf, in the deepeft of the river, and lend you His hand. Now, I believe your hell is dried up, and ye have only thefe two fhallow brooks, ficknefs and death, to pafs through; and ye have alfo a promife that Chrift fhall do more than meet you, even that He fhall come Himfelf, and go with you foot for foot, yea and bear you in His arms. O then! O then! for the joy that is fet before you; for the love of the Man (who is alfo " God over all, bleffed for ever"), that is ftanding upon the fhore to welcome you, run your race with patience. The Lord go with you. Your Lord will not have you, nor any of His fervants, to exchange for the worfe. Death in itfelf includeth both the death of the foul and the death of the body; but to God's children the bounds and the limits of death are abridged and drawn into a more narrow compafs. So that when ye die, a piece of death fhall only feize upon you, or the leaft part of you fhall die, and that is the diffolution of the body; for in Chrift ye are delivered from the fecond death; and, therefore, as one born of God, commit not fin (although ye cannot live and not fin), and that ferpent fhall but eat your earthly part. As for your foul, it is above the law of death. But it is fearful and dangerous to be a debtor and fervant to fin; for the count of fin ye will not be able to make good before God, except Chrift both count and pay for you.

I truft alfo, Madam, that ye will be careful to prefent to the Lord the prefent eftate of this decaying Kirk. For what fhall be concluded in Parliament anent* her, the Lord knoweth. Sure I

---

* " In reference to her,"—alluding to the known defign of Charles I. to enforce conformity to Epifcopacy. About the clofe of July, Charles I. refolved to come to Scotland to be crowned, and he wrote to that effect to the Privy Council, and indicted a Parliament to fit down at Edinburgh the 15th of September following. It is to that intended meeting of Parliament that Rutherford here refers. But it was not held.

am, the decree of a moſt fearful parliament in heaven is at the very
point of coming forth, becauſe of the ſins of the land.	For " we
have caſt away the law of the Lord, and deſpiſed the words of the
Holy One of Iſrael."*	" Judgment is turned away backward, and
juſtice ſtandeth afar off; truth is fallen in the ſtreets, and equity
cannot enter."†	Lo! the prophet, as if he had ſeen us and our
kirk, reſembleth ‡ *Juſtice* to be handled as an enemy holden out at
the ports of our city [ſo is ſhe baniſhed!], and *Truth* to a perſon ſickly
and diſeaſed, fallen down in a deadly ſwooning fit in the ſtreets, be-
fore he can come to an houſe.	" The prieſts have cauſed many to
ſtumble at the law, and have corrupted the covenant of Levi."§
" But what will they do in the end?"‖	Therefore give the Lord no
reſt for Zion.	Stir up your huſband, your brother, and all with
whom ye are in favour and credit, to ſtand upon the Lord's ſide
againſt Baal.	I have good hope that your huſband loveth the peace
and proſperity of Zion.	The peace of God be upon him, for his in-
tended courſes anent the eſtabliſhment of a powerful miniſtry in
this land.	Thus, not willing to weary your Ladyſhip further, I
commend you now, and always, to the grace and mercy of that
God who is able to keep you, that ye fall not.	The Lord Jeſus be
with your ſpirit.

Your Ladyſhip's ſervant at all dutiful obedience in Chriſt.

S. R.

Anworth, *July* 27, 1628.

---

* Iſa. v. 24.	† Iſa. lix. 14.	‡ Repreſenteth.
§ Mal. ii. 8.	‖ Jer. v. 31.

IV.—*To the Elect and Noble Lady, my* LADY KENMURE, *on occasion*
of the death of her infant daughter.

(*TRIBULATION THE PORTION OF GOD'S PEOPLE, AND INTENDED*
TO WEAN THEM FROM THE WORLD.)

ADAM,—Saluting your Ladyship with grace and mercy from God our Father, and from our Lord Jesus Christ, —I was sorry, at my departure, leaving your Ladyship in grief, and would still be grieved at it, if I were not assured that ye have One with you in the furnace, whose visage is like unto the Son of God. I am glad that ye have been acquainted from your youth with the wrestlings of God, and that ye get scarce liberty to swallow down your spittle, being casten* from furnace to furnace, knowing if ye were not dear to God, and if your health did not require so much of Him, He would not spend so much physic upon you. All the brethren and sisters of Christ must be conform to His image and copy in suffering.† And some do more vively‡ resemble the copy than others. Think, Madam, that it is a part of your glory to be enrolled among those whom one of the elders pointed out to John, "These are they which came out of great tribulation, and have washed their robes, and made them white in the blood of the Lamb."§ Behold your Forerunner going out of the world all in a lake of blood, and it is not ill to die as He did. Fulfil with joy the remnant of the grounds and remainders of the afflictions of Christ in your body. Ye have lost a child: nay, she is not lost to you who is found to Christ. She is not sent away, but only sent before, like unto a star, which going out of our sight doth not die and evanish, but shineth in another hemisphere. Ye see her not, yet she doth shine in another country. If her glass was but a short hour, what she wanteth of time that she hath gotten of

---

* Cast.   † Rom. viii. 29.   ‡ To the life, livingly, vividly.
§ Rev. vii. 14.

eternity; and ye have to rejoice that ye have now fome plenifhing*
up in heaven. Build your neft upon no tree here; for ye fee God
hath fold the foreft to death; and every tree whereupon we would
reft is ready to be cut down, to the end we may fly† and mount
up, and build upon the Rock, and dwell in the holes of the Rock.
What ye love befides Jefus, your hufband, is an adulterous lover.
Now it is God's fpecial blefling to Judah, that He will not let her
find her paths in following her ftrange lovers. "Therefore, behold
I will hedge up her way with thorns, and make a wall that fhe fhall
not find her paths. And fhe fhall follow after her lovers, but fhe
fhall not overtake them."‡ O thrice happy Judah, when God
buildeth a double ftone wall betwixt her and the fire of hell! The
world, and the things of the world, Madam, is the lover ye naturally affect,§ befide your own hufband Chrift. The hedge of thorns
and the wall which God buildeth in your way, to hinder you from
this lover, is the thorny hedge of daily grief, lofs of children, weaknefs of body, iniquity of the time, uncertainty of eftate, lack of
worldly comfort, fear of God's anger for old unrepented-of fins.
What lofe ye, if God twift and plait the hedge daily thicker? God
be blefled, the Lord will not let you find your paths. Return to
your firft hufband. Do not weary, neither think that death walketh towards you with a flow pace. Ye muft be riper ere ye be
fhaken. Your days are no longer than Job's, that were "fwifter
than a poft, and paffed away as the fhips of defire, and as the eagle
that hafteth for the prey." ‖ There is lefs fand in your glafs now
than there was yefternight. This fpan-length of ever-pofting time
will foon be ended. But the greater is the mercy of God, the more
years ye get to advife, upon what terms, and upon what conditions,
ye caft your foul in the huge gulf of never-ending eternity. The
Lord hath told you what ye fhould be doing till He come. "Wait
and haften," faith Peter, "for the coming of our Lord." All is

---

* Property, or furniture.

† In the earlier editions it is given "*fly*" throughout; not "*flee*."

‡ Hos. ii. 6, 7.   § Love, have affection to.   ‖ Job ix. 25, 26, margin.

night that is here, in refpect of ignorance and daily enfuing troubles, one always making way to another, as the ninth wave of the fea to the tenth; therefore figh and long for the dawning of that morning, and the breaking of that day of the coming of the Son of Man, when the fhadows fhall flee away. Perfuade yourfelf the King is coming; read His letter fent before Him, " Behold, I come quickly."* Wait with the wearied night-watch for the breaking of the eaftern fky, and think that ye have not a morrow. As the wife father faid, who, being invited againft to-morrow to dine with his friend, anfwered, "Thofe many days I have had no morrow at all." I am loth to weary you. Show yourfelf a Chriftian, by fuffering without murmuring, for which fin fourteen thoufand and feven hundred were flain.† In patience poffefs your foul. They lofe nothing who gain Chrift. Thus remembering my brother's and my wife's humble fervice to your Ladyfhip, I commend you to the mercy and grace of our Lord Jefus, affuring you that your day is coming, and that God's mercy is abiding you. The Lord Jefus be with your fpirit.

Yours in the Lord Jefus at all dutiful obedience,

S. R.

ANWOTH, *Jan.* 15, 1629.

V.—*To my* LADY KENMURE, *upon her removal with her hufband from the parifh of Anwoth.*

(CHANGES AND LOSS OF FRIENDS—THIS WORLD NO ABIDING-PLACE.)

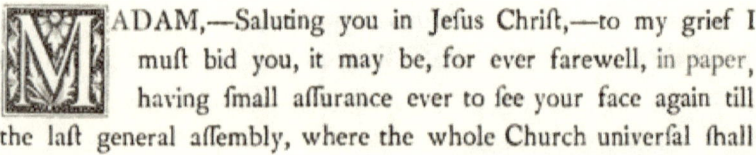

ADAM,—Saluting you in Jefus Chrift,—to my grief I muft bid you, it may be, for ever farewell, in paper, having fmall affurance ever to fee your face again till the laft general affembly, where the whole Church univerfal fhall meet; yet promifing, by His grace, to prefent your Ladyfhip and your burdens to Him who is able to fave you, and give you an inheritance with the faints, after a more fpecial manner than ever I have done before.*

Ye are going to a country where the Sun of righteoufnefs, in the Gofpel, fhineth not fo clearly as in this kingdom; but if ye would know where He whom your foul loveth doth reft, and where He feedeth at the noontide of the day, wherever ye be, get you forth by the footfteps of the flock, and feed yourfelf befide the fhepherds' tents;† that is, afk for fome of the watchmen of the Lord's city, who will tell you truly, and will not lie, where ye fhall find Him whom your foul loveth. I truft ye are fo betrothed in marriage to the true Chrift, that ye will not give your love to any falfe Chrift. Ye know not how foon your marriage-day will come; nay, is not eternity hard upon you? It were time, then, that ye had your wedding garment in readinefs. Be not fleeping at your Lord's coming. I pray God you may be upon your feet ftanding when He knocketh. Be not difcouraged to go from this country to another part of the Lord's earth : "The earth is His, and the fulnefs thereof."‡ This is the Lord's lower houfe; while we are lodged here, we have no affurance to lie ever in one chamber, but muft be content to remove from one corner of our Lord's nether houfe to another, refting in hope that, when we come up to the Lord's upper city, "Jerufalem that is above," we fhall remove no more, becaufe then we fhall be at home. And go wherefoever ye will, if your Lord go with you, ye are at home; and your lodging is ever taken before night, fo long as He who is Ifrael's dwelling-houfe is your home.§ Believe me, Madam, my mind is that ye are well lodged, and that in your houfe there are fair eafe-rooms‖ and pleafant lights, if ye can in faith lean down your head upon the breaft of Jefus

---

* Lord Kenmure and his lady refided at Rufco, in the parifh of Anwoth, during the firft two years of Rutherford's miniftry there; but they were now about to leave it. See a notice of this, Let. 147.

† Cant. i. 7, 8.   ‡ Pfalm xxiv. 1.   § Pfalm xc. 1.   ‖ Rooms for repofe.

Chrift: and till this be, ye fhall never get a found fleep. Jefus, Jefus, be your fhadow and your covering. It is a fweet foul-fleep to lie in the arms of Chrift, for His breath is very fweet.

Pray for poor friendlefs Zion. Alas! no man will fpeak for her now, although at home in her own country fhe hath good friends, her hufband Chrift, and His Father her Father-in-law. Befeech your hufband to be a friend to Zion, and pray for her.

I have received many and divers dafhes and heavy ftrokes, fince the Lord called me to the miniftry; but indeed I efteem your departure from us amongft the weightieft: but I perceive God will have us to be deprived of whatfoever we idolize, that He may have His own room. I fee exceeding fmall fruit of my miniftry, and would be glad to know of one foul to be my crown and rejoicing in the day of Chrift. Though I fpend my ftrength in vain, yet my labour is with my God.* I wifh and pray that the Lord would harden my face againft all, and make me to learn to go with my face againft a ftorm. Again I commend you, body and fpirit, to Him who hath loved us, and wafhed us from our fin in His own blood. Grace, grace, grace for ever be with you. Pray, pray continually.

Your Ladyfhip's at all dutiful obedience in Chrift,

S. R.

Anwoth, *Sept.* 14, 1629.

———◆———

VI.—*For* Marion M'Naught, *on occafion of the illnefs of his (Mr Rutherford's) wife.*

[MARION M'NAUGHT was daughter to the Laird of Kilquhanatie, in Kirkpatrick Durham (fee Let. 252), the reprefentative of an ancient family, now extinct, and connected alfo with the houfe of Kenmure, through her mother, Margaret Gordon, fifter to Lord Kenmure. She became the wife of William Fullerton, Provoft of Kirkcudbright, and was a woman extenfively known and held in honour by the moft eminent Chriftians and minifters of

---

* Ifa. xlix. 4.

her day, on account of her rare godlinefs and public fpirit. We find in *The Laft and Heavenly Speeches of Vifcount Kenmure*, that by the fpecial defire of that nobleman (who was her relative), fhe was in continual attendance on him as he lay on his deathbed. Her name is fometimes fpelt "M'Knaight," or "M'Knaichte," the modern "Macknight." She had three children—one daughter, Grizzel, and two fons, Samuel and William,—who are often affectionately remembered in Rutherford's letters to her. The following epitaph was infcribed on her tomb, in the churchyard of Kirkcudbright:—

" Marion M'Naught, fifter to John M'Naught of Kilquhanatie, an ancient
and honourable baron, and fpoufe to William Fullerton, Provoft of
Kirkcudbright, died April 1643, age 58.

> *Sexum animis, pietate genus, generofa, locumque*
> *Virtute exfuperans, conditur hoc tumulo.*"

The tombftone has fince been removed. It was only in 1860 that her houfe (in which the meeting with Blair and Rutherford took place) was pulled down. It ftood at the foot of the High Street, which was then the principal ftreet of the town.

A relative of this lady's hufband, Fullerton of Carlton (fee Let. 157), wrote on her the following acroftic:—

M More happy than imagined can be,
A And bleffed, are fuch as with heart fincere
R Refolve to cleave to Chrift, to live and die
I In Him, with Him, and for Him to appear.
O O what tranfcendant glory grows from grace!
N None but—no, not—the foul refinéd fhall

M' Make to appear; that life, that light, that peace,
K Known only to the pure poffeffors all.
N Now, *THOU*, by grace, art into glory gone,
A And gained the garland of eternal blifs,
I In feeing Him who, on that glorious throne,
C Created, uncreated, glory is.
H Heaven's quire did fing at thy converfion fweet,
T Time pofts thy final comforts to complete.

(*Append. to " Minute-Book of Committee of Covenanters.*")

(INWARD CONFLICT ARISING FROM OUTWARD TRIAL.)

LOVING AND DEAR SISTER,—If ever you would pleafure me, entreat the Lord for me, now when I am fo comfortlefs, and fo full of heavinefs, that I am not able to ftand under the burthen any longer. The Almighty hath doubled His ftripes upon me, for my wife is fo fore tormented night and day, that I have wondered why the Lord tarrieth fo long. My life is bitter unto me, and I fear the Lord be my contrair* party. It is (as I now know by experience) hard to keep fight of God in a ftorm, efpecially when He hides Himfelf, for the trial of His children. If He would be pleafed to remove His hand, I have a purpofe to feek Him more than I have done. Happy are they that can win away† with their foul. I am afraid of His judgments. I blefs my God that there is a death, and a heaven. I would weary to begin again to be a Chriftian, fo bitter is it to drink of the cup that Chrift drank of, if I knew not that there is no poifon in it. God give us not of it till we vomit again, for we have fick fouls when God's phyfic works not. Pray that God would not lead my wife into temptation. Woe is my heart, that I have done fo little againft the kingdom of Satan in my calling; for he would fain attempt to make me blafpheme God in His face. I believe, I believe, in the ftrength of Him who hath put me in His work, he fhall fail in that which he feeks. I have comfort in this, that my Captain, Chrift, hath faid, I muft fight and overcome the world,‡ and with a weak, fpoiled, weaponlefs devil, "the prince of this world cometh, and hath nothing in me."§ Defire Mr Robert‖ to remember me, if he love me. Grace, grace be with you, and all yours.

Remember Zion. There is a letter procured from the King by Mr John Maxwell to urge conformity, to give the communion at Chriftmas in Edinburgh. ¶ Hold faft that which you have, that no

---

* Contrary, *i.e.*, my adverfary.   † Efcape, get away from the world.
‡ John xvi. 33.   § John xiv. 30.
‖ Mr Robert Glendinning, minifter of Kirkcudbright.
¶ Mr· J. Maxwell here mentioned was at this time a minifter in Edinburgh, and afterwards became Bifhop of Rofs,—a man of talent, but devoid of principle, whofe aim was to fecure the favour of the notorious Laud, and forward his defigns for forcing Epifcopacy upon the Scottifh people. The letter above referred to was from the King, urging the adoption of the Englifh fervice.

man take the crown from you. The Lord Jefus be with your
fpirit.

Yours in the Lord,

S. R.

Anwoth, *Nov.* 17, 1629.

———◆———

VII.—*To my* Lady Kenmure.

*(THE EARNEST OF THE SPIRIT—COMMUNION WITH CHRIST—
FAITH IN THE PROMISES.)*

MADAM,—I have longed exceedingly to hear of your life
and health, and growth in the grace of God. I lacked
the opportunity of a bearer, in refpect I did not underftand of the hafty departure of the laft, by whom I might have
faluted your Ladyfhip, and therefore I could not write before this
time. I entreat you, Madam, let me have two lines from you concerning your prefent condition. I know ye are in grief and heavinefs;
and if it were not fo, ye might be afraid, becaufe then your way
fhould not be fo like the way that (our Lord faith) leadeth to the New
Jerufalem. Sure I am, if ye knew what were before you, or if ye
faw but fome glances of it, ye would with gladnefs fwim through
the prefent floods of forrow, fpreading forth your arms out of defire
to be at land. If God have given you the earneft of the Spirit, as
part of payment of God's principal fum, ye have to rejoice; for our
Lord will not lofe His earneft, neither will He go back or repent
Him of the bargain. If ye find at fome time a longing to fee God,
joy in the affurance of that fight, howbeit that feaft be but like the
Paffover, that cometh about only once a-year. Peace of confcience,
liberty of prayer, the doors of God's treafure caft up to the foul,
and a clear fight of Himfelf looking out, and faying, with a fmiling
countenance, "*Welcome to Me, afflicted foul;*" this is the earneft that
He giveth fometimes, and which maketh glad the heart, and is an
evidence that the bargain will hold. But to the end ye may get this

earneſt, it were good to come oft into terms of ſpeech with God, both in prayer and hearing of the word. For this is the houſe of wine, where ye meet with your Well-Beloved. Here it is where He kiſſeth you with the kiſſes of His mouth, and where ye feel the ſmell of His garments; and they have indeed a moſt fragrant and glorious ſmell. Ye muſt, I ſay, wait upon Him, and be often communing with Him, whoſe lips are as lilies, dropping ſweet-ſmelling myrrh, and by the moving thereof He will aſſuage your grief; for the Chriſt that ſaveth you is a ſpeaking Chriſt; the Church knoweth Him* by His voice, and can diſcern His tongue amongſt a thouſand. I ſay this to the end ye ſhould not love thoſe dumb maſks of antichriſtian ceremonies, that the Church,† where ye are for a time, hath caſt over the Chriſt whom your ſoul loveth. This is to ſet before you a dumb Chriſt. But when our Lord cometh, He ſpeaketh to the heart in the ſimplicity of the Goſpel.

I have neither tongue nor pen to expreſs to you the happineſs of ſuch as are in Chriſt. When ye have ſold all that ye have, and bought the field wherein this pearl is, ye will think it no bad mar-ket; for if ye be in Him, all His is yours, and ye are in Him; therefore, "becauſe He liveth, ye ſhall live alſo."‡ And what is that elſe, but as if the Son had ſaid, "I will not have heaven ex-cept My redeemed ones be with Me: they and I cannot live aſunder. Abide in Me, and I in you." § O ſweet communion, when Chriſt and we are through other,‖ and are no longer two! "Father, I will that thoſe whom Thou haſt given Me be with Me where I am, to behold My glory that Thou haſt given Me."¶ Amen, dear Jeſus, let it be according to that word. I wonder that ever your heart ſhould be caſt down, if ye believe this truth. I and they are not worthy of Jeſus Chriſt, who will not ſuffer forty years' trouble for Him, ſince they have ſuch glorious promiſes. But we fools believe thoſe promiſes as the man that read Plato's writings concerning the

---

* Cant. ii. 8.   † Epiſcopal.   ‡ John xiv. 19.
§ John xv. 4   ‖ Mixed up with each other.   ¶ John xvii. 24.

immortality of the foul: fo long as the book was in his hand he believed all was true, and that the foul could not die; but fo foon as
he laid by the book, he began to imagine that the foul is but a fmoke
or airy vapour, that perifheth with the expiring of the breath.   So
we at ftarts* do affent to the fweet and precious promifes; but laying afide God's book, we begin to call all in queftion.   It is faith
indeed, to believe without a pledge, and to hold the heart conftant
at this work; and when we doubt, to run to the law and to the
teftimony, and ftay there.   Madam, hold you here: here is your
Father's teftament,—read it; in it He hath left to you remiffion of
fins and life everlafting.   If all that ye have here be croffes and
troubles, down-caftings, frequent defertions, and departure of the
Lord, who is fuiting† you in marriage, courage!   He who is wooer
and fuitor fhould not be an houfehold man with you till ye and He
come up to His Father's houfe together.   He purpofeth to do you
good at your latter end,‡ and to give you reft from the days of adverfity.§   " It is good to bear the yoke of God in your youth."‖
" Turn in to your ftronghold as a prifoner of hope."¶   " For the
vifion is for an appointed time; but at the end it fhall fpeak, and not
lie: though it tarry, wait for it, becaufe it will furely come, it will not
tarry."**   Hear Himfelf faying, " Come, My people" (rejoice, He
calleth on you!), " enter thou into thy chambers, and fhut thy doors
about thee; hide thyfelf, as it were for a little moment, till the indignation be paft.††   Believe, then, believe and be faved; think
not hard if ye get not your will, nor your delights in this life; God
will have you to rejoice in nothing but Himfelf.   God forbid that
ye fhould rejoice in anything but in the crofs of Chrift.‡‡

Our Church, Madam, is decaying,—she is like Ephraim's cake;
" and grey hairs are here and there upon her, and fhe knoweth it
not."§§   She is old and grey-haired, near the grave, and no man
taketh it to heart.   Her wine is four and is corrupted.   Now if

---

* On occafions, fitfully.   † Wooing.   ‡ Deut. viii. 16.
§ Ps. xciv. 13.   ‖ Lam. iii. 27.   ¶ Zech. ix. 12.
** Hab. ii. 3.   †† Ifa. xxvi. 20.   ‡‡ Gal. vi. 14.
§§ Hos. vii. 9.

Phinehas's wife did live, fhe might travail in birth and die, to fee
the ark of God taken, and the glory depart from our Ifrael. The
power and life of religion is away. " Woe be to us ! for the day
goeth away, for the fhadows of the evening are ftretched out."*
Madam, Zion is the fhip wherein ye are carried to Canaan ; if fhe
fuffer fhipwreck, ye will be caft overboard upon death and life, to
fwim to land upon broken boards. It were time for us, by prayer,
to put upon† our mafter-pilot, Jefus, and to cry, " Mafter, fave us ;
we perifh." Grace, grace be with you. We would think it a
blefling to our kirk to fee you here ; but our fins withhold good
things from us. The great Meffenger of the Covenant preferve you
in body and fpirit.

Yours in the Lord,

S. R.

ANWOTH, *Feb.* 1, 1630.

VIII.—*For* MARION M'NAUGHT, *on occafion of his (Mr Rutherford's)*
wife's illnefs.

(*WRESTLINGS WITH GOD.*)

ISTRESS,—My love in Jefus Chrift remembered. I am
in good health ; honour to my Lord ; but my wife's
difeafe increafeth daily, to her great torment and pain
night and day. She has not been in God's houfe fince our communion, neither out of her bed. I have hired a man to Edinburgh to
Doctor Jeally and to John Hamilton.‡ I can hardly believe her
difeafe is ordinary, for her life is bitter to her ; fhe fleeps none, but
cries as a woman travailing in birth. What will be the event, He
that hath the keys of the grave knoweth. I have been many times,
fince I faw you, that I have befought the Lord to loofe her out of

---

* Jer. vi. 4. † Importune.

‡ Probably a relative of his wife, whofe name was Eupham Hamilton.

body, and to take her to her reſt. I believe the Lord's tide of afflictions will ebb again ; but at preſent I am exerciſed with the wrestlings of God, being afraid of nothing more than this, that God has
let looſe the tempter upon my houſe. " God rebuke him and his
inſtruments." Becauſe Satan is not caſt out but by faſting and
prayer, I entreat you remember our eſtate to our Lord, and entreat
all good Chriſtians whom ye know, but eſpecially your paſtor,* to
do the ſame. It becomes us ſtill to knock, and to lie at the Lord's
door, until we die knocking. If He will not open, it is more than
He has ſaid in His word. But He is faithful. I look not to win
away to my home without wounds and blood. Welcome, welcome
croſs of Chriſt, if Chriſt be with it. I have not a calm ſpirit in the
work of my calling here, being daily chaſtiſed ; yet God hath not
put out my candle, as He does to the wicked. Grace, grace be
with you and all yours.

Yours in the Lord,

S. R.

ANWOTH.

IX.—*For* MARION M'NAUGHT, *recommending a friend to her love.*

(PRAYERS ASKED.)

MISTRESS,—My love in Chriſt remembered. At the deſire of this bearer, whom I love, I thought to requeſt
you if ye can help his wife with your advice, for ſhe is
in a moſt dangerous and deadly-like condition. For I have thought
ſhe was changed in her carriage and life, this ſometime bypaſt, and
had hope that God would have brought her home ; and now, by
appearance, ſhe will depart this life, and leave a number of children
behind her. If ye can be entreated to help her, it is a work of
mercy. My own wife is ſtill in exceeding great torment night and

---

* The Rev. Mr Robert Glendinning, then miniſter of Kirkcudbright. His
grave-ſtone may be ſeen in the churchyard.

day. Pray for us, for my life was never fo wearifome to me. God hath filled me with gall and wormwood; but I believe (which holds up my head above the water), "It is good for a man," faith the Spirit of God, "that he bear the yoke in his youth."*

I do remember you. I pray you be humble and believe; and I entreat you in Jefus Chrift, pray for John Stuart and his wife, and defire your hufband to do the fame. Remember me heartily to Jean Brown. Defire her to pray for me and my wife : I do remember her. Forget not Zion. Grace, grace upon them, and peace, that pray for Zion. She is the fhip we fail in to Canaan. If fhe be broken on a rock, we will be caft overboard, to fwim to land betwixt death and life. The grace of Jefus be with your husband and children.

Yours in Chrift,

S. R.

Anwoth.

X.—*For* Marion M'Naught.

(SUBMISSION, PERSEVERANCE, AND ZEAL RECOMMENDED.)

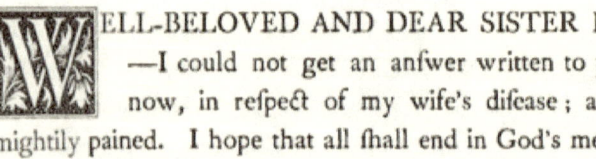

ELL-BELOVED AND DEAR SISTER IN CHRIST, —I could not get an anfwer written to your letter till now, in refpeɛt of my wife's difeafe ; and fhe is yet mightily pained. I hope that all fhall end in God's mercy. I know that an afflicted life looks very like the way that leads to the kingdom; for the Apoftle† hath drawn the line and the King's market-way, "through much tribulation, to the kingdom." The Lord grant us the whole armour of God.

Ye write to me concerning your people's difpofition, how that their hearts are inclined toward the man ye know, and whom ye defire moft earneftly yourfelf. He would moft gladly have the

---

* Lam. iii. 27.   † Acts xiv. 22 ; 1 Thefs. iii. 4.

Lord's call for tranfplantation; for he knows that all God's plants, fet by His own hand, thrive well; and if the work be of God, He can make a ftepping-ftone of the devil himfelf for fetting forward the work. For yourfelf, I would advife you to afk of God a fub-miffive heart. Your reward fhall be with the Lord, although the people be not gathered (as the prophet fpeaks); and fuppofe the word* do not profper, God fhall account you " a repairer of the breaches." And take Chrift caution,† ye fhall not lofe your reward. Hold your grip‡ fast. If ye knew the mind of the glorified in heaven, they think heaven come to their hand at an eafy market, when they have got it for three-fcore or four-fcore years wreftling with God. When ye are come thither, ye fhall think, " All I did, in refpect of my rich reward, now enjoyed of free grace, was too little." Now then, for the love of the Prince of your falvation, who is ftanding at the end of your way, holding up in His hand the prize and the gar-land to the race-runners, Forward, forward, faint not. Take as many to heaven with you as ye are able to draw. The more ye draw with you, ye fhall be the welcomer yourfelf. Be no niggard or fparing churl of the grace of God; and employ all your endea-vours for eftablifhing an honeft miniftry in your town, now when ye have fo few to fpeak a good word for you. I have many a grieved heart daily in my calling. I would be undone, if I had not accefs to the King's chamber of prefence, to fhow Him all the bufi-nefs. The devil rages, and is mad to fee the water drawn from his own mill; but would to God we could be the Lord's inftru-ments to build the Son of God's houfe.

Pray for me. If the Lord furnifh not new timber from Lebanon to build the houfe, the work will ceafe. I look to Him, who hath begun well with me. I have His handwrite, He will not change. Your daughter is well, and longs for a Bible. The Lord eftablifh you in peace. The Lord Jefus be with your fpirit.

Yours at all power in Chrift,

S. R.

ANWOTH.

---

* Work?   † Security.   ‡ Firm hold.

XI.—*To My* Lady Kenmure.

(GOD'S INEXPLICABLE DEALINGS WITH HIS PEOPLE WELL ORDERED — WANT OF ORDINANCES — CONFORMITY TO CHRIST — TROUBLES OF THE CHURCH — DEATH OF MR RUTHERFORD'S WIFE.)

MADAM,—Grace, mercy, and peace be multiplied upon you. I received your Ladyſhip's letter, in the which I perceive your caſe in this world ſmelleth of a fellow-ſhip and communion with the Son of God in His ſufferings. Ye cannot, ye muſt not, have a more pleaſant or more eaſy condition here, than He had, who "through afflictions was made perfect." * We may indeed think, Cannot God bring us to heaven with eaſe and proſperity? Who doubteth but He can? But His infinite wiſdom thinketh and decreeth the contrary; and we cannot ſee a reaſon of it, yet He hath a moſt juſt reaſon. We never with our eyes ſaw our own ſoul; yet we have a ſoul. We ſee many rivers, but we know not their firſt ſpring and original fountain; yet they have a beginning. Madam, when ye are come to the other ſide of the water, and have ſet down your foot on the ſhore of glorious eternity, and look back again to the waters and to your weariſome journey, and ſhall ſee, in that clear glaſs of endleſs glory, nearer to the bottom of God's wiſdom, ye ſhall then be forced to ſay, "If God had done otherwiſe with me than He hath done, I had never come to the enjoying of this crown of glory." It is your part now to believe, and ſuffer, and hope, and wait on; for I proteſt, in the preſence of that all-diſcerning eye, who knoweth what I write and what I think, that I would not want the ſweet experience of the conſolations of God for all the bitterneſs of affliction. Nay, whether God come to His children with a rod or a crown, if He come Himſelf with it, it is well. Welcome, welcome, Jeſus, what way ſoever Thou come, if we can get a ſight of Thee. And ſure I am,

---

* Heb. ii. 10.

it is better to be fick, providing Chrift come to the bed-fide and draw by* the curtains, and fay, " Courage, I am Thy falvation," than to enjoy health, being lufty and ftrong, and never to be vifited of God.

Worthy and dear lady, in the ftrength of Chrift, fight and overcome. Ye are now yourfelf alone, but ye may have, for the feeking, three always in your company, the Father, Son, and Holy Spirit. I truft they are near you. Ye are now deprived of the comfort of a lively miniftry ; fo was Ifrael in their captivity ; yet hear God's promife to them : " Therefore fay, Thus faith the Lord God, although I have caft them far off among the heathen, and although I have fcattered them among the countries, yet will I be to them as a little fanctuary in the countries where they fhall come."† Behold a fanctuary ! for a fanctuary, God Himfelf in the place and room of the temple of Jerufalem ! I truft in God, that, carrying this temple about with you, ye fhall fee Jehovah's beauty in His houfe.

We are in great fears of a great and fearful trial to come upon the kirk of God ; for thefe, who would build their houfes and nefts upon the afhes of mourning Jerufalem, have drawn our King upon hard and dangerous conclufions againft fuch as are termed Puritans, for the rooting of them out. Our prelates (the Lord take the keys of His houfe from thefe baftard porters !) affure us that, for fuch as will not conform,‡ there is nothing but imprifonment and deprivation. ‖ The fpoufe of Jefus will ever be in the fire ; but I truft in my God fhe fhall not confume, becaufe of the good-will of

---

* Afide.   † Ezek. xi. 16.   ‡ To the Englifh form of religious worfhip.

‖ The prelates, when the Courts of High Commiffion were erected in 1610, were invefted with the powers of imprifoning and depriving Nonconformifts. Nor had the bifhops failed, previous to the date of this letter, to exercife the exorbitant power thus granted them over the bodies and goods of loyal fubjects, not a few minifters having been deprived, imprifoned, and banifhed by the Courts of High Commiffion fimply for their nonconformity. In a paper entitled "The Grievances of the Minifters and other Profeffors given in by fome in their name to his Majefty, or to the Eftates," foon after Charles I. afcended the throne, it is complained, "That the bifhops, not being

Him who dwelleth in the Bush ; for He dwelleth in it with good-
will.   All forts of crying fins without controlment abound in our
land.   The glory of the Lord is departing from Ifrael, and the
Lord is looking back over His fhoulder, to fee if any one will fay,
" Lord, tarry," and no man requefteth Him to ftay.   Corrupt and
falfe doctrine is openly preached by the idol-fhepherds of the land.
For myfelf, I have daily griefs, through the difobedience unto, and
contempt of, the word of God.   I was fummoned before the High
Commiffion by a profligate perfon in this parifh, convicted of inceft.
In the bufinefs, Mr Alexander Colvill* (for refpect to your Lady-
fhip) was my great friend, and wrote a moft kind letter to me.
The Lord give him mercy in that day.   Upon the day of my
compearance, the fea and winds refufed to give paffage to the Bifhop
of St Andrews.†   I entreat your Ladyfhip, thank Mr Alexander
Colvill with two lines of a letter.

My wife now, after long difeafe and torment, for the fpace of a
year and a month, is departed this life.   The Lord hath done it ;
bleffed be His name.   I have been difeafed of a fever tertian for
the fpace of thirteen weeks, and am yet in the ficknefs, fo that I
preach but once on the Sabbath with great difficulty.   I am not
able either to vifit or examine the congregation.   The Lord Jefus
be with your fpirit.

Your Ladyfhip at all obedience,

S. R.

ANWOTH, *26th June*, 1630.

---

content with the titles and benefices of bifhopricks, encroached, againft their
own proteftations and promife, upon the jurifdiction ecclefiaftical, in accepting,
or rather procuring, power and commiffion from his Majefty to fine, confine,
decern upon fufpenfion, depofition, deprivation of minifters, and excommunication of whatfoever fubjects ; and that they have removed worthy men of the
miniftry from their calling for no other caufe but refufal of conformity to fome
ceremonies unknown till of late to our Kirk.—*Scots Apologet. Narrative*, pp.
322, 324.

* One of the judges.   † Archbifhop Spottifwoode.

XII.—*For* Marion M'Naught.

(GOD MIXETH THE CUP—THE WICKED HAVE THEIR REWARD
—FAITHFULNESS—FORBEARANCE—TRIALS.)

ELL-BELOVED AND DEAR SISTER,—My love in the Lord Jefus remembered. I underftand that you are ftill under the Lord's vifitation, in your former bufinefs with your enemies, which is God's dealing. For, till He take His children out of the furnace that knoweth how long they fhould be tried, there is no deliverance ; but after God's higheft and fulleft tide, that the fea of trouble is gone over the fouls of His children, then comes the gracious, long-hoped-for ebbing and drying up of the waters. Dear fifter, do not faint ; the wicked may hold the bitter cup to your head, but God mixeth it, and there is no poifon in it. They ftrike, but God moves the rod ; Shimei curfeth, but it is becaufe the Lord bids Him. I tell you, and I have it from Him before whom I ftand for God's people, that there is a decreet* given out, in the great court of the higheft heavens, that your prefent troubles fhall be difperfed as the morning cloud, and God fhall bring forth your righteoufnefs, as the light of the noon-tide of the day. Let me intreat you, in Chrift's name, to keep a good confcience in your proceedings in that matter, and beware of yourfelf : yourfelf is a more dangerous enemy than I, or any without you. Innocence and an upright caufe is a good advocate before God, and fhall plead for you, and win your caufe. And count much of your Mafter's approbation and His fmiling. He is now as the king that is gone to a far country. God feems to be from home (if I may fay fo), yet He fees the ill fervants, who fay, " Our Mafter deferreth His coming," and fo ftrike their fellowfervants. But patience, my beloved ; Chrift the King is coming home ; the evening is at hand, and He will afk an account of His

---

* Sentence.

fervants. Make a fair, clear count to Him. So carry yourfelf, as
at night you may fay, Mafter, I have wronged none; behold, you
have your own with advantage. O! your foul then will efteem
much of one of God's kiffes and embracements, in the teftimony of
a good confcience. The wicked, howbeit they be cafting many evil
thoughts, bitter words, and finful deeds behind their back, yet they
are, in fo doing, clerks to their own procefs, and doing nothing all
their life but gathering dittayes* againft themfelves; for God is
angry at the wicked every day. And I hope your prefent procefs
fhall be fighted† one day by Him, who knoweth your juft caufe;
and the bloody tongues, crafty foxes, double ingrained hypocrites,
fhall appear as they are before His majefty, when He fhall take the
mafk off their faces. And O, thrice happy fhall your foul be then,
when God finds you covered with nothing but the white robe of
the faints' innocence, and the righteoufnefs of Jefus Chrift.

You have been of late in the King's wine-cellar, where you were
welcomed by the Lord of the inn, upon condition that you would
walk in love. Put on love, and brotherly kindnefs, and long-fuffer-
ing; wait as long upon the favour and turned hearts of your enemies as your Chrift waited upon you, and as dear Jefus ftood at
your foul's door, with dewy and rainy locks, the long cold night.
Be angry, but fin not. I perfuade myfelf, that holy unction within
you, which teacheth you all things, is alfo faying, " Overcome evil
with good." If that had not fpoken in your foul, at the tears of
your aged paftor, you would not have agreed, and forgiven his
foolifh fon, who wronged you; but my Mafter bade me tell you,
God's bleffing fhall be upon you for it; and from Him I fay, Grace,
grace, grace, and everlafting peace be upon you. It is my prayer
for you, that your carriage may grace and adorn the Gofpel of that
Lord who hath graced you. I heard your hufband alfo was fick;
but I befeech you in the bowels of Jefus, welcome every rod of
God, for I find not in the whole book of God a greater note of
the child of God, than to fall down and kifs the feet of an angry

---

* Indictments.   † Narrowly infpected.

God; and when He feems to put you away from Him, and loofe your hands that grip* Him, to look up in faith, and fay, "I fhall not, I will not, be put away from Thee. Howbeit Thy Majefty draw to free Thyfelf of me, yet, Lord, give me leave to hold, and cleave unto Thyfelf." I will pray, that your hufband may return in peace. Your decreet comes from heaven; look up thither, for many (fays Solomon) feek the face of the ruler, but every man's judgment cometh of the Lord. And be glad that it is fo, for Chrift is the clerk of your procefs, and will fee that all go right; and I perfuade myfelf He is faying, "Yonder fervants of Mine are wronged; for My blood, Father, give them juftice." Think you not, dear fifter, but our High Prieft, our Jefus, the Mafter of requefts, prefents our bills of complaint to the great Lord Juftice? Yea, I believe it, fince He is our Advocate, and Daniel calls Him the Spokefman, whofe hand prefents all to the Father.

For other bufinefs, I fay nothing, while† the Lord give me to fee your face. I am credibly informed, that multitudes of England, and efpecially worthy preachers, and filenced preachers of London, are gone to New England; and I know one learned holy preacher, who hath written againft the Arminians, who is gone thither.‡ Our bleffed Lord Jefus, who cannot get leave to fleep with His

---

* Grafp, hold firm. † Till.

‡ The emigration of thefe preachers and of multitudes of the people to New England was the confequence of the perfecuting meafures purfued by Archbifhop Laud for enforcing conformity, in the profecution of his favourite fcheme of bringing the Church of England as near to that of Rome as could confort with his own fupremacy and that of his fovereign. Affected with the conftant perfecution of their party, and the reduction of their families to beggary, without any profpect of deliverance, Meffrs Higginfon and Skelton, with about three hundred and fifty private perfons, retired to America, and fettled in the Maffachufetts Bay, as their friends had formerly done at Plymouth. After landing, they entered into a folemn covenant to walk together in the fear of the Lord and in church-fellowfhip with one another. About feventy minifters and four thoufand planters are faid to have retired to that continent from the tyrannical rage of Laud and his agents.—*Brown's Britifh Churches*, vol. i., pp. 215-217.

spoufe in this land, is going to feek an inn where He will be better entertained. And what marvel? Wearied Jefus, after He had travelled from Geneva, by the miniftry of worthy Mr Knox, and was laid down in His bed, and reformation begun, and the curtains drawn, had not gotten His dear eyes well together, when irreverent bifhops came in, and with the din and noife of ceremonies, holy days, and other Romifh corruptions, they awake our Beloved Others came to His bed-fide, and drew the curtains, and put hands on His fervants, banifhed, deprived, and confined them ; and for the pulpit they got a ftool and a cold fire in the Blacknefs ; * and the nobility drew the covering off Him, and have made Him a poor naked Chrift, in fpoiling His fervant of the tithes and kirk-rents. And now there is fuch a noife of crying fins in the land, as the want of the knowledge of God, of mercy, and truth ; fuch fwearing, whoring, lying, and blood touching blood ; that Chrift is putting on His clothes, and. making Him,† like an ill-handled ftranger, to go to other lands. Pray Him, fifter, to lie down again with His beloved.

Remember my deareft love to John Gordon, to whom I will write when I am ftrong, and to John Brown, Griffel, Samuel, and William ; grace be upon them. As you love Chrift, keep Chrift's favour, and put not upon Him when He fleeps, to awake Him before He pleafe. The Lord Jefus be with your fpirit.

Your brother in Chrift,

S. R.

ANWOTH, *July* 21, 1630.

---

* Blacknefs Caftle, on the Forth, was ufed as a prifon.
† In the fenfe of appearing as if He would go ; Luke xxiv. 28.

(*JESUS A PATTERN OF PATIENCE UNDER SUFFERING.*)

WELL-BELOVED SISTER,—I have been thinking, fince my departure from you, of the pride and malice of your adverfaries; and ye may not (fince ye have had the Book of Pfalms fo often) take hardly with this; for David's enemies fnuffed at him, and through the pride of their heart faid, "The Lord will not require it."* I befeech you, therefore, in the bowels of Jefus, fet before your eyes the patience of your forerunner Jefus, who, when He was reviled, reviled not again; when He fuffered, He threatened not, but committed Himfelf to Him who judgeth right-eoufly.† And fince your Lord and Redeemer with patience received many a black ftroke on His glorious back, and many a buffet of the unbelieving world, and fays of Himfelf, "I gave My back to the fmiters, and My cheeks to them that plucked off the hair; I hid not My face from fhame and fpitting;"‡ follow Him, and think it not hard that you receive a blow with your Lord. Take part with Jefus of His fufferings, and glory in the marks of Christ. If this ftorm were over, you muft prepare yourfelf for a new wound; for, five thoufand years ago, our Lord proclaimed deadly war be-twixt the Seed of the Woman and the feed of the ferpent. And marvel not that one town cannot keep the children of God and the children of the devil, for one belly could not keep Jacob and Efau;§ one houfe could not keep peaceably together Ifaac, the fon of the promife, and Ifhmael, ‖ the fon of the handmaid. Be you upon Chrift's fide of it, and care not what flefh can do. Hold yourfelf faft by your Saviour, howbeit you be buffeted, and thofe that fol-low Him. Yet a little while and the wicked fhall not be. "We

---

* Ps. x. 13.   † 1 Pet. ii. 23.   ‡ Ifa. l. 6.
§ Gen. xxv. 22.   ‖ Gen. xxi. 10.

are troubled on every fide, yet not diftreffed ; we are perplexed, but not in defpair ; perfecuted, but not forfaken ; caft down, but not deftroyed."* If you can poffefs your foul in patience, their day is coming. Worthy and dear fifter, know to carry yourfelf in trouble ; and when you are hated and reproached, the Lord fhows it to you—" All this is come upon us, yet have we not forgotten Thee, neither have we dealt falfely in Thy covenant."† " Unlefs Thy law had been my delight, I had perifhed in mine affliction."‡ Keep God's covenant in your trials. Hold you by His bleffed word, and fin not. Flee anger, wrath, grudging, envying, fretting. Forgive an hundred pence to your fellow-fervant, becaufe your Lord hath forgiven you ten thoufand talents. For I affure you by the Lord, your adverfaries fhall get no advantage againft you, except you fin, and offend your Lord in your fufferings. But the way to overcome is by patience, forgiving and praying for your enemies, in doing whereof you heap coals upon their heads, and your Lord fhall open a door to you in your troubles. Wait upon Him, as the night watch waiteth for the morning. He will not tarry. Go up to your watch-tower, and come not down ; but by prayer, and faith, and hope, wait on. When the fea is full, it will ebb again ; and fo foon as the wicked are come to the top of their pride, and are waxed high and mighty, then is their change approaching. They that believe make not hafte.

Remember Zion, forget her not, for her enemies are many ; for the nations are gathered together againft her. "But they know not the thoughts of the Lord, neither underftand they His counfel : for He fhall gather them as the fheaves into the floor. Arife and threfh, O daughter of Zion."§ Behold, God hath gathered His enemies together, as fheaves to the threfhing. Let us ftay and reft upon thefe promifes. Now, again, I truft in our Lord you fhall by faith fuftain yourfelf, and comfort yourfelf in your Lord, and be ftrong in His power ; for you are in the beaten and common way to heaven

---

* 2 Cor. iv. 8, 9.   † Ps. xliv. 17.
‡ Ps. cxix. 92.   § Micah iv. 12, 13.

when you are under our Lord's croffes. You have reafon to rejoice in it, more than in a crown of gold ; and rejoice, and be glad
to bear the reproaches of Chrift. I reft, recommending you and
yours for ever to the grace and mercy of God.

Yours in Chrift,

S. R.

ANWOTH, *Feb.* 11, 1631.

XIV.—*For* MARION M'NAUGHT, *in the profpeƈl of a Communion feafon.*

(ABUNDANCE IN JESUS—THE RESTORATION OF THE JEWS— ENEMIES OF GOD.)

WELL-BELOVED IN THE LORD,—You are not un-
acquainted with the day of our Communion.* I entreat,
therefore, the aid of your prayers for that great work,
which is one of our feaft-days, wherein our Well-beloved Jefus rejoiceth, and is merry with His friends.

Good caufe have we to wonder at His love, fince the day of
His death was fuch a forrowful day to Him, even the day when
His mother, the kirk, crowned Him with thorns, and He had many
againft Him, and compeared His lone† in the fields againft them
all ; yet He delights with us to remember that day. Let us love
Him, and be glad and rejoice in His falvation. I am confident that
you fhall fee the Son of God that day, and I dare in His name invite
you to His banquet. Many a time you have been well entertained in
His houfe ; and He changes not upon His friends, nor chides them
for too great kindnefs. Yet I fpeak not this to make you leave off
to pray for me, who have nothing of myfelf, but in fo far as daily
I receive from Him, who is made of His Father a running-over
fountain, at which I and others may come with thirfty fouls, and

---

* The difpenfation of the Lord's Supper.

† Alone, no one with Him. Sometimes written, " His alone."

fill our veffels. Long hath this well been ftanding open to us. Lord Jefus, lock it not up again upon us. I am forry for our defolate kirk; yet I dare not but truft, fo long as there be any of God's loft money here He fhall not blow out the candle. The Lord make fair candlefticks in His houfe, and remove the blind lights.

I have been this time bypaft * thinking much of the incoming of the kirk of the Jews. Pray for them. When they were in their Lord's houfe, at their Father's elbow, they were longing for the incoming of their little fifter, the kirk of the Gentiles. They faid to their Lord, " We have a little fifter, and fhe hath no breafts: what fhall we do for our fifter in the day when fhe fhall be fpoken for ?"† Let us give them a meeting. What fhall we do for our elder fifter, the Jews? Lord Jefus, give them breafts. That were a glad day to fee us and them both fit down to one table, and Chrift at the head of the table. Then would our Lord come fhortly with his fair guard to hold His great court.

Dear fifter, be patient, for the Lord's fake, under the wrongs that you fuffer of the wicked. Your Lord fhall make you fee your defire on your enemies. Some of them fhall be cut off; " they fhall fhake off their unripe grapes as the vine, and caft off their flower as the olive :"‡ God fhall make them like unripe four grapes, fhaken off the tree with the blaft of God's wrath ; and therefore pity them, and pray for them. Others of them muft remain to exercife you. God hath faid of them, Let the tares grow up until harveft.§ It proves you to be your Lord's wheat. Be patient ; Chrift went to heaven with many a wrong. His vifage and countenance was all marred more than the fons of men. You may not be above your Mafter ; many a black ftroke received innocent Jefus, and He received no mends,‖ but referred them all to the great court-day, when all things fhall be righted. I defire to hear from you within a day or two, if Mr Robert remain in his purpofe to come and help us. God fhall give you joy of your children. I pray

---

* For fome time of late.   † Cant. viii. 8.   ‡ Job xv. 33.
§ Matt. xiii. 30.   ‖ Reparation.

for them by their names. I blefs you from our Lord, your hufband
and children. Grace, grace, and mercy be multiplied upon you.

Yours in the Lord for ever,

S. R.

ANWOTH, *May* 7, 1631.

XV.—*For* MARION M'NAUGHT, *on occafion of the threatened introduction of the Epifcopalian Service-Book.*

(TROUBLES OF THE CHURCH—PRIVATE WRONGS.)

ELL-BELOVED SISTER,—My love in Chrift remembered. I have received a letter from Edinburgh,
certainly informing me that the Englifh fervice, and the
organs, and King James' Pfalms, are to be impofed upon our kirk ;
and that the bifhops are dealing for a General Affembly. A. R.
hath confirmed the news alfo, and fays he fpoke with Sir William
Alexander,* who is to come down with his prince's warrant for
that effect. I am defired in the received letter to acquaint the beft-
affected about me with that ftorm : therefore I intreat you, and
charge you in the Lord's name, pray ; but do not communicate this
to any till I fee you. My heart is broken at the remembrance of
it, and it was my fear, and anfwereth to my laft letter except one,
that I wrote unto you. Dearly beloved, be not caften down, but
let us, as our Lord's doves, take us to our wings (for other armour
we have none), and flee into the hole of the rock. It is true A. R.
fays, the worthieft men in England are banifhed, and filenced, about
the number of fixteen or feventeen choice Gofpel preachers, and the
perfecution is already begun. Howbeit I do not write this unto you
with a dry face, yet I am confident in the Lord's ftrength, Chrift
and His fide fhall overcome; and you fhall be affured ; the kirk were
not a kirk, if it were not fo. As our dear Hufband, in wooing
His kirk, received many a black ftroke, fo His bride, in wooing Him,

---

* Sir W. Alexander of Menftrie, afterwards Earl of Stirling.

gets many blows, and in this wooing there are ftrokes upon both
fides.   Let it be fo.   The devil will not make the marriage go back,
neither can he tear the contraĉt ; the end fhall be mercy.   Yet
notwithftanding of all this, we have no warrant of God to leave off
all lawful means.   I have been writing unto you the counfels and
draughts* of men againft the kirk ; but they know not, as Micah
fays, the counfel of Jehovah.   The great men of the world may
make ready the fiery furnace for Zion ; but trow ye that they can
caufe the fire to burn ?   No.   He that made the fire, I truft, fhall
not fay amen to their decreets.   I truft in my Lord, that God hath
not fubfcribed their bill, and their conclufions have not yet paffed
our great King's feal.   Therefore, if ye think good, addrefs yourfelf
firft to the Lord, and then to A. R., anent the bufinefs that you know.

I am moft unkindly handled by the prefbytery; and (as if I had
been a ftranger, and not a member of that feat, to fit in judgment
with them) I was fummoned by their order as a witnefs againft B. A.
But they have got no advantage in that matter.   Other particulars
you fhall hear, God willing, at meeting.

Anent the matter betwixt you and I. E., I remember it to God.
I intreat you in the Lord, be fubmiffive to His will ; for the higher
that their pride mounts up, they are the nearer to a fall.   The Lord
will more and more difcover that man.   Let your hufband, in all
matters of judgment, take Chrift's part, for the defence of the poor
and needy, and the oppreffed, for the maintenance of equity and
juftice in the town.   And take you no fear.   He fhall take your part,
and then you are ftrong enough.   What ?   Howbeit you receive
indignities for your Lord's fake, let it be fo.   When He fhall put His
holy hand up to your face in heaven, and dry your face, and wipe
the tears from your eyes, judge ye if you will not have caufe then
to rejoice.   Anent other particulars, if you would fpeak with me,
appoint any of the firft three days of the next week in Carletoun,†

---

* What men draw up in forming plans.

† Carleton, in Galloway (see note at Let. 157), not far from Anwoth,
where Mr Fullerton, a true friend, refided.

when Carletoun is at home, and acquaint me with your defires. And remember me to God, and my deareft affection to your husband ; and for Zion's fake hold not your peace. The grace of our Lord Jefus Chrift be with you, and your hufband and children.

Yours in the Lord,

S. R.

ANWOTH, *June* 2, 1631.

XVI.—*For* MARION M'NAUGHT, *on occafion of a propofal to remove him from Anwoth.*

(BABYLON'S DESTRUCTION AND CHRIST'S COMING—THE YOUNG INVITED.)

ORTHY AND DEAR MISTRESS,—My deareft love in Chrift remembered. As to the bufinefs which I know you would fo fain have taken effect,* my earneft defire is, that you ftand ftill. Hafte not, and you fhall fee the falvation of God. The great Mafter Gardener, the Father of our Lord Jefus Chrift, in a wonderful providence, with His own hand (I dare, if it were for edification, fwear it), planted me here,† where, by His grace, in this part of His vineyard, I grow.—I dare not fay but Satan and the world (one of his pages whom he fends his errands) have faid otherwife. And here I will abide till the great Mafter of the Vineyard think fit to tranfplant me. But when He fees meet to loofe me at the root, and to plant me where I may be more ufeful, both as to fruit and fhadow, and when He who planted pulleth up that He may tranfplant, who dare put to their hand and hinder ? If they do, God fhall break their arm at the fhoulder blade, and do His turn. When our Lord is going weft, the devil and world go eaft ; and do you not know that it hath been ever this way betwixt God and the world—God drawing, and they

---

* So defire to fee accomplifhed.　　　　　　† At Anwoth.

holding, God " yea," and the world " nay?" But they fall on their back and are fruſtrate, and our Lord holdeth His grip.*

Wherefore doth the word ſay, that our Chriſt, the Goodman of this houſe, His dear kirk, hath feet like fine braſs, as if they burned in a furnace?† For no other cauſe but becauſe where our Lord ſetteth down His brazen feet, He will forward ; and whitherſoever He looketh, He will follow His look ; and His feet burn all under them, like as fire doth ſtubble and thorns. I think He hath now given the world a proof of His exceeding great power, when He is doing ſuch great things, wherein Zion is concerned, by the ſword of the Swediſh king,‡ as of a Gideon. As you love the glory of God, pray inſtantly § (yea engage all your praying acquaintance, and take their faithful promiſe to do the like) for this king, and every one that Zion's King armeth, to execute the written vengeance on Babylon. Our Lord hath begun to looſe ſome of Babylon's corner-ſtones. Pray to Him to hold on, for that city muſt fall, and the birds of the air and the beaſts of the earth muſt make a banquet of Babylon ; for He hath invited them to eat the fleſh of that whore, and to drink her blood. And the cup of the Lord's right hand ſhall be turned unto her, and ſhameful ſpewing ſhall be upon her glory. He whoſe word muſt ſtand hath ſaid, " 'Take this cup at the hand of the Lord, and drink and be drunken, and ſpew, and fall, and riſe no more." ‖ Our Jeſus is ſetting up Himſelf, as His Father's enſign, ¶ as God's fair white colours, that His ſoldiers may all flock about Him. Long, long may theſe colours ſtand. It is long ſince He diſplayed a banner againſt Babylon in the ſight of men and angels. Let us rejoice and triumph in our God. The victory is certain ; for when Chriſt and Babel wreſtle, then angels and ſaints may prepare themſelves to ſing, " Babylon the great is fallen, is fallen." Howbeit that Prince of renown, precious Jeſus, be now weeping and bleeding in His members, yet Chriſt will laugh again ; and it is time enough for us to laugh, when our Lord Chriſt

---

* Firm graſp.   † Rev. i. 15.   ‡ Guſtavus Adolphus.
§ Earneſtly.   ‖ Jer. xxv. 27.   ¶ Iſa. xi. 10.

laugheth,—and that will be fhortly. For when we hear of wars and rumours of wars, the Judge's feet are then before the door, and He muft be in heaven giving order to the angels to make themfelves ready, and prepare their hooks* and fickles for that great harveft. Chrift will be upon us in hafte; watch but a little, and ere long the fkies will rive,† and that fair lovely perfon, Jefus, fhall come in the clouds, freighted and loaded with glory. And then all thefe knaves and foxes that deftroyed the vines fhall call to the hills, and cry to the mountains to cover them, and hide them from the face of Him who fitteth upon the throne, and from the wrath of the Lamb.

Remember me to your hufband, and defire him from me to help Chrift, and to take His part, and in judgment fit ever befide Him, and receive a blow patiently for His fake; for He is worthy to be fuffered for, not only to blows, but alfo to blood. He fhall find that innocency and uprightnefs in judgment fhall hold its feet and make him happy, when jouking‡ will not do it. I fpeak this becaufe a perfon faid to me, "I pray God the country be not in worfe cafe now, when the provoft and bailies are agreed, than formerly,"—to whom I replied, "I truft the provoft is agreed with the man's perfon, but not with his faults." I pray for you, with my whole foul and defire, that your children may walk in the truth, and that the Lord may fhine upon them, and make their faces to fhine, when the faces of others fhall blufh. I dare promife them, in His name, whofe truth I preach, if they will but try God's fervice, that they fhall find Him the fweeteft Mafter that ever they ferved. And defire them from me but to try for a while the fervice of this bleffed Mafter, and then, if His fervice be not fweet, if it afford not what is pleafant to the foul's tafte, change Him upon trial, and feek a better. Chrift is an unknown Chrift to young ones; and therefore they feek Him not, becaufe they know Him not. Bid them come and fee, and feek a kifs of His mouth; and then they will find His mouth is fo fweet, that they will be ever-

---

* Reaping-hooks.   † Rend.

‡ Diffembling; properly, inclining the body forward to avoid a blow.

laftingly chained unto Him by their own confent. If I have any
credit with your children, I entreat them in Chrift's name to try
what truth and reality is in what I fay, and leave not His fervice
till they have found me a liar. I give you, your hufband, and
them, to His keeping, to whom I have,* and dare venture myfelf
and foul, even to our dear Friend Jefus Chrift, in whom I am,

Yours,

Anwotii.   S. R.

XVII.—*For* Marion M'Naught, *when in diftrefs as to profpects of
the Church.*

(*ARMINIANISM—CALL TO PRAYER—NO HELP BUT IN CHRIST.*)

WELL-BELOVED SISTER,—My deareft love in Chrift
remembered to you. Know that I am in great heavinefs for the pitiful cafe of our Lord's kirk. I hear the
caufe why Dr Burton† is committed to prifon is his writing and
preaching againft the Arminians. I therefore entreat the aid of
your prayers for myfelf, and the Lord's captives of hope, and for
Zion. The Lord hath let and daily lets me fee clearly, how deep
furrows Arminianifm and the followers of it fhall draw upon the
back of God's Ifrael (but our Lord cut the cords of the wicked !) ;
" Zion faid, 'The Lord hath forfaken me, and my Lord hath forgotten me."‡ " Zion weepeth fore in the night, and her tears are
upon her cheeks ; amongft all her lovers fhe hath none to comfort
her : all her friends have dealt treacheroufly with her ; they are become her enemies."§ " Our filver is become drofs, our wine
mixed with water."‖ " How is the gold become dim ! how is the
moft fine gold changed ! the ftones of the fanctuary are poured out

---

* To whom I have given, and dare venture to give.
† He refers to the cafe of Henry Burton, an able divine of the Church of
England, who wrote feveral vigorous pieces against Popery, and againft Mon-
tagu's " Appello Cæfarem." See Brook's " Lives of the Puritans."
‡ Ifa. xlix. 14.   § Lam. i. 2.   ‖ Ifa. i. 22.

in the top of every ftreet. The precious fons of Zion, comparable
to fine gold, how are they efteemed as earthen pitchers, the work
of the hands of the potter!"* It is time now for the Lord's fecret
ones, who favour the duft of Zion, to cry, "How long, Lord?"
and to go up to their watch-tower, and to ftay there, and not to
come down until the vifion fpeak; for it fhall fpeak.† In the mean
time, the juft fhall live by faith. Let us wait on and not weary. I
have not a thread to hang upon and reft, but this one, "Can a
woman forget her fucking child, that fhe fhould not have compaffion on the fon of her womb? Yea, fhe may forget, yet will I
not forget thee. Behold, I have graven thee upon the palms of My
hands; Thy walls are continually before Me."‡ For all outward
helps do fail; it is time therefore for us to hang ourfelves, as our
Lord's veffels, upon the nail that is faftened in a fure place. We
would make ftakes of our own faftening, but they will break. Our
Lord will have Zion on His own nail. Edom is bufy within us,
and Babel without us, againft the handful of Jacob's feed. It were
beft that we were upon Chrift's fide of it, for His enemies will get
the ftalks to keep,§ as the proverb is. Our greateft difficulty will
be to win upon the rock now, when the wind and waves of perfecution are fo lofty and proud. Let fweet Jefus take us by the
hand. Neither muft we think that it will be otherwife; for it is told
to the fouls under the altar, "That their fellow-fervants muft be
killed as they were."‖ Surely, it cannot be long to the day. Nay,
hear Him fay, "Behold, I come, My dear bride; think not long.¶
I fhall be at you at once. I hear you, and am coming." Amen;
even fo come, Lord Jefus, come quickly; for the prifoners of hope
are looking out at the prifon windows, to fee if they can behold the
King's ambaffador coming with the King's warrant and the keys.
I write not to you by guefs now, becaufe I have a warrant to fay
unto you, the garments of Chrift's fpoufe muft be once again dyed

---

* Lam. iv. 1, 2. † Hab. ii. 3. ‡ Ifa. xlix. 15, 16.
§ Nothing but the ftalks; none of the grain or fruit.
‖ Rev. vi. 11. ¶ To think long, is to long wearily for.

in blood, as long ago her Hufband's were. But our Father fees His bleeding Son. What I write unto you, fhow it to I. G. Grace, grace, grace and mercy be with you, your hufband, and children.

Yours in the Lord,

ANWOTH. S. R.

XVIII.—*For* MARION M'NAUGHT, *in the profpect of a Communion feafon.*

(*PRAYER SOLICITED—THE CHURCH'S PROSPECTS.*)

MISTRESS,—My love in Chrift as remembered. Our Communion is on Sabbath come * eight days. I will entreat you to recommend it to God, and to pray for me in that work. I have more fins upon me now than the laft time. Therefore I will befeech you in Chrift, feek this petition to me from God, that the Lord would give me grace to vow and perform new obedience. I have caufe to fuite† this of you; and fhow it to Thomas Carfon, Fergus and Jean Brown, for I have been and am exceedingly caft down, and am fighting againft a malicious devil, of whom I can win little ground. I would think a fpoil plucked from him, and his trufty fervant fin, a lawful and juft conqueft. And it were no fin to take from him, in the name of the Goodman of our houfe, our King Jefus. I invite you to the banquet. He faith, ye fhall be dearly welcome to Him. And I defire to believe (howbeit not without great fear) He fhall be as hearty in His own houfe as He has been before. For me, it is but fmall reckoning; but I would fain have our Father and Lord to break the great fair loaf, Chrift, and to diftribute His flain Son amongft the bairns‡ of His houfe. And that if any were a ftep-bairn, in refpect of comfort and fenfe, it were rather myfelf than His poor bairns.‡ Therefore bid our Well-beloved come to His garden and feed among the lilies.

---

* Sabbath that comes eight days after this.
† Urge this requeft. ‡ Children.

And as concerning Zion, I hope our Lord, who fent His angel[*]
with a meafuring line in his hand to meafure the length and breadth
of Jerufalem, in token He would not want a foot length or inch of
His own free heritage, fhall take order[†] with thofe who have taken
away many acres of His own land from Him.   And God will
build Jerufalem in the old fted[‡] and place where it was before.   In
this hope rejoice and be glad.   Chrift's garment was not dipt in
blood for nothing, but for His bride, whom He bought with
ftrokes.   I will defire you to remember my old fuits to God,
God's glory and the increafe of light, that I dry not up.   For
your town, hope and believe that the Lord will gather in His loofe
fheaves among you to His barn, and fend one with a well-toothed,
fharp hook, and ftrong gardies,[§] to reap His harveft.   And the
Lord Jefus be Hufbandman, and overfee the growing.   Remember my love to your hufband and to Samuel.   Grace upon you
and your children.   Lord, make them corner-ftones in Jerufalem,
and give them grace in their youth to take band[‖] with the fair
Chief Corner-ftone, who was hewed out of the mountain without
hands, and got many a knock with His Father's forehammer, and
endured them all, and the ftone did neither cleave nor break.
Upon that ftone make your foul to lie.   King Jefus be with your fpirit.

Your friend in his well-beloved Lord Jefus,

S. R.

Anwoth.

XIX.—*To my* Lady Kenmure.

*(ENCOURAGEMENT TO ABOUND IN FAITH FROM THE PROSPECT
OF GLORY—CHRIST'S UNCHANGEABLENESS.)*

ADAM,—Having faluted you in the Lord Jefus, I thought
it my duty, having the occafion of this bearer, to write
again unto your Ladyfhip, though I have no new pur-

---

[*] Zech. ii. 1, 2.   [†] Take meafures,—an old Englifh phrafe.
[‡] Situation, or fite.   [§] Arms; from the Gaelic "*gairdean*," an arm.
[‖] To unite themfelves to; *q.d.*, bind together.

pofe but what I wrote of before. Yet ye cannot be too often
awakened to go forward towards your city, fince your way is long,
and (for anything ye know) your day is fhort. And your Lord re-
quireth of you, as ye advance in years and fteal forward infenfibly
towards eternity, that your faith may grow and ripen for the Lord's
harveft. For the great Hufbandman giveth a feafon to His fruits that
they may come to maturity, and having gotten their fill of the tree,
they may then be fhaken and gathered in for ufe; whereas the
wicked rot upon the tree, and their branch fhall not be green, "He
fhall fhake off his unripe grape as the vine, and fhall caft off his
flower as the olive."* It is God's mercy to you, Madam, that
He giveth you your fill, even to loathing, of this bitter world, that
ye may willingly leave it, and, like a full and fatisfied banqueter,
long for the drawing of the table. And at laft, having trampled
under your feet all the rotten pleafures that are under fun and
moon, and having rejoiced as though ye rejoiced not, and having
bought as though ye poffeffed not,† ye may, like an old crazy fhip,
arrive at our Lord's harbour, and be made welcome, as one of thofe
who have ever had one foot loofe from the earth, longing for that
place where your foul fhall feaft and banquet for ever and ever
upon a glorious fight of the incomprehenfible Trinity, and where
ye fhall fee the fair face of the man Chrift, even the beautiful face
that was once for your caufe more marred than any of the vifages
of the fons of men,‡ and was all covered with fpitting and blood.
Be content to wade through the waters betwixt you and glory with
Him, holding His hand faft, for He knoweth all the fords. Howbeit ye may be ducked, but ye cannot drown, being in His company; and ye may all the way to glory fee the way bedewed with
His blood who is the Forerunner. Be not afraid, therefore, when
ye come even to the black and fwelling river of death, to put in
your foot and wade after Him. The current, how ftrong foever,
cannot carry you down the water to hell : the Son of God, His
death and refurrection, are ftepping-ftones and a ftay to you; fet

---

* Job xv. 33. † 1 Cor. vii. 30. ‡ Ifa. lii. 14.

down your feet by faith upon thefe ftones, and go through as on
dry land.   If ye knew what He is preparing for you, ye would be
too glad.   He will not (it may be) give you a full draught till you
come up to the well-head and drink, yea, drink abundantly, of the
pure river of the water of life, that proceedeth out from the throne
of God and of the Lamb.*   Madam, tire not, weary not; I dare
find you the Son of God caution,† when ye are got up thither, and
have caft your eyes to view the golden city, and the fair and never-
withering Tree of Life, that beareth twelve manner of fruits every
month, ye fhall then fay, " Four-and-twenty hours' abode in this
place is worth threefcore and ten years' forrow upon earth."   If
ye can but fay, that ye long earneftly to be carried up thither (as
I hope you cannot for fhame deny Him the honour of having wrought
that defire in your foul), then hath your Lord given you an earneft.
And, Madam, do ye believe that our Lord will lofe His earneft,
and rue of the bargain, and change His mind, as if He were a
man that can lie, or the fon of man that can repent?   Nay, He is
unchangeable, and the fame this year that He was the former year.
And His Son Jefus, who upon earth ate and drank with publicans
and finners, and fpake and conferred with whores and harlots, and
put up His holy hand and touched the leper's filthy fkin, and came
evermore nigh finners, even now in glory, is yet that fame Lord.
His honour, and His great court in heaven, hath not made Him forget His poor friends on earth.   In Him honours change not manners, and He doth yet defire your company.   Take Him for the
old Chrift, and claim ftill kindnefs to Him, and fay, " O it is fo;
He is not changed, but I am changed."   Nay, it is a part of His
unchangeable love, and an article of the new covenant, to keep you
that ye cannot difpone‡ Him, nor fell Him.   He hath not played
faft and loofe with us in the covenant of grace, fo that we may run
from Him at our pleafure.   His love hath made the bargain furer
than fo; for Jefus, as the cautioner, is bound for us.§   And it can-

---

* Rev. xxii. 1.   † Security.
‡ Difpofe of, make over.   § Heb. vii. 22.

not ftand with His honour to die in the borrows* (as we ufe to fay), and lofe thee, whom He muft render again to the Father when He fhall give up the kingdom to Him. Confent and fay " Amen" to the promifes, and ye have fealed that God is true, and Chrift is yours. This is an eafy market. Ye but look on with faith; for Chrift fuffered all, and paid all.

Madam, fearing I be tedious to your Ladyfhip, I muft ftop here, defiring always to hear that your Ladyfhip is well, and that ye have ftill your face up the mountain. Pray for us, Madam, and for Zion, whereof ye are a part. We expect a trial. God's wheat in this land muft go through Satan's sieve, but their faith fhall not fail. I am ftill wreftling in our Lord's work, and have been tried and tempted with brethren who look awry to the Gofpel. Now He that is able to keep you unto that day preferve your foul, body, and fpirit, and prefent you before His face with His own Bride, fpotlefs and blamelefs.

Your Ladyfhip to be commanded always in the Lord Jefus.

S. R.

ANWOTH, *Nov.* 26, 1631.

------------◆------------

XX.—*To my* LADY KENMURE.

(ASSURANCE OF CHRIST'S LOVE UNDER TRIALS—FULNESS OF CHRIST—HOPE OF GLORY.)

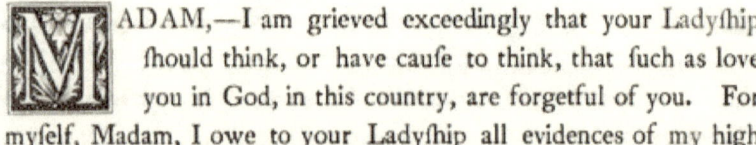ADAM,—I am grieved exceedingly that your Ladyfhip fhould think, or have caufe to think, that fuch as love you in God, in this country, are forgetful of you. For myfelf, Madam, I owe to your Ladyfhip all evidences of my high refpect (in the fight of my Lord, whofe truth I preach, I am bold to fay it) for His rich grace in you.

My Communion, put off till the end of a longfome and rainy

---

* Fail, when He has become fecurity. *Borrow* is " pledge."

harveft, and the prefbyterial exercife (as the bearer can inform your Ladyfhip), hindered me to fee you. And for my people's fake (finding them like hot iron, that cooleth being out of the fire, and that is pliable to no work), I do not ftir abroad ; neither have I left them at all, fince your Ladyfhip was in this country, fave at one time only, about two years ago. Yet I dare not fay but it is a fault, howbeit no defeét in my affeétion ; and I truft to make it up again, fo foon as poffibly I am able to wait upon you.

Madam, I have no new purpofe to write unto you, but of that which I think (nay, which our Lord thinketh) needful, that one thing, Mary's good part, which ye have chofen.* Madam, all that God hath, both Himfelf and the creatures, He is dealing and parting amongft the fons of Adam. There are none fo poor as that they can fay in His face, " He hath given them nothing." But there is no fmall odds betwixt the gifts given to lawful bairns,† and to baftards ; and the more greedy ye are in fuiting,‡ the more willing He is to give, delighting to be called open-handed. I hope your Ladyfhip laboureth to get affurance of the fureft patrimony, even God Himfelf. Ye will find in Chriftianity, that God aimeth, in all His dealings with His children, to bring them to a high contempt of, and deadly feud with the world, and to fet an high price upon Chrift, and to think Him One who cannot be bought for gold, and well worthy the fighting for. And for no other caufe, Madam, doth the Lord withdraw from you the childifh toys and the earthly delights that He giveth unto others, but that He may have you wholly to Himfelf. Think therefore of the Lord, as of one who cometh to woo you in marriage, when ye are in the furnace. He feeketh His anfwer of you in affliétion, to fee if ye will fay, Even fo I take Him. Madam, give Him this anfwer pleafantly, and in your mind do not fecretly grudge nor murmur. When He is ftriking you in love, beware to ftrike again : that is dangerous ; for thofe who ftrike again fhall get the laft blow.

If I hit not upon the right ftring, it is becaufe I am not ac-

---

* Luke x. 42.　　　　　† Children.　　　　　‡ Soliciting.

quainted with your Ladyſhip's preſent condition ; but I believe your
Ladyſhip goeth on foot, laughing, and putting on a good countenance before the world, and yet ye carry heavineſs about with you.
Ye do well, Madam, not to make them witneſſes of your grief, who
cannot be curers of it.   But be exceedingly charitable of your dear
Lord.   As there be ſome friends worldly of whom ye will not
entertain an ill thought, far more ought ye to believe good evermore
of your dear friend, that lovely fair perſon, Jeſus Chriſt.   The
thorn is one of the moſt curſed, and angry, and crabbed weeds that
the earth yieldeth, and yet out of it ſpringeth the roſe, one of the
ſweeteſt-ſmelled flowers, and moſt delightful to the eye, that the
earth hath.   Your Lord ſhall make joy and gladneſs out of your
afflictions ; for all His roſes have a fragrant ſmell.   Wait for the
time when His own holy hand ſhall hold them to your noſe ; and
if ye would have preſent comfort under the croſs, be much in prayer,
for at that time your faith kiſſeth Chriſt, and He kiſſeth the ſoul.
And oh ! if the breath of His holy mouth be ſweet, I dare be
caution,* out of ſome ſmall experience, that ye ſhall not be beguiled ;
for the world (yea, not a few number of God's children) know
not well what that is which they call a Godhead.   But, Madam,
come near to the Godhead, and look down to the bottom of the
well ; there is much in Him, and ſweet were that death to drown
in ſuch a well.   Your grief taketh liberty to work upon your mind,
when ye are not buſied in the meditation of the ever-delighting
and all-bleſſed Godhead.   If ye would lay the price ye give out
(which is but ſome few years pain and trouble) beſide the commodities ye are to receive, ye would ſee they are not worthy to be laid
in the balance together : but it is nature that maketh you look what
ye give out, and weakneſs of faith that hindereth you to ſee what
ye ſhall take in.   Amend your hope, and friſt† your faithful Lord
awhile.   He maketh Himſelf your debtor in the new covenant.   He
is honeſt ; take His word : " Affliction ſhall not ſpring up the
ſecond time."‡   " He that overcometh ſhall inherit all things."§

---

* Security.   † Put off your demand.   ‡ Nahum i. 9.   § Rev. xxi. 7.

Of all things, then, which ye want in this life, Madam, I am able to fay nothing, if that be not believed which ye have in Rev. iii. 5, 21 : " The overcomer fhall be clothed in white raiment. To the overcomer I will give to fit with Me in My throne, as I overcame, and am fet down with My Father in His throne." Confider, Madam, if ye are not high up now, and far ben* in the palace of our Lord, when ye are upon a throne in white raiment, at lovely Chrift's elbow. O thrice fools are we, who, like new-born princes weeping in the cradle, know not that there is a kingdom before them ! Then let our Lord's fweet hand fquare us and hammer us, and ftrike off the knots of pride, felf-love, and world-worfhip, and infidelity, that He may make us ftones and pillars in His Father's houfe.† Madam, what think ye to take binding‡ with the fair corner-ftone Jefus? The Lord give you wifdom to believe and hope your day is coming. I hope to be witnefs of your joy, as I have been a hearer and be-holder of your grief. Think ye much to follow the heir of the crown, who had experience of forrows, and was acquainted with grief ?§ It were pride to aim to be above the King's Son : it is more than we deferve, that we are equals in glory, in a manner. Now commending you to the deareft grace and mercy of God, I reft Your Ladyfhip's at all obedience in Chrift,

S. R.

Anwoth, *Jan.* 4, 1632.

XXI.—*To my* Lady Kenmure.

(SELF-DENIAL—HOPE OF CHRIST'S COMING—LOVING GOD FOR HIMSELF.)

MADAM,—Underftanding (a little after the writing of my laft letter) of the going of this bearer, I would not omit the opportunity of remembering your Ladyfhip,

---

* Got far into. " Ben" is the inner chamber. † Rev. iii. 12.
‡ To be united to; like " take band" in Let. 18. § Ifa. liii. 3.

ftill harping upon that ftring, which in our whole lifetime is never
too often touched upon, nor is our leffon well enough learned, that
there is a neceffity of advancing in the way to the kingdom of God,
of the contempt of the world, of denying ourfelf and bearing of our
Lord's crofs, which is no lefs needful for us than daily food.   And
among many marks that we are on this journey, and under fail toward heaven, this is one, when the love of God so filleth our hearts,
that we forget to love, and care not much for the having, or wanting of, other things ; as one extreme heat burneth out another.   By
this, Madam, ye know, ye have betrothed your foul in marriage to
Chrift, when ye do make but fmall reckoning of all other fuitors
or wooers ; and when ye can (having little in hand, but much in
hope) live as a young heir, during the time of his non-age and
minority, being content to be as hardly handled, and under as precife
a reckoning, as fervants, becaufe his hope is upon the inheritance.
For this caufe God's bairns* take well with fpoiling of their goods,
knowing in themfelves that they have in heaven a better and an
enduring fubftance.†   That day that the earth and the works
therein fhall be burned with fire,‡ your hidden hope and your life
fhall appear.   And therefore, fince ye have not now many years to
your endlefs eternity, and know not how foon the fky above your
head will rive, and the Son of man will be feen in the clouds of
heaven, what better and wifer courfe can ye take, than to think that
your one foot is here, and your other foot in the life to come, and
to leave off loving, defiring, or grieving for the wants that fhall be
made up when your Lord and ye fhall meet, and when ye fhall give
in your bill, that day, of all your wants here ? If your loffes be
not made up, ye have place to challenge the Almighty ; but it fhall
not be fo.   Ye fhall then rejoice with joy unfpeakable and full of
glory, and your joy fhall none take from you.§   It is enough, that
the Lord hath promifed you great things, only let the time of be-
ftowing them be in His own carving.   It is not for us to fet an hour-

---

* Children.   † Heb. x. 34.
‡ 2 Pet. iii. 10.   § 1 Pet i. 8 ; John xvi. 22.

glafs to the Creator of time.   Since He and we differ only in the
term of payment; fince He hath promifed payment, and we believe it,
it is no great matter.   We will put that in His own will, as the frank
buyer, who cometh near to what the feller feeketh, ufeth at laft to
refer the difference to his own will, and fo cutteth off the courfe of
mutual prigging.*   Madam, do not prigg with your frank-hearted
and gracious Lord about the time of the fulfilling of your joys.
It will be ; God hath faid it ; bide His harveft, wait upon His whitfunday.†   His day is better than your day ; He putteth not the
hook‡ in the corn till it be ripe and full-eared.   The great Angel
of the covenant bear you company, till the trumpet fhall found, and
the voice of the Archangel awaken the dead.   Ye fhall find it your
only happinefs, under whatever thing difturbeth and croffeth the
peace of your mind, in this life, to love nothing for itfelf, but only
God for Himfelf.   It is the crooked love of fome harlots, that they
love bracelets, ear-rings, and rings better than the lover that fendeth
them.   God will not fo be loved ; for that were to behave as
harlots, and not as the chafte fpoufe, to abate from our love when
thefe things are pulled away.   Our love to Him fhould begin on
earth, as it fhall be in heaven ; for the bride taketh not, by a thoufand
degrees, fo much delight in her wedding garment as fhe doth in her
bridegroom ; fo we, in the life to come, howbeit clothed with glory
as with a robe, fhall not be fo much affected with the glory that
goeth about us, as with the bridegroom's joyful face and prefence.
Madam, if ye can win§ to this here, the field is won ; and your mind,
for anything ye want, or for anything your Lord can take from
you, fhall foon be calmed and quieted.   Get Himfelf as a pawn,
and keep Him, till your dear Lord come and loofe the pawn, and
rue‖ upon you, and give you all again that He took from you, even
a thoufand talents for one penny.   It is not ill to lend God willingly,
who otherwife both will and may take from you againft your will.

---

* Higgling, chaffering.   † His term-day.
‡ His fickle.   In a fermon preached at Kirkmabreck, 1630, he fpeaks of
" Mowers with the fcythe and hook."
§ Get to.   ‖ Take pity upon.

It is good to play the usurer with Him, and take in, instead of ten of the hundred, an hundred of ten, often an hundred of one.

Madam, fearing to be tedious to you, I break off here, commending you (as I trust to do while I live), your person, ways, burdens, and all that concerneth you, to that Almighty who is able to bear you and your burdens. I still remember you to Him, who will cause you one day to laugh. I expect that, whatever ye can do, by word or deed, for the Lord's friendless Sion, ye will do it. She is your mother ; forget her not ; for the Lord intendeth to melt and try this land, and it is high time we were all upon our feet, and falling* about to try what claim we have to Christ. It is like the bridegroom will be taken from us, and then we shall mourn. Dear Jesus, remove not, else take us with Thee. Grace, grace be with you for ever. Your Ladyship at all dutiful obedience,

S. R.

Anwoth, 14*th Jan.* 1632.

———◆———

XXII.—To John Kennedy.†

(DELIVERANCE FROM SHIPWRECK—RECOVERY FROM THREAT-
ENED DEATH—USE OF TRIALS—REMEMBRANCE OF FRIENDS.)

Y LOVING AND MOST AFFECTIONATE BROTHER IN CHRIST,—I salute you with grace, mercy, and peace, from God our Father, and from our Lord Jesus Christ.

I promised to write to you, and although late enough, yet I now make it good. I heard with grief of your great danger of perishing by the sea, and of your merciful deliverance, with joy. Sure I am, brother, that Satan will leave no stone unrolled, as the proverb is, to roll you off your Rock, or at least to shake and unsettle you : for at that same time the mouths of wicked men were opened in hard speeches against you, by land, and the prince of the

---

* Searching about.   † See Let. 75.

power of the air was angry with you by fea. See then how much ye are obliged to that malicious murderer, who would beat you with two rods at one time ; but, bleffed be God, his arm is fhort ; if the fea and wind would have obeyed him, ye had never come to land. Thank your God, who faith, " I have the keys of hell and of death ;"* " I kill, and I make alive ;"† " The Lord bringeth down to the grave, and bringeth up."‡ If Satan were jailor, and had the keys of death and of the grave, they fhould be ftored with more prifoners. Ye were knocking at thefe black gates, and ye found the doors fhut ; and we do all welcome you back again.

I truft that ye know that it is not for nothing that ye are fent to us again. The Lord knew that ye had forgotten fomething that was neceffary for your journey ; that your armour was not as yet thick enough againft the ftroke of death. Now, in the ftrength of Jefus defpatch your bufinefs ; that debt is not forgiven, but frifted :§ death hath not bidden you farewell, but hath only left you for a fhort feafon. End your journey ere the night come upon you. Have all in readinefs againft the time that ye muft fail through that black and impetuous Jordan ; and Jefus, Jefus, who knoweth both thofe depths and the rocks, and all the coafts, be your pilot. The laft tide will not wait you for one moment. If ye forget anything, when your fea is full, and your foot in that fhip, there is no returning again to fetch it. What ye do amifs in your life to-day, ye may amend it to-morrow ; for as many funs as God maketh to arife upon you, ye have as many new lives ; but ye can die but once, and if ye mar, or fpill‖ that bufinefs, ye cannot come back to mend that piece of work again. No man finneth twice in dying ill ; as we die but once, fo we die but ill or well once. You fee how the number of your months is written in God's book ; and as one of the Lord's hirelings, ye muft work till the fhadow of the evening come upon you, and ye fhall run out your glafs even to the laft pickle¶ of fand. Fulfil your courfe with joy, for we take nothing

---

* Rev. i. 18.　　　　† Deut. xxxii. 39.　　　　‡ 1 Sam. ii. 6.
§ The payment put off.　　‖ Spoil or deftroy.　　　¶ Grain.

to the grave with us, but a good or evil confcience.　And, although the fky clear after this ftorm, yet clouds will engender another.

Ye contracted with Chrift, I hope, when firft ye began to follow Him, that ye would bear His crofs.　Fulfil your part of the contract with patience, and break not to Jefus Chrift.　Be honeft, brother, in your bargaining with Him; for who knoweth better how to bring up children than our God?　For (to lay afide His knowledge, of the which there is no finding out) He hath been practifed in bringing up His heirs thefe five thoufand years; and His bairns are all well brought up, and many of them are honeft men now at home, up in their own houfe in heaven, and are entered heirs to their Father's inheritance.　Now, the form of His bringing up was by chaftifements, fcourging, correcting, nurturing; and fee if He maketh exception of any of His bairns:* no, His eldeft Son and His Heir, Jefus, is not excepted.†　Suffer we muft; ere we were born, God decreed it; and it is eafier to complain of His decree than to change it.　It is true, terrors of confcience caft us down; and yet without terrors of confcience we cannot be raifed up again: fears and doubtings fhake us; and yet without fears and doubtings we would foon fleep, and lofe our grips‡ of Chrift. Tribulation and temptations will almoft loofen us to the root; and yet, without tribulations and temptations, we can now no more grow than herbs or corn without rain.　Sin, and Satan, and the world will fay, and cry in our ear, that we have a hard reckoning to make in judgment; and yet none of thefe three, except they lie, dare fay in our face that our fin can change the tenor of the new covenant.　Forward, then, dear brother, and lofe not your grips. Hold faft the truth: for the world, fell not one dram-weight of God's truth, efpecially now, when moft men meafure truth by time, like young feamen fetting their compafs by a cloud; for now time is father and mother to truth, in the thoughts and practices of our evil time.　The God of truth eftablifh us; for, alas! now there are none to comfort the prifoners of hope, and the mourners in

---

* Rev. iii. 19; Heb. xii. 7, 8.　† Heb. ii. 10.　‡ Grafp, firm hold.

Zion. We can do little, except pray and mourn for Jofeph in the ftocks. And let their tongue cleave to the roof of their mouth who forget Jerufalem now in her day; and the Lord remember Edom, and render to him as he hath done to us.

Now, brother, I fhall not weary you; but I entreat you to remember my deareft love to Mr David Dickfon, with whom I have fmall acquaintance; yet, I blefs the Lord, I know that he both prayeth and doeth for our dying kirk. Remember my deareft love to John Stuart, whom I love in Chrift; and fhow him from me, that I do always remember him, and hope for a meeting. The Lord Jefus eftablifh him more and more, though he be already a ftrong man in Chrift. Remember my heartieft affection in Chrift to William Rodger,* whom I alfo remember to God. I wifh that the firft news I hear of him and you, and all that love our common Saviour in thofe bounds, may be, that they are fo knit and linked, and kindly faftened in love with the Son of God, that ye may fay, "Now if ye would ever fo fain efcape out of Chrift's hands, yet love hath fo bound us, that we cannot get our hands free again; He hath fo ravifhed our hearts, that there is no loofening of His grips; the chains of His foul-ravifhing love are fo ftrong, that neither the grave nor death will break them." I hope, brother, yea, I doubt not of it, that ye lay me, and my firft entry to the Lord's vineyard, and my flock, before Him who hath put me into His work. As the Lord knoweth, fince firft I faw you, I have been mindful of you. Marion M'Naught doth remember moft heartily her love to you, and to John Stuart.† Bleffed be the Lord! that in God's mercy I found in this country fuch a woman, to whom Jefus is dearer than her own heart, when there be fo many that caft Chrift over their fhoulder. Good brother, call to mind the memory of your worthy father, now afleep in Chrift; and, as his cuftom was, pray continually, and wreftle, for the life of a

---

* Livingftone in his " Memor. Characteriftics" inferts, this godly man, a merchant in Ayr, after being for a time at Coleraine, in Ireland.

† See Let. 161, addreffed to him.

dying, breathlefs kirk. And defire John Stuart not to forget poor Zion; fhe hath few friends, and few to fpeak one good word for her.

Now I commend you, your whole foul, and body, and fpirit, to Jefus Chrift and His keeping, hoping that ye will live and die, ftand and fall, with the caufe of our Mafter, Jefus. The Lord Jefus Himfelf be with your fpirit.

Your loving brother in our Lord Jefus,

S. R.

ANWOTH, *Feb.* 2, 1632.

XXIII.—*To my* LADY KENMURE.

(EXHORTING TO REMEMBER HER ESPOUSAL TO CHRIST—TRI-BULATION A PREPARATION FOR THE KINGDOM—GLORY IN THE END.)

ADAM,—Your Ladyfhip will not (I know) weary nor offend, though I trouble you with many letters. The memory of what obligations I am under to your Lady-fhip, is the caufe of it.

I am poffibly impertinent in what I write, becaufe of my igno-rance of your prefent eftate; but for all that is faid, I have learned of Mr W. D.* that ye have not changed upon, nor wearied of your fweet Mafter, Chrift, and His fervice; neither were it your part to change upon Him who "refteth in His love." Ye are among honourable company, and fuch as affect grandeur and court. But, Madam, thinking upon your eftate, I think I fee an improvident wooer coming too late to feek a bride, becaufe fhe is contracted already, and promifed away to another; and fo the wooer's bufk-ing† and bravery (who cometh to you‡ as "who but he?") are in vain. The outward pomp of this bufy wooer, a beguiling world, is now coming in to fuit§ your foul too late, when ye have pro-

---

* Mr William Dalgleifh, minifter at Kirkmabreck.

† Decking, adorning.   ‡ A proverbial expreffion, as in Herkat's Poem, 84.

" Then came brave Glory paffing by,
With filks that whiftled, Who but he."

§ To woo.

mifed away your foul to Chrift many years ago. And I know, Madam, what anfwer ye may now juftly make to the late fuitor ; even this : " Ye are too long of coming ; my foul, the bride, is away already, and the contract with Chrift fubfcribed, and I cannot choofe, but I muft be honeft and faithful to Him." Honourable lady, keep your firft love, and hold the firft match with that foul-delighting, lovely Bridegroom, our fweet, fweet Jefus, fairer than all the children of men, " the Rofe of Sharon," and the faireft and fweeteft-fmelled rofe in all His Father's garden. There is none like Him ; I would not exchange one fmile of His lovely face with kingdoms. Madam, let others take their filly, fecklefs* heaven in this life. Envy them not ; but let your foul, like a tarrowing† and miflearned child, take the dorts‡ (as we ufe to fpeak), or caft at§ all things and difdain them, except one only : either Chrift or nothing. Your well-beloved, Jefus, will be content that ye be here devoutly proud, and ill to pleafe, as one that contemneth all hufbands but Himfelf. Either the King's Son, or no hufband at all ; this is humble, and worthy ambition. What have ye to do to dally with a whorifh and foolifh world ? Your jealous Hufband will not be content that ye look by ‖ Him to another : He will be jealous indeed, and offended, if ye kifs another but Himfelf. What weights do burden you, Madam, I know not ; but think it great mercy that your Lord from your youth hath been hedging in your outftraying affections, that they may not go a-whoring from Himfelf. If ye were His baftard, He would not nurture you fo. If ye were for the flaughter, ye would be fattened. But be content ; ye are His wheat, growing in our Lord's field ;¶ and if wheat, ye muft go under our Lord's threfhing-inftrument, in His barn-floor, and through His fieve,** and through His mill to be bruifed (as the Prince of your falvation, Jefus, was††), that ye may be found good bread in your Lord's houfe. Lord Jefus, blefs the fpiritual

---

* Pithlefs, worthlefs.   † Pettifh.   ‡ Get fulky.
§ Quarrel with, object to.   ‖ Paft.   ¶ Matt. xiii. 25, 38.
** Amos ix. 9.   †† Ifa. liii. 10.

hufbandry, and feparate you from the chaff, that dow not bide*
the wind.　I am perfuaded your glafs is fpending itfelf by little and
little ; and if ye knew who is before you, ye would rejoice in your
tribulations.　Think ye it a fmall honour to ftand before the throne
of God and the Lamb ? and to be clothed in white, and to be
called to the marriage fupper of the Lamb? and to be led to the
fountain of living waters, and to come to the Well-head, even God
Himfelf, and get your fill of the clear, cold, fweet, refrefhing water
of life, the King's own well ? and to put up your own finful hand
to the tree of life, and take down and eat the fweeteft apple in all
God's heavenly paradife, Jefus Chrift, your life and your Lord?
Up your heart! fhout for joy!　Your King is coming to fetch you
to His Father's houfe.

　　Madam, I am in exceeding great heavinefs, God thinking it beft
for my own foul thus to exercife me, thereby, it may be, to fit me
to be His mouth to others.　I fee and hear, at home and abroad,
nothing but matter of grief and difcouragement, which indeed
maketh my life bitter.　And I hope in God never to get my will
in this world.　And I expect ere long a fiery trial upon the Church ;
for as many men almoft in England and Scotland, as many falfe
friends to Chrift, and as many pulling and drawing to pull the
crown off His holy head ! and for fear that our Beloved ftay
amongft us (as if His room were more defirable than Himfelf),
men are bidding Him go feek His lodging.　Madam, if ye have
a part in filly, friendlefs Zion (as I know ye have), fpeak a word
on her behalf to God and man.　If ye can do nothing elfe, fpeak
for Jefus, and ye fhall thereby be a witnefs againft this declining age.
Now, from my very foul, laying and leaving you on the Lord, and
defiring a part in your prayers (as, my Lord knoweth, I remember
you), I deliver over your body, fpirit, and all your neceffities, to
the hands of our Lord, and remain for ever

　　　　Your Ladyfhip's in your fweet Lord Jefus and mine,

　　　　　　　　　　　　　　　　　　　　　　　S. R.

ANWOTH, *Feb.* 13, 1632.

----

* Cannot ftand.

(CHRIST AND HIS GARDEN—PROVISION OF ORDINANCES IN THE CHURCH—OUR CHILDREN.)

BELOVED MISTRESS,—My dearest love in Christ remembered to you. Know that Mr Abraham* showed me there is to be a meeting of the bishops at Edinburgh shortly. The caufes are known to themfelves. It is our part to hold up our hands for Zion. Howbeit, it is reported, they came fad from court. It is our Lord's wifdom, that His kirk fhould ever hang by a thread; and yet the thread breaketh not, being hanged upon Him who is the fure Nail in David's houfe,† upon whom all the veffels, great and fmall, do hang; and the Nail (God be thanked) neither crooketh nor can be broken. Jefus, that Flower of Jeffe fet without hands, getteth many a blaft, and yet withers not, because He is His Father's noble Rofe, cafting a fweet fmell through heaven and earth, and muft grow; and in the fame garden grow the faints, God's fair and beautiful lilies, under wind and rain, and all fun-burned, and yet life remaineth at the root. Keep within His garden, and you fhall grow with them, till the Great Hufbandman, our dear Mafter Gardener, come and tranfplant you from the lower part of His vineyard up to the higher, to the very heart of His garden, above the wrongs of the rain, fun, or wind. And then, wait upon the times of the blowing of the fweet fouth and north wind of His gracious Spirit, that may make you caft a fweet fmell in your Beloved's noftrils; and bid your Beloved come down to His garden, and eat of His pleafant fruits.‡ And He will come. You will get no more but this until you come up to the Well-head,

---

* Poffibly, this is Mr Abraham Henderfon, a ftaunch defender of Presbytery, who in 1605, prefifted, along with eight of his brethren, in convening at Aberdeen, in face of prohibition, in order to maintain a proteft in behalf of the Church's inherent right to meet in General Affembly. (See Forbes' Apolog. Narration,) p. 136.

† Ifa. xxii. 23.   ‡ Cant. iv. 16.

where you shall put up your hand and take down the apples of the tree of life, and eat under the shadow of that tree. These apples are sweeter up beside the tree than they are down here in this piece of a clay prison-house. I have no joy but in the thoughts of these times. Doubt not of your Lord's part and the spouse's part; she shall be in good case. That word shall stand, "I shall be as the dew to Israel: he shall grow up as the lily, and cast out his roots as Lebanon. His branches shall spread, his beauty shall be as the olive-tree, and his smell as Lebanon."* Christ shall set up His colours, and His ensign for the nations, and shall gather together the outcasts of Israel.† "Then the Lord said to me, Son of man, these dead bones are the whole house of Israel: behold, they say, Our bones are dried, our hope is lost; we are cut off for our parts. Therefore prophesy unto them, and say, Thus saith the Lord God, Behold, O My people, I will open your graves, and cause you come up out of your graves, and bring you into the land of Israel."‡ These promises are not wind, but the breast of our beloved Christ, which we must suck and draw comfort out of. Ye have cause to pity those poor creatures that stand out against Christ, and the building of His house. Silly men! they have but a feckless§ and silly heaven, nothing but meat and cloth, and laugh a day or two in the world, and then in a moment go down to the grave; and they shall not be able to hinder Christ's building. He that is Master of work will lead stones‖ to the wall over their belly.

And for that present tumult that the children of this world raise anent the planting of your town with a pastor, believe and stay upon God, as you still shame us all in believing. Go forward in the strength of the Lord; and I say from my Lord, before whom I stand, have your eyes upon none but the Lord of armies, and the Lord shall either let you see what you long to see, or then else fulfil your joy more abundantly another way. You and yours, and the

---

* Hos. xiv. 5, 6.　　　† Isa. xi. 12.　　　‡ Ezek. xxxvii. 11, 12.
§ No substance, or pith, in it, worthless.
‖ Carry (or cause to be carried) the stones for building His house.

children of God whom you care for in this town, fhall have as much
of the Son of God's fupper cut and laid upon your trenchers, be
who he will that carveth, as fhall feed you to eternal life.   And be
not caft down for all that is done : your reward is laid up with
God.   I hope to fee you laugh and leap for joy.   Will the temple
be built without din and tumult ?   No; God's ftones in His houfe
in Germany are laid with blood; and the Son of God no fooner
begins to chop and hew ftones with His hammer, but as foon the
fword is drawn.   If the work were of men, the world would fet
their fhoulders to yours; but, in Chrift's work, two or three muft
fight againft a Prefbytery (though His own court) and a city.   This
proveth that it is Chrift's errand, and therefore that it fhall thrive.
Let them lay iron chains crofs over the door,—ftay, and believe,
and wait, whill* the Lion of the tribe of Judah come.   And He
that comes from heaven clothed with the rainbow, and hath the
little book in His hand, when He taketh a grip† of their chains,
He will lay the door on the broadfide,‡ and come in, and go up to
the pulpit, and take the man with Him whom He hath chofen for
His work.   Therefore, let me hear from you, whether you be in
heavinefs, or rejoicing under hope, that I may take part of your
grief, and bear it with you, and get part of your joy, which is to
me alfo as my own joy.

　　And as to what are your fears anent the health or life of your
dear children, lay it upon Chrift's fhoulders : let Him bear all.
Loofe your grips† of them all; and when your dear Lord pulleth,
let them go with faith and joy.   It is a tried faith to kifs a Lord
that is taking from you.   Let them be careful, during the fhort time
that they are here, to run and get a grip of the prize.   Chrift is
ftanding in the end of their way, holding up the garland of endlefs
glory to their eyes, and is crying, " Run faft, and come and receive."
Happy are they (if their breath ferve them) to run and not to weary,
whill* their Lord, with His own dear hand, puts the crown upon
their head.   It is not long days, but good days, that make life glo-

---

* Till.　　　　　　† A firm hold.　　　　　　‡ Lay it flat.

rious and happy; and our dear Lord is gracious to us, who ſhort-
eneth and hath made the way to glory ſhorter than it was, ſo that
the crown that Noah did fight for five hundred years, children may
now obtain it in fifteen years.   And heaven is in ſome ſort better for
us now than it was to Noah, for the man Chriſt is there now,
who was not come in the fleſh in Noah's days.   You ſhall ſhow
this to your children, whom my ſoul in Chriſt bleſſeth, and entreat
them by the mercies of God, and the bowels of Jeſus Chriſt, to
covenant with Jeſus Chriſt to be His, and to make up the bond of
friendſhip betwixt their ſouls and their Chriſt, that they may have
acquaintance in heaven, and a friend at God's right hand.   Such a
friend at court is much worth.

 Now I take my leave of you, praying my Chriſt and your Chriſt
to fulfil your joy; and more graces and bleſſings from our ſweet
Lord Jeſus to your ſoul, your huſband's and children, than ever I
wrote of the letters of A, B, C, to you.   Grace, grace be with you.
   Yours in my ſweet Maſter, Jeſus Chriſt,

             S. R.

ANWOTH, *March* 9, 1632.

XXV.—*To a Gentlewoman at Kirkcudbright, excuſing himſelf from
viſiting.*

ISTRESS,—I beſeech you to have me excuſed if the daily
employments of my calling ſhall hinder me to ſee you
according as I would wiſh; for I dare not go abroad,
ſince many of my people are ſick, and the time of our Communion*
draweth near.   But frequent the company of your worthy and
honeſt-hearted paſtor, Mr Robert (Glendinning), to whom the
Lord hath given the tongue of the learned, to miniſter a word in
ſeaſon to the weary.   Remember me to him and to your huſband.
The Lord Jeſus be with your ſpirit.

   Your affectionate friend,

             S. R.

---

* The diſpenſing of the Lord's Supper.

(USE OF SICKNESS—REPROACHES—CHRIST OUR ETERNAL FEAST—FASTING.)

DEARLY BELOVED MISTRESS,—My love in Chrift remembered. You are not ignorant what our Lord in His love-vifitation hath been doing with your foul, even letting you fee a little fight of that dark trance* you muft go through ere you come to glory. Your life hath been near the grave, and you were at the door, and you found the door fhut and faft: your dear Chrift thinking it not time to open thefe gates to you till you have fought fome longer in His camp. And therefore He willeth you to put on your armour again, and to take no truce with the devil or this prefent world. You are little obliged to any of the two; but I rejoice in this, that when any of the two comes to fuit† your foul in marriage, you have an anfwer in readinefs to tell them,—"You are too long a-coming; I have many a year fince promifed my foul to another, even to my deareft Lord Jefus, to whom I muft be true." And therefore you are come back to us again to help us to pray for Chrift's fair bride, a marrow‡ dear to Him.

Be not caft down in heart to hear that the world barketh at Chrift's ftrangers, both in Ireland and in this land; they do it becaufe their Lord hath chofen them out of this world. And this is one of our Lord's reproaches, to be hated and ill-entreated by men. The filly ftranger, in an uncouth§ country, muft take with a fmoky inn and coarfe cheer, a hard bed, and a barking, ill-tongued hoft. It is not long to the day, and he will to his journey upon the morrow, and leave them all. Indeed, our fair morning is at hand, the day-ftar is near the rifing, and we are not many miles from home. What matters ill entertainment in the fmoky inns of this

---

* Paffage.   † Woo in marriage.   ‡ Companion.

§ *Unco*, in other editions; *i.e.*, ftrange. In his fermons, it is generally written "uncouth." Thus, "ftrange and uncouth to fee!" (On Zech. xi. 9.)

miferable life? We are not to ftay here, and we will be dearly
welcome to Him whom we go to. And I hope, when I fhall fee
you clothed in white raiment, wafhed in the blood of the Lamb,
and fhall fee you even at the elbow of your deareft Lord and Redeemer, and a crown upon your head, and following our Lamb and
lovely Lord whitherfoever He goeth,—you will think nothing of
all thefe days; and you fhall then rejoice, and no man fhall take
your joy from you. It is certain there is not much fand to run in
your Lord's fand-glafs, and that day is at hand; and till then your
Lord in this life is giving you fome little feafts.

It is true, you fee Him not now as you fhall fee Him then.
Your well-beloved ftandeth now behind the wall looking out at the
window,* and you fee but a little of His face. Then, you fhall fee
all His face and all the Saviour,—a long, and high, and broad Lord
Jefus, the lovelieft perfon among the children of men. O joy of
joys, that our fouls know there is fuch a great fupper preparing for
us even! Howbeit we be but half-hungered† of Chrift here, and
many a time dine behind noon,‡ yet the fupper of the Lamb will
come in time, and will be fet before us before we famifh and lofe our
ftomachs. You have caufe to hold up your heart in remembrance
and hope of that fair, long fummer day; for in this night of your
life, wherein you are in the body abfent from the Lord, Chrift's fair
moonlight in His word and facraments, in prayer, feeling, and holy
conference, hath fhined upon you, to let you fee the way to the
city. I confefs our diet here is but fparing; we get but taftings of
our Lord's comforts; but the caufe of that is not becaufe our
Steward, Jefus, is a niggard, and narrow-hearted, but becaufe our
ftomachs are weak, and we are narrow-hearted. But the great
feaft is coming, and the chambers of them made fair and wide to
take in the great Lord Jefus. Come in, then, Lord Jefus, to hungry
fouls gaping for thee! In this journey take the Bridegroom as you
may have Him, and be greedy of His fmalleft crumbs; but, dear

---

* Cant. ii. 9.   † Only half fed with.
‡ *Noon*, or a little before it, was then the ufual hour for dinner.

Miſtreſs, buy none of Chriſt's delicates-ſpiritual with ſin, or faſting againſt your weak body. Remember you are in the body, and it is the lodging-houſe; and you may not, without offending the Lord, ſuffer the old walls of that houſe to fall down through want of neceſſary food. Your body is the dwelling-houſe of the Spirit; and therefore, for the love you carry to the ſweet Gueſt, give a due regard to His houſe of clay. When He looſeth the wall, why not? Welcome Lord Jeſus! But it is a fearful ſin in us, by hurting the body by faſting, to looſe one ſtone or the leaſt piece of timber in it; for the houſe is not our own. The Bridegroom is with you yet; ſo faſt as that alſo you may feaſt and rejoice in Him. I think upon your magiſtrates; but He that is clothed in linen, and hath the writer's inkhorn by His ſide, hath written up their names in heaven already. Pray and be content with His will; God hath a council-houſe in heaven, and the end will be mercy unto you. For the planting of your town with a godly miniſter, have your eye upon the Lord of the harveſt. I dare promiſe you, God in this life ſhall fill your ſoul with the fatneſs of His houſe, for your care to ſee Chriſt's bairns fed. And your poſterity ſhall know it, to whom I pray for mercy, and that they may get a name amongſt the living in Jeruſalem; and if God portion them with His bairns, their rent is fair, and I hope it ſhall be ſo. The Lord Jeſus be with your ſpirit.

Yours ever in Chriſt,

S. R.

Anwoth, *Sept.* 19, 1632.

XXVII.—*To my* Lady Kenmure.

(LOVE TO CHRIST AND SUBMISSION TO HIS CROSS—BELIEVERS KEPT—THE HEAVENLY PARADISE.)

 ADAM,—Having ſaluted you with grace and mercy from God our Father, and from our Lord Jeſus Chriſt, I long both to ſee your Ladyſhip, and to hear how it goeth with you.

I do remember you, and prefent you and your neceffities to
Him who is able to keep you, and prefent you blamelefs before His
face with joy; and my prayer to our Lord is, that ye may be fick
of love for Him, who died of love for you,—I mean your Saviour
Jefus.   And O fweet were that ficknefs to be foul-fick for Him!
And a living death it were, to die in the fire of the love of that foul-
lover, Jefus!   And, Madam, if ye love Him, ye will keep His com-
mandments; and this is not one of the leaft, to lay your neck
cheerfully and willingly under the yoke of Jefus Chrift.   For I
truft your Ladyfhip did firft contract and bargain with the Son of
God to follow Him upon thefe terms, that by His grace ye fhould
endure hardfhip, and fuffer affliction, as the foldier of Chrift.   They
are not worthy of Jefus who will not take a blow for their Mafter's
fake.   As for our glorious Peace-maker, when He came to make
up the friendfhip betwixt God and us, God bruifed Him, and
ftruck Him; the finful world alfo did beat Him, and crucify Him;
yet He took buffets of both parties, and (honour to our Lord Jefus!)
He would not leave the field for all that, till He had made peace betwixt the parties.   I perfuade myfelf your fufferings are but like
your Saviour's (yea, incomparably lefs and lighter), which are
called but a bruifing of His heel;* a wound far from the heart.
Your life is hid with Chrift in God,† and therefore ye cannot be
robbed of it.   Our Lord handleth us, as fathers do their young
children; they lay up jewels in a place, above the reach of the
fhort arm of bairns, elfe bairns would put up their hands and take
them down, and lofe them foon: fo hath our Lord done with our
fpiritual life.   Jefus Chrift is the high coffer in the which our Lord
hath hid our life; we children are not able to reach up our arm fo
high as to take down that life and lofe it; it is in our Chrift's hand.
O long, long may Jefus be Lord Keeper of our life! and happy are
they that can, with the Apoftle,‡ lay their foul in pawn in the
hand of Jefus, for He is able to keep that which is committed in
pawn to Him againft that day.   Then, Madam, fo long as this life

---

* Gen. iii. 15.   † Col. iii. 3.   ‡ 2 Tim. i. 12.

is not hurt, all other troubles are but touches in the heel. I truft
ye will foon be cured.   Ye know, Madam, kings have fome fervants in their court that receive not prefent wages in their hand, but
live upon their hopes : the King of kings alfo hath fervants in His
court that for the prefent get little or nothing but the heavy crofs of
Chrift, troubles without and terrors within; but they live upon
hope; and when it cometh to the parting of the inheritance, they
remain in the houfe as heirs.   It is better to be fo than to get prefent payment, and a portion in this life, an inheritance in this world
(God forgive me, that I fhould honour it with the name of an inheritance, it is rather a farm-room !*), and then in the end to be
caften out of God's houfe, with this word, " Ye have received
your confolation, ye will get no more."   Alas! what get they?
The rich glutton's heaven.†   O but our Lord maketh it a filly‡
heaven!   " He fared well," faith our Lord, "and delicately every
day."   O no more? a filly heaven!   Truly no more, except that
he was clothed in purple, and that is all.   I perfuade myfelf,
Madam, ye have joy when ye think that your Lord hath dealt
more gracioufly with your foul.   Ye have gotten little in this life,
it is true indeed : ye have then the more to crave, yea, ye have all
to crave ; for, except fome taftings of the firft fruits, and fome kiffes
of His mouth whom your foul loveth, ye get no more.   But I cannot tell you what is to come.   Yet I may fpeak as our Lord doth
of it.   The foundation of the city is pure gold, clear as cryftal; the
twelve ports§ are fet with precious ftones ; if orchards and rivers
commend a foil upon earth, there is a paradife there, wherein groweth the tree of life, that beareth twelve manner of fruits every month,
which is feven fcore and four harvefts in the year ; and there is
there a pure river of water of life, proceeding out of the throne
of God and of the Lamb ; and the city hath no need of the light of
the fun or moon, or of a candle, for the Lord God Almighty and
the Lamb is the light thereof.   Madam, believe and hope for this,
till ye fee and enjoy.   Jefus is faying in the Gofpel, Come and fee ;

---

* Rented room, like a tenant's farm.   † Luke xvi. 25.   ‡ Poor.   § Gates.

and He is come down in the chariot of truth, wherein He rideth through the world, to conquer men's fouls,* and is now in the world faying, "Who will go with Me? will ye go? My Father will make you welcome, and give you houfe-room; for in My Father's houfe are many dwelling-places." Madam, confent to go with Him. Thus I reft, commending you to God's deareft mercy.

Yours in the Lord Jefus,

S. R.

Anwoth.

XXVIII.—*To my* Lady Kenmure, *after the death of a child.*

(THE STATE OF THE CHURCH, CAUSE FOR GOD'S DISPLEASURE— HIS CARE OF HIS CHURCH—THE JEWS—AFFLICTED SAINTS.)

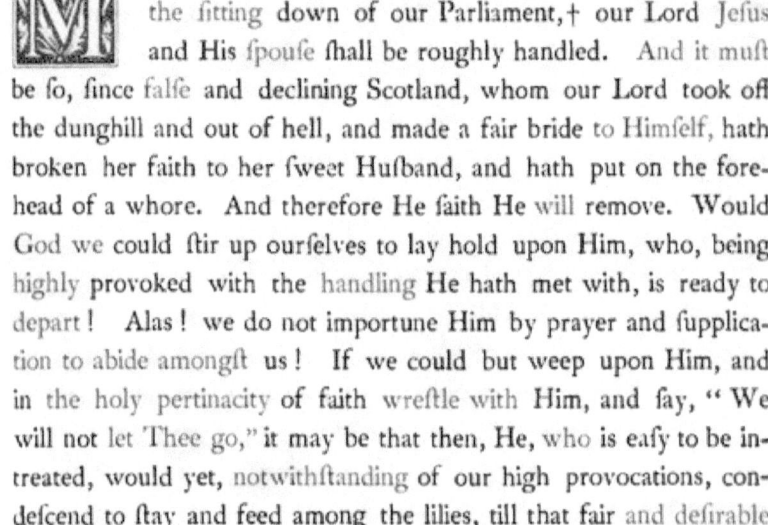

ADAM,—I am afraid now (as many others are) that, at the fitting down of our Parliament,† our Lord Jefus and His fpoufe fhall be roughly handled. And it muft be fo, fince falfe and declining Scotland, whom our Lord took off the dunghill and out of hell, and made a fair bride to Himfelf, hath broken her faith to her fweet Hufband, and hath put on the forehead of a whore. And therefore He faith He will remove. Would God we could ftir up ourfelves to lay hold upon Him, who, being highly provoked with the handling He hath met with, is ready to depart! Alas! we do not importune Him by prayer and fupplication to abide amongft us! If we could but weep upon Him, and in the holy pertinacity of faith wreftle with Him, and fay, " We will not let Thee go," it may be that then, He, who is eafy to be intreated, would yet, notwithftanding of our high provocations, condefcend to ftay and feed among the lilies, till that fair and defirable day break, and the fhadows flee away. Ah! what caufe of mourning is there, when our gold is become dim, and the vifage of our

---

* Ps. xlv. 4.

† The Parliament to be held at Edinburgh on 25th June of this year.

Nazarites, fometime* whiter than fnow, is now become blacker than a coal, and Levi's houfe, once comparable to fine gold, is now changed, and become like veffels in whom He hath no pleafure! Madam, think upon this, that when our Lord, who hath His handkerchief to wipe the face of the mourners in Zion, fhall come to wipe away all tears from their eyes, He may wipe yours alfo, in the paffing, amongft others. I am confident, Madam, that our Lord will yet build a new houfe to Himfelf, of our rejected and fcattered ftones, for our Bridegroom cannot want a wife. Can He live a widower? Nay, He will embrace both us, the little young fifter, and the elder fifter, the Church of the Jews; and there will yet be a day of it. And therefore we have caufe to rejoice, yea, to fing and fhout for joy. The Church hath been, fince the world began, ever hanging by a fmall thread, and all the hands of hell and of the wicked have been drawing at the thread. But, God be thanked, they only break their arms by pulling, but the thread is not broken; for the fweet fingers of Chrift our Lord have fpun and twifted it. Lord, hold the thread whole!

Madam, ftir up your hufband to lay hold upon the covenant, and to do good. What hath he to do with the world? It is not his inheritance. Defire him to make home† over, and put to his hand to lay one ftone or two upon the wall of God's houfe before he go hence. I have heard alfo, Madam, that your child is removed; but to have or want is beft, as He pleafeth. Whether fhe be with you, or in God's keeping, think it all one; nay, think it the better of the two by far that fhe is with Him. I truft in our Lord that there is fomething laid up and kept for you; for our kind Lord, who hath wounded you, will not be fo cruel as not to allay the pain of your green wound; and, therefore, claim Chrift ftill as your own, and own Him as your One thing. So refting, I recommend your Ladyfhip, your foul and fpirit, in pawn to Him who keepeth His Father's pawns, and will make an account of them faithfully, even to that faireft amongft the fons of men, our fweet Lord

---

* Once on a time.   † Homewards.

Jefus, the faireft, the fweeteft, the moft delicious Rofe of all His Father's great field. The fmell of that Rofe perfume your foul!

Your Ladyfhip, in his fweeteft Lord Jefus,

ANWOTH, *April* 1, 1633. S. R.

XXIX.—*For* MARION M'NAUGHT.

(*CHRIST WITH HIS PEOPLE IN THE FURNACE OF AFFLICTION— PRAYER.*)

EAR SISTER,—I longed much to have conferred with you at this time. I am grieved at anything in your houfe that grieveth you; and fhall, by my Lord's grace, fuit* my Lord to help you to bear your burden, and to come in behind you, and give you and your burdens a put† up the mountain. Know you not that Chrift wooeth His wife in the furnace? "Behold, I have refined thee, but not with filver; I have chofen thee in the furnace of affliction."‡ He cafteth His love on you when you are in the furnace of affliction. You might indeed be caften down if He brought you in and left you there; but when He leadeth you through the waters, think ye not that He has a fweet, foft hand? You know His love-grip§ already; you fhall be delivered, wait on. Jefus will make a road, and come and fetch home the captive. You fhall not die in prifon; but your ftrokes are fuch as were your Hufband's, who was wounded in the houfe of His friends. Strokes were not newings‖ to Him, and neither are they to you. But your winter night is near fpent; it is near-hand¶ the dawning. I will fee you leap for joy. The kirk fhall be delivered. This wildernefs fhall bud and grow up like a rofe. Chrift got a charter of Scotland from His Father; and who will bereave Him of His heritage, or put our Redeemer out of His mailing,* until His

---

* Entreat. † Pufh. ‡ Ifa. xlviii. 10.
§ Grafp, or firm hold. ‖ News, or new things. ¶ Nigh.
** *Mailing*, a farm; fo called from *mail*, rent.

tack be run out? I muſt have you praying for me: I am black
ſhamed for evermore now with Chriſt's goodneſs; and in private,
on the 17th and 18th of Auguſt, I got a full anſwer of my Lord
to be a graced miniſter, and a choſen arrow hidden in His own
quiver.   But know this, aſſurance is not keeped but by watching
and prayer; and, therefore, dear miſtreſs, help me.   I have gotten
now (honour to my Lord!) the gate * to open the ſlote,† and ſhut‡
the bar of His door; and I think it eaſy to get anything from the
King by prayer, and to uſe holy violence with Him.   Chriſt was in
Carſphairne § kirk, and opened the people's hearts wonderfully.
Jeſus is looking up that water;‖ and minting¶ to dwell amongſt
them.   I would we could give Him His welcome home to the
moors.   Now peace and grace be upon you and all yours.

Yours in Chriſt,

ANWOTH, *Aug.* 20, 1633.   S. R.

XXX.—*To my* LADY KENMURE.

*(RANK AND PROSPERITY HINDER PROGRESS—WATCHFULNESS
—CASE OF RELATIVES.)*

ADAM,—I determined, and was deſirous alſo, to have
ſeen your ladyſhip, but becauſe of a pain in my arm I
could not.   I know ye will not impute it to any un-
ſuitable forgetfulneſs of your Ladyſhip, from whom, at my firſt
entry to my calling in this country (and ſince alſo), I received ſuch
comfort in my affliction as I truſt in God never to forget, and ſhall

---

* Way.   † Bolt.

‡ Shut, or ſhute, or ſhoot.   Here it is to puſh back the bar ſo as to open
the door.

§ The village and church of *Carſphairn* ſtood not far from Kenmure Caſtle,
and very near Earlſton and Knockgray.   If one travels to it from the ſide of
Dalmellington, the road is ſolitary, dreary, bare, with ſteep, rocky hills on
either ſide of the glen.

‖ That river,—the Ken (?).   ¶ Making as if He would, trying.

labour by His grace to recompenfe in the only way poffible to me ; and that is, by prefenting your foul, perfon, houfe, and all your neceffities, in prayer to Him, whofe I hope you are, and who is able to keep you till that Day of Appearance, and to prefent you before His face with joy.

I am confident your Ladyfhip is going forward in the begun journey to your Lord and Father's home and kingdom. Howbeit ye want not temptations within and without. And who among the faints hath ever taken that caftle without ftroke of fword? the Chief of the houfe, our Elder Brother, our Lord Jefus, not being excepted, who won His own houfe and home, due to Him by birth, with much blood and many blows. Your Ladyfhip hath the more need to look to yourfelf, becaufe our Lord hath placed you higher than the reft, and your way to heaven lieth through a more wild and wafte wildernefs than the way of many of your fellow-travellers,— not only through the midft of this wood of thorns, the cumberfome world, but alfo through thefe dangerous paths, the vain-glory of it ; the confideration whereof hath often moved me to pity your foul, and the foul of your worthy and noble hufband. And it is more to you to win* heaven, being fhips of greater burden, and in the main fea, than for little veffels, that are not fo much in the mercy and reverence† of the ftorms, becaufe they may come quietly to their port by launching alongft the coaft. For the which caufe ye do much, if in the midft of fuch a tumult of bufinefs, and crowd of temptations, ye fhall give Chrift Jefus His own court and His own due place in your foul. I know and am perfuaded, that that lovely One, Jefus, is dearer to you than many kingdoms; and that ye efteem Him your Well-beloved, and the Standard-bearer among ten thoufand.‡ And it becometh Him full well to take the place

---

* Reach.

† "*Reverence*" occurs in Lets. 233 and 298 in the fenfe of " power," and is there fo explained by Jamiefon. It would be *q.d.*, " giving homage to the ftorms." A perfon ufed to fay, " I will not be in your reverence ;" *i.e.*, not fubmit to your dictation.

‡ Cant. v. 10.

and the board-head* in your foul before all the world. I knew and faw Him with you in the furnace of affliction; for there he wooed you to Himfelf, and chofe you to be His; and now He craveth no other hire of you but your love, and that He get no caufe to be jealous of you. And, therefore, dear and worthy lady, be like to the frefh river, that keepeth its own frefh tafte in the falt fea. This world is not worthy of your foul. Give it not a good-day when Chrift cometh in competition with it. Be like one of another country. Home! and ftay not; for the fun is fallen low, and nigh the tops of the mountains, and the fhadows are ftretched out in great length. Linger not by the way. The world and fin would train† you on, and make you turn afide. Leave not the way for them; and the Lord Jefus be at the voyage!

Madam, many eyes are upon you, and many would be glad your Ladyfhip fhould fpill‡ a Chriftian, and mar a good profeffor. Lord Jefus, mar their godlefs defires, and keep the confcience whole without a crack! If there be a hole in it, fo that it take in water at a leak,§ it will with difficulty mend again. It is a dainty, delicate creature, and a rare piece of the workmanfhip of your Maker; and therefore deal gently with it, and keep it entire, that amidft this world's glory your Ladyfhip may learn to entertain Chrift. And whatfoever creature your Ladyfhip findeth not to fmell of Him, may it have no better relifh to you than the white of an egg.

Madam, it is a part of the truth of your profeffion to drop words in the ears of your noble hufband continually, of eternity, judgment, death, hell, heaven, the honourable profeffion, the fins of his father's houfe. He muft reckon with God for his father's debt: forgetting of accounts payeth no debt. Nay, the intereft of a forgotten bond runneth up with God to intereft upon intereft. I knoweth he looketh homeward, and loveth the truth; but I pity him with my foul becaufe of his many temptations. Satan layeth

---

* Head of the dinner-table.　　† Draw, entice; the French "trainer."

‡ Spoil.　　　　　　　　　§ Spelt "leek" in old editions.

upon men a burden of cares above a load,* and maketh a pack-horfe of men's fouls when they are wholly fet upon this world. We owe the devil no fuch fervice. It were wifdom to throw off * that load into a mire, and caft all our cares over upon God.

Madam, think ye have no child. Subfcribe a bond to your Lord that fhe fhall be His if He take her; and thanks, and praife, and glory to His holy name fhall be the intereft for a year's loan of her. Look for croffes, and while it is fair weather mend the fails of the fhip.

Now, hoping your Ladyfhip will pardon my tedioufnefs, I re-commend your foul and perfon to the grace and mercy of our fweet Lord Jefus, in whom I am,

   Your Ladyfhip, at all dutiful obedience in Chrift,

             S. R.

ANWOTH, *Nov.* 15, 1633.

XXXI.—*To my* LADY KENMURE.

(*A UNION FOR PRAYER RECOMMENDED.*)

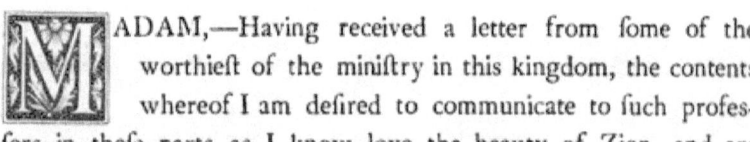

ADAM,—Having received a letter from fome of the worthieft of the miniftry in this kingdom, the contents whereof I am defired to communicate to fuch profes-fors in thefe parts as I know love the beauty of Zion, and are afflicted to fee the Lord's vineyard trodden under foot by the wild boars out of the wood, who lay it wafte, I could not but alfo defire your Ladyfhip's help to join with the reft, defiring you to impart it to my Lord your hufband, and if ye think it needful, I fhall write to his Lordfhip, as Mr. G. G.† fhall advertife me.

Know, therefore, that the beft affected of the miniftry have

---

* A burden above a load, or a load above a burden, is a phrafe for a very heavy weight.

† Mr George Gillefpie; fee Let. 144.

thought it convenient and neceſſary, at ſuch a time as this, that all who love the truth ſhould join their prayers together, and cry to God with humiliation and faſting. The times, which are agreed upon, are the two firſt Sabbaths of February next, and the ſix days intervening betwixt theſe Sabbaths, as they may conveniently be had, and the firſt Sabbath of every quarter. And the cauſes, as they are written to me, are theſe:

1. Beſides the diſtreſſes of the Reformed churches abroad, the many reigning ſins of uncleanneſs, ungodlineſs, and unrighteouſneſs in this land, the preſent judgments on the land, and many more hanging over us, whereof few are ſenſible, or yet know the right and true cauſe of them.

2. The lamentable and pitiful eſtate of a glorious church (in ſo ſhort a time, againſt ſo many bonds), in doctrine, ſacrament, and diſcipline, ſo ſore perſecuted, in the perſons of faithful paſtors and profeſſors, and the door of God's houſe kept ſo ſtrait by baſtard porters, inſomuch that worthy inſtruments, able for the work, are held at the door, the rulers having turned over religion into policy, and the multitude ready to receive any religion that ſhall be enjoined by authority.

3. In our humiliation, beſides that we are under a neceſſity of deprecating God's wrath, and vowing to God ſincerely new obedience, the weakneſs, coldneſs, ſilence, and lukewarmneſs of ſome of the beſt of the miniſtry, and the deadneſs of profeſſors, who have ſuffered the truth both ſecretly to be ſtolen away, and openly to be plucked from us, would be confeſſed.

4. Atheiſm, idolatry, profanity, and vanity, ſhould be confeſſed; our king's heart recommended to God; and God intreated, that He would ſtir up the nobles and the people to turn from their evil ways.

Thus, Madam, hoping that your Ladyſhip will join with others, that ſuch a work be not ſlighted, at ſuch a neceſſary time, when our kirk is at the overturning, I will promiſe to myſelf your help, as the Lord in ſecrecy and prudence ſhall enable you, that your Ladyſhip may rejoice with the Lord's people, when deliverance ſhall come; for true and ſincere humiliation come always ſpeed with God. And when authority, king, court, and churchmen oppofe the truth, what other armour have we but prayer and faith ? whereby, if we wreftle with Him, there is ground to hope that thofe who would remove the burdenfome ftone* out of its place, fhall but hurt their back, and the ftone fhall not be moved, at leaft not removed.

Grace, grace be with you, from Him who hath called you to the inheritance of the faints in light.

Your Ladyfhip's at all fubmiffive obedience in his fweet Lord Jefus.

S. R.

Anwoth, *Jan.* 23, 1634.

----------◆----------

XXXII.—*For* Marion M'Naught.

(*STATE AND PROSPECTS OF THE CHURCH—SATAN.*)

ISTRESS,—My love in Chrift remembered. I am in care and fear for this work of our Lord's, now near approaching, becaufe of the danger of the time ; and I dare not for my foul be filent, to fee my Lord's houfe burning, and not cry, "Fire, fire!" Therefore, feek from our Lord wifdom fpiritual, and not black policy, to fpeak with liberty our Lord's truth.—I am caft down, and would fain have accefs and prefence to The King that day, even howbeit I fhould break up iron doors. I believe you will not forget me ; and you will defire Jean Brown, Thomas Carfon, and Marion Carfon, to help me. Pray for well-cooked meat and an heartfome† Saviour, with joy crying, " Welcome in My Father's name."

I am confident Zion fhall be well ; the Bufh fhall burn and not confume, for the good will of Him that dwelt in the bufh. But the Lord is making on‡ a fire in Jerufalem, and purpofeth to blow the bellows, and to melt the tin and brafs, and bring out a

---

* Zech. xii. 3.   † Cheerful.   ‡ *Making on;* putting the fuel in order.

fair beautiful bride out of the furnace, that will be married over
again upon the new Hufband, and fing as in the days of her youth,
when the contract of marriage is written over again.   But I fear
the bride be hidden for a time from the dragon that purfueth the
woman with child.   But what, howbeit we go and lurk in the
wildernefs for a time ? for the Lord will take His kirk to the wildernefs, and fpeak to her heart.

Nothing cafteth me down, but only I fear the Lord will caft
down the fhepherd's tents, and feed His own in a fecret place.   But
let us, however matters frame,* caft over the affairs of the bride
upon the Bridegroom ; the government is upon His fhoulders, and
He dow† bear us all well enough.   That fallen ftar, the prince of the
bottomlefs pit, knoweth it is near the time when he fhall be tormented ; and now in his evening he has gathered his armies, to win
one battle or two, in the edge of the evening, at the fun going down.
And when our Lord has been watering His vineyards in France,
and Germany, and Bohemia, how can we think ourfelves Chrift's
fifter, if we be not like Him, and our other great fifters ?   I cannot
but think, feeing the ends of the earth are given to Chrift‡ (and
Scotland is the end of the earth, and fo we are in Chrift's charter-
tailzie§), but our Lord will keep His poffeffion.   We fall by promife
and law to Chrift.   He won us with the fweat of His brow, if I
may fay fo ; His Father promifed Him His liferent of Scotland.
Glory, glory to our King ! long may He wear His crown.   O
Lord, let us never fee another King !   O let Him come down like
rain upon the new-mown grafs !

I had you in remembrance on Saturday in the morning laft, in
a great meafure, and was brought, thrice on end,‖ in remembrance
of you in my prayer to God.   Grace, grace be your portion.

Yours in his fweet Lord Jefus,

S. R.

ANWOTH, *March* 2, 1634.

---

* Turn out ; fucceed.   † Is able to.   ‡ Ps. ii. 8.
§ Charter of entail.   ‖ In fucceffion.

(IN PROSPECT OF A COMMUNION SEASON.)

MISTRESS,—My love in Chrift remembered. Pleafe you underftand, to my grief, our Communion is delayed till Sabbath come eight days ; for the laird and lady hath earneftly defired me to delay it, becaufe the laird is fick, and he fears he be not able to travel, becaufe he has lately taken phyfic. The Lord blefs that work. Commend it to God as you love me, for I love not Satan's thorns caft in the Lord's way. The Lord rebuke him. I truft in God's mercy, Satan has gotten but a delay, but no free difcharge that his kingdom fhall not be hurt. Commend the laird to your God. I pray you advertife your people, that they be not difappointed in coming here. Show fuch of them as you love in Chrift, from me, that Jefus Chrift will be welcome, when He comes, in that He has fharpened their defires for eight days' fpace. Your daughter is well, I hope, every way. Forget not God's kirk ; they are but baftards, and not fons and daughters, that mourn not for Zion. Lord hear us ! No further. Jefus Chrift be with your fpirit. I fhall remember you and your new houfe. Lord Jefus go from the one houfe to the other.

Yours at all power in the Lord,

S. R.

Anwoth.

XXXIV.—*For* Marion M'Naught.

(PROSPECTS OF THE CHURCH—CHRIST'S CARE FOR THE CHILDREN OF BELIEVERS.)

WELL-BELOVED SISTER,—My old and deareft love in Chrift remembered. Know that I have been vifiting my Lady Kenmure. Her child is with the Lord. I

entreat you, vifit her, and defire the good-wife* of Barcapple to vifit her, and Knockbrecks (Mr Gordon), if you fee him in the town. My Lord her hufband is abfent, and I think fhe will be heavy. You know what Mr W. Dalgleifh and I defired you to deal for, at my Lord Kirkcudbright's hand. Send me word if you obtained anything at my Lord's hands, anent the giving up of our names to the High Commiffion; for I hear it is not for nothing that the Bifhop hath taken that courfe. Our Lord knows beft what is good for an old kirk that is fallen from her firft love, and hath forgotten her Hufband days without number. A trial is like to come on; but I am fure our Hufbandman Chrift fhall lofe chaff, but no corn at all. Yet there is a dry wind coming, but neither to fan nor to purge. Happy are they who are not blown away with the chaff, for we will but fuffer temptation for ten days; but thofe who are faithful to the death fhall receive the crown of life. I hear daily what hath been fpoken of myfelf, moft unjuftly and falfely; and no marvel,—the dragon, with the fwing of his tail, hath made the third part of the ftars to fall from heaven, and the fallen ftars would have many to fall with them. If ever Satan was busy, now, when he knoweth his time is fhort, he is bufy. "Yet a little while, and He that fhall come will come, and will not tarry." I know, ere it be long, the Lord fhall come and redd† all pleas betwixt us and our enemies. Now welcome, Lord Jefus, go faft.

Send me word about Grizel, your daughter, whom I remember in Chrift; and defire her to caft herfelf in His arms who was born of a woman, and, being the Ancient of days, was made a young weeping child. It was not for nothing that our brother Jefus was an infant. It was that He might pity infants of believers, who were to come out of the womb into the world. I believe our Lord Jefus fhall be waiting on, with mercy, mercy, mercy, to the end of that battle, and bring her through with life and peace, and

---

* Like " the good-man of the houfe," Luke xii. 39; one of the independent yeomanry of the day. *Barcaple* is in the ftewartry of Kircudbright, in the parifh of Tongueland.

† Settle, clear up.

a fign of God's favour. I will expeƐt advertifement from you, and efpecially if you fear her. Miftrefs, you remember that I faid to you anent your love to me and my brother, begun in Chrift ; you know we are here but ftrangers, and you have not yet found us a dry well, as others have been. Be not overcome of any fufpicion. I truft in God that the Lord, who knit us together, fhall keep us together. It is time now that the lambs of Jefus fhould all run together, when the wolf is barking at them ; yet I know, ere God's bairns want a crofs, their love amongst themfelves fhall be a crofs ; but our Lord giveth love for another end. I know you will, with love, cover infirmities ; and our Lord give you wifdom in all things. I think love hath broad fhoulders, and will bear many things, and yet neither faint nor fweat, nor fall under the burden.

Commend me to your hufband and dear Grizel. I think on her. Lord Jefus be in the furnace with her, and then fhe will but fmoke and not burn. Defire Mr Robert* to excufe my not feeing of him at his houfe. I have my own reafons therefor.† Grace, mercy, and peace be with you.

Yours in his fweet Lord Jefus,

S. R.

ANWOTH, *April* 25, 1634.

XXXV.—*To my* LADY KENMURE, *on the death of a child.*

(*GOD MEASURES OUR DAYS—BEREAVEMENTS RIPEN US FOR THE HARVEST.*)

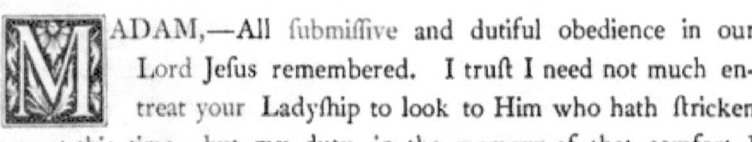

ADAM,—All fubmiffive and dutiful obedience in our Lord Jefus remembered. I truft I need not much entreat your Ladyfhip to look to Him who hath ftricken you at this time ; but my duty, in the memory of that comfort I found in your Ladyfhip's kindnefs, when I was no lefs heavy (in a cafe not unlike that), fpeaketh to me to fay fomething now. And I

---

* Mr Robert Glendinning, the minifter.

† For this; as in our metre verfion, Ps. cvi. 40, etc.

wifh I could eafe your Ladyfhip, at leaft with words. I am perfuaded your Phyfician will not flay you, but purge you, feeing He
calleth Himfelf the Chirurgeon, who maketh the wound and bindeth
it up again; for to lance a wound is not to kill, but to cure the
patient.* I believe faith will teach you to kifs a ftriking Lord; and
fo acknowledge the fovereignty of God (in the death of a child) to
be above the power of us mortal men, who may pluck up a flower
in the bud, and not be blamed for it. If our dear Lord pluck up
one of His rofes, and pull down four and green fruit before harveft,
who can challenge Him? For He fendeth us to His world, as men
to a market, wherein fome ftay many hours, and eat and drink, and
buy and fell, and pafs through the fair, till they be weary; and fuch
are thofe who live long and get a heavy fill of this life. And others
again come flipping in to the morning market, and do neither fit nor
ftand, nor buy nor fell, but look about them a little, and pafs
prefently home again; and thefe are infants and young ones, who
end their fhort market in the morning, and get but a fhort view of
the fair. Our Lord, who hath numbered man's months, and fet
him bounds that he cannot pafs,† hath written the length of our
market, and it is eafier to complain of the decree than to change it.

I verily believe, when I write this, your Lord hath taught your
Ladyfhip to lay your hand on your mouth. But I fhall be far from
defiring your Ladyfhip, or any others, to caft by a crofs, like an old
ufelefs bill that is only for the fire; but rather would wifh each
crofs were looked in the face feven times, and were read over and
over again. It is the meffenger of the Lord, and fpeaks fomething;
and the man of underftanding will hear the rod, and Him that hath
appointed it. Try what is the tafte of the Lord's cup, and drink
with God's blefling, that ye may grow thereby. I truft in God,
whatever fpeech it utter to your foul, this is one word in it,—" Behold, blefled is the man whom God correcteth;"‡ and that it faith
to you, " Ye are from home while here; ye are not of this world,

---

* Deut. xxxii. 39; 1 Sam. ii. 6; Job v. 18; Hos. vi. 1.
† Job xiv. 5.   ‡ Job v. 17.

as your Redeemer, Chrift, was not of this world." There is some-
thing keeping for you, which is worth the having. All that is here
is condemned to die, to pafs away like a fnow-ball before a fummer
fun ; and fince death took firft poffeffion of fomething of yours, it
hath been and daily is creeping nearer and nearer to yourfelf, howbeit with no noife of feet. Your Hufbandman and Lord hath lopped
off fome branches already ; the tree itfelf is to be tranfplanted to
the high garden. In a good time be it. Our Lord ripen your
Ladyfhip. All thefe croffes (and indeed, when I remember them,
they are heavy and many,—peace, peace be the end of them !) are
to make you white and ripe for the Lord's harveft-hook. I have
feen the Lord weaning you from the breafts of this world. It was
never His mind it fhould be your patrimony ; and God be thanked
for that. Ye look the liker one of the heirs. Let the moveables
go ; why not ? They are not yours. Faften your grips* upon
the heritage ; and our Lord Jefus make the charters fure, and give
your Ladyfhip to grow as a palm-tree on God's mount Zion ; howbeit fhaken with winds, yet the root is faft. This is all I can do,
to recommend your cafe to your Lord, who hath you written upon
the palms of His hand. If I were able to do more, your Ladyfhip
may believe me that gladly I would. I truft fhortly to fee your
Ladyfhip. Now He who hath called you, confirm and ftablifh your
heart in grace unto the Day of the Liberty of the Sons of God.

Your Ladyfhip at all fubmiffive obedience in his fweet Lord Jefus,

ANWOTH, *April* 29, 1634. **S. R.**

----◆----

XXXVI.—*For* MARION M'NAUGHT.

(*CHOICE OF A COMMISSIONER FOR PARLIAMENT.*)

ELL-BELOVED MISTRESS,—My love in Chrift re-
membered. I hear this day your town is to choofe a
commiffioner for the Parliament ; and I was written to

---

* Firm grafp.

from Edinburgh, to fee that good men fhould be chofen in your bounds. And I have heard this day that Robert Glendoning or John Ewart look to be chofen. I befeech you fee this be not. The Lord's caufe craveth other witneffes to fpeak for Him than fuch men ; and, therefore, let it not be faid that Kirkcudbright, which is fpoken of in this kingdom for their religion, hath fent a man to be their mouth that will fpeak againft Chrift. Such a time as this will not fall out once in half an age. I would intreat your hufband to take it upon him. It is an honourable and neceffary fervice for Chrift ; and fhew him that I wrote unto you for that effect. I fear William Glendoning hath not fkill and authority. I am in great heavinefs. Pray for me, for we muft take our life in our hand in this ill time. Let us ftir up ourfelves, to lay our Lord's bride and her wrongs before our Hufband and Lord. Lord Jefus be with your fpirit.

Yours in his fweet Lord Jefus,

S. R.

Anworth, *May* 20.

XXXVII.—*To my* Lady Kenmure.

(*ON THE DEATH OF LORD KENMURE—DESIGNS OF AND DUTIES OF AFFLICTION.*)

Y VERY NOBLE AND WORTHY LADY,—So oft as I call to mind the comforts that I myfelf, a poor friendlefs ftranger, received from your Ladyfhip here in a ftrange part of the country, when my Lord took from me the delight of mine eyes,* as the Word fpeaketh (which wound is not yet fully healed and cured), I truft your Lord fhall remember that, and give you comfort now at fuch a time as this, wherein your deareft Lord hath made you a widow, that ye may be a free

---

* Ezek. xxiv. 16.

woman for Chrift, who is now fuiting for marriage-love of you. And therefore, fince you lie alone in your bed, let Chrift be as a bundle of myrrh, to fleep and lie all the night betwixt your breafts,* and then your bed is better filled than before. And feeing, amongft all croffes fpoken of in our Lord's Word, this giveth you a particular right to make God your Hufband (which was not fo yours while your hufband was alive), read God's mercy out of this vifitation. And albeit I muft out of fome experience fay, the mourning for the hufband of your youth be, by God's own mouth, the heavieft worldly forrow ;† and though this be the weightieft burden that ever lay upon your back ; yet ye know (when the fields are emptied and your hufband now afleep in the Lord), if ye fhall wait upon Him who hideth His face for a while, that it lieth upon God's honour and truth to fill the field, and to be a Hufband to the widow. See and confider then what ye have loft, and how little it is. Therefore, Madam, let me intreat you, in the bowels of Chrift Jefus, and by the comforts of His Spirit, and your appearance before Him, let God, and men, and angels now fee what is in you. The Lord hath pierced the veffel ; it will be known whether there be in it wine or water. Let your faith and patience be feen, that it may be known your only beloved firft and laft hath been Chrift. And, therefore, now ware‡ your whole love upon Him ; He alone is a fuitable objeft for your love and all the affeftions of your foul. God hath dried up one channel of your love by the removal of your hufband. Let now that fpeat§ run upon Chrift. Your Lord and lover hath gracioufly taken out your hufband's name and your name out of the fummonfes that are raifed at the inftance of the terrible fin-revenging Judge of the world againft the houfe of the Kenmure. And I dare fay that God's hammering of you from your youth is only to make you a fair carved ftone in the high upper temple of the New Jerufalem. Your Lord never thought this world's vain painted glory a gift worthy of you ; and

---

* Cant. i. 13. † Joel i. 8. ‡ To *ware*, is to expend.
§ Flood; often written *fpait*. It is the Celtic *fpeid*, a great river-flood.

therefore would not beftow it on you, becaufe He is to propine *
you with a better portion. Let the moveables go ; the inheritance
is yours. Ye are a child of the houfe, and joy is laid up for you ;
it is long in coming, but not the worfe for that. I am now expect-
ing to fee, and that with joy and comfort, that which I hoped of
you fince I knew you fully, even that ye have laid fuch ftrength
upon the Holy One of Ifrael, that ye defy troubles, and that your
foul is a caftle that may be befieged, but cannot be taken. What
have ye to do here ? This world never looked like a friend upon
you. Ye owe it little love. It looked ever four-like upon you.
Howbeit ye fhould woo it, it will not match with you ; and
therefore never feek warm fire under cold ice. This is not a field
where your happinefs groweth ; it is up above, where there are a
great multitude, which no man can number, of all nations, and
kindreds, and people, and tongues, ftanding before the throne and
before the Lamb, clothed with white robes, and palms in their
hands.† What ye could never get here ye fhall find there. And
withall confider how in all thefe trials (and truly they have been
many) your Lord hath been loofing you at the root from perifhing
things, and hunting after you to grip‡ your foul. Madam, for the
Son of God's fake, let Him not mifs His grip,‡ but ftay and abide
in the love of God, as Jude faith. §

Now, Madam, I hope your Ladyfhip will take thefe lines in good
part ; and wherein I have fallen fhort and failed to your Ladyfhip,
in not evidencing what I was obliged to you more-than-undeferved
love and refpect, I requeft for a full pardon for it. Again, my
dear and noble lady, let me befeech you to lift up your head, for
the day of your redemption draweth near. And remember, that
ftar that fhined in Galloway is now fhining in another world. Now
I pray that God may anfwer, in His own ftyle, to your foul, and that
He may be to you the God of all confolations. Thus I remain,

Your Ladyfhip's at all dutiful obedience in the Lord,

ANWOTH, *Sept.* 14, 1634.   S. R.

---

* Prefent.   † Rev. vii. 9.   ‡ Take firm hold of.   § Jude ver. 21.

(*CHRIST'S CARE OF HIS CHURCH, AND HIS JUDGMENTS ON HER ENEMIES.*)

MISTRESS,—My deareſt love in Chriſt remembered. I entreat you charge your ſoul to return to reſt, and to glorify your deareſt Lord in believing; and know that for the good-will of Him that dwelleth in the buſh, the burning kirk ſhall not be conſumed to aſhes; but "Bleſſing ſhall come on the head of Joſeph, and upon the top of the head of him that was ſeparate from his brethren."* And are not the ſaints ſeparate from their brethren, and ſold and hated? "For the archers have ſorely grieved Joſeph, and ſhot at him and hated him; but his bow abode in ſtrength, and the arms of his hands were made ſtrong by the hands of the mighty God of Jacob."† From Him is the Shepherd and the Stone of Iſrael. The Stone of Iſrael ſhall not be broken in pieces; it is hammered upon by the children of this world, and we ſhall live and not die. Our Lord hath done all this, to ſee if we will believe, and not give over; and I am perſuaded you muſt of neceſ-ſity ſtick by your work. The eye of Chriſt hath been upon all this buſineſs; and He taketh good heed to who is for Him, and who is againſt Him. Let us do our part, as we would be approved of Chriſt. The Son of God is near to His enemies. If they were not deaf, they may hear the dinn of His feet; and He will come with a ſtart upon His weeping bairns, and take them on His knee, and lay their head in His boſom, and dry their watery eyes. And this day is faſt coming. "Yet a little time, and the viſion will ſpeak, it will not tarry."‡ Theſe queſtions betwixt us and our adverſaries will all be decided in yonder day, when the Son of God ſhall come, and redd all pleas;§ and it will be ſeen whether we or they have

---

* Deut. xxxiii. 16. † Gen. xlix. 23, 24. ‡ Hab. ii. 3.
§ Settle all diſputed caſes.

been for Chriſt, and who have been pleading for Baal. It is not known what we are now ; but when our Life ſhall appear in glory, then we ſhall ſee who laughs faſteſt that day. Therefore, we muſt poſſeſs our ſouls in patience, and go into our chamber and reſt, whill* the indignation be paſt. We ſhall not weep long when our Lord ſhall take us up, in the day that He gathereth His jewels. " They that feared the Lord ſpoke often one to another, and the Lord hearkened and heard it, and a book of remembrance was written before Him, for them that feared the Lord, and thought upon His name."† I ſhall never be of another faith, but that our Lord is heating a furnace for the enemies of His kirk in Scotland. It is true the ſpouſe of Chriſt hath played the harlot, and hath left her firſt Huſband, and the enemies think they offend not, for we have ſinned againſt the Lord ; but they ſhall get the devil to their thanks. The rod ſhall be caſt into the fire, that we may ſing as in the days of our youth. My dear friend, therefore, lay down your head upon Chriſt's breaſt. Weep not ; the Lion of the tribe of Judah will ariſe. The ſun is gone down upon the prophets, and our gold is become dim, and the Lord feedeth His people with waters of gall and wormwood ; yet Chriſt ſtandeth but behind the wall, His bowels are moved for Scotland. He waiteth, as Iſaiah ſaith, that He may ſhow mercy. If we could go home, and take our brethren with us, weeping with our face towards Zion, aſking the way thitherward, He would bring back our captivity. We may not think that God has no care of His honour, while men tread it under their feet ; He will cloth Himſelf with vengeance, as with a cloak, and appear againſt our enemies for our deliverance. Ye were never yet beguiled, and God will not now begin with you. Wreſtle ſtill with the angel of the covenant, and you ſhall get the bleſſing. Fight ! He delighteth to be overcome by wreſtling.

Commend me to Grizel. Deſire her to learn to know the ad-verſaries of the Lord, and to take them as her adverſaries, and to learn to know the right gate‡ into the Son of God. O but acquaint-

---

* Till.   † Mal. iii. 16.   ‡ Way to go to.

ance with the Son of God, to fay, " My Well-beloved is mine, and I am His," is a fweet and glorious courfe of life, that none know but thofe who are fealed and marked in the forehead with Chrift's mark, and the new name, that Chrift writeth upon His own. Grace, grace, and mercy be with you.

Yours in Chrift,

S. R.

ANWOTH, *Sept.* 25, 1634.

XXXIX.—*To my* LADY KENMURE.

(PREPARATION FOR DEATH AND ETERNITY).

MADAM,—All dutiful obedience in our Lord remembered. I know ye are now near one of thofe ftraits in which ye have been before. But becaufe your outward comforts are fewer, I pray Him, whofe ye are, to fupply what ye want another way. For howbeit we cannot win* to the bottom of His wife providence, who ruleth all; yet it is certain this is not only good which the Almighty hath done, but it is beft. He hath reckoned all your fteps to heaven; and if your Ladyfhip were through this water, there are the fewer behind; and if this were the laft, I hope your Ladyfhip hath learned by on-waiting to make your acquaintance with death, which being to the Lord, the woman's feed, Jefus, only a bloody heel and not a broken head,† cannot be ill to His friends, who get far lefs of death than Himfelf. Therefore, Madam, feeing ye know not but the journey is ended, and ye are come to the water-fide, in God's wifdom look all your papers and your counts, and whether ye be ready to receive the kingdom of heaven as a little child, in whom there is little haughtinefs and much humility. I would be far from difcouraging your Ladyfhip; but there is an abfolute neceffity that, near eternity, we look ere we leap, feeing no

---

* Get at.   † Gen. iii. 15.

man winneth back again to mend his leap. I am confident your Ladyfhip thinketh often upon it, and that your old Guide fhall go before you and take your hand. His love to you will not grow four, nor wear out of date, as the love of men, which groweth old and gray-haired often before themfelves. Ye have fo much the more reafon to love a better life than this, becaufe this world hath been to you a cold fire, with little heat to the body, and as little light, and much fmoke to hurt the eyes. But, Madam, your Lord would have you thinking it but dry breafts, full of wind and empty of food. In this late vifitation that hath befallen your Ladyfhip, ye have feen God's love and care, in fuch a meafure that I thought our Lord brake the fharp point off the crofs, and made us and your Ladyfhip fee Chrift take poffeffion and infeftment upon earth, of him who is now reigning and triumphing with the hundred forty and four thoufand who ftand with the Lamb on Mount Zion. I know the fweeteft of it is bitter to you; but your Lord will not give you painted croffes. He pareth not all the bitternefs from the crofs, neither taketh He the fharp edge quite from it; then* it fhould be of your waling† and not of His, which fhould have as little reason in it as it fhould have profit for us. Only, Madam, God commandeth you now to believe and caft anchor in the dark night, and climb up the mountain. He who hath called you, eftablifh you and confirm you to the end.

I had a purpofe to have vifited your Ladyfhip; but when I thought better upon it, the truth is, I cannot fee what my company would profit you; and this hath broken off my purpofe, and no other thing. I know many honourable friends and worthy profeffors will fee your Ladyfhip, and that the Son of God is with you, to whofe love and mercy, from my foul, I recommend your Ladyfhip, and remain,

Your Ladyfhip's at all dutiful obedience in his fweet Lord Jefus,

S. R.

ANWOTH, *Nov.* 29, 1634.

---

* In that cafe.   † Choofing, felecting.

XL.—*To my* Lady Kenmure.

(WHEN MR RUTHERFORD HAD THE PROSPECT OF BEING REMOVED FROM ANWOTH.)

MADAM,—My humble obedience in the Lord remembered. Know it hath pleafed the Lord to let me fee, by all appearance, that my labours in God's houfe here are at an end; and I muft now learn to fuffer, in the which I am a dull fcholar. By a ftrange providence, fome of my papers, anent the corruptions of this time, are come to the King's hand. I know, by the wife and well-affected I fhall be cenfured as not wife nor circumfpect enough; but it is ordinary, that that fhould be a part of the crofs of thofe who fuffer for Him. Yet I love and pardon the inftrument; I would commit my life to him, howbeit by him this hath befallen me. But I look higher than to him. I make no queftion of your Ladyfhip's love and care to do what ye can for my help, and am perfuaded that, in my adverfities, your Ladyfhip will wifh me well. I feek no other thing but that my Lord may be honoured by me in giving a teftimony. I was willing to do Him more fervice; but feeing He will have no more of my labours, and this land will thruft me out, I pray for grace to learn to be acquaint with mifery, if I may give fo rough a name to fuch a mark of thofe who fhall be crowned with Chrift. And howbeit I will poffibly prove a faint-hearted, unwife man in that, yet I dare fay I intend otherwife; and I defire not to go on the lee-fide or funny fide of religion, or to put truth betwixt me and a ftorm: my Saviour did not fo for me, who in His fuffering took the windy fide of the hill. No farther; but the Son of God be with you.

Your Ladyfhip's in the Lord Jefus,

S. R.

Anwoth, *Dec.* 5, 1634.

(*THE CHURCH'S TRIALS—COMFORT UNDER TEMPTATIONS—DELIVERANCE—A MESSAGE TO THE YOUNG.*)

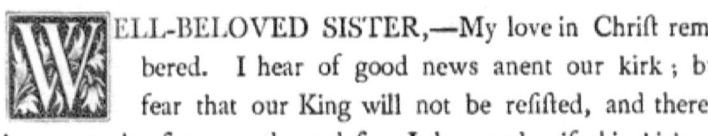ELL-BELOVED SISTER,—My love in Chrift remembered. I hear of good news anent our kirk ; but I fear that our King will not be refifted, and therefore let us not be fecure and carelefs. I do wonder if this kirk come not through our Lord's fan, fince there is fo much chaff in it ; howbeit I perfuade myfelf, the Son of God's wheat will not be blown away. Let us be putting on God's armour, and be ftrong in the Lord. If the devil and Zion's enemies ftrike a hole in that armour, let our Lord fee to that ;—let us put it on, and ftand. We have Jefus on our fide ; and they are not worthy fuch a Captain, who would not take a blow, at His back. We are in fight of His colours; His banner over us is love; look up to that white banner, and ftand, I perfuade you, in the Lord of victory.

My brother writeth to me of your heavinefs, and of temptations that prefs you fore. I am content it be fo : you bear about with you the mark of the Lord Jefus. So it was with the Lord's apoftle, when he was to come with the Gofpel to Macedonia :* his flefh had no reft ; he was troubled on every fide, and knew not what fide to turn him unto ; without were fightings, and within were fears. In the great work of our redemption, your lovely, beautiful, and glorious Friend and Well-beloved Jefus, was brought to tears and ftrong cries ; fo as His face was wet with tears and blood, arifing from a holy fear and the weight of the curfe. Take a drink of the Son of God's cup, and love it the better that He drank of it before you. There is no poifon in it. I wonder many times that ever a child of God fhould have a fad heart, confidering what their Lord is preparing for them.

* 2 Cor. vii. 5.

Is your mind troubled anent that bufinefs that we have now in hand in Edinburgh ?* I truft in my Lord, the Lord fhall in the end give to you your heart's defire ; even howbeit the bufinefs frame† not, the Lord fhall feed your foul, and all the hungry fouls in that town. Therefore I requeft you in the Lord, pray for a fubmiffive will, and pray as your Lord Jefus bids you, "Thy will be done on earth, as it is in heaven." And let it be that your faith be brangled‡ with temptations, believe ye that there is a tree in our Lord's garden that is not often fhaken with wind from all the four airts ?§ Surely there is none. Rebuke your foul, as the Lord's prophet doth : "Why art thou caft down, O my foul ? why art thou difquieted within me ?"‖ That was the word of a man who was at the very overgoing of the brae¶ and mountain ; but God held a grip of him. Swim through your temptations and troubles to be at that lovely, amiable perfon, Jefus, to whom your foul is dear. In your temptations run to the promifes : they be our Lord's branches hanging over the water, that our Lord's filly, half-drowned children may take a grip of them ; if you let that grip go, you will fall to the ground. Are you troubled with the cafe of God's kirk ? Our Lord will evermore have her betwixt the finking and the fwimming. He will have her going through a thoufand deaths, and through hell, as a cripple woman, halting, and wanting the power of her one fide,** that God may be her ftaff. That broken fhip will come to land, becaufe Jefus is the pilot. Faint not ; you fhall fee the falvation of God,—elfe fay, that God never fpake His word by my mouth ; and I had rather never have been born, ere it were fo with me. But my Lord hath fealed me. I dare not deny I have alfo been in heavinefs fince I came from you, fearing for my unthankfulnefs that I be deferted. But the Lord will be kind to me, whether I will or not. I repofe that†† much in His rich grace,

---

* Referring to the efforts then making by feveral eminent Prefbyterian minifters, to obtain redrefs from grievances inflicted by the prelatic party.

† Yet even if it turn out not fo (as in Let. 187); fucceed.

‡ Shaken.   § Quarters of the heavens.   ‖ Ps. xlii. 11.

¶ Hill-fide.   ** Micah iv. 6, 7.   †† So much.

that He will be loath to change upon me. As you love me, pray for me in this particular.

After advifing with Carletoun, I have written to Mr David Dickfon anent Mr Hugh M'Kail,* and defired him to write his mind to Carletoun, and Carletoun to Edinburgh, that they may particularly remember Mr Hugh to the Lord ; and I happened upon a convenient trufty bearer by God's wonderful providence. No further. I recommend you to the Lord's grace, and your hufband and children. The Lord Jefus be with your fpirit.

Yours in the Lord,

S. R.

EDINBURGH, 1634.

P.S.—MISTRESS,—I had not time to give my advice to your daughter Grizel ; you fhall carry my words therefore to her. Show her now, that in refpect of her tender age, fhe is in a manner as clean paper, ready to receive either good or ill ; and that it were a fweet and glorious thing for her to give herfelf up to Chrift, that He may write upon her His Father's name, and His own new name. And defire her to acquaint herfelf with the book of God ; the promifes that our Lord writes upon His own, and performeth in them and for them, are contained there. I perfuade you, when I think that fhe is in the company of fuch parents, and hath occafion to learn Chrift, I think Chrift is wooing her foul ; and I pray God fhe may not refufe fuch a hufband. And therefore I charge her, and befeech her by the mercies of God, by the wounds and blood of Him who died for her, by the word of truth, which fhe heareth, and can read, by the coming of the Son of God to judge the world, that fhe would fulfil your joy, and learn Chrift, and walk in Chrift. She fhall think this the truth of God many years after this ; and I will promife to myfelf, in refpect of the beginnings that I have feen, that fhe fhall give herfelf to Him that gave Himfelf for her. Let her begin at prayer ; for if fhe remember her Creator in the days

---

* See Let. 71.

of her youth, He will claim kindnefs to her in her old age. It fhall be a part of my prayers, that this may be effeftual in her, by Him who is able to do exceeding abundantly, to whofe grace again I recommend you, and her, and all yours.

XLII.—*To my* LADY KENMURE.

(*THE WORLD PASSETH AWAY—SPECIAL PORTIONS OF THE WORD FOR THE AFFLICTED—CALL TO KIRKCUDBRIGHT.*)

ADAM,—The caufe of my not writing to your Ladyfhip was not my forgetfulnefs of you, but the want of the opportunity of a convenient bearer; for I am under more than a fimple obligation to be kind (on paper, at leaft) to your Ladyfhip. I blefs our Lord, through Chrift, who hath brought you home again to your own country from that place,* where ye have feen with your eyes that which our Lord's truth taught you before, to wit, that worldly glory is nothing but a vapour, a fhadow, the foam of the water, or fomething lefs and lighter, even nothing; and that our Lord hath not without caufe faid in His Word, "The countenance," or fafhion, "of this world paffeth away,"†—in which place our Lord compareth it to an image in a looking-glafs, for it is the looking-glafs of Adam's fons. Some come to the glafs, and fee in it the pifture of *honour*,—and but a picture indeed, for true honour is to be great in the fight of God; and others fee in it the fhadow of *riches*,—and but a fhadow indeed, for durable riches ftand as one of the maids of Wifdom upon her left hand;‡ and a third fort fee in it the face of painted *pleafures*, and the beholders will not believe but the image they fee in this glafs is a living man, till the Lord come and break the glafs in pieces and remove the face, and then, like Pharaoh awakened, they fay, "And behold it was a dream." I know your Ladyfhip thinketh

---

* Edinburgh.　　　† 1 Cor. vii. 31.　　　‡ Prov. iii. 16.

1634.]   *LETTER XLII.*   129

yourfelf little in the common* of this world, for the favourable
afpeft of any of thefe three painted faces ; and bleffed be our Lord
that it is fo. The better for you, Madam ; they are not worthy to
be wooers, to fuit† in marriage your foul, that look to no higher
match than to be married upon painted clay. Know, therefore,
Madam, the place whither our Lord Jefus cometh to woo a bride,
it is even in the furnace : for if ye be one of Zion's daughters
(which I ever put beyond all queftion, fince I firft had occafion to
fee in your Ladyfhip fuch pregnant evidences of the grace of God),
the Lord, who hath His fire in Zion, and His furnace in Jerufalem,‡
is purifying you in the furnace. And therefore be content to live
in it, and every day to be adding and fewing-to a pafment§ to your
wedding garment, that ye may be at laft decored‖ and trimmed as
a bride for Chrift, a bride of His own bufking, beautified in the
hidden man of the heart. " Forgetting your father's houfe, fo fhall
the King greatly defire your beauty."¶   If your Ladyfhip be not
changed (as I hope ye are not), I believe ye efteem yourfelf to be
of thofe whom God hath tried thefe many years, and refined as
filver. But, Madam, I will fhew your Ladyfhip a privilege that
others want, and ye have, in this cafe. Such as are in profperity,
and are fatted with earthly joys, and increafed with children and
friends, though the Word of God is indeed written to fuch for
their inftruftion, yet to you, who are in trouble (fpare me, Madam,
to fay this), from whom the Lord hath taken many children, and
whom He hath exercifed otherwife, there are fome chapters, fome
particular promifes in the Word of God, made in a moft fpecial
manner, which fhould never have been yours, fo as they now are,
if you had your portion in this life, as others. And, therefore, all
the comforts, promifes, and mercies God offereth to the afflifted,
they are as fo many love-letters written to you. Take them to you,
Madam, and claim your right, and be not robbed. It is no fmall

---

* Under obligation to ; a phrafe derived from dining at a common table in
a college,—a privilege enjoyed by fpecial favour.

† Woo.   ‡ Ifa. xxxi. 9.   § Ornament, piece of lace.
‖ Adorned.   ¶ Ps. xlv. 11.

VOL. I.   I

comfort, that God hath written fome fcriptures to you, which He
hath not written to others. Ye feem rather in this to be envied
than pitied ; and ye are indeed in this, like people of another world,
and thofe that are above the ordinary rank of mankind, whom our
King and Lord, our Bridegroom Jefus, in His love-letter to His
well-beloved fpoufe, hath named befide all the reft. He hath
written comforts and His hearty commendations, in the 56th of
Ifaiah, vers. 4, 5 ; Pfalm cxlviii. 2, 3, to you. Read thefe and
the like, and think your God is like a friend that fendeth a letter to
a whole houfe and family, but fpeaketh in His letter to fome by
name, that are deareft to Him in the houfe. Ye are, then, Madam,
of the deareft friends of the Bridegroom. If it were lawful, I
would envy you, that God honoured you fo above many of His
dear children. Therefore, Madam, your part is, in this cafe (feeing
God taketh nothing from you but that which He is to fupply with
His own prefence), to defire your Lord to know His own room,
and take it even upon Him to come in, in the room of dead children. " Jehovah, know Thy own place, and take it to Thee," is
all ye have to fay.

Madam, I perfuade myfelf that this world is to you an unco*
inn ; and that ye are like a traveller, who hath his bundle upon his
back, and his ftaff in his hand, and his feet upon the door-threfhold.
Go forward, honourable and elect lady, in the ftrength of your
Lord (let the world bide at home and keep the houfe), with your
face toward Him, who longeth more for a fight of you than ye
can do for Him. Ere it be long, He will fee us. I hope to fee
you laugh as cheerfully after noon, as ye have mourned before
noon. The hand of the Lord, the hand of the Lord be with you
in your journey. What have ye to do here? This is not your
mountain of reft. Arife, then, and fet your foot up the mountain ;
go up out of the wildernefs, leaning upon the fhoulder of your
Beloved.† If ye knew the welcome that abideth you when ye
come home, ye would haften your pace ; for ye fhall fee your

---

* Strange.   † Cant. viii. 5.

Lord put up His own holy hand to your face, and wipe all tears from your eyes ; and I trow, then ye fhall have fome joy of heart.

Madam, paper willeth me to end before affection. Remember the eftate of Zion ; pray that Jerufalem may be as Zechariah pro-phefied, "a burdenfome ftone for all,"* that whofoever boweth down to roll the ftone out of the way, may hurt and break the joints of their back, and ftrain their arms, and disjoint their fhoulder-blades. And pray Jehovah that the ftone may lie ftill in its own place, and keep band† with the corner-ftone. I hope it fhall be fo ; He is a fkilled Mafter-builder who laid it.

I would, Madam, under great heavinefs be refrefhed with two lines from your Ladyfhip, which I refer to your own wifdom. Madam, I would feem undutiful not to fhow you, that great folici-tation is made by the town of Kirkcudbright for to have the ufe of my poor labours amongft them. If the Lord fhall call, and His people cry, who am I to refift ? But without His feen calling, and till the flock whom I now overfee be planted with one to whom I dare intruft Chrift's fpoufe, gold nor filver nor favour of men, I hope, fhall not loofe me. I leave your Ladyfhip, praying more earneftly for grace and mercy to be with you, and multiplied upon you, here and hereafter, than my pen can exprefs. The Lord Jefus be with your fpirit.

Your Ladyfhip's at all obedience in the Lord.

KIRKCUDBRIGHT.

XLIII.—*For* MARION M'NAUGHT.

(WHEN MR RUTHERFORD WAS IN DIFFICULTY AS TO ACCEPT-ING A CALL TO KIRKCUDBRIGHT, AND CRAMOND.)

UCH HONOURED AND DEAR MISTRESS,—My love in Chrift remembered. I am grieved at the heart to write anything to you to breed heavinefs to you ;

---

* Zech. xii. 3.   † Keep united with.

and what I have written, I wrote with much heavinefs. But I entreat you in Chrift's name, when my foul is under wreftlings, and feeking direction from our Lord (to whom His vineyard belongeth) whither I fhall go, give me liberty to advife, and try all airts* and paths, to fee whether He goeth before me and leadeth me. For if I were affured of God's call to your town, let my arm fall from my fhoulder-blade and lofe power, and my right eye be dried up, (which is the judgment of the idol fhepherd,†) if I would not swim through the water without a boat ere I fat His bidding.‡ But if ye knew my doubtings and fears in that, ye would fuffer with me. Whether they be temptations or impediments caft in by my God, I know not. But you have now caufe to thank God ; for feeing the Bifhop§ hath given you fuch a promife, he will give you an honeft man more willingly than he will permit me to come to you. And, as I ever entreated you, put the bufinefs out of your hand in the Lord's reverence ;‖ and try of Him, if ye have warrant of Him to feek no man in the world but one only, when there are choice of good men to be had. Howbeit they be too fcarce, yet they are. And what God faith to me in the bufinefs, I refolve by His grace to do ; for I know not what He will do with me. But God fhall fill you with joy ere this bufinefs be ended ; for I perfuade myfelf our Lord Jefus hath ftirred you up already to do good in the bufinefs, and ye fhall not lofe your reward.

I have heard your hufband and Samuel have been fick. The man who is called *the Branch* and *God's fellow*, who ftandeth before His Father, will be your ftay and help.¶ I would I were able to comfort your foul. But have patience, and ftand ftill ; he that believeth maketh not hafte. This matter of Cramond, caft in at this time, is either a temptation, having fallen out at this time ; or then**

---

* All points of the compafs.   † Zech. xi. 17.

‡ Failed promptly to obey Him, or do His bidding.

§ Referring to a promife made to the people of Kirkcudbright by the Bifhop of Galloway, to give them a man according to their own mind, provided they would not choofe Mr Rutherford.

‖ Power, difpofal. See Note, Lett. 30.   ¶ Zech. xiii. 7.   ** Or elfe.

it will clear all my doubts, and let you fee the Lord's will.   But I never knew my own part in the bufinefs till now.   I thought I was more willing to have embraced the charge in your town, than I am, or am able to win to.   I know ye pray that God would refolve me what to do ; and will interpret me, as love biddeth you, which " thinketh not ill, and believeth all things, and hopeth all things." Would ye have more than the Son of God ? and ye have Him already.   And ye fhall be fed by the carver of the meat, be he who he will ; and thofe who are hungry look more to the meat than to the carver.

I cannot fee you the next week.   If my lady come home, I muft vifit her.   The week thereafter will be a Prefbytery at Girthon.   God will difpofe of the meeting.   Grace upon you, and your feed, and hufband.   The Lord Jefus be with your fpirit.

Yours in Chrift,

ANWOTH.   S. R.

------◆------

XLIV.—*For* MARION M'NAUGHT.

(TROUBLES THREATENING THE CHURCH.)

WELL-BELOVED SISTER,—My love in Jefus Chrift remembered.   Your daughter is well, thanks be to God.   I truft in Him ye fhall have joy of her; the Lord blefs her.   I am now prefently going about catechifing.   The bearer is in hafte.   Forget not poor Zion; and the Lord remember you, for we fhall be fhortly winnowed.   Jefus, pray for us, that our faith fail not!   I would wifh to fee you a Sabbath with us, and we fhall ftir up one another, God willing, to feek the Lord; for it may be He hide Himfelf from us ere it be long.   Keep that which you have: ye will get more in heaven.   The Lord fend us to the fhore out of all the ftorms, with our filly fouls found and whole with us; for if liberty of confcience come, as is rumoured, the beft of us will be put to our wits to feek how to be freed.   But we fhall be like thofe who have their chamber to go in unto, fpoken of in

Ifaiah.* Read the place yourfelf, and keep you within your houfe whill† the ftorm be paffed. If you can learn a ditty‡ againft C., try, and caufe try, that ye may fee the Lord's righteous judgment upon the devil's inftruments. We are not much obliged to his kindnefs. I wifh all fuch wicked doers were cut off.

Thefe in hafte. I blefs you in God's name, and all yours. Your daughter defires a Bible and a gown. I hope fhe fhall ufe the Bible well, which if fhe do, the gown is the better beftowed. The Lord Jefus be with your fpirit.

Yours for ever in Chrift,

S. R.

Anwoth.

XLV.—*For* Marion M'Naught.

(IN THE PROSPECT OF THE COMMUNION, AND OF TRIALS TO THE CHURCH.)

ELL-BELOVED SISTER IN CHRIST,—You fhall underftand I have received a letter from Edinburgh, that it is fufpected that there will be a General Af-fembly, or then § fome meeting of the bifhops ; and that at this fynod there will be fome commiffioners chofen by the Bifhop ; which news have fo taken up my mind that I am not fo fettled for ftudies as I have been before, and therefore was never in fuch fear for the work. But becaufe it is written to me as a fecret, I dare not reveal it to any but to yourfelf, whom I know. And therefore, I entreat you, not for any comfort of mine, who am but one man, but for the glory and honour of Jefus Chrift, the Mafter of the banquet, be more earneft with God ; and, in general, fhow others of your Chriftian acquaintance my fears for myfelf. I can be content of fhame in that work, if my Lord and Mafter be honoured ; and therefore petition our Lord efpecially to fee to His own glory,

---

* Ifa. xxvi. 2c. † Till. ‡ Ground of charge. § Or if not that.

and to give bread to His hungry bairns, howbeit I go hungry away from the feaſt. Requeſt Mr Robert* from me, if he come not, to remember us to our Lord.

I have neither time, nor a free diſpoſed mind, to write to you anent your own caſe. Send me word if all your children and your huſband be well. Seeing they are not yours, but your dear Lord's, eſteem them but as borrowed, and lay them down at God's feet. Your Chriſt to you is better than they all. You will pardon my unaccuſtomed ſhort letter; and remember me and that honourable feaſt to our Lord Jeſus. He was with us before. I hope He will not change upon us; but I fear I have changed upon Him. But, Lord, let old kindneſs ſtand. Jeſus Chriſt be with your ſpirit.

Yours in his ſweet Lord Jeſus,

S. R.

Anwoth.

XLVI.—*To* Marion M'Naught.

(TOSSINGS OF SPIRIT—HER CHILDREN AND HUSBAND.)

WELL-BELOVED AND DEAR SISTER,—My tender affeċtion in Chriſt remembered. I left you in as great heavineſs as I was in ſince I came to this country; but I know you doubt not but that (as the truth is in Chriſt), my ſoul is knit to your ſoul, and to the ſoul of all yours; and I would, if I could, ſend you the largeſt part of my heart incloſed in this letter. But by fervent calling upon my Lord, I have attained ſome viċtory over my heart, which runneth often not knowing whither, and over my beguiling hopes, which I know now better than I did. I truſt in my Lord to hold aloof from the enticings of a ſeducing heart, by which I am daily coſened; and I mind not (by His grace who hath called me according to His eternal purpoſe) to come ſo far within the gripſ† of my fooliſh mind, grippinġ‡ about any folly com-ing its way, as the woodbine or ivy goeth about the tree.

---

* Mr Robert Glendinning.   † Graſp.   ‡ Graſping.

I adore and kifs the providence of my Lord, who knoweth well what is moft expedient for me, and for you and your children ; and I think of you as of myfelf, that the Lord, who in His deep wifdom turneth about all the wheels and turning of fuch changes, fhall alfo difpofe of that for the beft to you and yours. In the prefence of my Lord, I am not able, howbeit I would, to conceive amifs of you in that matter. Grace, grace for ever be upon you and your feed , and it fhall be your portion, in defpite of all the powers of darknefs. Do not make more queftion of this. But the Lord faw a nail in my heart loofe, and He hath now faftened it. Honour be to His Majefty.

I hear your fon is entered to the fchool. If I had known of the day, I would have begged from our Lord that He would have put the book in his hand with His own hand. I truft in my Lord it is fo ; and I conceive a hope to fee him a ftar, to give light in fome room of our Lord's houfe ; and purpofe, by the Lord's grace, as I am able (if our Lord call you to reft before me), when you are at your home, to do to the uttermoft of my power to help him every way in grace and learning, and his brothers, and all your children. And I hope you would expect that of me.

Further, you fhall know that Mr W. D.* is come home, who faith it is a miracle that your hufband, in this procefs before the Council, efcaped both difcredit and damage. Let it not be forgotten he was, in our apprehenfion, to our grief, caft down and humbled in the Lord's work, in that matter betwixt him and the bailie : now the Lord hath honoured him, and made him famous for virtue, honefty, and integrity, two feveral times, before the nobles of this kingdom. Your Lord liveth. We will go to His throne of grace again : His arm is not fhortened.

The King is certainly expected. Ill is feared ; we have caufe for our fins to fear that the Bridegroom fhall be taken from us. By our fins we have rent His fair garments, and we have ftirred up

---

* William Dalgleifh, minifter of Kirkdale and Kirkmabreck, adjoining the parifh of Anwoth.

and awakened our Beloved. Pray Him to tarry, or then* to take us with Him. It were good that we fhould knock and rap at our Lord's door. We may not tire to knock oftener than twice or thrice. He knoweth the knock of His friends.

I am ftill what I was ever to your dear children, tendering their foul's happinefs, and praying that grace, grace, grace, mercy, and peace from God, even God our Father, and from our Lord Jefus, may be their portion; and that now, while they are green and young, their hearts may take band† with Jefus, the Corner-ftone : and win once in, in our Lord and Saviour's houfe, and then they will not get leave to flit. Pray for me, and efpecially for humility and thankfulnefs. I have always remembrance of you, and your hufband, and dear children. The Lord Jefus be with your fpirit.

Yours evermore in my dear Lord Jefus and yours,

S. R.

ANWOTH.

XLVII.—*For* MARION M'NAUGHT.

(SUBMISSION TO GOD'S ARRANGEMENTS.)

ORTHY AND BELOVED MISTRESS,—My love in Chrift remembered. I have fent you a letter from Mr David Dick‡ concerning the placing of Mr Hugh M'Kail with themfelves; therefore I write to you now only to entreat you in Chrift not to be difcouraged thereat. Be fubmiffive to the will of your dear Lord, who knoweth beft what is good for your foul and your town both; for God can come over greater mountains than thefe, we believe; for He worketh His greateft works contrary to carnal reafon and means. " My ways are not," faith our Lord, "as your ways; neither are My thoughts as your thoughts."§   I am no whit put from my belief for all that. Be-

---

* Or elfe.   † Unite with.   ‡ Or Dickfon.   § Ifa. lv. 8.

lieve, pray, and ufe means. We fhall caufe Mr John Kerr, who conveyed myfelf to Lochinvar, to ufe means to feek a man, if Mr Hugh fail us. Our Lord has a little bride among you, and I truft He will fend one to woo her to our fweet Lord Jefus. He will not want His wife for the fuiting,* and He has means in abundance in His hand to open all the flots† and bars that Satan draws over the door. He cometh to His bride leaping over the mountains, and fkipping over the hills. His way to His fpoufe is full of ftones, mountains, and waters, yet He putteth in His foot and wadeth through. He will not want her; and therefore refrefh me with two words concerning your confidence and courage in our Lord, both about that, and about His own Zion; for He wooeth His wife in the Burning Bufh; and for the good-will of Him that dwelleth in the bufh, the bufh is not confumed. It is better to weep with Jerufalem in the forenoon, than to weep with Babel after noon, in the end of the day. Our day of laughter and rejoicing is coming. Yet a little while, and ye fhall fee the falvation of God. I long to fee you, and to hear how your children are, efpecially Samuel. Grace be their heritage and portion from the Lord, and the Lord be their lot, and then their inheritance fhall pleafe them well. Remember my love to your hufband. The Lord Jefus be with your fpirit.

Yours in his fweeteft Lord Jefus,

S. R.

Anwoth.

XLVIII.—*For* Marion M'Naught.

*(TROUBLES FROM FALSE BRETHREN—OCCURRENCES—
CHRIST'S COMING—INTERCESSION.)*

ELL-BELOVED SISTER,—I know you have heard of the fuccefs of our bufinefs in Edinburgh. I do every Prefbytery day fee the faces of my brethren fmiling

---

* Urging His requeft, wooing.   † Moveable bolts.

upon me, but their tongues convey reproaches and lies of me a hundred miles off, and have made me odious to the Bifhop of St Andrews, who faid to Mr W. Dalgleifh that minifters in Galloway were his informers. Whereupon no letter of favour could be procured from him for effectuating of our bufinefs ; only I am brought in the mouths of men, who otherwife knew me not, and have power (if God fhall permit) to harm me. Yet I entreat you, in the bowels of Chrift Jefus, be not caft down. I fear your forrow exceed becaufe of this ; and I am not fo careful for myfelf in the matter as for you. Take courage ;—your deareft Lord will light your candle, which the wicked would fain blow out ; and, as fure as our Lord liveth, your foul fhall find joy and comfort in this bufinefs. Howbeit you fee all the hounds in hell let loofe to mar it, their iron chains to our dear and mighty Lord are but ftraws, which He can eafily break. Let not this temptation ftick in your throat ; fwallow it, and let it go down ; our Lord give you a drink of the confolations of His Spirit, that it may digeft. You never knew one in God's book who put to their hand to the Lord's work for His kirk, but the world and Satan did bark againft them, and bite alfo where they had power. You will not lay one ftone on Zion's walls, but they will labour to caft it down again.

For myfelf, the Lord letteth me fee now greater evidence of a calling to Kirkcudbright than ever He did before ; and therefore pray, and poffefs your foul in patience. Thofe that were doers in the bufinefs have good hopes that it will yet go forward and profper. As for the death of the King of Sweden (which is thought to be too true), we can do nothing elfe but reverence our Lord, who doth not ordinarily hold Zion on her rock by the fword, and arm of flefh and blood, but by His own mighty and outftretched arm. Her King that reigneth in Zion yet liveth, and they are plucking Him round about to pull Him off His throne ; but His Father hath crowned Him, and who dare fay, "It is ill done"? The Lord's bride will be up and down, above the water fwimming and under the water finking, until her lovely and mighty Redeemer and Hufband fet His head through the fkies, and come with His fair

court to red* all their pleas, and give them the hoped-for inheritance : and then we fhall lay down our fwords and triumph, and
fight no more.   But do not think, for all this, that our Lord and
Chief Shepherd will want one weak fheep, or the fillieft dying
lamb, that He hath redeemed.   He will tell His flock and gather
them all together, and make a faithful account of them to the
Father who gave them to Him.   Let us learn to turn our eyes off
men, that our whorifh hearts doat not on them, and woo our old
Hufband, and make Him our darling.   For, "thus faith the Lord
to the enemies of Zion, Drink ye, and be drunk, and fpue, and fall,
and rife no more, becaufe of the fword that I fend amongft you.
And it fhall be, if they refufe to take the cup at thine hand to drink,
then fhalt thou fay to them, Thus faith the Lord of Hofts, Ye fhall
certainly drink."†   You fee our Lord brewing a cup of poifon for
His enemies, which they muft drink, and becaufe of this have fore
bowels and fick ftomachs, yea, burft.   But when Zion's captivity is
at an end, " the children of Ifrael fhall come, they and the children
of Judah together, going and weeping : they fhall go, and feek
the Lord their God.   They fhall afk the way to Zion, with their
faces thitherward, faying, Come, and let us join ourfelves to the
Lord in an everlafting covenant that fhall not be forgotten."‡   This
is fpoken to us, and for us, who with woe§ hearts afk, "What
is the way to Zion?"   It is our part who know how to go
to our Lord's door, and to knock by prayer, and how to lift
Chrift's flot,‖ and fhut the bar of His chamber door, to complain
and tell Him how the Lord handleth us, and how our King's
bufinefs goeth, that He may get up and lend them a blow, who are
tigging¶ and playing with Chrift and His fpoufe.   You have alfo,
dear Miftrefs, houfe troubles, in ficknefs of your hufband and bairns,
and in fpoiling of your houfe by thieves ; take thefe rods in patience
from your Lord.   He muft ftill move you from veffel to veffel, and
grind you as our Lord's wheat, to be bread in His houfe.   But

---

* Settle all difputes.   † Jer. xxv. 27, 28.   ‡ Jer. l. 4, 5.
§ Sorrowful.   ‖ Moveable bolt.   ¶ Dallying, toying.

when all thefe ftrokes are over your head, * what will ye fay to fee
your well-beloved Chrift's white and ruddy face, even His face
who is worthy to bear the colours among ten thoufand ?† Hope
and believe to the end. Grace for ever be multiplied upon you,
your hufband, and children.

Your own in his deareft Lord Jefus,

S. R.

EDINBURGH, *Dec.* 1634.

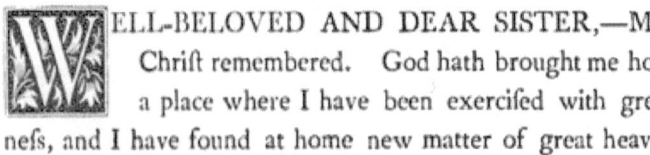

XLIX.—*To* MARION M'NAUGHT.

*(SPOILING OF GOODS—CALL TO KIRKCUDBRIGHT—THE LORD
REIGNETH.)*

WELL-BELOVED AND DEAR SISTER,—My love in
Chrift remembered. God hath brought me home from
a place where I have been exercifed with great heavinefs, and I have found at home new matter of great heavinefs, yet
dare not but in all things give thanks.

In my bufinefs in Edinburgh,‡ I have not finned nor wronged
my party,—by his own confeffion, and by the confeffion of his friends,
I have given of my goods for peace and the faving of my Lord's
truth from reproaches, which is dearer to me than all I have. My
mother is weak, and I think fhall leave me alone ; but I am not
alone, becaufe Chrift's Father is with me.

For your bufinefs anent your town I fee great evidence ; but
Satan and his inftruments are againft it, and few fet their fhoulders
to Chrift's fhoulder to help Him. But He will do all His lone ;
and I dare not but exhort you to believe, and perfuade you, that
the hungry in your city fhall be fed ; and as for the reft that want
a ftomach, the parings of God's loaf will fuffice them ; and, therefore, believe it fhall be well. I may not leave my mother to come
and confer with you of all particulars. I have given fuch directions

---

* Paft and gone.   † Cant. v. 10   ‡ See note, Let. 12.

to our dear friend as I can ; but the event is in our dear Lord's hands.

God's Zion abroad flouriſheth, and His arm is not ſhortened with us, if we could believe. There is ſcarcity and a famine of the word of God in Edinburgh. Your ſiſter Jane laboureth mightily in our buſineſs ; but hath not as yet gotten an anſwer from I. P. Mr A. C.* will work what he can. My Lady ſaith ſhe can do little, and that it ſuiteth not her nor her huſband well to ſpeak in ſuch an affair. I told her my mind plainly.

I long to know of your eſtate. Remember me heartily to your dear huſband. Grace be the portion of your bairns. I know you are mindful of the green wound of our ſiſter kirk in Ireland. Bid our Lord lay a plaiſter to it (He hath good ſkill to do ſo), and ſet others to work. Grace, grace upon your ſoul, and body, and all yours.

Yours in Chriſt,

S. R.

ANWOTH.

[The following brief note, addreſſed to Marion M'Naught, may be read as a ſort of poſtſcript to the foregoing, though generally printed as a ſeparate Letter.]

EAR MISTRESS,—I have not time this day to write to you ; but God, knowing my preſent ſtate and neceſſities of my calling, will, I hope, ſpare my mother's life for a time, for the which I have cauſe to thank the Lord. I entreat you, be not caſt down for that which I wrote before to you anent the planting of a miniſter in your town. Believe, and you ſhall ſee the ſalvation of God. I write this, becauſe when you ſuffer, my heart ſuffereth with you. I do believe your ſoul ſhall have joy in your labours and holy deſires for that work. Grace upon you, and your huſband, and children.

Yours ever in Chriſt.

ANWOTH.

---

* Probably Mr Alexander Colville, mentioned Let. 11.

I.—*For* MARION M'NAUGHT.

(CHRIST COMING AS CAPTAIN OF SALVATION—HIS CHURCH'S CONFLICT AND COVENANT—THE JEWS—LAST DAYS APOSTASY.)

WELL-BELOVED AND DEAR SISTER,—I know your heart is caſt down for the deſolation like to come upon this kirk, and the appearance that an hireling ſhall be thruſt in upon Chriſt's flock in that town ; but ſend a heavy heart up to Chriſt, it ſhall be welcome. Thoſe who are with the beaſt and the dragon, muſt make war with the Lamb ; "but the Lamb ſhall overcome them : for He is Lord of lords, and King of kings ; and they who are with Him are called, and choſen, and faithful."* Our ten days ſhall have an end ; all the former things ſhall be forgotten when we ſhall be up before the throne. Chriſt hath been ever thus in the world ; He hath always the defender's part, and hath been ſtill in the camp, fighting the Church's battles. The enemies of the Son of God will be fed with their own fleſh, and ſhall drink their own blood ; and therefore, their part of it ſhall at laſt be found hard enough : ſo that we may look forward and pity them. Until the number of the elect be fulfilled, Chriſt garments muſt be rolled in blood. He cometh from Edom, from the ſlaughter of His ene-mies, "clothed with dyed garments, glorious in His apparel, travel-ling in the greatneſs of His ſtrength." Who is this (ſaith he) that appears in this glorious poſture ? Our great He! that He who is mighty to ſave, whoſe glory ſhineth while He ſprinkleth the blood of His adverſaries, and ſtaineth all His raiment. The glory of His righteous revenges ſhineth forth in theſe ſtains.† But ſeeing our world is not here-away,‡ we poor children, far from home, muſt ſteal through many waters, weeping as we go, and withal believing that we do the Lord's faithfulneſs no wrong, ſeeing He hath ſaid,

* Rev. xvii. 14. † Iſa. lxiii. 1.
‡ In this quarter, in this preſent life's enjoyments.

"I, even I, am He that comforteth you : who art thou, that fhouldeft be afraid of a man that fhall die, and of the fon of man that fhall be made as grafs ?"* "When thou paffeft through the waters, I will be with thee ; and through the rivers, they fhall not overflow thee. When thou walkeft through the fire, thou fhalt not be burnt; neither fhall the flames kindle upon thee."†

There is a cloud gathering and a ftorm coming. This land fhall be turned upfide down ; and if ever the Lord fpake to me (think on it), Chrift's bride will be glad of a hole to hide her head in, and the dragon may fo prevail as to chafe the woman and her man-child over fea. But there fhall be a gleaning, two or three berries left in the top of the olive-tree, of whom God fhall fay, "Deftroy them not, for there is a bleffing in them." Thereafter there fhall be a fair fun-blink‡ on Chrift's old fpoufe, and a clear fky, and fhe fhall fing as in the days of her youth. The Antichrift and the great red dragon will lop Chrift's branches, and bring His vine to a low ftump, under the feet of thofe who carry the mark of the beaft ; but the Plant of Renown, the Man whofe name is the Branch, will bud forth again and bloffom as the rofe, and there fhall be fair white flourifhes§ again, with moft pleafant fruits, upon that tree of life. A fair feafon may He have! Grace, grace be upon that bleffed and beautiful tree! under whofe fhadow we fhall fit, and his fruit fhall be fweet to our tafte. But Chrift fhall woo His handful in the fire, and choofe His own in the furnace of affliction. But be it fo ; He dow‖ not, He will not flay His children. Love will not let Him make a full end. The covenant will caufe Him hold His hand. Fear not, then, faith the Firft and the Laft, He who was dead and is alive. We fee not Chrift fharpening and furbifhing His fword for His enemies ; and therefore our faithlefs hearts fay, as Zion did, "The Lord hath forfaken me." But God reproveth her, and faith, "Well, well, Zion, is that well faid ? Think again on it , you are in the wrong to Me. Can a

---

* Ifa. li. 12. †Ifa. xliii. 2. ‡ Gleam of funfhine.
§ Bloffoms. ‖ Can.

woman forget her fucking child, that fhe fhould not have compaffion on the fruit of her womb? Yea, fhe may; yet will I not forget thee. Behold, I have engraven thee upon the palms of My hands."* You break your heart and grow heavy, and forget that Chrift hath your name engraven on the palms of His hand in great letters. In the name of the Son of God, believe that buried Scotland, dead and buried with her dear Bridegroom, fhall rife the third day again, and there fhall be a new growth after the old timber is cut down. I recommend you, and your burdens and heavy heart, to the fupporting of His grace and good-will who dwelt in the Bufh, to Him who was feparated from His brethren. Try your hufband afar off, to fee if He can be induced to think upon going to America.

O to fee the fight, next to Chrift's Coming in the clouds, the moft joyful! our elder brethren the Jews and Chrift fall upon one another's necks and kifs each other! They have been long afunder; they will be kind to one another when they meet. O day! O longed-for and lovely day-dawn! O fweet Jefus, let me fee that fight which will be as life from the dead, Thee and Thy ancient people in mutual embraces.

Defire your daughter to clofe with Chrift upon terms of fuffering for Him; for the crofs is an old mealing† and plot of ground that lyeth to Chrift's houfe. Our dear Chief had aye that rent lying to His inheritance. But tell her the day is near the dawning, the fky is riving;‡ our Beloved will be on us, ere ever we be aware. The Antichrift, and death and hell, and Chrift's enemies and ours, will be bound and caft into the bottomlefs pit. The Lord Jefus be with your fpirit.

Yours in his fweet Lord Jefus,

S. R.

ANWOTH, *April* 22, 1635.

---

* Ifa. xlix. 15, 16. † Farm. It is written alfo "*mailing*." See Let. 29.
‡ Breaking, rending.

LI.—*To* MARION M'NAUGHT.

(PUBLIC TEMPTATIONS—THE SECURITY OF EVERY SAINT—
OCCURRENCES IN THE COUNTRY-SIDE.)

OVING AND DEAR SISTER,—For Zion's fake hold
not your peace, neither be difcouraged, for the ongoing
of this perfecution. Jehovah is in this burning Bufh.
The floods may fwell and roar, but our ark fhall fwim above the
waters ; it cannot fink, becaufe a Saviour is in it. Becaufe our Beloved was not let in by His fpoufe when He ftood at the door, with
His wet and frozen head, therefore He will have us to feek Him
awhile ; and while we are feeking, the watchmen who go about
the walls have ftricken the poor woman, and have taken away her
veil from her. But yet a little while and our Lord will come again.
Scotland's fky will clear again ; her moment muft go over. I dare
in faith fay and write, I am not dreaming ; Chrift is but feeking
(what He will have and make) a clean gliftering* bride out of the
fire. God fend Him His errand, but He cannot want what He feeks.
In the meantime, one way or other, He fhall find, or make a neft
for His mourning dove. What is this we are doing, breaking the
neck of our faith ? We are not come as yet to the mouth of the
Red Sea ; and howbeit we were, for His honour's fake, He muft
dry it up. It is our part to die gripping† and holding faft His faithful promife. If the Beaft fhould get leave to ride through the land,
to feal fuch as are his, he will not get one lamb with him, for thefe
are fecured and fealed as the fervants of God. In God's name, let
Chrift take His barn-floor, and all that is in it, to a hill, and winnow
it. Let Him fift His corn, and fweep His houfe, and feek His loft
gold. The Lord fhall cog‡ the rumbling wheels, or turn them ; for

---

* Glittering, fhining.　　　　　　　† Grafping, or clafping.

‡ Put a drag on ; it is to put a piece of wood edgewife between it and the
ground, to prevent it moving.

the remainder of wrath doth He reftrain.   He can loofe the belt of
kings ; to God, their belt, wherewith they are girt, is knit with a
fingle draw-knot.*

As for a paftor to your town, your confcience can bear you
witnefs you have done your part.   Let the Mafter of the vineyard
now fee to His garden, feeing you have gone on, till He hath faid,
" Stand ftill."   The will of the Lord be done.   But a trial is not,
to give up with God and believe no more.   I thank my God in
Chrift, I find the force of my temptation abated, and its edge blunted,
fince I fpoke to you laft.   I know not if the tempter be hovering,
until he find the dam gather again, and me more fecure ; but it hath
been my burden, and I am yet more confident the Lord will fuccour
and deliver.

I intend, God willing, that our Communion fhall be celebrated
the firft Sabbath after Pafch.†   Our Lord, that great Mafter of the
feaft, fend us one hearty and heartfome‡ fupper, for I look it fhall
be the laft.   But we expect, when the fhadows fhall flee away, and
our Lord fhall come to His garden, that He fhall feed us in green
paftures without fear.   The dogs fhall not then be hounded out
amongft the fheep.   I earneftly defire your prayers for affiftance at
our work, and put others with you to do the fame.   Remember
me to your hufband, and defire your daughter to be kind to Chrift,
and feek to win§ near Him ; He will give her a welcome into His
houfe of wine, and bring her into the King's chamber.   O how will
the fight of His face, and the fmell of His garments, allure and
ravifh the heart !   Now, the love of the lovely Son of God be with
you.

Yours in his fweet Jefus,

S. R.

Anwoth, 1635.

---

* Slip-knot, eafily loofened.   † Eafter, πασχα, Acts xii. 4.
‡ Cheerful, cheering.   § Get in.

LII.—*For* Marion M'Naught.

(IN THE PROSPECT OF HER HUSBAND BEING COMPELLED TO RECEIVE THE COMMAND OF THE PRELATES—SAINTS ARE YET TO JUDGE.)

WELL-BELOVED MISTRESS,—I charge you in the name of the Son of God, to reft upon your Rock, that is higher than yourfelf. Be not afraid of a man, who is a worm, nor of the fon of man, who fhall die. God be your fear. Encourage your hufband. I would counfel you to write to Edinburgh to fome advifed lawyers, to underftand what your hufband, as the head magiftrate, may do in oppofing any intruded minifter, and in his carriage toward the new prelate,* if he command him to imprifon or lay hands upon any, and, in a word, how far he may in his office difobey a prelate, without danger of law. For if the Bifhop come to your town, and find not obedience to his heart, it is like he will command the Provoft to affift him againft God and the truth. Ye will have more courage under the perfecution. Fear not ; take Chrift caution,† who faid, "There fhall not one hair of your head perifh."‡ Chrift will not be in your common § to have you giving out anything for Him, and not give you all incomes with advantage. It is His honour His fervants fhould not be herried ‖ and undone in His fervice. You were never honoured till now. And if your hufband be the firft magiftrate who fhall fuffer for Chrift's name in this perfecution, he may rejoice that Chrift hath put the firft garland on his head and upon yours. Truth will yet

---

* An attempt had been made by the Bifhop of Sydferff to force a minifter upon the people of Kirkcudbright, in room of Mr Glendinning, who had been fufpended, and ordered to be imprifoned, becaufe he would not conform to Epifcopacy. Provoft Fullarton (hufband of M. M'Naught), along with other magiftrates, would not imprifon Mr Glendinning, and this was the occafion of the above letter. See note at beginning of Let. 67.

† Surety. ‡ Luke xxi. 18. § Under obligation to. ‖ Pillaged cruelly.

keep the crown of the caufey* in Scotland. Chrift and truth are ftrong enough. They judge us now; we fhall one day judge them, and fit on twelve thrones and judge the twelve tribes. Believe, believe; for they dare not pray; they dare not look Chrift in the face. They have been falfe to Chrift, and He will not fit with† the wrong. Ye know it is not our caufe; for if we would quit our Lord, we might fleep for the prefent in a found fkin, and keep our place, means, and honour, and be dear to them alfo; but let us once put all we have over in Chrift's hand. Fear not for my papers; I fhall defpatch them, but ye will be examined for them. The Spirit of Jefus give you inward peace. Defire your hufband from me to prove honeft to Chrift; he fhall not be a lofer at Chrift's hand.

Yours ever in his fweet Lord Jefus,

ANWOTH, *July* 8, 1635.   S. R.

LIII.—*For* MARION M'NAUGHT.

(*ENCOURAGEMENT UNDER TRIAL BY PROSPECT OF BRIGHTER DAYS.*)

ISTRESS,—My love in Chrift remembered. Having appointed a meeting with Mr David Dickfon, and knowing that B. will not keep the Prefbytery, I cannot fee you now. Commend my journey to God. My foul bleffeth you for your laft letter. Be not difcouraged; Chrift will not want the Ifles-men. The Ifles fhall wait for His law. We are His inheritance, and He will fell no part of His inheritance. For the fins of this land, and our breach of the covenant, contempt of the Gofpel, and our defection from the truth, He hath fet up a burning furnace in our Mount Zion; but I fay it, and will bide by it, the grafs fhall yet grow green on our Mount Zion. There fhall be dew all the night upon the lilies, amongft which Chrift feedeth, until the day break, and the fhadows flee away. And the moth fhall eat up

---

* Appear openly with credit on the public ftreet.   † Bear in filence.

the enemies of Chrift. Let them make a fire of their own, and
walk in the light thereof, it fhall not let them fee to go to their
bed ; but they fhall lie down in forrow.* Therefore, rejoice and
believe. This in hafte. Grace, grace be with you and yours.

Yours in Chrift,

S. R.

ANWOTH.

LIV.—*For* MARION M'NAUGHT.

(*PUBLIC WRONGS—WORDS OF COMFORT.*)

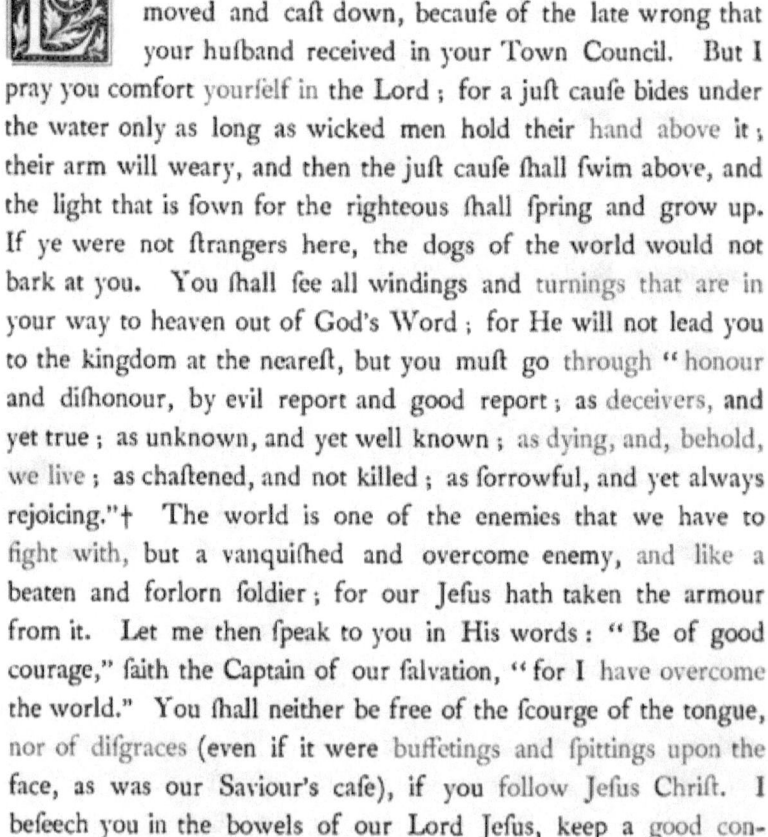

LOVING AND DEAR SISTER,—I fear that you be
moved and caft down, becaufe of the late wrong that
your hufband received in your Town Council. But I
pray you comfort yourfelf in the Lord ; for a juft caufe bides under
the water only as long as wicked men hold their hand above it ;
their arm will weary, and then the juft caufe fhall fwim above, and
the light that is fown for the righteous fhall fpring and grow up.
If ye were not ftrangers here, the dogs of the world would not
bark at you. You fhall fee all windings and turnings that are in
your way to heaven out of God's Word ; for He will not lead you
to the kingdom at the neareft, but you muft go through "honour
and difhonour, by evil report and good report ; as deceivers, and
yet true ; as unknown, and yet well known ; as dying, and, behold,
we live ; as chaftened, and not killed ; as forrowful, and yet always
rejoicing."† The world is one of the enemies that we have to
fight with, but a vanquifhed and overcome enemy, and like a
beaten and forlorn foldier ; for our Jefus hath taken the armour
from it. Let me then fpeak to you in His words : "Be of good
courage," faith the Captain of our falvation, "for I have overcome
the world." You fhall neither be free of the fcourge of the tongue,
nor of difgraces (even if it were buffetings and fpittings upon the
face, as was our Saviour's cafe), if you follow Jefus Chrift. I
befeech you in the bowels of our Lord Jefus, keep a good con-

---

* Ifa. l. 11.   † 2 Cor. vi. 8, 10.

ſcience, as I truſt you do.   You live not upon men's opinion ; gold
may be gold, and have the king's ſtamp upon it, when it is trampled
upon by men.   Happy are you, if, when the world trampleth upon
you in your credit and good name, yet you are the Lord's gold,
ſtamped with the King of heaven's image, and ſealed by the Spirit
unto the day of your redemption.   Pray for the ſpirit of love ; for
" love beareth all things ; it believeth all things, hopeth all things,
and endureth all things."*

And I pray you and your huſband, yea, I charge you before
God, and the Lord Jeſus Chriſt, and the elect angels, pray for
theſe your adverſaries, and read this to your huſband from me, and
let both of you put on, as the elect of God, bowels of mercies.
And, ſiſter, remember how many thouſands of talents of ſins your
Maſter hath forgiven you.   Forgive ye therefore your fellow-
ſervants one talent.   Follow God's command in this, and " ſeek
not after your own heart, and after your own eyes," in this matter,
as the Spirit ſpeaks.†   Aſk never the counſel of your own heart
here ; the world will blow up your heart now, and cauſe it ſwell,
except the grace of God cauſe it fall.   Jeſus, even Jeſus, the
Eternal Wiſdom of the Father, give you wiſdom.   I truſt God
ſhall be glorified in you.   And a door ſhall be opened unto you, as
to the Lord's priſoners of hope, as Zechariah ſpeaks.   It is a benefit
to you, that the wicked are God's fan to purge you.   And I hope
they ſhall blow away no corn, or ſpiritual graces, but only your
chaff.   I pray you in your purſuit, have ſo recourſe to the law of
men, that you wander not from the law of God.   Be not caſt
down : if you ſaw Him who, ſtanding on the ſhore, holding out
His arms to welcome you on land, you would not only wade
through a ſea of wrongs, but through hell itſelf to be at Him.   And
I truſt in God you ſee Him ſometimes.   The Lord Jeſus be with
your ſpirit, and all yours.

Your brother in the Lord,   S. R.

Anwoth.

---

* 1 Cor. xiii. 7.   † Num. xv. 39.

LV.—*To* Marion M'Naught.

(WHEN HE HAD BEEN THREATENED WITH PERSECUTION FOR PREACHING THE GOSPEL—THE SAINTS SHALL YET WIN THE DAY.)

ORTHY AND WELL-BELOVED MISTRESS,—My love in Chrift remembered. I know ye have heard of the purpofe of my adverfaries, to try what they can do againft me at this Synod for the work of God in your town when I was at your Communion. They intend to call me in queftion at the Synod for treafonable doctrine. Therefore help me with your prayers, and defire your acquaintance to help me alfo. Your ears heard how Chrift was there. If He fuffer His fervant to get a broken head in His own kingly fervice, and not either help or revenge the wrong, I never faw the like of it. There is not a night drunkard, time-ferving, idle, idol fhepherd to be fpoken againft : I am the only man ; and becaufe it is fo, and I know God will not help them left they be proud, I am confident their procefs fhall fall afunder. Only be ye earneft with God for hearing, for an open ear, and reading of the bill, that He may in heaven hear both parties, and judge accordingly. And doubt not, fear not ; they fhall not, who now ride higheft, put Chrift out of His kingly poffeffion in Scotland. The pride of man and his rage fhall turn to the praife of our Lord. It is an old feud, that the rulers of the earth, the dragon and his angels, have carried to the Lamb and His followers ; but the followers of the Lamb fhall overcome by the Word of God. And believe this, and wait on a little, till they have got their womb full of clay and gravel, and they fhall know (howbeit ftolen waters be fweet) Efau's portion is not worth his hunting. Commend me to your hufband, and fend me word how Grizel is. The Son of God lead her through the water. The Lord Jefus be with your fpirit.

Yours in his only, only Lord Jefus,

S. R.

Anwoth.

LVI.—*To My* Lady Kenmure.

(*REASONS FOR RESIGNATION—SECURITY OF SAINTS—THE END OF TIME.*)

ADAM,—I received your Ladyſhip's letter from J. G.[*] I thank our Lord ye are as well at leaſt as one may be who is not come home. It is a mercy in this ſtormy ſea to get a ſecond wind ; for none of the ſaints get a firſt, but they muſt take the winds as the Lord of the ſeas cauſeth them to blow, and the inn as the Lord and Maſter of the inns hath ordered it. If contentment were here, heaven were not heaven. Whoever ſeek the world to be their bed, ſhall at beſt find it ſhort and ill-made, and a ſtone under their ſide to hold them waking, rather than a ſoft pillow to ſleep upon. Ye ought to bleſs your Lord that it is not worſe. We live in a ſea where many have ſuffered ſhipwreck, and have need that Chriſt ſit at the helm of the ſhip. It is a mercy to win to heaven, though with much hard toil and heavy labour, and to take it by violence ill and well as it may be. Better go ſwimming and wet through our waters than drown by the way ; eſpecially now when truth ſuffereth, and great men bid Chriſt ſit lower and contraſt Himſelf in leſs bounds, as if He took too much room.

I expeſt our new prelate[†] ſhall try my ſitting. I hang by a thread, but it is (if I may ſpeak ſo) of Chriſt's ſpinning. There is no quarrel more honeſt or honourable than to ſuffer for truth. But the worſt is, that this kirk is like to ſink, and all her lovers and friends ſtand afar off ; none mourn with her, and none mourn for her. But the Lord Jeſus will not be put out of His conqueſt[‡] ſo ſoon in Scotland. It will be ſeen that the kirk and truth will riſe again within three days, and Chriſt again ſhall ride upon His white horſe ; howbeit His horſe ſeem now to ſtumble, yet he cannot fall. The fulneſs of Chriſt's harveſt in the end of the earth is not yet come in. I ſpeak not this becauſe I would have it ſo, but upon

---

[*] J. Gordon.   [†] Sydſerff.   [‡] Inheritance.

better grounds than my naked liking. But enough of this fad subject.

I long to be fully affured of your Ladyfhip's welfare, and that your foul profpereth, efpecially now in your folitary life, when your comforts outward are few, and when Chrift hath you for the very uptaking. I know His love to you is ftill running over, and His love hath not fo bad a memory as to forget you and your dear child, who hath two fathers in heaven, the one the Ancient of Days. I truft in His mercy He hath fomething laid up for him above, however it may go with him here. I know it is long fince your Ladyfhip faw this world turned your ftepmother and did for-fake you. Madam, ye have reafon to take in good part a lean dinner and fpare diet in this life, feeing your large fupper of the Lamb's preparing will recompenfe all. Let it go, which was never yours but only in fight, not in property. The time of your loan will wear fhorter and fhorter, and time is meafured to you by ounce weights ; and then I know your hope fhall be a full ear of corn and not blafted with wind. It may be your joy that your anchor is up within the vail, and that the ground it is caft upon is not falfe but firm. God hath done His part : I hope ye will not deny to fifh and fetch home all your love to Himfelf ; and it is but too narrow and fhort for Him if it were more. If ye were before pouring all your love (if it had been many gallons more) in upon your Lord, if drops fell by in the in-pouring, He forgiveth you. He hath done now all that can be done to win beyond it all, and hath left little to woo your love from Himfelf, except one only child. What is His purpofe herein He knoweth beft, who hath taken your foul in tutoring. Your faith may be boldly charitable of Chrift, that however matters go, the worft fhall be a tired travel-ler, and a joyful and fweet welcome home. The back of your winter night is broken. Look to the eaft, the day fky is breaking. Think not that Chrift lofeth time, or lingereth unfuitably. O fair, fair, and fweet morning ! We are but as fea paffengers. If we look right, we are upon our country coaft : our Redeemer is faft coming, to take this old worm-eaten world, like an old moth-eaten

garment, in His two hands, and to roll it up and lay it by Him.
Thefe are the laft days, and an oath is given, by God Himfelf, that
time fhall be no more ;* and when time itfelf is old and grey-haired,
it were good we were away. Thus, Madam, ye fee I am, as my
cuftom is, tedious in my lines. Your Ladyfhip will pardon it. The
Lord Jefus be with your fpirit.

Your Ladyfhip at all obedience in Chrift,

S. R.

Anwoth, *Jan.* 18, 1636.

LVII.—*For* Marion M‘Naught.

(IN THE PROSPECT OF REMOVAL TO ABERDEEN.)

ONOURED AND DEAREST IN THE LORD,—
Grace, mercy, and peace be to you. I am well, and
my foul profpereth. I find Chrift with me. I burden
no man; I want nothing; no face looketh on me but it laugheth
on me. Sweet, fweet is the Lord's crofs. I overcome my heavinefs. My Bridegroom's love-blinks† fatten my weary foul. I foon
go to my King's palace at Aberdeen. Tongue, and pen, and wit
cannot exprefs my joy.

Remember my love to Jean Gordon, to my fifter, Jean Brown,
to Grizel, to your hufband. Thus in hafte. Grace be with
you.

Yours in his only, only Lord Jefus,

S. R.

Edinburgh, *April 5,* 1636.

P.S.—My charge is to you to believe, rejoice, fing, and triumph.
Chrift has faid to me, Mercy, mercy, grace and peace for Marion
M‘Naught.

---

* Rev. x. 6.　　　　　　† Love-glances.

LVIII.—*To my* LADY KENMURE.

RIGHT HONOURABLE,—I´ cannot find a time for writing fome things I intended on Job, I have been fo taken up with the broils that we are encumbered with in our calling. For our prelate will have us either to fwallow our light over, and digeft it contrary to our ftomachs (howbeit we fhould vomit our confcience and all, in this troublefome conformity), or then * he will try if deprivation can convert us to the ceremonial faith.†

I write to your Ladyfhip, Madam, not as diftrufting your affection or willingnefs to help me, as your Ladyfhip is able by yourfelf or others, but to advertife you that I hang by a fmall thread. For our learned prelate, becaufe we cannot fee with his eyes fo far in a mill-ftone as his light doeth, will not follow his Mafter, meek Jefus, who waited upon the wearied and fhort-breathed in the way to heaven; and, where all fee not alike, and fome are weaker, He carrieth the lambs in His bofom, and leadeth gently thofe that are with young. But we muft either fee all the evil of ceremonies to be but as indifferent ftraws, or fuffer no lefs than to be caften out of the Lord's inheritance! Madam, if I had time I would write more at length, but your Ladyfhip will pardon me till a fitter occafion. Grace be with you and your child, and bear you company to your beft home.

Your Ladyfhip in his fweet Lord Jefus,

S. R.

ANWOTH, *June* 8, 1636.

---

* Or elfe.

† Referring to the attempts then made by the prelates to compel conformity to epifcopal forms.

[ALEXANDER GORDON of Earlston was defcended from the houfe of Gordon of Lochinvar, and the defignation of his family at firft was Gordon of Airds; but his great-grandfather, Alexander Gordon of Airds, having married Margaret, eldeft daughter of John Sinclair of Earlfton, the iffue of that union came to poffefs the lands of Earlfton.—(*Nifbet's Heraldry.*) His anceftors were at an early period brought to the knowledge of divine truth by fome of thofe difciples of Wickliff who itinerated in Scotland, preaching the pure doc- trines of the Gofpel; and they nobly vindicated the fincerity of their profeffion by the protection which they afforded to thefe devoted miffionaries, as well as by the zeal with which they laboured to propagate the faith. It is a tradition, that old Gordon of Airds imbibed Wickliffite views, when he was on a fort of embaffy to the Englifh Borderers, and that he propagated the truth by bringing home an Englifh Wickliffite to be tutor to his eldeft fon. Having obtained a New Teftament in the vulgar tongue, he read it at meetings which were held in the woods of Airds, in a fecluded fpot, at the junction of the Ken and the Dee, where the loch begins. So abundantly bleffed were fuch means, that the truth circulated rapidly through the whole province of Galloway. And at the very time when Patrick Hamilton fuffered martyrdom, on the laft day of February 1528, that province may be faid to have abjured Popery, and adopted the doctrines of the Reformation.

Earlfton, or *Erlifton*, or *Earlefton* (*Minute-book of Comm. of Covenanters*), is not far from Carfphairn. As you come from Dalry, you fee the roof of the ancient refidence among trees that furround it, and that grow up the flop- ing ridge at the foot of which it ftands. In front of the grim old tower, there is a fine lawn, a remnant of better days, and a linn not far off. It is not to be confounded with the *Earlfton* near Anwoth, in the parifh of Borgue, which is quite modern, having been built by a defcendant of this ancient family, and called after the name of the original property.

The grace of God, which had early chofen this family, continued to favour it for many generations. *Alexander Gordon*, Rutherford's friend, was worthy of his anceftors. Livingftone, in his *Characteriftics*, fpeaks of him as "a man of great fpirit, but much fubdued by inward exercife, and who attained the moft rare experience of downcafting and upholding;" and adds, "For wif- dom, courage, and righteoufnefs, he might have been a magiftrate in any part of the earth." In the ftruggle againft the attempts of the Court to introduce Prelacy into the Church of Scotland, he warmly efpoufed the fide of the Pref- byterians. In the end of July 1635, he was fummoned by the Bifhop of Glafgow to appear before the High Commiffion, for preventing the intrufion of an unpopular nominee of the Biſhop into a vacant pariſh. But Lord Lorn, afterwards the martyred Marquis of Argyle, having appeared with him before that court, and affirmed that what Earlſton had done was by his direction as patron of the pariſh, the matter was deferred to a future day. This letter of Rutherford to Earlſton, it is highly probable, refers to the vexatious proceedings inſtituted againſt him in regard to this matter. He was afterwards ſummoned by Sydſerff, Biſhop of Galloway, to appear before a High Commiſſion Court to be held at Wigtown. He did not make his appearance; but the Biſhop proceeded in his caſe, fined him five hundred merks, and baniſhed him to Montroſe. Earlſton, by the advice of Lord Lorn, gave in a repreſentation of his caſe to the Privy Council, who diſpenſed with his baniſhment upon the payment of his fine. Earlſton was a member of the Aſſembly which met at Glaſgow in 1638, having been a commiſſioner from the Preſbytery of Kirkcudbright. His name appears among the laſt of the members of Parliament in 1641, as member for the ſhire of Galloway. He was married to Elizabeth, daughter of John Gordon of Muirfad, by whom he had ſeveral children. His eldeſt ſon, William, who ſucceeded him, is retoured heir of his father on the 23d of January 1655. (*Inq. Retor. Abbrev.*, No. 264.) In the avenue leading to Earlſton, there is a very large old oak, ſtill ſhown as that in the thick foliage of which this William Gordon hid, and ſo eſcaped his purſuers, in the days of the perſecution.

(NO SUFFERING FOR CHRIST UNREWARDED—LOSS OF CHILDREN—CHRIST IN PROVIDENCE.)

MUCH HONOURED SIR,—I have heard of the mind and malice of your adverſaries againſt you. It is like they will extend the law they have, in length and breadth, anſwerable to their heat of mind. But it is a great part of your glory that the cauſe is not yours, but your Lord's whom you ſerve. And I doubt not but Chriſt will count it His honour to back His weak ſervant; and it were a ſhame for Him (with reverence to His holy name) that He ſhould ſuffer Himſelf to be in the common * of ſuch a poor man as ye are, and that ye ſhould give out for Him and not get in again. Write up your depurſments† for your Maſter Chriſt, and keep the account of what ye give out, whether name, credit, goods, or life, and ſuſpend your reckoning till nigh the evening; and remember that a poor weak ſervant of Chriſt

---

Under obligation to.   † Diſburſements.

wrote it to you, that ye fhall have Chrift, a King, caution* for your incomes and all your loffes. Reckon not from the forenoon. Take the Word of God for your warrant; and for Chrift's act of cautionary, howbeit body, life, and goods go for Chrift your Lord, and though ye fhould lofe the head for Him, yet " there fhall not one hair of your head perifh; in patience, therefore, poffefs your foul."† And becaufe ye are the firft man in Galloway called out and queftioned for the name of Jefus, His eye hath been upon you, as upon one whom He defigned to be among His witneffes. Chrift hath faid, " Alexander Gordon fhall lead the ring in witneffing a good confeffion," and therefore He hath put the garland of fuffer-ing for Himfelf firft upon your head. Think yourfelf fo much the more obliged to Him, and fear not; for He layeth His right hand on your head. He who was dead and is alive will plead your caufe, and will look attentively upon the procefs from the beginning to the end, and the Spirit of glory fhall reft upon you. " Fear none of thefe things which thou fhalt fuffer: behold, the devil fhall caft fome of you into prifon, that ye may be tried; and ye fhall have tribulation ten days: be thou faithful unto death, and I will give thee a crown of life."‡ This lovely One, Jefus, who alfo became the Son of man, that He might take ftrokes for you, write the crofs-fweetening and foul-fupporting fenfe of thefe words in your heart!

Thefe rumbling wheels of Scotland's ten days' tribulation are under His look who hath feven eyes. Take a houfe on your head, and flip yourfelf by faith in under Chrift's wings till the ftorm be over. And remember, when they have drunken us down, Jeru-falem will be a cup of trembling and of poifon.§ They fhall be fain to vomit out the faints; for Judah " fhall be a hearth of fire in a fheaf, and they fhall devour all the people round about, on the right hand and on the left." Woe to Zion's enemies! they have the worft of it; for we have writ ‖ for the victory. Sir, ye were never

---

* Security. † Luke xxi. 18, 19. ‡ Rev. ii. 10.
§ Zech. xii. 2, 6. ‖ A writing under His hand.

honourable till now. This is your glory, that Chrift hath put you
in the roll with Himfelf and with the reft of the witneffes who are
come out of great tribulation, and have wafhen their garments and
made them white in the blood of the Lamb. Be not caft down for
what the fervants of Antichrift caft in your teeth, that ye are a head
to and favourer of the Puritans, and leader to that fect. If your
confcience fay, "Alas! here is much din and little done" (as the proverb is), becaufe ye have not done fo much fervice to Chrift that way as
ye might and fhould, take courage from that fame temptation. For
your Lord Chrift looketh upon that very challenge* as an hungering defire in you to have done more than ye did; and that filleth
up the blank, and He will accept of what ye have done in that kind.
If great men be kind to you, I pray you overlook them; if they
fmile on you, Chrift but borroweth their face to fmile through them
upon His afflicted fervant. Know the well-head; and for all that,
learn the way to the well itfelf. Thank God that Chrift came to
your houfe in your abfence and took with Him fome of your children.
He prefumed that† much on your love, that ye would not offend;
and howbeit He fhould take the reft, He cannot come upon your
wrong fide. I queftion not, if they were children of gold, but ye
think them well beftowed upon Him.

Expound well thefe two rods on you, one in your houfe at
home, another on your own perfon abroad. Love thinketh no evil.
If ye were not Chrift's wheat, appointed to be bread in His houfe,
He would not grind you. But keep the middle line, neither defpife
nor faint.‡ Ye fee your Father is homely§ with you. Strokes of
a father evidence kindnefs and care; take them fo. I hope your
Lord hath manifefted Himfelf to you, and fuggefted thefe, or more
choice thoughts about His dealing with you. We are ufing our
weak moyen‖ and credit for you up at our own court, as we dow.¶
We pray the King to hear us, and the Son of Man to go fide for fide
with you, and hand in hand in the fiery oven, and to quicken and

---

* Rebuke, accufation. † So much, to that degree. ‡ Heb. xii. 5.
§ Familiar. ‖ Means, intereft. ¶ As we are able.

encourage your unbelieving heart when ye droop and defpond. Sir, to the honour of Chrift be it faid, my faith goeth with my pen now. I am prefently believing Chrift fhall bring you out. Truth in Scotland fhall keep the crown of the caufeway* yet. The faints fhall fee religion go naked at noon-day, free from fhame and fear of men. We fhall divide Shechem, and ride upon the high places of Jacob. Remember my obliged refpeƈts and love to Lady Kenmure and her fweet child.

　　　Yours ever in his fweet Lord Jefus,

　　　　　　　　　　　　　　　　　S. R.

ANWOTH, *July* 6, 1636.

------◆------

LX.—*To* MARION M‘NAUGHT.

(WHEN HE WAS UNDER TRIAL BY THE HIGH COMMISSION.)

Y DEAR AND WELL-BELOVED IN CHRIST,— I am yet under trial, and have appeared before Chrift's forbidden lords,† for a teftimony againft them. The Chancellor and the reft tempted me with queftions, nothing belonging to my fummons, which I wholly declined, notwithftanding of his threats. My newly printed book againft Arminians‡ was one challenge ; not lording the prelates§ was another. The moft part of the bifhops, when I came in, looked more aftonifhed than I, and heard me with filence. Some fpoke for me ; but my Lord ruled it fo as I am filled with joy in my fufferings, and I find Chrift's crofs fweet. What they intend againft the next day I know not. Be not fecure, but pray. Our Bifhop of Galloway faid, If the Commiffion fhould not give him his will of me (with an oath he faid), he would write to the King. The Chancellor fummoned me in judgment to appear

---

* Appear in public with triumph and honour.

† The Prelates, alluding to 1 Pet. v. 3.

‡ *Exercitat. Apol. pro Divinâ Gratiâ*, publifhed this year (1636) at Amfterdam.

§ Calling them " Lords."

that day eight days. My Lord has brought me a friend from the Highlands of Argyle, my Lord of Lorn,* who hath done as much as was within the compafs of his power. God gave me favour in his eyes. Mr Robert Glendinning is filenced, till he accepts a colleague. We hope to deal yet for him. Chrift is worthy to be entrufted. Your hufband will get an eafy and good way of his bufinefs. Ye and I both fhall fee the falvation of God upon Jofeph feparate from his brethren. Grace be with you.

S. R.

Edinburgh, 1636.

———◆———

LXI.—*To the truly Noble and Elect Lady, my* Lady Viscountess of Kenmure, *on the evening of his banifhment to Aberdeen.*

(HIS ONLY REGRETS—THE CROSS UNSPEAKABLY SWEET— RETROSPECT OF HIS MINISTRY.)

NOBLE AND ELECT LADY,—That honour that I have prayed for thefe fixteen years, with fubmiffion to my Lord's will, my kind Lord hath now beftowed upon me, even to fuffer for my royal and princely King Jefus, and for His kingly crown, and the freedom of His kingdom that His Father hath given Him. The forbidden lords† have fentenced me with deprivation, and confinement within the town of Aberdeen. I am charged in the King's name to enter againft the 20th day of Auguft next, and there to remain during the King's pleafure, as they have given it out. Howbeit Chrift's green crofs, newly laid upon me, be fomewhat heavy, while I call to mind the many fair days fweet and comfortable to my foul and to the fouls of many others, and how young ones in Chrift are plucked from the breaft, and the inherit-ance of God laid wafte; yet that fweet fmelled and perfumed crofs

---

* Brother to Lady Kenmure, afterwards the celebrated Marquis of Argyle. See Let. 61.   † Let. 60.

of Chrift is accompanied with fweet refrefhments, with the kiffes
of a King, with the joy of the Holy Ghoft, with faith that the Lord
hears the fighing of a prifoner, with undoubted hope (as fure as
my Lord liveth) after this night to fee daylight, and Chrift's fky
to clear up again upon me, and His poor kirk; and that in a
ftrange land, among ftrange faces, He will give favour in the eyes
of men to His poor oppreffed fervant, who dow* not but love
that lovely One, that princely One, Jefus, the Comforter of his
foul.   All would be well, if I were free of old challenges† for
guiltinefs, and for negleÉt in my calling, and for fpeaking too little
for my Well-beloved's crown, honour, and kingdom.   O for a day
in the affembly of the faints to advocate for King Jefus!   If my
Lord go on now to quarrels alfo, I die, I cannot endure it.   But I
look for peace from Him, becaufe He knoweth I dow* bear men's
feud, but I dow* not bear His feud.   This is my only exercife,
that I fear I have done little good in my miniftry; but I dare not
but fay, I loved the bairns of the wedding-chamber, and prayed
for and defired the thriving of the marriage, and coming of His
kingdom.

I apprehend no lefs than a judgment upon Galloway, and that
the Lord fhall vifit this whole nation for the quarrel of the Covenant.   But what can be laid upon me, or any the like of me, is too
light for Chrift.   Chrift dow* bear more, and would bear death and
burning quick, in His quick fervants, even for this honourable
caufe that I now fuffer for.   Yet for all my complaints (and He
knoweth that I dare not now diffemble), He was never fweeter and
kinder than He is now.   One kifs now is fweeter than ten long
fince; fweet, fweet is His crofs; light, light and eafy is His yoke.
O what a fweet ftep were it up to my Father's houfe through ten
deaths, for the truth and caufe of that unknown, and fo not half
well loved, Plant of Renown, the Man called the Branch, the Chief
among ten thoufands, the faireft among the fons of men!   O what
unfeen joys, how many hidden heart-burnings of love, are in the

---

* Can.   † Rebukes.

remnants of the fufferings of Chrift! My dear worthy Lady, I give it to your Ladyfhip, under my own hand, my heart writing as well as my hand,—welcome, welcome, fweet, fweet and glorious crofs of Chrift; welcome, fweet Jefus, with Thy light crofs. Thou haft now gained and gotten all my love from me; keep what Thou haft gotten! Only woe, woe is me, for my bereft flock, for the lambs of Jefus, that I fear fhall be fed with dry breafts. But I fpare now. Madam, I dare not promife to fee your Ladyfhip, becaufe of the little time I have allotted me; and I purpofe to obey the King, who hath power of my body; and rebellion to kings is unbefeeming Chrift's minifters. Be pleafed to acquaint my Lady Mar* with my cafe. I will look that your Ladyfhip and that good lady will be mindful to God of the Lord's prifoner, not for my caufe, but for the Gofpel's fake. Madam, bind me more, if more can be, to your Ladyfhip, and write thanks to your brother, my Lord of Lorn, for what he hath done for me, a poor unknown ftranger to his Lord-fhip. I fhall pray for him and his houfe, while I live. It is his honour to open his mouth in the ftreets, for his wronged and oppreffed Mafter Chrift Jefus. Now, Madam, commending your Ladyfhip and the fweet child to the tender mercies of mine own Lord Jefus, and His good-will who dwelt in the Bufh,

I am yours in his own fweeteft Lord Jefus,

S. R.

Edinburgh, *July* 28, 1636.

LXII.—*To the* Lady Culross, *on occafion of his banifhment to Aberdeen.*

[Elizabeth Melville, wife of James Colvill, the eldeft fon of Alexander, Commendator of Culrofs, was the daughter of Sir James Melville of Halhill, in Fife. Her father, an accomplifhed ftatefman, was ambaffador from Queen Mary to Queen Elizabeth, and a privy councillor to King James VI. He was alfo a man of piety, and, as Livingftone informs us, "profeffed he had got affurance from the Lord, that himfelf, wife, and all his children,

---

* See Let. to her, 140, and notice prefixed.

fhould meet in heaven." He died on the 13th of November 1617. Her mother was Chriftian, the feventh daughter of David Bofwell of Balmuto. (*Douglas's Peerage*, vol. ii.) Lady Culrofs held a high place among the eminent Chriftians of her day. Livingftone fays: "She was famous for her piety, and for her dream concerning her fpiritual condition, which fhe put in verfe, and was by others publifhed. Of all that ever I faw, fhe was moft unwearied in religious exercifes; and the more fhe enjoyed accefs to God therein fhe hungered the more." She was prefent at the Communion at Shotts in June 1636, when the fermon preached by Livingftone, on the Monday after the facrament, was the means, it is believed, of the converfion of not lefs than five hundred individuals. The night before had been fpent in prayer by a great number of Chriftians in a large room where fhe flept; and the minifter who fhould have preached on Monday having fallen fick, it was at her fuggeftion that the other minifters affifting on that occafion, to whom Livingftone was a ftranger, laid upon him the work of addreffing the people on Monday. There is a poem written by her entitled, "Ane Godlie Dream;" and there is ftill preferved a fonnet of her compofition, which fhe fent to Mr John Welfh when he was imprifoned in Blacknefs, 1605:—

"My dear brother, with courage bear the crofs,
   Joy fhall be joined with all thy forrow here.
High is thy hope, difdain this earthly drofs,
   Once fhall you fee the wifhed day appear.

"Now it is dark, thy fky cannot be clear,
   After the clouds it fhall be calm anon;
Wait on His will whofe blood hath bought thee dear:
   Extol His name, though outward joys be gone.

"Look to the Lord, thou art not left alone,
   Since He is thine, what pleafure canft thou take!
He is at hand, and hears thy every groan:
   End out thy fight, and fuffer for His fake.

"A fight moft bright thy foul fhall fhortly fee,
   When ftore of glore thy rich reward fhall be."
           —*Wodrow* MSS. Adv. Lib. Edin. vol. xxix.

(*CHALLENGES OF CONSCIENCE—THE CROSS NO BURDEN.*)

MADAM,—Your letter came in due time to me, now a prifoner of Chrift, and in bonds for the Gofpel. I am fentenced with deprivation and confinement within the town of Aberdeen. But O my guiltinefs, the follies of my youth, the neglects in my calling, and efpecially in not fpeaking more for the kingdom, crown, and fceptre of my royal and princely King Jefus, do fo ftare me in the face, that I apprehend anger in that which is a crown of rejoicing to the dear faints of God. This, before my compearance,* which was three feveral days, did trouble me, and burdeneth me more now ; howbeit Chrift, and in Him God reconciled, met me with open arms, and tryfted† me precifely at the entry of the door of the Chancellor's hall, and affifted me to anfwer, fo as the advantage that is is not theirs but Chrift's. Alas ! that is no caufe of wondering that I am thus borne down with challenges ;‡ for the world hath miftaken me, and no man knoweth what guiltinefs is in me fo well as thefe two, who keep my eyes now waking and my heart heavy, I mean, my heart and confcience, and my Lord, who is greater than my heart.

Shew your brother that I defire him, while he is on the watchtower, to plead with his mother, and to plead with this land, and fpare not to cry for my fweet Lord Jefus His fair crown, that the interdicted and forbidden lords§ are plucking off His royal head. If I were free of challenges‡ and a High Commiffion within my foul, I would not give a ftraw to go to my Father's houfe through ten deaths, for the truth and caufe of my lovely, lovely One, Jefus. But I walk in heavinefs now. If ye love me, and Chrift in me, my dear Lady, pray, pray for this only, that bygones betwixt my Lord and me may be bygones,‖ and that He would pafs from the fummons of His High Commiffion, and feek nothing from me, but what He will do for me and work in me. If your Ladyfhip knew me as I do myfelf, ye would fay, " Poor foul, no marvel." It is not my apprehenfion that createth this crofs to me ; it is too real, and hath fad and certain grounds. But I will not believe that God will take this advantage of me, when my back is at the wall. He who forbiddeth to add affliction to affliction, will He do it Himfelf ? Why fhould He purfue a dry leaf and ftubble ? Defire Him to fpare me

---

* Appearance at Court in obedience to a citation.

† Appointed a meeting with. ‡ Rebukes that I give myfelf.

§ The Prelates. ‖ All paft offences forgiven and forgotten.

now. Alfo the memory of the fair feast-days that Chrift and I had
in His banqueting-houfe of wine, and of the fcattered flock once committed to me, and now taken off my hand by Himfelf, becaufe I
was not fo faithful in the end as I was in the two firft years of my
entry, when fleep departed from my eyes, becaufe my foul was taken
up with a care for Chrift's lambs,—even thefe add forrow to my
forrow. Now my Lord hath only given me this to fay, and I write
it under mine own hand (be ye the Lord's fervant's witnefs), welcome, welcome, fweet, fweet crofs of Chrift ; welcome fair, fair,
lovely, royal King with Thine own crofs. Let us all three go to
heaven together. Neither care I much to go from the fouth of
Scotland to the north, and to be Chrift's prifoner amongft unco*
faces, in a place of this kingdom, which I have little reafon to be in
love with. I know Chrift fhall make Aberdeen my garden of delights. I am fully perfuaded that Scotland fhall eat Ezekiel's book,
that is written within and without, " lamentation, and mourning, and
woe."† But the faints fhall get a drink of the well that goeth
through the ftreets of the New Jerufalem, to put it down.‡ Thus
hoping that ye will think upon the poor prifoner of Chrift, I pray,
grace, grace be with you.

      Your Ladyfhip's in his fweet Lord Jefus,

                                 S. R.

EDINBURGH, *July* 30, 1636.

———◆———

LXIII.—*To* MR ROBERT CUNNINGHAM, *Minifter of the Gofpel at
Holywood, in Ireland.*

[MR ROBERT CUNNINGHAM was at firft for fome time employed as
chaplain to the Earl of Buccleuch's regiment in Holland. On the return of
the troops to Scotland, he removed to the north of Ireland, where he was admitted minifter of Holywood on the 9th of November 1615. " He was the
one man to my difcerning," fays Livingftone, " of all that ever I faw, who

---

* Strange.   † Ezek. ii. 10.
‡ Make it more pleafant to fwallow.

refembled moft the meeknefs of Jefus Chrift in his whole carriage, and was fo far reverenced by all, even the moft wicked, that he was oft troubled with that Scripture, ' Woe to you when all men fpeak well of you.'" He continued to labour in his charge, and in the furrounding diftrict, with great fuccefs, until, on the appointment of the Earl of Wentworth to be Lord Lieutenant of Ireland, the Prefbyterian minifters began to be molefted for their non-conformity. Owing to the fingular gentlenefs of Cunningham's difpofition, he was for fome time fubjected to lefs trouble than his brethren ; but at length, on the 12th of Auguft 1636, he and four other minifters, among whom was Mr Hamilton mentioned in the clofe of this letter, were formally depofed for refufing to fubfcribe certain canons, one of which was one enjoining kneeling at the Lord's Supper. Not long after, he and fome of his depofed brethren came over to Scotland ; but he did not long furvive his arrival, having been attacked with ficknefs at Irvine, where he died on the 29th of March 1637, fcarcely eight months after this letter was written. A little before he expired, while his wife was fitting on the front of his bed with her hand clafped in his, after committing to God by prayer his flock at Holywood, his friends and children, he faid, " And laft of all, I recommend to Thee this gentlewoman, who is no more my wife." His affectionate wife burfting into tears, he endeavoured by comfortable words to allay her grief ; and while in the act of fo doing, fell afleep in Jefus.]

(CONSOLATION TO A BROTHER IN TRIBULATION—HIS OWN DEPRIVATION OF MINISTRY—CHRIST WORTH SUFFERING FOR.)

ELL-BELOVED AND REVEREND BROTHER,— Grace, mercy, and peace be to you. Upon acquaintance in Chrift, I thought good to take the opportunity of writing to you. Seeing it hath feemed good to the Lord of the harveft to take the hooks* out of our hands for a time, and to lay upon us a more honourable fervice, even to fuffer for His name, it were good to comfort one another in writing. I have had a defire to fee you in the face ; yet now being the prifoner of Chrift, it is taken away. I am greatly comforted to hear of your foldier's ftately fpirit, for your princely and royal Captain Jefus our Lord, and for the grace of God in the reft of our dear brethren with you.

---

* The fickles for reaping.

You have heard of my trouble, I fuppofe. It hath pleafed our fweet Lord Jefus to let loofe the malice of thefe interdicted lords in His houfe to deprive me of my miniftry at Anwoth, and to confine me, eight fcore miles from thence, to Aberdeen ; and alfo (which was not done to any before) to inhibit* me to fpeak at all in Jefus' name, within this kingdom, under the pain of rebellion. The caufe that ripened their hatred was my book againft the Arminians, whereof they accufed me, on thefe three days I appeared before them. But, let our crowned King in Zion reign ! By His grace the lofs is theirs, the advantage is Chrift's and truth's. Albeit this honeft crofs gained fome ground on me, and my heavinefs and my inward challenges of confcience for a time were fharp, yet now, for the encouragement of you all, I dare fay it, and write it under my hand, " Welcome, welcome, fweet, fweet crofs of Chrift." I verily think the chains of my Lord Jefus are all overlaid with pure gold, and that His crofs is perfumed, and that it fmelleth of Chrift, and that the victory fhall be by the blood of the Lamb, and by the word of His truth, and that Chrift, lying on His back, in His weak fervants, and oppreffed truth, fhall ride over His enemies' bellies, and fhall " ftrike through kings in the day of His wrath."† It is time we laugh when He laugheth ; and feeing He is now pleafed to fit with‡ wrongs for a time, it becometh us to be filent until the Lord hath let the enemies enjoy their hungry, lean, and fecklefs§ paradife. Bleffed are they who are content to take ftrokes with weeping Chrift. Faith will truft the Lord, and is not hafty, nor headftrong ; neither is faith fo timorous as to flatter a temptation, or to bud‖ and bribe the crofs. It is little up or little down¶ that the Lamb and His followers can get no law-furety, nor truce with croffes ; it muft be fo, till we be up in our Father's houfe. My heart is woe** indeed for my mother Church, that hath played the harlot with many lovers. Her Hufband hath a mind to fell her for her horrible tranfgreffions ;

---

* Forbid.   † Ps. cx. 5.   ‡ To bear with in filence.
§ Worthlefs, no fubftance in it.   ‖ Try to gain by gift.
¶ Of little moment.   ** Sorrowful.

and heavy will the hand of the Lord be upon this backſliding nation. The ways of our Zion mourn ; her gold is become dim, her white Nazarites are black like a coal.   How ſhall not the children weep, when the Huſband and the mother cannot agree !   Yet I believe Scotland's ſky ſhall clear again; that Chriſt ſhall build again the old waſte places of Jacob ; that our dead and dry bones ſhall become one army of living men, and that our Well-beloved may yet feed among the lilies, until the day break and the ſhadows flee away.* My dear brother, let us help one another with our prayers.   Our King ſhall mow down His enemies, and ſhall come from Bozrah with His garments all dyed in blood.   And for our conſolation ſhall He appear, and call His wife Hephzibah, and His land Beulah ;† for He will rejoice over us and marry us, and Scotland ſhall ſay, " What have I to do any more with idols ?"   Only let us be faithful to Him that can ride through hell and death upon a windleſtrae,‡ and His horſe never ſtumble ; and let Him make of me a bridge over a water, ſo that His high and holy name may be glorified in me. Strokes with the ſweet Mediator's hand are very ſweet.   He was always ſweet to my ſoul ; but ſince I ſuffered for Him, His breath hath a ſweeter ſmell than before.   Oh that every hair of my head, and every member and every bone in my body, were a man to witneſs a fair confeſſion for Him !   I would think all too little for Him.   When I look over beyond the line, and beyond death, to the laughing ſide of the world, I triumph, and ride upon the high places of Jacob ; howbeit otherwiſe I am a faint, dead-hearted, cowardly man, oft borne down, and hungry in waiting for the marriage ſupper of the Lamb.   Nevertheleſs, I think it the Lord's wiſe love that feeds us with hunger, and makes us fat with wants and deſertions.

I know not, my dear brother, if our worthy brethren be gone to ſea or not.   They are on my heart and in my prayers.   If they be yet with you, ſalute my dear friend, John Stuart, my well-beloved brethren in the Lord, Mr Blair, Mr Hamilton, Mr Livingſton, and

---

* Song iv. 5, 6.   † Iſa. lxii. 4.   ‡ A ſtraw of dogs'-tail graſs.

Mr M'Clelland,* and acquaint them with my troubles, and entreat them to pray for the poor afflicted prisoner of Christ. They are dear to my soul. I seek your prayers and theirs for my flock : their remembrance breaketh my heart. I desire to love that people, and others my dear acquaintance in Christ, with love in God, and as God loveth them. I know that He who sent me to the west and south, sends me also to the north. I will charge my soul to believe and to wait for Him, and will follow His providence, and not go before it, nor stay behind it. Now, my dear brother, taking farewell in paper, I commend you all to the word of His grace, and to the work of His Spirit, to Him who holdeth the seven stars in His right hand, that you may be kept spotless till the day of Jesus our Lord.

I am your brother in affliction in our sweet Lord Jesus,

S. R.

From IRVINE, being on my journey to Christ's
Palace in Aberdeen, *August* 4, 1636.

LXIV.—*To* ALEXANDER GORDON *of Earlston.*

(HIS FEELINGS UPON LEAVING ANWOTH.)

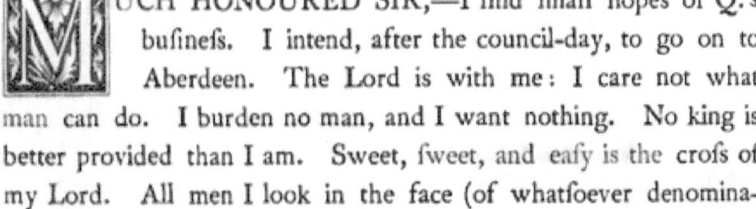

MUCH HONOURED SIR,—I find small hopes of Q.'s business. I intend, after the council-day, to go on to Aberdeen. The Lord is with me : I care not what man can do. I burden no man, and I want nothing. No king is better provided than I am. Sweet, sweet, and easy is the cross of my Lord. All men I look in the face (of whatsoever denomination, nobles and poor, acquaintance and strangers) are friendly to

---

* Correspondents to whom there are letters inserted in this volume, who having been obliged to remove from Scotland by the oppressive measures of the prelates, intended to proceed to New England. But the voyage proving disastrous, they ultimately returned to Ireland. There was a M'Lelland of Balmagachan, near Roberton, in the parish of Borgue; but this is not he. This was John M'Lelland, sometime minister of Kirkcudbright, a friend of R. Blair's.

me. My Well-beloved is fome* kinder and more warmly than ordinary, and cometh and vifiteth my foul. My chains are overgilded with gold. Only the remembrance of my fair days with Chrift in Anwoth, and of my dear flock (whofe cafe is my heart's forrow), is vinegar to my fugared wine. Yet both fweet and four feed my foul. No pen, no words, no ingine† can exprefs to you the lovelinefs of my only, only Lord Jefus. Thus, in hafte, making for my palace at Aberdeen, I blefs you, your wife, your eldeft fon, and other children. Grace, grace be with you.

Yours in his only, only Lord Jefus,

S. R.

EDINBURGH, *Sept.* 5, 1636.

LXV.—*To* ROBERT GORDON *of Knockbreck, on his way to Aberdeen.*

[ROBERT GORDON of Knockbrex, in the parifh of Borgue, which adjoins Anwoth, is, by Livingftone in his *Characterifics*, defcribed as "a fingle-hearted and painful Chriftian, much employed at parliaments and public meetings after the year 1638." He was a member of the famous Affembly which met at Glafgow in 1638, as commiffioner from the Prefbytery of Kirkcudbright. The precife date of his death is uncertain. But, on the 28th of July 1657, John Gordon, fon to John Gordon, who was fon to Alexander Gordon in Garloch, is retoured "heir of Robert Gordon of Knockbreck, his granduncle," in the lands of Knockbreck, &c. (*Inq. Retor. Abbrev. Kirkcudbright,* No. 274.) This retour enables us to correct fome miftakes which have been fallen into in reference to Knockbreck and his family. Stevenfon, in his edition of Livingftone's *Characterifics,* 1773, has added to Livingftone's account of Robert Gordon of Knockbreck the following fentence :—"They all three fuffered for religion. The two younger brothers were executed on one gibbet, and embracing each other in their arms, did fo expire." The two brothers to whom Stevenfon refers, John Gordon of Knockbreck, and Robert, who were executed at Edinburgh on the 7th of December 1666, for having been engaged in the rifing at Pentland (fee Let. 218), were the grandchildren of Alexander Gordon of Garloch, the brother of Robert Gordon of Knockbreck, to whom Rutherford addreffes this letter, and to whom one of them, John, in the above retour, was ferved heir. Others have made the fame

---

* Somewhat. † Power of mind. It is alfo written engine or ingyne. It is the Latin *ingenium.*

miſtake. *Robert Gordon of Knockbreck* was evidently only *their granduncle.* Their father's name was John, and he died many years before the martyrdom of his ſons.

Knockbrex ſtands over near the ſea-ſhore, amid thick woods, looking down on the opening of *Wigtown Bay.* But a modern manſion has taken the place of Gordon's reſidence.]

(HOW UPHELD ON THE WAY.)

Y DEAREST BROTHER,—I ſee Chriſt thinketh ſhame (if I may ſpeak ſo) to be in ſuch a poor man's common* as mine. I burden no man; I want nothing; no face hath gloomed upon me ſince I left you. God's ſun and fair weather conveyeth me to my time-paradiſe in Aberdeen. Chriſt hath ſo handſomely fitted for my ſhoulders this rough tree of the croſs, as that it hurteth me no ways. My treaſure is up in Chriſt's coffers; my comforts are greater than ye can believe; my pen ſhall lie for penury of words to write of them. God knoweth I am filled with the joy of the Holy Ghoſt. Only the memory of you, my deareſt in the Lord, my flock and others, keepeth me under, and from being exalted above meaſure. Chriſt's ſweet ſauce hath this four mixed with it; but O ſuch a ſweet and pleaſant taſte! I find ſmall hopes of Q.'s matter. Thus in haſte. Remember me to your wife, and to William Gordon. Grace be with you.

Yours in his only, only Lord Jeſus,

S. R.

EDINBURGH, *Sept.* 5, 1636.

———◆———

LXVI.—*To* ROBERT GORDON *of Knockbrex, after arriving at Aberdeen.*

(CHALLENGES OF CONSCIENCE—EASE IN ZION.)

EAR BROTHER,—Grace, mercy, and peace be to you. I am, by God's mercy, come now to Aberdeen, the place of my confinement, and ſettled in an honeſt man's houſe. I find the town's-men cold, general, and dry in their

* Under obligation to.

kindnefs; yet I find a lodging in the heart of many ftrangers. My challenges are revived again, and I find old fores bleeding of new; dangerous and painful is an undercotted* confcience; yet I have an eye to the blood that is phyfic for fuch fores. But, verily, I fee Chriftianity is conceived to be more eafy and lighter than it is; fo that I fometimes think I never knew anything but the letters of that name; for our nature contenteth itfelf with little in godlinefs. Our "Lord, Lord" feemeth to us ten "Lord, Lords." Little holi-nefs in our balance is much, becaufe it is our own holinefs; and we love to lay fmall burdens upon our foft natures, and to make a fair court-way to heaven. And I know it were neceffary to take more pains than we do, and not to make heaven a city more eafily taken than God hath made it. I perfuade myfelf that many runners fhall come fhort, and get a difappointment. Oh! how eafy is it to de-ceive ourfelves, and to fleep, and wifh that heaven may fall down in our laps! Yet for all my Lord's glooms,† I find Him fweet, gra-cious, loving, kind; and I want both pen and words to fet forth the fairnefs, beauty, and fweetnefs of Chrift's love, and the honour of this crofs of Chrift, which is glorious to me, though the world thinketh fhame thereof. I verily think that the crofs of Chrift would blufh and think fhame of thefe thin-fkinned worldlings, who are fo married to their credit that they are afhamed of the fufferings of Chrift. O the honour to be fcourged and ftoned with Chrift, and to go through a furious-faced death to life eternal! But men would have law-borrows‡ againft Chrift's crofs.

Now, my dear brother, forget not the prifoner of Chrift, for I fee very few here who kindly fear God. Grace be with you. Let my love in Chrift and hearty affection be remembered to your kind wife, to your brother John, and to all friends. The Lord Jefus be with your fpirit.

Yours in his only, only Lord Jefus,   S. R.

ABERDEEN, *Sept.* 20, 1636.

---

* Feftering under the fkin. Calderwood's Hift. v. 658.   † Frowns.
‡ Surety from injury; giving a pledge to the law not to injure.

[William Fullarton, as has been formerly noticed, was the huſband of Marion M'Naught. His religious principles were the ſame with thoſe of his excellent wife, and he was a man of virtue, integrity, and piety. He proved himſelf the patron of the oppreſſed in the caſe of Mr Robert Glendinning, the aged miniſter of Kirkcudbright ; to which caſe there is evident alluſion in this letter. Mr Glendinning having refuſed to conform to Prelacy, and to receive, as his aſſiſtant and ſucceſſor, a man whom Biſhop Sydſerff intruded upon him and the people of Kirkcudbright, the Biſhop ſuſpended him from his office, and ſentenced him to be impriſoned. Provoſt Fullarton, and the other magiſ-trates of the burgh (one of whom was Mr William Glendinning, ſon of the miniſter), indignant at ſuch tyrannical proceedings, refuſed to incarcerate their own paſtor, then nearly 80 years of age, and were determined, with the great body of the inhabitants of the town, to attend upon his miniſtry. Sydſerff, too proud and violent to allow his authority to be thus deſpiſed, cauſed Bailie Glendinning to be impriſoned in Kirkcudbright, and the other magiſtrates to be confined within the town of Wigtown, while he ſentenced the aged miniſter to remain within the bounds of his pariſh, and forbade him to exerciſe any part of his miniſterial functions. But he found it impoſſible, by all the means he could employ, to reduce theſe refractory magiſtrates to obedience. The firmneſs which Fullarton manifeſted on this occaſion is warmly commended by Rutherford.]

(*ENCOURAGEMENT TO SUFFER FOR CHRIST.*)

UCH HONOURED AND VERY DEAR FRIEND, —Grace, mercy, and peace be to you.—I am in good caſe, bleſſed be the Lord, remaining here in this unco* town, a priſoner for Chriſt and His truth. And I am not aſhamed of His croſs. My ſoul is comforted with the conſolations of His ſweet preſence, for whom I ſuffer.

I earneſtly entreat you to give your honour and authority to Chriſt, and for Chriſt ; and be not diſmayed for fleſh and blood, while you are for the Lord, and for His truth and cauſe. And howbeit we ſee truth put to the worſe for the time, yet Chriſt will

---

* Strange.

be a friend to truth, and will do* for thofe who dare hazard all that they have for Him and for His glory. Sir, our fair day is coming, and the court will change, and wicked men will weep after noon, and forer than the fons of God, who weep in the morning. Let us believe and hope for God's falvation.

Sir, I hope I need not write to you for your kindnefs and love to my brother,† who is now to be diftreffed for the truth of God as well as I am. I think myfelf obliged to pray for you, and your worthy and kind bed-fellow and children, for your love to him and me alfo. I hope your pains for us in Chrift fhall not be loft. Thus recommending you to the tender mercy and loving-kindnefs of God, I reft,

Your very loving and affectionate brother,

S. R.

ABERDEEN, *Sept.* 21, 1636.

LXVIII.—*To* JOHN FLEMING, *Bailiffe of Leith.*‡

[Of Mr Fleming nothing can be afcertained, unlefs it is he who is mentioned by Livingfton as being a merchant in Edinburgh, a man of note among the godly.]

(THE SWEETNESS AND FAITHFULNESS OF CHRIST'S LOVE.)

Y VERY WORTHY FRIEND,—Grace, mercy, and peace be to you. I received your letter. I blefs the Lord through Jefus Chrift, I find His word good, "I have chofen thee in the furnace of affliction."§—"I will be with

---

* Act fo as to undo them.

† His brother was a teacher in Kirkcudbright, and between him and Samuel there was a warm attachment, and ftrong mutual fympathies. He, too, fuffered perfecution for his adherence to the caufe of Prefbytery. For this, and his zealous fupport of Mr Glendinning, whom the Bifhop of Galloway treated with fuch cruelty, he was fummoned in November 1636 before the High Commiffion, and condemned to refign his charge, and remove from Kirkcudbright before the enfuing term of Whitfunday.

‡ Bailiffe is the modern " Bailie," the name for a city magiftrate.

§ Ifa. xlviii. 10.

him in trouble."* I never expected other† at Chrift's hand but much good and comfort ; and I am not difappointed. I find my Lord's crofs overgilded and oiled with comforts. My Lord hath now fhown me the white fide of His crofs. I would not exchange my weeping in prifon with the Fourteen Prelates'‡ laughter, amidft their hungry and lean joys. This world knoweth not the fweetnefs of Chrift's love ; it is a myftery to them.

At my firft coming here, I found great heavinefs, efpecially becaufe it had pleafed the prelates to add this gentle cruelty to my former fufferings (for it is gentle to them), to inhibit the minifters of the town to give me the liberty of a pulpit. I faid, What aileth Chrift at my fervice ? But I was a fool ; He hath chid Himfelf friends with me. If ye and others of God's children fhall praife His great name, who maketh worthlefs men witneffes for Him, my filence and fufferings fhall preach more than my tongue could do. If His glory be feen in me, I am fatisfied ; for I want for no kindnefs from Chrift. And, fir, I dare not fmother His liberality. I write it to you, that ye may praife, and defire your brother and others to join with me in this work.

This land fhall be made defolate. Our iniquities are full ; the Lord faith, we fhall drink, and fpue, and fall. Remember my love to your good kind wife. Grace be with you.

Yours in his fweet Lord Jefus,

S. R.

ABERDEEN, *Nov.* 13, 1636.

---

* Ps. xci. 15.   † Ought elfe.

‡ Referring probably to the number of prelates (confifting of two archbifhops and twelve bifhops), who were members of the High Commiffion by whom he was fentenced to imprifonment.

*(HIS ENJOYMENT OF CHRIST IN ABERDEEN—A SIGHT OF CHRIST
EXCEEDS ALL REPORTS—SOME ASHAMED OF HIM AND
HIS.)*

Y VERY HONOURABLE AND DEAR LADY,—
Grace, mercy, and peace be to you. I cannot forget
your Ladyſhip, and that ſweet child. I deſire to hear
what the Lord is doing to you and him. To write to me were
charity. I cannot but write to my friends, that Chriſt hath tryſted*
me in Aberdeen; and my adverſaries have ſent me here to be
feaſted with love banquets with my royal, high, high, and
princely King Jeſus. Madam, why ſhould I ſmother Chriſt's hon-
eſty? I dare not conceal His goodneſs to my ſoul; He looked
fremed† and unco-like‡ upon me when I came firſt here; but I
believe Himſelf better than His looks. I ſhall not again quarrel
Chriſt for a gloom, § now He hath taken the maſk off His face, and
faith, "Kiſs thy fill;" and what can I have more when I get great
heaven in my little arms? Oh how ſweet are the ſufferings of Chriſt
for Chriſt! God forgive them that raiſe an ill report upon the
ſweet croſs of Chriſt. It is but our weak and dim eyes, that look
but to the black ſide, that makes us miſtake. Thoſe who can take
that crabbed tree handſomely upon their back, and faſten it on
cannily,‖ ſhall find it ſuch a burden as wings unto a bird, or fails to
a ſhip. Madam, rue not of your having choſen the better part.
Upon my ſalvation, this is Chriſt's truth I now ſuffer for. If I
found but cold comfort in my ſufferings, I would not beguile others;
I would have told you plainly. But the truth is, Chriſt's crown,
His ſceptre, and the freedom of His kingdom, is that which is now

---

* Appointed to meet. † Like one who was no kinſman. ‡ Strange-like.
§ Frown. ‖ Quietly, and ſkilfully.

called in queftion; becaufe we will not allow that Chrift pay tribute and be a vaffal to the fhields of the earth, therefore the fons of
our mother are angry at us. But it becometh not Chrift to hold
any man's ftirrup. It were a fweet and honourable death to die
for the honour of that royal and princely King Jefus. His love is
a myftery to the world. I would not have believed that there was
fo much in Chrift as there is. "Come and fee" maketh Chrift to
be known in His excellency and glory. I wifh all this nation knew
how fweet His breath is. It is little to fee Chrift in a book, as
men do the world in a card.* They talk of Chrift by the book
and the tongue, and no more; but to come nigh Chrift, and haufe†
Him, and embrace Him, is another thing. Madam, I write to your
honour, for your encouragement in that honourable profeffion
Chrift hath honoured you with. Ye have gotten the funny fide of
the brae,‡ and the beft of Chrift's good things. He hath not given
you the baftard's portion; and howbeit ye get ftrokes and four
looks from your Lord, yet believe His love more than your own
feeling, for this world can take nothing from you that is truly
yours, and death can do you no wrong. Your rock doth not ebb
and flow, but your fea. That which Chrift hath faid, He will
bide by it. He will be your tutor. You fhall not get your charters
of heaven to play you with. It is good that ye have loft your
credit with Chrift, and that Lord Free-will fhall not be your tutor.
Chrift will lippen§ the taking you to heaven, neither to yourfelf,
nor any deputy, but only to Himfelf. Bleffed be your tutor. When
your Head fhall appear, your Bridegroom and Lord, your day
fhall then dawn, and it fhall never have an afternoon, nor an evening fhadow. Let your child be Chrift's; let him ftay befide you as
thy Lord's pledge, that you fhall willingly render again, if God
will.

Madam, I find folks here kind to me; but in the night, and
under their breath. My Mafter's caufe may not come to the crown

---

* Chart, map.   † Clofe with; clafp round the neck; *bals*, the neck, or throat.
‡ Of the hill; the comfortable and warm fituation.   § Entruft.

of the caufeway.*   Others are kind according to their fafhion. Many think me a ftrange man, and my caufe not good ; but I care not much for man's thoughts or approbation.   I think no fhame of the crofs.   The preachers of the town pretend great love, but the prelates have added to the reft this gentle cruelty (for fo they think of it), to difcharge me of the pulpits of this town.   The people murmur and cry out againft it ; and to fpeak truly (howbeit Chrift is moft indulgent to me otherwife), my filence on the Lord's day keeps me from being exalted above meafure, and from ftartling† in the heat of my Lord's love.   Some people affect‡ me, for the which caufe, I hear the preachers here purpofe to have my confinement changed to another place ; fo cold is northern love ; but Chrift and I will bear it. I have wreftled long with this fad filence.   I faid, what aileth Chrift at my fervice ? and my foul hath been at a pleading with Chrift, and at yea and nay.   But I will yield to Him, providing my fuffering may preach more than my tongue did ; for I give not Chrift an inch but for twice as good again.   In a word, I am a fool, and He is God.   I will hold my peace hereafter.

Let me hear from your Ladyfhip, and your dear child.   Pray for the prifoner of Chrift, who is mindful of your Ladyfhip.   Remember my obliged obedience to my good Lady Marr.   Grace, grace be with you.   I write and pray bleffings to your fweet child.

Yours in all dutiful obedience in his only Lord Jefus,

S. R.

Aberdeen, *Nov.* 22, 1636.

---

* Appear without fhame in public.
† *Startle*, as cattle do in hot weather, run up and down in an excited manner.
‡ Love.

(*EXERCISE UNDER RESTRAINT FROM PREACHING—THE DEVIL —CHRIST'S LOVING-KINDNESS—PROGRESS.*)

MADAM,—Grace, mercy, and peace be to you. I received your Ladyſhip's letter. It refreſhed me in my heavineſs. The bleſſing and prayer of a priſoner of Chriſt come upon you. Since my coming hither, Galloway ſent me not a line, except what my brother, Earleſton and his ſon did write. I cannot get my papers tranſported ; but, Madam, I want not kindneſs of one who hath the gate* of it. Chriſt (if He had never done more for me ſince I was born) hath engaged my heart, and gained my bleſſing in this houſe of my pilgrimage. It pleaſeth my Wellbeloved to dine with a poor priſoner, and the King's ſpikenard caſteth a fragrant ſmell. Nothing grieveth me, but that I eat my feaſts my lone, and that I cannot edify His ſaints. O that this nation knew what is betwixt Him and me ; none would ſcar† at the croſs of Chriſt ! My ſilence eats me up, but He hath told me He thanketh me no leſs, than if I were preaching daily. He ſees how gladly I would be at it ; and therefore my wages are going to the fore,‡ up in heaven, as if I were ſtill preaching Chriſt. Captains pay duly bedfaſt ſoldiers, howbeit they do§ not march, nor carry armour. "Though Iſrael be not gathered, yet ſhall I be glorious in the eyes of the Lord, and my God ſhall be my ſtrength."‖ My garland, "the baniſhed miniſter" (the term of Aberdeen), aſhameth me not. I have ſeen the white ſide of Chriſt's croſs ; how lovely hath He been to His oppreſſed ſervant ! "The Lord executeth judgment for the oppreſſed, He giveth food to the hungry : the Lord looſeth the priſoner ; the Lord raiſeth them that are bowed down :

---

* Way.   † Start aſide in fear.   ‡ Laid up in ſtore for my advantage.
§ Some editions read "dow,"—are not able.   ‖ Iſa. xlix. 5.

the Lord preferveth the ftranger."* If it were come to exchanging
of croffes, I would not exchange my crofs with any. I am well
pleafed with Chrift, and He with me ; I hope none fhall hear us.†
It is true for all this, I get my meat with many ftrokes, and am
feven times a-day up and down, and am often anxious and caft
down for the cafe of my oppreffed brother ; yet I hope the Lord
will be furety for His fervant. But now upon fome weak, very
weak experience, I am come to love a rumbling and raging devil
beft. Seeing we muft have a devil to hold the faints waking, I wifh
a cumberfome devil, rather than a fecure and fleeping one. At my
firft coming hither, I took the dorts‡ at Chrift, and took up a ftomach
againft Him ; I faid, He had caft me over the dike of the vineyard,
like a dry tree. But it was His mercy, I fee, that the fire did not
burn the dry tree ; and now, as if my Lord Jefus had done that
fault, and not I (who belied my Lord), He hath made the firft mends,§
and He fpake not one word againft me, but hath come again and
quickened my foul with His prefence. Nay, now I think the very
annuity‖ and cafualties of the crofs of Chrift Jefus my Lord, and
thefe comforts that accompany it, better than the world's fet-rent.‖
O how many rich off-fallings¶ are in my King's houfe! I am perfuaded, and dare pawn my falvation on it, that it is Chrift's truth I
now fuffer for. I know His comforts are no dreams ; He would not
put His feal on blank paper, nor deceive His afflicted ones that
truft in Him.

Your Ladyfhip wrote to me that ye are yet an ill fcholar.
Madam, ye muft go in at heaven's gates, and your book in your
hand, ftill learning. You have had your own large fhare of troubles,
and a double portion ; but it faith your Father counteth you not a
baftard ; full-begotten bairns are nurtured.** I long to hear of the
child. I write the bleffings of Chrift's prifoner and the mercies of

---

* Ps. cxlvi. 7-9.
† In Thomfon's edition this is explained by referring to Proverbs xiv. 10.
‡ Sulks.   § Firft repaired the injury, made up the quarrel.
‖ The quit-rent ; better than the world's full rent.   ¶ Odds and ends.
** Heb. xii. 8.   Legitimate children are put under difcipline.

God to him. Let him be Chrift's and yours betwixt you, but let Chrift be whole play-maker.* Let Him be the lender ; and you the borrower, not an owner.

Madam, it is not long fince I did write to your Ladyfhip that Chrift is keeping mercy for you ; and I bide by it ftill, and now I write it under my hand. Love Him dearly. Win† in to fee Him ; there is in Him that which you never faw. He is aye nigh ; He is a tree of life, green and bloſſoming, both fummer and winter. There is a nick‡ in Chriftianity, to the which whofoever cometh, they fee and feel more than others can do. I invite you of new to come to Him. " Come and fee," will fpeak better things of Him than I can do. " Come nearer" will fay much. God thought never this world a portion worthy of you. He would not even § you to a gift of dirt and clay ; nay, He will not give you Efau's portion, but re-ferves the inheritance of Jacob for you. Are ye not well married now ? Have you not a good hufband now ?

My heart cannot exprefs what fad nights I have had for the virgin daughter of my people. Woe is me, for my time is coming. " Behold, the day, behold, the day is come ; the morning hath gone forth, the rod hath bloſſomed, pride hath budded, violence is rifen up in a rod of wickednefs, the fun is gone down upon our prophets." A dry wind upon Scotland, but neither to fan nor to cleanfe ; but out of all queftion, when the Lord hath cut down the foreft, the after-growth of Lebanon fhall flourifh ; they fhall plant vines in our mountains, and a cloud fhall yet fill the temple. Now the bleſſing of our deareft Lord Jefus, and the bleſſing of him that is " feparate from his brethren," come upon you.

Yours, at Aberdeen, the prifoner of Chrift,

S. R.

ABERDEEN.

---

* Sole director of the play.   † Get in, in fpite of difficulty.
‡ Notch, degree, particular point.
§ A word for difparaging comparifon ; propofe as fit for you.

[Mr Hugh M'Kail was at this time minister of Irvine. Previous to his settlement in that parish, Rutherford, as we learn from some of the preceding letters to Marion M'Naught, was very desirous of seeing him settled assistant and successor to Mr Robert Glendinning, the aged minister of Kirkcudbright, and to him the people had an eye, but were disappointed, they having been anticipated by the parish of which he was now pastor. He and Mr William Cockburn were appointed by the General Assembly of 1644 to visit the north of Ireland for three months, with the view of promoting the interests of the Presbyterian Church in that country. He was ultimately translated to Edinburgh. In the unhappy controversy between the Resolutioners and Protesters, M'Kail took the side of the former; but he was among the more moderate of the party, and always showed a readiness to enter into healing measures. Baillie often refers to him in his letters. M'Kail died in the beginning of the year 1660, and was buried in the Greyfriars' churchyard, Edinburgh. (*Lamont's Diary*, p. 121.) He was the brother of Mr Matthew M'Kail of Bothwell, who was the father of the youthful Hugh M'Kail. Young Hugh was educated at Edinburgh, under the superintendence of this uncle, and nobly suffered martyrdom in 1666.]

(*CHRIST TO BE TRUSTED AMID TRIAL.*)

REVEREND AND DEAR BROTHER,—I thank you for your letter. I cannot but show you, that as I never expected anything from Christ, but much good and kindness, so He hath made me to find it in the house of my pilgrimage. And believe me, brother, I give it to you under mine own hand-writ, that whoso looketh to the white side of Christ's cross, and can take it up handsomely with faith and courage, shall find it such a burden as sails are to a ship, or wings to a bird. I find that my Lord hath overgilded that black tree, and hath perfumed it, and oiled it with joy and consolation. Like a fool, once I would chide and plead with Christ, and slander Him to others, of unkindness. But I trust in God, not to call His glooms* unkind again; for He hath taken from me my sackcloth; and I verily cannot tell you what a poor

---

* Frowns.

Joleph and prifoner (with whom my mother's children were angry)
doth now think of kind Chrift. I will chide no more, providing
He will quit me all by-gones ;* for I am poor. I am taught in this
ill weather to go on the lee-fide of Chrift, and to put Him in between
me and the ftorm ; and (I thank God) I walk on the funny fide of
the brae.† I write it, that ye may fpeak in my behalf the praifes of
my Lord to others, that my bonds may preach. O if all Scotland
knew the feafts, and love-blinks, and vifits that the prelates have
fent unto me ! I will verily give my Lord Jefus a free difcharge
of all that I, like a fool, laid to His charge, and beg Him pardon,
to the mends.‡ God grant that in my temptations I come not on
His wrong fide again, and never again fall a raving againft my
Phyfician in my fever.

Brother, plead with your mother while ye have time. A pulpit
would be a high feaft to me ; but I dare not fay one word againft
Him who hath done it. I am not out of the houfe as yet. My
fweet Mafter faith, I fhall have houfe-room at His own elbow ;
albeit their fynagogue will need-force§ to caft me out. A letter
were a work of charity to me. Grace be with you. Pray for me.

　　　　　　　　Your brother and Chrift's prifoner,

　　　　　　　　　　　　　　　　　　　　　　　S. R.

Aberdeen, *Nov.* 22, 1636.

·　　LXXII.—*To* William Gordon *of Roberton.*

[William Gordon of Roberton, in the parifh of Borgue in Galloway, to whom this letter is addreffed, was the father of William Gordon of
Roberton who joined with the Covenanters in the rifing at Pentland in 1666,
where he was killed, " to the great lofs of the country where he lived," fays
Wodrow, " and his own family, his aged father having no more fons." A
daughter of this venerable old man, named Mary, alfo fuffered much for non-
conformity at the hands of Claverhoufe and his friends. She was married to
John Gordon of Largmore (which is in Kells, near Kenmure Caftle), who

---

* Paft offences.　　　　　　　† Comfortable fide of the hill.
‡ To boot, to make all up.　　　§ Under plea of abfolute neceffity.

was alfo in the battle at Pentland, where he was feverely wounded, and who, returning to his own houfe, died in the courfe of a few days in confequence of the lofs of blood, and of lying in the fields some nights after the engagement. The old man, to whom this letter was written, did not long furvive the death of his fon and fon-in-law ; for, on the 8th of September 1668, Mary Gordon is retoured heir of William Gordon of Roberton, her father, in the lands of Rotraix, Roberton, Kingzeantoun, etc. (*Inq. Retor. Abbrev. Kirkcudbright.*)

(HOW TRIALS ARE MISIMPROVED—THE INFINITE VALUE OF CHRIST—DESPISED WARNINGS.)

DEAR BROTHER,—Grace, mercy, and peace be to you. So often as I think on our cafe, in our foldier's night-watch, and of our fighting life in the fields, while we are here, I am forced to fay, prifoners in a dungeon, condemned by a judge to want the light of the fun, and moon, and candle till their dying day, are no more, nay, not fo much, to be pitied as we are. For they are weary of their life, they hate their prifon ; but we fall to,* in our prifon, where we fee little, to drink ourfelves drunk with the night-pleafures of our weak dreams ; and we long for no better life than this. But at the blaft of the laft trumpet, and the fhout of the archangel, when God fhall take down the fhepherd's tent of this fading world, we fhall not have fo much as a drink of water, of all the dreams that we now build on. Alas ! that the fharp and bitter blafts on face and fides, which meet us in this life, have not learned us mortification, and made us dead to this world ! We buy our own forrow, and we pay dear for it, when we fpend out our love, our joy, our defires, our confidence, upon an handful of fnow and ice, that time will melt away to nothing, and go thirfty out of the drunken inn when all is done. Alas ! that we inquire not for the clear fountain, but are fo foolifh as to drink foul, muddy, and rotten waters, even till our bed-time. And then in the refurrection, when we fhall be awakened, our yefternight's four drink and fwinifh dregs fhall rift† up upon us ; and fick, fick, fhall many a foul be then. I know no wholefome fountain but one. I know not a thing

---

* Occupy ourfelves in.   † Be vomited up with violent retching.

worth the buying but heaven ; and my own mind is, if comparifon were made betwixt Chrift and heaven, I would fell heaven with my blefling, and buy Chrift. O if I could raife the market for Chrift, and heighten the market a pound for a penny, and cry up Chrift in men's eftimation ten thoufand talents more than men think of Him ! But they are fhaping Him, and crying Him down, and valuing Him at their unworthy halfpenny ; or elfe exchanging and bartering Chrift with the miferable old fallen houfe of this vain world. Or then * they lend Him out upon intereft, and play the ufurers with Chrift : becaufe they profefs Him, and give out before men that Chrift is their treafure and flock ; and, in the mean time, praife of men, and a name, and eafe, and the fummer fun of the Gofpel, is the ufury they would be at. So, when the trial cometh, they quit the flock for the intereft, and lofe all. Happy are they who can keep Chrift by Himfelf alone, and keep Him clean and whole, till God come and count with them. I know (that) in your hard and heavy trials long fince, ye thought well and highly of Chrift ; but, truly, no crofs fhould be old to us. We fhould not forget them becaufe years are come betwixt us and them, and caft them byhand† as we do old clothes. We may make a crofs old in time, new in ufe, and as fruitful as in the beginning of it. God is where and what He was feven years ago, whatever change may be in us. I fpeak not this as if I thought ye had forgotten what God did, to have your love long fince, but that ye may awake yourfelf in this fleepy age, and remember fruitfully of Chrift's firft wooing and fuiting of your love, both with fire and water, and try if He got His anfwer, or if ye be yet to give Him it. For I find in myfelf, that water runneth not fafter through a fieve than our warnings flip from us ; for I have loft and caften byhands† many fummons the Lord fent to me ; and therefore the Lord hath given me double charges, that I truft in God fhall not rive me.‡ I blefs His great name, who is no niggard in holding-in croffes upon me, but fpendeth largely His rods, that He may fave me from this perifhing

---

* Or, if they did not do this.   † Afide.   ‡ Rend in pieces.

world.   How plentiful God is in means of this kind is efteemed by many one of God's unkind mercies; but Chrift's crofs is neither a cruel nor unkind mercy, but the love-token of a father.   I am fure, a lover chafing us for our well,* and to have our love, fhould not be run away from, or fled from.   God fend me no worfe mercy than the fanctified crofs of Chrift portendeth, and I am fure I fhould be happy and bleffed.

Pray for me, that I may find houfe-room in the Lord's houfe to fpeak in His name.   Remember my deareft love in Chrift to your wife.   Grace, grace be unto you.

Yours in his fweet Lord Jefus,

S. R.

ABERDEEN, 1636.

LXXIII.—*To* EARLSTON, *Elder.*

" And they overcame the dragon by the blood of the Lamb, and by the word of their teftimony, and they loved not their lives unto the death."—REV. xii. 11.

(*CHRIST'S LIBERALITY—HIS OWN MISAPPREHENSIONS OF CHRIST.*)

MUCH-HONOURED SIR,—Grace, mercy, and peace be to you.   I long to fee you in paper, and to be refrefhed by you.   I cannot but defire you, and charge you to help me to praife Him who feedeth a poor prifoner with the fatnefs of His houfe.   O how weighty is His love!   O but there is much telling in Chrift's kindnefs!   The Amen, the Faithful and True Witnefs, hath paid me my hundred-fold, well told, and one to the hundred.   I complained of Him, but He is owing me nothing now. Sir, I charge you to help me to praife His goodnefs, and to proclaim to others my Bridegroom's kindnefs, whofe love is better than wine.   I took up an action againft Chrift, and brought† a plea

---

* Welfare, weal.

† Entered into a controverfy.   Old editions have "bought," by a misprint apparently.

againft His love, and libelled unkindnefs againft Chrift my Lord; and I faid, " This is my death; He hath forgotten me." But my meek Lord held His peace, and beheld me, and would not contend for the laft word of flyting;* and now He hath chided Himfelf friends with me. And now I fee He muft be God, and I muft be flefh. I pafs from my fummons;† I acknowledge He might have given me my fill of it, and never troubled Himfelf. But now He hath taken away the mafk; I have been comforted; He could not fmother His love any longer to a prifoner and a ftranger. God grant that I may never bring‡ a plea againft Chrift again, but may keep good quarters with Him. I want here no kindnefs,§ no love-tokens; but O wife is His love! for, notwithftanding of this hot fummer-blink, I am kept low with the grief of my filence. For His word is in me as a fire in my bowels; and I fee the Lord's vineyard laid wafte, and the heathen entered into the fanctuary: and my belly is pained, and my foul in heavinefs, becaufe the Lord's people are gone into captivity, and becaufe of the fury of the Lord, and that wind (but neither to fan nor purge) which is coming upon apoftate Scotland. Alfo I am kept awake with the late wrong done to my brother; but I truft ye will counfel and comfort him. Yet, in this mift, I fee and believe the Lord will heal this halting kirk, " and will lay her ftones with fair colours, and her foundations with fapphires, and will make her windows of agates, and her gates carbuncles." ‖ " And for brafs He will bring gold." He hath created the fmith that formed the fword; no weapon in war fhall profper againft us. Let us be glad and rejoice in the Lord, for His falvation is near to come. Remember me to your wife and your fon John. And I entreat you to write to me. Grace, grace be with you.

Yours in his only, only Lord Jefus,

S. R.

ABERDEEN, *Dec.* 30, 1636.

---

* Chiding.   † Do not enforce.
‡ Enter into controverfy with.   Old editions have " buy."
§ I am not in want of.   ‖ Ifa. liv. 11, 12.

"Thefe are they which came out of great tribulation, and have wafhed their robes, and made them white in the blood of the Lamb."—Rev. vii. 14.

(HIS OWN MISCONCEPTION OF CHRIST'S WAYS—CHRIST'S KINDNESS.)

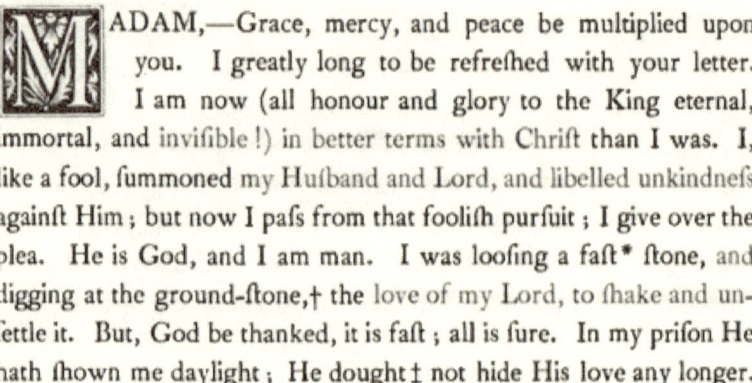

MADAM,—Grace, mercy, and peace be multiplied upon you. I greatly long to be refrefhed with your letter. I am now (all honour and glory to the King eternal, immortal, and invifible!) in better terms with Chrift than I was. I, like a fool, fummoned my Hufband and Lord, and libelled unkindnefs againft Him; but now I pafs from that foolifh purfuit; I give over the plea. He is God, and I am man. I was loofing a faft* ftone, and digging at the ground-ftone,† the love of my Lord, to fhake and un-fettle it. But, God be thanked, it is faft; all is fure. In my prifon He hath fhown me daylight; He dought‡ not hide His love any longer. Chrift was difguifed and mafked, and I apprehended it was not He, and He hath faid, "It is I, be not afraid;" and now His love is better than wine. O that all the virgins had part of the Bride-groom's love whereupon He maketh me to feed! Help me to praife. I charge you, Madam, help me to pay praifes; and tell others, the daughters of Jerufalem, how kind Chrift is to a poor prifoner. He hath paid me my hundred-fold; it is well told me, and one to the hundred. I am nothing behind with Chrift. Let not fools, becaufe of their lazy and foft flefh, raife a flander and an ill report upon the crofs of Chrift. It is fweeter than fair.

I fee grace groweth beft in winter. This poor perfecuted kirk, this lily amongft the thorns, fhall bloffom, and laugh upon the gardener; the hufbandman's blefling fhall light upon it. O if I

---

* Firm.   † Foundation-ftone.

‡ Was not able. *Dought* is the paft tenfe of "dow."

could be free of jealoufies * of Chrift, after this, and believe, and keep good quarters with my deareft Hufband! for He hath been kind to the ftranger. And yet in all this fair hot fummer weather, I am kept from faying, " It is good to be here," with my filence, and with grief to fee my mother wounded and her veil taken from her, and the fair temple caften down. And my belly is pained, my foul is heavy for the captivity of the daughter of my people, and becaufe of the fury of the Lord, and His fierce indignation againft apoftate Scotland. I pray you, Madam, let me have that which is my prayer here, that my fufferings may preach to the four quarters of this land ; and, therefore, tell others how open-handed Chrift hath been to the prifoner and the oppreffed ftranger. Why fhould I conceal it ? I know no other way how to glorify Chrift, but to make an open proclamation of His love, and of His foft and fweet kiffes to me in the furnace, and of His fidelity to fuch as fuffer for Him. Give it me under your hand, that ye will help me to pray and praife ; but rather to praife and rejoice in the falvation of God. Grace, grace be with you.

Yours in his deareft and only, only Lord Jefus,

S. R.

ABERDEEN, *Dec.* 30, 1636.

LXXV.—*To* JOHN KENNEDY, *Bailie of Ayr.*†

[JOHN KENNEDY was the fon of Hugh Kennedy, Provoft of Ayr. Hugh was an eminent Chriftian, and greatly inftrumental in promoting the caufe of religion in the place where he lived. To his religious character, John Welfh, minifter of Ayr, bore this high teftimony in a letter written to him from France : " Happy is that city, yea, happy is that nation that has a Hugh Kennedy in it. I have myfelf certainly found the anfwer of his prayers from the Lord in my behalf." On his death-bed, he was filled " with inexpreffible joy in the Holy Ghoft, beyond what it was poffible to comprehend." (Wodrow, in his Life of Boyd of Trochrig.) John, his fon, poffeffed much of the fpirit

---

* Sufpicions.   † Written " Bailiffe " in the old editions, as in Let. 68.

and character of his father. " He was," says Fleming (Fulfilling of the Scriptures), " as choice a Christian as was at that time." The same writer records
a remarkable escape from imminent peril at sea which Kennedy on one occasion
experienced ; but whether it was the deliverance to which Rutherford refers in
a subsequent letter, it is now impossible to ascertain. The case was shortly
this: John Stewart, Provost of Ayr, another of Rutherford's correspondents,
who had gone to France, having loaded a ship at Rochelle with various commodities for Scotland, proceeded to England by the nearest way, and thence
to Ayr. After waiting a considerable time for the arrival of his vessel, he was
told that it was captured by the Turks. This information, however, proved
to be incorrect, for it at length arrived in the roads ; upon hearing of which, ·
Kennedy, an intimate friend of Stewart, was so overjoyed, that he went out to
it in a small boat. But a storm suddenly arising, he was driven past the vessel,
and the general belief of the onlookers from the shore was that he and his boat
were swallowed up ; yea, the storm increased to such a degree of violence as to
threaten even the shipwreck of the vessel. Deeply affected at the apprehended
loss of his friend in such circumstances, Stewart shut himself up in entire seclu-
sion for three days ; but at last having gone to visit Kennedy's wife under her
supposed painful bereavement, Kennedy, who had been driven far away to
another part of the coast, but who had reached the land in safety, made his
appearance, to the great joy of his afflicted family and friends. Kennedy was
a member of the Scottish Parliament in the years 1644–5–6, for the burgh of
Ayr ; and is styled in the roll, " John Kennedy, Provost of Ayr." He was
also a member of the General Assemblies of 1642–3–4–6 and 7, and his name
appears among the ruling elders in the commission for the public affairs of the
kirk in all these years. His brother Hugh (also an elder of the Church) was
frequently a member of the General Assembly, and, as we learn from *Baillie's
Letters*, had an active share in the proceedings of the Covenanters during the
reign of Charles I. There are lineal descendants of this family in Ayr at this
day : one of them, like his ancestor, was lately Provost of the town.]

*(LONGING AFTER CLEARER VIEWS OF CHRIST—HIS LONG-
SUFFERING—TRYING CIRCUMSTANCES.)*

ORTHY AND DEAR BROTHER,—Grace, mercy,
and peace be to you. I long to see you in this northern
world on paper ; I know it is not forgetfulness that ye
write not. I am every way in good case, both in soul and body ;
all honour and glory be to my Lord. I want nothing but a further
revelation of the beauty of the unknown Son of God. Either I

know not what Chriftianity is, or we have ftinted a meafure of fo many ounce weights, and no more, upon holinefs ; and there we are at a ftand, drawing our breath all our life. A moderation in God's way now is much in requeft. I profefs that I have never taken pains to find out Him whom my foul loveth ; there is a gate* yet of finding out Chrift that I have never lighted upon. Oh, if I could find it out ! Alas, how foon are we pleafed with our own fhadow in a glafs ! It were good to be beginning in fad† earneft to find out God, and to feek the right tread of Chrift. Time, cuftom, and a good opinion of ourfelves, our good meaning, and our lazy defires, our fair fhows, and the world's gliftering luftres, and thefe broad paffments‡ and bufkings§ of religion, that bear bulk in the kirk, is that wherewith moft fatisfy themfelves. But a bed watered with tears, a throat dry with praying, eyes as a fountain of tears for the fins of the land, are rare to be found among us. Oh if we could know the power of godlinefs !

This is one part of my cafe ; and another is, that I, like a fool, once fummoned Chrift for unkindnefs, and complained of His ficklenefs and inconftancy, becaufe He would have no more of my fervice nor preaching, and had caften me out of the inheritance of the Lord. And now I confefs that this was but a bought plea,‖ and I was a fool. Yet He hath borne with me. I gave Him a fair advantage againft me, but love and mercy would not let Him take it ; and the truth is, now He hath chided Himfelf friends with me, and hath taken away the mafk, and hath renewed His wonted favour in fuch a manner that He hath paid me my hundred-fold in this life, and one to the hundred. This prifon is my banqueting-houfe ; I am handled as foftly and delicately as a dawted¶ child. I am nothing behind (I fee) with Chrift ; He can, in a month, make up a year's loffes. And I write this to you, that I may entreat, nay, adjure and charge you, by the love of our Well-beloved, to help me to praife ; and to

---

* Way, or manner. † Settled. ‡ Ornaments of lace, fewed on garments.
§ Deckings. ‖ Got up; not properly what I had to complain of.
¶ Much fondled, or doted upon.

tell all your Chriſtian acquaintance to help me, for I am as deeply drowned in His debt as any dyvour* can be.   And yet in this fair ſun-blink I have ſomething to keep me from ſtartling,† or being exalted above meaſure; His word is as fire ſhut up in my bowels, and I am weary with forbearing.   The miniſters in this town are ſaying that they will have my priſon changed into leſs bounds, be-cauſe they ſee God with me.   My mother hath borne me a man of contention, one that ſtriveth with the whole earth.   The late wrongs and oppreſſions done to my brother keep my ſails low; yet I defy croſſes to embark me in ſuch a plea againſt Chriſt as I was troubled with of late.   I hope to over-hope and over-believe my troubles.   I have cauſe now to truſt Chriſt's promiſe more than His gloom.‡

Remember my hearty affection to your wife.   My ſoul is grieved for the ſucceſs of our brethren's journey to New England; but God hath ſomewhat to reveal that we ſee not.   Grace be with you. Pray for the priſoner.

Yours, in his only Lord Jeſus,

S. R.

ABERDEEN, *Jan.* 1, 1637.

LXXVI.—*To* ROBERT GORDON *of Knockbrex.*

(BENEFIT OF AFFLICTION.)

Y DEAR BROTHER,—Grace, mercy, and peace be multiplied upon you.—I am almoſt wearying, yea, won-dering, that ye write not to me : though I know it is not forgetfulneſs.

As for myſelf, I am every way well, all glory to God.   I was before at a plea with Chriſt (but it was brought§ by me, and un-lawful), becauſe His whole providence was not yea and nay to my yea and nay, and becauſe I believed Chriſt's outward look better

---

* Bankrupt; or rather, debtor.   † Running wild, in high excitement.
‡ Frown.   § Got up.

than His faithful promife. Yet He hath in patience waited on, whill* I be come to myfelf, and hath not taken advantage of my weak apprehenfions of His goodnefs. Great and holy is His name ! He looketh to what I defire to be, and not to what I am. One thing I have learned. If I had been in Chrift, by way of adhefion only, as many branches are, I fhould have been burnt to afhes, and this world would have feen a fuffering minifter of Chrift (of fomething once in fhow) turned into unfavoury falt. But my Lord Jefus had a good eye that the tempter fhould not play foul play, and blow out Chrift's candle. He took no thought of my ftomach, and fretting and grudging humour, but of His own grace. When He burnt the houfe, He faved His own goods. And I believe that the devil and the perfecuting world fhall reap no fruit of me, but burnt afhes : for He will fee to His own gold, and fave that from being confumed with the fire.

Oh what owe I to the file, to the hammer, to the furnace of my Lord Jefus ! who hath now let me fee how good the wheat of Chrift is, that goeth through His mill, and His oven, to be made bread for His own table. Grace tried is better than grace, and it is more than grace ; it is glory in its infancy. I now fee that godlinefs is more than the outfide, and this world's paffments and their bufkings.† Who knoweth the truth of grace without a trial ? Oh how little getteth Chrift of us, but that which He winneth (to fpeak fo) with much toil and pains ! And how foon would faith freeze without a crofs ! How many dumb croffes have been laid upon my back, that had never a tongue to fpeak the fweetnefs of Chrift, as this hath ! When Chrift bleffeth His own croffes with a tongue, they breathe out Chrift's love, wifdom, kindnefs, and care of us. Why fhould I ftart at the plough of my Lord, that maketh deep furrows on my foul ? I know that He is no idle Hufbandman, He purpofeth a crop. O that this white, withered lea-ground‡ were made fertile to bear a crop for Him, by whom it is fo painfully dreffed ; and that this fallow-ground were broken up ! Why was

---

* Till.   † See laft letter.   ‡ Land left in grafs, not tilled.

I (a fool!) grieved that He put His garland and His rofe upon my head—the glory and honour of His faithful witneffes? I defire now to make no more pleas* with Chrift. Verily He hath not put me to a lofs by what I fuffer; He oweth me nothing; for in my bonds how fweet and comfortable have the thoughts of Him been to me, wherein I find a fufficient recompenfe of reward!

How blind are my adverfaries, who fent me to a banqueting-houfe, to a houfe of wine, to the lovely feafts of my lovely Lord Jefus, and not to a prifon, or place of exile! Why fhould I fmother my Hufband's honefty, or fin againft His love, or be a niggard in giving out to others what I get for nothing? Brother, eat with me, and give thanks. I charge you before God, that ye fpeak to others, and invite them to help me to praife! Oh, my debt of praife, how weighty it is, and how far run up! O that others would lend me to pay, and learn me to praife! Oh, I am a drowned dyvour!† Lord Jefus, take my thoughts for payments. Yet I am in this hot fummer-blink with the tear in my eye; for (by reafon of my filence) forrow, forrow hath filled me; my harp is hanged upon the willow-trees, becaufe I am in a ftrange land. I am ftill kept in exercife with envious brethren; my mother hath borne me a man of contention.

Write to me your mind anent Y. C.: I cannot forget him; I know not what God hath to do with him:—and your mind anent my parifhioners' behaviour, and how they are ferved in preaching; or if there be a minifter as yet thruft in upon them, which I defire greatly to know, and which I much fear.

Dear brother, ye are in my heart, to live and to die with you. Vifit me with a letter. Pray for me. Remember my love to your wife. Grace, grace be with you; and God, who heareth prayer, vifit you, and let it be unto you according to the prayers of

　　　　　　Your own brother, and Chrift's prifoner,

　　　　　　　　　　　　　　　　　　S. R.

ABERDEEN, *Jan.* 1, 1637.

---

* Controverfies.　　　　　　　　　† Debtor.

[LADY BOYD, whofe maiden name was Chriftian Hamilton, was the eldeft daughter of Thomas, firft Earl of Haddington. She was firft married to Robert, ninth Lord Lindfay of Byres, who died in 1616. To him fhe had a fon, John, tenth Lord Lindfay of Byres, and a daughter, Helen, married to Sir William Scott of Ardrofs. (*Douglas' Peerage*, vol. i.) She married for her fecond hufband, Robert, fixth Lord Boyd, who died in Auguft 1628. To him fhe had feveral children. Lady Boyd was diftinguifhed for piety, and a zealous Prefbyterian. Livingftone gives her a place among "fome of the profeffors in the Church of Scotland of his acquaintance, who were eminent for grace and gifts," eulogizes her as "a rare pattern of Chriftianity, grave, diligent, and prudent;" and adds, "She ufed every night to write what had been the cafe of her foul all the day, and what fhe had obferved of the Lord's dealing." In his Life he fpeaks of refiding for fome time, during the courfe of his miniftry, in the houfe of Kilmarnock, with "the worthy Lady Boyd."]

(*ABERDEEN—EXPERIENCE OF HIMSELF SAD—PRESSING FORWARDS.*)

MADAM,—Grace, mercy, and peace be unto you. The Lord hath brought me to Aberdeen, where I fee God in few. This town hath been advifed upon of purpofe for me; it confifteth either of Papifts, or men of Gallio's naughty* faith. It is counted wifdom in the moft, not to countenance a confined minifter; but I find Chrift neither ftrange nor unkind; for I have found many faces fmile upon me fince I came hither. I am heavy and fad, confidering what is betwixt the Lord and my foul, which none feeth but He. I find men have miftaken me; it would be no art (as I now fee) to fpin fmall,† and make hypocrify a goodly web, and to go through the market as a faint among men, and yet fteal quietly to hell, without obfervation: fo eafy is it to deceive men. I have difputed whether or no I ever knew anything of Chriftianity, fave the letters of that name. Men fee but as men, and they call ten twenty, and twenty an hundred; but O! to be

---

* Vile.   † Spin fine.

approved of God in the heart and in fincerity is not an ordinary mercy. My neglects while I had a pulpit, and other things where-of I am afhamed to fpeak, meet me now, fo as God maketh an honeft crofs my daily forrow. And, for fear of fcandal and ftum-bling, I muft hide this day of the law's pleading : I know not if this court kept within my foul be fenced* in Chrift's name. If certainty of falvation were to be bought, God knoweth, if I had ten earths, I would not prig† with God. Like a fool, I believed, under fuffering for Chrift, that I myfelf fhould keep the key of Chrift's treafures, and take out comforts when I lifted, and eat and be fat : but I fee now a fufferer for Chrift will be made to know himfelf, and will be holden at the door as well as another poor finner, and will be fain to eat with the bairns, and to take the by-board,‡ and glad to do fo. My blefling on the crofs of Chrift that hath made me fee this ! Oh ! if we could take pains for the king-dom of heaven ! But we fit down upon fome ordinary marks of God's children, thinking we have as much as will feparate us from a reprobate ; and thereupon we take the play and cry, " Holy day ! " and thus the devil cafteth water on our fire, and blunteth our zeal and care. But I fee heaven is not at the door ; and I fee, howbeit my challenges § be many, I fuffer for Chrift, and dare hazard my falvation upon it ; for fometimes my Lord cometh with a fair hour, and O ! but His love be fweet, delightful, and comfortable. Half a kifs is fweet ; but our doting love will not be content with a right to Chrift, unlefs we get poffeffion ; like the man who will not be content with rights‖ to bought land, except he get alfo the ridges and acres laid upon his back to carry home with him. How-ever it be, Chrift is wife ; and we are fools, to be browden ¶ and fond of a pawn in the loof of our hand.** Living on truft by faith may well content us. Madam, I know your Ladyfhip knoweth this, and that made me bold to write of it, that others might reap

---

* Conftituted by proclaiming its authority.   † Higgle.

‡ Sit at the fide-table with the children.   § Self-upbraidings.

‖ Title-deeds.   ¶ Eagerly and childifhly defirous.   ** Palm of the hand.

somewhat by my bonds for the truth ; for I fhould defire, and I
aim at this, to have my Lord well fpoken of and honoured, howbeit He fhould make nothing of me but a bridge over a water.
Thus, recommending your Ladyfhip, your fon, and children to
His grace, who hath honoured you with a name and room among
the living in Jerufalem, and wifhing grace to be with your Ladyfhip, I reft,

Your Ladyfhip's in his fweeteft Lord Jefus,

S. R.

ABERDEEN.

LXXVIII.—*To my* LORD BOYD.

[ROBERT, feventh LORD BOYD, the nobleman to whom this letter is
addreffed, was the only fon of Robert, fixth Lord Boyd, by Lady Chriftian
Hamilton, juft now noticed. His father (who was coufin of the famous
Robert Boyd of Trochrig, two miles from Girvan, under whom he ftudied
at Saumur) died in Auguft 1628, at the early age of 33. Young Robert was
ferved heir to his father the 9th of May 1629. His earthly courfe was, however, brief; for he died of a fever on the 17th of November 1640, aged about
24. He was married to Lady Anne Fleming, fecond daughter of John,
fecond Earl of Wigtown, but their union was without iffue. Lord Boyd
warmly efpoufed the fide of the Covenanters ; and, though not a member of
the General Affembly held at Glafgow in 1638, he attended its meetings and
took a deep intereft in its proceedings. Rutherford affectionately commends
and ftimulates his early zeal in behalf of the liberties of the Church.]

(ENCOURAGEMENT TO EXERTION FOR CHRIST'S CAUSE.)

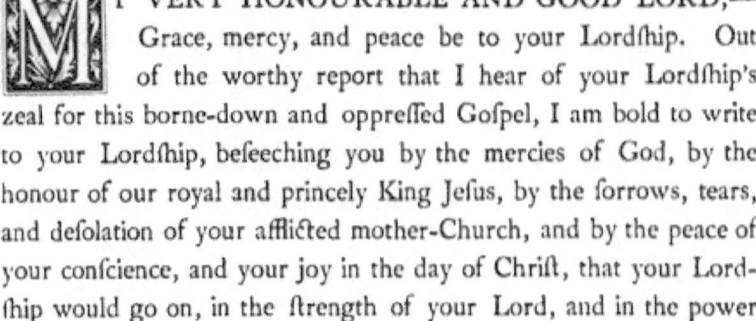

Y VERY HONOURABLE AND GOOD LORD,—
Grace, mercy, and peace be to your Lordfhip. Out
of the worthy report that I hear of your Lordfhip's
zeal for this borne-down and oppreffed Gofpel, I am bold to write
to your Lordfhip, befeeching you by the mercies of God, by the
honour of our royal and princely King Jefus, by the forrows, tears,
and defolation of your afflicted mother-Church, and by the peace of
your confcience, and your joy in the day of Chrift, that your Lordfhip would go on, in the ftrength of your Lord, and in the power
of His might, to beftir yourfelf, for the vindicating of the fallen

honour of your Lord Jefus. Oh, bleffed hands for evermore, that
fhall help to put the crown upon the head of Chrift again in Scotland ! I dare promife, in the name of our Lord, that this will faften
and fix the pillars and the ftakes of your honourable houfe upon
earth, if you lend and lay in pledge in Chrift's hand, upon fpiritual
hazard, life, eftate, houfe, honour, credit, moyen,* friends, the
favour of men (fuppofe kings with three crowns), fo being that ye
may bear witnefs, and acquit yourfelf as a man of valour and courage
to the Prince of your falvation, for the purging of His temple, and
fweeping out the lordly Diotrephefes, time-courting Demafes, corrupt
Hymeneufes and Philetufes, and other fuch oxen, that with their
dung defile the temple of the Lord. Is not Chrift now crying,
" Who will help Me ? who will come out with Me, to take part
with Me, and fhare in the honour of My victory over thefe Mine
enemies, who have faid, We will not have this man to rule over us ?"

My very honourable and dear Lord, join, join (as ye do) with
Chrift. He is more worth to you and your pofterity than this
world's May-flowers, and withering riches and honour, that fhall
go away as fmoke, and evanifh in a night vifion, and fhall, in one
half-hour after the blaft of the archangel's trumpet, lie in white
afhes. Let me befeech your Lordfhip to draw by the lap† of time's
curtain, and to look in through the window to great and endlefs
eternity, and confider, if a worldly price (fuppofe this little round
clay globe of this afhy and dirty earth, the dying idol of the fools
of this world, were all your own) can be given for one fmile of
Chrift's God-like and foul-ravifhing countenance. In that day when
fo many joints and knees of thoufand thoufands wailing fhall ftand
before Chrift, trembling, fhouting, and making their prayers to hills
and mountains to fall upon them, and hide them from the face of
the Lamb, oh, how many would fell lordfhips and kingdoms that
day, and buy Chrift ! But, oh, the market fhall be clofed and
ended ere then ! Your Lordfhip hath now a bleffed venture of
winning court with the Prince of the kings of the earth. He Him-

---

* Intereft.   † Draw afide the loofe fold.

felf weeping ; truth borne down and fallen in the ftreets, and an oppreffed Gofpel ; Chrift's bride with watery eyes and fpoiled of her veil, her hair hanging about her eyes, forced to go in ragged apparel ; the banifhed, alienated, and imprifoned prophets of God, who have not the favour of liberty to prophefy in fackcloth, all thefe, I fay, call for your help. Fear not worms of clay ; the moth fhall eat them as a garment. Let the Lord be your fear ; He is with you, and fhall fight for you ; and ye fhall make the heart of this your mother-Church to fing for joy. The Lamb and His armies are with you, and the kingdoms of the earth are the Lord's. I am perfuaded that there is not another gofpel, nor another faving truth, than that which ye now contend for. I dare hazard my heaven and falvation upon it, that this is the only faving way to glory.

Grace, grace, be with your Lordfhip.

Your Lordfhip's at all refpectful obedience in Chrift,

S. R.

Aberdeen, 1637.

LXXIX.—*To* Margaret Ballantyne.

[Probably this perfon was one of his Anwoth parifhioners.]

(*VALUE OF THE SOUL, AND URGENCY OF SALVATION.*)

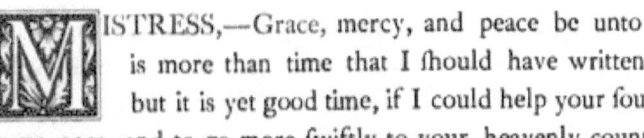

MISTRESS,—Grace, mercy, and peace be unto you.—It is more than time that I fhould have written to you ; but it is yet good time, if I could help your foul to mend your pace, and to go more fwiftly to your heavenly country. For truly ye have need to make all hafte, becaufe the inch of your day that remaineth will quickly flip away ; for whether we fleep or wake, our glafs runneth. The tide bideth no man. Beware of a beguile in the matter of your falvation. Woe, woe for evermore, to them that lofe that prize. For what is behind, when the foul is once loft, but that finners warm their bits of clay houfes at a fire of their own kindling, for a day or two (which doth rather fuffocate with its fmoke than warm them) ; and at length they lie down in

forrow, and are clothed with everlafting fhame! I would feek no
further meafure of faith to begin withal than to believe really and
ftedfaftly the doctrine of God's juftice, His all-devouring wrath,
and everlafting burning, where finners are burnt, foul and body,
in a river and great lake of fire and brimftone. Then they would
wifh no more goods than the thoufandth part of a cold fountain-
well to cool their tongues. They would then buy death with enduring of pain and torment for as many years as God hath created
drops of rain fince the creation. But there is no market of buying
or felling life or death there. Oh, alas! the greateft part of this
world run to the place of that torment rejoicing and dancing, eating,
drinking, and fleeping. My counfel to you is, that ye ftart in time
to be after Chrift; for if ye go quickly, Chrift is not far before
you; ye fhall overtake Him. O Lord God, what is fo needful as
this, "Salvation, falvation!" Fy upon this condemned and foolifh
world, that would give fo little for falvation! Oh, if there were
a free market for falvation proclaimed in that day when the trumpet
of God fhall awake the dead, how many buyers would be then!
God fend me no more happinefs than that falvation which the
blind world, to their eternal woe, letteth flip through their fingers.
Therefore, look if ye can give out your money (as Ifaiah fpeaketh *)
for bread, and lay Chrift and His blood in wadfet† for heaven. It is
a dry and hungry bairn's part of goods that Efaus are hunting for
here. I fee thoufands following the chafe, and in the purfuit of
fuch things, while in the meantime they lofe the blefling; and, when
all is done, they have caught nothing to roaft for fupper, but lie
down hungry. And, befides, they go to bed, when they die, without a candle; for God faith to them, "This ye fhall have at My
hand, ye fhall lie down in forrow."‡ And truly this is as ill-made
a bed to lie upon as one could wifh; for he cannot fleep foundly,
nor reft fweetly, who hath forrow for his pillow. Roufe, roufe
up, therefore, your foul, and fpeer§ how Chrift and your foul met
together. I am fure that they never got Chrift, who were not once

---

* Ifa. lv. 2.   † Mortgaged, pledged.   ‡ Ifa. l. 11.   § Afk.

fick at the yolk of the heart for Him. Too, too many whole fouls
think that they have met with Chrift, who had never a wearied
night for the want of Him : but, alas ! what richer are men, that
they dreamed the laft night they had much gold, and, when they
awoke in the morning, they found it was but a dream ? What
are all the finners in the world, in that day when heaven and earth
fhall go up in a flame of fire, but a number of beguiled dreamers ?
Every one fhall fay of his hunting and his conqueft,* " Behold, it was
a dream !" Every man in that day will tell his dream. I befeech
you, in the Lord Jefus, beware, beware of unfound work in the
matter of your falvation : ye may not, ye cannot, ye dow not want
Chrift. Then, after this day, convene all your lovers before your
foul, and give them their leave; and ftrike hands with Chrift, that
thereafter there may be no happinefs to you but Chrift, no hunting
for anything but Chrift, no bed at night, when death cometh, but
Chrift. Chrift, Chrift, who but Chrift ! I know this much of
Chrift, that He is not ill to be found, nor lordly of His love. Woe
had been my part of it for evermore, if Chrift had made a dainty of
Himfelf to me. But, God be thanked, I gave nothing for Chrift.
And now I proteft before men and angels that Chrift cannot be
exchanged, that Chrift cannot be fold, that Chrift cannot be weighed.
Where would angels, or all the world, find a balance to weigh Him
in ? All lovers blufh when ye ftand befide Chrift ! Woe upon
all love but the love of Chrift ! Hunger, hunger for evermore be
upon all heaven but Chrift ! Shame, fhame for evermore be upon
all glory but Chrift's glory. I cry death, death upon all lives but
the life of Chrift. Oh, what is it that holdeth us afunder ? O
that once we could have a fair meeting !

Thus recommending Chrift to you and you to Him, for evermore, I reft. Grace be with you.

Yours, in his fweet Lord Jefus,

S. R.

ABERDEEN, 1637.

---

* Acquifition ; what he has won.

(*HIS COMFORT UNDER TRIBULATIONS, AND THE PRISON A PALACE.*)

Y DEARLY BELOVED SISTER,—Grace, mercy, and peace be to you. I complain that Galloway is not kind to me in paper. I have received no letters thefe fixteen weeks but two. I am well. My prifon is a palace to me, and Chrift's banqueting-houfe. My Lord Jefus is as kind as they call Him. O that all Scotland knew my cafe, and had part of my feaft! I charge you in the name of God, I charge you to believe. Fear not the fons of men; the worms fhall eat them. To pray and believe now, when Chrift feems to give you a nay-fay,* is more than it was before. Die believing; die, and Chrift's promife in your hand. I defire, I requeft, I charge your hufband and that town,† to ftand for the truth of the Gofpel. Contend with Chrift's enemies; and I pray you fhow all profeffors (whom) you know my cafe. Help me to praife. The minifters here envy me; they will have my prifon changed. My mother hath born me a man of contention, and one that ftriveth with the whole earth. Remember my love to your hufband. Grace be with you.

Yours in the Lord,

S. R.

ABERDEEN, *Jan.* 3, 1637.

LXXXI.—*To* MR JOHN MEINE (*Jun.*)

[MR JOHN MEINE was the fon of John Meine, merchant in Edinburgh, "a folid and ftedfaft profeffor of the truth of God." His mother was Barbara Hamilton, a notice of whom fee at Let. 313. He was now, it would appear from an allufion in the clofe of this letter, a ftudent of theology, with a view to the holy miniftry.]

---

* A denial.   † Kirkcudbright.

WORTHY AND DEAR BROTHER,—Grace, mercy, and peace be to you. I have been too long in anfwering your letter, but other bufinefs took me up. I am here waiting, if the fair wind will turn upon Chrift's fails in Scotland, and if deliverance be breaking out to this overclouded and benighted kirk. O that we could contend, by prayers and fupplications, with our Lord for that effect! I know that He hath not given out His laft doom againft this land. I have little of Chrift, in this prifon, but groanings, and longings, and defires. All my ftock of Chrift is fome hunger for Him, and yet I cannot fay but I am rich in that. My faith, and hope, and holy practice of new obedience, are fcarce worth the fpeaking of. But bleffed be my Lord, who taketh me, light, and clipped, and naughty,* and fecklefs† as I am. I fee that Chrift will not prig‡ with me, nor ftand upon ftepping-ftones ;§ but cometh in at the broadfide‖ without ceremonies, or making it nice,¶ to make a poor, ranfomed one His own. O that I could feed upon His breathing, and kiffing, and embracing, and upon the hopes of my meeting and His! when love-letters fhall not go betwixt us, but He will be meffenger Himfelf! But there is required patience on our part, till the fummer-fruit in heaven be ripe for us. It is in the bud; but there be many things to do before our harveft come. And we take ill with it, and can hardly endure to fet our paper-face to one of Chrift's ftorms, and to go to heaven with wet feet, and pain, and forrow. We love to carry a heaven to heaven with us, and would have two fummers in one year, and no lefs than two heavens. But this will not do for us: one (and fuch a one!) may fuffice us well enough. The man, Chrift, got but one only, and fhall we have two?

---

* Of little value, like clipt coin; and worth naught.
† Pithlefs, unfubftantial.   ‡ Chaffer, higgle.
§ Require help of ftepping-ftones.   ‖ All at once, frankly.
¶ Being ill to pleafe.

Remember my love in Chrift to your father ; and help me with your prayers. If ye would be a deep divine, I recommend to you fanctification. Fear Him, and He will reveal His covenant to you. Grace be with you.

Yours, in his fweet Lord Jefus,

S. R.

ABERDEEN, *Jan.* 5, 1637.

✦

LXXXII.—*To* JOHN GORDON *of Cardonefs, Elder.*

[JOHN GORDON of Cardonefs, in the parifh of Anwoth, was defcended from Gordon of Lochinvar; but the degree of his defcent cannot now be afcertained, and little is known concerning him. His name appears the firft of **188** signatures attached to an unfuccefsful petition of the elders and parifhioners of Anwoth, prefented to the Commiffion of the General Affembly 1638, for Rutherford being continued minifter of that parifh, when counter applications were made by the city of Edinburgh and the Univerfity of St Andrews for the transference of his fervices. From Rutherford's letters to him, we learn that he was at this time far advanced in life. He was naturally a man of ftrong paffions, by which it would appear he had, in the previous part of his life, been led aftray.

The old caftle of *Cardonefs* ftands on a tongue of land, at the mouth of the river Fleet, about a mile from Gatehoufe. It is built on a rocky height, overhanging the public road, and looking toward the bay. You fee an old fquare-built tower, or fortalice, raifing its grey head from among the tall trees that now furround it. Tradition tells of an old proprietor, in league with Græme, the Border outlaw, and how, in confequence of his daring and God-defying deeds, the chief and his whole family perifhed in the *Black Loch*, in the parifh of Anwoth. Though not a defcendant, John Gordon feems to have been a man of like ftrong paffions with that old chieftain, till fubdued by grace.]

(WIN CHRIST AT ALL HAZARDS—CHRIST'S BEAUTY—A WORD
TO CHILDREN.)

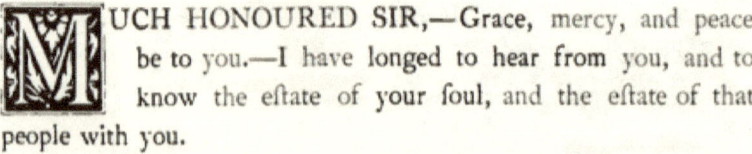

UCH HONOURED SIR,—Grace, mercy, and peace be to you.—I have longed to hear from you, and to know the eftate of your foul, and the eftate of that people with you.

I befeech you, Sir, by the falvation of your precious foul, and the mercies of God, to make good and fure work of your falvation, and try upon what ground-ftone* ye have builded. Worthy and dear Sir, if ye be upon finking fand, a ftorm of death, and a blaft, will loofe Chrift and you, and wafh you clofe off† the rock. Oh, for the Lord's fake, look narrowly to the work!

Read over your life, with the light of God's day-light and fun; for falvation is not caften down at every man's door. It is good to look to your compafs, and all ye have need of, ere you take fhipping; for no wind can blow you back again. Remember, when the race is ended, and the play either won or loft, and ye are in the utmoft circle and border of time, and fhall put your foot within the march‡ of eternity, and all your good things of this fhort night-dream fhall feem to you like the afhes of a bleeze§ of thorns or ftraw, and your poor foul fhall be crying, " Lodging, lodging, for God's fake!" then fhall your foul be more glad at one of your Lord's lovely and homely fmiles, than if ye had the charters of three worlds for all eternity. Let pleafures and gain, will and defires of this world, be put over into God's hands, as arrefted and fenced‖ goods that ye cannot intromit¶ with. Now, when ye are drinking the grounds of your cup, and ye are upon the utmoft end of the laft link of time, and old age, like death's long fhadow, is cafting a covering upon your days, it is no time to court this vain life, and to fet love and heart upon it. It is near after-fupper;** feek reft and eafe for your foul in God through Chrift.

Believe me, that I find it to be hard wreftling to play fair with Chrift, and to keep good quarters with Him, and to love Him in integrity and life, and to keep a conftant courfe of found and folid daily communion with Chrift. Temptations are daily breaking the thread of that courfe, and it is not eafy to caft a knot again; and many knots make evil work. Oh, how fair have many fhips been plying before the wind, that, in an hour's fpace, have been lying in

---

* Foundation.   † Completely off.   ‡ Border.
§ Sudden blazing, flame.   ‖ Guarded.   ¶ Meddle with.
** The time between fupper and bedtime; the very lateft part of the day.

the sea-bottom! How many profeffors caft a golden luftre, as if they were pure gold, and yet are, under that fkin and cover, but bafe and reprobate metal? And how many keep breath in their race many miles, and yet come fhort of the prize and the garland! Dear Sir, my foul would mourn in fecret for you, if I knew your cafe with God to be but falfe work. Love to have you anchored upon Chrift maketh me fear your tottering and flips. Falfe under-water, * not feen in the ground of an enlightened confcience, is dangerous; fo is often falling, and finning againft light. Know this, that thofe who never had fick nights or days in confcience for fin, cannot have but fuch a peace with God as will undercoat,† and break the flefh again, and end in a fad war at death. O how fearfully are thoufands beguiled with falfe hide,‡ grown over old fins, as if the foul were cured and healed!

Dear Sir, I always faw nature mighty, lofty, heady, and ftrong in you; and that it was more for you to be mortified and dead to the world, than for another common man. Ye will take a low ebb, and a deep cut, and a long lance, to go to the bottom of your wounds in faving humiliation, to make you a won prey for Chrift. Be humbled; walk foftly. Down, down, for God's fake, my dear and worthy brother, with your topfail. Stoop, ftoop! it is a low entry to go in at heaven's gate. There is infinite juftice in the party ye have to do with; it is His nature not to acquit the guilty and the finner. The law of God will not want one farthing of the finner. God forgetteth not both the cautioner and the finner; and every man muft pay, either in his own perfon (oh! Lord fave you from that payment!), or in his cautioner§ Chrift. It is violence to corrupt nature for a man to be holy, to lie down under Chrift's feet, to quit will, pleafure, worldly love, earthly hope, and an itching of heart after this farded‖ and over-gilded world, and to be content that Chrift trample upon all. Come in, come in to Chrift, and fee what ye want, and find it in Him. He is the fhort cut (as we ufed to fay), and the

---

* Bilge-water. † Fefter, after being fkinned over.
‡ Falfe fkin. § Surety. ‖ Painted.

neareſt way to an outgate* of all your burdens. I dare avouch that ye ſhall be dearly welcome to Him ; my ſoul would be glad to take part of the joy ye ſhould have in Him. I dare ſay that angels' pens, angels' tongues, nay, as many worlds of angels as there are drops of water in all the ſeas, and fountains, and rivers of the earth, cannot paint Him out to you. I think His ſweetneſs, ſince I was a priſoner, hath ſwelled upon me to the greatneſs of two heavens. Oh for a ſoul as wide as the utmoſt circle of the higheſt heaven that containeth all, to contain His love ! And yet I could hold little of it. O world's wonder ! Oh, if my ſoul might but lie within the ſmell of His love, ſuppoſe I could get no more but the ſmell of it ! Oh, but it is long to that day when I ſhall have a free world of Chriſt's love ! Oh, what a ſight to be up in heaven, in that fair orchard of the new paradiſe ; and to ſee, and ſmell, and touch, and kiſs, that fair Field-flower, that ever-green Tree of Life ! His bare ſhadow were enough for me ; a ſight of Him would be the earneſt of heaven to me. Fy, fy upon us ! that we have love lying ruſting beſide us, or, which is worſe, waſting upon ſome loathſome objeƈts, and that Chriſt ſhould lie His lone.† Wo, wo is me ! that ſin hath made ſo many madmen, ſeeking the fool's paradiſe, fire under ice, and ſome good and deſirable things, without and apart from, Chriſt. Chriſt, Chriſt, nothing but Chriſt, can cool our love's burning languor. O thirſty love ! wilt thou ſet Chriſt, the well of life, to thy head, and drink thy fill ? Drink, and ſpare not ; drink love, and be drunken with Chriſt ! Nay, alas ! the diſtance betwixt us and Chriſt is a death. Oh if we were claſped in other's‡ arms ! We ſhould never twin§ again, except heaven twinned and ſundered us ; and that cannot be.

I deſire your children to ſeek this Lord. Deſire them from me, to be requeſted, for Chriſt's ſake, to be bleſſed and happy, and to come and take Chriſt, and all things with Him. Let them beware of glaſſy and ſlippery youth, of fooliſh young notions, of worldly

---

* Outlet, eſcape from.   † Alone, and no one of us beſide Him.
‡ Each other's.   § Separate, be parted.

lufts, of deceivable gain, of wicked company, of curfing, lying, blas-
pheming, and foolifh talking. Let them be filled with the Spirit ;
acquaint themfelves with daily praying ; and with the ftore-houfe of
wifdom and comfort, the good word of God. Help the fouls of
the poor people. O that my Lord would bring me again among
them, that I might tell unco* and great tales of Chrift to them !
Receive not a ftranger to preach any other doctrine to them.

Pray for me, His prifoner of hope. I pray for you without
ceafing. I write my blefling, earneft prayers, the love of God, and
the fweet prefence of Chrift to you, and yours, and them. Grace,
grace, grace be with you.

Your lawful and loving paftor,

S. R.

ABERDEEN, 1637.

LXXXIII.—*To the* EARL OF LOTHIAN.

[WILLIAM, third EARL OF LOTHIAN, to whom this letter is addreffed,
was the eldeft fon of Robert, firft Earl of Ancrum ; and he acquired the title
of Earl of Lothian by his marriage with Anne Ker, Countefs of Lothian, the
eldeft daughter of Robert, fecond Earl of Lothian, to whofe eftates and titles
fhe fucceeded at his death in 1624. When the differences betwixt the King and
his Scottifh fubjects arofe in 1638, in confequence of the attempt of the former
to impofe on the latter the Anglo-Popifh Liturgy or Service Book, and other
innovations, this nobleman manifefted great zeal for the Covenant. He was
a member of the General Affembly which met at Glafgow that year, as elder
for the Prefbytery of Dalkeith. Hoftilities having again commenced in 1640,
his Lordfhip was in the Scottifh army that invaded England, defeated the
Royalifts at Newburn, and took poffeffion of Newcaftle, of which he was conftituted Governor, with a garrifon of 2000 men. In 1643 he was fent from Scotland by the Privy Council, with the approbation of Charles I., to make fome
propofitions to the Court of France relating to certain privileges of the Scottifh nation. In 1644 he commanded, with the Marquis of Argyle, the forces
fent againft the Marquis of Montrofe, whom he obliged to retreat, and then
delivered up his commiffion to the Committee of Eftates, who paffed an act
in approbation of his fervices. His Lordfhip was prefident of the Committee

---

* Strange.

defpatched by the Parliament to the King in December 1646, with their laft
propofitions, which were refufed. He protefted againft the raifing of an army
in 1648 to refcue the King from the hands of the Englifh, without receiving
from his Majefty affurance that he would fecure the religious liberties of his
Scottifh fubjects,—an attempt which was called the " Engagement." But
while refifting the arbitrary meafures of his princes, he was of fincere and ar-
dent loyalty. No fooner was it known that the Parliament of England intended to proceed againft Charles I. before the High Court of Juftice, than
he and other commiffioners were fent to remonftrate with them, in name of
the kingdom of Scotland, againft the violence and indignity which it was feared
they intended againft the facred perfon of the King. The Earl warned them
that the whole nation regarded the very thoughts of fuch a thing with the utmoft abhorrence ; and he took a folemn proteft againft their proceedings, for
which he was put under arreft, fent with a guard to Gravefend, and thence to
Scotland. On his return he received the thanks of Parliament for his conduct
on this occafion ; and, along with the Earl of Caffillis, was defpatched to Breda
in 1650 to invite King Charles to Scotland. His Lordfhip died in the year
1675. By Anne, Countefs of Lothian, he had five fons and nine daughters.]

*(ADVICE AS TO PUBLIC CONDUCT—EVERYTHING TO BE EN-
DURED FOR CHRIST.)*

IGHT HONOURABLE, AND MY VERY
WORTHY AND NOBLE LORD,—Out of the
honourable and good report that I hear of your Lordfhip's good-will and kindnefs, in taking to heart the honourable
caufe of Chrift, and His afflicted Church and wronged truth in this
land, I make bold to fpeak a word, on paper, to your Lordfhip, at
this diftance, which I truft your Lordfhip will take in good part.
It is to your Lordfhip's honour and credit, to put to your hand, as
ye do (all honour to God!), to the falling and tottering tabernacle
of Chrift, in this your mother-Church, and to own Chrift's wrongs
as your own wrongs. O bleffed hand, which fhall wipe and dry
the watery eyes of our weeping Lord Jefus, now going mourning
in fackcloth in His members, in His fpoufe, in His truth, and in the
prerogative royal of His kingly power ! He needeth not fervice
and help from men ; but it pleafeth His wifdom to make the wants
and loffes, the fores and wounds of His fpoufe, a field and an office-

houfe for the zeal of His fervants to exercife themfelves in. Therefore, my noble and dear Lord, go on, go on in the ftrength of the
Lord, againft all oppofition, to fide with wronged Chrift. The
defending, and warding of ftrokes off Chrift's bride, the King's
daughter, is like a piece of the reft of the way to heaven, knotty,
rough, ftormy, and full of thorns. Many would follow Chrift,
but with a refervation that, by open proclamation, Chrift would cry
down croffes, and cry up fair weather, and a fummer fky and fun,
till we were all fairly landed at heaven. I know that your Lordfhip
hath not fo learned Chrift; but that ye intend to fetch* heaven, fuppofe that your father were ftanding in your way, and to take it
with the wind on your face ; for fo both ftorm and wind were on
the fair face of your lovely Forerunner, Chrift, all His way. It is
poffible that the fuccefs anfwer not your defire in this worthy
caufe. What then? duties are ours, but events are the Lord's;
and I hope, if your Lordfhip, and others with you, will go on to
dive to the loweft ground and bottom of the knavery and perfidious
treachery to Chrift of the accurfed and wretched prelates, the
Antichrift's firft-born, and the firft-fruit of his foul womb, and
fhall deal with our Sovereign (law going before you) for the reafon-
able and impartial hearing of Chrift's bill of complaints, and fet
yourfelves fingly† to feek the Lord and His face, that your righteoufnefs fhall break through the clouds which prejudice hath drawn
over it, and that ye fhall, in the ftrength of the Lord, bring our
banifhed and departing Lord Jefus home again to His fanctuary.
Neither muft your Lordfhip advife with flefh and blood in this;
but wink, and in the dark, reach your hand to Chrift, and follow
Him. Let not men's fainting difcourage you ; neither be afraid of
men's canny‡ wifdom, who, in this ftorm, take the neareft fhore, and
go to the lee and calm fide of the Gofpel, and hide Chrift (if ever
they had Him) in their cabinets, as if they were afhamed of Him,
or as if Chrift were ftolen wares, and would blufh before the fun.

My very dear and noble Lord, ye have rejoiced the hearts of

---

* Make for heaven.   † With a fingle mind.   ‡ Prudent and kind.

many, that ye have made choice of Chrift and His Gofpel, whereas
fuch great temptations do ftand in your way. But I love your profeffion the better that it endureth winds. If we knew ourfelves
well, to want temptations is the greateft temptation of all. Neither
is father, nor mother, nor court, nor honour, in this over-luftred
world with all its paintry* and farding,† anything elfe, when they
are laid in the balance with Chrift, but feathers, fhadows, night-
dreams, and ftraws. Oh, if this world knew the excellency, fweetnefs, and beauty of that high and lofty One, that Faireft among the
fons of men, verily they would fee, that if their love were bigger
than ten heavens, all in circles beyond each other, it were all too
little for Chrift our Lord ! I hope that your choice will not repent
you, when life fhall come to that twilight betwixt time and eternity,
and ye fhall fee the utmoft border of time, and fhall draw the
curtain, and look into eternity, and fhall one day fee God take the
heavens in His hands, and fold them together, like an old holely‡
garment, and fet on fire this clay part of the creation of God, and
confume away into fmoke and afhes the idol-hope of poor fools,
who think that there is not a better country than this low country of
dying clay. Children cannot make comparifon aright betwixt this
life and that which is to come ; and, therefore, the babes of this
world, who fee no better, mould, in their own brain, a heaven of their
own coining, becaufe they fee no farther than the neareft fide of time.

I dare lay in pawn my hope of heaven, that this reproached
way is the only way of peace. I find it is the way that the Lord
hath fealed with His comforts now, in my bonds for Chrift ; and I
verily efteem and find chains and fetters for that lovely One, Chrift,
to be watered over with fweet confolations, and the love-fmiles of
that lovely Bridegroom, for whofe coming we wait. And when
He cometh, then fhall the blacks and whites of all men come before the fun ; then fhall the Lord put a final decifion upon the
pleas§ that Zion hath with her adverfaries. And as faft as time

---

* Painted things.   † Fine colouring.
‡ Full of holes ; worn out.   § Matters of controverfy.

posteth away (which neither sitteth, nor standeth, nor sleepeth), as fast is our hand-breadth of this short winter-night flying away, and the sky of our long-lasting day drawing near its breaking.

Except your Lordship be pleased to plead for me against the tyranny of prelates, I shall be forgotten in this prison ; for they did shape my doom according to their new, lawless canons, which is, that a deprived minister shall be utterly silenced, and not preach at all ; which is a cruelty, contrary to their own former practices.

Now, the only wise God, the very God of peace, confirm, strengthen, and establish your Lordship upon the stone laid in Zion, and be with you for ever.

Your Lordship's at all respectful obedience in his sweet Lord Jesus,

S. R.

ABERDEEN, 1637.

———————◆———————

LXXXIV.—*To* JEAN BROWN.

[JEAN BROWN was the mother of the well-known Mr John Brown, minister of Wamphray in Annandale, who, after the restoration of Charles II., was ejected from his charge and banished from the King's dominions for his opposition to Prelacy. As may be gathered from Rutherford's letters to her, she was a woman of intelligence and piety.]

(*THE JOYS OF THIS LIFE EMBITTERED BY SIN—HEAVEN AN OBJECT OF DESIRE—TRIAL A BLESSED THING.*)

MISTRESS,—Grace, mercy, and peace be unto you. I long to hear how your soul prospereth. I earnestly desire your on-going toward your country. I know that ye see your day melteth away by little and little, and that in a short time ye shall be put beyond time's bounds ; for life is a post that standeth not still, and our joys here are born weeping, rather than laughing, and they die weeping. Sin, sin, this body of sin and corruption embittereth and poisoneth all our enjoyments. Oh that I were where I shall sin no more ! Oh to be freed of these

chains and iron fetters, which we carry about with us! Lord,
loofe the fad prifoners! Who of the children of God have not
caufe to fay, that they have their fill of this vain life? and, like a full
and fick ftomach, to wifh at mid-fupper that the fupper were ended,
and the table drawn, that the fick man might win * to bed, and enjoy
reft ? We have caufe to tire at mid-fupper of the beft meffes that
this world can drefs up for us ; and to cry to God, that He would
remove the table and put the fin-fick fouls to reft with Himfelf.
Oh for a long play-day with Chrift, and our long-lafting vacance†
of reft! Glad may their fouls be that are fafe over the frith,‡
Chrift having paid the fraught.§ Happy are they who have paffed
their hard and wearifome time of apprenticefhip, and are now free-
men and citizens in that joyful, high city, the New Jerufalem.

Alas ! that we fhould be glad of and rejoice in our fetters, and
our prifon-houfe, and this dear inn, a life of fin, where we are
abfent from our Lord, and fo far from our home. O that we
could get bonds and law-furetyfhip of our love, that it faften not
itfelf on thefe clay-dreams, thefe clay-fhadows, and worldly vanities!
We might be oftener feeing what they are doing in heaven, and our
hearts more frequently upon our fweet treafure above. We fmell
of the fmoke of this lower houfe of the earth, becaufe our hearts
and our thoughts are here. If we could haunt‖ up with God, we
fhould fmell of heaven and of our country above; and we fhould
look like our country, and like ftrangers, or people not born or
brought up hereaway. ¶ Our croffes would not bite** upon us
if we were heavenly-minded. I know of no obligation which the
faints have to this world, feeing we fare but upon the fmoke of it ;
and, if there be any fmoke in the houfe, it bloweth upon our eyes.
All our part of the table is fcarce worth a drink of water ; and
when we are ftricken, we dare not weep, but fteal our grief away
betwixt our Lord and us, and content ourfelves with ftolen forrow

---

* Get into.　　† Vacation, holidays.　　　‡ The ftrait, or eftuary.
§ Freight.　　‖ " Haunt," frequent God's prefence up above this world.
¶ In this quarter.　　　　** Leave the mark of their teeth.

behind backs. God be thanked that we have many things that ſo ſtroke us againſt the hair that we may pray, " God keep our better home, God bleſs our Father's houſe ; and not this ſmoke, that bloweth us to ſeek our beſt lodging." I am ſure that this is the beſt fruit of the croſs, when we, from the hard fare of the dear* inn, cry the more that God would ſend a fair wind, to land us, hungered and oppreſſed ſtrangers, at the door of our Father's houſe, which now is made, in Chriſt, our kindly heritage. Oh ! then, let us pull up the ſtakes and ſtoups† of our tent, and take our tent on our back, and go with our flitting to our beſt home ; for here we have no continuing city.

I am waiting in hope here, to ſee what my Lord will do with me. Let Him make of me what He pleaſeth ; providing He make glory to Himſelf out of me, I care not. I hope, yea, I am now ſure, that I am for Chriſt, and all that I can or may make is for Him. I am His everlaſting dyvour,‡ and ſtill ſhall be ; for, alas, I have nothing for Him, and He getteth but little ſervice of me ! Pray for me, that our Lord would be pleaſed to give me houſe-room, that I may ſerve Him in the calling which He hath called me unto. Grace be with you.

Yours, in his ſweet Lord Jeſus,

S. R.

ABERDEEN, 1637.

LXXXV.—*To* JOHN KENNEDY, *Bailie of Ayr.*

(THE REASONABLENESS OF BELIEVING UNDER ALL AFFLIC-TION—OBLIGATIONS TO FREE GRACE.)

ORTHY AND WELL-BELOVED BROTHER,— Grace, mercy, and peace be unto you.—I am yet wait-ing what our Lord will do for His afflicted Church, and

---

* Where proviſion is dear, or coſtly.   † Poſts.

‡ Debtor. Bankrupt is the meaning preferred by ſome; but that is not neceſſarily implied. In one of his ſermons Rutherford has, " As we ſay to dyvours, Pay me, or ſay ye will not !"

for my re-entry to my Lord's house. O that I could hear the
forfeiture of Chrift (now caften out of His inheritance) recalled and
taken off by open proclamation ; and that Chrift were reftored to
be a freeholder and a landed heritor in Scotland ; and that the
courts fenced* in the name of the baftard prelates (their godfather,
the Pope's, bailiffs and fheriffs) were cried down ! Oh how fweet
a fight were it to fee all the tribes of the Lord in this land fetching
home again our banifhed King, Chrift, to His own palace, His
fanctuary, and His throne ! I fhall think it mercy to my foul, if
my faith will out-watch all this winter-night, and not nod nor flumber
till my Lord's fummer-day dawn upon me. It is much if faith and
hope, in the fad nights of our heavy trial, efcape with a whole fkin,
and without crack or crook. I confefs that unbelief hath not reafon
to be either father or mother to it,† for unbelief is always an irra-
tional thing ; but how can it be, but that fuch weak eyes as ours
muft caft water in a great fmoke, or that a weak head fhould not
turn giddy when the water runneth deep and ftrong ? But God be
thanked that Chrift in His children can endure a ftrefs and a
ftorm, howbeit foft nature would fall down in pieces. O that I had
that‡ confidence as to reft on this, though He fhould grind me into
fmall powder, and bray me into duft, and fcatter the duft to the four
winds of heaven, that my Lord would gather up the powder, and
make me up a new veffel again, to bear Chrift's name to the world !
I am fure that love, bottomed and feated upon the faith of His love
to me, would defire and endure this, and would even claim and
threep§ kindnefs upon Chrift's ftrokes, and kifs His love-glooms, ‖
and both fpell and read falvation upon the wounds made by Chrift's
fweet hands. O that I had but a promife made from the mouth
of Chrift, of His love to me ! and then, howbeit my faith were as
tender as paper, I think longing, and dwining, ¶ and greening** of
fick defires would caufe it to bide†† out the fiege till the Lord came

---

* Conftituted and opened.   † Unbelief has not its origin in *reafon.*
‡ Such.   § Perfevere in vehement affertion.   ‖ Frowns.
¶ Pining.   ** Longing after greedily.   †† Continue to bear or hold out.

to fill the foul with His love. And I know alfo, that in that cafe faith would bide* green and fappy at the root, even at mid-winter, and ftand out againft all ftorms. However it be, I know that Chrift winneth heaven in defpite of hell.

But I owe as many praifes and thanks to free grace as would lie betwixt me and the utmoft border of the higheft heaven, fuppofe ten thoufand heavens were all laid above other. But oh! I have nothing that can hire or bud† grace; for if grace would take hire, it were no more grace. But all our ftability, and the ftrength of our falvation, is anchored and faftened upon free grace; and I am fure that Chrift hath by His death and blood caften the knot fo faft, that the fingers of the devils and hell-fulls of fins cannot loofe it. And that bond of Chrift (that never yet was, nor ever fhall, nor can be regiftrated‡) ftandeth furer than heaven, or the days of heaven, as that fweet pillar of the covenant whereon we all hang. Chrift, with all his little ones under His two wings and in the com-pafs or circle of His arms, is fo fure, that, caft Him and them into the ground§ of the fea, He fhall come up again and not lofe one. An odd one cannot, nor fhall be loft in the telling.‖

This was always God's aim, fince Chrift came into the play betwixt Him and us, to make men dependent creatures; and, in the work of our falvation, to put created ftrength, and arms and legs of clay, quite out of play, and out of office and court. And now God hath fubftituted in our room and accepted His Son, the Mediator, for us and all that we can make. If this had not been, I would have fkinked¶ over and foregone my part of paradife and falva-tion, for a breakfaft of dead, moth-eaten earth; but now I would not give it, nor let it go for more than I can tell. And truly they are filly fools, and ignorant of Chrift's worth, and fo full ill-trained and tutored, who tell Chrift and heaven over the board for two feathers or two ftraws of the devil's painted pleafures, only luftred on the outer fide. This is our happinefs now, that our reckonings

---

* Continue to hold out.   † Bribe.   ‡ Protefted.   § Bottom.
‖ Counting up.   ¶ Renounced by a formal farewell.

at night, when eternity fhall come upon us, cannot be told. We
fhall be so far gainers, and fo far from being fuper-expended (as the
poor fools of this world are, who give out their money, and get in
but black hunger), that angels cannot lay our counts, nor fum our
advantage and incomes.   Who knoweth how far it is to the bottom
of our Chrift's fulnefs, and to the ground* of our heaven?   Who
ever weighed Chrift in a pair of balances?   Who hath feen the
foldings and plies, and the heights and depths of that glory which is
in Him, and kept for us?   O for such a heaven as to ftand afar off,
and fee, and love and long for Him, whill† time's thread be cut, and
this great work of creation diffolved, at the coming of our Lord !

Now to His grace I recommend you.   I befeech you alfo to pray
for a re-entry to me into the Lord's houfe, if it be His good will.

Yours in his fweet Lord Jefus,

S. R.

Aberdeen, *Jan.* 6, 1637.

———◆———

LXXXVI.——*To my* Lord Craighall.

[Sir John Hope, Lord Craighall, was the eldeft fon of Sir Thomas
Hope (Lord Advocate of Scotland in the time of James VI. and Charles I.),
and Elizabeth, daughter of John Bennet of Wallyford. His property, Craighall, is in the parifh of Inverefk, near Edinburgh. Sir Thomas was the moft
eminent lawyer of his day, and was firft brought into notice by the ability
with which he defended the caufe of John Forbes, John Welfh, and the
other minifters who were tried for high treafon at Linlithgow, on account of
their holding a General Affembly at Aberdeen in 1605. John, fecond baronet
of Craighall, followed the profeffion of law, and quickly rofe to diftinction and
influence. He was admitted a Lord of Seffion 27th July 1632, and became
Prefident of the Court. In 1645 he was appointed one of the Privy Council.
He was an elder of the Church, and his name appears on the roll of members
of the General Affemblies 1645-1649, and of the commiffions which thefe
Affemblies appointed, and invefted with full powers for profecuting, advancing, and bringing to a happy conclufion, the work of uniformity in religion in
all his Majefty's dominions. He was married to Margaret, daughter of Sir

———————————

* Bottom.   † Till.

Archibald Murray of Blackbarony. This lady died on the 3d of October 1641. His father, in his publifhed Diary, has the following entry of that date in reference to the event : " About 9 of the night, my dear daughter D. M. Murray, fpoufe to my fon Craighall, deceafed in child-bed, fhe and the bairn in her womb. God in mercy pity me, and my fon, and his children, for it is a fore ftroke" (p. 152). Lord Craighall died at Edinburgh near the end of April 1654. He had a daughter, Mary, who became the wife of William Gordon of Earlfton, and two fons, Sir Thomas and Sir Archibald. *(Douglas' Peerage.)*]

(EPISCOPALIAN CEREMONIES—HOW TO ABIDE IN THE TRUTH —DESIRE FOR LIBERTY TO PREACH CHRIST.)

Y LORD,—I received Mr L.'s* letter with your Lord-fhip's, and his learned thoughts in the matter of cere-monies. I owe refpect to the man's learning, for that I hear him to be oppofed to Arminian herefies. But, with reverence of that worthy man, I wonder to hear fuch popifh-like expreffions as he hath in his letter, as, " Your Lordfhip may fpare doubtings, when the King and Church have agreed in the fettling of fuch orders ; and the Church's direction in things indifferent and circum-ftantial (as if indifferent and circumftantial were all one!) fhould be the rule of every private Chriftian." I only viewed the papers two hours' fpace, the bearer haftening me to write. I find the worthy man not fo feen† in this controverfy as fome turbulent men of our country, whom he calleth "refufers of conformity ;" and let me fay it, I am more confirmed in non-conformity, when I fee fuch a great wit play the agent‡ fo flenderly. But I will lay the blame on the weaknefs of the caufe, not on the meannefs of Mr L.'s learning. I

---

* Who is here meant cannot now be well afcertained. It could not be Mr Robert Leighton, afterwards Archbifhop of Glafgow, as he was then abroad, and not ordained. Perhaps it may have been Mr Loudian, of whom Baillie fays, " He has written fomewhat againft our courfes (at leaft for kneeling) againft Rutherford. They fay he is dead alfo. I much regrate it : he was an excellent philofophe, found and orthodoxe, oppofite to Canterbury's way, al-beit too conform. I counfelled oft Glafgow to have him for their Divinity Lecturer." (*Baillie's Letters and Journals*, i. 77.)

† Converfant with.   ‡ Advocate?

have been, and ftill am confident, that Britain* cannot anfwer one argument, *a fcandalo :* and I longed much to hear Mr L. fpeak to the caufe ; and I would fay, if fome ordinary divine had anfwered as Mr L. doth, that he underftood not the nature of a fcandal ; but I dare not vilify that worthy man fo. I am now upon the heat of fome other employment. I fhall (but God willing) anfwer this, to the fatisfying of any not prejudiced.

I will not fay that every one is acquainted with the reafon in my letter, from God's prefence and bright fhining face in fuffering for this caufe. Ariftotle never knew the medium of the conclufion : and Chrift faith few know it.† I am fure that confcience ftanding in awe of the Almighty, and fearing to make a little hole in the bottom for fear of under-water,‡ is a ftrong medium to hold off an erroneous conclufion in the leaft wing, or lith,§ of fweet, fweet truth, that concerneth the royal prerogative of our kingly and higheft Lord Jefus. And my witnefs is in heaven, that I faw neither pleafure, nor profit, nor honour, to hook me, or catch me, in entering into prifon for Chrift, but the wind on my face for the prefent. And if I had loved to fleep in a whole fkin, with the eafe and prefent delight that I faw on this fide of fun and moon, I fhould have lived at eafe, and in good hopes to fare as well as others. The Lord knoweth that I preferred preaching of Chrift, and ftill do, to anything, next to Chrift Himfelf. And their new canons took my one, my only joy, from me, which was to me as the poor man's one ewe, that had no more! And, alas ! there is little lodging in their hearts for pity or mercy, to pluck out a poor man's one eye for a thing indifferent ; *i.e.,* for knots of ftraw, and things (as they mean ‖) off the way to heaven. I defire not that my name take journey, and go a pilgrim to Cambridge, for fear I come into the ears of authority. I am fufficiently burnt already.

In the mean time, be pleafed to try if the Bifhop of St Andrews, ¶

---

* All the Divines in Britain.   † Rev. ii. 17, "hidden manna."   ‡ Bilge-water.

§ *Joint.* In a fermon at Kirkmabreck, 1634, he fpeaks of "the fhoulder-blade being *out of lith.*"

‖ As they reckon, or think.   ¶ John Spottifwood.

and Glafgow* (Galloway's† ordinary), will be pleafed to abate
from the heat of their wrath, and let me go to my charge. Few
know the heart of a prifoner ; yet I hope that the Lord will hew
His own glory out of as knotty timber as I am. Keep Chrift, my
dear and worthy Lord. Pretended paper-arguments from‡ angering
the mother-Church, (that can reel, and nod, and ftagger,) are not of
fuch weight as peace with the Father, and Hufband. Let the wife
gloom, § I care not, if the Hufband laugh.

Remember my fervice to my Lord your father, and mother, and
lady. Grace be with you.

Yours at all obedience in Chrift,

S. R.

Aberdeen, *Jan.* 24, 1637.

LXXXVII.—*To* Elizabeth Kennedy.

[Elizabeth Kennedy was the fifter of Hugh Kennedy, Provoft of
Ayr, and a woman as eminent for piety and prayer as her brother. Wodrow
records an anecdote of her which illuftrates the devotional character of Christians in her time, and their faith in the power of prayer. Being much afflicted
with the ftone, fhe was advifed to fubmit to a furgical operation. Several
meetings for prayer took place among the godly at Ayr in reference to her
cafe in particular. When the furgeon came to perform the operation, one of
thefe meetings was held in her own houfe, and the people continued fo long
in prayer, as nearly to exhauft his patience; but before they had concluded,
the ftone diffolved, and without furgical aid fhe obtained immediate relief.
(*Wodrow's Analecta*, vol. ii.)]

(*DANGER OF FORMALITY—CHRIST WHOLLY TO BE LOVED—*
OTHER OBJECTS OF LOVE.)

ISTRESS,—Grace, mercy, and peace be to you.—I have
long had a purpofe of writing unto you, but I have
been hindered. I heartily defire that ye would mind

---

* James Law was the ordinary or official deputy of the Bifhop.

† Thomas Sydferff, Bifhop of Galloway.

‡ Arguments drawn from the risk of provoking.   § Frown.

your country, and confider to what airt* your foul fetteth its face ;
for all come not home at night who fuppofe that they have fet their
face heavenward.   It is a woful thing to die, and mifs heaven, and
to lofe houfe-room with Chrift at night : it is an evil journey where
travellers are benighted in the fields.   I perfuade myfelf that thoufands
fhall be deceived and afhamed of their hope.   Becaufe they caft their
anchor in finking fands, they muft lofe it.   Till now I knew not the
pain, labour, nor difficulty that there is to win† at home : nor did
I underftand fo well, before this, what that meaneth, " The righteous fhall fcarcely be faved."   Oh, how many a poor profeffor's
candle is blown out, and never lighted again !   I fee that ordinary
profeffion, and to be ranked amongft the children of God, and to
have a name among men, is now thought good enough to carry profeffors to heaven.   But certainly a name is but a name, and will
never bide‡ a blaft of God's ftorm.   I counfel you not to give your
foul or Chrift reft, nor your eyes fleep, till ye have gotten fomething
that will bide‡ the fire, and ftand out the ftorm.   I am fure, that if
my one foot were in heaven, and if then He fhould fay, " Fend §
thyfelf, I will hold my grips‖ of thee no longer," I fhould go no
farther, but prefently fall down in as many pieces of dead nature.

They are happy for evermore who are over head and ears in
the love of Chrift, and know no ficknefs but love-ficknefs for
Chrift, and feel no pain but the pain of an abfent and hidden Well-
beloved.   We run our fouls out of breath, and tire them, in cours-
ing and galloping after our night-dreams (fuch are the rovings of
our mifcarrying hearts), to get fome created good thing in this life,
and on this fide of death.   We would fain ftay and fpin out a
heaven to ourfelves, on this fide of the water ; but forrow, want,
changes, croffes, and fin, are both woof and warp in that ill-fpun
web.   O how fweet and dear are thofe thoughts that are ftill
upon the things which are above ! and how happy are they who
are longing to have little fand in their glafs, and to have time's

---

* Quarter of the fky.   † Get to.   ‡ Continue to endure.
§ Take care of.   ‖ Grafp.

thread cut, and can cry to Chrift, "Lord Jefus, have over :* come
and fetch the dreary† paffenger!" I wifh that our thoughts were
more frequently than they are upon our country. Oh but heaven
cafteth a fweet fmell afar off to thofe who have fpiritual fmelling!
God hath made many fair flowers; but the faireft of them all is
heaven, and the Flower of all flowers is Chrift. Oh! why do we
not fly up to that lovely One? Alas, that there is fuch a fcarcity
of love, and of lovers, to Chrift amongft us all! Fie, fie upon us,
who love fair things, as fair gold, fair houfes, fair lands, fair pleafures, fair honours, and fair perfons, and do not pine and melt
away with love to Chrift! Oh! would to God I had more love
for His fake! O for as much as would lie betwixt me and heaven,
for His fake! O for as much as would go round about the earth,
and over the heaven, yea, the heaven of heavens, and ten thoufand
worlds, that I might let all out upon fair, fair, only fair Chrift!
But, alas! I have nothing for Him, yet He hath much for me. It
is no gain to Chrift that He getteth my little, fecklefs,‡ fpan-length
and hand-breadth of love.

If men would have fomething to do with their hearts and their
thoughts, that are always rolling up and down (like men with oars
in a boat), after finful vanities, they might find great and fweet employment to their thoughts upon Chrift. If thofe frothy, fluctuating,
and reftlefs hearts of ours would come all about Chrift, and look
into His love, to bottomlefs love, to the depth of mercy, to the
unfearchable riches of His grace, to inquire after and fearch into the
beauty of God in Chrift, they would be fwallowed up in the depth
and height, length and breadth of His goodnefs. Oh, if men would
draw the curtains, and look into the inner fide of the ark, and behold how the fulnefs of the Godhead dwelleth in Him bodily! Oh!
who would not fay, "Let me die, let me die ten times, to fee a fight
of Him"? Ten thoufand deaths were no great price to give for
Him. I am fure that fick, fainting love would heighten the market,
and raife the price to the double for Him. But, alas! if men and

---

* Be done.   † Sorrowful.   ‡ Unfubftantial, worthlefs.

angels were rouped,* and fold at the deareft price, they would not all buy a night's love, or a four-and-twenty-hours' fight of Chrift! Oh, how happy are they who get Chrift for nothing! God fend me no more, for my part of paradife, but Chrift: and furely I were rich enough, and as well heavened as the beft of them, if Chrift were my heaven.

I can write no better thing to you, than to defire you, if ever ye laid Chrift in a count, to take Him up and count over again: and weigh Him again and again: and after this have no other to court your love, and to woo your foul's delight, but Chrift. He will be found worthy of all your love, howbeit it fhould fwell upon you from the earth to the uppermoft circle of the heaven of heavens. To our Lord Jefus and His love I commend you.

Yours in his fweet Lord Jefus,

S. R.

ABERDEEN, 1637.

———————◆———————

LXXXVIII.—*To* JANET KENNEDY.

[This feems to be the wife of Mr John Ferguſhill; fee Let. 112.]

(*CHRIST TO BE KEPT AT EVERY SACRIFICE—HIS INCOMPARABLE LOVELINESS.*)

MISTRESS,—Grace, mercy, and peace be unto you. Ye are not a little obliged to His rich grace, who hath feparated you for Himfelf, and for the promifed inheritance with the saints in light, from this condemned and guilty world. Hold faft Chrift, contend for Him; it is a lawful plea† to go to holding and drawing for Chrift; and it is not poffible to keep Chrift peaceably, having once gotten Him, except the devil were dead. It muft be your refolution to fet your face againft Satan's northern tempefts and ftorms, for falvation. Nature would have heaven to come to us while fleeping in our beds. We

---

* Sold by public auction.   † Controverfy.

would all buy Chrift, fo being we might make price ourfelves.
But Chrift is worth more blood and lives than either ye or I have
to give Him. When we fhall come home, and enter to the poffeffion
of our Brother's fair kingdom, and when our heads fhall find the
weight of the eternal crown of glory, and when we fhall look back
to pains and **fufferings, then fhall we fee life and** forrow to be lefs
than one ftep or ftride from a prifon to glory; **and that** our little
inch of time-fuffering is not worthy of our firft night's welcome-
home to heaven. Oh, what then fhall be the weight of every one
of Chrift's kiffes! Oh, how weighty, and of what worth fhall every
one of Chrift's love-fmiles be! Oh, when once He fhall thruft a
wearied traveller's head betwixt His bleffed breafts, the poor foul
will think one kifs of Chrift hath fully paid home forty or fifty
years' wet feet, and all its fore hearts, and light* fufferings it had
in following after Chrift! Oh, thrice-blinded fouls, whofe hearts
are charmed and bewitched with dreams, fhadows, fecklefs things,
night-vanities, and night-fancies of a miferable life of fin! Shame
on us who fit ftill, fettered with the **love and** liking of the loan
of a piece of dead clay! Oh, poor fools, **who** are beguiled with
painted things, and this world's fair weather, and fmooth promifes,
and rotten, worm-eaten hopes! May not the devil laugh to fee us
give out our **fouls, and get** in but corrupt and counterfeit pleafures
of fin? O for a **fight of** eternity's glory, and a little tafting **of**
the Lamb's marriage-fupper! Half a draught, or a drop of the
wine of confolation, that is up at our banqueting-houfe, out of
Chrift's own hand, would **make our** ftomachs loathe the brown
bread and the four drink of a miferable life. Oh, how **far are we**
bereaved of wit, to chafe, and hunt, and run, till our fouls be out
of breath, after a condemned **happinefs** of our own making! And
do we not fit far in our own light, to make it a matter of bairn's
play, to fkink and drink over† paradife, and the heaven that Chrift

---

* 2 Cor. iv. 17.

† Skink is formally to renounce his part in a thing; "*and drink over,*"
drink the health of the buyer over the concluded bargain.

did fweat for, even for a blaft of fmoke, and for Efau's morning breakfaft ? O that we were out of ourfelves, and dead to this world, and this world dead and crucified to us !   And, when we fhould be clofe* out of love and conceit of any mafked and farded† lover whatfoever, then Chrift would win and conquer to Himfelf a lodging in the inmoft yolk of our heart.   Then Chrift fhould be our night-fong and morning-fong : then the very noife and din of our Well-beloved's feet, when He cometh, and His firft knock or rap at the door, fhould be as news of two heavens to us. O that our eyes and our foul's fmelling fhould go after a blafted and fun-burnt flower, even this plaftered, fair-outfided‡ world : and then we have neither eye nor fmell for the Flower of Jeffe, for that Plant of renown, for Chrift, the choiceft, the faireft, the fweeteft rofe that ever God planted ! Oh, let fome of us die to fmell the fragrance of Him; and let my part of this rotten world be forfeited and fold for evermore, providing I may anchor my tottering foul upon Chrift ! I know that it is fometimes at this, " Lord, what wilt Thou have for Chrift ?"   But, O Lord, canft Thou be budded,§ and propined‖ with any gift for Chrift? O Lord, can Chrift be fold? or rather, may not a poor needy finner have Him for nothing? If I can get no more, oh, let me be pained to all eternity, with long-ing for Him ! The joy of hungering for Chrift fhould be my heaven for evermore.   Alas, that I cannot draw fouls and Chrift together ! But I defire the coming of His kingdom, and that Chrift, as I affuredly hope He will, would come upon withered Scotland, as rain upon the new-mown grafs. Oh, let the King come ! Oh, let His kingdom come ! Oh, let their eyes rot in their eye-holes,¶ who will not receive Him home again to reign and rule in Scotland. Grace, grace be with you.

Yours in his fweet Lord Jefus,

S. R.

ABERDEEN, 1637.

---

* Quite out.   † Embellifhed, painted.   ‡ That has a fair external.
§ Bribed.   ‖ Prefented with.   ¶ Zech. xiv. 12.

LXXXIX.—*To my Well-beloved and Reverend Brother,*
Mr Robert Blair.

[Mr Robert Blair was born at Irvine in 1593. After completing his education at the College of Glafgow, he there held for feveral years the office of Regent, during which time he was licenfed as a probationer for the holy miniftry. Having a ftrong defire to go to France, he was encouraged to this by M. Bafnage, a French Proteftant minifter who vifited Scotland in 1622. But Providence ordered his lot otherwife. He was induced to accept of the charge of Bangor, in Ireland, and was admitted in the year 1623. Here he laboured with great diligence and fuccefs; and there being in the fame part of the country feveral other devout minifters, by mutual excitement and co-operation, they were inftrumental in producing in the north of Ireland a change upon an ignorant and irreligious people, much refembling the effects of the preaching of the Gofpel in the apoftolic age. But this good work was not allowed to go on unoppofed. In the autumn of 1631 he was fufpended from his miniftry by the Bifhop of Down; in May 1632 he was depofed; and in November 1634 folemnly excommunicated; and all this fimply for non-conformity. In thefe circumftances, he and fome other minifters fimilarly fituated, together with a confiderable number of people, formed the purpofe of going to New England, and actually embarked in 1636; but the tempeftuous ftate of the weather forced them to return. He then came over to Scotland, and in 1638 became minifter of Ayr, from which by a fentence of the General Affembly he was foon tranflated to St Andrew's, where he and Rutherford lived in the warmeft friendfhip until the controverfy between the Refolutioners and Protefters arofe, which in fome degree difturbed their mutual good underftanding. Rutherford was a ftrong Protefter: Blair endeavoured to remain neutral. He regretted the extremes, as he conceived, to which both parties went; and, with Mr James Durham of Glafgow, endeavoured to reftore harmony between them, but without fuccefs. Towards the end of September 1661 he was fummoned before the Privy Council for a fermon he had preached, in which he dwelt on fuffering for righteoufnefs' fake, and bore teftimony to the covenanted Reformation, as well as againft the defections of the times. His anfwers to the Council proving unfatisfactory, he was fentenced to be confined to his own houfe. He was afterwards permitted to retire to Muffelburgh. He next removed to Kirkcaldy, and from thence to Meikle Coufton, in the parifh of Aberdour, where he died on the 27th of April 1666.]

(*GOD'S ARRANGEMENTS SOMETIMES MYSTERIOUS.*)

EVEREND AND DEARLY BELOVED BROTHER,
—Grace, mercy, and peace from God our Father, and
from our Lord Jefus Chrift, be unto you.

It is no great wonder, my dear brother, that ye be in heavinefs
for a feafon, and that God's will (in croffing your defign and defires
to dwell amongft a people whofe God is the Lord) fhould move you.
I deny not but ye have caufe to inquire what His providence fpeaketh
in this to you ; but God's directing and commanding Will can by
no good logic be concluded from events of providence. The Lord
fent Paul on many errands for the fpreading of His Gofpel, where
he found lions in his way. A promife was made to His people of
the Holy Land, and yet many nations were in the way, fighting
againft, and ready to kill them that had the promife, or to keep
them from poffeffing that good land which the Lord their God had
given them. I know that ye have moft to do with fubmiffion of
fpirit ; but I perfuade myfelf that ye have learned, in every condition
wherein ye are caft, therein to be content, and to fay, " Good is
the will of the Lord, let it be done." I believe that the Lord
tacketh His fhip often to fetch the wind, and that He purpofeth to
bring mercy out of your fufferings and filence, which (I know
from mine own experience) is grievous to you. Seeing that He
knoweth our willing mind to ferve Him, our wages and ftipend is
running to the fore* with our God, even as fome fick foldiers get
pay, when they are bedfaft and not able to go to the field with
others. " Though Ifrael be not gathered, yet fhall I be glorious
in the eyes of the Lord, and my God fhall be my ftrength."† And
we are to believe it fhall be thus ere all the play be played. " The

---

* Into account for your advantage. † Ifa. xlix. 5.

violence done to me and to my flefh be upon Babylon " (and the great whore's lovers), " fhall the inhabitant of Zion fay ; and my blood be upon Chaldea, fhall Jerufalem fay."* And, " Behold, I will make Jerufalem a cup of trembling to all the people round about, when they fhall be in the fiege both againft Judah and againft Jerufalem. And in that day will I make Jerufalem a burden-fome ftone for all people : they that burden themfelves with it fhall be broken in pieces, though all the people of the earth be gathered together againft it."† When they have eaten and fwallowed us up, they fhall be fick, and vomit us out living men again ; the devil's ftomach cannot digeft the Church of God. Suffering is the other half of our miniftry, howbeit the hardeft ; for we would be content that our King Jefus fhould make an open proclamation, and cry down croffes, and cry up joy, gladnefs, eafe, honour, and peace. But it muft not be fo ; through many afflictions we muft enter into the kingdom of God. Not only by them, but through them, muft we go ; and wiles will not take us paft the crofs. It is folly to think to fteal to heaven with a whole fkin.

For myfelf, I am here a prifoner confined in Aberdeen, threatened to be removed to Caithnefs, becaufe I defire to edify in this town ; and am openly preached againft in the pulpits in my hearing, and tempted with difputations by the doctors, efpecially by D. B.‡ Yet I am not afhamed of the Lord Jefus, His garland, and His crown. I would not exchange my weeping with the painted laughter of the fourteen prelates. At my firft coming here I took the dorts§ at Chrift, and would, forfooth, fummon Him for unkindnefs. I fought a plea‖ of my Lord, and was toffed with challenges¶ whether He loved me or not ; and difputed over again all that He had done to

---

* Jer. li. 35.   † Zech. xii. 2, 3.

‡ Dr Robert Barron, Profeffor of Divinity in the Marifchal College of Aberdeen, one of the learned doctors of that city, whofe difpute, in 1638, with Alexander Henderfon, David Dickfon, and Andrew Cant, on the fub-ject of the Covenant, excited at the time fo much attention.

§ Sulks, pet.   ‖ A quarrel.   ¶ Upbraiding, queftioning.

me, becaufe His word was a fire fhut up in my bowels, and I was
weary with forbearing, becaufe I faid I was caſt out of the Lord's
inheritance. But now I fee that I was a fool. My Lord mifkent *
all, and did bear with my foolifh jealoufies ; and mifkent * that ever
I wronged His love. And now He is come again with mercy under
His wings. I pafs from my (oh witlefs!) fummons: He is God,
I fee, and I am man. Now it hath pleafed Him to renew His love
to my foul, and to dawt† His poor prifoner. Therefore, dear
brother, help me to praife, and fhow the Lord's people with you
what He hath done to my foul, that they may pray and praife.
And I charge you, in the name of Chriſt, not to omit it. For this
caufe I write to you, that my fufferings may glorify my royal King,
and edify His Church in Ireland. He knoweth how one of Chriſt's
love coals hath burnt my foul with a defire to have my bonds to
preach His glory, whofe crofs I now bear. God forgive you if you
do it not ; but I hope the Lord will move your heart, to proclaim
in my behalf the fweetnefs, excellency, and glory of my royal King.
It is but our foft flefh that hath raifed a flander on the crofs of
Chriſt : I fee now the white fide of it ; my Lord's chains are all
over-gilded. Oh, if Scotland and Ireland had part of my feaſt!
And yet I get not my meat but with many ſtrokes. There are
none here to whom I can fpeak: I dwell in Kedar's tents. Refrefh
me with a letter from you. Few know what is betwixt Chriſt and
me.

Dear brother, upon my falvation, this is His truth that we fuffer
for. Chriſt would not feal a blank charter to fouls. Courage,
courage! joy, joy for evermore! O joy unfpeakable and glorious!
O for help to fet my crowned King on high! O for love to Him
who is altogether lovely,—that love which many waters cannot
quench, neither can the floods drown !

I remember you, and bear your name on my breaſt to
Chriſt. I befeech you, forget not His afflicted prifoner. Grace,
mercy, and peace be with you. Salute in the Lord, from

---

* Overlooked.   † Dote upon, fondle.

me, Mr Cunningham, Mr Livingſtone, Mr Ridge,* Mr Colwart,† &c.

Your brother, and fellow-priſoner,

S. R.

Aberdeen, *Feb.* 7, 1637.

XC.—*To his Reverend and Dear Brother*, Mr John Livingstone.

[John Livingstone (the ſon of Alexander Livingſtone, firſt miniſter at Monyabroch or Kilſyth, and afterwards at Lanark) was born at Monyabroch on the 21ſt of January 1603. At the College of Glaſgow, where he received his education, he enjoyed the advantage of having as his regent for two years the famous Robert Blair, for whom he continued ever after to retain the higheſt veneration. He was firſt ſettled miniſter at Killinchie, in Ireland, towards the cloſe of the year 1630, but had not laboured above twelve months in that charge when he was ſuſpended by the Biſhop of Down, for nonconformity. Being afterwards depoſed, and finally excommunicated, to enjoy religious liberty he accompanied Mr Blair and others in their intended emigration to America; but, with the reſt, was forced by the adverſe ſtate of the weather to return. Shortly after, when on a viſit to the weſt of Scotland, he received calls from two pariſhes, Stranraer and Stewarton. By the advice of his friends, whom he conſulted, he preferred the call from the former pariſh, and his induction took place on the 5th of July 1638. Here he continued in the aſſiduous diſcharge of his paſtoral functions until 1648, when, by the ſentence of the General Aſſembly, he was tranſlated to the pariſh of Ancrum, in the Preſbytery of Jedburgh. Upon the death of Charles I., he was ſent to the Hague, and afterwards to Breda, as one of the commiſſioners from the

---

* Mr John Ridge was an Engliſh miniſter, whom oppoſition to ceremonial impoſitions on conſcience led to leave his native country for Ireland. He was admitted to the vicarage of Antrim on the 7th of July 1619, in which he laboured with ſucceſs for many years; but being at length depoſed by Henry Leſlie, the Biſhop of Down, for non-conformity, he came over to Irvine, where he died.

† Mr Henry Colwart was alſo a native of England; and, like Mr Ridge, left the land of his birth, and went to Ireland. He was admitted to the paſtoral charge of Oldſtone in 1630; but being alſo depoſed by Biſhop Leſlie for refuſing to ſubmit to the innovations of Prelacy, he came over to Scotland, and was admitted miniſter of Paiſley, where he died.

Church of Scotland to treat with his fon Charles II., whofe character he had
the penetration to difcover. In the controverfy between the Refolutioners and
Protefters, Livingftone took the fide of the latter, but was diffatisfied with
the violence manifefted by his party. After the reftoration of Charles II.,
being fummoned to appear before the Privy Council on the 11th of December
1662, he appeared, and, declining to engage to obferve the anniverfary of the
death of Charles I., and to take the oath of allegiance in the precife way in
which it was dictated to him, he was fentenced to quit his native land within
two months. Having repaired to Rotterdam, he preached occafionally to the
Scottifh congregation there, and devoted the remainder of his life to the culti-
vation of Biblical literature. He died in that city on the 9th of Auguft 1672,
in the feventieth year of his age.

It was this fame Livingftone that was fo bleffed in awakenings. By a fermon which he preached in 1630 at the Kirk-of-Shotts, on the Monday after
the difpenfation of the Lord's Supper, five hundred fouls, it is believed, were
converted. On a fimilar occafion, at Holywood, in the north of Ireland, he
was the inftrument of awakening double that number to inquiry after falvation.]

(RESIGNATION—ENJOYMENT—STATE OF THE CHURCH.)

MY REVEREND AND DEAR BROTHER,—Grace,
mercy, and peace be to you. I long to hear from you,
and to be refrefhed with the comforts of The Bride of
our Lord Jefus in Ireland. I fuffer with you in grief, for the dafh
that your defires to be at New England have received of late; but if
our Lord, who hath fkill to bring up His children, had not feen it your
beft, it would not have befallen you. Hold your peace, and ftay
yourfelves upon the Holy One of Ifrael. Hearken to what He hath
faid in croffing of your defires; He will fpeak peace to His people.

I am here removed from my flock, and filenced, and confined
in Aberdeen, for the teftimony of Jefus. And I have been confined
in fpirit alfo with defertions and challenges. I gave in a bill of
quarrels, and complaints of unkindnefs againft Chrift, who feemed
to have caft me over the dyke of the vineyard as a dry tree, and
feparated me from the Lord's inheritance; but high, high and loud
praifes be to our royal crowned King in Zion, that He hath not
burnt the dry branch. I fhall yet live, and fee His glory.

Your mother-Church, for her whoredom, is like to be caft off.

The bairns may break their hearts to fee fuch chiding betwixt the hufband and the wife. Our clergy is upon a reconciliation with the Lutherans; and the Doctors are writing books, and drawing up a common confeffion, at the Council's command. Our Service Book is proclaimed with found of trumpet. The night is fallen down upon the prophets! Scotland's day of vifitation is come. It is time for the bride to weep, while Chrift is a-faying that He will choofe another wife. But our fky will clear again; the dry branch of cut-down Lebanon will bud again and be glorious, and they fhall yet plant vines upon our mountains.

Now, my dear brother, I write to you for this end, that ye may help me to praife; and feek help of others with you, that God may be glorified in my bonds. My Lord Jefus hath taken the withered, dry ftranger, and His prifoner broken in heart, into His houfe of wine. Oh, oh if ye, and all Scotland, and all our brethren with you, knew how I am feafted! Chrift's honey-combs drop comforts. He dineth with His prifoner, and the King's fpikenard cafteth a fmell. The devil cannot get it denied that we fuffer for the apple of Chrift's eye, His royal prerogatives, as King and Lawgiver. Let us not fear or faint. He will have His Gofpel once again rouped* in Scotland, and have the matter going to voices, to fee who will fay, "Let Chrift be crowned King in Scotland." It is true that Antichrift ftirreth his tail; but I love a rumbling and raging devil in the kirk (fince the Church militant cannot or may not want a devil to trouble her), rather than a fubtle or fleeping devil. Chrift never yet got a bride without ftroke of fword. It is now nigh the Bridegroom's entering into His chamber;—let us awake and go in with Him.

I bear your name to Chrift's door; I pray you, dear brother, forget me not. Let me hear from you by a letter; and I charge you, fmother not Chrift's bounty towards me. I write what I have found of Him in the houfe of my pilgrimage. Remember my love to all our brethren and fifters there.

---

* Set up to fale by auction, once more.

The Keeper of the vineyard watch for His befieged city, and for you.

Your brother, and fellow-fufferer,

S. R.

Aberdeen, *Feb.* 7, 1637.

———◆———

XCI.—*To* Mr Ephraim Melvin.

[Ephraim Melvin, or Melville, was firft ordained minifter of Queensferry, and afterwards tranflated to Linlithgow, where he died. His miniftry was fignally bleffed of God for bringing many to the faving know-ledge of the truth, among whom were fome who afterwards became eminent minifters of the Gofpel in their day. One of thefe was the famous Mr James Durham of Glafgow. Happening, with his pious wife, a daughter of the laird of Duntervie, to pay a vifit to her mother, alfo a religious woman, in Queensferry, when the facrament of the Lord's Supper was to be obferved in that place, his mother-in-law, upon the Saturday, defired him to go with her to hear fermon. Being then a ftranger to true religion, he was difinclined to go, and faid, with a tone of indifference, "that he had not come there to hear fermon;" but upon being preffed, to gratify his pious relative, he went. The difcourfe which he heard, though plain and ordinary, was delivered with an affection and earneftnefs that arrefted the attention of Durham, and fo impreffed him, that on coming home he faid to his mother-in-law, "Your minifter preached very ferioufly, and I fhall not need to be preffed to go to hear to-morrow." Accordingly he went, and Mr Melvin choofing for his text thefe words, "To you which believe, He is precious," 1 Peter ii. 7, opened up the precioufnefs of Chrift with fuch unction and ferioufnefs, that it proved, by the power of the Holy Spirit, the means of his converfion. In that fermon he firft clofed with Chrift, and took his feat at the Lord's Table, though to that day he had been an abfolute ftranger to believing. He was accuftomed afterwards to call Mr Melvin his father, when he fpoke of him or to him. Melvin, by a fermon which he preached at Stewarton, when a probationer and chaplain to the excellent Lady Boyd, was alfo the inftrument of converting Mr John Stirling in the fourteenth or fixteenth year of his age, an excellent and ufeful minifter in his day, though lefs known than Durham. "Some fay alfo," remarks Wodrow, "that he was a fpiritual father to Mr John Dury of Dalmeny, who was much efteemed of in his time, as having a taking and foaring gift of preaching, much like Mr William Guthrie's gift." When Rutherford heard of Melvin's death, he is reprefented to have faid, " And is Ephraim dead ? He was an interpreter among a thoufand." (*Wodrow's Anal.*, vol. iii.)]

(*THE IDOLATRY OF KNEELING AT THE COMMUNION.*)

EVEREND AND DEAR BROTHER,—I received your letter, and am contented, with all my heart, that our acquaintance in our Lord continue.

I am wreftling as I dow,* up the mount with Chrift's crofs : my Second† is kind and able to help.

As for your queftions, becaufe of my manifold diftractions, and letters to multitudes, I have not time to anfwer them. What fhall be faid in common for that fhall be imparted to you ; for I am upon thefe queftions. Therefore fpare me a little, for the Service Book would take a great time. But I think ; Sicut deofculatio religiofa imaginis, aut etiam elementorum, eft in fe idololatria externa, etfi intentio deofculandi, tota, quanta in actu eft, feratur in Deum πρω-τοτυπὸν ; ita, geniculatio coram pane, quando, nempe, ex inftituto, totus homo externus et internus verfari debeat circa elementaria figna, eft adoratio relativa, et adoratio ipfius panis. Ratio : Intentio ado-randi objectum materiale, non eft de effentiâ externæ adorationis, ut patet in deofculatione religiosâ. Sic geniculatio coram imagine Babylonicâ eft externa adoratio imaginis, etfi tres pueri mente inten-diffent adorare Jehovam. Sic, qui ex metu folo, aut fpe pretii, aut inanis gloriæ, geniculatur coram aureo vitulo Jeroboami (quod ab ipfo rege, qui nullâ religione inductus, fed libidine dominandi tantum, vitulum erexit, factitatum effe, textus fatis luculenter clamat), adorat vitulum externâ adoratione ; efto quod putaret vitulum effe meram creaturam, et honore nullo dignum : quia geniculatio, five nos no-lumus, five volumus, ex inftituto Dei et naturæ, in actu religiofo, eft fymbolum religiofæ adorationis. Ergo, ficut panis fignificat cor-pus Chrifti, etfi abfit actus omnis noftræ intentionis ; fic religiofa geniculatio, fublatâ omni intentione humanâ, eft externa adoratio panis, coram quo adoramus, ut coram figno vicario et repræfentativo

---

* I am able.   † Chrift, who is my helper, at my fide.

Dei. [As the religious homage done to an image, or even to elements, is in itself an external act of idolatry, in so far as the act is concerned, although the *intention* of such homage may be directed to God the Great First Cause,—so the act of kneeling to a piece of bread, seeing that, according to the ordinance, the whole man, internal and external, ought to be engaged in the elementary signs, is a relative act of worship and an adoration of the bread itself. The reason is : an *intention* to worship a material object is not of the essence of external adoration, as appears in a religious act of homage.   Thus, the bending of the knee before the Babylonish image is an external act of worship, even though the three youths had no intention to worship any but the true God ; and in like manner, those who, from fear or the hope of reward or vain-glory, bend the knee to Jeroboam's golden calf (which the text clearly enough proclaims to have been done by the king himself, from no religious motive but the mere desire to rule), do pay adoration to the calf by the external act, although, no doubt, they may suppose the calf a mere created object and unworthy of honour,—because the act of homage, whether we mean it or not, is, from the ordinance of God and nature, a symbol of worship.   Therefore, as the bread denotes the body of Christ (even though that idea be not present to the mind), so in like manner, kneeling, when used as a religious service, is the external adoration of that bread, in presence of which we bow as before the delegated representative of God, be our intention what it may.]

Thus recommending you to God's tender mercy, I desire that you would remember me to God.   Sanctification will settle you most in the truth.

Grace be with you, Brother in Christ Jesus,

S. R.

ABERDEEN, 1637.

XCII.—*To* ROBERT GORDON *of Knockbrex.*

(VISITS OF CHRIST—THE THINGS WHICH AFFLICTION TEACHES.)

Y VERY WORTHY AND DEAR FRIEND,— Grace, mercy, and peace be to you. Though all Galloway fhould have forgotten me, I would have expected a letter from you ere now; but I will not expound it to be forgetfulnefs of me.

Now, my dear brother, I cannot fhow you how matters go betwixt Chrift and me. I find my Lord going and coming feven times a day. His vifits are fhort; but they are both frequent and fweet. I dare not for my life think of a challenge of my Lord. I hear ill tales, and hard reports of Chrift, from The Tempter and my flefh; but love believeth no evil. I may fwear that they are liars, and that apprehenfions make lies of Chrift's honest and unalterable love to me. I dare not fay that I am a dry tree, or that I have no room at all in the vineyard; but yet I often think that the fparrows are bleffed, who may refort to the houfe of God in Anwoth, from which I am banifhed.

Temptations, that I fuppofed to be ftricken dead and laid upon their back, rife again and revive upon me; yea, I fee that while I live, temptations will not die. The devil feemeth to brag and boaft as much as if he had more court with Chrift than I have; and as if he had charmed and blafted my miniftry, that I fhall do no more good in public. But his wind fhaketh no corn.* I will not believe that Chrift would have made fuch a mint† to have me to Himfelf, and have taken fo much pains upon me as He hath done, and then flip fo eafily from poffeffion, and lofe the glory of what He hath done. Nay, fince I came to Aberdeen, I have been taken up to fee the new land, the fair palace of the Lamb; and will Chrift let me fee heaven, to break my heart, and never give it to me? I fhall not think my Lord Jefus giveth a dumb earneft, or putteth His feals to

---

* Does no harm.   † An effort expreffive of intention.

blank paper, or intendeth to put me off with fair and falſe promiſes.
I ſee that now which I never ſaw well before. (1.) I ſee faith's
neceſſity in a fair day is never known aright; but now I miſs nothing
ſo much as faith.   Hunger in me runneth to fair and ſweet promiſes;
but when I come, I am like a hungry man that wanteth teeth, or a
weak ſtomach having a ſharp appetite that is filled with the very
ſight of meat, or like one ſtupified with cold under the water, that
would fain come to land, but cannot grip anything caſten* to him.
I can let Chriſt grip* me, but I cannot grip Him.   I love to be
kiſſed, and to ſit on Chriſt's knee; but I cannot ſet my feet to the
ground, for afflictions bring the cramp upon my faith.   All that I
dow do† is to hold out a lame faith to Chriſt, like a beggar holding
out a ſtump, inſtead of an arm or leg, and cry, " Lord Jeſus, work
a miracle!"   Oh, what would I give to have hands and arms to
grip* ſtrongly, and fold heartſomely about Chriſt's neck, and to have
my claim made good with real poſſeſſion!   I think that my love to
Chriſt hath feet in abundance, and runneth ſwiftly to be at Him, but
it wanteth hands and fingers to apprehend Him.   I think that I would
give Chriſt every morning my bleſſing, to have as much faith as I have
love and hunger; at leaſt, I miſs faith more than love or hunger.

(2.) I ſee that mortification, and to be crucified to the world, is
not ſo highly accounted of by us as it ſhould be.   Oh, how heavenly a
thing it is to be dead, and dumb, and deaf to this world's ſweet muſic!
I confeſs it hath pleaſed His Majeſty to make me laugh at the children,
who are wooing this world for their match.   I ſee men lying about
the world, as nobles about a king's court; and I wonder what they
are all doing there.   As I am at this preſent, I would ſcorn to
court ſuch a feckleſs‡ and petty princeſs, or buy this world's kindneſs
with a bow of my knee.   I ſcarce now either hear or ſee what it is
that this world offereth me; I know that it is little which it can
take from me, and as little that it can give me.   I recommend mortification to you above anything; for, alas! we but chaſe feathers
flying in the air, and tire our own ſpirits for the froth and over-

---

* Take faſt hold of anything flung to him.   † Am able to do.   ‡ Worthleſs.

gilded clay of a dying life. One fight of what my Lord hath let me fee within this fhort time is worth a world of worlds.

(3.) I thought courage, in the time of trouble for Chrift's fake, a thing that I might **take up** at my foot. I thought that the very remembrance of the honefty of the caufe would be enough. **But I** was a fool in **fo thinking.** I have much ado now to win to* one fmile. But I fee that joy groweth up in heaven, and it is above our fhort arm. **Chrift** will be fteward and difpenfer Himfelf, and none elfe but **He**; therefore, now, I count much of one dramweight of fpiritual **joy.** One fmile of Chrift's face is now to me as a kingdom; and yet **He is** no niggard to me of comforts. Truly I have no caufe to **fay** that I am pinched with penury, or that the confolations of Chrift are dried up : for He hath poured down rivers upon **a dry** wildernefs the like of me, to my admiration ; and in my very fwoonings, He holdeth up my head, and ftayeth me with flagons of wine, and comforteth me with apples. My houfe and bed are ftrewed **with** kiffes of love. Praife, praife with me. Oh, if ye and I betwixt **us could** lift up Chrift upon His throne, howbeit all Scotland fhould **caft Him down to** the ground !

My brother's cafe toucheth me near. **I hope** that ye will be kind **to him, and give him your beft** counfel.

Remember **my love to your brother, to** your wife, and G. M.† Defire him to be faithful, and to repent of his hypocrify ; and fay that I wrote it to you. I wifh him falvation. Write to me **your** mind anent C. E. and **C. Y., and their wives, and I. G., or any** others in my parifh. I fear that I am forgotten amongft **them** ; but I cannot forget them.

The prifoner's prayers and bleffings come upon **you. Grace,** grace be with you.

Your brother, in the Lord Jefus,

S. R.

ABERDEEN, *Feb.* 9, 1637.

---

* To get at.

† All thofe whofe initials are given are underftood to have been parifhioners of his at Anwoth.

*(GOD'S DEALINGS WITH SCOTLAND—THE EYE TO BE
DIRECTED HEAVENWARD.)*

ADAM,—Grace, mercy, and peace be to your Ladyſhip.
—I long to hear from you.

I am here waiting, if a good wind, long looked for,
will at length blow into Chriſt's ſails, in this land. But I wonder
if Jeſus be not content to ſuffer more yet in His members and cauſe,
and in the beauty of His houſe, rather than He ſhould not be avenged
upon this land. I hear that many worthy men, who ſee more in
the Lord's dealings than I can take up with my dim ſight, are of
a contrary mind, and do believe that the Lord is coming home again
to His houſe in Scotland. I hope He is on His journey that way;
yet I look not but that He will feed this land with their own blood,
before He eſtabliſh His throne amongſt us.

I know that your honour is not looking after things hereaway.*
Ye have no great cauſe to think that your ſtock and principal is
under the roof of theſe viſible heavens; and I hope that ye would
think yourſelf a beguiled and cozened ſoul if it were ſo. I ſhould
be ſorry to counſel your Ladyſhip to make a covenant with time,
and this life; but rather deſire you to hold in fair generals, and
afar off from this ill-founded heaven that is on this ſide of the water.
It ſpeaketh ſomewhat when our Lord bloweth the bloom off our
daft† hopes in this life, and loppeth the branches off our worldly
joys, well nigh the root, on purpoſe that they ſhould not thrive.
Lord, ſpill‡ my fool's heaven in this life, that I may be ſaved for
ever. A forfeiture of the ſaint's part of the yolk and marrow of
ſhort-laughing worldly happineſs, is not ſuch a real evil as our
blinded eyes conceive.

---

* In this quarter, this preſent world.
† Blows off the bloſſom from our fooliſh hopes.　　　　　　‡ Spoil, mar.

I am thinking long* now for fome deliverance more than before. But I know I am in an error. It is poffible I am not come to that meafure of trial which the Lord is feeking in His work. If my friends in Galloway would effectually do† for my deliverance, I fhould exceedingly rejoice ; but I know not but the Lord hath a way whereof He will be the only reaper of praifes.

Let me know with the bearer how the child is. The Lord be his father and tutor, and your only comforter. There is nothing here, where I am, but profanity and atheifm. Grace, grace, be with your Ladyfhip.

Your Ladyfhip's, at all obliged obedience, in Chrift,

                                        S. R.

ABERDEEN, *Feb.* 13, 1637.

XCIV.—*To the Noble and Chriftian Lady, the* VISCOUNTESS OF KENMURE.

(*THE TIMES—CHRIST'S SWEETNESS IN TROUBLE—LONGING AFTER HIM.*)

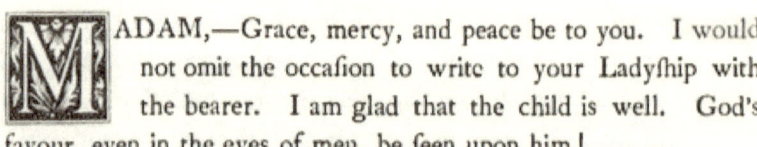

MADAM,—Grace, mercy, and peace be to you. I would not omit the occafion to write to your Ladyfhip with the bearer. I am glad that the child is well. God's favour, even in the eyes of men, be feen upon him !

I hope that your Ladyfhip is thinking upon thefe fad and woful days wherein we now live, when our Lord, in His righteous judgment, is fending the kirk the gate‡ fhe is going to Rome's brothelhoufe to feek a lover of her own, feeing that fhe hath given up with Chrift her Hufband. Oh, what fweet comfort, what rich falvation, is laid up for thofe who had rather wafh and roll their garments in their own blood, than break out§ from Chrift by apoftacy ! Keep yourfelf in the love of Chrift, and ftand far aback from

---

* Am longing.   † Act for, make exertions.   ‡ The way.   § *Off*, probably.

the pollutions of the world.   Side not with thefe times, and hold off
from coming nigh the figns of a confpiracy with thofe that are now
come out againft Chrift, that ye may be one kept for Chrift only.
I know that your Ladyfhip thinketh upon this, and how you may
be humbled for yourfelf and this backfliding land ; for I avouch,
that wrath from the Lord is gone out againft Scotland.   I think aye
the longer the better of my royal and worthy Mafter.   He is become a new Well-beloved to me now, in renewed confolations, by
the prefence of the Spirit of grace and glory.   Chrift's garments fmell
of the powder of the merchant, when He cometh out of His ivory
chambers.   O, His perfumed face, His fair face, His lovely and
kindly kiffes, have made me, a poor prifoner, fee that there is more
to be had of Chrift in this life than I believed !   We think all is
but a little earneft, a four-hours,* a fmall tafting, that we have, or
that is to be had, in this life (which is true compared with the inheritance); but yet I know it is more : it is the kingdom of God within
us.   Wo, wo is me, that I have not ten loves for that one Lord
Jefus ; and that love faileth, and drieth up in loving Him ; and that
I find no way to fpend my love defires, and the yolk of my heart
upon that faireft and deareft One.   I am far behind with my narrow
heart.   O, how ebb† a foul have I to take in Chrift's love ! for
let worlds be multiplied, according to angels' underftanding, in
millions, whill‡ they weary themfelves, thefe worlds would not
contain the thoufandth part of His love.   O, if I could yoke in§
amongft the thick‖ of angels, and feraphims, and now glorified
faints, and could raife a new love-fong of Chrift, before all the
world !   I am pained with wondering at new-opened treafures in
Chrift.   If every finger, member, bone, and joint, were a torch
burning in the hotteft fire in hell, I would that they could all fend
out love praifes, high fongs of praife for evermore, to that Plant of
Renown, to that royal and high Prince, Jefus my Lord.   But alas !
His love fwelleth in me, and findeth no vent.   Alas ! what can a

---

* Afternoon meal.   † Shallow.   ‡ Till.
§ Join in with energy.   ‖ The crowd.

dumb prifoner do or fay for Him! O for an ingine* to write a book of Chrift and His love! Nay, I am left of Him bound and chained with His love. I cannot find a loofed foul to lift up His praifes, and give them out to others. But oh! my day-light hath thick clouds; I cannot fhine in His praifes. I am often like a fhip plying about to feek the wind: I fail at great leifure, and cannot be blown upon that lovelieft Lord. Oh, if I could turn my fails to Chrift's right airth,† and that I had my heart's wifhes of His love! But I but mar His praifes: nay, I know no comparifon of what Chrift is, and what His worth is. All the angels, and all the glorified, praife Him not fo much as in halves. Who can advance Him, or utter all His praifes? I want nothing: unknown faces favour me: enemies muft fpeak good of the truth: my Mafter's caufe pur-chafeth commendations.

The hopes of my enlargement, from appearances, are cold. My faith hath no bed to fleep upon but omnipotency. The good-will of the Lord, and His fweeteft prefence, be with you and that child. Grace and peace be yours.

Your Ladyfhip's, in all duty in his fweet Lord Jefus,

S. R.

Aberdeen, 1637.

XCV.—*To the Right Honourable and Chriftian Lady, the* Viscountess of Kenmure.

(CHRIST'S CROSS SWEET—HIS COMING TO BE DESIRED— JEALOUS OF ANY RIVAL.)

ADAM,—Grace, mercy, and peace be to your Ladyfhip. I would not omit to write a line with this Chriftian bearer; one in your Ladyfhip's own cafe, driven near to Chrift, in and by her affliction. I wifh that my friends in Gallo-

---

* Power or faculty.   † Point of the compafs.

way forget me not. However it be, Chrift is fo good, I will have
no other tutor, fuppofe I could have wale* and choice of ten thoufand
befide. I think now five hundred heavy hearts for Him too little.
I wifh that Chrift, now weeping, fuffering, and contemned of men,
were more dear and defirable to many fouls than He is. I am
fure that if the faints wanted† Chrift's crofs, fo profitable, and fo
fweet, they might, for the gain and glory of it, wifh it were lawful
either to buy or borrow His crofs. But it is a mercy that the
faints have it laid to their hand for nothing ; for I know no fweeter
way to heaven than through free grace and hard trials together ;
and one of thefe cannot well want another.

Oh that time would poft fafter, and haften our looked-for communion with that faireft, faireft among the fons of men ! Oh that
the day would favour us and come, and put Chrift and us into each
other's arms ! I am fure that a few years will do our turn, and the
foldier's hour-glafs will foon run out. Madam, look to your lamp,
and look for your Lord's Coming, and let your heart dwell aloof
from that fweet child. Chrift's jealoufy will not admit of two equal
loves in your Ladyfhip's heart. He muft have one, and that the
greateft ; a little one to a creature may and muft fuffice a foul married to Him. " Thy Maker is thine Hufband."‡ I would wifh you
well, and my obligations thefe many years byegone§ fpeak no lefs to
me ; but more I can neither wifh, nor pray, nor defire for your
Ladyfhip, than Chrift fingled and waled‖ out from all created good
things, or Chrift howbeit wet in His own blood, and wearing a
crown of thorns. I am fure that the faints, at their beft, are but
ftrangers to the weight and worth of the incomparable fweetnefs of
Chrift. He is fo new, fo frefh in excellency every day of new, to
thofe that fearch more and more in Him, as if heaven could furnifh
us as many new Chrifts (if I may fo fpeak) as there are days betwixt Him and us ; and yet He is one and the fame. Oh, we love
an unknown lover when we love Chrift !

---

* Liberty of felecting from a ftore.　† Were deftitute of.　‡ Ifa. liv. 5.
§ Paffed.　　　　　　　　　　　　　‖ Selected.

Let me hear how the child is every way. The prayers of a prifoner of Chrift be upon him. Grace for evermore, even whill* glory perfect it, be with your Ladyfhip.

Yours, in his fweet Lord Jefus,

S. R.

ABERDEEN, 1637.

XCVI.—*To the Noble and Chriftian Lady, the* VISCOUNTESS OF KEMMURE.

(CHRIST ALL WORTHY—ANWOTH.)

ADAM,—Notwithftanding the great hafte of the bearer, I would blefs your Ladyfhip on paper, defiring, that fince Chrift hath ever envied that the world fhould have your love by Him,† that ye give yourfelf out for Chrift, and that ye may be for no other. I know none worthy of you but Chrift.

Madam, I am either fuffering for Chrift—and this is either the fure and good way—or I have done with heaven, and fhall never fee God's face, which, I blefs Him, cannot be.

I write my blefling to that fweet child, that ye have borrowed from God. He is no heritage to you, but a loan : love him as folks do borrowed things. My heart is heavy for you.

They fay that the kirk of Chrift hath neither fon nor heir, and therefore that her enemies fhall poffefs her. But I know that fhe is not that‡ ill-friended ;§ her Hufband is her heir, and fhe His heritage.

If my Lord would be pleafed, I fhould defire that fome be dealt with, for my return to Anwoth. But if that never be, I thank God Anwoth is not heaven ; preaching is not Chrift. I hope to wait on.

Let me hear how your child is, and your Ladyfhip's mind and hopes of him ; for it would eafe my heart to know that he is well.

---

* Till.   † More than He, or to the fetting Him afide.
‡ So.   § Deftitute of friends.

I am in good terms with Chrift; but oh, my guiltinefs! Yet He bringeth not pleas betwixt Him and me to the ftreets, and before the fun.

Grace, grace for ever more be with your Ladyfhip.

Your Ladyfhip's at all obedience in Chrift,

S. R.

Aberdeen, 1637.

* * *

XCVII.—*To* Alexander Gordon *of Earlston.*

(CHRIST ENDEARED BY BITTER EXPERIENCES—SEARCHINGS OF HEART—FEARS FOR THE CHURCH.)

MUCH HONOURED SIR,—Grace, mercy, and peace be to you. I received your letter, which refrefhed me. Except from your fon, and my brother, I have feen few letters from my acquaintance in that country; which maketh me heavy. But I have the company of a Lord who can teach us all to be kind, and hath the right gate* of it. Though, for the prefent, I have feven ups and downs every day, yet I am abundantly comforted and feafted with my King and Well-beloved daily. It pleafeth Him to come and dine with a fad prifoner, and a folitary ftranger. His fpikenard cafteth a fmell. Yet my fweet hath fome four mixed with it, wherein I muft acquiefce; for there is no reafon that His comforts be too cheap, feeing they are delicates. Why fhould He not make them fo to His own? But I verily think now, that Chrift hath led me up to a nick† in Chriftianity that I was never at before; I think all before was but childhood and bairn's play. Since I departed from you, I have been fcalded, whilft‡ the fmoke of hell's fire went in at my throat, and I would have bought peace with a thoufand years' torment in hell; and I have been up alfo, after thefe deep down-caftings and forrows, before the Lamb's

---

* Way. † A point. ‡ Till.

white throne, in my Father's inner court, the Great King's dining-
hall. And Chrift did caft a covering of love on me. He hath caften
a coal into my foul, and it is fmoking among the ftraw and keeping
the hearth warm. I look back to what I was before, and I laugh
to fee the fand-houfes I built when I was a child.

At firft the remembrance of the many fair feaft-days with my
Lord Jefus in public, which are now changed into filent Sabbaths,
raifed a great tempeft, and (if I may fpeak fo) made the devil ado *
in my foul. The devil came in, and would prompt me to make a
plea† with Chrift, and to lay the blame on Him as a hard mafter.
But now thefe mifts are blown away, and I am not only filenced as
to all quarrelling, but fully fatisfied. Now, I wonder that any man
living can laugh upon the world, or give it a hearty good-day.
The Lord Jefus hath handled me fo, that, as I am now difpofed, I
think never to be in this world's commons‡ again for a night's lodging. Chrift beareth me good company. He hath eafed me, when
I faw it not, lifting the crofs off my fhoulders, fo that I think it to
be but a feather, becaufe underneath are everlafting arms. God
forbid it come to bartering or niffering§ of croffes ; for I think my
crofs fo fweet, that I know not where I would get the like of it.
Chrift's honey-combs drop fo abundantly, that they fweeten my gall.
Nothing breaketh my heart, but that I cannot get the daughters of
Jerufalem to tell them of my Bridegroom's glory. I charge you in
the name of Chrift, that ye tell all that ye come to of it ; and yet it
is above telling and underftanding. Oh, if all the kingdom were as
I am, except my bonds ! They know not the love-kiffes that my
only Lord Jefus wafteth on a dawted‖ prifoner. On my falvation,
this is the only way to the New City. I know that Chrift hath no
dumb feals. Would he put His privy-feal upon blank paper ? He
hath fealed my fufferings with His comforts. I write this to confirm you. I write now what I have feen as well as heard. Now
and then my filence burneth up my fpirit ; but Chrift hath faid,

---

* Aftir. See Let. 181, note.   † Controverfy.   ‡ Under obligation to.
§ Exchanging.   ‖ Fondled.

" Thy ftipend is running up with intereft in heaven, as if thou wert preaching ;" and this from a King's mouth rejoiceth my heart. At other times I am fad, dwelling in Kedar's tents.

There are none (that I yet know of) but two perfons in this town that I dare give my word for. And the Lord hath removed my brethren and my acquaintance far from me ; and it may be, that I fhall be forgotten in the place where the Lord made me the inftrument to do fome good. But I fee that this is vanity in me ; let Him make of me what He pleafeth, if He make falvation out of it to me. I am tempted and troubled, that all the fourteen prelates* fhould have been armed of God againft me only, while the reft of my brethren are ftill preaching. But I dare not fay one word but this, " It is good, Lord Jefus, becaufe Thou haft done it."

Wo is me for the virgin-daughter ! wo is me for the defolation of the virgin-daughter of Scotland ! Oh, if my eyes were a fountain of tears, to weep day and night for that poor widow-kirk, that poor miferable harlot ! Alas, that my Father hath put-to† the door on my poor harlot-mother ! Oh for‡ that cloud of black wrath, and fury of the indignation of the Lord, that is hanging over the land !

Sir, write to me, I befeech you. I pray you alfo be kind to my afflicted brother. Remember my love to your wife ; and the prayer and blefling of the prifoner of Chrift be on you. Frequent your meetings for prayer and communion with God : they would be fweet meetings to me.

    Yours, in his fweet Lord Jefus,

               S. R.

ABERDEEN, *Feb.* 16, 1637.

XCVIII.—*To the Worthy and much Honoured* Mr ALEXANDER
COLVILLE *of Blair.*

[ALEXANDER COLVILLE of Blair (which is in the parish of Carnock, Fifefhire) early commended himfelf to the gratitude of Rutherford by be-

---

* See note Lct. 68.   † Shut.   ‡ Alas! for.

friending him under prelatic perfecutions. When Rutherford in 1630 was fummoned before the High Commiffion Court, this gentleman, being one of the judges, fo exerted himfelf in his behalf, that his influence, together with the abfence of the Archbifhop of St Andrews (whom the tempeftuous ftate of the weather prevented from attending), occafioned the defertion of the diet, and put a ftop to the proceedings againft the obnoxious minifter. (See *Letter* XI.) As we learn from this letter, he alfo fhowed much kindnefs to Rutherford's brother on his trial before the High Commiffion in November 1636, for his non-conformity and zealous fupport of Mr Glendinning, the injured minifter of Kirkcudbright. Colville was an elder of the Church, and his name appears on the roll of the members of the General Affemblies 1645, 1646, 1648, and 1649, and of the Commiffions appointed by thefe Affemblies. In the roll he is ftyled " Mr Alexander Colville, Juftice-Depute." We find him after this, in co-operation with another individual, delating Mr Robert Bruce, minifter of Ballagray, of which they were parifhioners, on the ground that they were not edified by his doctrine.]

(INCREASING EXPERIENCE OF CHRIST'S LOVE—GOD WITH HIS SAINTS.)

MUCH HONOURED SIR,—Grace, mercy, and peace be to you. The bearer hereof, Mr R. F., is moft kind to me ; I defire you to thank him. But none is fo kind as my only royal King and Mafter, whofe crofs is my garland. The King dineth with His prifoner, and His fpikenard cafteth a fmell. He hath led me up to fuch a pitch and nick* of joyful communion with Himfelf, as I never knew before. When I look back to by-gones,† I judge myfelf to have been a child at A, B, C, with Chrift. Worthy Sir, pardon me, I dare not conceal it from you ; it is as a fire in my bowels. (In His prefence who feeth me I speak it !) I am pained, pained with the love of Chrift; He hath made me fick, and wounded me. Hunger for Chrift outrunneth faith ; I mifs faith more than love. Oh, if the three kingdoms would come and fee ! Oh, if they knew His kindnefs to my foul ! It hath pleafed Him to bring me to this, that I will not ftrike fails to this world, nor flatter it, nor adore this clay idol that fools worfhip. As I am now difpofed, I think that I fhall neither borrow

---

* Degree.   † Things paffed, former attainments.

nor lend* with it ; and yet I get my meat from Chrift with nurture;†
for feven times a-day I am lifted up, and caften down.   My dumb
Sabbaths burden my heart, and make it bleed.   I want not fearful
challenges, and jealoufies‡ fometimes of Chrift's love, that He hath
caften me over the dyke § of the vineyard as a dry tree.   But this is
my infirmity.   By His grace I take myfelf‖ in thefe ravings.   It is
kindly ¶ that faith and love both be fick, and fevers are kindly to
moft joyful communion with Chrift.

Ye are bleffed who avouch Chrift openly before The Prince of
this kingdom, whofe eyes are upon you.   It is your glory to lift
Him up on His throne, to carry His train, and bear up the hem of
His robe royal.   He hath an hiding-place for Mr Alexander Colville againft the ftorm : go on, and fear not what man can do. The
faints feem to have the worft of it (for apprehenfion can make a lie
of Chrift and His love) ; but it is not fo.   Providence is not rolled
upon unequal and crooked wheels ; all things work together for the
good of thofe who love God, and are called according to His purpofe.
Ere it be long, we fhall fee the white fide of God's providence.

My brother's cafe hath moved me not a little.   He wrote to
me your care and kindnefs. Sir, the prifoner's bleffings and prayers,
I truft, fhall not go paft you.   He that is able to keep you, and to
prefent you before the prefence of His face with joy, eftablifh your
heart in the love of Chrift.

Yours, in his fweet Lord Jefus,

S. R.

ABERDEEN, *19th Feb.* 1637.

* * *

XCIX.—*To* EARLSTON, *Younger.*

[WILLIAM GORDON, to whom this letter is addreffed, was the eldeft fon
of Alexander Gordon of Earlfton, formerly noticed (Let. 59).   He exhi-

---

* That is, have no dealings with it.
† Difcipline ; fuch as a child gets when training.
‡ Queftionings and fufpicions.   § The dry wall.   ‖ Retract my word.
¶ According to nature.

bited in youth much of the piety and public fpirit of his father, which Rutherford, in his correfpondence with him, is careful to ftrengthen. His well-known attachment to the caufe of Prefbytery rendered him early obnoxious to Charles II. and the Malignant party. When that monarch came to Scotland in 1651, and held a Parliament, Gordon (like many other gentlemen within the kingdom) was fined for his compliance with the Englifh; and on his refufing to pay the fine, foldiers were fent out to extract it by compulfion from his tenants, who were almoft ruined by the driving away of their cattle and the robbing of their houfes. He was again fined by Middleton, in the Parliament 1662. But ftill further: he was fummoned before the Privy Council; and on the 1st of March 1664, fentence of banifhment from the kingdom was pronounced upon him for keeping conventicles, and for refufing to engage to refrain from fuch meetings in all time coming. He accordingly left the kingdom. Whither he went we have not difcovered; but the Council, on being petitioned, granted him licenfe to return until the 15th of March enfuing, at the fame time requiring him to " depart and remain forth of the kingdom the faid day, in cafe the faid Lords give order therefor." (*Deer. Seer. Council, Regifter Houfe, Edin.*) After this he remained at home, but had not long to live. He died a martyr in the caufe of religious freedom, of which he had proved a noble defender during life. Coming up to join the forces of the Covenanters at Bothwell, in the beginning of the year 1679, after the defeat (either on the day of it, or the day after), he was met near the place by a party of Englifh dragoons, who, upon his refufing to furrender, killed him on the fpot. " Thus fell," fays Howie, in the *Scots Worthies*, "a renowned Gordon, one whofe character at prefent I am in no capacity to defcribe; only I may venture to fay, that he was a gentleman of good parts and endowments; a man devoted unto religion and godlinefs, and a prime fupporter of the Prefbyterian intereft in that part of the country where he lived." He was married to Mary, daughter of Sir John Hope, fecond baronet of Craighall, and Prefident of the Court of Seffion, by his wife Margaret, daughter of Sir Archibald Murray of Blackbarony. His eldeft fon, Alexander, fucceeded him.]

(*CHRIST'S WAYS MISUNDERSTOOD—HIS INCREASING KINDNESS —SPIRITUAL DELICACY—HARD TO BE DEAD TO THE WORLD.*)

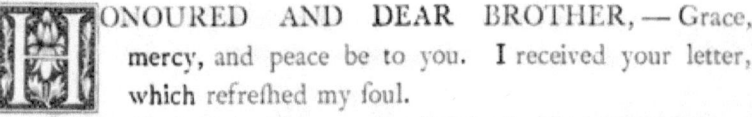 ONOURED AND DEAR BROTHER, — Grace, mercy, and peace be to you. I received your letter, which refrefhed my foul.

I thank God that the court is clofed; I think fhame of my part of it. I pafs now from my unjuft fummons of unkindnefs libelled againft Chrift my Lord. He is not fuch a Lord and Mafter

as I took Him to be ; verily He is God, and I am duſt and aſhes.
I took Chriſt's glooms * to be as good as Scripture ſpeaking wrath ;
but I have ſeen the other ſide of Chriſt, and the white ſide of His
croſs now. I behoved to come to Aberdeen to learn a new myſtery
in Chriſt, that His promiſe is better to be believed than His looks,
and that the devil can cauſe Chriſt's glooms * to ſpeak a lie to a
weak man. Nay, verily, I was a child before : all by-gones† are but
bairn's play. I would I could begin to be a Chriſtian in ſad‡ earneſt.
I need not blame Chriſt if I be not one, for He hath ſhowed me
heaven and hell in Aberdeen. But the truth is, for all my ſorrow,
Chriſt is nothing in my debt, for comforts have refreſhed my ſoul.
I have heard and ſeen Him in His ſweetneſs, ſo as I am almoſt ſaying, it is not He that I was wont to meet with. He ſmileth more
cheerfully, His kiſſes are more ſweet and ſoul-refreſhing than the
kiſſes of the Chriſt I ſaw before were, though He be the ſame. Or
rather, the King hath led me up to a meaſure of joy and communion
with my Bridegroom that I never attained to before, ſo that often I
think that I will neither borrow nor lend with this world.§ I will
not ſtrike ſail to croſſes, nor flatter them to be quit of them, as I
have done. Come all croſſes, welcome, welcome ! ſo that I may
get my heartful of my Lord Jeſus. I have been ſo near Him, that
I have ſaid, " I take inſtruments that this is the Lord. Leave a
token behind Thee, that I may never forget this." Now, what can
Chriſt do more to dawt‖ one of His poor priſoners ? Therefore,
Sir, I charge you in the name of my Lord Jeſus, praiſe with me,
and ſhow unto others what He hath done unto my ſoul. This is
the fruit of my ſufferings, that I deſire Chriſt's name may be ſpread
abroad in this kingdom, in my behalf. I hope in God not to ſlander
Him again. Yet in this, I get not my feaſts without ſome mixture
of gall ; neither am I free of old jealouſies, for He hath removed
my lovers and friends far from me ; He hath made my congregation deſolate, and taken away my crown. And my dumb Sabbaths
are like a ſtone tied to a bird's foot, that wanteth not wings,—they

---

* Frowns.   † The paſt matters.   ‡ Settled.   § Let. 98.   ‖ Dote upon, fondle.

feem to hinder me to fly, were it not that I dare not fay one word, but, " Well done, Lord Jefus."

We can, in our profperity, fport ourfelves, and be too bold with Chrift ; yea, be that * infolent, as to chide with Him ; but under the water we dare not fpeak. I wonder now of my fometime† boldnefs, to chide and quarrel Chrift, to nickname providence when it ftroked me againft the hair ; for now, fwimming in the waters, I think my will is fallen to the ground‡ of the water : I have loft it. I think that I would fain let Chrift alone, and give Him leave to do with me what He pleafeth, if He would fmile upon me. Verily, we know not what an evil it is to fpill§ and indulge ourfelves, and to make an idol of our will. I was once that I would not eat except I had waled‖ meat ; now I dare not complain of the crumbs and parings under His table. I was once that I would make the houfe ado,¶ if I faw not the world carved and fet in order to my liking ; now I am filent when I fee God hath fet fervants on horfeback, and is fattening and feeding the children of perdition. I pray God, that I may never find my will again. Oh, if Chrift would fubject my will to His, and trample it under His feet, and liberate me from that lawlefs lord !

Now, Sir, in your youth gather faft ; your fun will mount to the meridian quickly, and thereafter decline. Be greedy of grace. Study above anything, my dear brother, to mortify your lufts. Oh, but pride of youth, vanity, luft, idolizing of the world, and charming pleafures, take long time to root them out ! As far as ye are advanced in the way to heaven, as near as ye are to Chrift, as much progrefs as ye have made in the way of mortification, ye will find that ye are far behind, and have moft of your work before you. I never took it to be fo hard to be dead to my lufts and to this world. When the day of vifitation cometh, and your old idols come weeping about you, ye will have much ado** not to break your heart :

---

* So.   † Former.   ‡ Bottom.   § Spoil.
‖ Carefully felected.   ¶ Aftir.
** Troublefome occupation.   " *Ado*" here is a noun ; in the phrafe, " make the houfe ado," it is an adjective.

it is beft to give up in time with them, fo as ye could at a call quit your part of this world for a **drink of water, or a thing of** nothing. Verily I have feen the beft of this world, a moth-eaten, threadbare coat : I purpofe to lay it afide, being now old and **full of** holes. O for my houfe above, not made with hands !

Pray for Chrift's prifoner : and **write to me.** Remember my love to your mother. **Defire her, from me, to make ready for re-** moving ; the Lord's **tide will not bide her :** and to feek an heavenly mind, that her heart **may be often there.** Grace be with you.

Yours, and Chrift's prifoner,

S. R.

ABERDEEN, *Feb.* 20, 1637.

C.—*To the* LADY CARDONESS.

(*THE ONE THING NEEDFUL—CONSCIENTIOUS ACTING IN THE WORLD—ADVICE UNDER DEJECTING TRIALS.*)

MY DEARLY BELOVED, AND LONGED-FOR IN THE **LORD,**—Grace, mercy, and peace be to you.— I long to hear how your foul profpereth, and how the kingdom of Chrift thriveth in you. I exhort you and befeech you in the bowels of Chrift, **faint not, weary not.** There is a great neceffity of heaven ; ye muft needs have it. All other things, as houfes, lands, children, hufband, friends, country, credit, health, wealth, honour, may be wanted ; but heaven is your one thing neceffary, the good part that fhall not be taken from you. See that ye buy the field where **the pearl is.** Sell all, and make a purchafe of falvation. Think it not eafy ; for it is a fteep afcent to eternal glory : many are lying dead by the way, that were flain with fecurity.

I have now been led by my Lord Jefus to fuch a nick* in Chriftianity, as I think little of former things. Oh what I want ! I want fo many things, that **I am almoft afking if I** have anything

---

* Degree, point.

at all. Every man thinketh he is rich enough in grace, till he
take out his purfe, and tell his money, and then he findeth his pack
but poor and light in the day of a heavy trial. I found that I had
not to bear my expenfes ; and I fhould have fainted, if want and
penury had not chafed me to the ftore-houfe of all.

I befeech you make confcience of your ways. Deal kindly, and
with confcience, with your tenants. To fill a breach, or a hole,
make not a greater breach in the confcience. I wifh plenty of love
to your foul. Let the world be the portion of baftards, make it
not yours. After the laft trumpet is blown, the world and all its
glory will be like an old houfe that is burnt to afhes, and like an
old fallen caftle, without a roof. Fy, fy upon us, fools ! who
think ourfelves debtors to the world ! My Lord hath brought me
to this, that I would not give a drink of cold water for this world's
kindnefs. I wonder that men long after, love, or care for thefe
feathers. It is almoft an unco* world to me. To think that men
are fo mad as to block† with dead earth ! To give out confcience,
and get in clay again, is a ftrange bargain !

I have written my mind at length to your hufband. Write to
me again his cafe. I cannot forget him in my prayers ; I am looking.‡ Chrift hath fome claim to him. My counfel is, that ye bear
with him when paffion overtaketh him : " A foft anfwer putteth
away wrath." Anfwer him in what he fpeaketh, and apply yourfelf
in the fear of God to him ; and then ye will remove a pound
weight of your heavy crofs, that way, and fo it fhall become light.

When Chrift hideth Himfelf, wait on, and make din till He return ; it is not time then to be careleffly patient. I love to be grieved
when He hideth His fmiles. Yet believe His love in a patient on-
waiting and believing in the dark. Ye muft learn to fwim and hold
up your head above the water, even when the fenfe of His prefence
is not with you to hold up your chin. I truft in God that He will
bring your fhip fafe to land. I counfel you to ftudy fanctification,
and to be dead to this world. Urge kindnefs on Knockbrex.

---

* Strange.   † Bargain.   ‡ For an anfwer, Ps. v. 3.

Labour to benefit by his company; the man is acquainted with Chrift.

I beg the help of your prayers, for I forget not you. Counfel your hufband to fulfil my joy, and to feek the Lord's face. Show him, from me, that my joy and defire is to hear that he is in the Lord. God cafteth him often in my mind : I cannot forget him. I hope Chrift and he have fomething to do together. Blefs John from me. I write bleffings to him, and to your hufband, and to the reft of your children. Let it not be faid, " I am not in your houfe," through neglect of the Sabbath exercife.

Your lawful and loving paftor in his only, only Lord,

S. R.

ABERDEEN, *Feb.* 20, 1637.

---◆---

CI.—*To* JONET MACCULLOCH.

[No doubt this lady was one of the *Maccullochs* of *Ardwell*, a refidence near Anwoth, next to Cardonefs, and to this day in poffeffion of the fame family. The Letter, 284, to Mr Thomas Macculloch of *Nether Ardwell*, re- lates apparently to another of the fame houfe. The houfe is very pleafantly fituated near the mouth of the Fleet. The old manfion-houfe of Ardwell, or Ardwall, bore the name " Nether Ardwell;" it occupied a fpot about a hundred yards diftant from the prefent manfion, lying toward the fhore, a little below where the bay has received the waters of the Fleet. " Higher Ardwell" was toward the north: a farm near Bufhy Bield (Rutherford's old manfe, which was originally a manfion-houfe) ftill bears that name. The family of the Maccullochs, who were intimate with Rutherford, ftill retain the property. They are an ancient family; for William Macculloch got a feu- charter of the lands of Nether Ardwell from his coufin, or uncle, Macculloch of Cardonefs and Myreton, in 1587. It is the wife of this William Mac- culloch, in all probability, of whom the following lines fpeak, on the tomb at the fouth fide of the raifed pile in the old Churchyard :—

  " Dumb, fenfelefs ftatue of a painted ftone,
   What means this boaft ? Thy captive is but clay.
   Thou gaineft nothing but fome lifelefs bones ;
   Her choiceft part, her foul, triumphs for aye.
   Then, gazing friends, do not her death deplore ;
   You lofe, while fhe doth gain for evermore.

" Margrat Maklellan, goodwife of Ardwell, departed this life 1620. Ætatis fuæ 31."

We may add, the grand-daughter of this lady, to whom the lines on the monument refers, was mother of the martyr, John Bell of Whytefide.]

(CHRIST'S SUFFICIENCY—STEDFASTNESS IN THE TRUTH.)

EAR SISTER,—Grace, mercy, and peace be to you.— I long to hear how your foul profpereth.

I am as well as a prifoner of Chrift can be, feafted and made fat with the comforts of God. Chrift's kiffes are made fweeter to my foul than ever they were. I would not change my Mafter with all the kings of clay upon the earth. Oh! my Well beloved is altogether lovely, and loving. I care not what flefh can do.

I perfuade my foul that I delivered the truth of Chrift to you. Slip not from it, for any bofts* or fear of men. If ye go againft the truth of Chrift that I now fuffer for, I fhall bear witnefs againft you in the day of Chrift.

Sifter, faften your grips† faft on Chrift. Follow not the guifes‡ of this finful world. Let not this clay portion of earth take up your foul : it is the portion of baftards, and ye are a child of God ; and, therefore, feek your Father's heritage. Send up your heart to fee the dwelling-houfe and fair rooms in the New City. Fy, fy upon thofe who cry, " Up with the world, and down with confcience and heaven !" We have bairn's wits, and therefore we cannot prize Chrift aright. Counfel your hufband, and mother, to make them ready for eternity. That day is drawing nigh.

Pray for me, the prifoner of Chrift. I cannot forget you.

Your lawful paftor and brother,

S. R.

ABERDEEN, *Feb.* 20, 1637.

---

* Threatened blows; often written *boift*. † Your hold.

‡ Ways; *mapper*, (French).

[Knockgray is a farm-like houfe, enclofed by trees, at the foot of the hills of Carfphairn. It is on your right hand, coming from Earlfton to Carfphairn, after paffing the little hill of Dundeuch. " Alexander Gordon of Knockgray," fays Livingftone, who perfonally knew him, " was a rare Chriftian in his time. His chief, the Laird of Lochinvar, put him out of his land moftly for his religion; yet, being thereafter reftored by that man's fon, Lord Vifcount of Kenmure, he told me the Lord had bleffed him, fo as he had ten thoufand fheep." (*Select Biograph.* vol. i.) From what Rutherford fays in a fubfequent letter addreffed to him—" Chrift's ways were known to you long before I (who am but a child) knew anything of Him,"—it may be concluded that he was much older than Rutherford. As, therefore, Rutherford was born about the year 1600, and Gordon many years before, there is reafon to believe that the following act of Privy Council may refer to Gordon's fon, and not to himfelf: " Ordaining the baillies of the Canongate to fet at liberty Alexander Gordon, defigned of Knockgray, in regard they find he is not an heritor, that he is an old dying man, and has renounced in the King's favours, or his donator, any lands he had the time of the rebellion, and has given bond to appear when called." (*Decr. Secr. Conc.*) At any rate the venerable old man, to whom this act refers, was apprehended in his own houfe by one Captain Stuart ; by whom alfo he feems to have been carried to Edinburgh, and there incarcerated. Alexander, his fon (the grandfon of Rutherford's correfpondent), had alfo his own fhare of perfecution under the intolerant reign of Charles II. He fuffered much by garrifons put into his houfe, by the houfehold articles which they carried away, and by the forfeiture of his property, which was gifted to Lord Livingftone. (*Wodrow, MSS.,* vol. xxxvii.)]

(GROUNDS OF PRAISE—AFFLICTION TEMPTS TO MISREPRESENT CHRIST—IDOLS.)

EAR BROTHER,—Grace, mercy, and peace be to you. I long to hear how your foul profpereth. I expected letters from you ere now.

As for myfelf, I am here in good cafe, well feafted with a great King. At my coming here, I was that bold * as to take up a jealoufy†

---

* Bold to fuch an extent that.   † Sufpicion.

of Chrift's love. I faid I was caft over the dyke of the Lord's vineyard, as a dry tree ; but I fee that if I had been a withered branch,
the fire would have burned me long ere now. Bleffed be His high
name, who hath kept fap in the dry tree. And now, as if Chrift
hath done the wrong, He hath made the mends, and hath mifkent*
my ravings ; for a man under the water cannot well command his
wit, far lefs his faith and love. Because it was a fever, my Lord
Jefus forgave me that amongft the reft. He knoweth that in our
afflictions we can find a fpot in the faireft face that ever was, even
in Chrift's face. I would not have believed that a gloom† fhould
have made me to mifken‡ my old Mafter ; but we muft be whiles §
fick. Sicknefs is but kindly‖ to both faith and love. But O how
exceedingly is a poor dawted ¶ prifoner obliged to fweet Jefus ! My
tears are fweeter to me than the laughter of the Fourteen Prelates
is to them. The worft of Chrift, even His chaff, is better than the
world's corn.

Dear Brother, I befeech you, I charge you in the name and
authority of the Son of God, to help me to praife His Highnefs ;
and I charge you, alfo, to tell all your acquaintance, that my Mafter
may get many thanks. Oh, if my hairs, all my members, and all
my bones, were well-tuned tongues, to fing the high praifes of my
great and glorious King ! Help me to lift Chrift up upon His
throne, and to lift Him up above the thrones of the clay-kings, the
dying fceptre-bearers of this world. The prifoner's bleffing, the
bleffing of him that is feparate from his brethren, be upon them
all who will lend me a lift in this work. Show this to that people
with you to whom I fometimes preached.

Brother, my Lord hath brought me to this, that I will not
flatter the world for a drink of water. I am no debtor to clay ;
Chrift hath made me dead to that. I now wonder that ever I was
fuch a child, long fince, as to beg at fuch beggars ! Fy upon us,
who woo fuch a black-fkinned harlot, when we may get fuch a

---

* Overlooked, as if He did not know. † Frown. ‡ Overlook.
§ At times. ‖ Quite natural. ¶ Fondled.

fair, fair match in heaven! Oh that I could give up this clay-idol, this mafked, painted, over-gilded dirt, that Adam's fons adore! We make an idol of our will. As many lufts in us, as many gods; we are all godmakers. We are like to lofe Chrift, the true God, in the throng of thofe new and falfe gods. Scotland hath caft her crown off her head; the virgin-daughter hath loft her garland. Wo, wo to our harlot-mother. Our day is coming; a time when women fhall wifh they had been childlefs, and fathers fhall blefs mifcarrying wombs and dry breafts: many houfes great and fair fhall be defolate. This kirk fhall fit on the ground all the night, and the tears fhall run down her cheeks. The fun hath gone down upon her prophets. Bleffed are the prifoners of hope, who can run into their ftronghold, and hide themfelves for a little, till the indignation be overpaft.

Commend me to your wife, your daughters, your fon-in-law, and to A. T. Write to me the cafe of your kirk. Grace be with you.

I am much moved for my brother. I entreat for your kindnefs and counfel to him.

Yours, in his fweet Lord Jefus,

S. R.

ABERDEEN, *Feb.* 23, 1637.

CIII.—To the LADY CARDONESS, Elder.

(CHRIST AND HIS CAUSE RECOMMENDED—HEAVENLY-MINDED-NESS—CAUTION AGAINST COMPLIANCES—ANXIETY ABOUT HIS PARISH.)

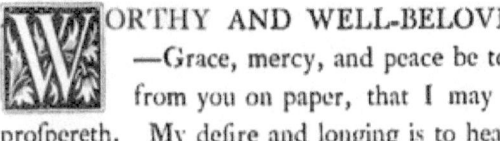

ORTHY AND WELL-BELOVED IN THE LORD, —Grace, mercy, and peace be to you. I long to hear from you on paper, that I may know how your foul profpereth. My defire and longing is to hear that ye walk in the truth, and that ye are content to follow the defpifed, but moft lovely Son of God.

I cannot but recommend Him unto you, as your Hufband, your Well-Beloved, your Portion, your Comfort, and your Joy. I fpeak this of that lovely One, becaufe I praife and commend the ford (as we ufe to fpeak) as I find it. He hath watered with His fweet comforts an oppreffed prifoner. He was always kind to my foul; but never fo kind as now, in my greateft extremities. I dine and fup with Chrift. He vifiteth my foul with the vifitations of love, in the night-watches.

I perfuade my foul that this is the way to heaven, and His own truth I now fuffer for. I exhort you in the name of Chrift to con-tinue in the truth which I delivered unto you. Make Chrift fure to your foul; for your day draweth nigh to an end. Many flide back now, who feemed to be Chrift's friends, and prove difhoneft to Him; but be ye faithful to the death, and ye fhall have the crown of life. This fpan-length of your days (whereof the Spirit of God fpeaketh,*) shall, within a fhort time, come to a finger-breadth, and at length to nothing. O how fweet and comfortable will the feaft of a good confcience be to you, when your eye-ftrings fhall break, your face wax pale, and the breath turn cold, and your poor foul come fighing to the windows of the houfe of clay of your dying body, and fhall long to be out, and to have the jailor to open the door, that the prifoner may be fet at liberty! Ye draw nigh the water-fide: look your accounts; afk for your Guide to take you to the other fide. Let not the world be your portion; what have ye to do with dead clay? Ye are not a baftard, but a lawfully be-gotten child; therefore, fet your heart on the inheritance. Go up beforehand, and fee your lodging. Look through all your Father's rooms in heaven: in your Father's houfe are many dwelling-places. Men take a fight of lands ere they buy them. I know that Chrift hath made the bargain already; but be kind to the houfe ye are going to, and fee it often. Set your heart on things that are above, where Chrift is at the right hand of God.

Stir up your hufband to mind his own country at home.

---

* Ps xxxix. 5.

Counfel him to deal mercifully with the poor people of God under him. They are Chrift's, and not his ; therefore, defire him to fhow them merciful dealing and kindnefs, and to be good to their fouls. I defire you to write to me. It may be that my parifh forget me ; but my witnefs is in heaven that I dow* not, I do not, forget them. They are my fighs in the night, and my tears in the day. I think myfelf like a hufband plucked from the wife of his youth. O Lord, be my Judge : what joy would it be to my foul to hear that my miniftry hath left the Son of God among them, and that they are walking in Chrift ! Remember my love to your fon and daughter. Defire them from me to feek the Lord in their youth, and to give Him the morning of their days. Acquaint them with the word of God and prayer.

Grace be with you. Pray for the prifoner of Chrift ; in my heart I forget you not.

Your lawful and loving paftor, in his only Lord Jefus,

S. R.

ABERDEEN, *March* 6, 1637.

------------◆------------

CIV.—*To the Right Honourable and Chriftian Lady, my*
LADY VISCOUNTESS OF KENMURE.

*(PAINS-TAKING IN THE KNOWLEDGE OF CHRIST—UNUSUAL
ENJOYMENT OF HIS LOVE—NOT EASY TO BE A CHRISTIAN
—FRIENDS MUST NOT MISLEAD.)*

MADAM,—Grace, mercy, and peace be to you.—I am re-frefhed with your letter. The right hand of Him to whom belong the iffues from death hath been gracious to that fweet child. I dow not,* I do not, forget him and your Ladyfhip in my prayers.

Madam, for your own cafe. I love careful, and withal, *doing*

---

* Cannot.

complaints of want of practice; becaufe I obferve many who think it holinefs enough to complain, and fet themfelves at nothing; as if to fay "I am fick" could cure them. They think complaints a good charm for guiltinefs. I hope that ye are wreftling and ftruggling on, in this dead age, wherein folks have loft tongue, and legs, and arms for Chrift. I urge upon you, Madam, a nearer communion with Chrift, and a growing communion. There are curtains to be drawn by* in Chrift, that we never faw, and new foldings of love in Him. I defpair that ever I fhall win to the far end of that love, there are fo many plies† in it. Therefore, dig deep; and fweat, and labour, and take pains for Him; and fet by as much time in the day for Him as you can. He will be won with labour.

I, His exiled prifoner, fought Him, and He hath rued‡ upon me, and hath made a moan for me, as He doth for His own;§ and I know not what to do with Chrift. His love furroundeth and furchargeth me. I am burdened with it; but Oh how fweet and lovely is that burden! I dow‖ not keep it within me. I am fo in love with His love, that if His love were not in heaven, I fhould be unwilling to go thither. Oh, what weighing, and what telling is in Chrift's love! I fear nothing now fo much as the lofing ¶ of Chrift's crofs, and of the love-fhowers that accompany it. I wonder what He meaneth, to put fuch a flave at the board-head,** at His own elbow. Oh that I fhould lay my black mouth to fuch a fair, fair, fair face as Chrift's! But I dare not refufe to be loved. The caufe is not in me, why He hath looked upon me, and loved me, for He got neither bud†† nor hire of me; it coft me nothing, it is goodcheap‡‡ love. O the many pound-weights of His love, under which I am fweetly preffed!

Now, Madam, I perfuade you, that the greateft part but play with Chriftianity; they put it by-hand§§ easily. I thought it had

---

* Afide. † Folds. ‡ Grieved for. § Jer. xxxi. 20; Hos. xi. 8. ‖ Cannot.
¶ The fear to be deprived of it. Former editions give "*laughing*," which feems a mifprint.
** Head of the table. †† Bribe. ‡‡ Very cheap
§§ Put it paft, and are done with it.

been an eafy thing to be a Chriftian, and that to feek God had been
at the next door ; but O the windings, the turnings, the ups and
the downs that He hath led me through ! And I fee yet much way
to the ford. He fpeaketh with my reins in the night-feafon ; and
in the morning, when I awake, I find His love-arrows, that He fhot
at me, fticking in my heart. Who will help me to praife ? Who
will come to lift up with me, and fet on high, His great love ? And
yet I find that a fire-flaught* of challenges will come in at mid-
fummer, and queftion me. But it is only to keep a finner in order.

As for friends, I will not think the world to be the world if
that well go not dry. I truft, in God, to ufe the world as a canny†
or cunning mafter doth a knave fervant (at leaft God give me grace
to do fo!) : he giveth him no handling nor credit, only he intrufteth
him with common errands, wherein he cannot play the knave. I
pray God that I may not give this world the credit of my joys,
and comforts, and confidence. That were to put Chrift out of
His office. Nay, I counfel you, Madam, from a little experience,
let Chrift keep the great feal, and intruft Him fo as to hing‡ your
veffels, great and fmall, and pin your burdens, upon the Nail
faftened in David's houfe.§ Let me not be well, if ever they get
the tutoring of my comforts. Away, away with irrefponfal‖ tutors
that would play me a flip, and then Chrift would laugh at me, and
fay, " Well-wared ;¶ try again ere you truft." Now wo is me,
for my whorifh mother, the Kirk of Scotland ! Oh, who will
bewail her !

Now the prefence of the great Angel of the Covenant be with
you and that fweet child.

Yours in his fweet Lord Jefus,

S. R.

ABERDEEN, *March 7, 1637.*

---

* Fire-flake, or flafh of lightning.   † Prudent.   ‡ Hang.
§ Ifa. xxii. 23.   ‖ Irrefponfible.   ¶ Well-deferved.

CV.—*To a Gentlewoman, upon the death of her Husband.*

(RESIGNATION UNDER BEREAVEMENT—HIS OWN ENJOYMENT OF CHRIST'S LOVE.)

MISTRESS,—Grace, mercy, and peace be to you.

I cannot but rejoice, and withal be grieved, at your cafe. It hath pleafed the Lord to remove your hufband (my friend, and this kirk's faithful profeffor *) foon to his reft; but fhall we be forry that our lofs is his gain, feeing his Lord would want his company no longer? Think not much of fhort fummons; for, feeing he walked with his Lord in his life, and defired that Chrift fhould be magnified in him at his death, ye ought to be filent and fatisfied. When Chrift cometh for His own, He runneth faft: mercy, mercy to the faints goeth not at leifure. Love, love in our Redeemer is not flow; and withal He is homely† with you, who cometh at His own hand to your houfe, and intromitteth,‡ as a friend, with anything that is yours. I think He would fain borrow and lend with you. Now he fhall meet with the folacious§ company, the fair flock and bleffed bairn-teme‖ of the firft-born, banqueting at the marriage fupper of the Lamb. It is a mercy that the poor wandering fheep get a dyke-fide in this ftormy day, and a leaking fhip a fafe harbour, and a fea-fick paffenger a found and foft bed afhore. Wrath, wrath, wrath from the Lord is coming upon this land that he hath left behind him. Know, therefore, that the wounds of your Lord Jefus are the wounds of a lover, and that He will have compaffion upon a fad-hearted fervant; and that Chrift hath faid, He will have the hufband's room in your heart. He loved you in your firft hufband's time, and He is but wooing you ftill. Give Him heart and chair, houfe and all. He will not be made companion with any other. Love is full of jealoufies: He will have all your

---

* Confeffor?   † Familiar.   ‡ Intermeddleth.
§ Full of confolation.   ‖ Family by one mother.

love ; and who fhould get it but He ? I know that ye allow it upon Him. There are comforts both fweet and fatisfying laid up for you : wait on. Frift* Chrift ; He is an honeft debtor.

Now for mine own cafe. I think fome poor body would be glad of a dawted prifoner's leavings.† I have no fcarcity of Chrift's love : He hath wafted more comforts upon His poor banifhed fervant than would have refrefhed many fouls. My burden was once fo heavy, that one ounce weight would have caften the balance, and broken my back ; but Chrift faid, " Hold, hold !" to my forrow, and hath wiped a bluthered‡ face, which was foul with weeping. I may joyfully go my Lord's errands, with wages in my hands. Deferred hopes need not make me dead-fweir§ (as we ufed to fay) : my crofs is both my crofs and my reward. Oh that men would found His high praife ! I love Chrift's worft reproaches, His glooms,‖ His crofs, better than all the world's plaftered glory. My heart is not longing to be back again from Chrift's country ; it is a fweet foil I am come to. I, if any in the world, have good caufe to fpeak much good of Him. Oh, hell were a good-cheap ¶ price to buy Him at ! Oh, if all the three kingdoms were witneffes to my pained, pained foul, overcome with Chrift's love !

I thank you moft kindly, my dear fifter, for your love to, and tender care of, my brother. I fhall think myfelf obliged to you if ye continue his friend. He is more to me than a brother now, being engaged to fuffer for fo honourable a Mafter and caufe.

Pray for Chrift's prifoner ; and grace, grace be with you.

Yours in his fweet Lord Jefus,

S. R.

ABERDEEN, *March* 7, 1637.

---

* Give Him credit to a future day.
† What an over-indulged prifoner leaves after his feaft is over.
‡ Blurred with tears. § Extremely lazy. ‖ Frowns. ¶ Very cheap.

CVI.—*To the Right Honourable and Chriſtian Lady, my*
LADY KENMURE.

*(WEAK ASSURANCE—GRACE DIFFERENT FROM LEARNING—
SELF-ACCUSATIONS.)*

ADAM,—Upon the offered opportunity of this worthy
bearer, I could not omit to anſwer the heads of your
letter.

1ſtly, I think not much to ſet down on paper ſome good things
anent Chriſt (that ſealed and holy thing),* and to feed my ſoul with
raw wiſhes to be one with Chriſt ; for a wiſh is but broken and
half love.   But verily to obey this, " Come and ſee," is a harder
matter !   Oh, I have rather ſmoke than fire, and gueſſings rather
than real aſſurances of Him.   I have little or nothing to ſay, that I
am as one who hath found favour in His eyes ; but there is ſome
pining and miſmannered† hunger, that maketh me miſcall‡ and
nickname Chriſt as a changed Lord.   But alas ! it is ill-flitten.§   I
cannot believe without a pledge.   I cannot take God's word without a caution, ‖ as if Chriſt had loſt and ſold His credit, and were
not in my books reſponſal, ¶ and law-biding.**   But this is *my* way ;
for *His* way is, " After that ye believed, ye were ſealed with that
Holy Spirit of promiſe."††

2dly, Ye write, " that I am filled with knowledge, and ſtand
not in need of theſe warnings."   But certainly my light is dim when
it cometh to handy-grips.‡‡   And how many have full coffers, and
yet empty bellies !   Light, and the ſaving uſe of light, are far different.   Oh, what need then have I to have the aſhes blown away
from my dying-out fire !   I may be a bookman, and (yet) be an idiot
and ſtark fool in Chriſt's way !   Learning will not beguile Chriſt.

---

* Luke i. 35.   † That makes a man unmannerly.
‡ Give wrong names to.   § A miſplaced rebuke.
‖ Security given.   ¶ Reſponſible.   ** Able to face the law.
†† Eph. i. 13.   ‡‡ Cloſe grappling.

The Bible beguiled the Pharifees, and fo may I be mifled. Therefore, as night-watchers hold one another waking by fpeaking to one
another, fo have we need to hold one another on foot : fleep ftealeth
away the light of watching, even the light that reproveth fleeping.
I doubt not but more would fetch* heaven, if they believed not
heaven to be at the next door. The world's negative holinefs—' no
adulterer, no murderer, no thief, no cozener,'—maketh men believe
they are already glorified faints. But the fixth chapter to the Hebrews
may affright us all, when we hear that men may take (a tafte) of the
gifts and common graces of the Holy Spirit, and a tafte of the powers
of the life to come, to hell with them. Here is reprobate filver,
which yet feemeth to have the King's image and fuperfcription upon it!

3*dly*, I find you complaining of yourfelf. And it becometh a
finner fo to do. I am not againft you in that. Senfe of death is a
fib friend,† and of kin and blood to life ; the more fenfe, the more
life ; the more fenfe of fin, the lefs fin. I would love my pain, and
forenefs, and my wounds, howbeit thefe fhould bereave me of my
night's fleep, better than my wounds without pain. Oh how fweet
a thing it is to give Chrift His handful of broken arms and legs, and
disjointed bones !

4*thly*, Be not afraid for little grace. Chrift foweth His living
feed, and He will not lofe His feed. If He have the guiding of my
ftock and ftate, it fhall not mifcarry. Our fpilled‡ works, loffes,
deadnefs, coldnefs, wretchednefs, are the ground upon which the
Good Hufbandman laboureth.

5*thly*, Ye write, " that His compaffions fail not, notwithftanding
that your fervice to Chrift mifcarrieth." To which I anfwer :

God forbid that there were buying and felling, and blocking§
for as good again, betwixt Chrift and us ; for then free grace might
go to play, and a Saviour fing dumb,‖ and Chrift go to fleep. But
we go to heaven with light fhoulders ; and all the bairn-teme, ¶ and

---

* Make for ; Lett. 83.   † Near relative.   ‡ Spoiled.
§ Bargaining.   ‖ Be filenced.

¶ Family. Peden ufes the word thus: " The Church fhall come forth with
a bonny bairn-teme at her back."

the veffels great and fmall that we have, are faftened upon the fure Nail.* The only danger is, that we give grace more to do than God giveth it ; that is, by turning His grace into wantonnefs.

6*thly,* Ye write, that "few fee your guiltinefs, and that ye cannot be free with many, as with me." I anfwer : Bleffed be God, that Chrift and we are not heard before men's courts. It is at home, betwixt Him and us, that pleas are taken away.

Grace be with you.

Yours, in his fweet Lord Jefus,

S. R.

ABERDEEN.

CVII.—*To the Right Honourable and Chriftian Lady, my* LADY BOYD.

(*CONSCIOUSNESS OF DEFECTS NO ARGUMENT OF CHRIST BEING UNKNOWN—HIS EXPERIENCE IN EXILE.*)

MADAM,—Grace, mercy, and peace be to you, from God our Father, and from our Lord Jefus Chrift.

I cannot but thank your Ladyfhip for your letter, that hath refrefhed my foul. I think myfelf many ways obliged to your Ladyfhip for your love to my afflicted brother, now embarked with me in that fame caufe. His Lord hath been pleafed to put him on truth's fide. I hope that your Ladyfhip will befriend him with your counfel and countenance in that country, where he is a ftranger. And your Ladyfhip needeth not fear but your kindnefs to His own will be put up into Chrift's accounts.

Now, Madam, for your Ladyfhip's cafe. I rejoice exceedingly that the Father of lights hath made you fee that there is a nick† in Chriftianity, which ye contend to be at ; and that is, to quit the right eye, and the right hand, and to keep the Son of God. I hope your defire is to make Him your garland, and that your eye looketh

---

* Ifa. xxii. 23, 24.   † A degree or point.

up the mount, which certainly is nothing but the new creature. Fear not, Chrift will not caft water upon your fmoking coal ; and then, who elfe dare do it if He fay nay ? Be forry at corruption, and be not fecure. That companion lay with you in your mother's womb, and was as early friends with you as the breath of life. And Chrift will not have it otherwife ; for He delighteth to take up fallen bairns, and to mend broken brows. Binding up of wounds is His office. *

Firft, I am glad that Chrift will get employment of His calling in you. Many a whole foul is in heaven which was fickerer† than ye are. He is content that ye lay broken arms and legs on His knee, that He may fpelk‡ them. *Secondly*, hiding of His face is wife love. His love is not fond, doting, and reafonlefs, to give your head no other pillow whill§ ye be in at heaven's gates, but to lie between His breafts, and lean upon His bofom. Nay, His bairns muft often have the frofty cold fide of the hill, and fet down both their bare feet among thorns. His love hath eyes, and, in the meantime, is looking on. Our pride muft have winter weather to rot it. But I know that Chrift and ye will not be heard ; ‖ ye will whifper it over betwixt yourfelves, and agree again. For the anchor-tow¶ abideth faft within the vail ; the end of it is in Chrift's ten fingers : who dare pull, if He hold ? " I, the Lord thy God, will hold thy right hand, faying, Fear not, I will help thee. Fear not, Jacob."** The fea-fick paffenger fhall come to land ; Chrift will be the firft to meet you on the fhore. I hope that your Ladyfhip will keep the King's highway. Go on (in the ftrength of the Lord), in hafte, as if ye had not leifure to fpeak to the innkeepers by the way. He is over beyond time, on the other fide of the water, who thinketh long†† for you.

For my unfaithful felf, Madam, I muft fay a word. At my

---

* Ifa. lxi. 1.
‡ Support by fplinters or trufs.
‖ No one will ever hear the chiding.
** Ifa. xli. 13, 14.

† Stronger.
§ Till.
¶ Cable.
†† Longeth for.

firſt coming hither, the devil made many a black lie of my Lord Jeſus, and ſaid the court was changed, and he was angry, and would give an evil ſervant his leave at mid-term.* But He gave me grace not to take my leave. I refolved to bide ſummons,† and ſit, howbeit it was ſuggeſted and ſaid, "What ſhould be done with a withered tree, but over the dyke with it?" But now, now (I dare not, I dow‡ not keep it up!), who is feaſted as His poor exiled priſoner? I think ſhame of the board-head§ and the firſt meſs, and the royal King's dining-hall, and that my black hand ſhould come upon ſuch a Ruler's table. But I cannot mend it; Chriſt muſt have His will: only He paineth my foul ſo ſometimes with His love, that I have been nigh to paſs modeſty, and to cry out. He hath left a ſmoking, burning coal in my heart, and gone to the door Himſelf, and left me and it together. Yet it is not de-ſertion; I know not what it is, but I was never ſo ſick for Him as now. I durſt not challenge my Lord, if I got no more for heaven; it is a dawting‖ croſs. I know He hath other things to do than to play with me, and to trindle¶ an apple with me, and that this feaſt will end. O for inſtruments** in God's name, that this is He! and that I may make uſe of it, when, it may be, a near friend within me will ſay, and when it will be ſaid by a challenging†† devil, "Where is thy God?" Since I know that it will not laſt, I deſire but to keep broken meat. But let no man after me ſlander Chriſt for His croſs.

The great Lord of the Covenant, who brought from the dead the great Shepherd of His ſheep, by the blood of the eternal cove-nant eſtabliſh you, and keep you and yours to His appearance.

Yours in his ſweet Lord Jeſus,

S. R.

ABERDEEN, *March* 7, 1637.

---

* Diſcharge His ſervant, turn him off.
‡ Cannot.
‖ That has fondneſs in it.
** A law phraſe; taking documents in proof of a thing.
†† Accuſing, upbraiding.

† Obey the citation.
§ Head of the table.
¶ Trundle.

CVIII.—*To the* LADY KASKIBERRY.

[This lady was wife to *James Schoneir* of *Kaſkeberrie*, or Kaſkeberrian, in Fife. His name occurs as elder to the General Aſſembly in 1647, and he was ruling elder in the Preſbytery of Kirkcaldy. (*Lamont's Diary*, 1650.) His lady died in 1655, and was buried in Kinglaſſie church. (*Do.*)]

(GRATITUDE FOR KINDNESS—CHRIST'S PRESENCE FELT.)

MADAM,—Grace, mercy, and peace be to you.—I long to hear how your Ladyſhip is. I know not how to requite your Ladyſhip's kindneſs; but your love to the ſaints, Madam, is laid up in heaven. I know it is for your well-beloved Chriſt's ſake that ye make His friends ſo dear to you, and concern yourſelf ſo much in them.

I am, in this houſe of pilgrimage, every way in good caſe: Chriſt is moſt kind and loving to my ſoul. It pleaſeth Him to feaſt, with His unſeen conſolations, a ſtranger and an exiled priſoner; and I would not exchange my Lord Jeſus with all the comfort out of heaven. His yoke is eaſy, and His burden is light.

This is His truth which I now ſuffer for; for He hath ſealed it with His bleſſed preſence. I know that Chriſt ſhall yet win the day, and gain the battle in Scotland. Grace be with you.

Yours in his ſweet Lord Jeſus,

S. R.

ABERDEEN, *March* 7, 1637.

CIX.—*To the* LADY EARLSTON.

[This was probably Lady Earlſton, ſenior, as may be inferred from Ruther-ford's reminding her that her "afternoon ſun will ſoon go down." Her maiden name was Elizabeth Gordon, ſhe being the daughter of John Gordon of Muir-fad, in Kirkmabreck, next pariſh to Anwoth (the ſame who was afterwards deſigned of Penningham), the ſecond ſon of Sir John Gordon of Lochinvar, and brother to Sir John Gordon of Lochinvar, father of firſt Lord Kenmure. (*Niſbet's Heraldry*, vol. i.) Sir John Gordon was married to Jean Glendonning. (*Minutes of Com. of Cor.*, p. 29.)]

(FOLLOWING CHRIST NOT EASY—CHILDREN NOT TO BE OVER-LOVED—JOY IN THE LORD.)

ISTRESS,—Grace, mercy, and peace be to you.—I long to hear how your ſoul proſpereth. I exhort you to go on in your journey ; your day is ſhort, and your afternoon ſun will ſoon go down. Make an end of your accounts with your Lord ; for death and judgment are tides that bide* no man. Salvation is ſuppoſed to be at the door, and Chriſtianity is thought an eaſy taſk ; but I find it hard, and the way ſtrait and narrow, were it not that my Guide is content to wait on me, and to care for a tired traveller. Hurt not your conſcience with any known ſin. Let your children be as ſo many flowers borrowed from God : if the flower die or wither, thank God for a ſummer loan of them, and keep good neighbourhood, to borrow and lend† with Him. Set your heart upon heaven, and trouble not your ſpirit with this clay-idol of the world, which is but vanity, and hath but the luſtre of the rainbow in the air, which cometh and goeth with a flying March ſhower. Clay is the idol of baſtards, not the inheritance of the children.

My Lord hath been pleaſed to make many unknown faces laugh upon me, and hath made me well content of a borrowed fireſide, and a borrowed bed. I am feaſted with the joys of the Holy Ghoſt, and my royal King beareth my charges honourably. I love the ſmell of Chriſt's ſweet breath better than the world's gold. I would I had help to praiſe Him.

The great Meſſenger of the Covenant, the Son of God, eſtabliſh you on your Rock, and keep you to the day of His coming.

              Yours in his ſweet Lord Jeſus,

                                S. R.

ABERDEEN, *March* 7, 1637.

---

     * Wait for.   † To be on good terms.

[David Dickson or Dick, born in 1583, was the only fon of Mr John Dickfon, a pious and wealthy merchant in Glafgow. After finifhing his ftudies at the Univerfity of Glafgow, he was admitted Profeffor of Philofophy in that Univerfity, a fituation which he held for eight years. In 1618 he was ordained minifter of Irvine, where he laboured with much acceptance and fuccefs. In 1622, refufing to practife the ceremonies then impofed upon the Church by the Perth Articles, he was fummoned by James Law, Archbifhop of Glafgow, to appear before the High Commiffion Court. Dickfon appeared, but declined the authority of the Court in ecclefiaftical matters. The refult was, that he was deprived of his charge at Irvine, and banifhed to Turriff, in Aberdeenfhire. There he was employed every Sabbath by the incumbent of the parifh. Yielding to the folicitations of the Earl of Eglinton and the town of Irvine, the Bifhop granted him liberty to return to his old charge about the end of July 1623. He refumed his paftoral duties with increafed ardour; and in addition to his Sabbath labours, preached every Monday (the market-day of Irvine), for the benefit of the rural population. Great numbers, particularly from the neighbouring parifh of Stewarton, attending thefe meetings, the refult was the famous Stewarton Revival, which lafted from 1623 to 1630. After the renewal of the National Covenant, in 1638, Dickfon, who was then diftinguifhed as a leader, in conjunction with Alexander Henderfon and Andrew Cant, was fent on a miffion to Aberdeen, to explain the Covenant to the inhabitants who were hoftile to it, when the celebrated controverfy between the three commiffioners and the doctors of Aberdeen, on the fubject, took place. In 1642 he was appointed Profeffor of Divinity in the Univerfity of Glafgow, in which office he was affociated with the celebrated Robert Baillie. He was afterwards tranflated to the fame office in the Univerfity of Edinburgh. In the differences between the Refolutioners and Protefters, he took the fide of the former; but on feeing how matters went upon the reftoration of Charles II., is reported to have faid to one who vifited him on his deathbed, that the Protefters were the trueft prophets. He died in December 1662. Dickfon was a man of more than ordinary talents, of extenfive theological acquirements, of a very intrepid fpirit, and a popular preacher. He was the author of various works, which have been highly efteemed.]

(GOD'S DEALINGS—THE BITTER SWEETENED—NOTES ON
SCRIPTURE.)

REVEREND AND DEAREST BROTHER,—What
joy have I out of heaven's gates, but that my Lord Jefus
be glorified in my bonds? Bleffed be ye of the Lord
who contribute anything to my obliged and indebted praifes. Dear
brother, help me, a poor dyvour,* to pay the intereft; for I cannot
come nigh to render the principal. It is not jeft nor fport which
maketh me to fpeak and write as I do: I never before came to that
nick† or pitch of communion with Chrift that I have now attained
to. For my confirmation, I have been thefe two Sabbaths or
three in private, taking inftruments‡ in the name of God, that my
Lord Jefus and I have kiffed each other in Aberdeen, the houfe of
my pilgrimage. I feek not an apple to play me with (He knoweth,
whom I ferve in the fpirit!) but a feal. I but beg earneft, and am
content to fufpend and frift§ glory whill‖ fupper-time. I know
that this world will not laft with me; for my moon-light is noon-
day light, and my four hours¶ above my feafts when I was a
preacher; at which time, alfo, I was embraced very often in His
arms. But who can blame Chrift to take me on behind Him (if I
may fay fo), on His white horfe, or in His chariot, paved with love,
through a water? Will not a father take his little dawted Davie**
in his arms, and carry him over a ditch or a mire? My fhort legs
could not ftep over this lair,†† or finking mire; and, therefore, my
Lord Jefus will bear me through. If a change come, and a dark
day (fo being that He will keep my faith without flaw or crack), I
dare not blame Him, howbeit I get no more whill‖ I come to
heaven. But ye know that the phyfic behoved to have fugar: my
faith was fallen afwoon,‡‡ and Chrift but held up a fwooning man's

---

* Debtor.   † Degree.
‡ The documents that prove the matter fettled.   § Poftpone for a time.
‖ Till.   ¶ Slight afternoon refrefhment.   ** His fondled boy, or pet.
†† Sinking bog.   ‡‡ Into a fwoon.

head. Indeed, I pray not for a dawted* bairn's diet: He knoweth that I would have Chrift, four or fweet,—any way, fo being it be Chrift indeed. I ftand not now upon pared apples, or fugared difhes, but I cannot blame Him to give, and I muft gape and make a wide mouth. Since Chrift will not pantry† up joys, He muft be welcome who will not bide away. I feek no other fruit than that He may be glorified. He knoweth that I would take hard fare to have His name fet on high.

I blefs you for your counfel. I hope to live by faith, and fwim without a mafs or bundle of joyful fenfe under my chin ; at leaft to venture, albeit I fhould be ducked.

Now for my cafe: I think that the council fhould be effayed, and the event referred to God ;—duties are ours, and events are God's.

I fhall go through yours upon the Covenant at leifure, and write to you my mind thereanent ; ‡ and anent the Arminian contraft betwixt the Father and the Son. I befeech you, fet to,§ to go through Scripture.‖ Yours on the Hebrews is in great requeft with all who would be acquainted with Chrift's Teftament. I purpofe, God willing, to fet about Hofea, and to try if I can get it to the prefs here.

It refrefheth me much that ye are fo kind to my brother. I hope your counfel will do him good. I recommend him to you, fince I am fo far from him. I am glad that the dying fervant of God,

---

* Fondled.   † Lock up in the pantry, or cupboard.

‡ Regarding this.   § Set about, begin.

‖ Rutherford feems here to allude to a plan of furnifhing fhort commentaries on the whole Bible, which was fuggefted and fet on foot by Dickfon at the beginning of the feventeenth century. "The Hebrews," as is mentioned in this letter, together with "The Pfalms" and "Matthew," were undertaken by Dickfon; and "Hofea," which Rutherford here intimates his intention to undertake, but never accomplifhed, was contributed by Hutchifon inftead of him. In the Preface to one of the earlieft editions of the Letters, a complaint is made that fome one was fecreting a MS. commentary of Rutherford's, upon *Ifaiah*.

famous and faithful Mr Cunningham, fealed your miniftry before he
fell afleep.

Grace, grace be with you.

Yours in his fweet Lord Jefus,

S. R.

ABERDEEN, *March* 7, 1637.

CXI.—*To* JEAN BROWN.

(CHRIST'S UNTOLD PRECIOUSNESS—A WORD TO HER BOY.)

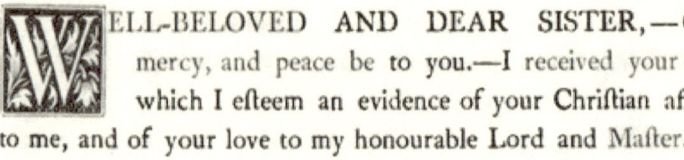

WELL-BELOVED AND DEAR SISTER,—Grace,
mercy, and peace be to you.—I received your letter,
which I efteem an evidence of your Chriftian affection
to me, and of your love to my honourable Lord and Mafter. My
defire is, that your communion with Chrift may grow, and that
your reckonings may be put by-hand* with your Lord ere you
come to the water-fide.

Oh, who knoweth how fweet Chrift's kiffes are! Who hath
been more kindly embraced and kiffed than I, His banifhed prifoner?
If the comparifon could ftand, I would not exchange Chrift with
heaven itfelf. He hath left a dart and arrow of love in my foul,
and it paineth me till He come and take it out. I find pain of thofe
wounds, becaufe I would have poffeffion. I know now that this
worm-eaten apple, the plaftered, rotten world, which the filly
children of this world are beating, and buffeting, and pulling each
other's ears for, is a portion for baftards, good enough; and that it is
all they have to look for. I am not offended that my adverfaries ftay
at home at their own firefide, with more yearly rent than I. Should
I be angry that the Goodman of this houfe of the world cafteth a
dog a bone to hurt his teeth? He hath taught me to be content
with a borrowed firefide, and an unco† bed; and I think I have
loft nothing, the income is fo great. O what telling is in Chrift!

---

* Put afide, as finifhed and over.   † Strange.

O how weighty is my fair garland, my crown, my fair fupping-hall in glory, where I fhall be above the blows and buffeting of prelates! Let this be your defire, and let your thoughts dwell much upon that bleffednefs that abideth you in the other world. The fair fide of the world will be turned to you quickly, when ye fhall fee the crown. I hope that ye are near your lodging. Oh, but I would think myfelf bleffed, for my part, to win* to the houfe before the fhower come on ; for God hath a quiver full of arrows to fhoot at and fhower down upon Scotland.

Ye have the prayers of a prifoner of Chrift. I defire Patrick to give Chrift his young love, even the flower of it ; and to put it by all others. It were good to ftart foon to the way ; he fhould thereby have a great advantage in the evil day. Grace be with you.

Yours in his only Lord Jefus,

S. R.

ABERDEEN, *March* 7, 1637.

CXII.—*To* MR JOHN FERGUSHILL.

[MR JOHN FERGUSHILL's mother was Janet Kennedy, fifter or near relative to Hugh Kennedy of Ayr. He was at this time minifter of Ochiltree, a parifh in the centre of Ayrfhire, in the diftrict of Kyle. When Mr Robert Blair was tranflated from Ayr to St Andrews by the General Affembly, 1639, Fergufhill was, by the fame Affembly, appointed his fucceffor. He died in 1644. He is mentioned by Livingftone, as one of the "many of the godly and able minifters" in Scotland. He was a member of the famous Glafgow Affembly 1638. Lady Gaitgirth's manfion was near Ochiltree; fee Let. 187.]

(THE ROD UPON GOD'S CHILDREN—PAIN FROM A SENSE OF CHRIST'S LOVE—HIS PRESENCE A SUPPORT UNDER TRIALS —CONTENTEDNESS WITH HIM ALONE.)

EVEREND AND WELL-BELOVED IN THE LORD,—I was refrefhed with your letter. I am forry for that lingering and longfome vifitation that is

---

* Reach in fpite of difficulty.

upon your wife; but I know that ye take it as the mark of a lawfully begotten child, and not of a baftard, to be under your Father's rod. Till ye be in heaven, it will be but foul weather; one fhower up and another down. The lintel-ftone and pillars of the New Jerufalem fuffer more knocks of God's hammer and tool than the common fide-wall ftones. And if twenty croffes be written for you in God's book, they will come to nineteen, and then at laft to one, and after that to nothing, but your head fhall lie betwixt Chrift's breafts for evermore, and His own foft hand fhall dry your face, and wipe away your tears. As for public fufferings for His truth, your Mafter alfo will fee to thefe. Let us put Him into His own office, to comfort and deliver. The gloom* of Chrift's crofs is worfe than itfelf.

I cannot keep up what He hath done to my foul. My dear brother, will I not get help of you to praife, and to lift Chrift up on high? He hath pained me with His love, and hath left a love-arrow in my heart, that hath made a wound, and fwelled me up with defires, fo that I am to be pitied for want of real poffeffion. Love would have the company of the party loved; and my greateft pain is the want of Him, not of His joys and comforts, but of a near union and communion.

This is His truth, I am fully perfuaded, which I now fuffer for; for Chrift hath taken upon Him to be witnefs to it by His fweet comforts to my foul; and fhall I think Him a falfe witnefs? or that He would fubfcribe blank paper? I thank His high and dreadful name for what He hath given. I hope to keep His feal and His pawn till He come and loofe it Himfelf. I defy hell to put me off it. But He is Chrift, and He hath met with His prifoner; and I took inftruments in His own hand, † that it was He, and none other for Him. When the devil fenceth a baftard-court‡ in my Lord's ground, and giveth me forged fummons, it will be my fhame to mis-

---

* The frown imagined to be in it.
† Took documents that proved the matter fettled.
‡ Opens and conftitutes an unauthorized court.

believe, * after fuch a fair broad feal. And yet Satan and my apprehenfion fometimes make a lie of Chrift, as if He hated me. But I
dare believe no evil of Chrift. If He would cool my love-fever
for Himfelf with real prefence and poffeffion, I would be rich ; but
I dare not be miflearned,† and feek more in that kind, howbeit it
be no fhame to beg at Chrift's door. I pity my adverfaries. I
grudge not that my Lord keepeth them at their own firefide, and
hath given me a borrowed firefide : let the Goodman of the houfe
caft the dog a bone, why fhould I take offence ? I rejoice that the
broken bark fhall come to land, and that Chrift will, on the fhore,
welcome the fea-fick paffenger. We have need of a great ftock
againft this day of trial that is coming. There is neither chaff nor
corn in Scotland, but it fhall once ‡ pafs through God's fieve. Praife,
praife, and pray for me ; for I cannot forget you. I know that ye
will be friendly to my afflicted brother, who is now embarked in
the fame caufe with me. Let him have your counfel and comforts.

Remember my love in Chrift to your wife ; her health is coming, and her falvation fleepeth not. Ye have the prayers and bleffing
of a prifoner of Chrift. Sow faft, deal bread plentifully. The
pantry-door will be locked on the bairns, in appearance, ere long.
Grace, grace, be with you.

Yours in his fweet Lord Jefus,

S. R.

ABERDEEN, *March* 7, 1637.

CXIII.—*To his Reverend and Dear Brother*, MR ROBERT DOUGLAS.

[ROBERT DOUGLAS, one of the ableft and moft refpected minifters of the
Church of Scotland in his day, was the illegitimate fon of one Mr Douglas, who
was believed to have been a baftard child of Queen Mary, by Sir G. Douglas,
Governor of Lochleven Caftle, born when fhe was prifoner there. He was thus
the grandfon of Queen Mary (*Wodrow's Analecta*, iv. 226). Having finifhed
his preparations for the miniftry, he was ordained to be chaplain for the forces

---

* Not to believe truly.   † Ill-bred, indifcreet.   ‡ Some time or other.

that ferved under the celebrated Guftavus of Sweden. Continuing in this fituation for a confiderable time, he attracted the notice of the Swedifh monarch, who held his character and talents in high eftimation. It is faid that, in one of Guftavus' engagements, furveying the battle from an eminence, and obferving fomething wrong in the left wing of Guftavus army which threatened to prove difaftrous, he either went perfonally, or fent a meffenger to acquaint the commanding officer with the circumftance, and that this information led to victory. When he left the army, Guftavus parted with him reluctantly, pronouncing him to be a man of the moft diftinguifhed abilities he had ever known. "There," fays he, "is a man who, for wifdom and prudence, might be a counfellor to any king in Europe. He might be a moderator to any affembly in the world; and he might be a general to conduct any army, for his fkill in military affairs" (*Ibid.* iv. 221). During this period, he committed to memory the greater part of the Bible, having almoft no other book to read. Returning to his own country, he was admitted colleague to Mr James Simfon, minifter of Kirkaldy, in 1630. Thence he was tranflated to Edinburgh in 1641. For a time he was deceived by the duplicity of James Sharp, but at laft he detected his real character; and when the traitor (fhortly before he went up to London to be confecrated Archbifhop) happened to meet with him, and addreffed him as "Brother," the good man, difgufted at his hypocrify, exclaimed, "Brother! no more brother! James, if my confcience had been of the make of yours, I could have been Bifhop of St Andrews fooner than you." (*Analecta*, vol. iii. p. 130.) In 1669 he was admitted indulged minifter at Pencaitland, where he died at an advanced age in 1674, and was buried in Edinburgh. (*Ibid.* vol. i. p. 337; *Wodrow's Hiftory*, vol. ii. p. 133.)]

(GREATNESS OF CHRIST'S LOVE REVEALED TO THOSE WHO SUFFER FOR HIM.)

Y VERY REVEREND AND DEAR BROTHER, —Grace, mercy, and peace be to you.—I long to fee you on paper. I cannot but write you, that this which I now fuffer for is Chrift's truth ; becaufe He hath been pleafed to feal my fufferings with joy unfpeakable and glorious. I know that He will not put His feal upon blank paper ; Chrift hath not dumb feals, neither will He be a witnefs to a lie. I befeech you, my dear brother, to help me to praife, and to lift Chrift up on His throne above the fhields of the earth. I am aftonifhed and confounded at the greatnefs of His kindnefs to fuch a finner. I know that Chrift

and I fhall never be even ;* I fhall die in His debt. He hath left an arrow in my heart that paineth me for want of real poffeffion ; and hell cannot quench this coal of God's kindling. I wifh no man to flander Chrift or His crofs for my caufe ; for I have much caufe to fpeak much good of Him. He hath brought me to a nick† and degree of communion with Himfelf that I knew not before. The din and gloom‡ of our Lord's crofs is more fearful and hard than the crofs itfelf. He taketh the bairns in His arms when they come to a deep water; at leaft, when they lofe ground, and are put to fwim, then His hand is under their chin.

Let me be helped by your prayers ; and remember my love to your kind wife. Grace be with you.

Your brother, and Chrift's prifoner,

S. R.

ABERDEEN, *March* 7, 1637.

------◆------

CXIV.—*To the much Honoured* WILLIAM RIGG, *of Athernie, in Fife, near Leven.*

[WILLIAM RIGG of Athernie, in the capacity of one of the bailies of Edinburgh, " gave great evidence (fays Livingftone) that he had the fpirit of a magiftrate beyond many, being a terror to all evil-doers." He took an active part againft all attempts to introduce Prelacy, and contributed liberally to the printing of fuch books as " croffed the courfe of Conformity." In March 1624, a committee of the Privy Council, by the authority of the King, deprived Rigg of his office, fined him in fifty thoufand pounds Scots, and ordered him to be warded in Blacknefs Caftle till the fum was paid, and afterwards to be confined in Orkney. This fentence, however, was afterwards mitigated. He was diftinguifhed above moft for devoting a large portion of his income to religious purpofes. Such was his liberality, that one faid, " To my certain knowledge, he fpends yearly more on pious ufes than all my eftate is

---

* Be quits, have accounts fairly balanced.

† Explained by the next word, " degree," which probably has crept into the text from the margin. So in Let. 110, " pitch."

‡ The noife made about the crofs, and the frown.

worth; and mine will be towards 8 or 9000 merks (about L.350) in the year."
He was a man of much prayer, and generally commenced with deep and bitter
complaints and confeffion of fin, but ended with unfpeakable affurance, and
joy and thankfgiving. His death took place on the 2d of January 1644, and
is thus recorded by Sir Thomas Hope, in his Diary (p. 201): "This day,
my worthy coufin, William Rigg of Athernie, departed, at his houfe of
Athernie, having taken bed on Sunday of before, and died on the third day.
The Lord prepare me; for this, next to my deareft fon, is a heavy ftroke."]

*(SUSTAINING POWER OF CHRIST'S LOVE—SATAN'S OPPOSITION
—YEARNINGS FOR CHRIST HIMSELF—FEARS FOR THE
CHURCH.)*

MUCH HONOURED SIR,—Grace, mercy, and peace
be to you. I received your long-looked-for and fhort
letter. I would that ye had fpoken more to me, who
ftand in need. I find Chrift, as ye write, aye the longer the better;
and therefore cannot but rejoice in His falvation, who hath made my
chains my wings, and hath made me a king over my croffes, and over
my adverfaries. Glory, glory, glory to His high, high and holy
name! Not one ounce, not one grain-weight more is laid on me
than He hath enabled me to bear; and I am not fo much wearied
to fuffer as Zion's haters are to perfecute. Oh, if I could find a
way, in any meafure, to ftrive to be even with* Chrift's love! But
that I muft give over. Oh, who would help a dyvour† to pay
praifes to the King of faints, who triumpheth in His weak fervants!

I fee that if Chrift but ride upon a worm or feather, His horfe
will neither ftumble nor fall. The worm Jacob is made by Him a
new, fharp threfhing inftrument, having teeth, to threfh the mountains, and beat them fmall, and to make the hills as chaff, and to
fan them fo as the wind fhall carry them away, and the whirlwind
fhall fcatter them.‡ Chrift's enemies are but breaking their own
heads in pieces, upon the Rock laid in Zion; and the ftone is not
removed out of its place. Faith hath caufe to take courage from
our very afflictions; the devil is but a whetftone to fharpen the

---

* Be quits; repay in full.   † Debtor.   ‡ Ifa. xli. 14-16.

faith and patience of the saints. I know that he but heweth and polisheth stones, all this time, for the New Jerusalem.

But in all this, three things have much moved me, since it hath pleased my Lord to turn my moon-light into day-light. *First*, He hath yoked* me to work, to wrestle with Christ's love; of† longing wherewith I am sick, pained, fainting, and like to die because I cannot get Himself; which I think a strange sort of desertion. For I have not Himself, whom if I had, my love-sickness would cool, and my fever go away: at least, I should know the heat of the fire of complacency, which would cool the scorching heat of the fire of desire. (And yet I have no penury of His love!) And so I dwine,‡ I die, and He seemeth not to rue§ on me. I take instruments in His hand, ‖ that I would have Him, but I cannot get Him; and my best cheer is black hunger. I bless Him for that feast.

Secondly, Old challenges¶ now and then revive, and cast all down. I go halting and sighing, fearing there be an unseen process yet coming out, and that heavier than I can answer. I cannot read distinctly my surety's act of cautionary** for me in particular, and my discharge; and sense, rather than faith, assureth me of what I have; so unable am I to go but by a hold. I could, with reverence of my Lord, forgive Christ, if He would give me as much faith as I have hunger for Him. I hope the pardon is now obtained, but the peace is not so sure to me as I would wish. Yet, one thing I know, there is not a way to heaven but the way which He hath graced me to profess and suffer for.

Thirdly, Wo, wo is me for the virgin-daughter of Scotland, and for the fearful desolation and wrath appointed for this land! And yet all are sleeping, eating and drinking, laughing and sporting, as if all were well. O our dim gold! our dumb, blind pastors! The sun is gone down upon them, and our nobles bid Christ fend††

---

* Engaged, bound me in a pressing way.
† I am sick of longing for which.   ‡ Pine.   § Take pity on.
‖ Take documents in evidence.   ¶ Self-upbraidings, or rebukes.
** Suretyship.   †† Provide for, shift for.

for Himfelf, if He be Chrift. It were good that we fhould learn in time the way to our ftronghold.

Sir, howbeit not acquainted, remember my love to your wife. I pray God to eftablifh you.

Yours in his fweet Lord Jefus,

S. R.

ABERDEEN, *March* 9, 1637.

CXV.—*To* Mr ALEXANDER HENDERSON.

[ALEXANDER HENDERSON, the well-known hero of the Second Reformation, was born in the year 1583, and received his education at the Univerfity of St Andrews. After having taught for feveral years a clafs of philofophy and rhetoric in that Univerfity, he obtained a prefentation to the parifh of Leuchars, in 1612. Being at that time unimpreffed with fpiritual truth, he was a defender of the principles and meafures of the prelatic party in the Church. His fettlement was on thefe accounts fo unpopular, that on the day of his ordination the church-doors were fecured by the people, and the members of Prefbytery, together with the prefentee, were obliged to break in by the window. But his foul was foon after vifited by the Holy Spirit, and underwent an entire change. He became Leader in effecting that revolution in the ecclefiaftical affairs of Scotland which commenced about the year 1637. He was Moderator of the famous Affembly which met at Glafgow in 1638, and by that Affembly was tranflated to Edinburgh. In the civil war, Henderfon was appointed by the Covenanters to act as one of their commiffioners in treating with his Majefty Charles I. In 1642, he was delegated by the Commiffion of the General Affembly to fit as one of their commiffioners in the Weftminfter Affembly of Divines, which kept him in London for feveral years. He died on the 12th of Auguft 1646, in the 63d year of his age, fhortly after his return from England. Baillie, in his fpeech to the General Affembly in the following year, pronounced him, "the faireft ornament after Mr John Knox, of incomparable memory, that ever the Church of Scotland did enjoy."]

(*SADNESS BECAUSE CHRIST'S HEADSHIP NOT SET FORTH—HIS CAUSE ATTENDED WITH CROSSES—THE BELIEVER SEEN OF ALL.*)

Y REVEREND AND DEAR BROTHER,—I received your letters. They are as apples of gold to me; for with my fweet feafts (and they are above the

deferving of fuch a finner, high and out of meafure), I have fadnefs
to ballaft me, and weight* me a little. It is but His boundlefs
wifdom which hath taken the tutoring of His witlefs child ; and He
knoweth that to be drunken with comforts is not fafeft for our
ftomachs. However it be, the din and noife and glooms† of Chrift's
crofs are weightier than itfelf. I proteft to you (my witnefs is in
heaven), that I could wifh many pound-weights added to my crofs,
to know that by my fufferings Chrift were fet forward in His kingly
office in this land. Oh, what is my fkin to His glory ; or my loffes,
or my fad heart, to the apple of the eye of our Lord and His beloved
Spoufe, His precious truth, His royal privileges, the glory of manifefted juftice in giving of His foes a dafh, the teftimony of His faithful fervants, who do glorify Him, when He rideth upon poor, weak
worms, and triumpheth in them ! I defire you to pray, that I may
come out of this furnace with honefty, and that I may leave Chrift's
truth no worfe than I found it ; and that this moft honourable caufe
may neither be ftained nor weakened.

As for your caufe, my reverend and deareft brother, ye are the
talk of the north and fouth ; and looked to, fo as if ye were all
cryftal glafs. Your motes and duft would foon be proclaimed, and
trumpets blown at your flips. But I know that ye have laid help
upon One that is mighty. Intruft not your comforts to men's airy
and frothy applaufe, neither lay your down-caftings on the tongues
of falt‡ mockers and reproachers of godlinefs. " As deceivers, and
yet true ; as unknown, and yet well known."§ God hath called you
to Chrift's fide, and the wind is now in Chrift's face in this land ;
and feeing ye are with Him, ye cannot expect the lee-fide,‖ or the
funny fide of the brae. But I know that ye have refolved to take
Chrift upon any terms whatfoever. I hope that ye do not rue,¶
though your caufe be hated, and prejudices are taken up againft it.

---

* Burden, deprefs.   † Frowns.
‡ Bitter, farcaftic ?   In Jamiefon's Dict. we have it fignifying " trouble-
fome."   § 2 Cor. vi. 8, 9.
‖ The fheltered fide of the hill.   ¶ Repent of it.

The fhields of the world think our Mafter cumberfome wares, and
that He maketh too great din, and that His cords and yokes make
blains, and deep fcores in their neck. Therefore they kick. They
fay, " This man fhall not reign over us."

Let us pray one for another. He who hath made you a chofen
arrow in His quiver, hide you in the hollow of His hand !

I am yours, in his fweet Lord Jefus,

S. R.

ABERDEEN, *March* 9, 1637.

CXVI.—*To the Right Honourable my* LORD LOUDON.

[JOHN CAMPBELL, firft Earl of Loudon, and the fon of Sir James
Campbell of Lawers, was a man of diftinguifhed talents, and of a very decided
character. In the hiftory of his country he makes no fmall figure as a ftrenu-
ous opponent of the attempts made by Charles I. to impofe Prelacy and arbitrary power on Scotland. He was a member of the General Affembly which
met at Glafgow in 1638, in the bufinefs of which he took an active part.
When the King, diffatisfied with the proceedings of this Affembly, put himfelf at the head of an army to reduce his Scottifh fubjects to fubmiffion,
Loudon had a leading hand in the meafures then adopted for preferving the
religion and liberties of Scotland, according to the ecclefiaftical and civil laws
of the kingdom. In the fkirmifh at Newburn, where the King's forces were
defeated by the Scottifh army, he commanded a brigade of horfe. In 1641,
when peace was reftored between the King and his Scottifh fubjects, Loudon
was made Lord Chancellor of Scotland, a fituation which he held till after
the execution of Charles I., and the calling home of Charles II. by the Scots in
1650. Malignants being again brought into places of power and truft, he
demitted his office. He continued, however, ftrongly to adhere to the caufe
of Charles, in confequence of which he was excepted from Cromwell's act of
indemnity, and his eftates forfeited. But all that he had fuffered for the royal
caufe did not recommend him to the favour of the unprincipled government
of Charles II. His name is in the lift of Middleton's fines (impofed upon
the gentlemen of Ayrfhire in 1662) for L.12,000. He felt convinced that,
fhould his life be fpared, he would fall an early victim to the vengeance of his
enemies, and often exhorted his pious lady to befeech the Lord that he might
not live to the next feffion of Parliament, elfe he would fhare the fame fate with
the Marquis of Argyle. His wifh was granted ; for he died at Edinburgh,
March 15, 1662. Rutherford's " Divine Right of Church Government and

Excommunication," printed at London in 1646, is dedicated to this nobleman, who was then Chancellor of the Univerfity of St Andrews. His fon James, fecond Earl of Loudon, was fubjected to no fmall perfecution under the dominancy of Prelacy; and, feeking refuge in Holland, took up his refidence at Leyden, where he died on the 29th of October 1684.]

(*BLESSEDNESS OF ACTING FOR CHRIST—HIS LOVE TO HIS PRISONER.*)

Y VERY NOBLE AND HONOURABLE LORD,— Grace, mercy, and peace be to you.—I make bold to write to your Lordfhip, that you may know the honourable caufe which ye are graced* to profefs is Chrift's own truth. Ye are many ways blefled of God, who have taken upon you to come out to the ftreets with Chrift on your forehead, when fo many are afhamed of Him, and hide Him (as it were) under their cloak, as if He were a ftolen Chrift. If this faithlefs generation, and efpecially the nobles of this kingdom, thought not Chrift dear wares, and religion expenfive, hazardous, and dangerous, they would not flip from His caufe as they do, and ftand looking on with their hands folded behind their back when louns† are running with the fpoil of Zion on their back, and the boards of the Son of God's tabernacle. Law and juftice are to be had by any, efpecially for money and moyen ;‡ but Chrift can get no law, good-cheap§ or dear. It were the glory and honour of you, who are the nobles of this land, to plead for your wronged Bridegroom and His opprefled fpouse, as far as zeal and ftanding law will go with you. Your ordinary logic from the event, " that it will do no good to the caufe, and, therefore, filence is beft till the Lord put to His own hand," is not (with reverence to your Lordfhip's learning) worth a ftraw. Events are God's. Let us do,‖ and not plead againft God's office. Let Him fit at His own helm, who moderateth all events. It is

---

* Allufion to Luke i. 28, κεχαριτωμένη, " graced, highly favoured."

† Rogues, worthlefs fcoundrels.   ‡ Means, influence.

§ Gratis.   ‖ Act.

not a good courfe to complain that we cannot get a providence of gold, when our lazinefs, cold zeal, temporizing, and faithlefs fearfulnefs fpilleth * good providence.

Your Lordfhip will pardon me : I am not of that mind, that tumults or arms is the way to put Chrift on His throne ; or that Chrift will be ferved and truth vindicated, only with the arm of flefh and blood. Nay, Chrift doth His turn with lefs din, than with garments rolled in blood. But I would that the zeal of God were in the nobles to do their part for Chrift ; and I muft be pardoned to write to your Lordfhip thus.

I dow not,† I dare not, but fpeak to others what God hath done to the foul of His poor, afflicted exile-prifoner. His comfort is more than I ever knew before. He hath fealed the honourable caufe which I now fuffer for, and I fhall not believe that Chrift will put His amen and ring‡ upon an imagination. He hath made all His promifes good to me, and hath filled up all the blanks with His own hand. I would not exchange my bonds with the plaftered joy of this whole world. It hath pleafed Him to make a finner the like of me an ordinary banqueter in His houfe-of-wine, with that royal, princely One, Chrift Jefus. O what weighing, O what telling is in His love ! How fweet muft He be, when that black and burdenfome tree, His own crofs, is fo perfumed with joy and gladnefs ! Oh for help to lift Him up by praifes on His royal throne ! I feek no more than that His name may be fpread abroad in me, that meikle§ good may be fpoken of Chrift on my behalf ; and this being done, my loffes, place, ftipend, credit, eafe, and liberty, fhall all be made up to my full contentment and joy of heart.

I fhall be confident that your Lordfhip will go on in the ftrength of the Lord, and keep Chrift, and avouch Him, that He may read your name publicly before men and angels. I fhall entreat your Lordfhip to exhort and encourage that nobleman, your chief, ‖ to

---

* Spoils. † I cannot.

‡ As if fealing it by His ring as in marriage, or as Efth. iii. 10.

§ Much. ‖ The Earl of Argyle.

do the fame.   But I am wo* that many of you find a new wifdom,
which deferveth not fuch a name.   It were better that men would
fee that their wifdom be holy, and their holinefs wife.

I muft be bold to defire your Lordfhip to add to your former
favours to me (for the which your Lordfhip hath a prifoner's blefs-
ing and prayers), this, that ye would be pleafed to befriend my
brother, now fuffering for the fame caufe ; for as he is to dwell
nigh your Lordfhip's bounds, your Lordfhip's word and countenance
may help him.

Thus recommending your Lordfhip to the faving grace and
tender mercy of Chrift Jefus our Lord, I reft, your Lordfhip's
obliged fervant in Chrift,

S. R.

ABERDEEN, *March* 9, 1637.

———————◆———————

CXVII.—*To* MR WILLIAM DALGLEISH, *Minifter of the Gofpel.*

[Mr WILLIAM DALGLEISH was minifter of the conjunct parifhes of
Anwoth, Kirkdale, and Kirkmabreck.† He preached at Anwoth only every
alternate week; but fo abundantly bleffed were his labours to the people, that
when he furrendered (*quoad facra*) the charge of Anwoth to Rutherford, upon
its being formed into a diftinct parochial charge, not only many of the humbler
clafs of the parifhioners, but the proprietors too, had embraced the doctrines of
the Gofpel.   Dalgleifh ftrictly adhered to Prefbyterian principles, and on that
account was fubjected to trouble.   Upon the death of Andrew Lamb, the
tolerant Bifhop of Galloway, in 1634, and the elevation of Thomas Sydferff,
Bifhop of Brechin, a man of the moft intolerant character, to the vacant fee,
the prelate immediately threatened Rutherford and Dalgleifh with a profecution
before the High Commiffion Court, as appears from a letter written at that
time by Rutherford to Marion M'Naught, referring to a requeft which he and
Dalgleifh had made to her to ufe her influence in inducing Lord Kirkcudbright

———————

* Grieved.

† *Barholm Caftle* is in this parifh, and was the fpot where John Knox was
fecreted previous to his efcape for the Continent.   His fignature was long
fhown on the wall of one of the rooms.   You fee the old walls, covered with
ivy, on the right of the road as you are going from Kirkdale to Creetown.
The modern *Barholm* is a fine manfion, on the other fide of Creetown.

to extend to them his protection. (See *Let.* 34.) Next year, he was deprived of his charge as minifter of the united parifhes of Kirkdale* and Kirkmabreck. In 1637, when Epifcopacy began to be the lofing caufe, he returned
to his flock. His name appears on the roll of the members of the famous
Affembly which met at Glafgow in 1638; and in 1639 he was tranflated to
Cramond, as fucceffor to Mr William Colville, afterwards Principal of the
Univerfity of Edinburgh; to whom he appears to have been related, as the
name of his wife was Elizabeth Colville. He was the intimate friend of the
well-known Alexander Henderfon, who by his latter will ordained his executor
" to deliver to my dear acquaintance Mr John Duncan, at Culrofs, and Mr
William Dalgleifh, minifter at Cramond, all my manufcripts and papers which
are in my ftudy, and that belong to me any where elfe; and after they have
received them, to deftroy or preferve and keep them, as they fhall judge convenient for their own private or the public good." In 1662, Dalgleifh was
ejected for non-conformity, and died before the Revolution. Rutherford often
preached at Kirkmabreck. We have notes of feveral fermons in print, as
preached by him there, at Communions.]

(CHRIST'S KINDNESS—DEPENDENCE ON PROVIDENCE—
CONTROVERSIES.)

REVEREND AND DEAR BROTHER,—Grace, mercy,
and peace be to you.—I am well. My Lord Jefus is
kinder to me than ever He was. It pleafeth Him to
dine and fup with His afflicted prifoner. A King feafteth me, and
His fpikenard cafteth a fweet fmell. Put Chrift's love to the trial,
and put upon it our burdens, and then it will appear love indeed.
We employ not His love, and therefore we know it not. I verily
count the fufferings of my Lord more than this world's luftred†
and over-gilded glory. I dare not fay but my Lord Jefus hath fully
recompenfed my fadnefs with His joys, my loffes with His own
prefence. I find it a fweet and rich thing to exchange my forrows
with Chrift's joys, my afflictions with that fweet peace I have with
Himfelf.

---

* The modern manfion of Kirkdale looks acrofs the bay to Wigton, and
is seen peering out on the paffer-by from its high platform above the road.
Kirkmabreck was a pendicle of the abbey of *Dundrennan*, which is about
feven miles from Kirkcudbright. (Nicolfon's *Scotland.*)

† Shining by art.

Brother, this is His own truth I now fuffer for.   He hath fealed my fufferings with His own comforts, and I know that He will not put His feal upon blank paper.   His feals are not dumb nor delufive, to confirm imaginations and lies.   Go on, my dear brother, in the ftrength of the Lord, not fearing man who is a worm, nor the fon of man that fhall die.   Providence hath a thoufand keys, to open a thoufand fundry doors for the deliverance of His own, when it is even come to a *conclamatum eft*.*   Let us be faithful, and care for our own part, which is to do and fuffer for Him, and lay Chrift's part on Himfelf, and leave it there.   Duties are ours, events are the Lord's.   When our faith goeth to meddle with events, and to hold a court (if I may fo fpeak) upon God's providence, and beginneth to fay, " How wilt Thou do this and that ? " we lofe ground.   We have nothing to do there.   It is our part to let the Almighty ex-ercife His own office, and fteer His own helm.   There is nothing left to us, but to fee how we may be approved of Him, and how we may roll the weight of our weak fouls in well-doing upon Him who is God Omnipotent : and when that we thus effay mifcarrieth, it will be neither our fin nor crofs.

Brother, remember the Lord's word to Peter ; " Simon, loveft thou Me ?—Feed My fheep."   No greater teftimony of our love to Chrift can be, than to feed carefully and faithfully His lambs.

I am in no better neighbourhood with the minifters here than before : they cannot endure that any fpeak of me, or to me.   Thus I am, in the mean time, filent, which is my greateft grief.   Dr Barron† hath often difputed with me, efpecially about Arminian con-

---

* " All is over!"

† Barron was a branch of the family of Kinnaird in Fifefhire, and educated at St Andrews.   He afterwards became minifter in the parifh of Keith; in 1624 was appointed to a charge in Aberdeen; and 1625 nominated Profeffor of Divinity in Marifchal College there.   He was a determined opponent of Rutherford, Dickfon, and others, and was obliged to refign the chair and retire to Berwick, where he died in 1639.   *Vide* Funeral Sermon by Patrick Forbes, publifhed by the Spotteswoode Society, p. 27, and Baillie's Letters, i. 221.

troverfies, and for the ceremonies. Three yokings* laid him by; and I have not been troubled with him fince. Now he hath ap- pointed a difpute before witneffes; I truft that Chrift and truth will do for themfelves.

I hope, brother, that ye will help my people; and write to me what ye hear the Bifhop is to do with them. Grace be with you.

Your brother in bonds,

S. R.

ABERDEEN.

CXVIII.—*To* MR HUGH MACKAIL, *Minifter of the Gofpel at Irvine.*

(CHRIST'S BOUNTIFUL DEALINGS—JOY IN CHRIST THROUGH THE CROSS.)

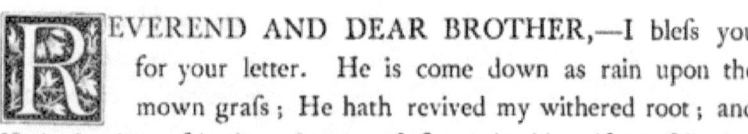EVEREND AND DEAR BROTHER,—I blefs you for your letter. He is come down as rain upon the mown grafs; He hath revived my withered root; and He is the dew of herbs. I am moft fecure in this prifon : falvation is for walls in it; and what think ye of thefe walls? He maketh the dry plant to bud as the lily, and to bloffom as Lebanon :—the great Hufbandman's bleffing cometh down upon the plants of righteoufnefs. Who may fay this, my dear brother, if I, His poor exiled ftranger and prifoner, may not fay it? Howbeit all the world fhould be filent, I cannot hold my peace. Oh how many black accounts have Chrift and I rounded over together in the houfe of my pilgrimage! and how fat a portion He hath given to a hungry foul! I had rather have Chrift's four-hours,† than have dinner and fupper both in one from any other. His dealing, and the way of His judgments, are paft finding out. No preaching, no book, no learning, could give me that which it behoved me to come and get in this town. But what of all this, if I were not mifted,‡ and

---

* Contefts, oufets.   † Afternoon refrefhment, which was very flight.
‡ Like one in a mift.

confounded, and aftonifhed how to be thankful, and how to get Him praifed for evermore! And, what is more, He hath been pleafed to pain me with His love, and my pain groweth through want of real poffeffion.

Some have written to me, that I am poffibly too joyful of the crofs ; but my joy overleapeth the crofs, it is bounded and terminated upon Chrift. I know that the fun will overcloud and eclipfe, and that I fhall again be put to walk in the fhadow : but Chrift muft be welcome to come and go, as He thinketh meet. Yet He would be more welcome to me, I trow, to come than to go. And I hope He pitieth and pardoneth me, in cafting apples to me at fuch a fainting time as this. Holy and bleffed is His name! It was not my flattering of Chrift that drew a kifs from His mouth. But He would fend me as a fpy into this wildernefs of fuffering, to fee the land and try the ford ; and I cannot make a lie of Chrift's crofs. I can report nothing but good both of Him and it, left others fhould faint. I hope, when a change cometh, to caft anchor at midnight upon the Rock which He hath taught me to know in this day-light ; whither I may run, when I muft fay my leffon without book, and believe in the dark. I am fure it is fin to tarrow* at Chrift's good meat, and not to eat when He faith, " Eat, O well-beloved, and drink abundantly." If He bear me on His back, or carry me in His arms over this water, I hope for grace to fet down my feet on dry ground, when the way is better. But this is flippery ground : my Lord thought good I fhould go by a hold, and lean on my Well-beloved's fhoulder. It is good to be ever taking from Him. I defire that He may get the fruit of praifes, for dawting† and thus dandling me on His knee : and I may give my bond of thankfulnefs, fo being I have Chrift's back-bond ‡ again for my relief, that I fhall be ftrengthened by His powerful grace to pay my vows to Him. But, truly, I find that we have the advantage of the brae upon our

---

* To be pettifh at.   † Fondling.

‡ A bond given after a former bond, declaring the perfon who gave the firft bond free.

enemies : we are more than conquerors through Him who loved us ; and they know not wherein our ſtrength lieth.

Pray for me. Grace be with you.

Your brother in Chriſt,

S. R.

CXIX.—*To* Mr DAVID DICKSON.

(JOYFUL EXPERIENCE—CUP OVERFLOWING IN EXILE.)

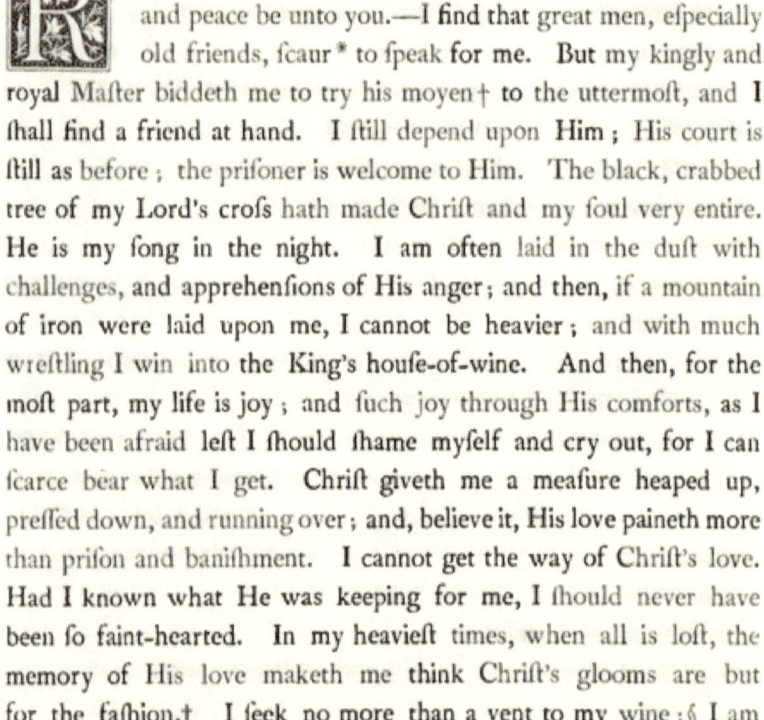

EVEREND AND DEAR BROTHER,—Grace, mercy, and peace be unto you.—I find that great men, eſpecially old friends, ſcaur* to ſpeak for me. But my kingly and royal Maſter biddeth me to try his moyen† to the uttermoſt, and I ſhall find a friend at hand. I ſtill depend upon Him ; His court is ſtill as before ; the priſoner is welcome to Him. The black, crabbed tree of my Lord's croſs hath made Chriſt and my ſoul very entire. He is my ſong in the night. I am often laid in the duſt with challenges, and apprehenſions of His anger; and then, if a mountain of iron were laid upon me, I cannot be heavier ; and with much wreſtling I win into the King's houſe-of-wine. And then, for the moſt part, my life is joy ; and ſuch joy through His comforts, as I have been afraid leſt I ſhould ſhame myſelf and cry out, for I can ſcarce bear what I get. Chriſt giveth me a meaſure heaped up, preſſed down, and running over; and, believe it, His love paineth more than priſon and baniſhment. I cannot get the way of Chriſt's love. Had I known what He was keeping for me, I ſhould never have been ſo faint-hearted. In my heavieſt times, when all is loſt, the memory of His love maketh me think Chriſt's glooms are but for the faſhion.‡ I ſeek no more than a vent to my wine ;§ I am

---

* Are afraid, boggle at. † Means or intereſt.

‡ Frowns for form's ſake. § Alluding to Job xxxii. 19.

fmothered and ready to burft for want of vent. Think not much
of perfecution. It is before you; but it is not as men conceive of
it. My fugared crofs forceth me to fay this to you, ye fhall have
waled* meat. The fick bairn is ofttime the fpilled† bairn; ye fhall
command all the houfe. I hope that ye help a tired prifoner to
praife and pray. Had I but the annual of annual‡ to give to my
Lord Jefus, it would eafe my pain. But, alas! I have nothing to
pay, He will get nothing of poor me; but I am wo that I have
not room enough in my heart for fuch a ftranger. I am not caft
down to go farther north. I have good caufe to work for my
Mafter, for I am well paid beforehand; I am not behind, howbeit
I fhould not get one fmile more till my feet be up within the King's
dining-hall.

I have gone through yours upon the Covenant; § it hath edified
my foul, and refrefhed a hungry man. I judge it fharp, fweet,
quick, and profound. Take me at my word, I fear that it get no
lodging in Scotland.

The brethren of Ireland write not to me; chide with them for
that. I am fure that I may give you and them a commiffion (and
I will abide by it), that you tell my Beloved that I am fick of love.
I hope in God to leave fome of my ruft and fuperfluities in Aberdeen. I cannot get a houfe in this town wherein to leave drink-
filver‖ in my Mafter's name, fave one only. There is no fale for
Chrift in the north; He is like to lie long on my hand, ere any
accept Him. Grace be with you.

Yours, in his fweet Lord Jefus,

S. R.

ABERDEEN.

---

* The beft, felected.   † The fpoilt child.
‡ The fmalleft return, the quit-rent of a quit-rent.
§ Therapeutica Sacra; feu de curandis cafibus confcientiæ circa regenera-
tionem per Fœderum Divinorum applicationem.
‖ A token of regard for kindnefs fhown.

[Matthew Mowat, fon to the Laird of Bufbie (Lett. 133), was minifter of Kilmarnock. He was one of the feven leading minifters in the weft whom the Parliament, after the reftoration of Charles II., brought before them with the view of extorting their acquiefcence in the eftablifhment of Prelacy; which, if effected, it was apprehended would have an influence in leading others to comply. They were all put in prifon, and refufing (though feveral times brought before the Parliament), to take the oath of allegiance without explanation, inasmuch as it involved the oath of fupremacy, they were more feverely treated. Livingftone defcribes Mowat as "one of a meek, fweet difpofition, ftraight and zealous for the truth." Rutherford, who highly valued him, fays in one of his letters, "I cannot fpeak to a man fo fick of love to Chrift as Mr Matthew Mowat;" and in another, "I am greatly in love with Mr Matthew Mowat, for I fee him really ftampt with the image of God." The time of his death is unknown. Some additional notices of him are to be found in Wodrow's *Analecta*, vol. iii.]

(*PLENITUDE OF CHRIST'S LOVE—NEED TO USE GRACE ARIGHT —CHRIST THE RANSOMER—DESIRE TO PROCLAIM HIS GOS-PEL—SHORTCOMINGS AND SUFFERINGS.*)

REVEREND AND DEAR BROTHER,—I am a very far miftaken man. If others knew how poor my ftock was, they would not think upon the like of me, but with compaffion. For I am as one kept under a ftrict tutor; I would have more than my tutor alloweth me. But it is good that a bairn's wit is not the rule which regulateth my Lord Jefus. Let Him give what He will, it fhall aye be above merit, and my ability to gain therewith. I would not wifh a better ftock, whill* heaven be my ftock, than to live upon credit at Chrift's hands, daily borrowing. Surely, running-over love (that vaft, huge, boundlefs love of Chrift that there is telling† in for man and angels!) is the only thing I moft fain would be in hands with. He knoweth that I have little but the love of that love; and that I fhall be happy, fuppofe I never get another heaven but only an eternal, lafting, feaft of that

---

* Till.   † Which will try the fkill of men and angels to eftimate.

love. But suppose my wishes were poor, He is not poor : Christ, all the seasons of the year, is dropping sweetness. If I had vessels, I might fill them ; but my old, riven,* and running-out dish, even when I am at the Well, can bring little away. Nothing but glory will make tight and fast our leaking and rifty† vessels. Alas! I have skailed‡ more of Christ's grace, love, faith, humility, and godly sorrow, than I have brought with me. How little of the sea can a child carry in his hand ! As little dow§ I take away of my great Sea, my boundless and running-over Christ Jesus.

I have not lighted upon the right gate‖ of putting Christ to the bank, and making myself rich with Him. My misguiding and childish trafficking with that matchless Pearl, that heaven's Jewel, the Jewel of the Father's delights, hath put me to a great loss. O that He would take a loan of me, and my stock, and put His name in all my bonds, and serve Himself heir to the poor, mean, portion which I have, and be accountable for the talent Himself! Gladly would I put Christ into my room to guide all ; and let me be but a servant to run errands, and act by His direction. Let me be His interdicted ¶ heir. Lord Jesus, work upon my minority, and let Him win a pupil's blessing. Oh, how would I rejoice to have this work of my salvation legally fastened upon Christ ! A back-bond** of my Lord Jesus that it should be forthcoming to the orphan, would be my happiness. Dependency on Christ were my surest way ; if Christ were my foundation, I were sure enough. I thought the guiding of grace had been no art ;†† I thought it would come of will ; but I would spill‡‡ my own heaven yet, if I had not burdened Christ with all. I but lend my bare name to the sweet covenant ; Christ, behind and before, and on either side, maketh all sure. God will not take an Arminian cautioner.§§ Freewill is a weather-cock, turning at a serpent's tongue, a tutor that cowped‖‖ our Father Adam, unto us ; and brought down the house ; and

---

* Rent.   † Full of rents.   ‡ Spilled.   § Am able to.   ‖ Way.
¶ Forbidden by interdict to enter a possession in the meantime.
** See Let. 118.   †† Required no skill, but would come as I chose.
‡‡ Mar.   §§ Surety.   ‖‖ Overturned, upset.

fold the land ; and fent the father, and mother, and all the bairns
through the earth to beg their bread.   Nature in the Gofpel hath
but a cracked credit.   Oh, well to* my poor foul for evermore, that
my Lord called grace to the council, and put Chrift Jefus, with
free merits and the blood of God, foremoft in the chafe to draw
finners after a Ranfomer !   Oh, what a fweet block† was it by
way of buying and felling, to give and tell down a ranfom for grace
and glory to dyvours !‡   Oh, would to my Lord that I could caufe
paper and ink to fpeak the worth and excellency, the high and
loud praifes of a Brother-ranfomer !   The Ranfomer needeth not
my report, but, oh, if He would take it, and make ufe of it !   I
fhould be happy if I had an errand to this world, but for fome few
years, to fpread proclamations, and outcries, and love-letters of the
highnefs, the highnefs for evermore, the glory, the glory for evermore, of the Ranfomer, whofe clothes were wet and dyed in blood !
albeit, after I had done that, my foul and body fhould go back to
their mother *Nothing* that their Creator brought them once out from,
as from their beginning.   But why fhould I pine away, and pain
myfelf with wifhes ? and not believe, rather, that Chrift will hire
fuch an outcaft as I am, a mafterlefs § body, put out of the houfe
by the fons of my mother, and give me employment and a calling,
one way or other, to fet out Chrift and His wares to country
buyers, and propofe Chrift unto, and prefs Him upon fome poor
fouls, that fainer than their life would receive Him ?

     You complain heavily of " your fhortcoming in practice, and
venturing on fuffering for Chrift."   You have many marrows.||
For the firft, I would put you off a fenfe of wretchednefs.   Hold
on ! Chrift never yet flew a fighing, groaning child : more of that
would make you won goods, ¶ and a meet prey for Chrift.   Alas !
I have too little of it, for venturing on fuffering.   I had not fo much
free gear** when I came to Chrift's camp as to buy a fword.   I

---

* It has been well for my foul.   † Bargain drawn up.   ‡ Debtors.
§ None to own him as under his care. || Many to match you.
¶ Goods already got.   ** Money.

wonder* that Chrift fhould not laugh at fuch a foldier. I am no
better yet ; but faith liveth and fpendeth upon our Captain's charges,
who is able to pay for all. We need not pity Him, He is rich
enough.

Ye defire me alfo " Not to miftake Chrift under a mafk." I
blefs you, and thank God for it. But alas ! mafked or bare-faced,
kiffing or glooming, I miftake Him : yea, I miftake Him the far-
theft when the mafk is off ; for then I play me with His fweetnefs.
I am like a child that hath a gilded book, that playeth with the
ribbons and the gilding, and the picture on the firft page, but readeth
not the contents of it. Certainly, if my defires to my Well-beloved
were fulfilled, I could provoke devils, and croffes, and the world,
and temptations to the field ; but oh ! my poor weaknefs maketh
me lie behind the bufh and hide me.

Remember my fervice and my bleffing to my Lord. I am
mindful of him as I am able. Defire him from a prifoner, to come
and vifit my good Mafter, and feel but the fmell of His love. It
fetteth him† well, howbeit he be young, to make Chrift his garland. I could not wifh him in a better cafe, than in a fever of
love-ficknefs for Chrift.

Remember my bonds. The Lord Jefus be with your fpirit.

Yours in his fweet Lord Jefus,

S. R.

ABERDEEN, 1637.

---◆---

CXXI.—*To* WILLIAM HALLIDAY.

[The name " Halliday" occurs on the tombftones of the old churchyard
of Anwoth. No doubt this correfpondent was one of his flock at Anwoth.
One of the name lies buried in the old churchyard, with the following infcription on her tombftone :—

" *Margaret Halliday*, fpoufe of John Bell in Archland, 1631. O death,

---

* In old editions, it is " *a* wonder," as if in way of exclamation.
† It becomes him.

I will be thy death ! Now is Chrift rifen from the dead, and is the firft fruits of them that . . ." (broken off.)

Archland is the fame place as *Henton*, in the parifh of Anwoth, a notice of which is given at Letter 219, addreffed to this John Bell.]

(*DILIGENCE IN SECURING SALVATION.*)

OVING FRIEND,—I received your letter.—I wifh that ye take pains for falvation. Miftaken grace, and fomewhat like converfion which is not converfion, is the faddeft and moft doleful thing in the world. Make fure of falvation, and lay the foundation fure, for many are beguiled. Put a low price upon the world's clay ; but a high price upon Chrift. Temptations will come , but if they be not made welcome by you, ye have the beft of it. Be jealous over yourfelf and your own heart, and keep touches* with God. Let Him not have a faint and feeble foldier of you. Fear not to back Chrift, for He will conquer and overcome. Let no man fcaur† at Chrift, for I have no quarrels at His crofs ; He and His crofs are two good guefts, and worth the lodging. Men would fain have Chrift good-cheap ;‡ but the market will not come down. Acquaint yourfelf with prayer. Make Chrift your Captain and your armour. Make confcience of finning§ when no eye feeth you. Grace be with you.

Yours, in Chrift Jefus,

ABERDEEN.　　　　　　　　　　　　　　　　　　S. R.

CXXII.—*To a Gentlewoman, after the death of her Hufband.*

(*VANITY OF EARTHLY POSSESSIONS—CHRIST A SUFFICIENT PORTION—DESIGN OF AFFLICTION.*)

EAR AND LOVING SISTER,—I know that ye are minding your fweet country, and not taking your inn, the place of your banifhment, for your home. This

---

* Keep faith with. It is an old Englifh phrafe for "exact performance of agreement."

† Boggle at, go off in fear.　　　　　　　　　　　　　　‡ Gratis.

§ Be confcientious as to finning.

life is not worthy to be the thatch, or outer wall, of the paradife of your Lord Jefus, that He did fweat for to you, and that He keepeth for you. Short, and filly, and fand-blind were our hope, if it could not look over the water to our beft heritage, and if it ftayed only at home about the doors of our clay houfe.

I marvel not, my dear fifter, that ye complain that ye come fhort of your old wreftlings which ye had for a bleffing ; and that now you find it not fo. Bairns are but hired to learn their leffon when they firft go to fchool. And it is enough that thofe who run a race fee the gold only at the ftarting-place ; and poffibly they fee little more of it, or nothing at all till they win to the rinks-end, * and get the gold in the looft† of their hand. Our Lord maketh delicates and dainties of His fweet prefents and love-vifits to His own : but Chrift's love, under a veil, is love. If ye get Chrift, howbeit not the fweet and pleafant way ye would have Him, it is enough ; for the Well-beloved cometh not our way ; He muft wale His own gate‡ Himfelf. For worldly things, feeing there are meadows and fair flowers in your way to heaven, a fmell in the by-going§ is fufficient. He that would reckon and tell all the ftones in his way, in a journey of three or four hundred miles, and write up in his count-book‖ all the herbs and the flowers growing in his way, might come fhort of his journey. You cannot ftay, in your inch of time, to lofe your day (feeing that you are in hafte, and the night and your afternoon will not bide ¶ you), in fetting your heart on this vain world. It were your wifdom to read your account-book,‖ and to have in readinefs your bufinefs, againft the time you come to death's water-fide. I know that your lodging is taken ; your forerunner, Chrift, hath not forgotten that ; and therefore you muft fet yourfelf to your " one thing," which you cannot well want.

In that our Lord took your hufband to Himfelf, I know it was that He might make room for Himfelf. He cutteth off your love to the creature, that ye might learn that God only is the right owner

---

* Get to the end of the courfe.   † Palm of the hand.
‡ Select His own way.   § In the paffing by.   ‖ Journal.   ¶ Wait for.

of your love. Sorrow, lofs, fadnefs, death, are the worft of things that are, except fin. But Chrift knoweth well what to make of them, and can put His own in the crofs's common,* that we fhall be obliged to affliction, and thank God who taught us to make our acquaintance with fuch a rough companion, who can hale us to Chrift. You muft learn to make your evils your great good; and to fpin comforts, peace, joy, communion with Chrift, out of your troubles, which are Chrift's wooers, fent to fpeak for you† to Himfelf. It is eafy to get good words, and a comfortable meffage from our Lord, even from fuch rough ferjeants as divers temptations. Thanks to God for croffes! When we count and reckon our loffes in feeking God, we find that godlinefs is great gain. Great partners of a fhipful of gold are glad to fee the fhip come to the harbour;— furely we, and our Lord Jefus together, have a fhipful of gold coming home, and our gold is in that fhip. Some are fo in love, or, rather, in luft, with this life, that they fell their part of the fhip for a little thing. I would counfel you to buy hope, but fell it not, and give not away your croffes for nothing. The infide of Chrift's crofs is white and joyful, and the far-end of the black crofs is a fair and glorious heaven of eafe. And feeing Chrift hath faftened heaven to the far-end of the crofs, and He will not loofe the knot Himfelf, and none elfe can (for when Chrift cafteth‡ a knot, all the world cannot loofe it), let us then count it exceeding joy when we fall into divers temptations.

Thus recommending you to the tender mercy and grace of our Lord, I reft, your loving brother,

S. R.

ABERDEEN.

———◆———

CXXIII.—*To* JOHN GORDON *of Cardonefs, Younger.*

[JOHN GORDON of Cardonefs, younger, like his father, previoufly noticed (Let. 82), was naturally a man of ftrong paffions. Judging from this letter, he

---

* Put you under deep obligations to the crofs.
† See 1 Kings ii. 18.   ‡ Tieth.

appears not only to have been neglectful of religion, but to have freely indulged in the follies and vices of youth. Rutherford warns him of his sin and danger with much freedom and affectionate earnestness; and these warnings, it is to be hoped, were not in vain. He was in the Covenanters' army in England in 1644, as appears from a letter of his preserved among the Wodrow MSS. It is dated "Sunderland, 28th March 1644," and is addressed to Mr Thomas Wylie. It is written in a religious strain. After referring to the success of the army, and to the account of this drawn up by Mr Robert Douglas, it contains in the close the following passage:—"I entreat you be kind to my wife, and deal with her neither to take my absence, nor the form of coming from her, in evil part; for, in God's presence, public duties and nothing else removed me, or marred the form of my removal. Be earnest with her that she seek a nearer acquaintance with Christ: and fail not to pray for her and her family, and me." (*Wodrow MSS.*, vol. xxix. 4to.)]

(REASONS FOR BEING EARNEST ABOUT THE SOUL, AND FOR RESIGNATION.)

ONOURED AND DEAR BROTHER,—I wrote of late to you : multitudes of letters burden me now. I am refreshed with your letter.

I exhort you in the bowels of Christ, set to work for your soul. And let these bear weight with you, and ponder them seriously : 1*st*, Weeping and gnashing of teeth in utter darkness, or heaven's joy. 2*dly*, Think what ye would give for an hour, when ye shall lie like dead, cold, blackened clay. 3*dly*, There is sand in your glass yet, and your sun is not gone down. 4*thly*, Consider what joy and peace are in Christ's service. 5*thly*, Think what advantage it will be to have angels, the world, life and death, crosses, yea, and devils, all for you, as the King's serjeants and servants, to do your business. 6*thly*, To have mercy on your seed, and a blessing on your house. 7*thly*, To have true honour, and a name on earth that casteth a sweet smell. 8*thly*, How ye will rejoice when Christ layeth down your head under His chin, and betwixt His breasts, and drieth your face, and welcometh you to glory and happiness. 9*thly*, Imagine what pain and torture is a guilty conscience ; what slavery to carry the devil's dishonest loads. 10*thly*, Sin's joys are but night-dreams, thoughts, vapours, imaginations, and shadows. 11*thly*,

What dignity it is to be a fon of God. 12*thly*, Dominion and mastery over temptations, over the world and fin. 13*thly*, That your enemies fhould be the tail, and you the head.

For your bairns, now at reft, I fpeak to you and your wife (and caufe her read this). 1*ft*, I am a witnefs for Barbara's glory in heaven. 2*dly*, For the reft, I write it under my hand, there are days coming on Scotland when barren wombs, and dry breafts, and childlefs parents fhall be pronounced bleffed. They are, then, in the lee of the harbour ere the ftorm come on. 3*dly*, They are not loft to you that are laid up in Chrift's treafury in heaven. 4*thly*, At the refurrection, ye fhall meet with them; thither they are fent before, but not fent away. 5*thly*, Your Lord loveth you, who is homely* to take and give, borrow and lend. 6*thly*, Let not bairns be your idols; for God will be jealous, and take away the idol, becaufe He is greedy of your love wholly.

I blefs you, your wife, and children. Grace for evermore be with you.

Your loving paftor,

S. R.

ABERDEEN.

CXXIV.—*To* JOHN GORDON *of Cardonefs, Elder.*

(CALL TO EARNESTNESS ABOUT SALVATION—INTRUSION OF MINISTERS.)

ONOURABLE, AND DEAREST IN THE LORD,— Your letter hath refrefhed my foul. My joy is fulfilled if Chrift and ye be faft together. Ye are my joy and my crown. Ye know that I have recommended His love to you. I defy the world, Satan, and fin. His love hath neither brim nor bottom in it. My deareft in Chrift, I write my foul's defire to you. Heaven is not at the next door. I find Chriftianity to be a hard tafk; fet to in your evening. We would all keep both Chrift and our

---

* Acts the part of a familiar friend.

right eye, our right hand and foot ; but it will not do with us. I befeech you, by the mercies of God, and your compearance* before Chrift, look Chrift's account-book† and your own together, and collate them.   Give the remnant of your time to your foul.   This great idol-god, the world, will be lying in white afhes on the day of your compearance ;* and why fhould night-dreams, and day-fhadows, and water-froth, and May-flowers run away with your heart ?   When we win to the water-fide, and black death's river-brink, and put our foot into the boat, we fhall laugh at our folly. Sir, I recommend unto you the thoughts of death, and how ye would wifh your foul to be when ye fhall lie cold, blue, ill-fmelling clay.

For any hireling to be intruded, I, being the King's prifoner, can-not fay much ; but, as God's minifter, I defire you to read Acts i. 15, 16, to the end, and Acts vi. 2–5, and ye fhall find that God's people fhould have a voice in choofing church-rulers and teachers. I fhall be forry if, willingly, ye fhall give way to his unlawful intru-fion upon my labours.   The only wife God direct you.

   God's grace be with you.

Your loving paftor,

S. R.

Aberdeen.

❖

CXXV.—To the Lady Forret.

[Lady Forret was, we fuppofe, a " faint in Cæfar's houfehold ;" for Lord Forret (originally Mr David Balfour), was one of Lauderdale's friends, appointed to watch the outed minifters in Fife.   See *Blair's Life*, by Row.]

(SICKNESS A KINDNESS—CHRIST'S GLOOMS BETTER THAN THE WORLD'S JOYS.)

ORTHY MISTRESS,—Grace, mercy, and peace be to you.—I long to hear from you.   I hear Chrift hath been that‡ kind as to vifit you with ficknefs, and to bring

---

* Appearing in court in obedience to a fummons.
† Journal of tranfactions.   ‡ So very kind.

you to the door of the grave : but ye found the door ſhut (bleſſed be His glorious name!) whill* ye be riper for eternity. He will have more ſervice of you ; and, therefore, He seeketh of you that henceforth ye be honeſt to your new Huſband, the Son of God. We have all idol-love, and are whoriſhly inclined to love other things beſide our Lord ; and, therefore, our Lord hunteth for our love more ways than one or two. Oh that Chriſt had His own of us ! I know He will not want you, and that is a ſweet wilfulneſs in His love : and ye have as good cauſe, on the other part, to be headſtrong and peremptory in your love to Chriſt, and not to part, nor divide your love betwixt Him and the world. If it were more, it is little enough, yea, too little for Chriſt.

I am now, every way, in good terms with Chriſt. He hath ſet a baniſhed priſoner as a ſeal on His heart, and as a bracelet on His arm. That crabbed and black tree of the croſs laugheth upon me now ; the alarming noiſe of the croſs is worse than itſelf. I love Chriſt's glooms† better than the world's worm-eaten joys. Oh, if all the kingdom were as I am, except theſe bonds ! My loſs is gain ; my ſadneſs joyful ; my bonds, liberty ; my tears comfortable. This world is not worth a drink of cold water. Oh, but Chriſt's love caſteth a great heat ! Hell, and all the ſalt ſea, and the rivers of the earth, cannot quench it.

I remember you to God ; ye have the prayers of a priſoner of Chriſt. Grace, grace, be with you.

                 Yours, in his ſweet Lord Jeſus,

                                     S. R.

ABERDEEN, *March* 9, 1637.

---

* Till.   † Frowns.

*(ADHERENCE TO DUTY AMIDST OPPOSITION—POWER OF
CHRIST'S LOVE.)*

LOVING AND DEAR SISTER,—Grace, mercy, and
peace be to you. Your letter hath refreſhed my ſoul.
You ſhall not have my advice to make haſte to go out
of that town ; for if you remove out of Kirkcudbright, they will
eaſily undo all. You are at God's work, and in His way there.
Be ſtrong in the Lord ; the devil is weaker than you are, becauſe
ſtronger is He that is in you than he that is in the world. Your
care of and love ſhowed towards me, now a priſoner of Chriſt, is
laid up for you in heaven, and you ſhall know that it is come up in
remembrance before God.

Pray, pray for my deſolate flock ; and give them your counſel,
when you meet with any of them. It ſhall be my grief to hear that
a wolf enter in upon my labours ; but if the Lord permit it, I am
ſilent. My ſky ſhall clear, for Chriſt layeth my head in His boſom,
and admitteth me to lean there. I never knew before what His
love was in ſuch a meaſure. If He leave me, He leaveth me in
pain, and ſick of love ; and yet my ſickneſs is my life and health.
I have a fire within me , I defy all the devils in hell and all the
prelates in Scotland, to caſt water on it.

I rejoice at your courage and faith. Pray ſtill, as if I were on
my journey to come and be your paſtor. What iron gates or bars
are able to ſtand it out againſt Chriſt ? for when He bloweth, they
open to Him.

I remember your huſband. Grace, grace, be with you.

Yours, in his ſweet Lord Jeſus,

S. R.

ABERDEEN, *March* 11, 1637.

CXXVII.—*To* JOHN CARSEN.

[JOHN CARSEN was the fon of Andrew Carfen, merchant and burgefs of Kirkcudbright. He was retoured heir of his father 13th May 1635.—*Inquir. Gener. No.* 2121. There are ftill feveral of the name in Kirkcudbright, and it is found often in the churchyard. There is " Bailie John Carfen" in the " Minute-book of Comm. of Covenanters," along with Bailie Ewart ; and is called " Carfen of *Senwick.*"]

(*NOTHING WORTH THE FINDING, BUT CHRIST.*)

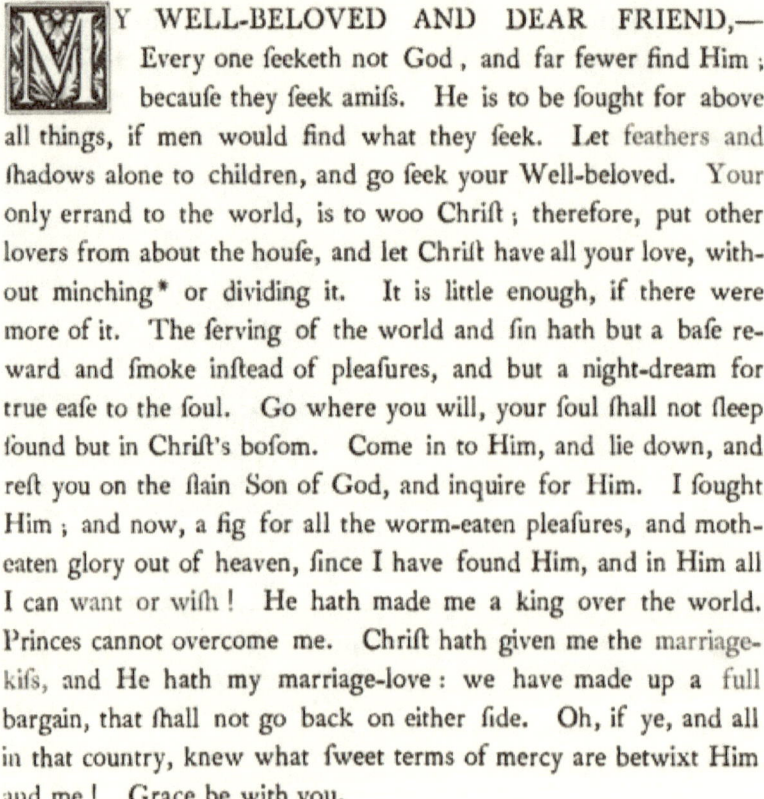Y WELL-BELOVED AND DEAR FRIEND,— Every one feeketh not God , and far fewer find Him ; becaufe they feek amifs. He is to be fought for above all things, if men would find what they feek. Let feathers and fhadows alone to children, and go feek your Well-beloved. Your only errand to the world, is to woo Chrift ; therefore, put other lovers from about the houfe, and let Chrift have all your love, without minching* or dividing it. It is little enough, if there were more of it. The ferving of the world and fin hath but a bafe reward and fmoke inftead of pleafures, and but a night-dream for true eafe to the foul. Go where you will, your foul fhall not fleep found but in Chrift's bofom. Come in to Him, and lie down, and reft you on the flain Son of God, and inquire for Him. I fought Him ; and now, a fig for all the worm-eaten pleafures, and moth-eaten glory out of heaven, fince I have found Him, and in Him all I can want or wifh ! He hath made me a king over the world. Princes cannot overcome me. Chrift hath given me the marriage-kifs, and He hath my marriage-love : we have made up a full bargain, that fhall not go back on either fide. Oh, if ye, and all in that country, knew what fweet terms of mercy are betwixt Him and me ! Grace be with you.

Yours, in his fweet Lord Jefus,

ABERDEEN, *March* 11, 1637.   S. R.

---

* Cutting into fmall pieces.

CXXVIII.—*To the* EARL OF CASSILLIS.

[JOHN KENNEDY, fixth EARL OF CASSILLIS, was the fon of Gilbert Kennedy, mafter of Caffillis (which is fix miles from AYR), third fon of Gilbert, fourth Earl of Caffillis. He was ferved heir to his uncle, John, fifth Earl of Caffillis, in 1616. His Lordfhip was a perfon of confiderable talents, of great virtue, and a zealous Covenanter. Having ftudied under Dr Cameron, Principal of the College of Glafgow, a great defender of abfolute government, he could not yield to fome claufes in the firft draught of The Covenant, which feemed to vindicate the ufe of defenfive arms againft the King; but he agreed to the Covenant as it now ftands. He fat in the Glafgow Affembly, 1638, being returned as elder by the Prefbytery of AYR; and was one of the three ruling elders fent to the Affembly of Divines at Weftminfter in 1643. He was one of the commiffioners who, in March 1650, went from Scotland to Breda, to treat with Charles II., and who returned 23d June that year, bringing his Majefty along with them. He attended at the crowning of Charles at Scoone, January 1, 1651. So ftrongly attached was he to the royal family, that when Cromwell, at one time, fummoned him to a meeting, inftead of attending it, he, along with fome minifters and his chaplain, kept a day of fafting and prayer in his family. Such was his hoftility to the meafures of the court, in eftablifhing Prelacy and in ejecting the Prefbyterian minifters from their charges for non-conformity, that he would fcarce ever pay ftipend to any of the curates intruded into their places till he got a charge of horning. Wodrow defignates him " the great and worthy Earl of Caffillis." " I have this account," fays he, " of the Earl of Caffillis, that he was fingularly pious, and a man of a very high fpirit, who carried with a great ftate and majefty. His carriage in his family was moft exemplary and religious. He was very much in fecret duty, and had his hours wherein none had accefs to him. Upon the Sabbath his carriage was fingular. He ufually wrote the fermon, and at night caufed his chaplain to examine all his fervants and his children, even after they were pretty big, upon the fermon; and every one behoved to give their notes; and after all, many times he took out his own papers and read to them. When at Edinburgh, Lauderdale fent a fervant to him upon a Sabbath night, telling him he was coming to wait on him. Prefently he called Mr Violant, his chaplain, and ordered him to go out and meet Lauderdale, and tell him that if he defigned a Sabbath day's vifit he was very welcome, but he would difcourfe upon no other thing with him but what was fuitable to the day. Lauderdale came up, and difcourfed with him,—as he could very well do,—only upon points of divinity." (*Wodrow's Analecta.*) His Lordfhip died at his own houfe in the Weft in 1668.

The manfion is a peculiar edifice, near Dalrymple. It is on the banks of the Doon, and embofomed in wood, with the hill called *The Dounans* facing the houfe. It is a confufed pile of building. A long avenue of fine old trees leads up to it.]

(HONOUR OF TESTIFYING FOR CHRIST.)

Y VERY NOBLE AND HONOURABLE LORD,
—I make bold (out of the honourable and Chriftian report I hear of your Lordfhip, having no other thing to fay but that which concerneth the honourable caufe which the Lord hath enabled your Lordfhip to profefs) to write this, that it is your Lordfhip's crown, your glory, and your honour, to fet your fhoulder under the Lord's glory, now falling to the ground, and to back Chrift now, when fo many think it wifdom to let Him fend* for Himfelf. The fhields of the earth ever did, and do ftill believe that Chrift is a cumberfome neighbour, and that it is a pain to hold up His yeas and nays. They fear that He take their chariots, and their crowns, and their honour from them ; but my Lord ftandeth in need of none of them all. But it is your glory to own Chrift and His buried truth ; for, let men fay what they pleafe, the plea with Zion's enemies in this day of Jacob's trouble is, if Chrift fhould be King, and no mouth fpeak laws but His ? It concerneth the apple of Chrift's eye, and His royal privileges, what is now debated ; and Chrift's kingly honour is come to yea and nay. But let me be pardoned, my dear and noble Lord, when I befeech you by the mercies of God, by the comfort of the Spirit, by the wounds of our dear Saviour, by your compearance† before the Judge of quick and dead, to ftand for Chrift, and to back Him.‡ Oh, if the nobles had done their part, and been zealous for the Lord ! it had not been as it is now. But men think it wifdom to ftand befide Chrift till His head be broken, and fing dumb.§ There is a time coming when Chrift will have a thick‖ court, and He will be the glory of

---

* Provide for, fhift for.   † Appearing when fummoned.
‡ Help, fecond Him in what He does.   § Be reduced to filence.
‖ Crowded.

Scotland; and He will make a diadem, a garland, a feal upon His heart, and a ring upon His finger, of thofe who have avouched Him before this faithlefs generation. Howbeit, ere that come, wrath from the Lord is ordained for this land.

My Lord, I have caufe to write this to your Lordfhip; for I dare not conceal His kindnefs to the foul of an afflicted, exiled prifoner. Who hath more caufe to boaft in the Lord than fuch a finner as I, who am feafted with the confolations of Chrift, and have no pain in my fufferings, but the pain of foul-ficknefs of love for Chrift, and forrow that I cannot help to found aloud the praifes of Him who hath heard the fighing of the prifoner, and is content to lay the head of His opprefled fervant in His bofom, under His chin, and let Him feel the fmell of His garments? It behoved me to write this, that your Lordfhip might know that Chrift is as good as He is called; and to teftify to your Lordfhip, that the caufe, which your Lordfhip now profeffeth before the faithlefs world, is Chrift's, and that your Lordfhip fhall have no fhame of it.

Grace be with you.

Your Lordfhip's obliged fervant,

S. R.

ABERDEEN, *March* 13, 1637.

* * *

CXXIX.—*To* MR ROBERT GORDON, *Bailie of Ayr.*

[ROBERT GORDON was a merchant in Ayr. In Paterfon's *Hiftory of the County of Ayr*, he and his partner merchants are mentioned as having, in 1644, fupplied the Scots army in Ireland, at a certain price, with a large quantity of meal and beans. He was coufin to John, Vifcount of Kenmure, whofe " Laft and Heavenly Speeches and Glorious Departure " were publifhed by Ruther-ford, and to which there is a reference in the beginning of this letter. This appears from the following quotations from thefe Speeches:—" To a coufin (Robert Gordon, bailie of Ayr), he faid, ' Robert, I know you have light and underftanding; and though you have no need to be inftructed by me, yet have you need to be incited'" (p. 94). Gordon was frequently a member of the Town Council of Ayr. In the Records, he appears in 1631 as Dean of Guild, and in 1632 as Bailie. In 1638, and 1647, he held the office of Pro-

voſt.   He was a man of piety, and a zealous ſupporter of the Preſbyterian
cauſe.   In an old parchment copy of the National Covenant 1638 (in the
poſſeſſion of Hugh Cowan, Eſquire, Ayr), Gordon's ſignature appears, as
well as the ſignatures of the other members of the Town Council, ſome of
whom were Rutherford's correſpondents, as John Kennedy, John Oſburn,
and John Stewart.   The above copy of the National Covenant is ſigned by
Rothes, Montroſe, and other men of rank, being one of the copies ſent at that
time by the Covenanters from Edinburgh to the various burghs throughout
the country to be ſubſcribed.]

(CHRIST ABOVE ALL.)

WORTHY SIR,—Grace, mercy, and peace be to you.—I
long to hear from you on paper.   Remember your
chief's ſpeeches* on his death-bed.   I pray you, ſir, ſell
all, and buy the Pearl.   Time will cut you from this world's glory;
look what will do you good, when your glaſs ſhall be run out.
And let Chriſt's love bear moſt court in your ſoul, and that court
will bear down the love of other things.   Chriſt ſeeketh your help
in your place; give Him your hand.   Who hath more cauſe to encourage others to own Chriſt than I have? for He hath made me
ſick of love, and left me in pain to wreſtle with His love.   And love
is like to fall afwoon through His abſence.   I mean not that He
deſerteth me, or that I am ebb† of comforts; but this is an unco‡
pain.   O that I had a heart and a love to render to Him back
again!   Oh, if principalities and powers, thrones and dominions,
and all the world would help me to praiſe!   Praiſe Him in my
behalf.

Remember my love to your wife.   I thank you moſt kindly
for your love to my brother.   Grace be with you.

Yours, in his ſweet Lord Jeſus,

S. R.

ABERDEEN, *March* 13, 1637.

---

* The words of Lord Kenmure.   † At a low tide in reſpect of.
‡ Strange.

(*CHRIST'S LOVE—THE THREE WONDERS—DESIRES FOR HIS SECOND COMING.*)

RACE, mercy, and peace be to you. Your not writing to me cannot bind me up from remembering you now and then, that at leaſt ye may be a witneſs, and a third man, to behold on paper what is betwixt Chriſt and me. I was in His eyes like a young orphan, wanting known parents, caſten out in the open fields; either Chriſt behoved to take me up, and to bring me home to His houſe and fireſide, elſe I had died in the fields. And now I am homely* with Chriſt's love, ſo that I think the houſe mine own, and the Maſter of the houſe mine alſo. Chriſt inquired not, when He began to love me, whether I was fair, or black, or ſun-burnt; love taketh what it may have. He loved me before this time, I know; but now I have the flower of His love; His love is come to a fair bloom, like a young roſe opened up out of the green leaves; and it caſteth a ſtrong and fragrant ſmell. I want nothing but ways of expreſſing Chriſt's love. A full veſſel would have a vent. Oh, if I could ſmoke out, and caſt out coals, to make a fire in many breaſts of this land! Oh! it is a pity that there were not many impriſoned for Chriſt, were it for no other purpoſe than to write books and love-ſongs of the love of Chriſt. This love would keep all created tongues of men and angels in exerciſe, and buſy night and day, to ſpeak of it. Alas! I can ſpeak nothing of it, but wonder at three things in His love :—*Firſt,* freedom. Oh that lumps of ſin ſhould get ſuch love for nothing! *Secondly,* the ſweetneſs of His love. I give over either to ſpeak or write of it; but thoſe that feel it, may better bear witneſs what it is. But it is ſo ſweet, that, next to

---

* At home with, on no ceremony with.

Chrift Himfelf, nothing can match it. Nay, I think that a foul
could live eternally bleffed only on Chrift's love, and feed upon no
other thing. Yea, when Chrift in love giveth a blow, it doeth a
foul good; and it is a kind of comfort and joy to it to get a cuff *
with the lovely, fweet, and foft hand of Jefus. And, *thirdly,* what
power and ftrength are in His love! I am perfuaded it can climb
a fteep hill, with hell upon its back; and fwim through water and
not drown; and fing in the fire, and find no pain; and triumph in
loffes, prifons, forrows, exile, difgrace, and laugh and rejoice in
death. O for a year's leafe of the fenfe of His love without a
cloud, to try what Chrift is! O for the coming of the Bridegroom! O, when fhall I fee the Bridegroom and the Bride meet
in the clouds, and kifs each other! O, when will we get our day,
and our heart's fill of that love! O, if it were lawful to complain
of the famine of that love, and want of the immediate vifion of God!
O time, time! how doft thou torment the fouls of thofe that would
be fwallowed up of Chrift's love, becaufe thou moveft fo flowly!
Oh, if He would pity a poor prifoner, and blow love upon me, and
give a prifoner a tafte or draught of that fweetnefs, which is glory
as it were begun, to be a confirmation that Chrift and I fhall have
our fill of each other for ever! Come hither, O love of Chrift,
that I may once kifs thee before I die! What would I not give to
have time, that lieth betwixt Chrift and me, taken out of the way,
that we might once meet! I cannot think but that, at the firft
fight I fhall fee of that moft lovely and faireft face, love will come
out of His two eyes, and fill me with aftonifhment. I would but
defire to ftand at the outer fide of the gates of the New Jerufalem,
and look through a hole of the door, and fee Chrift's face. A
borrowed vifion in this life would be my borrowed and begun
heaven, whill† the long, long-looked-for day dawn. It is not for
nothing that it is faid, "Chrift in you the hope of glory."‡ I will
be content of no pawn of heaven but Chrift Himfelf; for Chrift,
poffeffed by faith here, is young heaven, and glory in the bud. If

---

* A blow.   † Till.   ‡ Col. i. 27.

I had that pawn, I would bide horning* and hell both, ere I gave
it again. All that we have here is fcarce the picture of glory.
Should not we young bairns long and look for the expiring of our
minority? It were good to be daily begging propines† and love-
gifts, and the Bridegroom's favours; and, if we can do no more, to
feek crumbs, and hungry dinners of Chrift's love, to keep the tafte
of heaven in our mouth whill‡ fupper-time. I know it is far after
noon, and nigh the marriage-fupper of the Lamb; the table is
covered already. O Well-beloved, run, run faft! O fair day,
when wilt thou dawn! O fhadows, flee away! I think hope and
love, woven through other,§ make our abfence from Chrift fpiritual
torment. It is a pain to wait on; but hope that maketh not afhamed
fwalloweth up that pain. It is not unkindnefs that keepeth Chrift
and us fo long afunder. What can I fay to Chrift's love? I think
more than I can fay. To confider, that when my Lord Jefus may
take the air (if I may fo fpeak), and go abroad, yet He will be
confined and keep the prifon with me! But, in all this fweet communion with Him, what am I to be thanked for? I am but a
fufferer. Whether I will or not, He will be kind to me; as if He
had defied my guiltinefs to make Him unkind, He fo beareth His
love in on me. Here I die with wondering, that juftice hindereth
not love; for there are none in hell, nor out of hell, more unworthy
of Chrift's love. Shame may confound and fcaur‖ me once to hold
up my black mouth to receive one of Chrift's undeferved kiffes. If
my innerfide were turned out, and all men faw my vilenefs, they
would fay to me, "It is a fhame for thee to ftand ftill whill‡ Chrift
kifs thee and embrace thee." It would feem to become me rather
to run away from His love, as afhamed at my own unworthinefs;
nay, I may think fhame to take heaven, who have fo highly provoked my Lord Jefus. But feeing Chrift's love will fhame me, I
am content to be fhamed. My defire is, that my Lord would give

---

* A legal demand for payment of a debt, under threat of imprifonment if
difregarded. It ufed to be made with three blafts of a horn in the market-
place.

   † Prefents.   ‡ Till.   § Through one another.   ‖ Make afraid.

me broader and deeper thoughts, to feed myſelf with wondering at
His love. I would I could weigh it, but I have no balance for it.
When I have worn my tongue to the ſtump, in praiſing of Chriſt,
I have done nothing to Him. I muſt let Him alone, for my
withered arms will not go about His high, wide, long, and broad
love. What remaineth, then, but that my debt to the love of Chriſt
lie unpaid for all eternity? All that are in heaven are black-ſhamed*
with His love as well as I. We muſt all be dyvours† together ;
and the bleſſing of that houſeful, or heavenful, of dyvours† ſhall
reſt for ever upon Him. Oh, if this land and nation would come
and ſtand beſide His inconceivable and glorious perfections, and
look in, and love, and adore! Would to God I could bring in
many lovers to Chriſt's houſe! But this nation hath forſaken the
Fountain of living waters. Lord, caſt not water on Scotland's coal.
Wo, wo will be to this land, becauſe of the day of the Lord's fierce
anger that is ſo faſt coming.

Grace be with you.

Your affectionate brother, in our Lord Jeſus,

S. R.

ABERDEEN.

CXXXI.—*To* JEAN BROWN.

(HIS WISDOM IN OUR TRIALS—REJOICE IN TRIBULATION.)

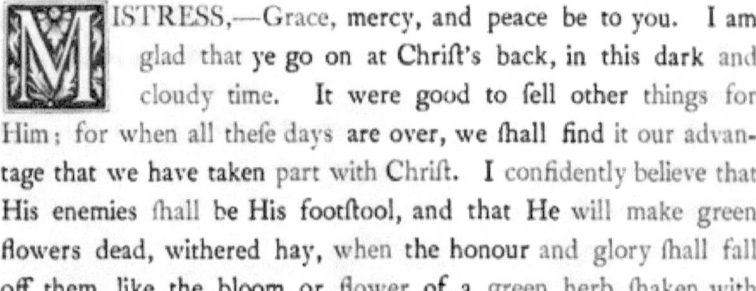 ISTRESS,—Grace, mercy, and peace be to you. I am
glad that ye go on at Chriſt's back, in this dark and
cloudy time. It were good to ſell other things for
Him ; for when all theſe days are over, we ſhall find it our advantage that we have taken part with Chriſt. I confidently believe that
His enemies ſhall be His footſtool, and that He will make green
flowers dead, withered hay, when the honour and glory ſhall fall
off them, like the bloom or flower of a green herb ſhaken with

---

* Made black with ſhame.   † Debtors.

the wind. It were not wifdom for us to think that Chrift and the Gofpel would come and fit down at our firefide ; nay, but we muft go out of our own warm houfes, and feek Chrift and His Gofpel. It is not the funny fide of Chrift that we muft look to, and we muft not forfake Him for want of that; but muft fet our face againft what may befall us in following on, till He and we be through the briers and bufhes, on the dry ground. Our foft nature would be borne through the troubles of this miferable life in Chrift's arms ; and it is His wifdom, who knoweth our mould, that His bairns go wet-fhod and cold-footed to heaven. Oh, how fweet a thing were it for us to learn to make our burdens light, by framing our hearts to the burden, and making our Lord's will a law!

I find Chrift and His crofs not fo ill* to pleafe, nor yet fuch troublefome guefts, as men call them ; nay, I think patience fhould make the water which Chrift giveth us good wine, and His drofs good metal. And we have caufe to wait on ; for, ere it be long, our Mafter will be at us, and bring this whole world out, before the fun and daylight, in their blacks and whites. Happy are they who are found watching. Our fand-glafs is not fo long as we need to weary ; time will eat away and root out our woes and forrow. Our heaven is in the bud, and growing up to an harveft. Why then fhould we not follow on, feeing our fpan-length of time will come to an inch? Therefore I commend Chrift to you, as your laft-living, and longeft-living Hufband, and the ftaff of your old age. Let Him now have the reft of your days. And think not much of a ftorm upon the fhip that Chrift faileth in : there fhall no paffenger fall overboard ; but the crazed fhip and the fea-fick paffengers fhall come to land fafe.

I am in as fweet communion with Chrift as a poor finner can be ; and am only pained that HE hath much beauty and fairnefs, and *I* little love ; HE great power and mercy, and *I* little faith ; HE much light, and *I* bleared eyes. O that I faw Him in the fweetnefs of His love, and in His marriage-clothes, and were over head and ears in love

---

* Difficult.

with that princely one, Chrift Jefus my Lord! Alas, my riven* difh, and the running-out veffel, can hold little of Chrift Jefus!

I have joy in this, that I would not refufe death before† I put Chrift's lawful heritage in men's tryfting; and what know I, if they would have pleafed both Chrift and me? Alas, that this land hath put Chrift to open rouping,‡ and to an "Any man bids more?" Bleffed are they who would hold the crown on His head, and buy Chrift's honour with their own loffes.

I rejoice to hear that your fon John§ is coming to vifit Chrift, and tafte of His love. I hope that he will not lofe his pains, nor rue of that choice. I had always (as I faid often to you) a great love to dear Mr John Brown, becaufe I thought I faw Chrift in him more than in his brethren. Fain would I write to him, to ftand by my fweet Mafter; and I wifh ye would let him read my letter, and the joy I fhall have if he will appear for, and fide with, my Lord Jefus. Grace be with you.

> Yours, in his fweet Jefus,
>
> S. R.

ABERDEEN, *March* 13, 1637.

------◆------

CXXXII.—*To* JEAN MACMILLAN.

[There were Macmillans at Dalfhangan, near Carfphairn, noted as Covenanters. But the name is a common one, and this correfpondent was probably an Anwoth parifhioner.]

(*STRIVE TO ENTER IN.*)

LOVING SISTER,—Grace, mercy, and peace be to you. I cannot come to you to give you my counfel; and howbeit I would come, I cannot ftay with you. But I be-

---

* Rent, cracked.

† I would die, ere ever I would put Chrift's property at the difpofal of men who may choofe to appoint their own times.

‡ Public fale by auƈtion.

§ This was he who was afterwards fo well known as an eminent Chriftian, Brown of Wamphray.

feech you to keep Chrift, for I did what I could to put you within grips* of Him. I told you Chrift's teftament and latter-will plainly, and I kept nothing back that my Lord gave me ; and I gave Chrift to you with good will. I pray you to make Him your own, and go not from that truth which I taught you, in one hair-breadth. That truth will fave you if you follow it. Salvation is not an eafy thing, and foon gotten. I often told you that few are faved, and many damned : I pray you to make your poor foul fure of falvation, and the feeking of heaven your daily tafk. If ye never had a fick night and a pained foul for fin, ye have not yet lighted upon Chrift. Look to the right marks of having clofed with Chrift. If ye love Him better than the world, and would quit all the world for Him, then that faith the work is found. Oh, if ye faw the beauty of Jefus, and fmelled the fragrance of His love, you would run through fire and water to be at Him! God fend you Him.

Pray for me, for I cannot forget you. Grace be with you.

Your loving paftor,

S. R.

ABERDEEN, 1637.

---◆---

CXXXIII.—*To the* LADY BUSBIE.

[LADY BUSBIE is probably the mother-in-law of R. Blair, Rutherford's intimate friend. R. Blair married Catherine, daughter of Hugh Montgomery, Laird of Bufbie, near Glafgow, in 1635.]

(*COMPLETE SURRENDER TO CHRIST—NO IDOLS—TRIALS DIS-COVER SINS—A FREE SALVATION—THE MARRIAGE SUPPER.*)

MISTRESS,—Grace, mercy, and peace be to you.—I am glad to hear that Chrift and ye are one, and that ye have made Him your " one thing," whereas many are painfully toiled in feeking many things, and their many things are

---

* Reach, grafp.

nothing. It is only beft that ye fet yourfelf apart, as a thing laid up and out of the gate,* for Chrift alone; for ye are good for no other thing than Chrift; and He hath been going about you thefe many years, by afflictions, to engage you to Himfelf. It were a pity and a lofs to fay Him nay. Verily I could wifh that I could fwim through hell, and all the ill weather in the world, and Chrift in my arms. But it is my evil and folly, that except Chrift come unfent for, I dow† not go to feek Him: when He and I fall a-reckoning, we are both behind, He in payment, and I in counting; and fo marches‡ lie ftill unredd,§ and accounts uncleared betwixt us. Oh that He would take His own blood for counts and mifcounts, ‖ that I might be a free man, and none had any claim to me but only, only Jefus. I will think it no bondage to be rouped, ¶ comprifed,** and poffeffed by Chrift as His bondman.

Think well of the vifitation of your Lord; for I find one thing, which I faw not well before, that when the faints are under trials, and well humbled, little fins raife great cries and war-fhouts in the confcience; and in profperity, confcience is a pope, to give difpenfa-tions, and let out and in, and give latitude and elbow-room to our heart. Oh, how little care we for pardon at Chrift's hand, when we make difpenfations! And all is but bairns' play, till a crofs without beget a heavier crofs within, and then we play no longer with our idols. It is good ftill†† to be fevere againft ourfelves; for we but transform God's mercy into an idol, and an idol that hath a difpenfation to give, for the turning of the grace of God into wantonnefs. Happy are they who take up God, wrath, juftice, and fin, as they are in themfelves; for we have mifcarrying light, that parteth with the child, when we have good refolutions only. But, God be thanked, that falvation is not rolled upon our wheels.

Oh, but Chrift hath a faving eye! falvation is in His eyelids! When He firft looked on me, I was faved; it coft Him but a look

---

* Out of the way.   † Cannot.   ‡ Boundaries.   § Undefined.
‖ Erroneous reckonings.   ¶ Set up to public fale by auction.
** Seized for debt.   †† Always.

to make hell quit of me! Oh, but merits, free merits, and the dear blood of God, were the beſt gate* that ever we could have gotten out of hell! Oh what a ſweet, oh what a ſafe and ſure way is it, to come out of hell leaning on a Saviour! That Chriſt and a ſinner ſhould be one, and have heaven betwixt them, and be halvers of ſalvation, is the wonder of ſalvation. What more humble could love be? And what an excellent ſmell doth Chriſt caſt on His lower garden, where there grow but wild flowers, if we ſpeak by way of compariſon. But there is nothing but perfeċt garden flowers in heaven, and the beſt pleniſhing† that is there is Chriſt. We are all obliged to love heaven for Chriſt's ſake. He graceth heaven, and all His Father's houſe, with His preſence. He is a Roſe that beautifieth all the upper garden of God; a leaf of that Roſe of God for ſmell is worth a world. O that He would blow His ſmell upon a withered and dead ſoul! Let us, then, go on to meet with Him, and to be filled with the ſweetneſs of His love. Nothing will hold Him from us. He hath decreed to put time, ſin, hell, devils, men, and death out of the way, and to rid‡ the rough way betwixt us and Him, that we may enjoy one another. It is ſtrange and wonderful, that He would think long§ in heaven without us; and that He would have the company of ſinners to ſolace and delight Himſelf withal in heaven. And now the ſupper is abiding us. Chriſt, the Bridegroom, with deſire is waiting on, till the bride, the Lamb's wife, be buſked‖ for the marriage, and the great hall be redd¶ for the meeting of that joyful couple. Oh, fools! what do we here? and why ſit we ſtill? Why ſleep we in the priſon? Were it not beſt to make us wings, to flee up to our bleſſed Match, our Marrow,** and our fellow Friend?

I think, Miſtreſs, that ye are looking thereaway,†† and that this is your ſecond or third thought. Make forward; your Guide waiteth on you.

---

* Way, manner.   † Furniture of a houſe.   ‡ Annihilate.
§ Have a longing heart.   ‖ Decked with ornaments.   ¶ Cleared out.
** Partner.   †† To that quarter.

· I cannot but blefs you for your care and kindnefs to the faints. God give you to find mercy, in that day of our Lord Jefus; to whofe faving grace I recommend you.

Yours, in our Lord Jefus,

S. R.

ABERDEEN, 1637.

------◆------

CXXXIV.—*To* JOHN EWART, *Bailie of Kirkcudbright.*

[JOHN EWART's name often occurs in the " Minute Book of Comm. of Covenanters," as refiding in Kirkcudbright. He is underftood to be the father of the John Ewart who was fentenced to banifhment, 1663, for refufing to take part in quelling a tumult raifed at the intrufion of a curate in room of the ejected minifter of Kirkcudbright.—(*Wodrow's Hiſt.*) A defcendant of his at Stranraer has a fmall filver cup, which has been handed down as once belonging to his anceftors.]

(THE CROSS NO BURDEN—NEED OF SURE FOUNDATION.)

Y VERY WORTHY AND DEAR FRIEND,—I cannot but moft kindly thank you for the expreffions of your love. Your love and refpect to me is a great comfort to me.

I blefs His high and glorious name, that the terrors of great men have not affrighted me from openly avouching the Son of God. Nay, His crofs is the fweeteft burden that ever I bare; it is fuch a burden as wings are to a bird, or fails are to a fhip, to carry me forward to my harbour. I have not much caufe to fall in love with the world; but rather to wifh that He who fitteth upon the floods would bring my broken fhip to land, and keep my confcience fafe in thefe dangerous times; for wrath from the Lord is coming on this finful land.

It were good that we prifoners of hope know of our ftronghold to run to, before the ftorm come on; therefore, Sir, I befeech you by the mercies of God, and comforts of His Spirit, by the blood of your Saviour, and by your compearance * before the fin-revenging Judge of the world, keep your garments clean, and ftand for the truth of Chrift, which ye profefs. When the time fhall come that your eye-ftrings fhall break, your face wax pale, your breath grow cold, and this houfe of clay fhall totter, and your one foot fhall be over the march,† in eternity, it will be your comfort and joy that ye gave your name to Chrift. The greateft part of the world think heaven at the next door, and that Chriftianity is an eafy tafk ; but they will be beguiled. Worthy Sir, I befeech you, make fure work of falvation. I have found by experience, that all I could do hath had much ado‡ in the day of my trial ; and, therefore, lay up a fure foundation for the time to come.

I cannot requite you for your undeferved favours to me and my now afflicted brother. But I truft to remember you to God. Remember me heartily to your kind wife.

Yours, in his only Lord Jefus,

S. R.

ABERDEEN, *March* 13, 1637.

------◆------

CXXXV.—*To* WILLIAM FULLERTON, *Provoft of Kirkcudbright.*

(*FEAR NOT THEM WHO KILL THE BODY—UNEXPECTED FAVOUR.*)

MUCH HONOURED SIR,—Grace, mercy, and peace be to you. I am much obliged to your love in God. I befeech you, Sir, let nothing be fo dear to you as Chrift's truth, for falvation is worth all the world ; and, therefore, be not afraid of men that fhall die. The Lord will do for you § in your fuffering for Him, and will blefs your houfe and feed ; and ye have God's promife, that ye fhall have His prefence in fire, water, and in feven tribulations. Your day fhall wear to an end, and your

---

* Appearance in court in obedience to a fummons.   † Boundary.
‡ My utmoft ftrength is hard put to.   § Act for.

fun go down. In death it will be your joy that ye have ventured all ye have for Chrift; and there is not a promife of heaven made but to fuch as are willing to fuffer for it. It is a caftle taken by force. This earth is but the clay portion of baftards; and, therefore, no wonder that the world fmile on its own; but better things are laid up for His lawfully-begotten bairns, whom the world hateth.

I have experience to fpeak this; for I would not exchange my prifon and fad nights with the court, honour, and eafe of my adverfaries. My Lord is pleafed to make many unknown faces to laugh upon me, and to provide a lodging for me; and He Himfelf vifiteth my foul with feafts of fpiritual comforts. Oh how fweet a Mafter is Chrift! Bleffed are they who lay down all for Him.

I thank you kindly for your love to my diftreffed brother. Ye have the bleffing and prayers of the prifoner of Chrift to you, your wife and your children.

Remember my love and bleffing to William and Samuel. I defire them in their youth to feek the Lord, and to fear His great name; to pray twice a-day, at leaft, to God, and to read God's word; to keep themfelves from curfing, lying, and filthy talking.

Now the only wife God, and the prefence of the Son of God, be with you all.

Yours in his fweet Lord Jefus,

S. R.

ABERDEEN, *March* 13, 1637.

CXXXVI.—*To* ROBERT GLENDINNING, *Minifter of Kirkcudbright.*

(*PREPARE TO MEET THY GOD—CHRIST HIS JOY.*)

Y DEAR FRIEND,—Grace, mercy, and peace be to you. I thank you moft kindly for your care of me, and your love and refpective * kindnefs to my brother in

---

* Perhaps this word means kindnefs that had refpect to his fpecial needs.

his diftrefs. I pray the Lord that ye may find mercy in the day of Chrift ; and I entreat you, Sir, to confider the times which ye live in, and that your foul is more worth to you than the whole world, which, in the day of the blowing of the Laft Trumpet, fhall lie in white afhes, as an old caftle burned to nothing. And remember that judgment and eternity is before you. My dear and worthy friend, let me entreat you in Chrift's name, and by the falvation of your foul, and by your compearance* before the dreadful and fin-revenging Judge of the world, to make your accounts ready. Redd† them ere ye come to the water-fide ; for your afternoon will wear fhort, and your fun fall low and go down ; and ye know that this long time your Lord hath waited on you. Oh how comfortable a thing it will be to you, when time fhall be no more, and your foul fhall depart out of the house of clay to vaft and endlefs eternity, to have your foul dreffed up, and prepared for your Bridegroom! No lofs is comparable to the lofs of the foul ; there is no hope of re-gaining that lofs. Oh how joyful would my foul be to hear that ye would ftart to the gate,‡ and contend for the crown, and leave all vanities, and make Chrift your garland ! Let your foul put away your old lovers, and let Chrift have your whole love.

I have fome experience to write of this to you. My witnefs is in heaven, that I would not exchange my chains and bonds for Chrift, and my fighs, for ten worlds' glory. I judge this clay-idol, which Adam's fons are rouping§ and felling their fouls for, not worth a drink of cold water. Oh, if your foul were in my foul's ftead, how fick would ye be of love for that faireft One, that Faireft among the fons of men ! May-flowers, and morning vapour, and fummer mift, pofteth not fo faft away as thefe worm-eaten pleafures which we follow. We build caftles in the air, and night-dreams are our daily idols that we doat on. Salvation, falvation is our only neceffary thing. Sir, call home your thoughts to this work, to inquire for your Well-beloved. This earth is the portion

---

* Appearing in court.   † Settle ; fet in order.
‡ Begin with alacrity the journey.   § Setting up to auction

of baftards : feek the Son's inheritance, and let Chrift's truth be dear to you.

I pawn* my falvation on it, that this is the honour of Chrift's kingdom which I now fuffer for (and this world, I hope, fhall not come between me and my garland); and that this is the way to life. When ye and I fhall lie lumps of pale clay upon the ground, our pleafures, that we now naturally love, fhall be lefs than nothing in that day. Dear brother, fulfil my joy, and betake you to Chrift without further delay. Ye will be fain at length to feek Him, or do infinitely worfe. Remember my love to your wife. Grace be with you.

Yours, in his fweet Lord Jefus,

S. R.

Aberdeen, *March* 13, 1637.

CXXXVII.—*To* William Glendinning.

[William Glendinning was the fon of Mr Robert Glendinning, minifter of Kirkcudbright. A fhort time before this letter was written, he was ordered to be imprifoned in Kirkcudbright by Bifhop Sydferff, for refufing to incarcerate his father, whom that intolerant prelate had fufpended from his office, and had ordered to be imprifoned, becaufe he would neither conform to Epifcopacy, nor admit as his affiftant a creature of the Bifhop. He was a member of the General Affembly of Glafgow 1638, being returned by the burgh of Kirkcudbright, of which he was then Provoft. During the fubfe-quent years, he was frequently a member of the General Affembly; and his name appears as a member of Parliament for the burgh of Kirkcudbright, and fent by the Committee of Eftates, in 1644, 1645, and 1646.]

(PERSEVERANCE AGAINST OPPOSITION.)

ELL-BELOVED AND DEAR BROTHER,—Grace, mercy, and peace be to you. I thank you moft kindly for your care and love to me, and in particular to my

---

* Pledge.

brother, in his diftrefs in Edinburgh.*   Go on through your waters
without wearying; your Guide knoweth the way; follow Him, and
caft your cares and temptations upon Him.   And let not worms,
the fons of men, affright you; they fhall die, and the moth fhall
eat them.   Keep your garland; there is no lefs at the ftake, in this
game betwixt us and the world, than our confcience and falvation.
We have need to take heed to the game, and not to yield to them.
Let them take other things from us; but here, in matters of confcience, we muft hold and draw† with kings, and fet ourfelves in
terms of oppofition with the fhields of the earth.   O the fweet communion, for evermore, that hath been between Chrift and His
prifoner !   He wearieth not to be kind.   He is the faireft fight I
fee in Aberdeen, or in any part that ever my feet were in.

Remember my hearty kindnefs to your wife.   I defire her to
believe, and lay her cares on God, and make faft work of falvation.
Grace be with you.

Yours, in his only Lord Jefus,

S. R.

Aberdeen, *March* 13, 1637.

---

* Rutherford here refers to the trial of his brother George, fchoolmafter
and reader in Kirkcudbright, before the High Commiffion, at Edinburgh, in
November the preceding year, for his non-conformity and zealous fupport of
Mr Robert Glendinning, the perfecuted minifter of Kirkcudbright.   As previoufly noticed (Let. 67), he was condemned to refign his charge, and to remove from Kirkcudbright before the enfuing term of Whitfunday.   When
at Edinburgh, and on his trial, he experienced much kindnefs from feveral
of the correfpondents of our author, who, in his letters to them, makes the
moft heartfelt grateful acknowledgments.   After his ejection, "he feems,"
fays Murray, "to have taken refuge in Ayrfhire; for in a letter to Lord
Loudon, Rutherford fpeaks of his brother as being nigh his Lordfhip's
bounds; and every individual whom he addreffed on his behalf (after his removal from Kirkcudbright), was connected with that county.   The kindnefs
and the frequency with which, in his letters, he fpeaks of him, do honour to
his heart."—*Life of Rutherford,* p. 93.

† We muft ftruggle with.

CXXXVIII.—*To* Mr HUGH HENDERSON.

[HUGH HENDERSON was firſt miniſter of Dalry, a pariſh in the diſtrict of
Cunningham, Ayrſhire, and afterwards of Dumfries. The firſt inſtance in
which we meet with his name as miniſter of Dalry is in 1643, when he was
nominated as one of the eight miniſters whom the General Aſſembly appointed
to viſit Ireland by pairs, and to continue there for three months ſucceſſively,
to inſtruct, comfort, and encourage the Preſbyterians in that country, who had
been deprived of their miniſters through the tyranny of the prelates. In 1645
he was appointed by the General Aſſembly chaplain to Colonel Stuart's regiment; and in 1648 tranſlated to Dumfries, by a ſentence of the Aſſembly.
Shortly after the reſtoration of Charles II., he, and all the miniſters of the
Preſbytery of Dumfries, were, by the order of the King's Commiſſioner, carried priſoners to Edinburgh, for having, on various grounds, agreed not to
obſerve the 29th day of May as a religious anniverſary, in commemoration of
the King's birth and reſtoration. But he and the reſt, with the exception of
two, at laſt yielded ſo far as to engage ſimply to preach on that day, knowing
it would be the day of their ordinary weekly ſermon; upon which they were
diſmiſſed. This engagement ſeems hardly compatible with ſtraightforwardneſs
and ſtedfaſtneſs to principle, as it was ſomething like a diſingenuous attempt to
make it appear that they were complying with the ſtatute of Parliament, when
they were merely diſcharging a profeſſional duty. Henderſon exhibited more
conſiſtency and ſtedfaſtneſs the ſubſequent year, when he preferred being expelled
from his charge to conforming to Prelacy. He was ejected in the cloſe of the
year 1662, by the Earl of Middleton. After this, Henderſon frequently
preached in his own houſe in Galloway.]

*(TRIALS SELECTED BY GOD—PATIENCE—LOOKING FOR THE
JUDGE.)*

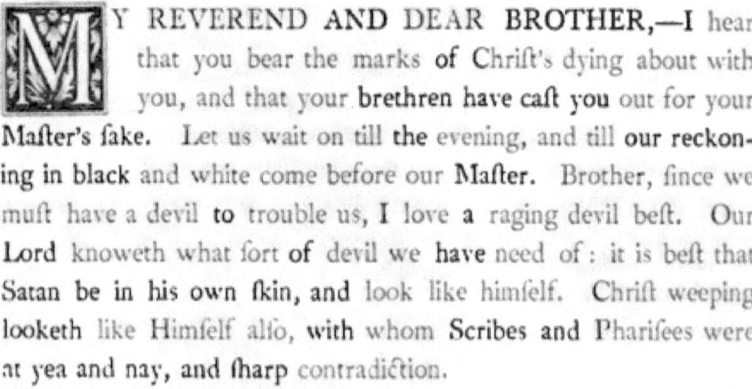 Y REVEREND AND DEAR BROTHER,—I hear
that you bear the marks of Chriſt's dying about with
you, and that your brethren have caſt you out for your
Maſter's ſake. Let us wait on till the evening, and till our reckoning in black and white come before our Maſter. Brother, ſince we
muſt have a devil to trouble us, I love a raging devil beſt. Our
Lord knoweth what ſort of devil we have need of : it is beſt that
Satan be in his own ſkin, and look like himſelf. Chriſt weeping
looketh like Himſelf alſo, with whom Scribes and Phariſees were
at yea and nay, and ſharp contradiction.

Ye have heard of the patience of Job. When he lay in the aſhes, God was with him, clawing and curing his ſcabs, and letting out his boils, comforting his foul; and He took him up at laſt. That God is not dead yet: He will ſtoop and take up fallen bairns. Many broken legs ſince Adam's days hath He ſpelked,* and many weary hearts hath He refreſhed. Bleſs Him for comfort. Why? None cometh dry from David's well. Let us go among the reſt, and caſt down our toom† buckets into Chriſt's ocean, and ſuck conſolations out of Him. We are not ſo ſore ſtricken, but we may fill Chriſt's hall with weeping. We have not gotten our anſwer from Him yet. Let us lay up our broken pleas to a full ſea, and keep them till the day of Chriſt's Coming. We and this world will not be even‡ till then: they would take our garment from us; but let *us* hold and *them* draw.

Brother, it is a ſtrange world if we laugh not. I never ſaw the like of it, if there be not " paiks the man,"§ for this contempt done to the Son of God. We muſt do as thoſe who keep the bloody napkin to the Bailie,‖ and let him ſee blood; we muſt keep our wrongs to our Judge, and let Him ſee our bluddered¶ and foul faces. Priſoners of hope muſt run to Chriſt, with the gutters** that tears have made on their cheeks.

Brother, for myſelf, I am Chriſt's dawted†† one for the preſent; and I live upon no deaf‡‡ nuts, as we uſe to ſpeak. He hath opened fountains to me in the wilderneſs. Go, look to my Lord Jeſus: His love to me is ſuch, that I defy the world to find either brim or bottom to it. Grace be with you.

Your brother, in his ſweet Lord Jeſus,

S. R.

ABERDEEN, *March* 13, 1637.

---

* Truſſed up, bound with ſplinters.   † Empty.   ‡ Be quits.

§ " *Paiks*" is *blows*.   " Be the man ſoundly beaten;" an expreſſion uſed to intimate what the man deſerved.

‖ The magiſtrate who was to judge the caſe.   ¶ Blurred.

** The marks left by the tears that ran down and ſoiled the face.

†† Fondled.   ‡‡ No kernel in them.

[JOHN ELPHINSTON, fecond LORD BALMERINOCH, was the only fon of the firft marriage of the Honourable Sir James Elphinfton, firft Lord Balmerinoch. He diftinguifhed himfelf in 1633 for his oppofition to the meafures of the Court in favour of Prelacy, and particularly for oppofing in Parliament the Act concerning the King's prerogative in impofing apparel on churchmen, and the Act ratifying the Acts previoufly made for fettling and advancing the eftate of bifhops. Soon after he was libelled and condemned to death as guilty of treafon. However, after a long and fevere imprifonment, he at laft obtained from his Majefty a free though reluctant pardon. True to his former principles, he ftill continued to oppofe the meafures then purfued by Government, and particularly the attempts to introduce the Service Book into Scotland. He was a member of the Glafgow Affembly 1638, being returned as elder for the Prefbytery of Edinburgh. "His Lordfhip," fays Wood, "was, without exception, the beft friend the Covenanters had, as he not only affifted that party with his advice on all occafions, but alfo fupplied them with large fums of money, by which he irreparably injured the very ample fortune he inherited from his father. He lived in habits of ftrict friendfhip with the chief leaders of the Prefbyterians, and was particularly intimate with Sir Archibald Johnfton of Warrifton. He had fo ftrong a fenfe of juftice, that having reafon to fufpect his father had made too advantageous a purchafe of the lands of Balumby, in the county of Forfar, he, of his own accord, gave 10,000 merks to the heir of that eftate, by way of compenfation."—(*Wood's Cramond.*) He died fuddenly in 1649, at the time when Charles II. was proclaimed King of Scotland, and when commiffioners were to be fent to Holland to treat with him, of which his Lordfhip was chofen to be one.—(*Lamont's Diary*, p. 1.)]

(*HIS HAPPY OBLIGATIONS TO CHRIST—EMPTINESS OF THE WORLD.*)

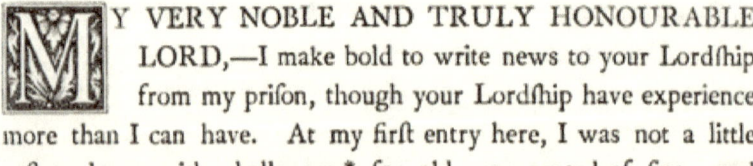 Y VERY NOBLE AND TRULY HONOURABLE LORD,—I make bold to write news to your Lordfhip from my prifon, though your Lordfhip have experience more than I can have. At my firft entry here, I was not a little caften down with challenges,* for old, unrepented-of fins; and

---

* Self-upbraidings.

Satan and my own apprehenfions made a lie of Chrift, that He hath caften a dry, withered tree over the dyke of the vineyard. But it was my folly, bleffed be His great name, the fire cannot burn the dry tree. He is pleafed now to feaft the exiled prifoner with His lovely prefence; for it fuiteth Chrift well to be kind, and He dineth and fuppeth with fuch a finner as I am. I am in Chrift's tutoring here. He hath made me content with a borrowed firefide, and it cafteth as much heat as mine own. I want nothing but real poffef-fion of Chrift; and He hath given me a pawn of that alfo, which I hope to keep till He come Himfelf to loofe the pawn. I cannot get help to praife His high name. He hath made me king over my loffes, imprifonment, banifhment; and only my dumb Sabbaths ftick in my throat. But I forgive Chrift's wifdom in that. I dare not fay one word; He hath done it, and I will lay my hand upon my mouth. If any other hand had done it to me, I could not have borne it.

Now, my Lord, I muft tell your Lordfhip that I would not give a drink of cold water for this clay idol, this plaftered world. I teftify, and give it under my own hand, that Chrift is moft worthy to be fuffered for. Our lazy flefh, which would have Chrift to cry down croffes by open proclamation, hath but raifed a flander upon the crofs of Chrift. My Lord, I hope that ye will not forget what He hath done for your foul. I think that ye are in Chrift's count-book, as His obliged debtor.

Grace, grace be with your fpirit.

Your Lordfhip's obliged fervant,

S. R.

ABERDEEN, *March* 13, 1637.

CXL.—*To my* LADY MAR, *Younger.*

[LADY MAR, *Younger*, whofe maiden name was Chriftian Hay (being the daughter of Francis, ninth Earl of Errol), was the wife of John Erfkine, eighth Earl of Mar. She became a widow in 1654, his Lordfhip having died in that year. She had to him a fon, John, who became ninth Earl of Mar, and a daughter, Elizabeth, who was married to Archibald, Lord Napier. Lord James Erfkine of Grange, one of the fenators of the College of Juftice, who lived in the beginning of the laft century, was the great-grandfon of this lady.—(*Douglas' Peerage*, vol. ii., p. 216; *Crawford's Hiftory of the Shire of Renfrew*, p. 112.) Lady Mar, *fenior*, from whom fhe is diftinguifhed, was Lady Mary Stewart, daughter of Efme, Duke of Lennox, fecond wife of John, Lord Erfkine, feventh Earl of Mar. She died in the houfe of Sir Thomas Hope, in the Cowgate, Edinburgh, and was buried at Alloa, 11th May 1644.—(*Sir Thomas Hope's Diary*, p. 205.) It was for her that, in 1625, the book of devotion, called, "*The Countefs of Mar's Sanctuary, or Arcadia*," was drawn up—a little work of which only two copies were known to be in exiftence, till reprinted this year, 1862, at Edinburgh.]

(*NO EXCHANGE FOR CHRIST.*)

 Y VERY NOBLE AND DEAR LADY,—Grace, mercy, and peace be to you. I received your Lady-fhip's letter, which hath comforted my foul. God give you to find mercy in the day of Chrift.

I am in as good terms and court with Chrift as an exiled, op-preffed prifoner of Chrift can be. I am ftill welcome to His houfe; He knoweth my knock, and letteth in a poor friend. Under this black, rough tree of the crofs of Chrift, He hath ravifhed me with His love, and taken my heart to heaven with Him. Well and long may He brook* it. I would not niffer† Chrift with all the joys that man or angel can devife befide Him. Who hath fuch caufe to fpeak honourably of Chrift as I have? Chrift is King of all croffes, and He hath made His faints little kings under Him; and He can ride and triumph upon weaker bodies than I am (if any can be weaker), and His horfe will neither fall nor ftumble.

Madam, your Ladyfhip hath much ado with Chrift, for your foul, hufband, children, and houfe. Let Him find much employ-ment for His calling with you; for He is fuch a friend as delighteth to be burdened with fuits and employments; and the more ye lay

---

* Poffefs, enjoy.   † Exchange.

on Him, and the more homely* ye be with Him, the more welcome.
O the depth of Chrift's love! It hath neither brim nor bottom.
Oh, if this blind world faw His beauty! When I count with Him
for His mercies to me, I muft ftand ftill and wonder, and go away
as a poor dyvour,† who hath nothing to pay. Free forgivenefs is
payment. I would that I could get Him fet on high; for His love
hath made me fick, and I die except I get real poffeffion.

Grace, grace be with you.

Your Ladyfhip's, at all obedience in Chrift,

S. R.

ABERDEEN, *March* 13, 1637.

CXLI.—*To* JAMES MACADAM.

[John Livingftone (*Hiftor. Relation*), along with Marion M'Naught and
other fuch, mentions John Macadam and Chriftian Macadam of Waterhead,
near Carfphairn, as eminent Chriftians. The perfon to whom this letter is
addreffed may have been one of that family. The famous road engineer in
our day, Macadam, was born at Waterhead, defcended from this ancient
family.

It feems that the Chriftian Macadam mentioned above was afterwards
Lady Cardonefs; and becaufe of her connection with this correfpondent of
Rutherford's, we may give the infcription on her tomb. The tomb is part of
the enclofed pile clofe to the old Anwoth church. The infcription is on the
north fide of the pile:—

" Chriftian M'Adam, Lady Cardynes. Departed 16th June of 1628.
Ætatis fuæ, 33.

" Ye gazers on the trophy of a tomb,
Send out one groan for want of her whofe life,
Twice born on earth, now is in earth's womb;
Lived long a virgin, now a fpotlefs wife.
Church keeps her godly life, the tomb her corpfe,
And earth her precious name. Who then does lofe?
Her hufband? No, fince heaven her foul doth gain."

---

* At home, familiar.   † Debtor.

(THE KINGDOM TAKEN BY FORCE.)

MY VERY DEAR AND WORTHY FRIEND,—
Grace, mercy, and peace be to you. I long to hear of your growing in grace, and of your advancing in your journey to heaven. It will be the joy of my heart to hear that ye hold your face up the brae,* and wade through temptations without fearing what man can do. Chrift fhall, when He arifeth, mow down His enemies, and lay bulks† (as they ufe to fpeak) on the green, and fill the pits with dead bodies.‡ They fhall lie like handfuls of withered hay, when He arifeth to the prey. Salvation, falvation is the only neceffary thing. This clay idol, the world, is not to be fought; it is a morfel not for you, but for hunger-bitten baftards. Contend for falvation. Your Mafter, Chrift, won heaven with ftrokes: it is a befieged caftle; it muft be taken with violence. Oh, this world thinketh heaven but at the next door, and that godlinefs may fleep in a bed of down till it come to heaven! But that will not do it.

For myfelf, I am as well as Chrift's prifoner can be; for by Him I am mafter and king of all my croffes. I am above the prifon, and the lafh of men's tongues; Chrift triumpheth in me. I have been caften down, and heavy with fears, and haunted with challenges. I was fwimming in the depths, but Chrift had His hand under my chin all the time, and took good heed that I fhould not lofe breath; and now I have gotten my feet again, and there are love-feafts of joy, and fpring-tides of confolation betwixt Chrift and me. We agree well; I have court with Him; I am ftill welcome to His houfe. Oh, my fhort arms cannot fathom His love! I befeech you, I charge you, to help me to praife. Ye have a prifoner's prayers, therefore forget me not.

* The flope, or hillfide.
† Carcafes; properly, the *trunk*, or *bulk* of the man. Some write it "houks;" but "*bulks*" is in all the old editions.
‡ Ps. cx. 6; "the places."

I defire Sibylla to remember me dearly to all in that parifh who know Chrift, as if I had named them.

Grace, grace be with you.

    Yours, in his fweet Lord Jefus,

           S. R.

ABERDEEN, *March* 13, 1637.

CXLII.—*To my very dear Brother*, WILLIAM LIVINGSTONE.

[Probably one of his Anwoth parifhioners. There are Livingftones in that neighbourhood to this day.]

(*COUNSEL TO A YOUTH.*)

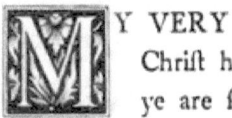Y VERY DEAR BROTHER,—I rejoice to hear that Chrift hath run away with your young love, and that ye are fo early in the morning matched with fuch a Lord; for a young man is often a dreffed lodging for the devil to dwell in. Be humble and thankful for grace; and weigh it not fo much by weight, as if it be true. Chrift will not caft water on your fmoking coal; He never yet put out a dim candle that was lighted at the Sun of Righteoufnefs. I recommend to you prayer and watching over the fins of your youth; for I know that miffive* letters go between the devil and young blood. Satan hath a friend at court in the heart of youth; and there pride, luxury, luft, revenge, forgetfulnefs of God, are hired as his agents. Happy is your foul if Chrift man† the houfe, and take the keys Himfelf, and command all, as it fuiteth Him full well to rule all wherever He is. Keep Chrift, and entertain Him well. Cherifh His grace; blow upon your own coal; and let Him tutor you.

Now for myfelf: know that I am fully agreed with my Lord. Chrift hath put the Father and me into each other's arms. Many a fweet bargain He made before, and He hath made this among the

---

* Letters empowering a perfon to act.

† Man the houfe, means act as the goodman of the houfe, attending to vifitors.

reft. I reign as king over my croffes. I will not flatter a temptation, nor give the devil a good word : I defy hell's iron gates. God
hath paffed over my quarrelling of Him at my entry here, and now
He feedeth and feafteth with me.

Praife, praife with me ; and let us exalt His name together.

Your brother in Chrift,

S. R.

Aberdeen, *March* 13, 1637.

CXLIII.—*To* William Gordon *of Whitepark.*

[This may be a fon of George Gordon, who is recorded as heir to the
eftate of " Whytpark," March 20, 1628. It was in the Parifh of Anwoth.]

(*NOTHING LOST BY TRIALS—LONGING FOR CHRIST HIMSELF,
BECAUSE OF HIS LOVE.*)

WORTHY SIR,—Grace, mercy, and peace be unto you.
I long to hear from you. I am here the Lord's prifoner
and patient, handled as foftly by my Phyfician as if I
were a fick man under a cure. I was at hard terms with my Lord,
and pleaded with Him, but I had the worft fide. It is a wonder
that He fhould have fuffered the like of me to have nicknamed the
Son of His love, Chrift, and to call Him a changed Lord, who
hath forfaken me. But mifbelief* hath never a good word to
fpeak of Chrift. The drofs of my crofs gathered a fcum of fears in
the fire—doubtings, impatience, unbelief, challenging of Providence
as fleeping, and as not regarding my forrow ; but my goldfmith,
Chrift, was pleafed to take off the fcum, and burn it in the fire.
And, bleffed be my Refiner, He hath made the metal better, and
furnifhed new fupply of grace, to caufe me hold out weight ; and I
hope that He hath not loft one grain-weight by burning His fervant.

---

* Erroneous faith.

Now His love in my heart cafteth a mighty heat; He knoweth
that the defire I have to be at Himfelf paineth me. I have fick
nights and frequent fits of love-fevers for my Well-beloved.
Nothing paineth me now but want of His prefence. I think it long
till day. I challenge time as too flow in its pace, that holdeth my
only fair one, my love, my Well-beloved, from me. Oh, if we
were together once! I am like an old crazed fhip that hath endured many ftorms, and that would fain be in the lee of the fhore,
and feareth new ftorms; I would be that* nigh heaven, that the
fhadow of it might break the force of the ftorm, and the crazed
fhip might win to land.† My Lord's fun cafteth a heat of love and
beam of light on my foul. My bleffing thrice every day upon the
fweet crofs of Chrift! I am not afhamed of my garland, "the
banifhed minifter," which is the term of Aberdeen. Love, love
defieth reproaches. The love of Chrift hath a corflet of proof on
it, and arrows will not draw blood of it. We are more than conquerors through the blood of Him that loved us.‡ The devil and
the world cannot wound the love of Chrift. I am further from
yielding to the courfe of defection than when I came hither. Sufferings blunt not the fiery edge of love. Caft love into the floods
of hell, it will fwim above. It careth not for the world's bufked§
and plaftered offers. It hath pleafed my Lord fo to line my heart
with the love of my Lord Jefus, that, as if the field were already
won, and I on the other fide of time, I laugh at the world's golden
pleafures, and at this dirty idol which the fons of Adam worfhip.
This worm-eaten god is that which my foul hath fallen out of love
with.

Sir, ye were once my hearer: I defire now to hear from you
and your wife. I falute her and your children with bleffings. I
am glad that ye are ftill handfafted‖ with Chrift. Go on in your
journey, and take the city by violence. Keep your garments clean.
Be clean virgins to your hufband the Lamb. The world fhall fol-

---

* So nigh.　　　† Get to.　　　‡ Romans viii. 37.
§ Decked with ornaments.　　　‖ Betrothed to by joining hands.

low you to heaven's gates : and ye would not wifh it to go in with you. Keep faft Chrift's love. Pray for me, as I do for you.

The Lord Jefus be with your fpirit.

Yours, in his fweet Lord Jefus,

S. R.

ABERDEEN, *March* 13, 1637.

CXLIV.—*To* Mr GEORGE GILLESPIE.

[GEORGE GILLESPIE was the fon of Mr John Gillefpie, fometime minifter of the Gofpel at Kirkcaldy. He was licenfed to preach the Gofpel fome time prior to 1638; and in April, that year, was ordained minifter of Wemyfs. In 1642, by a fentence of the General Affembly, he was tranflated to one of the churches in Edinburgh, where he continued till his death. Gillefpie poffeffed talents of the higheft order; and fo much were thefe appreciated, that he was one of the four minifters fent as commiffioners from the Church of Scotland to the Weftminfter Affembly in 1643. There he attracted general notice, by the cogency of argument, and the rare learning which he fhowed in pleading the caufe of **Prefbytery**, and oppofing Eraftianifm. At one of the meetings of that Affembly, when the learned Selden had delivered a long and an elaborate difcourfe in favour of Eraftianifm, to which none feemed prepared to reply, Gillefpie, who was ftill a young man, was obferved to be writing. A venerable friend went to his chair, and afked if he had taken notes, but found that he had written nothing except thefe words, frequently repeated, " Give light, Lord." His friend urged him to anfwer. Gillefpie at laft rofe, and in an extempore fpeech refuted Selden with a power of reafoning and an amount of learning which excited the admiration of all prefent. Selden himfelf is faid to have obferved, after hearing this reply, " That young man, by a fingle fpeech, has fwept away the labour and the learning of ten years of my life!" Gillefpie died in December 1648, in the 36th year of his age. During his laft illnefs he enjoyed little comfort, but was ftrong in the faith of adherence to the divine promifes—a fubject on which he infifted much in his fermons. When afked if he had any comfort, he faid, " No; but though the Lord allow me no comfort, yet I will *believe* that my Beloved is mine, and that I am His." To two minifters, who afked what advice he had to give them, he anfwered : " I have little experience of the miniftry, having been in it only nine years ; but I can fay that I have got more affiftance in the work of preaching from prayer than ftudy ; and much more help from the affiftance of the Spirit than from books." And yet he was known to have been an indefatigable ftudent. He is the author of various works, which are chiefly controverfial, fuch as "The Englifh Popifh Ceremonies," and "Aaron's Rod Bloffoming."]

(SUSPICIONS OF CHRIST'S LOVE REMOVED—THREE DESIRES.)

REVEREND AND DEAR BROTHER,—I received your letter. As for my cafe, brother, I blefs His glorious name, that my loffes are my gain, my prifon a palace, and my fadnefs joyfulnefs. At my firft entry, my apprehenfions fo wrought upon my crofs, that I became jealous* of the love of Chrift, as being by Him thruft out of the vineyard, and I was under great challenges ;† as, ordinarily,‡ melted gold cafteth forth a droffy fcum, and Satan and our corruption form the firft words that the heavy crofs fpeaketh, and fay, "God is angry, He loveth you not." But our apprehenfions are not canonical ;§ they indite lies of God and Chrift's love. But fince my fpirit was fettled, and the clay has fallen to the bottom of the well, I fee better what Chrift was doing. And now my Lord is returned with falvation under His wings. Now I want little of half a heaven, and I find Chrift every day fo fweet, comfortable, lovely, and kind, that three things only trouble me : 1*ft*, I fee not how to be thankful, or how to get help to praife that Royal King, who raifeth up thofe that are bowed down. 2*d*, His love paineth me, and woundeth my foul, fo that I am in a fever for want of real prefence. 3*d*, An exceffive defire to take inftruments‖ in God's name, that this is Chrift and His truth, which I now fuffer for ; yea, the apple of the eye of Chrift's honour, even the fovereignty and royal privileges of our King and Lawgiver, Chrift. And, therefore, let no man fcaur at Chrift's crofs, or raife an ill report upon Him or it ; for He beareth the fufferer and it both.

I am here troubled with the difputes of the great doctors (efpecially with Dr B.¶) in Ceremonial and Arminian controverfies,

---

* Sufpicious.　† Rebukes.　‡ Ufually.　§ Authentic Scripture.
‖ Take documents to atteft the matter.　¶ Dr Robert Barron.

for all are corrupt here ; but, I thank God, with no detriment to
the truth, or difcredit to my profeffion.   So, then, I fee that Chrift
can triumph in a weaker man* nor I ; and who can be more weak ?
But His grace is fufficient for me.

Brother, remember **our old covenant, and** pray for me, **and**
write to me your cafe.   The Lord Jefus be with your fpirit.

Yours, in his fweet Lord Jefus,

S. R.

ABERDEEN, *March* 13, 1637.

CXLV.—*To* JEAN GORDON.

(GOD THE SATISFYING PORTION—ADHERENCE TO CHRIST.)

Y VERY DEAR **AND** LOVING SISTER,—Grace,
mercy, and peace be to you.—I long to hear from you.
I exhort you to fet up the brae† to the King's city,
that muft be taken by violence.   **Your afternoon's fun is** wearing
low.   Time will eat up your frail life, like a worm gnawing at the
root of a May-flower.   Lend Chrift your heart.   Set Him as a feal
there.   Take Him in within, and let the world and children ftand
at the door.   They are not yours ; make‡ you and them for your
proper owner, **Chrift.**   It is good that He is your Hufband and
their Father.   What miffing can there be **of** a dying man, when
God filleth His chair ?   Give hours of the day to **prayer.**   Fafh §
Chrift (if I may fpeak fo), and importune Him ; be often at His
gate ; give His door no reft.   I can tell you that He will be found.
Oh what fweet fellowfhip is betwixt Him and me!   I am imprifoned,
but He is not imprifoned.   He hath fhamed me with His kindnefs.
He hath **come to my prifon, and** run away with my heart and all
my love.   Well may He brook ‖ it !   I wifh that my love get never

---

* Than.   † Pufh up the hill.

‡ This feems to mean, mould, fafhion yourfelf and them.

§ Trouble ; by being importunate.   ‖ Poffefs, enjoy.

an owner but Chrift. Fy, fy upon old lovers, that held us fo long afunder! We fhall not part now. He and I fhall be heard, before He win out of my grips.* I refolve to wreftle with Chrift, ere I quit Him. But my love to Him hath caften my foul into a fever, and there is no cooling of my fever, till I get real poffeffion of Chrift. O ftrong, ftrong love of Jefus, thou haft wounded my heart with thine arrows! Oh pain! Oh pain of love for Chrift! Who will help me to praife?

Let me have your prayers. Grace be with you.

Yours, in his fweet Lord Jefus,

S. R.

ABERDEEN, *March* 13, 1637.

CXLVI.—*To* MR JAMES BRUCE, *Minifter of the Gofpel.*

[MR JAMES BRUCE was minifter of Kingfbarns, in the Prefbytery of St Andrews. He was admitted in 1630. Prelacy and the Englifh ceremonies had then, for a confiderable time, been impofed upon the Church of Scotland. But Bruce, like many other of her minifters, being in principle decidedly favourable to Prefbytery, refufed to practife the ceremonies. He was, however, overlooked, and permitted to continue in his charge, the Bifhops at that time removing very few, becaufe, the introduced ceremonies being fo unpopular, it was judged dangerous and impolitic to enforce a rigid and univerfal compliance with them. Bruce made an early public appearance againft the attempts of the court to impofe the Anglo-Popifh liturgy, or Service-book, in 1637. He was a member of the Glafgow Affembly, 1638. He died at Kingfbarns, May 26, 1662, when the ftorm of perfecution was about to break upon the Church of Scotland, being thus taken away from the evil to come.]

(MISJUDGING OF CHRIST'S WAYS.)

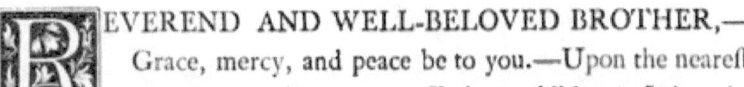 EVEREND AND WELL-BELOVED BROTHER,— Grace, mercy, and peace be to you.—Upon the neareft acquaintance (that we are Father's children), I thought good to write to you. My cafe in my bonds for the honour of my

---

* Grafp.

royal Prince and King, Jefus is as good as becometh the witnefs of fuch a fovereign King. At my firft coming hither, I was in great heavinefs, wreftling with challenges;* being burdened in heart (as I am yet), for my filent Sabbaths, and for a bereaved people, young ones new-born, plucked from the breaft, and the children's table drawn.† I thought I was a dry tree caft over the dyke of the vineyard. But my fecret conceptions of Chrift's love, at His fweet and long-defired return to my foul, were found to be a lie of Chrift's love, forged by the tempter and my own heart. And I am perfuaded it was fo. Now there is greater peace and fecurity within than before ; the court is raifed and difmiffed, for it was not fenced‡ in God's name. I was far miftaken who fhould have fummoned Chrift for unkindnefs ; mifted§ faith, and my fever, conceived amifs of Him. Now, now, He is pleafed to feaft a poor prifoner, and to refrefh me with joy unfpeakable and glorious ! fo as the Holy Spirit is witnefs that my fufferings are for Chrift's truth ; and God forbid that I fhould deny the teftimony of the Holy Spirit and make Him a falfe witnefs. Now, I teftify under my hand, out of fome fmall experience, that Chrift's caufe, even with the crofs, is better than the king's crown ; and that His reproaches are fweet, His crofs perfumed, the walls of my prifon fair and large, my loffes gain.

I defire you, my dear brother, to help me to praife, and to remember me in your prayer to God. Grace, grace be with you.

Yours, in our Lord Jefus,

S. R.

ABERDEEN, *March*, 14, 1637.

CXLVII.—*To* JOHN GORDON, *at Rufco, in Parifh of Anwoth, Galloway.*

[The old tower, or caftle, ftill ftands on a gentle flope, three miles from Anwoth, but uninhabited. It was at this old manfion (Rufco) that Robert

---

* Self-upbraidings.   † Removed.   ‡ Opened and conftituted.
§ That has a mift between it and its object.

Campbell, laird of Kinzeancleugh, the friend of John Knox, died of fever, in 1574, when on a visit to Gordon of Lochinvar, "expressing his confidence of victory, and his desire to depart and be with Christ."]

(PRESSING INTO HEAVEN—A CHRISTIAN NO EASY ATTAIN-
MENT—SINS TO BE AVOIDED.

MY WORTHY AND DEAR BROTHER,—Misspend not your short sand-glass, which runneth very fast; seek your Lord in time. Let me obtain of you a letter under your hand, for a promise to God, by His grace, to take a new course of walking with God. Heaven is not at the next door; I find it hard to be a Christian. There is no little thrusting and thringing* to thrust in at heaven's gates; it is a castle taken by force; —" Many shall strive to enter in, and shall not be able."

I beseech and obtest you in the Lord, to make conscience of rash and passionate oaths, of raging and sudden avenging anger, of night drinking, of needless companionry,† of Sabbath-breaking, of hurting any under you by word or deed, of hating your very enemies. " Except ye receive the kingdom of God as a little child," and be as meek and sober-minded as a babe, " ye cannot enter into the kingdom of God." That is a word which should touch you near, and make you stoop and cast yourself down, and make your great spirit fall. I know that this will not be easily done, but I re-commend it to you, as you tender your part of the kingdom of heaven.

Brother, I may, from new experience, speak of Christ to you. Oh, if ye saw in Him what I see! A river of God's unseen joys have flowed from bank to brae‡ over my soul since I parted with you. I wish that I wanted part, so being ye might have; that your soul might be sick of love for Christ, or rather satiated with Him. This clay-idol, the world, would seem to you then not worth a fig; time will eat you out of possession of it. When the eye-strings break, and the breath groweth cold, and the imprisoned soul looketh

---

* Pressing urgently.   † Associating with companions; companionships.

‡ Rising high above ordinary limits.

out of the windows of the clay-houfe, ready to leap out into eternity, what would you then give for a lamp full of oil? Oh feek it now.

I defire you to correct and curb banning,* fwearing, lying, drinking, Sabbath-breaking, and idle fpending of the Lord's day in abfence from the kirk, as far as your authority reacheth in that parifh.

I hear that a man is to be thruft into that place, to the which I have God's right. I know that ye fhould have a voice by God's word in that (Acts i. 15, 16, to the end; vi. 3-5). Ye would be loath that any prelate fhould put you out of your poffeffion earthly; and this is your right. What I write to you, I write to your wife. Grace be with you.

Your loving paftor,

S. R.

ABERDEEN, *March* 14, 1637.

CXLVIII.—*To the* LADY HALLHILL.

[LADY HALLHILL, whofe maiden name was Learmonth, was the wife of Sir James Melville of Hallhill, in Fife, the fon of Sir James Melville of Hallhill, a privy counfellor to King James VI., and an accomplifhed ftatefman and courtier in his day, who died in 1617.—(*Douglas' Peerage*, vol. ii.) Confequently, this lady was fifter-in-law to Lady Culrofs, formerly noticed. Livingftone, who was perfonally acquainted with her, defcribes her as "eminent for grace and gifts; and whofe "memory was very precious and refrefhing" to him.]

(*CHRIST'S CROSSES BETTER THAN EGYPTS TREASURES.*)

EAR AND CHRISTIAN LADY,—Grace, mercy, and peace be to you.—I longed much to write to your Ladyfhip; but now, the Lord offering a fit occaffion, I would not omit to do it.

I cannot but acquaint your Ladyfhip with the kind dealing of Chrift to my foul, in this houfe of my pilgrimage, that your Lady-

---

* Smaller oaths.

fhip may know that He is as good as He is called. For at my firft
entry into this trial (being caften down and troubled with challenges
and jealoufies * of His love, whofe name and teftimony I now bear
in my bonds), I feared nothing more than that I was caften over
the dyke of the vineyard, as a dry tree. But, bleffed be His great
name, the dry tree was in the fire, and was not burnt; His dew
came down and quickened the root of a withered plant. And now
He is come again with joy, and hath been pleafed to feaft His exiled
and afflicted prifoner with the joy of His confolations. Now I
weep, but am not fad; I am chaftened, but I die not; I have lofs,
but I want nothing; this water cannot drown me, this fire cannot
burn me, becaufe of the good-will of Him that dwelt in The Bufh.
The worft things of Chrift, His reproaches, His crofs, are better
than Egypt's treafures. He hath opened His door, and taken into
His houfe-of-wine a poor finner, and hath left me fo fick of love
for my Lord Jefus, that if heaven were at my difpofing, I would
give it for Chrift, and would not be content to go to heaven, except
I were perfuaded that Chrift were there. I would not give, nor
exchange, my bonds for the prelates' velvets; nor my prifon for
their coaches; nor my fighs for all the world's laughter. This
clay-idol, the world, hath no great court† in my foul. Chrift hath
come and run away to heaven with my heart and my love, fo that
neither heart nor love is mine : I pray God, that Chrift may keep
both without reverfion.‡ In my eftimation, as I am now difpofed,
if my part of this world's clay were rouped§ and fold, I would
think it dear of a drink of water. I fee Chrift's love is fo kingly, that
it will not abide a marrow;‖ it muft have a throne all alone in
the foul. And I fee that apples beguile bairns, howbeit they be
worm-eaten. The moth-eaten pleafures of this prefent world make
bairns believe ten is a hundred, and yet all that are here are but
fhadows. If they would draw by ¶ the curtain that is hung betwixt

---

* Self-upbraidings and fufpicions.　　† No great influence.
‡ Without there being any one to poffefs it after Him.　§ Set up to public fale·
‖ A companion on equal terms.　　¶ Draw afide.

them and Chrift, they fhould fee themfelves fools who have fo long miſkenned* the Son of God. I feek no more, next to heaven, than that He may be glorified in a prifoner of Chrift; and that in my behalf many would praife His high and glorious name who heareth the fighing of the prifoner.

Remember my fervice to the laird, your hufband; and to your fon, my acquaintance. I wifh that Chrift had His young love, and that in the morning he would ftart to the gate,† to feek that which the world knoweth not, and, therefore, doth not feek it.

The grace of our Lord Jefus Chrift be with you.

Yours, in his fweet Lord Jefus,

S. R.

ABERDEEN, *March* 14, 1637.

CXLIX.—*To the much honoured* JOHN OSBURN, *Provoft of Ayr.*

[Of JOHN OSBURN, merchant in Ayr, and at this time chief magiftrate of that burgh, little is now known. He died about the clofe of the year 1653, or beginning of the following year, as appears from his fon David being re-toured his heir on 17th January 1654.—(*Inq. Gener.* No. 3884.) He had a daughter, Jane, who was married to Robert Kelfo of Halrig and Kelfoland, the reprefentative of one of the moft ancient families of Ayrfhire, to whom fhe had two fons, John, furveyor of the cuftoms at Port-Glafgow, and William of Dalkeith, writer to the fignet. Their father appears on the lift of the gentlemen in Ayrfhire, whom Middleton fined, in 1662.]

(ADHERENCE TO CHRIST—HIS APPROBATION WORTH ALL WORLDS.

MUCH HONOURED SIR,—Grace, mercy, and peace be to you.—Upon our fmall acquaintance, and the good report I hear of you, I could not but write to you. I have nothing to fay, but that Chrift, in that honourable place He hath put you in, hath intrufted you with a dear pledge, which is His own glory; and hath armed you with His fword to keep the

---

* Miftaken through ignorance.　　† Set out on his journey with alacrity.

pledge, and make a good account of it to God. Be not afraid of men. Your Mafter can mow down His enemies, and make withered hay of fair flowers. Your time will not be long; after your afternoon will come your evening, and after evening, night. Serve Chrift. Back Him; let His caufe be your caufe; give not an hairbreadth of truth away; for it is not yours, but God's. Then, fince ye are going, take **Chrift's teftificate** * with you out of this life —" Well done, good and faithful fervant!" His " well done " is worth a fhipful of " Good-days " and earthly honours. I have caufe to fay this, becaufe I find Him truth itfelf. In my fad days, Chrift laugheth cheerfully, and faith, " All will be well!" Would to God that all this kingdom, and all that know God, knew what is betwixt Chrift and me in this prifon—what kiffes, embracements, and love communions! I take His crofs in my arms with joy; I blefs it, I rejoice in it. Suffering for Chrift is my garland. I would not exchange Chrift for ten thoufand worlds! nay, if the comparifon could ftand, I would not exchange Chrift with heaven.

Sir, pray for me, and the prayers and bleffing of a prifoner of Chrift meet you in all your ftraits. Grace be with you.

Yours, in Chrift Jefus, his Lord,

S. R.

ABERDEEN, *March* 14, 1637.

CL.—*To his loving Friend*, JOHN HENDERSON.   [See Let. 208.]

(*CONTINUING IN CHRIST—PREPAREDNESS FOR DEATH.*)

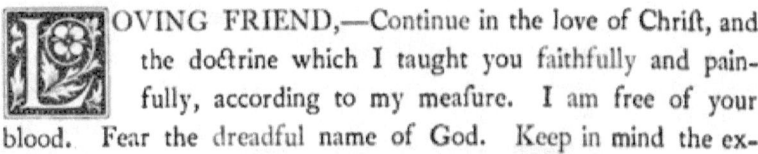

OVING FRIEND,—Continue in the love of Chrift, and the doctrine which I taught you faithfully and painfully, according to my meafure. I am free of your blood. Fear the dreadful name of God. Keep in mind the ex-

---

* Teftimonial, or certificate of character.

aminations* which I taught you, and love the truth of God. Death, as faft as time fleeth, chafeth you out of this life ; it is poffible that ye may make your reckoning with your Judge before I fee you. Let falvation be your care, night and day, and fet afide hours and times of the day for prayer. I rejoice to hear that there is prayer in your houfe. See that your fervants keep the Lord's day. This dirt and god of clay (I mean the vain world) is not worth the feeking.

An hireling paftor is to be thruft in upon you, in the room to which I have Chrift's warrant and right. Stand to your liberties, for the word of God alloweth you a vote in choofing your paftor.

What I write to you, I write to your wife. Commend me heartily to her. The grace of God be with you.

Your loving Friend and Paftor,

S. R.

ABERDEEN, *March* 14, 1637.

———•———

CLI.—*To* JOHN MEINE, *Senior.*

[JOHN MEINE, merchant in Edinburgh, was a man of enlightened piety, and a decided Prefbyterian. His zeal and fteadfaftnefs in maintaining Prefbyterian principles, expofing him to the refentment of the court and prelates, he was, on different occafions, the object of their perfecution. Having, with other citizens of Edinburgh, encouraged Nonconforming minifters, by accompanying them to the court when dragged before the High Commiffion, he was, without citation, trial, or conviction, banifhed to Wigtown by the Privy Council, according to the orders of the king. But the execution of the fentence was fufpended. In regard to the Perth Articles, he would make no compromife. In 1624, when the Town Council, Seffion, and citizens of Edinburgh, convened, according to an ancient cuftom obferved among them from the time of the Reformation, to remove fuch grounds of difference as might have arifen, before uniting in the celebration of the Lord's Supper, Meine ftrongly pleaded that the ordinance fhould be folemnifed without kneeling, a ceremony with which (he faid) he could not comply. On account of his zeal in this matter, he was fummoned before the Privy Council. The refult was, that in

---

* Perhaps (fee in Let. 166) his inftructions on the Catechifm are meant.

June that year, Meine was fentenced by the Council to be confined within the town of Elgin. About the beginning of January next year, he obtained liberty for a few days to come home to vifit his family. He was afterwards ordered to return to his place of confinement; but James VI. dying on the 27th of March that year, an end was put to his trouble for a time. Living-ftone, defcribing him in his Memorable Characteriftics, fays, "He ufed, fummer and winter, to rife about three in the morning, and always fing fome pfalm as he put on his clothes. He fpent till fix o'clock alone in religious ex-ercifes, and at fix worfhipped God with his family, and then went to his fhop." Meine was married to Barbara Hamilton, fifter to the firft wife of the famous Robert Blair.]

(*ENJOYMENT OF GOD'S LOVE—NEED OF HELP—BURDENS.*)

EAR BROTHER,—Grace, mercy, and peace be to you. —I wonder that ye fent me not an anfwer to my laft letter, for I ftand in need of it. I am in fome piece of court* with our great King, whofe love would caufe a dead man to fpeak, and live. Whether my court* will continue or not, I cannot well fay; but I have His ear frequently, and (to His glory only I fpeak it), no penury of the love-kiffes of the Son of God. He thinketh good to caft apples to me in my prifon to play withal, left I fhould think long† and faint. I muft give over all attempts to fathom the depth of His love. All I can do is, but to ftand befide His great love, and look and wonder. My debts of thank-fulnefs affright me; I fear that my creditor get a dyvour-bill‡ and ragged account.‡

I would be much the better of help. Oh, for help! and that ye would take notice of my cafe. Your not writing to me maketh me think ye fuppofe that I am not to be bemoaned, becaufe He fendeth comfort. But I have pain in my unthankfulnefs, and pain in the feeling of His love, whill§ I am fick again for real prefence and real poffeffion of Chrift. Yet there is no gowked‖ (if I may fo fpeak), nor fond love in Chrift. He cafteth me down fometimes for

---

* Have fomething like influence. † Yearn wearily.
‡ A bankrupt debtor's account; torn and incomplete. § Till.
‖ Foolifh; love that puts the perfon in a foolifh pofition.

old faults ; and I know that He knoweth well that fweet comforts
are swelling, and, therefore forrow muft take a vent to the wind.

My dumb Sabbaths are undercoating* wounds. The condition
of this oppreffed kirk, and my brother's cafe (I thank you and your
wife for your kindnefs to him), hold my fore fmarting, and keep
my wounds bleeding. But the groundwork ftandeth fure. Pray
for me. Grace be with you. Remember me to your wife.

Yours, in his fweet Lord Jefus,

S. R.

ABERDEEN, *March* 14, 1637.

CLII.—*To* MR THOMAS GARVEN.

[This correfpondent was one of the minifters of Edinburgh. Letters 165
and 247, are alfo addreffed to him.]

(A PRISONER'S JOYS—LOVE OF CHRIST—THE GOOD PART—
HEAVEN IN SIGHT.)

 EVEREND AND DEAR BROTHER,—I blefs you
for your letter ; it was a fhower to the new-mown grafs.
The Lord hath given you the tongue of the learned.
Be fruitful and humble.

It is poffible that ye may come to my cafe, or the like ; but the
water is neither fo deep, nor the ftream fo ftrong, as it is called.
I think my fire is not fo hot ; my water is dry land, my lofs rich
lofs. Oh, if† the walls of my prifon be high, wide, and large, and
the place fweet ! No man knoweth it, no man, I fay, knoweth it,
my dear brother, fo well as He and I ; no man can put it down in
black and white as my Lord hath fealed it in my heart. My poor
ftock hath grown fince I came to Aberdeen ; and if any had known
the wrong I did, in being jealous of fuch an honeft lover as Chrift,
who withheld not His love from me, they would think the more of
it. But I fee, He muft be above me in mercy. I will never ftrive

---

* Feftering under the fkin.

† " *Oh if;*" *q. d.*, What will you fay if I tell you that the walls of my
prifon are, etc.

with Him ; to think to recompenfe Him is folly.   If I had as many
angels' tongues, as there have fallen drops of rain fince the creation,
or as there are leaves of trees in all the forefts of the earth, or ftars
in the heaven, to praife, yet my Lord Jefus would ever be behind
with me.*   We will never get our accounts fitted.   A pardon muft
clofe the reckoning ; for His comforts to me in this honourable
caufe have almoft put me beyond the bounds of modefty ; howbeit
I will not let every one know what is betwixt us.   Love, love (I
mean Chrift's love), is the hotteft coal that ever I felt.   Oh, but
the fmoke of it be hot !   Caft all the falt fea on it, it will flame ;
hell cannot quench it ; many many waters will not quench love.
Chrift is turned over to His poor prifoner in a mafs and globe of
love.   I wonder that He fhould wafte fo much love upon such a
wafter as I am ; but He is no wafter, but abundant in mercy.   He
hath no niggard's alms, when He is pleafed to give.   Oh that I
could invite all the nation to love Him !   Free grace is an unknown
thing.   This world hath heard but a bare name of Chrift, and no
more.   There are infinite plies in His love that the faints will never
win† to unfold ; I would it were better known, and that Chrift got
more of His own due than He doth.

Brother, ye have chofen the good part, who have taken part
with Chrift.   Ye will fee Him win the field, and fhall get part of
the fpoil when He divideth it.   They are but fools who laugh at
us ; for they fee but the backfide of the moon, yet our moonlight
is better than their twelve-hours'‡ fun.   We have gotten the New
Heavens, and, as a pledge of that, the Bridegroom's love-ring.   The
children of the wedding-chamber have caufe to fkip and leap for
joy ; for the marriage-fupper is drawing nigh, and we find the four-
hours'§ fweet and comfortable.   O time, be not flow !   O fun,
move fpeedily, and haften our banquet !   O Bridegroom, be like a
roe or a young hart upon the mountains !   O Well-beloved, run
faft, that we may once‖ meet !

---

* Never get me to come up to His due.   † Folds that faints will not get at.
‡ Noon of the day ; their fun at his beft.
§ The flight meal taken in the afternoon.   ‖ Some time or other.

Brother, I reftrain myfelf for want of time. Pray for me; I hope to remember you. The good-will of Him who dwelt in the bufh, the tender mercies of God in Chrift, enrich you. Grace be with you.

Yours, in his fweet Lord Jefus,

S. R.

ABERDEEN, *March* 14, 1637.

CLIII.—*To* BETHAIA AIRD.

[The name *Aird* is not uncommon in the hiftory of the Church. *Mr Wm. Aird* was a noted minifter in Edinburgh in Livingftone's days. Wodrow's Hiftory mentions *Aird* of Muirkirk, and alfo *John Aird* of Milton. In the memoir of Walter Pringle of Greenknow, we find *James Aird* was his intimate friend. But whether this correfpondent was related to any of them, we know not. She may have been fimply an Anwoth parifhioner.]

(UNBELIEF UNDER TRIALS—CHRIST'S SYMPATHY.)

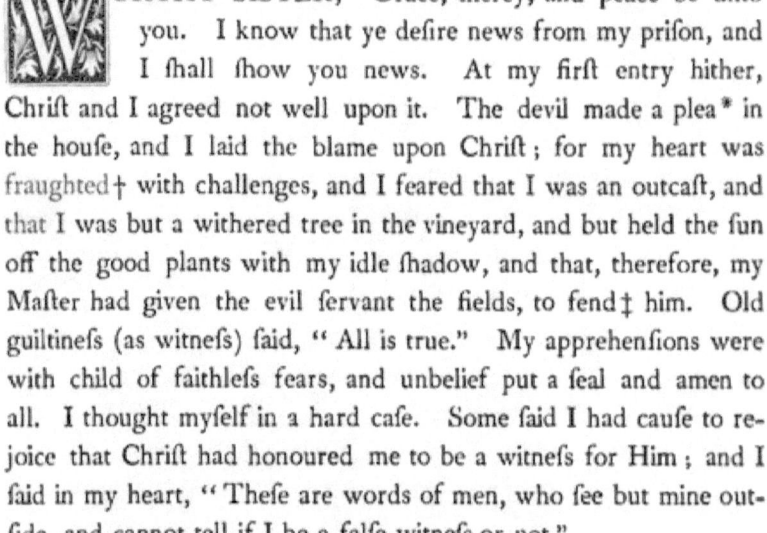 ORTHY SISTER,—Grace, mercy, and peace be unto you. I know that ye defire news from my prifon, and I fhall fhow you news. At my firft entry hither, Chrift and I agreed not well upon it. The devil made a plea* in the houfe, and I laid the blame upon Chrift; for my heart was fraughted† with challenges, and I feared that I was an outcaft, and that I was but a withered tree in the vineyard, and but held the fun off the good plants with my idle fhadow, and that, therefore, my Mafter had given the evil fervant the fields, to fend‡ him. Old guiltinefs (as witnefs) faid, "All is true." My apprehenfions were with child of faithlefs fears, and unbelief put a feal and amen to all. I thought myfelf in a hard cafe. Some faid I had caufe to rejoice that Chrift had honoured me to be a witnefs for Him; and I faid in my heart, "Thefe are words of men, who fee but mine outfide, and cannot tell if I be a falfe witnefs or not."

---

* Controverfy, difpute.   † Fully filled with felf-upbraidings.
‡ To fhift for himfelf in the fields; caft him out.

If Chriſt had in this matter been as wilful and ſhort* as I was, my faith had gone over the brae,† and broken its neck. But we were well met,—a haſty fool, and a wiſe, patient, and meek Saviour. He took no law-advantage of my folly, but waited on till my ill-blood was fallen, and my drumbled‡ and troubled well began to clear. He was never a whit angry at the fever-ravings of a poor tempted ſinner; but He mercifully forgave, and came (as it well becometh Him), with grace and new comfort, to a ſinner who deſerved the contrary. And now He is content to kiſs my black mouth, to put His hand into mine, and to feed me with as many conſolations as would feed ten hungry ſouls. Yet I dare not ſay that He is a waſter of comforts, for no leſs would have borne me up ; one grain-weight leſs would have caſten § the balance.

Now, who is like to that royal King, crowned in Zion! Where ſhall I get a ſeat for real Majeſty to ſet Him on ? If I could ſet Him as far above the heaven as thouſand thouſands of heights deviſed by men and angels, I ſhould think Him but too low. I pray you, for God's ſake, my dear ſiſter, to help me to praiſe. His love hath neither brim nor bottom ; His love is like Himſelf, it paſſeth all natural underſtanding. I go to fathom it with my arms ; but it is as if a child would take the globe of ſea and land in his two ſhort arms. Bleſſed and holy is His name! This muſt be His truth which I now ſuffer for ; for He would not laugh upon a lie, nor be witneſs with His comforts to a night-dream.

I entreat for your prayers ; and the prayer and bleſſing of a priſoner of Chriſt be upon you. Grace be with you.

Yours in his ſweet Lord Jeſus,

S. R.

ABERDEEN, *March* 14, 1637.

---

* Short-tempered ; haſty.   † Fallen over the hill.
‡ Diſturbed, made muddy.   § Turned the ſcale.

CLIV.—*To* Alexander Gordon *of Knockgray, near Carfphairn.*

(*PROSPECTIVE TRIALS.*)

EAR BROTHER,—I have not leifure to write to you. Chrift's ways were known to you long before I, who am but a child, knew anything of Him. What wrong and violence the prelates may, by God's permiffion, do unto you, for your trial, I know not; but this I know, that your ten days' tribulation will end. Contend to the laft breath for Chrift. Banifhment out of thefe kingdoms is determined againft me, as I hear; this land dow* not bear me. I pray you, to recommend my cafe and bonds to my brethren and fifters with you. I intruft more of my fpiritual comfort to you and them that way, my dear brother, than to many in this kingdom befides. I hope that ye will not be wanting to Chrift's prifoner.

Fear nothing; for I affure you that Alexander Gordon of Knockgray fhall win away,† and get his foul for a prey. And what can he then want that is worth the having? Your friends are cold (as ye write); and fo are thofe in whom I trufted much. Our Hufband doth well in breaking our idols in pieces. Dry wells fend us to the fountain. "My life is not dear to me, fo being I may fulfil my courfe with joy." I fear that ye muft remove, if your new hireling will not bear your difcountenancing of him; for the prelate is afraid that Chrift get you; and that he hath no will to.

Grace be with you.

Yours in his fweet Lord and Mafter,

S. R.

Aberdeen, 1637.

---

* Is not able to.   † Get away from this world.

CLV.—*To* Grizzel Fullerton.

[Grizzel Fullerton was the daughter of William Fullerton, Provoſt of Kirkcudbright, and Marion M'Naught. See Let. 6.]

(THE ONE THING NEEDFUL—CHRIST'S LOVE.)

DEAR SISTER,—I exhort you in the Lord, to ſeek your one thing, Mary's good part, that ſhall not be taken from you. Set your heart and ſoul on the children's inheritance. This clay-idol, the world, is but for baſtards, and ye are His lawfully-begotten child. Learn the way (as your dear mother hath done before you) to knock at Chriſt's door. Many an alms of mercy hath Chriſt given to her, and hath abundance behind to give to you. Ye are the ſeed of the faithful, and born within the covenant ; claim your right. I would not exchange Chriſt Jeſus for ten worlds of glory. I know now (bleſſed be my Teacher !) how to ſhute* the lock, and unbolt my Well-beloved's door ; and He maketh a poor ſtranger welcome when He cometh to His houſe. I am ſwelled up and ſatisfied with the love of Chriſt, that is better than wine. It is a fire in my ſoul ; let hell and the world caſt water on it, they will not mend themſelves. I have now gotten the right gate† of Chriſt. I recommend Him to you above all things. Come and find‡ the ſmell of His breath ; ſee if His kiſſes be not ſweet. He deſireth no better than to be much made of ; be homely§ with Him, and ye ſhall be the more welcome ; ye know not how fain Chriſt would have all your love. Think not this is imagination and bairns' play, which we make din for.‖ I would not ſuffer for it, if it were ſo. I dare pawn my heaven for it, that it is the way to glory. Think much of truth, and abhor theſe ways deviſed by men in God's worſhip.

---

* Shove back. † Way of dealing with. ‡ Feel; or find out.
§ At home with; familiar. ‖ Make ſo much noiſe about.

The grace of Chrift be with you.
                    Yours, in his fweet Lord Jefus,

                                                    S. R.

ABERDEEN, *March* 14, 1637.

CLVI.—*To* PATRICK CARSEN.

[This was, perhaps, the fon of John Carfen, formerly noticed. See
Let. 127.]

(*EARLY DEVOTEDNESS TO CHRIST.*)

DEAR AND LOVING FRIEND,—I cannot but, upon
the opportunity of a bearer, exhort you to refign the
love of your youth to Chrift; and in this day, while
your fun is high and your youth ferveth you, to feek the Lord and
His face. For there is nothing out of heaven fo neceffary for you as
Chrift. And ye cannot be ignorant but your day will end, and the
night of death fhall call you from the pleafures of this life: and a
doom given out in death ftandeth for ever—as long as God liveth!
Youth, ordinarily, is a poft and ready fervant for Satan, to run
errands; for it is a neft for luft, curfing, drunkennefs, blafpheming
of God, lying, pride, and vanity. Oh, that there were fuch an
heart in you as to fear the Lord, and to dedicate your foul and
body to His fervice! When the time cometh that your eye-ftrings
fhall break, and your face wax pale, and legs and arms tremble,
and your breath fhall grow cold, and your poor foul look out at
your prifon houfe of clay, to be fet at liberty; then a good confcience, and your Lord's favour, fhall be worth all the world's glory.
Seek it as your garland and crown.
        Grace be with you.
                    Yours, in his fweet Lord Jefus,

                                                    S. R.

ABERDEEN, *March* 14, 1637.

CLVII.—*To* CARLETON.

[Livingſtone, in his Characteriſtics, mentions two perſons of this name: "Fullerton of Carleton, in Galloway, a grave and cheerful Chriſtian;" and "Cathcart of Carleton, in Carrick, an old, experienced Chriſtian," in much repute among the religious of his day, for his ſkill in ſolving caſes of conſcience, and dealing with perſons under ſpiritual affliction. But it ſeems clear that Rutherford's correspondent was *John Fullerton of Carleton*, in the pariſh of Borgue. For, in Let. 15, he is ſpoken of as in Galloway. In the "Minutes of Comm. of Covenanters," we find the following eſtates put ſide by ſide, all of them a few miles from Anwoth, viz., "*Roberton* and *Carleton*, Caillie and Rufco, Carfluth and Caffincarrie." His lady's name appears prefixed to Let. 256.

This, too, was the Carleton that wrote the Acroſtic on Marion M'Naught (ſee note on Let. 5). He was author of a poem—"*The Turtle Dove*, under the abſence and preſence of her only *Choice*. 1664,"—dedicated by the author to Lady Jane Campbell, Viſcounteſs Kenmure, with whom he was connected. The only copy known is in poſſeſſion of Mr Nicholſon, Kirkcudbright. He alſo wrote "A Manifeſto of the Kingdom of Scotland in favour of the League and Covenant," in verſe. (See "Minutes of Comm. of Covenanters.")]

(INCREASING SENSE OF CHRIST'S LOVE—RESIGNATION— DEADNESS TO EARTH—TEMPTATIONS—INFIRMITIES.)

MUCH HONOURED SIR,—I will not impute your not writing to me to forgetfulneſs. However, I have One above who forgetteth me not—nay, He groweth in His kindneſs. It hath pleaſed His holy Majeſty to take me from the pulpit, and teach me many things, in my exile and priſon, that were myſteries to me before.

I ſee His bottomleſs and boundleſs love and kindneſs, and my jealouſies and ravings, which, at my firſt entry into this furnace, were ſo fooliſh and bold, as to ſay to Chriſt, who is truth itſelf, in His face, "Thou lieſt." I had well nigh loſt my grips.* I wondered if it was Chriſt or not; for the miſt and ſmoke of my per-

---

* Firm hold.

turbed heart made me miftake my Mafter, Jefus. My faith was
dim, and hope frozen and cold; and my love, which caufed
jealoufies, had fome warmnefs, and heat, and fmoke, but no flame
at all. (Yet I was looking for fome good of Chrift's old claim to
me.) I thought I had forfeited all my rights. But the tempter
was too much upon my counfels, and was ftill blowing the coal.
Alas! I knew not well before how good fkill my Interceffor and
Advocate, Chrift, hath of pleading, and of pardoning me fuch follies.
Now He is returned to my foul with healing under His wings; and
I am nothing behind with Chrift* now; for He hath overpaid me,
by His prefence, the pain I was put to by on-waiting, and any little
lofs that I fuftained by my witneffing againft the wrongs done to
Him. I trow it was a pain to my Lord to hide Himfelf any longer.
In a manner, He was challenging† His own unkindnefs, and repented
Him of His glooms.‡   And now, what want I on earth that Chrift
can give to a poor prifoner? Oh, how fweet and lovely is He now!
Alas! that I can get none to help me to lift up my Lord Jefus
upon His throne, above all the earth.

2*dly*, I am now brought to fome meafure of fubmiffion, and I
refolve to wait till I fee what my Lord Jefus will do with me. I
dare not now nickname, or fpeak one word againft, the all-feeing
and over-watching providence of my Lord. I fee that providence
runneth not on broken wheels. But I, like a fool, carved a providence for my own eafe, to die in my neft, and to fleep ftill till my
grey hairs, and to lie on the funny fide of the mountain, in my
miniftry at Anwoth. But now I have nothing to fay againft a
borrowed firefide, and another man's houfe, nor Kedar's tents,
where I live, being removed far from my acquaintance, my lovers,
and my friends. I fee that God hath the world on His wheels, and
cafteth it as a potter doth a veffel on the wheel. I dare not fay
that there is any inordinate or irregular motion in providence. The
Lord hath done it. I will not go to law with Chrift, for I would
gain nothing of that.

---

* Chrift has paid me all my claim.   † Rebuking.   ‡ Frowns.

3*dly*, I have learned fome greater mortification, and not to mourn after, or feek to fuck, the world's dry breafts. Nay, my Lord hath filled me with fuch dainties, that I am like to a full banqueter, who is not for common cheer. What have I to do to fall down upon my knees, and worfhip mankind's great idol, the world ? I have a better God than any claygod : nay, at prefent, as I am now difpofed, I care not much to give this world a difcharge of my life-rent of it, for bread and water. I know that it is not my home, nor my Father's houfe ; it is but His foot-ftool, the outer clofe* of His houfe, His out-fields and muir-ground. Let baftards take it. I hope never to think myfelf in its common,† for honour or riches. Nay, now, I fay to laughter, " Thou art madnefs."

4*thly*, I find it to be moft true, that the greateft temptation out of hell, is, to live without temptations. If my waters fhould ftand, they would rot. Faith is the better of the free air, and of the fharp winter ftorm in its face. Grace withereth without adverfity. The devil is but God's mafter fencer, to teach us to handle our weapons.

5*thly*, I never knew how weak I was, till now when He hideth Himfelf, and when I have Him to feek, feven times a day. I am a dry and withered branch, and a piece of dead carcafs, dry bones, and not able to ftep over a ftraw. The thoughts of my old fins, are as the fummons of death to me , and my late brother's cafe hath ftricken me to the heart. When my wounds are clofing, a little ruffle‡ caufeth them to bleed afrefh ; fo thin-fkinned is my foul, that I think it is like a tender man's fkin that may touch nothing. Ye fee how fhort I would fhoot of the prize, if His grace were not fufficient for me.

Wo is me for the day of Scotland ! Wo, wo is me for my harlot-mother ; for the decree is gone forth ! Women of this land fhall call the childlefs and mifcarrying wombs blefled. The anger of the Lord is gone forth, and fhall not return, till He perform the purpofe of His heart againft Scotland. Yet He fhall make Scotland

---

* The lane, or paffage, forming the entry to the houfe.

† Under obligation to.   ‡ It is written " rifle," in old editions.

a new, sharp instrument, having teeth to thresh the mountains, and fan the hills as chaff.

The prisoner's blessing be upon you.

　　　　　　　　　　Yours, in his sweet Lord Jesus,

　　　　　　　　　　　　　　　　　　　　　　S. R.

Aberdeen, *March* 14, 1637.

CLVIII.—*To the* Lady Busbie.　[See Let. 133.]

*(CHRIST ALL-WORTHY AND BEST AT OUR LOWEST—SINFULNESS
OF THE LAND—PRAYERS.)*

MISTRESS,—I know that ye are thinking sometimes what Christ is doing in Zion, and that the haters of Zion may get the bottom of our cup, and the burning coals of our furnace that we have been tried in, those many years bygone. Oh, that this nation would be awakened to cry mightily unto God, for the setting up of a new tabernacle to Christ in Scotland. Oh, if this kingdom knew how worthy Christ were of His room ! His worth was ever above man's estimation of Him.

And for myself I am pained at the heart, that I cannot find myself disposed to leave myself and go wholly into Christ. Alas, that there should be one bit of me out of Him, and that we leave too much liberty and latitude for ourselves, and our own ease, and credit, and pleasures, and so little room for all-love-worthy Christ ! Oh, what pains and charges it costeth Christ ere He get us ! and when all is done, we are not worth the having. It is a wonder that He should seek the like of us. But love overlooketh blackness and fecklessness ;* for if it had not been so, Christ would never have made so fair and blessed a bargain with us as the covenant of grace is. I find that in all our sufferings Christ is but redding marches,† that every one of us may say, " Mine, and thine ;" and

---

* Worthless, uselessness.　　　　　　† Settling the boundaries.

that men may know by their croffes, how weak a bottom nature is
to ftand upon in trial; that the end which our Lord intendeth, in
all our fufferings, is to bring grace into court * and requeft, amongft
us.   I fhould fuccumb and come fhort of heaven, if I had no more
than my own ftrength to fupport me ; and if Chrift fhould fay to
me, "Either do or die," it were eafy to determine what fhould
become of me.   The choice were eafy, for I behoved to die if
Chrift fhould pafs by with ftraitened bowels ; and who then
would take us up in our ftraits ?   I know we may fay that Chrift
is kindeft in His love, when we are at our weakeft ; and that if
Chrift had not been to the fore,† in our fad days, the waters had
gone over our foul.   His mercy hath a fet period, and appointed
place, how far and no farther the fea of affliction fhall flow, and
where the waves thereof fhall be ftayed.   He prefcribeth how
much pain and forrow, both for weight and meafure, we muft
have.   Ye have, then, good caufe to recall your love from all lovers,
and give it to Chrift.   He who is afflicted in all your afflictions,
looketh not on you in your fad hours with an infenfible heart or
dry eyes.

  All the Lord's faints may fee that it is loft love which is beftowed upon this perifhing world.   Death and judgment will make
men lament that ever their mifcarrying hearts carried them to lay
and lavifh out their love upon falfe appearances and night-dreams.
Alas ! that Chrift fhould fare the worfe, becaufe of His own goodnefs in making peace and the Gofpel to ride together ; and that we
have never yet weighed the worth of Chrift in His ordinances, and
that we are like to be deprived of the well, ere we have tafted the
fweetnefs of the water.   It may be that with watery eyes, and a
wet face, and wearied feet, we feek Chrift, and fhall not find Him.
Oh, that this land were humbled in time, and by prayers, cries,
and humiliation, would bring Chrift in at the Church-door again,
now when His back is turned toward us, and He is gone to the
threfhhold, and His one foot, as it were, is out of the door !   I am

---

* Into favour.   † If Chrift had not been exifting ftill.

fure that His departure is our deferving ; we have bought it with
our iniquities ; for even the Lord's own children are fallen afleep,
and, alas ! profeffors are made all of fhows and fafhions, and are
not at pains to recover themfelves again. Every one hath his fet
meafure of faith and holinefs, and contenteth himfelf with but a
ftinted meafure of godlinefs, as if that were enough to bring him to
heaven. We forget that as our gifts and light grow, fo God's gain
and the intereft of His talents, fhould grow alfo ; and that we cannot pay God with the old ufe and wont (as we ufe to fpeak) which
we gave Him feven years ago ; for this were to mock the Lord,
and to make price with Him as we lift. Oh, what difficulty is there
in our Chriftian journey, and how often come we fhort of many
thoufand things that are Chrift's due ! and we confider not, how
far our dear Lord is behind with us.

Miftrefs, I cannot render you thanks, as I would, for your
kindnefs to my brother, an oppreffed ftranger ; but I remember
you unto the Lord as I am able. I entreat you to think upon me,
His prifoner, and pray that the Lord would be pleafed to give me
room to fpeak to His people in His name.

Grace, grace be with you.

Yours in his fweet Lord and Mafter,

S. R.

ABERDEEN, 1637.

CLIX.—*To* JOHN FLEMING, *Bailie of Leith.*

(*DIRECTIONS FOR CHRISTIAN CONDUCT*).

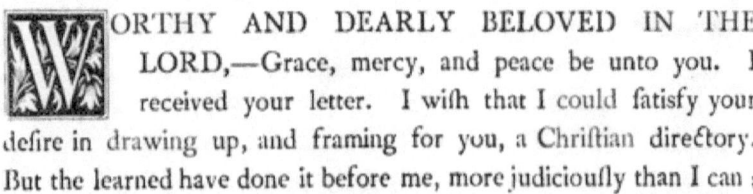

ORTHY AND DEARLY BELOVED IN THE
LORD,—Grace, mercy, and peace be unto you. I
received your letter. I wifh that I could fatisfy your
defire in drawing up, and framing for you, a Chriftian directory.
But the learned have done it before me, more judicioufly than I can ;

efpecially Mr Rogers,* Greenham,† and Perkins.‡   Notwithftanding, I fhall fhow you what I would have been at myfelf; howbeit
I came always fhort of my purpofe.

1. That hours of the day, lefs or more time, for the word and
prayer, be given to God, not fparing the twelfth hour, or mid-day,
howbeit it fhould then be the fhorter time.

2. In the midft of worldly employments, there fhould be fome
thoughts of fin, death, judgment, and eternity, with at leaft a word
or two of ejaculatory prayer to God.

3. To beware of wandering of heart in private prayers.

4. Not to grudge, howbeit ye come from prayer without fenfe of
joy. Down-cafting, fenfe of guiltinefs, and hunger, are often beft for us.

5. That the Lord's-day, from morning to night, be fpent always
either in private or public worfhip.

6. That words be obferved, wandering and idle thoughts be
avoided, fudden anger and defire of revenge, even of fuch as perfecute the truth, be guarded againft; for we often mix our zeal with
our wild-fire.

---

* Dr Daniel Rogers, a Puritan divine, author of a treatife called " David's
Coft; or, What it will coft to ferve God aright;" " A Practical Catechifm;"
" Naaman the Syrian," and others.   He was born in 1573, educated at Cambridge, fuffered from the perfecution of Laud, and died in 1652, at the age of
eighty.   He was a man of great talents, deep humility and devotion, but of a
temper fo bold that a friend faid of him, " He had grace enough for *two* men,
but not enough for himfelf."

† Richard Greenham, a Puritan, who was born in 1531, and died of the
plague 1591.   He was the author of feveral fermons and practical treatifes.   (See
Brooke's Lives of the Puritans, vol. ii., pp. 448.)

‡ Dr Wm. Perkins, an Englifh divine, who lived in the end of the fixteenth
century, and was the author of feveral practical and doctrinal treatifes; among
others, the one here referred to, " A Cafe of Confcience, and Thirteen Principles of Religion," publifhed after his death.   He was a ftrict Calvinift, and
took part in the controverfy againft Arminianifm.   He ufed fo to apply the
terrors of the law to the confcience, that oftentimes his hearers fell down before
him.   It was alfo faid that he pronounced the word " *Damnation*" with fuch
an emphafis and pathos as left a doleful echo in the ear long after.   He wrote
on all his books, " Thou art a minifter of the Word: mind thy bufinefs."

7. That known, difcovered, and revealed fins, that are againft the confcience, be efchewed, as moft dangerous preparatives to hardnefs of heart.

8. That in dealing with men, faith and truth in covenants and trafficking be regarded, that we deal with all men in fincerity; that confcience be made of idle and lying words; and that our carriage be fuch, as that they who fee it may fpeak honourably of our fweet Mafter and profeffion.

9. I have been much challenged,* 1. For not referring all to God as the laft end; that I do not eat, drink, fleep, journey, fpeak, and think for God. 2. That I have not benefited by good company; and that I left not fome word of conviction, even upon natural and wicked men, as by reproving fwearing in them; or becaufe of being a filent witnefs to their loofe carriage; and becaufe I intended not in all companies to do good. 3. That the woes and calamities of the Kirk, and of particular profeffors, have not moved me. 4. That at the reading of the life of David, Paul, and the like, when it humbled me, I (coming fo far fhort of their holinefs) laboured not to imitate them, afar off at leaft, according to the meafure of God's grace. 5. That unrepented fins of youth were not looked to, and lamented for. 6. That fudden ftirrings of pride, luft, revenge, love of honours, were not refifted and mourned for. 7. That my charity was cold. 8. That the experiences I had of God's hearing me, in this and the other particular, being gathered, yet in a new trouble I had always (once at leaft) my faith to feek, as if I were to begin at A, B, C, again. 9. That I have not more boldly contradicted the enemies fpeaking againft the truth, either in public church meetings, or at tables, or ordinary conference. 10. That in great troubles I have received falfe reports of Chrift's love, and misbelieved Him in His chaftening; whereas the event hath faid, " All was in mercy;" 11. Nothing more moveth me, and weighteth† my foul,

---

* Rebuked.

† Weighed down with fadnefs. " Death did not weight the martyrs when it was laid on them," occurs in one of his fermons.

than that I could never from* my heart, in my profperity, fo wreftle
in prayer with God, nor be fo dead to the world, fo hungry and fick
of love for Chrift, fo heavenly-minded, as when ten ftone-weight of
a heavy crofs was upon me. 12. That the crofs extorted vows of
new obedience, which eafe hath blown away, as chaff before the
wind. 13. That practice was fo fhort and narrow, and light fo long
and broad. 14. That death hath not been often meditated upon.
15. That I have not been careful of gaining others to Chrift.
16. That my grace and gifts bring forth little or no thankfulnefs.

There are fome things, alfo, whereby I have been helped : as,
1. I have been benefited by riding alone a long journey, in giving
that time to prayer. 2. By abftinence, and giving days to God. 3.
By praying for others; for by making an errand to God for them,
I have gotten fomething for myfelf. 4. I have been really confirmed, in many particulars, that God heareth prayers ; and, therefore, I ufed to pray for anything, of how little importance foever.
5. He enabled me to make no queftion, that this mocked way,
which is nicknamed, is the only way to heaven.

Sir, thefe and many more occurrences in your life, fhould be
looked unto; and, 1. Thoughts of Atheifm fhould be watched
over, as, " If there be a God in heaven ?" which will trouble and
affault the beft, at fome times. 2. Growth in grace fhould be cared
for above all things ; and falling from our firft love mourned for.
3. Confcience made of praying for the enemies, who are blinded.

Sir, I thank you moft kindly for the care of my brother, and of
me alfo. I hope it is laid up for you, and remembered in heaven.

I am ftill afhamed with Chrift's kindnefs to fuch a finner as I
am. He hath left a fire in my heart, that hell cannot caft water on,
to quench or extinguifh it. Help me to praife, and pray for me ,
for ye have a prifoner's blefling and prayers.

Remember my love to your wife. Grace be with you. Yours
in Chrift Jefus,

ABERDEEN, *March* 15, 1637.   S. R.

---

* Should probably be "*from;*" though it is " for," in other editions.

CLX.—*To* ALEXANDER GORDON *of Earlston.*

(*HUNGERING AFTER CHRIST HIMSELF RATHER THAN HIS
LOVE.*)

UCH HONOURED AND WORTHY SIR,—Grace,
mercy, and peace be unto you.—I long to hear from
you. I have received few letters fince I came hither ;
I am in need of a word. A dry plant fhould have fome watering.

My cafe betwixt Chrift my Lord, and me, ftandeth between
love and jealoufy, faith and fufpicion of His love ; it is a marvel He
keepeth houfe with me. I make many pleas* with Chrift, but He
maketh as many agreements with me. I think His unchangeable
love hath faid, "I defy thee to break Me and change Me." If
Chrift had fuch changeable and new thoughts of my falvation as I
have of it, I think I fhould then be at a fad lofs. He humoureth
not a fool like me in my unbelief, but rebuketh me, and fathereth
kindnefs upon me. Chrift is more like the poor friend and needy
prifoner begging love, than I am. I cannot, for fhame, get Chrift
faid "nay" of my whole love, for He will not want His errand for
the feeking. God be thanked that my Bridegroom tireth not of
wooing. Honour to Him! He is a wilful fuitor of my foul.
But as love is His, pain is mine, that I have nothing to give Him.
His account-book is full of my debts of mercy, kindnefs, and free
love towards me. Oh that I might read with watery eyes! Oh
that He would give me the intereft of intereft to pay back! Or
rather, my foul's defire is, that He would comprife† my perfon, foul
and body, love, joy, confidence, fear, forrow, and defire, and drive‡
the poind, and let me be rouped,§ and fold to Chrift, and taken
home to my creditor's houfe and firefide.

---

* Quarrels.   † Arreft by a civil procefs, by writ.
‡ Drive away the cattle that has been feized, is the primary meaning of the term.
§ Set up by public auction to fale.

The Lord knoweth that, if I could, I would fell myfelf without reverfion to Chrift. O fweet Lord Jefus, make a market, and overbid all my buyers! I dare fwear, that there is a myftery in Chrift which I never faw; a myftery of love. Oh, if He would lay by* the lap of the covering that is over it, and let my greening† foul fee it! I would break the door, and be in upon Him, to get a wombful of love; for I am an hungered and famifhed foul. O, fir, if you, or any other, would tell Him how fick my foul is, dying for want of a hearty draught of Chrift's love! Oh, if I could dote (if I may make ufe of that word in this cafe) as much upon Himfelf as I do upon His love! It is a pity that Chrift Himfelf fhould not rather be my heart's choice, than Chrift's manifefted love. It would fatisfy me, in fome meafure, if I had any bud‡ to give for His love. Shall I offer Him my praifes? Alas! He is more than praifes. I give it over to get Him exalted according to His worth, which is above what can be known.

Yet all this time I am tempting Him, to fee if§ there be both love and anger in Him againft me. I am plucked from His flock (dear to me!), and from feeding His lambs; I go, therefore, in fackcloth, as one who hath loft the wife of His youth. Grief and forrow are fufpicious, and fpew out againft Him the fmoke of jealoufies; and I fay often, "Show me wherefore Thou contendeft with me. Tell me, O Lord: read the procefs againft me." But I know that I cannot anfwer His allegations; I fhall lofe the caufe when it cometh to open pleading. Oh, if I could force my heart to believe dreams to be dreams! Yet when Chrift giveth my fears the lie, and faith to me, "Thou art a liar," then I am glad. I refolve to hope to be quiet, and to lie on the brink on my fide, till the water fall and the ford be ridable.‖ And, howbeit there be pain upon me, in longing for deliverance that I may fpeak of Him in the great congregation, yet I think there is joy in that pain and on-waiting; and I even re-joice that He putteth me off for a time, and fhifteth me. Oh, if I

---

* Put afide.   † Earneftly longing.   ‡ Bribe.
§ As if I wifhed to find out.   ‖ Can be croffed on horfeback

could wait on for all eternity, howbeit I fhould never get my foul's
defire, fo being He were glorified! I would wifh my pain and my
miniftry could live long to ferve Him; for I know that I am a clay
veffel, and made for His ufe. Oh, if my very broken fherds could
ferve to glorify Him! I defire Chrift's grace to be willingly content,
that my hell (excepting His hatred and difpleafure, which I put out
of all play, for fubmiffion to this is not called for) were a preaching
of His glory to men and angels for ever and ever! When all is
done, what can I add to Him? or what can fuch a clay-fhadow as
I do? I know that He needeth not me. I have caufe to be grieved,
and to melt away in tears, if I had grace to do it (Lord, grant it to
me!), to fee my Well-beloved's fair face fpitted upon by dogs, to
fee loons* pulling the crown off my royal King's head; to fee
my harlot-mother and my fweet Father agree fo ill, that they are
going to fkail† and give up houfe. My Lord's palace is now a neft
of unclean birds. Oh, if harlot, harlot Scotland, would rue‡ upon
her provoked Lord, and pity her good Husband, who is broken
with her whorifh heart! But thefe things are hid from her eyes.

I have heard of late of your new trial by the Bifhop of Galloway.§ Fear not clay, worms' meat. Let truth and Chrift get no
wrong in your hand. It is your gain if Chrift be glorified; and
your glory to be Chrift's witnefs. I perfuade you, that your fufferings are Chrift's advantage and victory; for He is pleafed to reckon
them fo. Let me hear from you. Chrift is but winning a clean
kirk out of the fire; He will win this play. He will not be in your
common‖ for any charges ye are at in His fervice. He is not poor,

---

* Worthlefs fcoundrels.   † To part; break up and difperfe.   ‡ Repent.

§ The Bifhop of Galloway held this year a High Commiffion Court in
Galloway, in which, befides fining fome gentlemen, and confining the magis-
trates of Kirkcudbright to Wigtown, for matters of nonconformity, he fined
Gordon of Earlfton for his abfence, five hundred merks (about L.28), and fentenced him to be confined to Montrofe. (*Baillie's Letters and Journals.*) This,
no doubt, is the "new trial by the Bifhop of Galloway," to which Rutherford refers. See notice of Alexander Gordon of Earlfton, Let. 59.

‖ Under obligation to.

to fit in your debt; He will repay an hundred-fold more, it may be, even in this life.

The prayers and bleffings of Chrift's prifoner be with you.

Your brother, in his fweet Lord Jefus,

ABERDEEN, 1637.   S. R.

CLXI.—*To* JOHN STUART, *Provoſt of Ayr.*

[JOHN STUART, Provoft of Ayr, is defcribed by Livingftone as " a godly and zealous Chriftian of a long ftanding," for he had, from his earlieft years, been impreffed with a fenfe of religion. Inheriting, after the death of his father, confiderable property, he largely applied it to benevolent purpofes. Such was his difintereftednefs and love to thofe who were the friends of Chrift and His truth, that he called a number of them whofe diftreffed and ftraitened condition he knew, to meet with him in Edinburgh, and after fome time fpent in prayer, told them he had brought a little money to lend to each of them, which they were not to offer to pay back till he required it, at the fame time requiring them to promife not to make this known during his life. Not long after (the plague raging with feverity in Ayr, and trade becoming, in confe-quence, much depreffed) he himfelf fell into pecuniary difficulties, which made him at that time remove from the country. Borrowing a little money, he went over to France, and coming to Rochelle, loaded a fhip with falt and other commodities, which he purchafed upon credit at a very cheap rate, there having been little or no trading there for a long time. He then returned the neareft way to England, and thence to Ayr, in expectation of the fhip's re-turn. After waiting long he was informed that it was taken by the Turks, which, confidering the lofs which others in that cafe would fuftain, much afflicted him. But it at laft arrived in the road; and it was on this occafion that his friend John Kennedy, going out to the veffel in a fmall boat, was driven away by a ftorm. (See notice of Kennedy, Letter 75.) Stuart having fold the commodities which he brought from France, not only was enabled by the profits to pay all his debts, but cleared twenty thoufand merks. (*Fleming's Fulfilling of the Scriptures.*) He joined with Mr Blair, Mr Livingftone, and others, in their intended emigration to New England; but they were forced, from the tempeftuous ftate of the weather, to return. This good man was much afflicted on his death-bed. One day he faid, " I teftify, that except when I flept, or was in bufinefs, I was not thefe ten years without thoughts of God, fo long as I would be in going from my own houfe to the crofs; and yet I doubt myfelf, and am in great agony, yea, at the brink of defpair." But a day or two before he died, all his doubts were difpelled; and to Mr Fergufon, the pious minifter of Ayr, he faid, referring to his ftruggle with

temptations at that time, "I have been fighting and working out my falvation with fear and trembling, and now I blefs God it is perfected, fealed, confirmed, and all fears are gone."]

(COMMERCIAL MISFORTUNES—SERVICE-BOOK—BLESSEDNESS
OF TRIAL.)

UCH HONOURED SIR,—Grace, mercy, and peace
be unto you. I long to hear from you, being now
removed from my flock, and the prifoner of Chrift at
Aberdeen. I would not have you to think it ftrange that your
journey to New England hath gotten fuch a dafh.* It indeed hath
made my heart heavy; yet I know it is no dumb providence, but a
fpeaking one, whereby our.Lord fpeaketh His mind to you, though
for the prefent ye do not well underftand what He faith. However it
be, He who fitteth upon the floods hath fhown you His marvellous
kindnefs in the great depths. I know that your lofs is great, and
your hope is gone far againft you; but I entreat you, fir, expound
aright our Lord's laying all hindrances in the way. I perfuade myfelf that your heart aimeth at the footfteps of the flock, to feed
befide the fhepherds' tents, and to dwell befide Him whom your
foul loveth; and that it is your defire to remain in the wildernefs,
where the Woman is kept from the Dragon, And this being your
defire, remember that a poor prifoner of Chrift faid it to you, that
that mifcarried journey is with child to you of mercy and confolation; and fhall bring forth a fair birth, on which the Lord will
attend. Wait on; "He that believeth maketh not hafte."†

I hope that ye have been afking what the Lord meaneth, and
what further may be His will, in reference to your return. My
dear brother, let God make of you what He will, He will end all
with confolation, and will make glory out of your fufferings; and
would you wifh better work? This water was in your way to
heaven, and written in your Lord's book; ye behoved to crofs it,
and, therefore, kifs His wife and unerring providence. Let not the
cenfures of men, who fee but the outfide of things, and fcarce well

---

* See note at Let. 63.   † Ifa. xxviii. 16.

that, abate your courage and rejoicing in the Lord. Howbeit your
faith feeth but the black fide of providence; yet it hath a better
fide, and God will let you fee it.   Learn to believe Chrift better
than His ftrokes, Himfelf and His promifes better than His glooms.*
Dafhes and difappointments are not canonical Scripture; fighting
for the promifed land feemed to cry to God's promife, "Thou
lieft." If our Lord ride upon a ftraw, His horfe fhall neither
ftumble nor fall. "For we know that all things work together for
good to them that love God;"† *ergo*, fhipwreck, loffes, &c., work
together for the good of them that love God.   Hence I infer, that
loffes, difappointments, ill-tongues, lofs of friends, houfes, or country,
are God's workmen, fet on work to work out good to you, out of
everything that befalleth you.   Let not the Lord's dealing feem
harfh, rough, or unfatherly, becaufe it is unpleafant.   When the
Lord's bleffed will bloweth acrofs your defires, it is beft, in humility,
to ftrike fail to Him, and to be willing to be led any way our Lord
pleafeth.   It is a point of denial of yourfelf, to be as if ye had not
a will, but had made a free difpofition of it to God, and had fold it
over to Him; and to make ufe of His will for your own is both
true holinefs, and your eafe and peace. Ye know not what the
Lord is working out of this, but ye fhall know it hereafter.

And what I write to you, I write to your wife. I compaffionate her cafe, but entreat her not to fear nor faint. This journey is
a part of her wildernefs to heaven and the promifed land, and there
are fewer miles behind.   It is nearer the dawning of the day to
her than when fhe went out of Scotland. I fhould be glad to hear
that ye and fhe have comfort and courage in the Lord.

Now, as concerning our Kirk; our Service-book is ordained,
by open proclamation and found of trumpet, to be read in all the
kirks of the kingdom.‡   Our prelates are to meet this month about

---

* Frowns.   † Rom. viii. 28.

‡ The Service-book, or Liturgy, at this time impofed upon Scotland, was
juft that of England, but containing numerous alterations. The Act of Privy
Council, enjoining the ufe of the Service-book, is dated 20th December 1636;
and it was next day proclaimed at the crofs of Edinburgh: but it was not

our Canons,* and for a reconciliation betwixt us and the Lutherans.
The Profeffors of Aberdeen **Univerfity** are charged to draw up the
Articles of an uniform Confeffion ; but reconciliation with Popery
is **intended.** This is the **day of** Jacob's vifitation ; the ways of
Zion mourn, our gold **is become** dim, **the** fun is gone down upon
our prophets. A **dry wind, but neither to fan** nor to cleanfe, is
coming upon this land ; **and all our ill** is coming from the multiplied tranfgreffions of this land, and from the friends and lovers of
Babel among us. "The violence done to me and to my flefh be
upon **thee,** Babylon, fhall the inhabitant **of Zion fay** ; and, **My
blood upon** the inhabitants of Chaldea, fhall Jerufalem fay."†

---

publifhed till towards the end of May **1637.** Its title is, "The Booke of
Common **Prayer** and Adminiftration **of the** Sacraments and other parts of
Divine Service, **for the use of the Church** of Scotland. Edinburgh, 1637."
This book was extremely obnoxious to the great body of the minifters and
people of Scotland, both from the manner of its introduction, which was by
the fole authority of the King, without the Church having been even confulted
in the **matter, and** from the doctrines which **it contained, in** which it approached nearer to the Roman miffal than the Englifh liturgy. It was drawn
up by **James** Wedderburn, Bifhop of Dunblane, and John Maxwell, Bifhop
of Rofs, with the affiftance of Sydferff, Bifhop of Galloway, and Ballenden,
Bifhop of Aberdeen. It **was** revifed by Archbifhop Laud, and Wren,
Bifhop of Norwich. Kirkton mentions that he faw the original copy corrected by Laud's own hands, and that all his corrections approached towards
Popery and the Roman miffal. (*Kirkton's Hiftory,* p. 30.)

* The Book of Canons was, in obedience to the King's orders, drawn up
b/ four of the Scottifh bifhops,—Sydferff of Galloway, Maxwell of **Rofs,**
Ballenden of Aberdeen, and Whiteford of Dunblane. After being fubmitted
to Archbifhop Laud and two other Englifh prelates for revifal, it received
the Royal fanction, and became law in **1635.** This book, like the Service-
book which followed **it, was** extremely **unpopular** in Scotland, becaufe it was
impofed folely by **Royal** authority, and from the nature of the canons themfelves, which prefcribed **a** variety of ceremonial and fuperftitious rites in the
obfervance of **baptifm** and the Lord's Supper; invefted bifhops with uncon-
trollable power; inculcated the doctrine of the King's fupremacy in matters
ecclefiaftical as well as civil,—affirming that no meeting of General Affembly
could be held unlefs called by the King's authority ; and introduced other innovations equally arbitrary and obnoxious.

† Jer. li. 35

Now for myfelf : I was three days before the High Commiffion, and accufed of treafon preached againft our King. (A minifter being witnefs, went well nigh to fwear it.) God hath faved me from their malice. 1/t, They have deprived me of my miniftry ; 2*dly*, Silenced me, that I exercife no part of the minifterial function within this kingdom, under the pain of rebellion ; 3*dly*, Confined my perfon within the town of Aberdeen, where I find the minifters working for my confinement in Caithnefs or Orkney, far from them, becaufe fome people here (willing to be edified) refort to me. At my firft entry, I had heavy challenges* within me, and a court fenced† (but I hope not in Chrift's name), wherein it was afferted that my Lord would have no more of my fervices, and was tired of me ; and, like a fool, I fummoned Chrift alfo for unkindnefs. My foul fainted, and I refufed comfort, and faid, " What ailed Chrift at me ? for I defired to be faithful in His houfe." Thus, in my rov-ings‡ and miftakings, my Lord Jefus beftowed mercy on me, who am lefs than the leaft of all faints. I lay upon the duft, and bought a plea from Satan againft Chrift, and He was content to fell it. But at length Chrift did fhow Himfelf friends with me, and in mercy pardoned and paffed my part of it, and only complained that a court fhould be holden in His bounds without His allowance. Now I pafs from my compearance ;§ and, as if Chrift had done the fault, He hath made the mends, ‖ and returned to my foul ; fo that now His poor prifoner feedeth on the feafts of love. My adverfaries know not what a courtier I am now with my Royal King, for whofe crown I now fuffer. It is but our foft and lazy flefh that hath raifed an ill report of the crofs of Chrift. O fweet, fweet is His yoke ! Chrift's chains are of pure gold ; fufferings for Him are perfumed. I would not give my weeping for the laughing of all the fourteen prelates ;¶ I would not exchange my fadnefs with the world's joy. O lovely, lovely Jefus, how fweet muft thy kiffes

---

* Upbraidings. † Conftituted. ‡ Wanderings, like one out of his mind.
§ Appearing in court in obedience to legal citation.
‖ Made up for the wrong.
¶ *Fourteen* was the number of bifhops in Scotland.

be, when thy crofs fmelleth fo fweetly! Oh, if all the three kingdoms had part of my love-feaft, and of the comfort of a dawted*
prifoner!

Dear Brother, I charge you to praife for me, and to feek help
of our acquaintance there to help me to praife. Why fhould I
fmother Chrift's honefty to me? My heart is taken up with this,
that my filence and fufferings may preach. I befeech you in the
bowels of Chrift, to help me to praife. Remember my love to
your wife, to Mr Blair, and Mr Livingftone, and Mr Cunningham.
Let me hear from you, for I am anxious what to do. If I faw a
call for New England, I would follow it. Grace be with you.

Yours in our Lord Jefus,

S. R.

ABERDEEN, 1637.

CLXII.—*To* JOHN STUART, *Provoft of Ayr.*

(*THE BURDEN OF A SILENCED MINISTER—SPIRITUAL SHORTCOMINGS.*)

UCH HONOURED AND DEAREST IN CHRIST,
—Grace, mercy, and peace from God our Father, and
from our Lord Jefus Chrift, be upon you.

I expected the comfort of a letter to a prifoner from you, ere
now. I am here, Sir, putting off† a part of my inch of time; and
when I awake firft in the morning (which is always with great
heavinefs and fadnefs), this queftion is brought to my mind, "Am
I ferving God or not?" Not that I doubt of the truth of this
honourable caufe wherein I am engaged; I dare venture into
eternity, and before my Judge, that I now fuffer for the truth: becaufe that I cannot endure that my Mafter, who is a freeborn King,
fhould pay tribute to any of the fhields or potfherds of the earth.
Oh that I could hold the crown upon my princely King's head with

---

* Fondled.   † Spending.

my finful **arm**, howbeit it fhould be ftruck from me in that fervice,
from the fhoulder-blade.   But my clofed mouth, my dumb Sabbaths, the memory of my communion with Chrift, in many fair, fair
days in Anwoth, whereas now my Mafter getteth no fervice of my
tongue as then, hath almoft broken my faith in two halves.   Yet
in my deepeft apprehenfions of His anger, I fee through a cloud
that I am wrong ; and He, in love to my foul, hath taken up the
controverfy betwixt faith and apprehenfions, and a decreet* is paffed
on Chrift's fide of it, and I fubfcribe the decreet.*   The Lord is
equal in His ways, but my guiltinefs often overmaftereth my believing.   I have not been well known : for except as to open out-
breakings, I want nothing of what Judas and Cain had ; only He
hath been pleafed to prevent me in mercy, and to caft me into a
fever of love for Himfelf, and His abfence maketh my fever moft
painful.   And befide, He hath vifited my foul and watered it with
His comforts.   But yet I have not what I would.   The want of
real and felt poffeffion is my only death.   I know that Chrift pitieth
me in this.

The great men, my friends, that did† for me, are dried up like
winter-brooks of water.   All fay, " No dealing for that man ; his
beft will be to be gone out of the kingdom."   So I fee they tire of
me.   But, believe me, I am moft gladly content that Chrift breaketh
all my idols in pieces.   It hath put a new edge upon my blunted love
to Chrift ; I fee that He is jealous of my love, and will have all to
Himfelf.   In a word, thefe fix things are my burden : 1. I am not
in the vineyard as others are ; it may be, becaufe Chrift thinketh me
a withered tree, not worth its room.   But God forbid ! 2. Woe,
woe, woe is coming upon my harlot-mother, this apoftate Kirk !
The time is coming when we fhall wifh for doves' wings to flee and
hide us.   Oh, for the defolation of this land ! 3. I fee my dear
Mafter Chrift going His lone‡ (as it were), mourning in fackcloth.
His fainting friends fear that King Jefus fhall lofe the field.   But

---

* A fentence of the Court.   † Acted for me.
‡ Going lonely, by himfelf ; Ps. cii. ;.

He muſt carry the day. 4. My guiltineſs and the ſins of youth are come up againſt me, and they would come into the plea in my ſufferings, as deſerving cauſes in God's juſtice ; but I pray God, for Chriſt's ſake, that He may never give them that room. 5. Woe is me, that I cannot get my royal, dreadful, mighty, and glorious Prince of the kings of the earth ſet on high. Sir, ye may help me and pity me in this ; and bow your knee, and bleſs His name, and deſire others to do it, that He hath been pleaſed, in my ſufferings, to make Atheiſts, Papiſts, and enemies about me ſay, " It is like that God is with this priſoner." Let hell and the powers of hell (I care not) be let looſe againſt me to do their worſt, ſo being that Chriſt, and my Father, and His Father, be magnified in my ſufferings. 6. Chriſt's love hath pained me : for howbeit His preſence hath ſhamed me, and drowned me in debt, yet He often goeth away when my love to Him is burning. He ſeemeth to look like a proud wooer, who will not look upon a poor match that is dying of love. I will not ſay He is lordly. But I know He is wiſe in hiding Himſelf from a child and a fool, who maketh an idol and a god of one of Chriſt's kiſſes, which is idolatry. I fear that I adore His comforts more than Himſelf, and that I love the apples of life better than the tree of life.

Sir, write to me. Commend me to your wife. Mercy be her portion. Grace be with you.

Yours, in his deareſt Lord Jeſus,

S. R.

ABERDEEN, 1637.

CLXIII.—*To* JOHN STUART, *Provoſt of Ayr.*

*(VIEW OF TRIALS PAST—HARD THOUGHTS OF CHRIST—CROSSES
—HOPE.)*

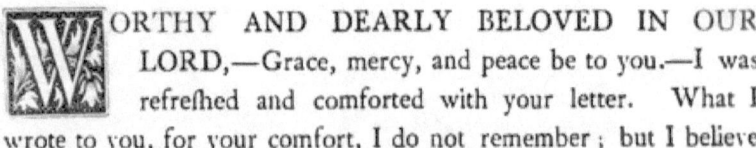

ORTHY AND DEARLY BELOVED IN OUR LORD,—Grace, mercy, and peace be to you.—I was refreſhed and comforted with your letter. What I wrote to you, for your comfort, I do not remember ; but I believe

that love will prophefy homeward,* as it would have it. I wifh that
I could help you to praife His great and holy name who keepeth
the feet of His faints, and hath numbered all your goings. I know
that our deareft Lord will pardon and pafs by our honeft errors and
miftakes, when we mind His honour ; yet I know that none of you
have feen the other half, and the hidden fide, of your wonderful return home to us again. I am confident ye fhall yet fay, that God's
mercy blew your fails back to Ireland again.†

Worthy and dear Sir, I cannot but give you an account of my
prefent eftate, that ye may go an errand for me to my high and
royal Mafter, of whom I boaft all the day. I am as proud of His
love (nay, I blefs myfelf, and boaft more of my prefent lot) as any
poor man can be of an earthly king's court, or of a kingdom. *Firft*,
I am very often turning both the fides of my crofs, efpecially my
dumb and filent Sabbaths ; not becaufe I defire to find a crook or
defect in my Lord's love, but becaufe my love is fick with fancies
and fear. Whether or not the Lord hath a procefs leading againft
my guiltinefs, that I have not yet well feen, I know not. My defire is to ride fair, and not to fpark‡ dirt (if, with reverence to Him,
I may be permitted to make ufe of fuch a word) in the face of my
only, only Well-beloved ; but fear of guiltinefs is a talebearer be-

---

* In its own favour.

† Some of those who had embarked in that voyage had important work to
perform in Scotland. The minifters, after their return coming over to this
country, were settled in various parifhes; Meffrs Blair at Ayr, Livingftone
at Stranraer, M'Clelland at Kirkcudbright, and Hamilton at Dumfries.
They were zealous promoters of the fubfcribing of the National Covenant,
and of other meafures by which the triumph of the Prefbyterian Church in
Scotland was ultimately fecured; and all of them were chofen members of the
celebrated Affembly held at Glafgow in 1638, in the proceedings of which
they took a prominent part. Speaking of their return, Row of Ceres fays,
" Neither the prelates and conformifts, nor they themfelves, knew that within
a year the Lord would not only root out the prelates in Scotland, and, after
that, out of England and Ireland, but make fome of them, efpecially Meffrs
Blair, Livingftone, and M'Clelland, to be very inftrumental in the work of
reformation."—*Life of Robert Blair* (Wodrow Society).

‡ Caufe fparks of dirt to be fquirted.

twixt me and Chrift, and is ftill whifpering ill tales of my Lord, to
weaken my faith. I had rather that a cloud went over my comforts
by thefe meffages, than that my faith fhould be hurt; for, if my
Lord get no wrong by me, verily I defire grace not to care what
become of me. I defire to give no faith nor credit to my forrow,
that can make a lie of my beft friend Chrift. Woe, woe be to them
all who fpeak ill of Chrift! Hence thefe thoughts awake with me
in the morning, and go to bed with me. Oh, what fervice can a
dumb body do in Chrift's houfe! Oh, I think the word of God is
imprifoned alfo! Oh, I am a dry tree! Alas, I can neither plant
nor water! Oh, if my Lord would make but dung of me, to fatten
and make fertile His own corn-ridges in Mount Zion! Oh, if I
might but fpeak to three or four herdboys* of my worthy Mafter, I
would be fatisfied to be the meaneft and moft obfcure of all the
paftors in this land, and to live in any place, in any of Chrift's bafeft
outhoufes! But he faith, " Sirrah, I will not fend you; I have no
errands for you thereaway."† My defire to ferve Him is fick of
jealoufy, left He be unwilling to employ me. *Secondly*, This is
feconded by another; Oh! all that I have done in Anwoth, the
fair work that my Mafter began there, is like a bird dying in the
fhell; and what will I then have to fhow of all my labour, in the
day of my compearance‡ before Him, when the Mafter of the vineyard calleth the labourers, and giveth them their hire? *Thirdly*,
But truly, when Chrift's fweet wind is in the right airth, § I repent,
and I pray Chrift to take law-burrows∥ of my quarrelous¶ unbelieving fadnefs and forrow. Lord, rebuke them that put ill betwixt a
poor fervant like me and his good Mafter. Then I fay, whether
the black crofs will or not, I muft climb on hands and feet up to
my Lord. I am now ruing from my heart that I pleafured the
law (my old dead hufband) fo far as to apprehend wrath in my

---

* Boys, like David, keeping the fheep or cattle.   † In thofe places.
‡ Appearance, becaufe fummoned.   § Quarter.
∥ Pledge, fuch as the law demands from a man that he will not injure his
neighbour.
¶ Querulous, or quarrelfome rather.

fweet Lord Jefus. I had far rather take a hire to plead for the grace of God, for I think myfelf Chrift's fworn debtor; and the truth is (to fpeak of my Lord what I cannot deny), I am over head and ears, drowned in many obligations to His love and mercy.

He handleth me fome time fo, that I am afhamed almoft to feek more for a four-hours,* but to live content (till the marriage-fupper of the Lamb) with that which He giveth. But I know not how greedy and how ill† to pleafe love is. For either my Lord Jefus hath taught me ill manners, not to be content with a feat, except my head lie in His bofom, and except I be fed with the fatnefs of His houfe; or elfe I am grown impatiently dainty, and ill to pleafe, as if Chrift were obliged, under this crofs, to do no other thing but bear me in His arms, and as if I had claim by merit for my fuffering for Him. But I wifh He would give me grace to learn to go on my own feet, and to learn to do without His comforts, and to give thanks and believe, when the fun is not in my firmament, and when my Well-beloved is from home, and gone another errand. Oh, what fweet peace have I, when I find that Chrift holdeth and I draw; when I climb up and He fhuteth‡ me down; when I grip § Him and embrace Him, and He feemeth to loofe the grips § and flee away from me! I think there is even a fweet joy of faith, and contentednefs, and peace, in His very tempting unkindnefs, becaufe my faith faith, "Chrift is not in fad earneft with me, but trying if I can be kind to His mafk and cloud that covereth Him, as well as to His fair face." I blefs His great name that I love His vail which goeth over His face, whill‖ God fend better; for faith can kifs God's tempting reproaches when He nicknameth a finner, "A dog, not worthy to eat bread with the bairns."¶ I think it an honour that Chrift mifcalleth** me, and reproacheth me. I will take that well of Him, howbeit I would not bear it well if another fhould be that homely;†† but becaufe I am His own (God be thanked), He may ufe me as He pleafeth. I muft fay, the faints

---

* A flight afternoon's meal.   † Difficult.   ‡ Shoveth, pufheth.   § Grafp.
‖ Till.   ¶ Mark vii. 27, 28.   ** Gives me by-names.   †† So familiar.

have a sweet life between them and Christ. There is much sweet
solace of love between Him and them, when He feedeth among the
lilies, and cometh into His garden, and maketh a feast of honey-
combs, and drinketh His wine and His milk, and crieth, " Eat, O
friends: drink, yea, drink abundantly, O well-beloved." One hour
of this labour is worth a shipful of the world's drunken and muddy
joy; nay, even the gate* to heaven is the sunny side **of the** brae,
and the very garden of the world. For the men of this world have
their own unchristened and profane crosses; and woe be to them and
their cursed crosses both; for their ills are salted with God's vengeance, and our ills seasoned with our Father's blessing. So that they
are no fools who choose Christ, and sell all things for Him. **It is**
no bairns' market, nor a blind block ;† we know well what we get,
and what **we** give.

Now, for any resolution to go to any other kingdom, I dare not
speak one word.‡ My **hopes** of enlargement **are** cold, my hopes of
re-entry to my Master's ill-dressed vineyard again are far colder.
I have no seat for my faith to sit on, but **bare omnipotency, and
God's holy arm** and good-will. **Here I desire to** stay, and ride at

---

* This seems to mean, " The very way (gate) to heaven is pleasant."

† Bargain.

‡ At present the prospects of the Church were so dark, that Rutherford
appears sometimes to have entertained the idea of removing to another country,
should he succeed in obtaining his liberty. In a preceding letter to Stuart,
he names New England, then an asylum for multitudes who were persecuted
for conscience sake, as a place to which he would willingly go, provided he
could see the call of Providence. And some of his friends about this time
were desirous that he might be honourably and usefully employed abroad.
Robert Baillie, in a letter to Mr William Spang, minister at Campvere, dated
January 29, 1637, says, " Alwayes I take the man [Rutherford] to be among
the most learned and best ingynes of our nation. I think he were verie able for
some profession in your colledges of Utreck, Groninge, or Rotterdame; for
our King's dominions, there is no appearance he will ever gett living into them.
If you could quietly procure him a calling, I think it were a good service to
God to relieve one of his troubled ministers; a good to the place he came to,
for he is both godlie and learned; yea, I think by time he might be ane ornament to our natione."—*Baillie's Letters and Journals*, vol. i., **p. 9.**

anchor, and winter, whill* God fend fair weather again, and be pleafed to take home to His houfe my harlot-mother. Oh, if her hufband would be that† kind, as to go and fetch her out of the brothel-houfe, and chafe her lovers to the hills! But there will be fad days ere it come to that. Remember my bonds. Grace be with you.

Yours, in our Lord Jefus,

S. R.

Aberdeen, 1637.

CLXIV.—*To* Ninian Mure [fee Let. 191], *one of the family of Caſſincarrie.*

[We do not know more of *Ninian Mure* than that he was a parifhioner of Anwoth. The name "*Mure*" is found on feveral tombs in the old church-yard, of which the oldeſt and moſt intereſting is the following, on the eaſt fide of the enclofed pile :—

> "Walking with God in purity of life,
> In Chriſt I died, and endit all my ſtrife.
> For in my faul Chriſt here did dwell by grace ;
> Now dwells my faul in glory of His face.
> Therefore my body ſhall not here remain,
> But to full glory furely rife again."
>
> "*Marion Mure*, goodwife of Cullindock,
> Departed this life, anno 1612."

(A YOUTH ADMONISHED.)

LOVING FRIEND,—I received your letter. I entreat you now, in the morning of your life, to feek the Lord and His face. Beware of the follies of dangerous youth, a perilous time for your foul. Love not the world. Keep faith and truth with all men in your covenants and bargains. Walk with God, for He feeth you. Do nothing but that which ye may and would do if your eye-ſtrings were breaking, and your breath

---

* Till.   † So really kind.

growing cold. Ye heard the truth of God from me, my dear heart,
follow it, and forfake it not. Prize Chrift and falvation above all
the world. To live after the guife* and courfe of the reft of the
world will not bring you to heaven; without faith in Chrift, and
repentance, ye cannot fee God. Take pains for falvation; prefs
forward toward the mark for the prize of the high calling. If ye
watch not againft evils night and day, which befet you, ye will come
behind.† Beware of lying, fwearing, uncleannefs, and the reft of
the works of the flefh; becaufe "for thefe things the wrath of
God cometh upon the children of difobedience." How fweet foever
they may feem for the prefent, yet the end of thefe courfes is the
eternal wrath of God, and utter darknefs, where there is weeping
and gnafhing of teeth. Grace be with you.

> Your loving paftor,
>
>   S. R.

Aberdeen, 1637.

* * *

CLXV.—*To* Mr Thomas Garven.

[Thomas Garven, one of the minifters of Edinburgh. R. Blair's Life,
by Row, tells of his being banifhed from the town by the King in 1662, for
his adherence to Prefbytery.]

(PERSONAL INSUFFICIENCY—GRACE FROM CHRIST ALONE—
LONGINGS AFTER HIM.)

REVEREND AND DEAR BROTHER,—Grace, mercy,
and peace be to you. I am forry that what joy and
forrow drew from my imprifoned pen in my love-fits
hath made you and many of God's children believe that there is
fomething in a broken reed the like of me. Except that Chrift's
grace hath bought fuch a fold body, I know not what elfe any may
think of me, or expect from me. My ftock is lefs (my Lord

---

* Manner.   † 1 Cor. i. 7; fall fhort, or be wanting in.

knoweth that I fpeak truth) than many believe. My empty founds have promifed too much. I fhould be glad to lie under Chrift's feet, and kep* and receive the off-fallings, or the old pieces of any grace, that fall from His fweet fingers to forlorn finners. I lie often, unco†-like, looking at the King's windows. Surely I am unworthy of a feat in the King's hall-floor; I but often look afar off, both feared and fremmed-like,‡ to that faireft face, fearing He bid me look away from Him. My guiltinefs rifeth up upon me, and I have no anfwer for it. I offered my tongue to Chrift, and my pains in His houfe: and what know I what it meaneth, when Chrift will not receive my poor propine?§ When love will not take, we ex-pone‖ that it will neither take nor give, borrow nor lend. Yet Chrift hath another fea-compafs which He faileth by, than my fhort and raw thoughts. I leave His part of it to Himfelf. I dare not expound His dealing as forrow and mifbelief often dictate to me. I look often with bleared and blind eyes to my Lord's crofs; and when I look to the wrong fide of His crofs, I know that I mifs a ftep and flide. Surely, I fee that I have not legs of my own for carrying me to heaven: I muft go in at heaven's gates, borrowing ftrength from Chrift.

I am often thinking, "Oh, if He would but give me leave to love Him, and if Chrift would but open up His wares, and the in-finite plies, and windings, and corners of His foul-delighting love, and let me fee it, backfide and forefide; and give me leave but to ftand befide it, like a hungry man befide meat, to get my fill of wonder-ing, as a preface to my fill of enjoying!" But, verily, I think that my foul eyes would defile His fair love to look to it. Either my hunger is over humble (if that may be faid), or elfe I confider not what honour it is to get leave to love Chrift. Oh, that He would pity a prifoner, and let out a flood upon the dry ground! It is nothing to him to fill the like of me; one of His looks would do

---

* Catch up when falling. † Strange.

‡ Like one who has no bond of relationfhip to the perfon.

§ Prefent held out. ‖ Expound the meaning to be.

me meikle* world's good, and Him no ill. I know that I am not at a point yet with Chriſt's love : I am not yet fitted for ſo much as I would have of it. My hope ſitteth neighbour with meikle black† hunger : and certainly I dow‡ not but think that there is more of that love ordained for me than I yet comprehend, and that I know not the weight of the penſion which the King will give me. I ſhall be glad if my hungry bill get leave to lie beſide Chriſt, waiting on an anſwer. Now I ſhould be full and rejoice, if I got a poor man's alms of that ſweeteſt love ; but I confidently believe that there is a bed made for Chriſt and me, and that we ſhall take our fill of love in it. And I often think, when my joy is run out, and at the loweſt ebb, that I would ſeek no more than my rights paſſed the King's great ſeal,§ and that theſe eyes of mine could ſee Chriſt's hand at the pen.

If your Lord call you to ſuffering, be not diſmayed ; there ſhall be a new allowance of the King for you when you come to it. One of the ſofteſt pillows Chriſt hath is laid under His witneſſes' head, though often they muſt ſet down their bare feet among thorns. He hath brought my poor ſoul to deſire and wiſh, " Oh that my aſhes, and the powder I ſhall be diſſolved into, had well-tuned tongues to praiſe Him !"

Thus in haſte, deſiring your prayers and praiſes, I recommend you to my ſweet, sweet Maſter, my honourable Lord, of whom I hold all. Grace be with you.

Your own, in his ſweet Lord Jeſus,

S. R.

ABERDEEN, 1637.

---

* As much as having a world's good things.
† Much of terrible hunger.   ‡ Cannot.
§ Things I am to get, handed to me in the ſhape of title-deeds from the King.

(*A GOOD CONSCIENCE—CHRIST KIND TO SUFFERERS—
RESPONSIBILITY—YOUTH.*)

MUCH HONOURED SIR,—I long to hear how your foul profpereth. I wonder that ye write not to me: for the Holy Ghoft beareth me witnefs, that I cannot, I dare not, I do* not forget you, nor the fouls of thofe with you, who are redeemed by the blood of the great Shepherd. Ye are in my heart in the night-watches; ye are my joy and crown in the day of Chrift. O Lord, bear me witnefs, if my foul thirfteth for anything out of heaven, more than for your falvation. Let God lay me in an even balance, and try me in this.

Love heaven; let your heart be on it. Up, up, and vifit the new Land and view the fair City, and the white Throne, and the Lamb, the bride's Hufband in His Bridegroom's clothes, fitting on it. It were time that your foul caft itfelf, and all your burdens, upon Chrift. I befeech you by the wounds of your Redeemer, and by your compearance† before Him, and by the falvation of your foul, lofe no time; run faft, for it is late. God hath fworn by Himfelf, who made the world and time, that time fhall be no more.‡ Ye are now upon the very border of the other life. Your Lord cannot be blamed for not giving you warning. I have taught the truth of Chrift to you, and delivered unto you the whole counfel of God; and I have ftood before the Lord for you, and I will yet ftill ftand. Awake, awake to do righteoufly. Think not to be eafed of the burdens and debts that are on your houfe by opprefling any, or being rigorous to thofe that are under you. Remember how I endeavoured to walk before you in this matter, as an example. " Behold, here am I, witnefs againft me, before the Lord

---

* " *Dow* not," in old editions; but we have given it "*do* not;" for " cannot" is the fame as " dow not."

† Appearing in obedience to a fummons.   ‡ Rev. x. 6.

and His Anointed : whofe ox or whofe afs have I taken ?   Whom
have I defrauded ?   Whom have I oppreffed ?"*   Who knoweth
how my foul feedeth upon a good confcience, when I remember
how I fpent this body in feeding the lambs of Chrift ?

At my firft entry hither, I grant, I took a ftomach againft my
Lord, becaufe He had caften me over the dyke of the vineyard, as
a dry tree, and would have no more of my fervice.   My dumb
Sabbaths broke my heart, and I would not be comforted.   But now
He whom my foul loveth is come again, and it pleafeth Him to feaft
me with the kiffes of His love.   A King dineth with me, and His
fpikenard cafteth a fweet fmell.   The Lord is my witnefs above,
that I write my heart to you.   I never knew, by my nine years'
preaching, fo much of Chrift's love, as He has taught me in Aberdeen, by fix months' imprifonment.   I charge you in Chrift's name
to help me to praife; and fhow that people and country the
loving-kindnefs of the Lord to my foul, that fo my fufferings may
fomeway preach to them when I am filent.   He hath made me to
know now better than before, what it is to be crucified to the world.
I would not now give a drink of cold water for all the world's
kindnefs.   I owe no fervice to it : I am not the flefh's debtor.   My
Lord Jefus hath dawted† His prifoner, and hath thoughts of love
concerning me.   I would not exchange my fighs with the laughing
of adverfaries.   Sir, I write this to inform you, that ye may know
that it is the truth of Chrift I now fuffer for, and that He hath
fealed my fuffering with the comforts of His Spirit on my foul ;
and I know that He putteth not His feal upon blank paper.

Now, fir, I have no comfort earthly, but to know that I have
efpoufed, and fhall prefent a bride to Chrift in that congregation.
The Lord hath given you much, and therefore He will require
much of you again.   Number your talents, and fee what you have
to render back.   Ye cannot be enough perfuaded of the fhortnefs
of your time.   I charge you to write to me, and in the fear of God
to be plain with me, whether or not ye have made your falvation

---

* 1 Sam. xii. 3.   † Fondled.

fure. I am confident, and hope the beft; but I know that your reckonings with your Judge are many and deep. Sir, be not beguiled, negleçt not your one thing,* your one neceffary thing,† the good part that fhall not be taken from you. Look beyond time: things here are but moonfhine. They have but children's wit who are delighted with fhadows, and deluded with feathers flying in the air.

Defire your children, in the morning of their life, to begin and feek the Lord, and to remember their Creator in the days of their youth,‡ to cleanfe their way, by taking heed thereto, according to God's word.§ Youth is a glaffy age. Satan finds a fwept chamber, for the moft part, in youthhood, and a garnifhed lodging for himfelf and his train. Let the Lord have the flower of their age; the beft facrifice is due to Him. Inftruçt them in this, that they have a foul, and that this life is nothing in comparifon of eternity. They will have much need of God's conduçt in this world, to guide them by‖ thofe rocks upon which moft men fplit; but far more need when it cometh to the hour of death, and their compearance before Chrift. Oh that there were fuch an heart in them, to fear the name of the great and dreadful God, who hath laid up great things for thofe that love and fear Him! I pray that God may be their portion. Show others of my parifhioners, that I write to them my beft wifhes, and the bleffings of their lawful paftor. Say to them from me, that I befeech them, by the bowels of Chrift, to keep in mind the doçtrine of our Lord and Saviour Jefus Chrift, which I taught them; that fo they may lay hold on eternal life, ftriving together for the faith of the Gofpel, and making fure falvation to themfelves. Walk in love, and do righteoufnefs; feek peace; love one another. Wait for the coming of our Mafter and Judge. Receive no doçtrine contrary to that which I delivered to you. If ye fall away, and forget it, and that Catechifm which I taught you, and fo forfake your own mercy, the Lord be Judge betwixt you and me. I take heaven and earth to witnefs, that fuch fhall eternally perifh. But if they ferve the Lord, great will their reward

---

* Phil. iii. 13.   † Luke x. 42.   ‡ Eccles. xii. 1.   § Ps. cxix. 9.   ‖ Paft.

·be when they and I ſhall ſtand before our Judge. Set forward up the mountain, to meet with God ; climb up, for your Saviour calleth on you. It may be that God will call you to your reſt, when I am far from you ; but ye have my love, and the deſires of my heart for your ſoul's welfare. He that is holy, keep you from falling, and eſtabliſh you, till His own glorious appearance.

Your affectionate and lawful paſtor,

S. R.

ABERDEEN, 1637.

CLXVII.—*To my* LADY BOYD. [Let. 107.]

(*LESSONS LEARNED IN THE SCHOOL OF ADVERSITY.*)

ADAM,—Grace, mercy, and peace from God our Father, and from our Lord Jeſus Chriſt, be multiplied upon you.

I have reaſoned with your ſon* at large ; I rejoice to ſee him ſet His face in the right airth,† now when the nobles love the ſunny ſide of the Goſpel beſt, and are afraid that Chriſt want ſoldiers, and ſhall not be able to do for Himſelf.

Madam, our debts of obligation to Chriſt are not ſmall ; the freedom of grace and of ſalvation is the wonder of men and angels. But mercy in our Lord ſcorneth hire. Ye are bound to lift Chriſt on high, who hath given you eyes to diſcern the devil now coming out in his whites, and the idolatry and apoſtaſy of the time, well waſhen‡ with fair pretences ; but the ſkin is black and the water foul. It were art, I confeſs, to waſh a black devil, and make him white.

I am in ſtrange ups and downs, and ſeven times a-day I loſe ground. I am put often to ſwimming ; and again my feet are ſet on the Rock that is higher than myſelf. He hath now let me ſee four things which I never ſaw before : 1ſt, That the Supper ſhall be great cheer, that is up in the great hall with the Royal King of

---

* Lord Boyd. See notice of him, Let. 78.   † Quarter.
‡ Waſhed ; whitened over.

glory, when the four-hours,* the standing drink,* in this dreary wildernefs, is so sweet. When He bloweth a kiss afar off to His poor heart-broken mourners in Zion, and sendeth me but His hearty commendations till we meet, I am confounded with wonder to think what it shall be, when the Fairest among the sons of men shall lay a King's sweet soft cheek to the sinful cheeks of poor sinners. O time, time, go swiftly, and hasten that day! Sweet **Lord Jesus**, post! come, flying like a young hart or a roe upon the mountains of separation. I think that **we** should tell† the hours carefully, and look often **how low the sun is.** For love hath no " Ho ! "‡ it is pained, pained in itself, till it come into grips § with the party **beloved.**

2*dly.* I find Christ's absence **to be love's sickness and love's death.** The wind that bloweth out of the airth where my Lord Jesus reigneth is sweet-smelled, soft, joyful, and heartsome‖ to a soul burnt with absence. It is a painful battle for a soul sick of love to fight with absence and delays. Christ's " Not yet" is a stounding¶ of all the joints and liths** of the soul. A nod of His head, when He is under a mask, **would be half a pawn.**†† To say, " Fool, what aileth thee ? He is coming," **would be life to a dead man.** I am often in my dumb Sabbaths **seeking a new plea**‡‡ with my Lord Jesus (God forgive me!), and I care not if there be not two or three ounce-weight of black wrath in **my cup.**

3*dly.* **For** the third thing, I have **seen my abominable vilenefs ;** if I were well known, there would **none in this kingdom ask how I** do. Many take my **ten to be a hundred, but I am a deeper hypo-**crite, and shallower professor, than every **one believeth.** God knoweth I feign not. But I think my reckonings on **the one page** written in great letters, **and His mercy to such a forlorn § and

---

* When even the slight afternoon meal and the cup handed to one at the door is so sweet.

† Count. ‡ Cessation ; cry to halt. § Grasp. ‖ Cheering.

¶ A dull stroke that comes suddenly and vibrates through the body.

** Joints; the one word explains the other. " Joist" was in the margin of old editions.

†† A pledge. ‡‡ Quarrel ; controversy. §§ Lost prodigal debtor.

wretched dyvour on the other, to be more than a miracle. If I could get my finger-ends upon a full aſſurance, I trow that I would grip* faſt; but my cup wanteth not gall. And, upon my part, deſpair might be almoſt excuſed, if every one in this land ſaw my inner ſide. But I know that I am one of them who have made great ſale, and a free market, to free grace. If I could be ſaved, as I would fain believe, ſure I am that I have given Chriſt's blood, His free grace, and the bowels of His mercy, a large field to work upon; and Chriſt hath manifeſted His art, I dare not ſay to the uttermoſt (for He can, if He would, forgive all the devils and damned reprobates, in reſpeĉt of the wideneſs of His mercy), but I ſay to an admirable degree.

4thly. I am ſtricken with fear of unthankfulneſs. This apoſtate Kirk hath played the harlot with many lovers. They are ſpitting in the face of my lovely King, and mocking Him, and I dow† not mend it; and they are running away from Chriſt in troops, and I dow† not mourn and be grieved for it. I think Chriſt lieth like an old forcaſten‡ caſtle, forſaken of the inhabitants; all men run away now from Him. Truth, innocent truth, goeth mourning and wringing her hands in ſackcloth and aſhes. Woe, woe, woe is me, for the virgin daughter of Scotland! Woe, woe to the inhabitants of this land! for they are gone back with a perpetual backſliding.

Theſe things take me ſo up, that a borrowed bed, another man's fireſide, the wind upon my face (I being driven from my lovers and dear acquaintance, and my poor flock), find no room in my ſorrow. I have no ſpare or odd ſorrow for theſe; only I think the ſparrows and ſwallows that build their neſts in the kirk of Anwoth, bleſſed birds. Nothing hath given my faith a harder back-ſet§ till it crack again, than my cloſed mouth. But let me be miſerable myſelf alone; God keep my dear brethren from it. But ſtill I keep breath; and when my royal, and never, never-enough-praiſed King returneth to

---

* Graſp.   † Am not able.   ‡ Not uſed; caſt off.

§ A thruſt back. In a ſermon at Anwoth, 1630, on Zech. xiii. 7, he ſays,
" God gives a back-ſet and fall under temptation."

His finful prifoner, I ride upon the high places of Jacob. I divide Shechem,* I triumph in His ftrength. If this kingdom would glorify the Lord in my behalf! I defire to be weighed in God's even balance in this point, if I think not my wages paid to the full. I fhall crave no more hire of Chrift.

Madam, pity me in this, and help me to praife Him ; for whatever I be, the chief of finners, a devil, and a moft guilty devil, yet it is the apple of Chrift's eye, His honour and glory, as the Head of the Church, that I fuffer for now, and that I will go to eternity with.

I am greatly in love with Mr M. M.;† I fee him ftamped with the image of God. I hope well of your fon, my Lord Boyd.

Your Ladyfhip and your children have a prifoner's prayers. Grace be with you.

Your Ladyfhip's, at all obedience in Chrift,

ABERDEEN, *May* 1, 1637·   S. R.

------◆------

CLXVIII.—*To his reverend and dear Brother*, MR DAVID DICKSON.

(*CHRIST'S INFINITE FULNESS.*)

Y REVEREND AND DEAR BROTHER,—I fear that ye have never known me well. If ye faw my inner fide, it is poffible that ye would pity me, but you would hardly give me either love or refpect : men miftake me the whole length of the heavens. My fins prevail over me, and the terrors of their guiltinefs. I am put often to afk, if Chrift and I did ever fhake hands together in earneft. I mean not that my feaft-days are quite gone, but I am made of extremes. I pray God that ye never have the woful and dreary experience of a clofed mouth ; for then ye fhall judge the fparrows, that may fing on‡ the church of Irvine, bleffed birds. But my foul hath been refrefhed and watered,

---

* Pfalm lx. 6.

† Mr Matthew Mowat, minifter of Kilmarnock. See notice of him, Let. 120.

‡ *On*, not "*in*," as in old editions.

when I hear of your courage and zeal for your never-enough-praifed, praifed Mafter, in that ye put the men of God, chafed out of Ireland, to work.* Oh, if I could confirm you! I darefay, in God's prefence, "That this fhall never haften your fuffering, but will be David Dickfon's feaft **and fpeaking joy,** that while he had time and leifure, he put many to work, **to lift up** Jefus, his fweet Mafter, high in the fkies." O man of God, go on, go on ; be valiant for that Plant of renown, for that Chief among ten thoufands, for that Prince of the kings of the earth. It is but little that I know of **God** ; yet this I dare write, that Chrift will be glorified in **David** Dickfon, howbeit Scotland be not gathered.

I am pained, pained, that I have not more to give my fweet Bridegroom. His comforts to me are not dealt with a niggard's hand ; but I would fain learn not to idolize comfort, fenfe, joy, and fweet, felt prefence. All thefe are but creatures, and nothing but the kingly robe, the gold ring, and the bracelets of the Bridegroom ; the Bridegroom Himfelf is better than **all the** ornaments that are about Him. Now, I would not fo much have thefe as God Himfelf, and to be fwallowed up of love to Chrift. I fee that in delighting in a communion with Chrift, we may make more gods than one. But, however, all was but bairns' play between Chrift and me, till now. If one would have fworn unto me, I would not have

---

* When Mr **Robert Blair** and Mr John Livingftone, who had been depofed in Ireland by the Bifhop of Down, were obliged to leave that country, to avoid falling into the hands of the Government, which had given orders for their apprehenfion, on account of their preaching in their own private houfes, they came over to Irvine in 1637, to Mr Dickfon. Dickfon had been advifed by fome refpectable gentlemen not to employ them to preach, left the bifhops, who were then zealous in urging on minifters the ufe of the Service-book, fhould thereby take occafion to remove him from his miniftry. " But," faid Dickfon, " I dare not be of their opinion, nor follow their counfel, fo far as to difcountenance thefe worthies, now when they are fuffering for holding faft the name of Chrift, and every letter of that bleffed name, as not to employ them as in former times. Yea, I would think my fo doing would provoke the Lord, fo that I might upon another account be depofed, and not have fo good a confcience."--(*Life of Robert* **Blair.**)

believed what may be found in Chrift. I hope that ye pity my pain that * much, in my prifon, as to help me yourfelf, and to caufe others help me, a dyvour,† a finful wretched dyvour, to pay fome of my debts of praife to my great King. Let my God be judge and witnefs, if my foul would not have fweet eafe and comfort, to have many hearts confirmed in Chrift, and enlarged with His love, and many tongues fet on work to fet on high my royal and princely Well-beloved. Oh that my fufferings could pay tribute to fuch a king! I have given over wondering at His love; for Chrift hath manifefted a piece of art upon me, that I never revealed to any living. He hath gotten fair and rich employment, and fweet fale, and a goodly market for His honourable calling of fhowing mercy, on me the chief of finners. Every one knoweth not fo well as I do, my wofully-often broken covenants. My fins againft light, working‡ in the very act of finning, have been met with admirable mercy: but, alas! he will get nothing back again, but wretched unthank-fulnefs. I am fure, that if Chrift pity anything in me next to my fin, it is pain of love for an armful and foulful of Himfelf, in faith, love, and begun fruition. My forrow is, that I cannot get Chrift lifted off the duft in Scotland, and fet on high, above all the fkies, and heaven of heavens.

Yours, in his fweet Lord Jefus,

ABERDEEN, *May* 1, 1637.   S. R.

CLXIX.—*To the* LAIRD OF CARLETON.

(GOD'S WORKING INCOMPREHENSIBLE—LONGING AFTER ANY DROP OF CHRIST'S FULNESS.)

ORTHY SIR,—Grace, mercy, and peace be to you. I received your letter, and am heartily glad that our Lord hath begun to work for the apparent delivery

---

* So greatly.   † Debtor; bankrupt.

‡ The fenfe feems to be, "My fins againft light, which was at work even when I was in the act of finning."

of this poor oppreſſed Kirk. Oh that ſalvation would come for Zion !

I am for the preſent hanging by hope, waiting what my Lord will do with me, and if it will pleaſe my ſweet Maſter to ſend me amongſt you again, and keep out a hireling from my poor people and flock. It were my heaven till I come home, even to ſpend this life in gathering in ſome to Chriſt. I have ſtill great heavineſs for my ſilence, and my forced ſtanding idle in the market, when this land hath ſuch a plentiful, thick harveſt. But I know that His judgments, who hath done it, paſs finding out. I have no knowledge to take up the Lord in all His ſtrange ways, and paſſages of deep and unſearchable providences. For the Lord is before me, and I am ſo bemiſted* that I cannot follow Him ; He is behind me, and following at the heels, and I am not aware of Him ; He is above me, but His glory ſo dazzleth my twilight of ſhort knowledge, that I cannot look up to Him. He is upon my right hand, and I ſee Him not ; He is upon my left hand, and within me, and goeth and cometh, and His going and coming are a dream to me ; He is round about me, and compaſſeth all my goings, and ſtill I have Him to ſeek. He is every way higher, and deeper, and broader than the ſhallow and ebb† handbreadth of my ſhort and dim light can take up ; and, therefore, I would that my heart could be ſilent, and ſit down in the learnedly-ignorant wondering at the Lord, whom men and angels cannot comprehend. I know that the noon-day light of the higheſt angels, who ſee Him face to face, ſeeth not the borders of His infiniteneſs. They apprehend God near hand ;‡ but they cannot comprehend Him. And, therefore, it is my happineſs to look afar off, and to come near to the Lord's back parts, and to light my dark candle at His brightneſs, and to have leave to ſit and content myſelf with a traveller's light, without the clear viſion of an enjoyer. I would ſeek no more till I were in my country, than a little watering and ſprinkling of a withered ſoul, with ſome half out-breakings and half

---

* Involved in a miſt. † Low, ſhallow.
‡ They have to do with God near at hand.

out-lookings of the beams, and fmall ravifhing fmiles of the faireft
face of a revealed and believed-on Godhead.   A little of God would
make my foul bankfull. *   Oh that I had but Chrift's odd off-fallings ; that He would let but the meaneft of His love-rays and love-
beams fall from Him, fo as I might gather and carry them with me !
I would not be ill † to pleafe with Chrift, and vailed vifions of Chrift ;
neither would I be dainty in feeing and enjoying of Him : a kifs of
Chrift blown over His fhoulder, the parings and crumbs of glory
that fall under His table in heaven, a fhower like a thin May-mift
of His love, would make me green, and fappy, and joyful, till the
fummer-fun of an eternal glory break up. ‡   Oh that I had anything
of Chrift !   Oh that I had a fip, or half a drop, out of the hollow
of Chrift's hand, of the fweetnefs and excellency of that lovely One !
Oh that my Lord Jefus would rue upon me, and give me but the
meaneft alms of felt and believed falvation !   Oh, how little were
it for that infinite fea, that infinite fountain of love and joy, to fill
as many thoufand thoufand little veffels (the like of me) as there
are minutes of hours fince the creation of God !   I find § it true that
a poor foul, finding § half a fmell of the Godhead of Chrift, hath
defires (paining and wounding the poor heart fo with longings to be
up at Him) that make it fometimes think, "Were it not better never
to have felt anything of Chrift, than thus to lie dying twenty deaths,
under thefe felt wounds, for the want of Him ?"   Oh, where is He ?
O Faireft, where dwelleft Thou ?   O never-enough admired Godhead, how can clay win ‖ up to Thee ? how can creatures of yefterday be able to enjoy Thee ?   Oh, what pain is it, that time and fin
fhould be fo many thoufand miles betwixt a loved and longed-for
Lord and a dwining ¶ and love-fick foul, who would rather than
all the world have lodging with Chrift !   Oh, let this bit of love of
ours, this inch and half-fpan length of heavenly longing, meet with
Thy infinite love !   Oh, if the little I have were fwallowed up with
the infinitenefs of that excellency which is in Chrift !   Oh that we

---

* Like a river, full up to its bank.   † Difficult.   ‡ Song ii. 17.
§ Experience, or feel.   ‖ Get up.   ¶ Pining.

little ones were in at the greateft Lord Jefus! Our wants fhould foon be fwallowed up with His fulnefs.

Grace, grace be with you.

Yours in his fweet Lord Jefus,

S. R.

ABERDEEN, *May* 10, 1637.

CLXX.—*To* ROBERT GORDON *of Knockbrex.*

(*LONGING FOR CHRIST'S GLORY—FELT GUILTINESS—LONGING FOR CHRIST'S LOVE—SANCTIFICATION.*)

DEAR BROTHER,—Grace, mercy, and peace be to you. I received your letter from Edinburgh.

I would not wifh to fee another heaven, whill* I get mine own heaven, but a new moon like the light of the fun, and a new fun like the light of feven days fhining upon my poor felf, and the Church of Jews and Gentiles, and upon my withered and funburnt mother, the Church of Scotland, and upon her fifter Churches, England and Ireland; and to have this done, to the fetting on high of our great King! It mattereth† not, howbeit I were feparate from Chrift, and had a fenfe of ten thoufand years' pain in hell, if this were. O bleffed nobility! Oh, glorious, renowned gentry! Oh, bleffed were the tribes in this land to wipe my Lord Jefus' weeping face, and to take the fackcloth of Chrift's loins, and to put His kingly robes upon Him! Oh, if the Almighty would take no lefs‡ wager of me than my heaven to have it done! But my fears are ftill for wrath once§ upon Scotland. But I know that her day will clear up, and that glory fhall be upon the top of the mountains, and joy at the voice‖ of the married wife, once again. Oh that our Lord would make us to contend, and plead, and wreftle by prayers and tears, for our Hufband's reftoring of His forfeited heritage in Scotland.

---

* Till.   † *Mattereth?* In other editions it is " *maketh.*"
‡ Pledge.   § Some time or other.   ‖ " *Noife,*" in old editions.

Dear brother, I am for the prefent in no fmall battle, betwixt
felt guiltinefs, and pining longings and high fevers for my Well-
beloved's love! Alas! I think that Chrift's love playeth the
niggard to me, and I know it is not for fcarcity of love. There is
enough in Him, but my hunger prophefieth of in-holding and
fparingnefs in Chrift; for I have but little of Him, and little of His
fweetnefs. It is a dear fummer with me; yet there is fuch joy in
the eagernefs and working of hunger for Chrift, that I am often at
this, that if I had no other heaven than a continual hunger for
Chrift, fuch a heaven of ever-working hunger were ftill a heaven
to me. I am fure that Chrift's love cannot be cruel; it muft be a
ruing, a pitying, a melting-hearted love; but fufpenfion of that love
I think half a hell, and the want of it more than a whole hell.
When I look to my guiltinefs, I fee that my falvation is one of our
Saviour's greateft miracles, either in heaven or earth. I am fure I
may defy any man to fhow me a greater wonder. But, feeing I
have no wares, no hire, no money for Chrift, He muft either take
me with want, mifery, corruption, or then* want me. Oh, if He
would be pleafed to be compaffionate and pitiful-hearted to my
pining fevers of longing for Him; or then* give me a real pawn†
to keep, out of His own hand, till God fend a meeting betwixt Him
and me! But I find neither as yet. Howbeit He who is abfent be
not cruel nor unkind, yet His abfence is cruel and unkind. His
love is like itfelf; His love is *His* love; but the covering and the
cloud, the vail and the mafk of His love, is more wife than kind, if
I durft fpeak my apprehenfions. I lead no procefs now againft the
fufpenfion and delay of God's love; I would with all my heart
frift till a day‡ ten heavens, and the fweet manifeftations of His
love. Certainly I think that I could give Chrift much on His word;
but my whole pleading is about intimated and borne-in affurance of
His love. Oh, if He would perfuade me of§ my heart's defire of

---

* Or elfe.   † A pledge.   ‡ Defer to a day that might be named.
§ Convince me that He intends to gratify my heart's defire.

His love at all, He fhould have the term-day of payment at His own cowing.* But I know that raving unbelief fpeaketh its pleafure, while it looketh upon guiltinefs and this body of corruption. Oh how loathfome and burdenfome is it to carry about a dead corpfe, this old carrion of corruption! Oh how fteadable† a thing is a Saviour, to make a finner rid of His chains and fetters!

I have now made a new queftion, whether Chrift be more to be loved, for giving Sanctification or for **free Juftification.** And I hold that He is more **and moft** to be loved for fanctification. It is in fome refpect greater love in Him to fanctify, than to juftify ; for He maketh us moft like Himfelf, in His own effential portraiture and image, in fanctifying us. Juftification doth but make us happy, which is to **be like angels only.** Neither is it fuch a mifery to lie a condemned man, and under unforgiven guiltinefs, as to ferve fin, and work the works of the devil ; and, therefore, I think fanctification cannot be bought : **it is above** price. God be thanked for ever, that Chrift was a told-down price for fanctification. Let a finner, if poffible, **lie in** hell for ever, if He make him truly holy ; and let him lie there burning in love to God, rejoicing in the Holy Ghoft, hanging upon Chrift by faith and hope,—that is heaven in the heart and bottom of hell!

Alas! I find a very thin harveft here, and few to be faved. Grace, grace be with you.

Yours, in his lovely and longed-for Lord Jefus,

S. R.

Aberdeen, 1637.

———————◆———————

CLXXI.—*To the* Laird of Moncrieff.

[Sir John Moncrieff, of that ilk, was the eldeft fon of William Moncrieff of that ilk, by his wife Anne, daughter of Robert Murray of Abercarnie. He married, firft, Anne, daughter of David Beaton of Creich, and, fecondly,

---

* Cutting out ; as we fay, "at His own carving." † Available ; ferviceable.

Lady Mary Murray, daughter of William, second Earl of Tullibardin. He was a zealous Covenanter, and a ruling elder in the parish of Carnbee, in which he resided. His name appears in the list of the General Assembly's Commission for the public affairs of the Church, in the years 1646 and 1648 ; and he was an active member of the Presbytery of St Andrews, as appears from the minutes of that Presbytery. He died about the close of the year 1650, or beginning of the year 1651. Lady Leyes, to whom reference is made in this letter, was his third sister Jean, who was married to Hay of Leyes· (*Douglas' Baronage of Scotland*, p. 46).]

(CONCERT IN PRAYER—STEDFASTNESS TO CHRIST—GRIEF MISREPRESENTS CHRIST'S GLORY.)

MUCH HONOURED SIR,—Grace, mercy, and peace be to you. Although not acquainted, yet at the desire of your worthy sister, the Lady Leys, and upon the report of your kindness to Christ and His oppressed truth, I am bold to write to you, earnestly desiring you to join with us (so many as in these bounds profess Christ), to wrestle with God, one day of the week, especially the Wednesday, for mercy to this fallen and decayed Kirk, and to such as suffer for Christ's name ; and for your own necessities, and the necessities of others, who are by covenant engaged in that business. For we have no other armour in these evil times but prayer, now when wrath from the Lord is gone out against this backsliding land. For ye know we can have no true public fasts, neither are the true causes of our humiliation ever laid before the people.

Now, very worthy Sir, I am glad in the Lord, that the Lord reserveth any of your place, or of note, in this time of common apostasy, to come forth in public to bear Christ's name before men, when the great men think Christ a cumbersome neighbour, and that religion carrieth hazards, trials, and persecutions with it. I persuade myself that it is your glory and your garland, and shall be your joy in the day of Christ, and the standing of your house and seed, to inherit the earth, that you truly and sincerely profess Christ. Neither is our King, whom the Father hath crowned in Mount Zion, so weak, that He cannot do for Himself and His own cause. I verily believe that they are bleffed who can hold the crown upon His head, and carry up the train of His robe royal, and that He fhall be victorious, and triumph in this land. It is our part to back our royal King, howbeit there was not fix in all the land to follow Him. It is our wifdom now to take up, and difcern the devil and the antichrift coming out in their whites, and the apoftasy and idolatry of this land wafhen * with foul waters. I confefs that it is art to wafh the devil till his fkin be white.

For myfelf, Sir, I have bought a plea† againft Chrift, fince I came hither, in judging my princely Mafter angry at me, becaufe I was caft out of the vineyard as a withered tree, my dumb Sabbaths working me much forrow. But I fee now that forrow hath not eyes to read love written upon the crofs of Chrift; and, therefore, I pafs from my rafh plea. Woe, woe is me, that I fhould have received a flander of Chrift's love to my foul! And for all this, my Lord Jefus hath forgiven all, as not willing to be heard‡ with fuch a fool; and is content to be, as it were, confined with me, and to bear me company, and to feaft a poor oppreffed prifoner. And now I write it under my hand, worthy Sir, that I think well and honourably of this crofs of Chrift. I wonder that He will take any glory from the like of me. I find when he but fendeth His hearty commendations to me, and but bloweth a kifs afar off, I am confounded with wondering what the fupper of the Lamb will be, up in our Father's dining-palace of glory, fince the four-hours§ in this difmal wildernefs, and (when in prifons and in our fad days), a kifs of Chrift, are fo comfortable. Oh, how fweet and glorious fhall our cafe be, when that Faireft among the fons of men will lay His fair face to our now finful faces, and wipe away all tears from our eyes! O time, time, run fwiftly and haften this day! O fweet Lord Jefus, come flying like a roe or a young hart! Alas! that we,

---

* Wafhed.　　　　　　　　† Got up a quarrel.

‡ Not willing to be heard difputing with fuch a fool.

§ The flight afternoon's meal is fo refrefhing,—

　　　　" If fuch the fweetnefs of the ftream,
　　　　What muft the fountain be?"

blind fools, are fallen in love with moonfhine and fhadows. How fweet is the wind that bloweth out of the airth* where Chrift is! Every day we may fee fome new thing in Chrift; His love hath neither brim nor bottom. Oh, if I had help to praife Him! He knoweth that if my fufferings glorify His name, and encourage others to ftand faft for the honour of our fupreme Lawgiver, Chrift, my wages then are paid to the full. Sir, help me to love that never-enough-praifed Lord. I find now, that the faith of the faints, under fuffering for Chrift, is fair before the wind, and with full fails carried upon Chrift. And I hope to lofe nothing in this furnace but drofs; for Chrift can triumph in a weaker man than I am, if there be any fuch. And when all is done, His love paineth me, and leaveth me under fuch debt to Chrift, as I can neither pay principal nor intereft. Oh, if He would comprife† myfelf, and if I were fold to Him as a bondman, and that He would take me home to His houfe and firefide; for I have nothing to render to Him! Then, after me, let no man think hard of Chrift's fweet crofs; for I would not exchange my fighs with the painted laughter of all my adverfaries. I defire grace and patience to wait on, and to lie upon the brink, till the water fill and flow. I know that He is faft coming.

Sir, ye will excufe my boldnefs: and, till it pleafe God that I fee you, ye have the prayers of a prifoner of Chrift; to whom I recommend you, and in whom I reft.

Yours, at all obedience in Chrift,

S. R.

ABERDEEN, *May* 14, 1637.

---

* Point of the compafs.   † Arreft me by writ.

CLXXII.—*To* JOHN CLARK (*fuppofed to be one of his Parifhioners at Anwoth*).

(*MARKS OF DIFFERENCE BETWIXT CHRISTIANS AND REPROBATES.*)

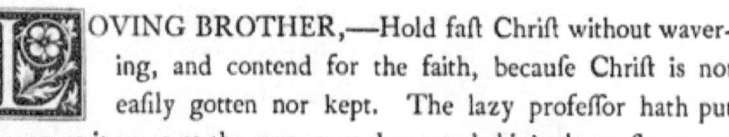

OVING BROTHER,—Hold faft Chrift without wavering, and contend for the faith, becaufe Chrift is not eafily gotten nor kept. The lazy profeffor hath put heaven as it were at the very next door, and thinketh to fly up to heaven in his bed, and in a night-dream ; but, truly, that is not fo eafy a thing as moft men believe. Chrift Himfelf did fweat ere He wan * this city, howbeit He was the freeborn heir. It is Chriftianity, my Heart, to be fincere, unfeigned, honeft, and upright-hearted before God, and to live and ferve God, fuppofe there was not one man nor woman in all the world dwelling befide you, to eye you. Any little grace that ye have, fee that it be found and true.

Ye may put a difference betwixt you and reprobates, if ye have thefe marks :—1. If ye prize Chrift and His truth fo as ye will fell all and buy Him ; and fuffer for it. 2. If the love of Chrift keepeth you back from finning, more than the law, or fear of hell. 3. If ye be humble, and deny your own will, wit, credit, eafe, honour, the world, and the vanity and glory of it. 4. Your profeffion muft not be barren, and void of good works. · 5. Ye muft in all things aim at God's honour ; ye muft eat, drink, fleep, buy, fell, fit, ftand, fpeak, pray, read, and hear the word, with a heart-purpofe that God may be honoured. 6. Ye muft fhow yourfelf an enemy to fin, and reprove the works of darknefs, fuch as drunkennefs, fwearing, and lying, albeit the company fhould hate you for fo doing. 7. Keep in mind the truth of God, that ye heard me teach, and have nothing to do with the corruptions and new guifes entered into the houfe of God. 8. Make confcience of your calling, in covenants, in buying and felling. 9. Acquaint yourfelf with daily

---

* Won ; obtained poffeffion of.

praying; commit all your ways and actions to God, by prayer, supplication, and thankfgiving; and count not much of being mocked; for Chrift Jefus was mocked before you.

Perfuade yourfelf, that this is the way of peace and comfort which I now fuffer for. I dare go to death and into eternity with it, though men may poffibly fee another way. Remember me in your prayers, and the ftate of this oppreffed Church. Grace be with you.

Your foul's well-wifher,

Aberdeen.   S. R.

CLXXIII.—*To* Cardoness, *the Younger.* [Let. 123.]

(*WARNING AND ADVICE AS TO THINGS OF SALVATION.*)

MUCH HONOURED SIR,—I long to hear whether or not your foul be hand-fafted* with Chrift. Lofe your time no longer : flee the follies of youth : gird up the loins of your mind, and make you ready for meeting the Lord. I have often fummoned you, and now I fummon you again, to compear† before your Judge, to make a reckoning of your life. While ye have time, look upon your papers, and confider your ways. Oh that there were fuch an heart in you, as to think what an ill confcience will be to you, when ye are upon the border of eternity, and your one foot out of time! Oh then, ten thoufand thoufand floods of tears cannot extinguifh thefe flames, or purchafe to you one hour's releafe from that pain! Oh, how fweet a day have ye had! But this is a fair-day‡ that runneth faft away. See how ye have fpent it, and confider the neceffity of falvation! and tell me, in the fear of God, if ye have made it fure. I am perfuaded, that ye have a confcience that will be fpeaking fomewhat to you. Why will ye die, and deftroy yourfelf? I charge you in Chrift's name,

---

* Betrothed by joining hands.   † Appear in obedience to a fummons.
‡ A market-day.

to roufe up your confcience, and begin to indent* and contract with
Chrift in time, while falvation is in your offer. This is the accepted
time, this is the day of falvation. Play the merchant ; for ye cannot
expect another market-day when this is done. Therefore, let me
again befeech you to " confider, in this your day, the things that
belong to your peace, before they be hid from your eyes." Dear
Brother, fulfil my joy, and begin to feek the Lord while He may
be found. Forfake the follies of deceiving and vain youth : lay hold
upon eternal life. Whoring, night-drinking, and the miffpending
of the Sabbath, and neglecting of prayer in your houfe, and refufing
of an offered falvation, will burn up your foul with the terrors of
the Almighty, when your awakened confcience fhall flee in your
face. Be kind and loving to your wife : make confcience of cherifh-
ing her, and not being rigidly auftere. Sir, I have not a tongue to
exprefs the glory that is laid up for you in your Father's houfe, if
ye reform your doings, and frame your heart to return to the Lord.
Ye know that this world is but a fhadow, a fhort-living creature,
under the law of time. Within lefs than fifty years, when ye look
back to it, ye fhall laugh at the evanifhing vanities thereof, as feathers
flying in the air, and as the houfes of fand within the fea-mark,
which the children of men are building. Give up with courting
of this vain world : feek not the baftard's moveables, but the fon's
heritage in heaven. Take a trial of Chrift. Look unto Him, and
His love will fo change you, that ye fhall be taken with Him, and
never choofe to go from Him. I have experience of His fweetnefs,
in this houfe of my pilgrimage here. My Witnefs, who is above,
knoweth that I would not exchange my fighs and tears with the
laughing of the fourteen prelates. There is nothing that will make
you a Chriftian indeed, but a tafte of the fweetnefs of Chrift.
" Come and fee," will fpeak beft to your foul. I would fain hope
good of you. Be not difcouraged at broken and fpilled† refolutions ; but to it, and to it again ! Woo about Chrift, till ye get your
foul efpoufed as a chafte virgin to Him. Ufe the means of profit-

---

* Put your name to a paper containing articles of agreement.   † Marred.

ing with your confcience, pray in your family, and read the word. Remember how our Lord's day was fpent when I was among you. It will be a great challenge* to you before God, if ye forget the good that was done within the walls of your houfe on the Lord's day ; and if ye turn afide after the fafhions of this world, and if ye go not in time to the kirk, to wait on the public worfhip of God, and if ye tarry not at it, till all the exercifes of religion be ended. Give God fome of your time both morning and evening, and after-noon ; and in fo doing, rejoice the heart of a poor oppreffed prifoner. Rue upon† your own foul, and from your heart fear the Lord.

Now He that brought again from the dead the great Shepherd of His fheep, by the blood of the eternal covenant, eftablifh your heart with His grace, and prefent you before His prefence with joy.

Your affectionate and loving paftor,

S. R.

ABERDEEN, 1637.

CLXXIV.—*To my* Lord Craighall. [Let. 86.]

(*IDOLATRY CONDEMNED.*)

Y LORD,—Grace, mercy, and peace be to you. I am not only content, but I exceedingly rejoice, that I find any of the rulers of this land, and efpecially your Lordfhip, fo to affect‡ Chrift and His truth, as that ye dare, for His name, come to yea and nay with monarchs in their face. I hope that He who hath enabled you for that, will give more, if ye fhow yourfelf courageous, and (as His word fpeaketh), "a man in the ftreets," for the Lord.§ But I pray your Lordfhip, give me leave to be plain with you, as one who loveth both your honour and your foul. I verily believe that there was never idolatry at Rome, never idolatry condemned in God's word by the prophets, if religious

---

* Caufe of felf-upbraiding. † Have pity upon. ‡ Love. § Jerem. v. 1.

kneeling before a confecrated creature, ftanding in room of Chrift crucified in that very act, and that for reverence of the elements, (as our Act cleareth), be not idolatry.* Neither will your *intention* help, which is not of the effence of worfhip ; for then, Aaron faying, " To-morrow fhall be a feaft for Jehovah," that is, for the golden calf, fhould not have been guilty of idolatry : for he *intended* only to decline the lafh of the people's fury, not to honour the calf. Your intention to honour Chrift is nothing, feeing that religious kneeling, by God's inftitution, doth neceffarily import religious and divine adoration, fuppofe that our intention were both dead and fleeping ; otherwife, kneeling before the image of God and directing prayer to God were lawful, if our intention go right. My Lord, I cannot in thefe bounds difpute ; but if Cambridge and Oxford, and the learning of Britain, will anfwer this argument, and the argument from active fcandal, which your Lordfhip feemeth to ftand upon, I will turn a formalift, and call myfelf an arrant fool (by doing what I have done) in my fuffering for this truth. I do much re-verence Mr L.'s† learning ; but, my Lord, I will anfwer what he writeth in that, to pervert you from the truth ; elfe repute me, be-fide an hypocrite, an afs alfo. I hope ye fhall fee fomething upon that fubject (if the Lord permit), that no fophiftry in Britain fhall anfwer. Courtiers' arguments, for the moft part, are drawn from their own fkin, and are not worth a ftraw for your confcience. A Marquis' or a King's word, when ye ftand before Chrift's tribunal, fhall be lighter than the wind. The Lord knoweth that I love your true honour, and the ftanding of your houfe ; but I would not that your honour or houfe were eftablifhed upon fand, and hay, and ftubble.

But let me, my very dear and worthy Lord, moft humbly be-feech you, by the mercies of God, by the confolations of His Spirit, by the dear blood and wounds of your lovely Redeemer, by the falvation of your foul, by your compearance before the awful face of a fin-revenging and dreadful Judge, not to fet in comparifon together your foul's peace, Chrift's love, and His kingly honour

---

* See Let. xcii.   † Probably Mr Loudian. Let. 86, note.

now called in queſtion, with your place, honour, houſe, or eaſe, that an inch of time will make out of the way. I verily believe that Chriſt is now begging a teſtimony of you, and is ſaying, " And will ye alſo leave Me ?" It is poſſible that the wind ſhall not blow ſo fair for you all your life, for coming out and appearing before others to back and countenance Chriſt, the faireſt among the ſons of men, the Prince of the kings of the earth, " Fear ye not the reproach of men, neither be afraid of their revilings : for the moth ſhall eat them up like a garment, and the worm ſhall eat them like wool."* When the Lord will begin, He will make an end, and mow down His adverſaries ; and they ſhall lie before Him like withered hay, and their bloom be ſhaken off them. Conſider how many thouſands in this kingdom ye ſhall cauſe to fall and ſtumble, if ye go with them ; and that ye ſhall be out of the prayers of many who do now ſtand before the Lord for you and your houſe. And further ; when the time of your accounts cometh, and your one foot ſhall be within the border of eternity, and the eyeſtrings ſhall break, and the face wax pale, and the poor ſoul ſhall look out at the windows of the houſe of clay, longing to be out, and ye ſhall find yourſelf arraigned before the Judge of quick and dead, to anſwer for your putting to your hand, with the reſt confederated againſt Chriſt, to the over-turning of His ark, and the looſing of the pins of Chriſt's tabernacle in this land, and ſhall certainly ſee yourſelf mired† in a courſe of apoſtaſy—then, then, a king's favour and your worm-eaten honour ſhall be miſerable comforters to you ! The Lord hath enlightened you with the knowledge of His will ; and as the Lord liveth, they lead you and others to a communion with great Babel, the mother of fornications. God ſaid of old, and continueth to ſay the ſame to you, " Come out of her, My people, leſt ye be partakers of her plagues." Will ye, then, go with them, and ſet your lip to the whore's golden cup, and drink of the wine of the wrath of God Almighty with them ? Oh, poor hungry honour ! Oh ! curſed pleaſure ! and, oh, damnable eaſe, bought with the loſs of God !

---

* Iſa li. 7, 8.   † Plunged in mire.

How many will pray for you! what a sweet presence shall ye find of Christ under your sufferings, if ye will lay down your honours and place at the feet of Christ. What a fair recompense of reward! I avouch before the Lord that I am now showing you a way how the house of Craighall may stand on sure pillars. If ye will set it on rotten pillars, ye cruelly **wrong** your posterity. **Ye have** the word of a King for an hundred-fold more in this **life** (if it be good for you), and for life everlasting also. Make not Christ a liar, in distrusting His promise. **Kings of** clay cannot back you when you stand before Him. A straw for them and their hungry heaven, that standeth on this side **of time**! A fig for the day's smile of a worm! **Consider who** have gone before you to eternity, and would have **given a** world for a new occasion of avouching that truth. It is true they call it not substantial, and we are made a scorn to those **that are at** ease, for suffering these things for it. But it is not time to judge of our losses by the morning; stay till the evening, and we will count with the best of them.

I have found by experience, since the time of my imprisonment (**my witness is** above), that Christ is sealing this honourable cause with another and a nearer fellowship than ever I knew before; and **let God weigh me in** an even balance in this, if I would exchange **the cross of Christ or His truth, with** the fourteen prelacies, or what else **a King can give.** My dear Lord, venture to take the wind on your face for **Christ.** I believe that if He should come from heaven in His own person, and seek the charters of **Craighall** from you, and a dismission of your place, and ye saw **His face**, ye would fall down at His feet and say, "**Lord Jesus, it is** too little for Thee." If any man think it not a truth to die **for, I am against him.** I dare **go** to eternity with it, that this day the honour of our Lawgiver and King, in the government **of** His own free kingdom (who should pay tribute to no dying king), **is** the true state of the question. My Lord, be ye upon Christ's side of it, and take the word of a poor prisoner, nay, the Lord Jesus be surety for it, that ye have incomparably **made the** wisest choice. For my own part, I have so **been** in this prison, that I would be half-ashamed to seek more till I be up at the Well-head. Few know in this world the fweetnefs of Chrift's breath, the excellency of His love, which hath neither brim nor bottom. The world hath raifed a flander upon the crofs of Chrift, becaufe they love to go to heaven by dry land, and love not fea-ftorms. But I write it under my hand (and would fay more, if poffibly a reader would not deem it hypocrify), that my obligation to Chrift for the fmell of His garments, for His love-kiffes thefe thirty weeks, ftandeth fo great, that I fhould (and I defire alfo to choofe to), fufpend my falvation, to have many tongues loofed in my behalf to praife Him. And, fuppofe in perfon I never entered within the gates of the New Jerufalem, yet fo being Chrift may be fet on high, and I had the liberty to caft my love and praifes for ever over the wall to Chrift, I would be filent and content. But oh, He is more than my narrow praifes! Oh time, time, flee fwiftly, that our communion with Jefus may be perfected!

I wifh that your Lordfhip would urge Mr L. to give his mind in the ceremonies ; and be pleafed to let me fee it as quickly as can be, and it fhall be anfwered.

To His rich grace I recommend your Lordfhip, and fhall remain,

Yours, at all refpectful obedience in Chrift,

S. R.

ABERDEEN, *June* 8, 1637.

CLXXV.—*To* JOHN LAURIE.

(CHRIST'S LOVE—A RIGHT ESTIMATE OF HIM—HIS GRACE.)

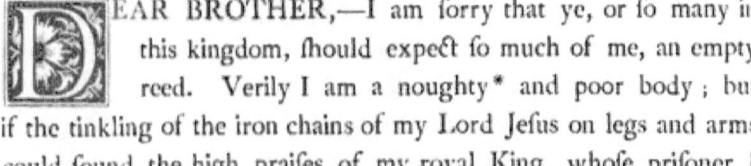DEAR BROTHER,—I am forry that ye, or fo many in this kingdom, fhould expect fo much of me, an empty reed. Verily I am a noughty* and poor body ; but if the tinkling of the iron chains of my Lord Jefus on legs and arms could found the high praifes of my royal King, whofe prifoner I

---

* Some underftand this as meaning, "Being nought," or nothing. It is, however, written "naughty," evil, in old editions.

am, oh, how would my joy run over! If my Lord would bring edification to one foul by my bonds, I am fatisfied. But I know not what I can do to fuch a princely and beautiful Well-beloved ; He is far behind with me.* Little thanks to me, to fay to others that His wind bloweth on me, who am but withered and dry bones ; but, fince ye defire me to write to you, either help me to fet Chrift on high, for His running-over love, in. that the heat of His fweet breath hath melted a frozen heart ; elfe† I think that ye do nothing for a prifoner.

I am fully confirmed, that it is the honour of our Lawgiver which I fuffer for now. I am not afhamed to give out letters of recommendation of Chrift's love to as many as will extol the Lord Jefus and His Crofs. If I had not failed this fea-way to heaven, but had taken the land-way, as many do, I fhould not have known Chrift's fweetnefs in fuch a meafure. But the truth is, let no man thank me, for I caufed not Chrift's wind to blow upon me. His love came upon a withered creature, whether I would or not ; and yet by coming it procured from me a welcome. A heart of iron, and iron doors, will not hold Chrift out. I give Him leave to break iron locks and come in, and that is all. And now I know not whether pain of love for want of poffeffion, or forrow that I dow‡ not thank Him, paineth me the moft ; but both work upon me. For the firft : oh that He would come and fatisfy the longing foul, and fill the hungry foul with thefe good things! I know indeed that my guiltinefs may be a bar in His way ; but He is God, and ready to forgive. And for the other : woe, woe is me, that I cannot find a heart to give back again my unworthy little love for His great fea-full of love to me! Oh that He would learn§ me this piece of gratitude! Oh that I could have leave to look in through the hole of the door, to fee His face and fing His praifes! or could break up one of His chamber-windows, to look in upon His delighting beauty, till my Lord fend more! · Any little communion with Him,

---

* He has fo fully paid me.   † Unlefs ye do this.

‡ Cannot.   § Teach. It is the German, *lehren.*

one of His love-looks, fhould be my begun heaven. I know that
He is not lordly, neither is the Bridegroom's love proud, though I
be black, and unlovely, and unworthy of Him. I would feek but
leave, and withal grace, to fpend my love upon Him. I counfel you
to think highly of Chrift, and of free, free grace, more than ye did
before ; for I know that Chrift is not known amongft us. I think
that I fee more of Chrift than ever I faw ; and yet I fee but little of
what may be feen. Oh that He would draw by* the curtains, and
that the King would come out of His gallery and His palace, that
I might fee Him! Chrift's love is young glory and young heaven ;
it would foften hell's pain to be filled with it. What would I refufe to fuffer, if I could get but a draught of love at my heart's
defire! Oh, what price can be given for Him? Angels cannot
weigh Him. Oh, His weight, His worth, His fweetnefs, His over-
paffing beauty! If men and angels would come and look to that
great and princely One, their ebbnefs† could never take up His
depth, their narrownefs could never comprehend His breadth,
height, and length. If ten thoufand thoufand worlds of angels
were created, they might all tire themfelves in wondering at His
beauty, and begin again to wonder of new. Oh that I could win‡
nigh Him, to kifs His feet, to hear His voice, to feel the fmell of
His ointments! But oh, alas, I have little, little of Him! Yet I
long for more.

Remember my bonds, and help me with your prayers ; for I
would not niffer§ or exchange my fad hours with the joy of my
velvet adverfaries. Grace be with you.

Yours in his fweet Lord Jefus,

S. R.

Aberdeen, *June* 10, 1637.

---

* Afide. † Shallownefs. ‡ Get near.

§ Barter. Perhaps "*or exchange*" have been put into the text from the
margin.

(A CHRISTIAN'S CONFESSION OF UNWORTHINESS—DESIRE FOR CHRIST'S HONOUR—PRESENT CIRCUMSTANCES.)

ORTHY AND MUCH HONOURED,—Grace, mercy, and peace be to you. I received your letter from my brother, to which I now anfwer particularly.

I confefs two things of myfelf: 1*ft*, Woe, woe is me, that men fhould think there is anything in me! He is my witnefs, before whom I am as cryftal, that the fecret houfe-devils that bear me too often company, and that this fink of corruption which I find within, make me go with low fails. And if others faw what I fee, they would look by* me, but not to me.

2*dly*, I know that this fhower of His free grace behoved to be on me, otherwife I fhould have withered. I know, alfo, that I have need of a buffeting tempter, that grace may be put to exercife, and I kept low.

Worthy and dear brother in the Lord Jefus, I write that from my heart which ye now read. 1*ft*, I avouch that Chrift, and fweating and fighing under His crofs, is fweeter to me by far, than all the kingdoms in the world could poffibly be. 2*dly*, If you, and my deareft acquaintance in Chrift, reap any fruit by my fuffering, let me be weighed in God's even balance, if my joy be not fulfilled. What am I, to carry the marks of fuch a great King! But, howbeit I am a fink and finful mafs, a wretched captive of fin, my Lord Jefus can hew heaven out of worfe timber than I am; if worfe can be. 3*dly*, I now rejoice with joy unfpeakable and glorious, that I never purpofed to bring Chrift, or the leaft hoof or hair-breadth of truth, under tryfting.† I defired to have and keep Chrift all alone,

---

* Paft; as Paul "failed *by* Ephefus," *i.e.*, paft; Acts xx. 16.

† To bring under man's arrangement the fmalleft part of Chrift's truth.

and that He fhould never rub clothes with that black-fkinned harlot
of Rome. I am now fully paid home, fo that nothing aileth me for
the prefent, but love-ficknefs for a real poffeffion of my faireft
Well-beloved. I would give Him my bond under my faith and
hand, to frift * heaven an hundred years longer, fo being He would
lay His holy face to my fometimes wet cheeks. Oh, who would
not pity me, to know how fain I would have the King fhaking the
tree of life upon me, or letting me into the well of life with my old
difh, that I might be drunken with the fountain here in the houfe of
my pilgrimage! I cannot, nay, I would not, be quit of Chrift's
love. He hath left the mark behind where he gripped.† He
goeth away and leaveth me and His burning love to wreftle together,
and I can fcarce win‡ my meat of His love, becaufe of His abfence.
My Lord giveth me but hungry half-kiffes, which ferve to feed
pain and increafe hunger, but do not fatisfy my defires ; His dieting
of my foul for this race maketh me lean. I have gotten the wale §
and choice of Chrift's croffes, even the tythe and the flower of the
gold of all croffes, to bear witnefs to the truth ; and herein find I
liberty, joy, accefs, life, comfort, love, faith, fubmiffion, patience,
and refolution to take delight in on-waiting. And withal, in my
race, He hath come near me, and let me fee the gold and crown.
What, then, want I but fruition and real enjoyment, which is referved to my country?‖ Let no man think he fhall lofe at Chrift's
hands in fuffering for Him. 4thly, As for thefe prefent trials, they
are moft dangerous ; for people are ftolen off their feet with well-
wafhen ¶ and white-fkinned pretences of indifferency. But it is the
power of the great antichrift working in this land. Woe, woe,
woe be to apoftate Scotland! There is wrath, and a cup of the
red wine of the wrath of God Almighty in the Lord's hand, that
they fhall drink and fpue, and fall and not rife again. The ftar
called " Wormwood and gall," is fallen into the fountains and

---

* Defer.　　† Grafp.　　‡ Get enough out of His love to feed me.
§ Selecteft part.　　　　　‖ Till I reach the heavenly country.
¶ Wafhed, in order that their blacknefs may not appear.

rivers, and hath made them bitter. The fword of the Lord is fur-
bifhed againft the idol-fhepherds of the land. Women fhall blefs
the barren womb and mifcarrying breaft ; all hearts fhall be faint,
and all knees fhall tremble. An end is coming ; the leopard and
the lion fhall watch over our cities ; houfes great and fair fhall be
defolate without an inhabitant. The Lord hath faid, " Pray not for
this people, for I have taken My peace from them." Yet the Lord's
third part fhall come through the fire, as refined gold for the treafure of the Lord, and the outcafts of Scotland fhall be gathered
together again, and the wildernefs fhall bloffom as the flower, and
bud, and grow as the rofe of Sharon ; and great fhall be the glory
of the Lord upon Scotland. 5*thly*, I am here affaulted with the
learned and pregnant wits of this kingdom. But, all honour be to
my Lord, truth but laughs at bemifted* and blind fcribes, and dif-
puters of this world ; and God's wifdom confoundeth them, and
Chrift triumpheth in His own ftrong truth, that fpeaketh for itfelf.
6*thly*, I doubt not but my Lord is preparing me for heavier trials.
I am moft ready at the good pleafure of my Lord, in the ftrength
of His grace, for anything He will be pleafed to call me to ; neither
fhall the black-faced meffenger, Death, be holden at the door, when
it fhall knock. If my Lord will take honour of the like of me, how
glad and joyful will my foul be ! Let Chrift come out with me to
a hotter battle than this, and I will fear no flefh. I know that my
Mafter fhall win the day, and that He hath taken the ordering of
my fufferings into His own hand. 7*thly*, As for my deliverance that
mifcarrieth ; I am here, by my Lord's grace, to lay my hand on my
mouth, to be filent, and wait on. My Lord Jefus is on His journey
for my deliverance ; I will not grudge that He runneth not fo faft
as I would have Him. On-waiting till the fwelling rivers fall, and
till my Lord arife as a mighty man after ftrong wine, will be my
beft. I have not yet refifted to blood. 8*thly*, Oh, how often am
I laid in the duft, and urged by the tempter (who can ride his own
errands upon our lying apprehenfions) to fin againft the unchangeable

---

* Bewildered in mift.

love of my Lord ! When I think upon the fparrows and fwallows that build their nefts in the kirk of Anwoth, and of my dumb Sabbaths, my forrowful, bleared eyes look afquint upon Chrift, and prefent Him as angry. But in this trial (all honour to our princely and royal King !) faith faileth fair before the wind, with topfail up, and carrieth the paffenger through. I lay inhibitions upon my thoughts, that they receive no flanders of my only, only Beloved. Let Him even fay out of His own mouth, " There is no hope ;" yet I will die in that fweet beguile,* " It is not fo, I fhall fee the falvation of God." Let me be deceived really, and never win to dry land ; it is my joy to believe under the water, and to die with faith in my hand, gripping† Chrift. Let my conceptions of Chrift's love go to the grave with me, and to hell with me ; I may not, I dare not quit them. I hope to keep Chrift's pawn : if He never come to loofe it, let Him fee to His own promife. I know that prefumption, howbeit it be made of ftoutnefs, will not thus be wilful in heavy trials.

Now my deareft in Chrift, the great Meffenger of the Covenant, the only wife and all-fufficient Jehovah, eftablifh you to the end. I hear that the Lord hath been at your houfe, and hath called home your wife to her reft. I know, Sir, that ye fee the Lord loofing the pins of your tabernacle, and wooing your love from this plaftered and over-gilded world, and calling upon you to be making yourfelf ready to go to your Father's country, which fhall be a fweet fruit of that vifitation. Ye know, " to fend the Comforter," was the King's word when He afcended on high. Ye have claim to, and intereft in, that promife.

Remember my love in Chrift to your father. Show him that it is late and black night with him. His long lying at the water-fide is that he may look his papers ere he take fhipping, and be at a point for his laft anfwer before his Judge and Lord.

All love, all mercy, all grace and peace, all multiplied faving confolations, all joy and faith in Chrift, all ftability and confirm-

---

* Delufion.   † Grafping.

ing ſtrength of grace, and the good-will of Him that dwelt in The Buſh, be with you.

Your unworthy brother, in his ſweet Lord Jeſus,

ABERDEEN, *June* 15, 1637. S. R.

CLXXVII.—*To* MARION M'NAUGHT.

(CHRIST SUFFERING IN HIS CHURCH—HIS COMING—OUT-POURINGS OF LOVE FROM HIM.)

ORTHY AND DEAREST IN THE LORD,—I ever loved (ſince I knew you) that little vineyard of the Lord's planting in Galloway; but now much more, ſince I have heard that He who hath His fire in Zion, and His furnace in Jeruſalem, hath been pleaſed to ſet up a furnace amongſt you with the firſt in this kingdom. He who maketh old things new, ſeeing Scotland an old, droſſy, and ruſted Kirk, is beginning to make a new, clean bride of her, and to bring a young, chaſte wife to Himſelf out of the fire. This fire ſhall be quenched, ſo ſoon as Chriſt has brought a clean ſpouſe through the fire! Therefore, my dearly beloved in the Lord, fear not a worm. "Fear not, worm Jacob."* Chriſt is in that plea, and ſhall win the plea. Charge an unbelieving heart, under the pain of treaſon againſt our great and royal King Jeſus, to dependence by faith, and quiet on-waiting on our Lord. Get you into your chambers, and ſhut the doors about you. In, in with ſpeed to your ſtronghold, ye priſoners of hope. Ye doves, fly into Chriſt's windows till the indignation be over, and the ſtorm be paſt. Glorify the Lord in your ſufferings, and take His banner of love, and ſpread it over you. Others will follow you, if they ſee you ſtrong in the Lord. Their courage will take life from your Chriſtian carriage. Look up and ſee who is coming! Lift up your head, He is coming to ſave, in garments dyed in blood, and travelling in the greatneſs of His ſtrength. I laugh, I ſmile, I leap for joy, to ſee Chriſt coming to

---

* Job xxv. 6, and Iſaiah xli. 14.

fave you fo quickly. Oh, fuch wide fteps Chrift taketh! Three or four hills are but a ftep to Him ; He fkippeth over the mountains. Chrift hath fet a battle betwixt His poor weak faints and His enemies. He waleth* the weapons for both parties, and faith to the enemies, "Take you a fword† of fteel, law, authority, parliaments, and kings upon your fide ; that is your armour." And He faith to His faints, "I give you a fecklefs tree-fword in your hand, and that is fuffering, receiving of ftrokes, fpoiling of your goods ; and with your tree-fword ye fhall get and gain the victory." Was not Chrift dragged through the ditches of deep diftreffes and great ftraits ? And yet Chrift, who is your Head, hath won‡ through with His life, howbeit not with a whole fkin. Ye are Chrift's members, and He is drawing His members through the thorny hedge up to heaven after Him. Chrift one day will not have fo much as a pained toe ; but there are great pieces and portions of Chrift's myftical body not yet within the gates of the great high city, the New Jerufalem ; and the dragon will ftrike at Chrift, fo long as there is one bit or member of Chrift's body out of heaven. I tell you, Chrift will make new work out of old, forcaften§ Scotland, and gather the old broken boards of His tabernacle, and pin them and nail them together. Our bills and fupplications are up in heaven ; Chrift hath coffers full of them. There is mercy on the other fide of this His crofs ; a good anfwer to all our bills is agreed upon.

I muft tell you what lovely Jefus, fair Jefus, King Jefus hath done to my foul. Sometimes He fendeth me out a ftanding drink,‖ and whifpereth a word through the wall ; and I am well content of kindnefs at the fecond hand : His bode¶ is ever welcome to me, be what it will. But at other times He will be meffenger Himfelf, and

---

* Selecteth.

† In old editions, "word;" but the contraft, "tree-fword," fword of wood, inftead of fteel, fhows the true reading.

‡ Get.   § Caft off.

‖ A cup handed to one as he ftood at the door of a friend without difmounting. It is like the ftirrup-cup.

¶ Offer made in order to bargain.

I get the cup of falvation out of His own hand (He drinking to me), and we cannot reft till we be in other's arms. And oh, how fweet is a frefh kifs from His holy mouth ! His breathing that goeth before a kifs upon my poor foul is fweet, and hath no fault but that it is too fhort. I am carelefs, and ftand not much on this, howbeit loins, and back, and fhoulders, and head fhould rive* in pieces in ftepping up to my Father's houfe. I know that my Lord can make long, and broad, and high, and deep glory to His name, out of this bit fecklefs† body ; for Chrift looketh not what ftuff He maketh glory out of.

My dearly beloved, ye have often refrefhed me. But this is put up in my Mafter's account ; ye have Him debtor for me. But if ye will do anything for me (as I know ye will) now in my ex-tremity, tell all my dear friends that a prifoner is fettered and chained in Chrift's love (Lord, never loofe the fetters !) ; and ye and they together take my heartieft commendations to my Lord Jefus, and thank Him for a poor friend.

I defire your hufband to read this letter. I fend him a pri-foner's blefling. I will be obliged to him, if he will be willing to fuffer for my dear Mafter. Suffering is the profeffor's golden gar-ment ; there fhall be no loffes on Chrift's fide of it. Ye have been witneffes of much joy betwixt Chrift and me at communion feafts, the remembrance whereof (howbeit I be feafted in fecret) holeth‡ my heart ; for I am put from the board-head‡ and the King's firft mefs to His by-board.§ And His broken meat is sweet unto me ; I thank my Lord for borrowed crumbs, no lefs than when I feafted at the communion table at Anwoth and Kirkcudbright. Pray that I may get one day of Chrift in public, fuch as I have had long fince, before my eyes be clofed. Oh that my Mafter would take up

---

* Be rent in pieces.   † Worthlefs.

‡ " Holleth." It is properly " holeth," makes a hole in my heart. It is ufed for making a hole for inferting railings or bars. So in Let. 197, and in a fermon preached before the Houfe of Commons, 1644, on Dan. vi. 26, he fpeaks of " a threadbare cloak, ragged and holed," p. 45.

§ Head of the table, the place of honour. The by-board, or fide-table, for children or the like.

houſe again, and lend me the keys of His wine-cellar again , and God ſend me borrowed drink till then !

Remember my love to Chriſt's kinſmen with you. I pray for Chriſt's Father's bleſſing to them all. Grace be with you ; a priſoner's bleſſing be with you. I write it and abide by it, God will be glorious in Marion M'Naught, when this ſtormy blaſt ſhall be over. O woman beloved of God, believe, rejoice, be ſtrong in the Lord ! Grace is thy portion.

Your brother, in his ſweet Lord Jeſus,

ABERDEEN, *June* 15, 1637.   S. R.

CLXXVIII.—*To* LADY CULROSS. [Let. 74.]

*(CHRIST'S MANAGEMENT OF TRIALS—WHAT FAITH CAN DO—
CHRIST NOT EXPERIENCE—PRAYERS.)*

ADAM,—Grace, mercy, and peace be to you. I dare not ſay that I wonder that ye have never written to me in my bonds, becauſe I am not ignorant of the cauſe ; yet I could not but write to you.

I know not whether joy or heavineſs in my ſoul carrieth it away. Sorrow, without any mixture of ſweetneſs, hath not often love-thoughts of Chriſt ; but I ſee that the devil can inſinuate himſelf, and ride his errands upon the thoughts of a poor diſtreſſed priſoner. I am woe* that I am making Chriſt my unfriend,† by ſeeking pleas‡ againſt Him, becauſe I am the firſt in the kingdom put to utter ſilence, and becauſe I cannot preach my Lord's righteouſneſs in the great congregation. I am, notwithſtanding, the leſs ſolicitous how it go, if there be not wrath in my cup. But I know that I but claw my wounds when my Phyſician hath forbidden me. I would believe in the dark upon luck's head,§ and take my hazard of Chriſt's good-will, and reſt on this, that in my fever my Phyſician

---

* Sorry.   † Leſs than friend.
‡ Occaſions of quarrel.   § On the chance of winning.

is at my bedfide, and that He fympathizeth with me when I figh.
My borrowed houfe, and another man's bed and firefide, and other
loffes, have no room in my forrow ; a greater heat to eat out a lefs
fire, is a good remedy for fome burning.   I believe that when Chrift
draweth blood, He hath fkill to cut the right vein ; and that He
hath taken the whole ordering and difpofing of my fufferings.   Let
Him tutor me, and tutor my croffes, as He thinketh good.   There
is no danger nor hazard in following fuch a guide, howbeit He
fhould lead me through hell, if I could put faith foremoft, and fill
the field with a quiet on-waiting, and believing to fee the falvation of
God.   I know that Chrift is not obliged to let me fee both the fides
of my crofs, and turn it over and over that I may fee all.   My faith
is richer to live upon credit, and Chrift's borrowed money, than to
have much on hand.   Alas! I have forgotten that faith in times
paft hath ftopped a leak in my crazed bark, and hath filled my fails
with a fair wind.   I fee it a work of God that experiences are all
loft, when fummons of improbation,* to prove our charters of Chrift
to be counterfeits, are raifed againft poor fouls in their heavy trials.

But let me be a finner, and worfe than the chief of finners, yea,
a guilty devil, I am fure that my Well-beloved is God.   And when
I fay that Chrift is God, and that my Chrift is God, I have faid all
things, I can fay no more.   I would that I could build as much on
this, " My Chrift is God," as it would bear ; I might lay all the
world upon it.   I am fure, that Chrift untried, and untaken-up in
the power of His love, kindnefs, mercies, goodnefs, wifdom, long-
fuffering, and greatnefs, is the rock that dim-fighted travellers dafh
their foot againft, and fo ftumble fearfully.   But my wounds are
foreft, and pain me moft, when I fin againft His love and mercy.
And if He would fet me and my confcience by the ears together, and
refolve not to red the plea, but let us deal it betwixt us, my fpitting
upon the fair face of Chrift's love and mercies by my jealoufies,†

---

* Actions raifed with the view of fhowing that the perfons had no right to
what they claimed.

† Sufpicions.

unbelief, and doubting, would be enough to fink me. Oh, oh, I am convinced! O Lord, I ftand dumb before Thee for this! Let me be mine own judge in this, and I take a dreadful doom upon me for it. For I ftill mifbelieve, though I have feen that my Lord hath made my crofs as if it were all cryftal, fo as I can fee through it Chrift's fair face and heaven ; and that God hath honoured a lump of finful flefh and blood the like of me,* to be Chrift's honourable lord-prifoner. I ought to efteem the walls of the thieves' hole† (if I were fhut up in it), or any ftinking dungeon, all hung with tapeftry, and moft beautiful, for my Lord Jefus ; and yet, I am not fo fhut up but that the fun fhineth upon my prifon, and the fair wide heaven is the covering of it. But my Lord, in His fweet vifits, hath done more ; for He maketh me to find that He will be a confined prifoner with me. He lieth down and rifeth up with me ; when I figh, He figheth ; when I weep, He fuffereth with me ; and I confefs that here is the bleffed iffue of my fufferings already begun, that my heart is filled with hunger and defire to have Him glorified in my fufferings.

Bleffed be ye of the Lord, Madam, if ye would help a poor dyvour, and caufe others of your acquaintance in Chrift to help me to pay my debt of love, even real praifes to Chrift my Lord. Madam, let me charge you in the Lord, as ye fhall anfwer to Him, to help me in this duty (which He hath tied about my neck with a chain of fuch fingular expreffions of His loving-kindnefs), to fet on high Chrift ; to hold in my honefty at His hands,‡ for I have nothing to give to Him. Oh that He would arreft and comprife§ my love and my heart for all! I am a dyvour, who have no more free goods in the world for Chrift fave that ; it is both the whole heritage I have, and all my moveables befides. Lord, give the thirfty man a drink. Oh, to be over the ears in the well! Oh, to be fwattering ‖ and fwimming over head and ears in Chrift's love! I

---

* A man fuch as I am.   † Prifon.

‡ In order hereby to keep up my character with Him.

§ *Arreft*, is apprehended by force ; *comprife*, is doing fo by writ of law.

‖ Fluttering and moving awkwardly in water, as ducks do.

would not have Chrift's love entering into me, but I would enter into it, and be fwallowed up of that love. But I fee not myfelf here; for I fear I make more of His love than of Himfelf; whereas Himfelf is far beyond and much better than His love. Oh, if I had my finful arms filled with that lovely one Chrift! Bleffed be my rich Lord Jefus, who fendeth not away beggars from His houfe with a toom* difh. He filleth the veffels of fuch as will come and feek. We might beg ourfelves rich (if we were wife) if we could hold out our withered hands to Chrift, and learn to fuit† and feek, afk and knock. I owe my falvation for Chrift's glory, I owe it to Chrift; and defire that my hell, yea, a new hell, feven times hotter than the old hell, might buy praifes before men and angels to my Lord Jefus; providing always that I were free of Chrift's hatred and difpleafure. What am I, to be forfeited and fold in foul and body, to have my great and royal King fet on high and extolled above all? Oh, if I knew how high to have Him fet, and all the world far, far beneath the foles of His feet? Nay, I deferve not to be the matter of His praifes, far lefs to be an agent in praifing of Him. But He can win His own glory out of me, and out of worfe than I (if any fuch be), if it pleafe His holy majefty fo to do. He knoweth that I am not now flattering Him.

Madam, let me have your prayers, as ye have the prayers and bleffing of him that is feparated from His brethren. Grace, grace be with you.

Your own, in his fweet Lord Jefus,

S. R.

ABERDEEN, *June* 15, 1637.

———◆———

CLXXIX.—*To his reverend and loving Brother*, MR JOHN NEVAY.

[MR JOHN NEVAY, or NEAVE, as he fpelt his name, was minifter of Newmills, in the parifh of Loudon, and chaplain to the Earl of Loudon. In all the queftions which divided the Covenanters in his day, he adhered to what

_____

* Empty.   † Urge a requeft.

may be called the ftrict party, being oppofed to the Public Refolutions. After
the reftoration of Charles II., Nevay, in 1662, was obliged to fubfcribe an
engagement to remove forth of the king's dominions before the ift of February, and not to return under pain of death. He reached Holland, and
lived for fome time in Rotterdam. But, on the 26th of July 1670, a letter of
Charles II. was laid before the affembled States of Holland, accufing Nevay and
other two minifters, Mr Robert Trail and Mr Robert M'Ward (who was
fecretary to Rutherford at the Weftminfter Affembly, and who firft edited his
" Letters"), all refiding within the jurifdiction of the States, of writing and
publifhing *pafquils* againft his Majefty's Government. It would, however,
appear that he ftill continued at Rotterdam, and died there. Wodrow defcribes him as "a perfon of very confiderable parts, and bright piety." Robert
M'Ward, in 1677, thus writes: "Oh! when I remember that burning and
fhining light, worthy and warm Mr Livingftone, who ufed to preach as
within the fight of Chrift, and the glory to be revealed; *acute and diftinct
Nevay;* judicious and neat Simfon; fervent, ferious, and zealous Trail;—
when I remember, I fay, that all thefe great luminaries are now fet and removed by death from our people, and out of our pulpit, in fo fhort a time,
what matter of forrow prefents itfelf to my eye!" Nevay cultivated the art
of poetry, and is the author of a paraphrafe (called by Wodrow "a handfome
paraphrafe") of the Song of Solomon in Latin verfe. The General Affembly
entertained fo high an opinion of his poetical talents, that they appointed him,
in Auguft 1647, along with three other minifters, to revife Rous' metrical
verfion of the Pfalms. The portion affigned to him for revifal was the laft
thirty pfalms of that verfion. After his death, a volume of fermons, preached
by him on the Covenant of Grace, was publifhed. His fon married Sarah
Van Brakel, whofe poetical compofitions are favourably exhibited in her
elegy upon a popular preacher, and who was a kind friend to the Britifh
refugees.]

*(CHRIST'S LOVE SHARPENED IN SUFFERING—KNEELING AT
THE COMMUNION—POSTURES AT ORDINANCES.)*

EVEREND AND DEAR BROTHER,— Grace,
mercy, and peace be to you. I received yours of
April 11, as I did another of March 25, and a letter
for Mr Andrew Cant.*

---

* Mr Andrew Cant was at this time minifter of Pitfligo, in Buchan,
Aberdeenfhire. He had been previoufly minifter of Alford. In 1639, he was
removed from Pitfligo to Newbottle; and in 1640, to the New Town of Aber-

I am not a little grieved that our mother Church is running fo quickly to the brothel-houfe, and that we are hiring lovers, and giving gifts to the Great Mother of Fornications.* Alas, that our hufband is like to quit us fo fhortly! It were my part (if I were able), when our Hufband is departing, to ftir up myfelf to take hold of Him, and keep Him in this land ; for I know Him to be a fweet fecond,† and a lovely companion to a poor prifoner.

I find that my extremity hath fharpened the edge of His love and kindnefs, fo that He feemeth to devife new ways of expreffing the fweetnefs of His love to my foul. Suffering for Chrift is the very element wherein Chrift's love liveth, and exercifeth itfelf, in cafting out flames of fire, and fparks of heat, to warm fuch a frozen heart as I have. And if Chrift weeping in fackcloth be fo fweet, I cannot find any imaginable thoughts to think what He will be, when we clay-bodies (having put off mortality) fhall come up to the marriage-hall and great palace, and behold the King clothed in His robes royal, fitting on His throne. I would defire no more for my heaven beneath the moon, while I am fighing in this houfe of clay, but daily renewed feafts of love with Chrift, and liberty now and then to feed my hunger with a kifs of that faireft face, that is like the fun in his ftrength at noon-day. I would willingly fubfcribe an ample refignation to Chrift of the fourteen prelacies of this land, and of all the moft delightful pleafures on earth, and forfeit my part of this clay god, this earth, which Adam's foolifh children wor- fhip, to have no other exercife than to lie on a love-bed with Chrift,

---

deen, where he became Profeffor of Theology in Marifchal College. In this fituation he continued till the year after the reftoration of Charles II. Ruther- ford's *Lex Rex* having then, by the orders of the State, been publicly burnt, and the author himfelf fummoned before Parliament to anfwer an accufation of high treafon, Cant, indignant at fuch ungenerous treatment of a great and good man, condemned it in one of his fermons. Being accufed of treafon for this, before the magiftrates, he demitted his charge, and came to dwell with his fon at Liberton. In 1663, he was formally depofed from his charge by the Bifhop and Synod of Aberdeen, and died not long after, aged feventy-nine. He is the author of a treatife on " The Titles of our Bleffed Saviour."

* Rev. xvii. 5. † Helper.

and fill this hungered and famished soul with kissing, embracing,
and real enjoying of the Son of God; and I think that then I might
write to my friends, that I had found the Golden World, and look
out and laugh at the poor bodies who are slaying one another for
feathers.   For verily, brother, since I came to this prison, I have
conceived a new and extraordinary opinion of Christ, which I had
not before.   For, I perceive, we frist* all our joys to Christ, till He
and we be in our own house above, as married parties, thinking
that there is nothing of it here to be sought or found, but only hope
and fair promises; and that Christ will give us nothing here but
tears, sadness, and crosses; and that we shall never feel the smell of
the flowers of that high garden of paradise above, till we come there.
Nay, but I find that it is possible to find young glory, and a young
green paradise of joy, even here.   I know that Christ's kisses will
cast a more strong and refreshful smell of incomparable glory and
joy in heaven than they do here; because a drink of the well of life,
up at the well's head, is more sweet and fresh by far than that
which we get in our borrowed, old, running-out vessels, and our
wooden dishes here.   Yet I am now persuaded it is our folly to
frist* all till the term-day, seeing abundance of earnest† will not
diminish anything of our principal sum.   We dream of hunger in
Christ's house while we are here, although he alloweth feasts to all
the bairns within God's household.   It were good, then, to store
ourselves with more borrowed kisses of Christ, and with more borrowed visits, till we enter heirs to our new inheritance, and our
Tutor put us in possession of our own when we are past minority.
O that all the young heirs would seek more, and a greater, and
a nearer communion with my Lord Tutor, the prime heir of all,
Christ!   I wish that, for my part, I could send you, and that
gentleman who wrote his commendations to me, into the King's
innermost cellar and house of wine, to be filled with love.   A drink
of this love is worth the having indeed.   We carry ourselves but too
nicely with Christ our Lord; and our Lord loveth not niceness, and

---

* Defer to another time.   † Foretaste of what is to be got.

dryness, and unconess,* in friends. Since need-force† that we muſt be in Chriſt's common,‡ then let us be in His common ; for it will be no otherwiſe.

Now, for my preſent caſe in my impriſonment : deliverance (for any appearance that I ſee) looketh cold-like. § My hope, if it looked to or leaned upon men, would wither ſoon at the root, like a May flower. Yet I reſolve to eaſe myſelf with on-waiting on my Lord, and to let my faith ſwim where it loſeth ground. I am under a neceſſity either of fainting (which I hope my Maſter, of whom I boaſt all the day, will avert), or then‖ to lay my faith upon Omni-potency, and to wink and ſtick by my grip.¶ And I hope that my ſhip ſhall ride it out, ſeeing Chriſt is willing to blow His ſweet wind in my ſails, and mendeth and cloſeth the leaks in my ſhip, and ruleth all. It will be ſtrange if a believing paſſenger be caſten over-board.

As for your maſter, my lord and my lady,** I ſhall be loath to forget them. I think my prayers (ſuch as they are) are debt due to him ; and I ſhall be far more engaged to his Lordſhip, if he be faſt for Chriſt (as I hope he will) now when ſo many of his coat and quality ſlip from Chriſt's back, and leave Him to fend†† for Himſelf.

I entreat you to remember my love to that worthy gentleman, A. C., who ſaluted me in your letter : I have heard that he is one of my Maſter's friends, for the which cauſe I am tied to him. I wiſh that he may more and more fall in love with Chriſt.

Now for your queſtion :—As far as I rawly conceive, I think that God is praiſed two ways : 1ſt. By a *concional* profeſſion of His highneſs before men, ſuch as is the very hearing of the word, and receiving of either of the ſacraments ; in which acts by profeſſion, we give out to men, that He is our God with whom we are in

---

* Reſerve ; behaving as if ſtrangers. † Of pure neceſſity.
‡ Under obligation to. § The fire gone out, hopeleſs.
‖ Or, as an alternative. ¶ Shut the eyes, and keep firm hold, in ſpite of peril.
** John Campbell, firſt Earl of Loudon, and his lady, Margaret Campbell, Baroneſs of Loudon, daughter of George Campbell, maſter of Loudon.
†† Shift for, provide.

covenant, and our Lawgiver. Thus eating and drinking in the Lord's Supper, is an annunciation and profeffion before men, that Chrift is our flain Redeemer. Here, becaufe God fpeaketh to us, not we to Him, it is not a formal thankfgiving, but an annunciation or predication of Chrift's death—*concional,** not *adorative*—neither hath it God for the immediate objeft, and therefore no kneeling can be here.

2dly. There is another praifing of God, *formal*, when we are either formally bleffing God, or fpeaking His praifes. And this I take to be twofold :—1. When we direftly and formally direft praifes and thankfgiving to God. This may well be done kneeling, in token of our recognizance of His highnefs ; yet not fo but that it may be done ftanding or fitting, efpecially feeing joyful elevation (which fhould be in praifing) is not formally fignified by kneeling. 2. When we fpeak good of God, and declare His glorious nature and attributes, extolling Him before men, to excite men to conceive highly of Him. The former I hold to be worfhip every way im- mediate, elfe I know not any immediate worfhip at all ; the latter hath God for the fubjeft, not properly the objeft, feeing the predi- cation is directed to men immediately, rather than to God ; for here we fpeak *of* God by way of praifing, rather than *to* God. And, for my own part, as I am for the prefent minded, I fee not how this can be done kneeling, feeing it is *prædicatio Dei et Chrifti, non laudatio aut benedictio Dei.* [A preaching of God and Chrift, and not of praifing or bleffing of God.] But obferve, that it is formal praifing of God, and not merely concional, as I diftinguifhed in the firft member ; for, in the firft member, any fpeaking of God, or of His works of creation, providence, and redemption, is indireft and concional* praifing of Him, and formally preaching, or an aft of teaching, not an aft of predication of His praifes. For there is a difference betwixt the fimple relation of the virtues of a thing (which is formally teaching), and the extolling of the worth of a thing by way of commendation, to caufe others to praife with us.

---

* An act in which we addrefs men, not one in which we adore.

Thus recommending you to God's grace,* I reſt, yours, in his
ſweet Lord Jeſus,

ABERDEEN, *June* 15, 1637. S. R.

CLXXX.—*To the much Honoured* JOHN GORDON *of Cardoneſs,
the Elder.*

(*LONGINGS FOR THOSE UNDER HIS FORMER MINISTRY—DE-
LIGHT IN CHRIST AND HIS APPEARING—PLEADING WITH
HIS FLOCK.*)

UCH HONOURED, AND DEAREST IN MY
LORD,—Grace, mercy, and peace be to you. My
ſoul longeth exceedingly to hear how matters go betwixt you and Chriſt ; and whether or not there be any work of
Chriſt in that pariſh, that will bide the trial of fire and water. Let
me be weighed of my Lord in a juſt balance, if your ſouls lie not
weighty upon me. Ye go to bed and ye riſe with me : thoughts
of your ſoul, my deareſt in our Lord, depart not from me in my
ſleep. Ye have a great part of my tears, ſighs, ſupplications, and
prayers. Oh, if I could buy your ſoul's ſalvation with any ſuffering whatſoever, and that ye and I might meet with joy up in the
rainbow, when we ſhall ſtand before our Judge ! Oh, my Lord,
forbid that I have any hard thing to depone† againſt you in that
day ! Oh that He who quickeneth the dead would give life to
my ſowing among you ! What joy is there (next to Chriſt) that
ſtandeth on this ſide of death, which would comfort me more, than
that the ſouls of that poor people were in ſafety, and beyond all
hazard of being loſt !

Sir, ſhow the people this ; for when I write to you, I think I
write to you all, old and young. Fulfil my joy, and ſeek the Lord.
Sure I am, that once I diſcovered my lovely, royal, princely Lord

---

* In ſome modern editions, it is " ſweet grace ; " but not ſo in the earlieſt.
† To ſtate as a witneſs does.

Jesus to you all.   Woe, woe, woe shall be your part of it for evermore, if the Gospel be not the favour of life to you.   As many sermons as I preached, as many sentences as I uttered, as many points of dittay* shall there be, when the Lord shall plead with the world, for the evil of their doings.   Believe me, I find heaven a city hard to be won.   " The righteous shall scarcely be saved." Oh, what violence of thronging† will heaven take !   Alas ! I see many deceiving themselves ; for we will all to heaven now !   Every foul dog, with his foul feet, will in at the nearest, to the new and clean Jerusalem.   All say they have faith ; and the greatest part in the world know not, and will not consider, that a slip in the matter of their salvation is the most pitiable slip that can be ; and that no loss is comparable to this loss.   Oh, then, see that there be not a loose pin in the work of your salvation ; for ye will not believe how quickly the Judge will come.   And for yourself, I know that death is waiting, and hovering, and lingering at God's command.   That ye may be prepared, then, ye had need to stir your time, and to take eternity and death to your riper advisement.   A wrong step, or a wrong stot,‡ in going out of this life, in one property, is like the sin against the Holy Ghost, and can never be forgiven, because ye cannot come back again through the last water to mourn for it. I know your accounts are many, and will take telling and laying, and reckoning betwixt you and your Lord.   Fit your accounts, and order them.   Lose not the last play, whatever ye do, for in that play with death your precious soul is the prize : for the Lord's sake spill § not the play, and lose not such a treasure.   Ye know that, out of love which I had to your soul, and out of desire which I had to make an honest account of you, I testified my displeasure and disliking of your ways very often, both in private and public.   I am not now a witness of your doings, but your Judge is always your witness.   I beseech you by the mercies of God, by the salva-

---

* Indictment.   " Your *dittay* is burnt," (*i.e.* there is now no charge against you), occurs in Kenmure's Dying Speeches.

† Pressing in, as is done in a crowd.   ‡ Rebound, stumble.   § Spoil, mar.

tion of your foul, by your comfort when your eye-ftrings fhall break, and the face wax pale, and the foul fhall tremble to be out of the lodging of clay, and by your compearance before your awful Judge, after the fight of this letter to take a new courfe with your ways, and now, in the end of your day, make fure of heaven. Examine yourfelf if ye be in good earneft in Chrift ; for fome are partakers of the Holy Ghoft, and tafte of the good word of God, and of the powers of the life to come, and yet have no part in Chrift at all.* Many think they believe, but never tremble : the devils are farther on than thefe.† Make fure to yourfelf that ye are above ordinary pro-feffors. The fixth part of your fpan-length and hand-breadth of days is fcarcely before you. Hafte, hafte, for the tide will not bide.‡ Put Chrift upon all your accounts and your fecrets. Better it is that you give Him your accounts in this life, out of your own hand, than that, after this life, He take them from you. I never knew fo well what fin was as fince I came to Aberdeen, howbeit I was preaching of it to you. To feel the fmoke of hell's fire in the throat for half-an-hour ; to ftand befide a river of fire and brimftone broader than the earth ; and to think to be bound hand and foot, and caften into the midft of it quick, and then to have God locking the prifon-door, never to be opened for all eternity ! Oh how it will fhake a con-fcience that hath any life in it ! I find the fruits of my pains to have Chrift and that people once§ fairly met, now meet my foul in my fad hours. And I rejoice that I gave fair warning of all the corruptions now entering into Chrift's houfe ; and now many a fweet, fweet, foft kifs, many perfumed, well-fmelled kiffes, and em-bracements have I received of my royal Mafter. He and I have had much love together. I have for the prefent a fick dwining‖ life, with much pain, and much love-ficknefs for Chrift. Oh, what would I give to have a bed made to my wearied foul in His bofom ! I would frift¶ heaven for many years, to have my fill of Jefus in this life, and to have occafion to offer Chrift to my people, and to

---

* Heb. vi. 4, 5.　　　　　　　　† James ii. 19.　　　‡ Wait.

§ One time or other ; or, once for all.　　‖ Pining.　　¶ Defer.

woo many people to Chrift. I cannot tell you what fweet pain
and delightfome torments are in Chrift's love ; I often challenge *
time, that holdeth us fundry. I profefs to you, I have no reft, I
have no eafe, whill† I be over head and ears in love's ocean. If
Chrift's love (that fountain of delight) were laid as open to me as I
would wifh, oh, how I would drink, and drink abundantly ! oh,
how drunken would this my foul be ! I half call His abfence cruel ;
and the mafk and vail on Chrift's face a cruel covering, that hideth
fuch a fair, fair face from a fick foul. I dare not challenge * Himfelf, but His abfence is a mountain of iron upon my heavy heart.
Oh, when fhall we meet ? Oh, how long is it to the dawning of
the marriage-day ! O fweet Lord Jefus, take wide fteps ; O my
Lord, come over mountains at one ftride ! O my Beloved, be like a
roe or a young hart on the mountains of Separation.‡ Oh, if He
would fold the heavens together like an old cloak, and fhovel time
and days out of the way, and make ready in hafte the Lamb's wife
for her Hufband ! Since He looked upon me, my heart is not mine
own ; He hath run away to heaven with it. I know that it was not
for nothing that I fpake fo meikle§ good of Chrift to you in public.
Oh, if the heaven, and the heaven of heavens, were paper, and the
fea ink, and the multitude of mountains pens of brafs, and I able to
write that paper, within and without, full of the praifes of my
faireft, my deareft, my lovelieft, my fweeteft, my matchlefs, and
my moft marrowlefs‖ and marvellous Well-beloved ! Woe is me,
I cannot fet Him out to men and angels ! Oh, there are few tongues
to fing love-fongs of His incomparable excellency ! What can I,
poor prifoner, do to exalt Him ? or what courfe can I take to extol
my lofty and lovely Lord Jefus ? I am put to my wits' end, how
to get His name made great. Blefled they who would help me in
this ! How fweet are Chrift's back parts ? Oh, what then is His
face ? Thofe that fee His face, how dow¶ they get their eye
plucked off Him again ! Look up to Him and love Him. Oh,

---

* Rebuke, upbraid.　† Till.　‡ " *Bether*" means " feparation," Song ii. 17.
§ Much.　　　　　‖ Unequalled, peerlefs.　　　¶ Can they.

love and live! It were life to me if you would read this letter to that people, and if they did profit by it. Oh, if I could caufe them to die of love for Jefus! Charge them, by the falvation of their fouls, to hang about Chrift's neck, and take their fill of His love, and follow Him as I taught them. Part by no means with Chrift. Hold faft what ye have received. Keep the truth once delivered. If ye or that people quit it in an hair, or in a hoof, ye break your confcience in twain; and who then can mend it, and caft a knot* on it? My deareft in the Lord, ftand faft in Chrift; keep the faith; contend for Chrift. Wreftle for Him, and take men's feud for God's favour; there is no comparifon betwixt thefe. O that the Lord would fulfil my joy, and keep the young bride that is at Anwoth to Chrift.

And now, whoever they be that have returned to the old vomit fince my departure, I bind upon their back, in my Mafter's name and authority, the long-lafting, weighty vengeance and curfe of God. In my Lord's name I give them a doom of black, unmixed, pure wrath, which my Mafter will ratify and make good, when we ftand together before Him, except they timeoufly† repent and turn to the Lord. And I write to thee, poor mourning and broken-hearted believer, be thou who thou wilt, of the free falvation, Chrift's fweet balm for thy wounds, O poor humble believer! Chrift's kiffes for thy watery cheeks! Chrift's blood of atonement for thy guilty foul! Chrift's heaven for thy poor foul, though once banifhed out of paradife! And my Mafter will make good my word ere long. Oh that people were wife! Oh that people were wife! Oh that people would fpeer‡ out Chrift, and never reft whill§ they find Him. Oh, how my foul will mourn in fecret, if my nine years' pained head, and fore breaft, and pained back, and grieved heart, and private and public prayers to God, will all be for nothing among that people! Did my Lord Jefus fend me but to fummon you

---

* Tie, to keep from flipping.

† In good time, foon. See the metre verfion of Ps. cxix. 148.

‡ Afk queftions about.   § Till.

before your Judge, and to leave your fummons at your houfes? Was I fent as a witnefs only to gather your dittays?* Oh, may God forbid! Often did I tell you of a fan of God's word† to come among you, for the contempt of it. I told you often of wrath, wrath from the Lord, to come upon Scotland; and yet I bide by my Mafter's word. It is quickly coming! defolation for Scotland, becaufe of the quarrel of a broken covenant.

Now, worthy Sir, now my dear people, my joy, and my crown in the Lord, let Him be your fear. Seek the Lord, and His face: fave your fouls. Doves! flee to Chrift's windows. Pray for me, and praife for me. The bleffing of my God, the prayers and bleffing of a poor prifoner, and your lawful paftor, be upon you.

Your lawful and loving paftor,

S. R.

ABERDEEN, *June* 16, 1637.

CLXXXI.—*To* EARLSTON, *the younger.*

DANGERS OF YOUTH—CHRIST THE BEST PHYSICIAN—FOUR REMEDIES AGAINST DOUBTING — BREATHINGS AFTER CHRIST'S HONOUR.

UCH HONOURED AND WELL-BELOVED IN THE LORD,—Grace, mercy, and peace be to you. Your letters give a dafh to my lazinefs in writing.

I muft firft tell you, that there is not fuch a glaffy, icy, and flippery piece of way betwixt you and heaven, as Youth; and I have experience to fay with me here, and to feal what I affert. The old afhes of the fins of my youth are new fire of forrow to me. I have feen the devil, as it were, dead and buried, and yet rife again, and be a worfe devil than ever he was; therefore, my brother, beware of a green young devil, that hath never been buried. The devil in

* Indictments.

† Should not this be *wind*, not "*word*;" alluding to Jer. iv. 12?

his flowers (I mean the hot, fiery lufts and paffions of youth) is
much to be feared : better yoke* with an old grey-haired, withered,
dry devil.   For in youth he findeth dry fticks, and dry coals, and a
hot hearth-ftone ; and how foon can he with his flint caft† fire, and
with his bellows blow it up, and fire the houfe ! Sanctified thoughts,
thoughts made confcience of, and called in, and kept in awe, are
green fuel that burn not, and are a water for Satan's coal.   Yet I
muft tell you, that the whole faints now triumphant in heaven, and
ftanding before the throne, are nothing but Chrift's forlorn‡ and
beggarly dyvours.   What are they but a pack of redeemed finners?
But their redemption is not only paft the feals, but completed ; and
yours is on the wheels, and in doing.

All Chrift's good bairns go to heaven with a broken brow, and
with a crooked leg.   Chrift hath an advantage of you, and I pray
you to let Him have it ; He will find employment for His calling in
you.   If it were not with you as ye write, grace fhould find no fale
nor market in you ; but ye muft be content to give Chrift fomewhat
to do.   I am glad that He is employed that way.   Let your bleeding foul and your fores be put in the hand of this expert Phyfician ;
let young and ftrong corruptions and His free grace be yoked
together, and let Chrift and your fins deal it betwixt them.   I fhall
be loath to put you off your fears, and your fenfe of deadnefs : I
wifh it were more.   There be fome wounds of that nature, that
their bleeding fhould not be foon ftopped.   Ye muft take a houfe
befide the Phyfician.   It will be a miracle if ye be the firft fick man
whom He put away uncured, and worfe than He found you. Nay,
nay, Chrift is honeft, and in that is flyting-free§ with finners. " Him
that cometh unto Me I will in no wife caft out."‖   Take ye that.
It cannot be prefumption to take that as your own, when you find
that your wounds ftound¶ you.   Prefumption is ever whole at the

---

* Set to, enter into conflict.   † Strike.   ‡ Loft, prodigal debtors.

§ " I am flyting free with him," is a proverb; *q. d.*, He has nothing to
fay to me, and I am free to chide with him for his faults.

‖ John vi. 37.

¶ Shoot pain through you.

heart, and hath but the truant* ſickneſs, and groaneth only for the
faſhion.   Faith hath ſenſe of ſickneſs, and looketh, like a friend, to
the promiſes ; and, looking to Chriſt therein, is glad to ſee a known
face.   Chriſt is as full a feaſt as ye can have to hunger.   Nay,
Chriſt, I ſay, is not a full man's leavings.   His mercy ſendeth always
a letter of defiance to all your ſins, if there were ten thouſand more
of them.

I grant you that it is a hard matter for a poor hungry man to
win his meat† upon hidden Chriſt : for then the key of His pantry-
door, and of the houſe of wine, is a-ſeeking and cannot be had.   But
hunger muſt break through iron locks.   I bemoan them not who
can make a din, and all the fields ado,‡ for a loſt Saviour.   Ye
muſt let Him hear it (to ſay ſo) upon both ſides of His head, when
He hideth Himſelf ; it is no time then to be bird-mouthed § and
patient.   Chriſt is rare indeed, and a delicacy to a ſinner.   He is a
miracle, and a world's wonder, to a ſeeking and a weeping ſinner ;
but yet ſuch a miracle as ſhall be ſeen by them who will come and
ſee.   The ſeeker and ſigher, is at laſt a ſinger and enjoyer ; nay,
I have ſeen a dumb man get alms from Chriſt.   He that can tell
his tale, and ſend ſuch a letter to heaven as he hath ſent to Aberdeen, it is very like he will come ſpeed‖ with Chriſt.   It bodeth
God's mercy to complain heartily for ſin.   Let wreſtling be with
Chriſt till He ſay, " How is it, ſir, that I cannot be quit of your bills,
and your miſleared ¶ cries ?" and then hope for Chriſt's bleſſing ;
and His bleſſing is better than ten other bleſſings.   Think not ſhame
becauſe of your guiltineſs ; neceſſity muſt not bluſh to beg.   It
ſtandeth you hard to want Chriſt ; and, therefore, that which idle
on-waiting cannot do, miſnurtured** crying and knocking will do.

---

* Pretended, like ſchoolboys' pretences for play.   † Earn his livelihood.

‡ In a ſermon preached at Kirkcudbright, on Rev. xix. 11, he ſuppoſes the
courtiers ſaying to Daniel, " *What need ye make all the fields ado with your
prayers ?*"   The word means " aſtir."   Cattle are ſaid to do this when bel-
lowing for their mates.

§ Mealy-mouthed.   ‖ Succeed.

¶ Ill-taught ; unmannerly.   ** Undiſciplined, unſubdued.

And for doubtings, becaufe you are not as you were long fince with your Mafter : confider three things. 1*ft*, What if Chrift had fuch tottering thoughts of the bargain of the new covenant betwixt you and Him, as you have? 2*dly*, Your heart is not the compafs which Chrift faileth by. He will give you leave to fing as you pleafe, but He will not dance to your daft* fpring. It is not referred to you and your thoughts, what Chrift will do with the charters betwixt you and Him. Your own mifbelief hath torn them ; but He hath the principal in heaven with Himfelf. Your thoughts are no parts of the new covenant ; dreams change not Chrift. 3*dly*, Doubtings are your fins ; but they are Chrift's drugs, and ingredients that the Phyfician maketh ufe of for the curing of your pride. Is it not fuitable for a beggar to fay at meat, " God reward the winners ?"† for then he faith that he knoweth who beareth the charges of the houfe. It is alfo meet that ye fhould know, by experience, that faith is not nature's ill-gotten baftard, but your Lord's free gift, that lay in the womb of God's free grace. Praifed be the Winner !‡ I may add a 4*thly*, In the paffing of your bill and your charters, when they went through the Mediator's great feal, and were concluded, faith's advice was not fought. Faith hath not a vote befide Chrift's merits : blood, blood, dear blood, that came from your Cautioner's§ holy body, maketh that fure work. The ufe, then, which ye have of faith now (having already clofed with Jefus Chrift for juftification) is, to take out a copy of your pardon ; and fo ye have peace with God upon the account of Chrift. For, fince faith apprehendeth pardon, but never payeth a penny for it, no marvel that falvation doth not die and live, ebb or flow, with the working of faith. But becaufe it is your Lord's honour to believe His mercy and His fidelity, it is infinite goodnefs in our Lord, that mifbelief giveth a dafh to our Lord's glory, and not to our falvation. And fo, whoever want (yea, howbeit God here bear with the want of what we are obliged to

---

* Foolifh fprightly air ; or tune.   † Thofe who got this for us.

‡ He who got it for us.   § The furety.

give Him, even the glory of His grace by believing), yet a poor
covenanted finner wanteth not.   But if guiltinefs were removed,
doubtings would find no friend, nor life ; and yet faith is to believe
the removal of guiltinefs in Chrift.   A reafon why ye get lefs now
(as ye think) than before, as I take it, is, becaufe, at our firft converfion, our Lord putteth the meat in young bairns' mouths with
His own hand ; but when we grow to fome further perfection, we
muft take heaven by violence, and take by violence from Chrift
what we get.   And He can, and doth hold, becaufe He will have us
to draw.   Remember now that ye muft live upon violent plucking.
Lazinefs is a greater fault now than long fince.   We love always
to have the pap put in our mouth.

Now for myfelf ; alas! I am not the man I go for in this nation ;
men have not juft weights to weigh me in.   Oh, but I am a filly,
fecklefs* body, and overgrown with weeds ; corruption is rank and
fat in me.   Oh, if I were anfwerable to this holy caufe, and to that
honourable Prince's love for whom I now fuffer!   If Chrift fhould refer the matter to me (in His prefence I fpeak it), I might think fhame
to vote my own falvation.   I think Chrift might fay, " Thinkeft thou
not fhame to claim heaven, who doeft fo little for it ? "   I am very
often fo, that I know not whether I fink or fwim in the water.   I
find myfelf a bag of light froth.   I would bear no weight (but vanities and nothings weigh in Chrift's balance) if my Lord caft not in
borrowed weight and metal, even Chrift's righteoufnefs, to weigh
for me.   The ftock I have is not mine own ; I am but the merchant
that trafficketh with other folks' goods.   If my creditor, Chrift,
fhould take from me what He hath lent, I fhould not long keep the
caufeway ;† but Chrift hath made it mine and His.   I think it man-
hood to play the coward, and jouk‡ in the lee-fide of Chrift ; and
thus I am not only faved from my enemies, but I obtain the victory.
I am fo empty, that I think it were an alms-deed in Chrift, if He
would win a poor prifoner's bleffing for evermore, and fill me with

---

* Pithlefs, worthlefs.   † Appear in open ftreet unabafhed.
‡ Bend my body on the fide where there is fhelter from the wind.

His love. I complain that when Chrift cometh, He cometh always
to fetch fire;* He is ever in hafte, He may not tarry; and poor I
(a beggarly dyvour†) **get** but a ftanding vifit and a ftanding kifs,
and but, "How doeft thou?" in the by-going.‡ I dare not fay He
is lordly, becaufe He is made a King **now** at the right hand of God;
or is grown mifkenning§ and dry‖ to His poor friends : for He cannot make more of His kiffes than they are worth. But I think it
my happinefs to love **the love of** Chrift : and **when** He goeth away,
the memory **of His fweet** prefence is like a feaft **in a dear** fummer.
I have comfort in this, that my foul defireth that every hour of my
imprifonment were a company of heavenly tongues to praife Him on
my behalf, howbeit my **bonds** were prolonged for many hundred
years. Oh that I could be the man who could procure my Lord's
glory to flow like a full fea, and blow like a mighty wind upon all
the four airths¶ of Scotland, England, and Ireland ! Oh, if I
could write a **book of** His praifes ! O Faireft among the fons of
men, why ftayeft thou fo long away? O heavens, move faft ! O
time, run, run, and haften the marriage-day! for love is tormented
with delays. O angels, O feraphims, who ftand before Him, O
bleffed fpirits who now fee His face, fet Him on high ! for when ye
have worn your harps in His praifes, all is too little, and is nothing,
to caft the fmell of the praife of that fair Flower, the fragrant Rofe
of Sharon, through **many worlds** !

Sir, take my hearty **commendations** to Him, and tell Him that I
am fick of love.

Grace be with you.

Yours in his fweet Lord Jefus,

S. R.

ABERDEEN, *June* 16, 1637.

---

* As fteel from flint ? † Debtor. ‡ In paffing by.
§ Apt to overlook, as if not knowing. ‖ Referved. ¶ Quarters.

(*JOY IN GOD—TRIALS WORK OUT GLORY TO CHRIST.*)

DEAREST AND TRULY HONOURED BROTHER,
—Grace, mercy, and peace be to you.   I have feen no
letter from you fince I came to Aberdeen.   I will not
interpret it to be forgetfulnefs.   I am here in a fair prifon : Chrift
is my fweet and honourable fellow-prifoner, and I His fad and joyful lord-prifoner,* if I may fpeak fo.   I think this crofs becometh
me well, and is fuitable to me in refpeÆt of my duty to fuffer for
Chrift, howbeit not in regard of my deferving to be thus honoured.
However it be, I fee that Chrift is ftrong, even lying in the duft, in
prifon, and in banifhment.   Loffes and difgraces are the wheels of
Chrift's triumphant chariot.   In the fufferings of His own faints, as
He intendeth their good, fo He intendeth His own glory, and that
is the butt His arrows fhoot at.   And Chrift fhooteth not at rovers,†
He hitteth what He purpofeth to hit ; therefore He doth make His
own fecklefs‡ and weak nothings, and thofe who are the contempt
of men, "a new fharp threfhing inftrument, having teeth, to threfh
the mountains, and beat them fmall, and to make the hills as chaff,
and to fan them."§   What harder ftuff, or harder grain for
threfhing out, than high and rocky mountains?   But the faints
are God's threfhing inftruments, to beat them all into chaff.   Are
we not God's leem‖ veffels? and yet when they caft us over
a houfe we are not broken into fherds.   We creep in under our
Lord's wings in the great fhower, and the water cannot come

---

* In Luther's ftyle, he playfully fpeaks of himfelf as if raifed to nobility
among prifoners.

† At random.   ‡ Worthlefs.   § Ifa. xli. 15, 16.

‖ Earthen ; from *limus?*   He fpeaks of " the potter having the dominion of
art over the leamy pot," in a fermon on Dan. vi. 26.   It is conneÆted with
" *loam.*"

through thofe wings. It is folly then for men to fay, "This is not Chrift's plea, He will lofe the wad-fee;* men are like to beguile Him:" that were indeed a ftrange play. Nay, I dare pledge my foul, and lay it in pawn on Chrift's fide of it, and be half-tiner,† half-winner with my Mafter! Let fools laugh the fool's laughter, and fcorn Chrift, and bid the weeping captives in Babylon "fing us one of the fongs of Zion, play a fpring‡ to cheer up your fad-hearted God!" We may fing upon luck's-head§ beforehand, even in our winter-ftorm, in the expectation of a fummer fun, at the turn of the year. No created powers in hell, or out of hell, can mar the mufic of our Lord Jefus, nor fpoil our fong of joy. Let us then be glad, and rejoice in the falvation of our Lord; for faith had never yet caufe to have wet cheeks, and hanging down brows, or to droop or die. What can ail faith, feeing Chrift fuffereth Himfelf (with reverence to Him be it fpoken) to be commanded by it, and Chrift commandeth all things? Faith may dance becaufe Chrift fingeth; and we may come into the choir, and lift our hoarfe and rough voices, and chirp, and fing, and fhout for joy with our Lord Jefus. We fee oxen go to the fhambles, leaping and ftartling;‖ we fee God's fed oxen, prepared for the day of flaughter, go dancing and finging down to the black chambers of hell; and why fhould we go to heaven weeping, as if we were like to fall down through the earth for forrow? If God were dead (if I may fpeak fo, with reverence of Him who liveth for ever and ever), and Chrift buried, and rotten among the worms, we might have caufe to look like dead folks; but "the Lord liveth, and bleffed be the Rock of our falvation."¶ None have right to joy but we; for joy is fown for us, and an ill fummer or harveft will not fpill** the crop. The children of this world have much robbed joy that is not well-come.†† It is no good fport they laugh at: they fteal joy, as it were, from

---

* Pledge; the fum paid in hiring, as a pledge of engagement.
† Half-lofer.   ‡ A fprightly air.   § On the chance of winning.
‖ Running to and fro in an excited manner.   ¶ Ps. xviii. 46.
** Mar.   †† Got in a right way.

God ; for He commandeth them to mourn and howl.*   Then let us
claim our leel-come† and lawfully conqueſſed† joy.

My dear brother, I cannot but ſpeak what I have felt ; ſeeing
my Lord Jeſus hath broken a box of ſpikenard upon the head of
His poor priſoner, and it is hard to hide a ſweet ſmell.   It is a pain
to ſmother Chriſt's love ; it will be out whether we will or not.   If
we did but ſpeak according to the matter, a croſs for Chriſt ſhould
have another name ; yea, a croſs, eſpecially when He cometh with
His arms full of joys, is the happieſt hard tree that ever was laid
upon my weak ſhoulder.   Chriſt and His croſs together are ſweet
company, and a bleſſed couple.   My priſon is my palace, my ſorrow
is with child of joy, my loſſes are rich loſſes, my pain eaſy pain, my
heavy days are holy and happy days.   I may tell a new tale of
Chriſt to my friends.   Oh, if I could make a love ſong of Him,
and could commend Chriſt, and tune His praiſes aright !   Oh, if I
could ſet all tongues in Great Britain and Ireland to work, to help
me to ſing a new ſong of my Well-beloved !   Oh, if I could be a
bridge over a water for my Lord Jeſus to walk upon, and keep His
feet dry !   Oh, if my poor bit heaven could go betwixt my Lord
and blaſphemy, and diſhonour !   (Upon condition He loved me).
Oh that my heart could ſay this word, and abide by it for ever !
Is it not great art and incomparable wiſdom in my Lord, who can
bring forth ſuch fair apples out of this crabbed tree of the croſs ?
Nay, my Father's never-enough admired providence can make a
fair face‡ out of a black devil.   Nothing can come wrong to my
Lord in His ſweet working.   I would even fall found aſleep in
Chriſt's arms, and my ſinful head on His holy breaſt, while He
kiſſeth me ; were it not that often the wind turneth to the north,
and whiles§ my ſweet Lord Jeſus is ſo that He will neither give nor

---

* James v. i.

† Purchaſed, or obtained by induſtry, not inherited. *Leel-come*, is what
has come to us in a found way, honeſt and true.

‡ This ſeems the true reading, though " feaſt " is in other editions.

§ At times.

take, borrow nor lend with me. I complain that He is not focial ;
I half call Him proud and lordly of His company, and nice of
His looks, which yet is not true. It would content me to give,
howbeit He fhould not take. I fhould be content to want His
kiffes at fuch times, providing He would be content to come near-
hand, and take my werfh,* dry, and fecklefs† kiffes. But at that
time He will not be entreated, but let a poor foul ftand ftill and
knock, and never let-on‡ him that He heareth ; and then the old
leavings, and broken meat, and dry fighs, are greater cheer than I
can tell. All I have then is, that howbeit the law and wrath have
gotten a decreet§ againft me, I can yet lippen‖ that meikle good in
Chrift as to get a fufpenfion,¶ and to bring my caufe in reafoning
again before my Well-beloved. I defire but to be heard, and at
laft He is content to come and agree the matter with a fool, and
forgive freely, becaufe He is God. Oh, if men would glorify Him,
and tafte of Chrift's fweetnefs !

Brother, ye have need to be bufy with Chrift for this whorifh
Kirk ; I fear left Chrift caft water upon Scotland's coal. Nay, I
know that Chrift and His wife will be heard : He will plead for the
broken covenant. Arm you againft that time.

Grace be with you.

Yours, in his fweet Lord Jefus,

Aberdeen, *June* 16, 1637.   S. R.

------◆------

CLXXXIII.—*To* Mr J—— R——.

[It is highly probable that the individual to whom this letter is addreffed
was John Row, fon of John Row, minifter of Carnock, and grandfon of John
Row the reformer, and contemporary of Knox. In 1632 he was appointed
mafter of the Grammar School of Perth, in which fituation he continued for
fome years. The year after his appointment, he was in fome danger of expul-
fion, for refufing to join in the obfervance of the Lord's Supper after the man-

---

* Infipid, no falt in them.   † No worth in them.   ‡ Seem to notice.
§ Sentence of court.   ‖ Truft that there is fo much good.
¶ An act fufpending final execution of fentence.

ner enjoined by the Perth Articles. At the time when this letter was written, he appears to have been expofed to a fimilar danger. In 1641 he was ordained minifter of St Nicholas Church, Aberdeen; and in 1652 was elevated to be Principal of King's College. Row was a man of learning, and was the author of the firft Hebrew grammar printed in Scotland. He died in 1646.]

(CHRIST THE PURIFIER OF HIS CHURCH—SUBMISSION TO HIS WAYS.)

EAR BROTHER,—Grace, mercy, and peace be unto you. Upon the report which I hear of you, without any further acquaintance, except our ftraiteft bonds in our Lord Jefus, I thought good to write unto you, hearing of your danger to be thruft out of the Lord's houfe for His name's fake. Therefore, my earneft and humble defire to God is, that ye may be ftrengthened in the grace of God, and, by the power of His might, to go on for Chrift, not ftanding in awe of a worm that fhall die. I hope that ye will not put your hand to the ark to give it a wrong touch,* and to overturn it, as many now do, when the archers are fhooting fore at Jofeph, whofe bow fhall abide in its ftrength. We owe to our royal King and princely Mafter a teftimony. Oh, how bleffed are they who can ward a blow off Chrift, and His borne-down truth! Men think Chrift a gone† man now, and that He fhall never get up His head again; and they believe that His court‡ is failed, becaufe He fuffereth men to break their fpears and fwords upon Him, and the enemies to plough Zion, and make long and deep their furrows on her back. But it would not be fo, if the Lord had not a fowing for His ploughing. What can He do, but melt an old droffy Kirk, that He may bring out a new bride out of the fire again? I think that Chrift is juft now repairing His houfe, and exchanging His old veffels with new veffels, and is going through this land, and taking up an inventory and a roll of fo many of Levi's fons, and good profeffors, that He may make them

* In old editions, "totch;" and explained to be a fudden pufh, fuch a pufh, too, as fets the objeft in motion. The allufion is to 2 Sam. vi. 6.

† Whofe caufe is utterly hopelefs, ruined.   ‡ His power and influence.

new work * for the Second Temple ; and whatfoever fhall be found not to be for the work, fhall be caften over the wall. When the houfe fhall be builded, He will lay by † His hammers, as having no more to do with them. It is poffible that He may do worfe to them than lay them by ; and I think the vengeance of the Lord, and the vengeance of His temple, fhall be upon them.

I defire no more than to keep weight when I am paft the fire ; ‡ and I can now, in fome weak meafure, give Chrift a teftimonial § of a lovely and loving companion under fuffering for Him. I faw Him before, but afar off. His beauty, to my eye-fight, groweth. A fig, a ftraw for a ten worlds' plaftered glory, and for childifh fha-dows, the idol of clay (this god, the world) that fools fight for ! If I had a leafe of Chrift of my own dating (for whoever once cometh nigh-hand, ‖ and taketh a hearty look of Chrift's inner fide, fhall never wring nor wreftle themfelves out of His love-grips ¶ again), I would reft contentedly in my prifon, yea, in my prifon without light of fun or candle, providing Chrift and I had a love-bed, not of mine, but of Chrift's own making, that we might lie together among the lilies, till the day break and the fhadows flee away. Who knoweth how fweet a drink of Chrift's love is ! Oh, but to live on Chrift's love is a king's life ! The worft things of Chrift, even that which feemeth to be the refufe of Chrift, His hard crofs, His black crofs, is white and fair ; and the crofs receiveth a beautiful luftre and a perfumed fmell from Jefus. My dear brother, fcaur ** not at it.

While ye have time to ftand upon the watch-tower and fpeak, contend with this land. Plead with your harlot-mother, who hath been a treacherous half-marrow †† to her hufband Jefus. For I would think liberty to preach one day, the root and top of my defires ; and would feek no more of the bleffings that are to be had on this

---

* See p. 456. † Caft afide.
‡ Lofe nothing when I am paffed through the fire, even if I fhould not gain.
§ An atteftation, that He is. ‖ Near. ¶ Love-grafp.
** Boggle, be afraid. †† A married partner.

fide of time, till I be over the water, than to fpend this my crazy clay-houfe in His fervice, and faving of fouls. But I hold my peace, becaufe He hath done it. My fhallow and ebb* thoughts are not the compafs which Chrift faileth by. I leave His ways to Himfelf, for they are far, far above me : only I would contend with Chrift for His love, and be bold to make a plea with Jefus, my Lord, for a heart-fill of His love ; for there is no more left to me. What ftandeth beyond the far end† of my fufferings, and what fhall be the event, He knoweth, and I hope, to my joy, will make me know, when God will unfold His decrees concerning me. For there are windings, and tos and fros, in His ways, which blind bodies like us cannot fee.

Thus much for farther acquaintance ; fo, recommending you, and what is before you, to the grace of God, I reft,

Your very loving brother in his fweet Lord Jefus,

S. R.

ABERDEEN, *June* 16, 1637.

CLXXXIV.—*To* Mr WILLIAM DALGLEISH.   [Let. 117.]

(THE FRAGRANCE OF THE MINISTRY—A REVIEW OF HIS PAST AND PRESENT SITUATION, AND OF HIS PROSPECTS.)

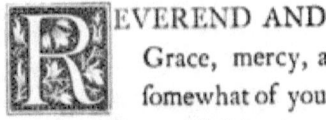
EVEREND AND WELL-BELOVED BROTHER,— Grace, mercy, and peace be unto you. I have heard fomewhat of your trials in Galloway. I blefs the Lord, who hath begun firft in that corner to make you a new kirk to Himfelf. Chrift hath the lefs ado behind, when He hath refined you.

Let me entreat you, my dearly beloved, to be faft to Chrift. My witnefs is above, my deareft brother, that ye have added much joy to me in my bonds, when I hear that ye grow in the grace and zeal of God for your Mafter. Our miniftry, whether by preaching or fuffering, will caft a fmell through the world both of heaven and

---

* Shallow.   † The farther end, the final iffue.

hell.* I perfuade you, my dear brother, that there is nothing out of heaven, next to Chriſt, dearer to me than my miniſtry ; and the worth of it, in my eſtimation, is ſwelled, and paineth me exceedingly. Yet I am content, for the honour of my Lord, to ſurrender it back again to the Lord of the vineyard. Let Him do with it, and me both, what He thinketh good. I think myſelf too little for Him.

And, let me ſpeak to you, how kind a fellow-priſoner is Chriſt to me ! Believe me, this kind of croſs (that would not go by† my door, but would needs viſit me) is ſtill the longer the more welcome to me. It is true, my ſilent Sabbaths have been, and ſtill are, as glaſſy ice, whereon my faith can ſcarce hold its feet, and I am often blown on my back, and off my feet, with a ſtorm of doubting ; yet truly, my bonds all this time caſt a mighty and rank ſmell of high and deep love in Chriſt. I cannot, indeed, ſee through my croſs to the far end ;‡ yet I believe I am in Chriſt's books, and in His decree (not yet unfolded to me), a man triumphing, dancing, and ſinging, on the other ſide of the Red Sea, and laughing and praiſing the Lamb, over beyond time, ſorrow, deprivation, prelates' indignation, loſſes, want of friends, and death. Heaven is not a fowl flying in the air (as men uſe to ſpeak of things that are uncertain) ; nay, it is well paid for. Chriſt's compriſement§ lieth on‖ glory for all the mourners in Zion, and ſhall never be looſed. Let us be glad and rejoice, that we have blood, loſſes, and wounds, to ſhow our Maſter and Captain at His appearance, and what we ſuffered for His cauſe.

Woe is me, my dear brother, that I ſay often, " I am but dry bones, which my Lord will not bring out of the grave again ;" and that my faithleſs fears ſay, " Oh, I am a dry tree, that can bear no fruit ; I am a uſeleſs body, who can beget no children to the Lord in His houſe !" Hopes of deliverance look cold and uncertain, and afar off, as if I had done with it. It is much for Chriſt (if I may

---

* 2 Cor. ii. 15, 16. † Paſs by. ‡ To the final iſſue.

§ Apprehending as by legal proceſs.

‖ " *To lie on,*" is for a thing to be a matter of duty or obligation, or of legal ſecurity. Chriſt has laid His compriſ ment on glory ; He hath taken care that the mourners in Zion be ſecured in poſſeſſion of glory.

fay fo) to get law-borrows* of my forrow, and of my quarrelous†
heart. Chrift's love playeth me fair play. I am not wronged at
all ; but there is a tricking and falfe heart within me, that ftill
playeth Chrift foul play. I am a cumberfome neighbour to Chrift :
it is a wonder that He dwelleth befide the like of me. Yet I often
get the advantage of the hill above my temptations, and then I defpife temptation, even hell itfelf, and the ftink of it, and the inftruments of it, and am proud of my honourable Mafter. And I refolve,
whether contrary winds will or not, to fetch‡ Chrift's harbour ; and
I think a wilful and ftiff contention with my Lord Jefus for His
love very lawful. It is fometimes hard to me to win my meat§
upon Chrift's love, becaufe my faith is fick, and my hope withereth,
and my eyes wax dim ; and unkind and comfort-eclipfing clouds
go over the fair and bright Sun, Jefus ; and then, when I and
temptation tryft‖ the matter together, we fpill all through unbelief.
Sweet, fweet for evermore would my life be, if I could keep faith
in exercife ! But I fee that my fire cannot always caft light ; I have
even a " poor man's hard world,"¶ when He goeth away. But furely,
fince my entry hither, many a time hath my fair fun fhined without
a cloud : hot and burning hath Chrift's love been to me. I have
no vent to the expreffion of it ; I muft be content with ftolen and
fmothered defires of Chrift's glory. Oh, how far is His love behind the hand with me !** I am juft like a man who hath nothing
to pay his thoufands of debt : all that can be gotten of him is to
feize upon his perfon. Except Chrift would feize upon myfelf, and
make the readieft payment that can be of my heart and love to
Himfelf, I have no other thing to give Him. If my fufferings could
do beholders good, and edify His Kirk, and proclaim the incomparable worth of Chrift's love to the world, oh, then would my
foul be overjoyed, and my fad heart be cheered and calmed !

---

* Pledge given to the law, that the man will not injure his neighbour.
† Ready to find fault.   ‡ Make for.   § Get a livelihood.
‖ As by appointment, bring it to our meeting.
¶ A proverbial faying.   ** Far from receiving what I owe to it.

Dear brother, I cannot tell what is become of my labours among that people! If all that my Lord builded by me be caſten down, and the bottom be fallen out of the profeſſion of that pariſh, and none ſtand by Chriſt, whoſe love I once preached as clearly and plainly as I could (though far below its worth and excellence) to that people ; if ſo, how can I bear it ! And if another make a foul harveſt, where I have made a painful and honeſt ſowing, it will not ſoon digeſt with me. But I know that His ways paſs finding out. Yet my witneſs, both within me and above me, knoweth. And my pained breaſt upon the Lord's day at night, my deſire to have had Chriſt awful, and amiable, and ſweet to that people, is now my joy. It was my deſire and aim to make Chriſt and them one ; and, if I ſee my hopes die in the bud, ere they bloom* a little, and come to no fruit, I die with grief. O my God, ſeek not an account of the violence done to me by my brethren, whoſe ſalvation I love and deſire. I pray that they and I be not heard as contrary parties in the day of our compearance† before our Judge, in that proceſs, led by them againſt my miniſtry which I received from Chriſt. I know that a little inch, and leſs than the third part of this ſpan-length and hand-breadth of time, which is poſting away, will put me without the ſtroke, and above the reach of either brethren or foes ; and it is a ſhort-laſting injury done to me, and to my pains in that part of my Lord's vineyard. Oh, how ſilly‡ an advantage is my deprivation to men, ſeeing that my Lord Jeſus hath many ways to recover His own loſſes, and is irreſiſtible to compaſs His own glorious ends, that His lily may grow amongſt thorns, and His little kingdom exalt Himſelf, even under the ſwords and ſpears of contrary powers!

But, my dear brother, go on in the ſtrength of His rich grace, whom ye ſerve. Stand faſt for Chriſt. Deliver the goſpel off your hand, and your miniſtry to your Maſter, with a clean and undefiled conſcience. Looſe not a pin of Chriſt's tabernacle. Do not ſo much as pick with your nail at one board or border of the ark.

---

* Bloſſom.
† Appearance in obedience to legal citation.   ‡ Pitiful.

Have no part or dealing, upon any terms, in a hoof,* in a clofed
window,† or in a bowing of your knee, in cafting down of the
temple. But be a mourning and fpeaking witnefs againft them who
now ruin Zion. Our Mafter will be on us all now in a clap,‡
ere ever we wit.§ That day will difcover all our whites and our
blacks, concerning this controverfy of poor oppreffed Zion. Let
us make our part of it good, that it may be able to abide the fire,
when hay and ftubble fhall be burned to afhes. Nothing, nothing,
I fay, nothing, but found fanctification can abide the Lord's fan.
I ftand to my teftimony that I preached often of Scotland.—" Lamentation, mourning, and woe abideth thee, O Scotland ! O Scotland! the fearful quarrel of a broken covenant ftandeth good with
thy Lord !"

Now, remember my love to all my friends, and to my parifhioners, as if I named each of them particularly. I recommend you,
and God's people, committed by Chrift to your truft, to the rich
grace of our all-fufficient Lord. Remember my bonds. Praife my
Lord, who beareth me up in my fufferings. As ye find occafion,
according to the wifdom given you, fhow our acquaintance what
the Lord hath done to my foul. This I feek not, verily, to hunt
my own praife, but that my fweeteft and deareft Mafter may be
magnified in my fufferings. I reft,

Yours, in his fweet Lord Jefus,

S. R.

Aberdeen, June 16, 1637.

---

* Referring to Exod. x. 26.   † Referring to Dan. vi. 10.
‡ Suddenly, like a clap of thunder.   § Know, are aware.

(*LONGING TO BE RESTORED TO HIS CHARGE.*)

EARLY BELOVED IN OUR LORD JESUS CHRIST,—Grace, mercy, and peace be to you. Few know the heart of a stranger and prisoner. I am in the hands of mine enemies. I would that honest and lawful means were essayed for bringing me home to my charge, now when Mr A. R. and Mr H. R. are restored. It concerneth you of Galloway most, to use supplications and addresses for this purpose, and try if by fair means I can be brought back again. As for liberty, without I be restored to my flock, it is little to me ; for my silence is my greatest prison. However it be, I wait for the Lord ; I hope not to rot in my sufferings : Lord, give me submission to wait on. My heart is sad that my days flee away, and I do no service to my Lord in His house, now when His harvest and the souls of perishing people require it. But His ways are not like my ways, neither can I find Him out. Oh that He would shine upon my darkness, and bring forth my morning light from under the thick cloud that men have spread over me ! Oh that the Almighty would lay my cause in a balance and weigh me, if my soul was not taken up,[*] when others were sleeping, how to have Christ betrothed with a bride, in that part of the land ! But that day that my mouth was most unjustly and cruelly closed, the bloom fell off my branches, and my joy did cast the flower. Howbeit, I have been casting myself under God's feet, and wrestling to believe under a hidden and covered Lord ; yet my fainting cometh before I eat, and my faith hath bowed with the fore cast,[†] and under this almost insupportable weight ! Oh that it break not ! I dare not say that the Lord hath put out my candle, and hath casten water upon my poor coal, and broken the stakes of my tabernacle ; but I have tasted bitterness,

---

[*] Occupied busily.   [†] Lot ; fate, as we say.

and eaten gall and wormwood, fince that day on which my Mafter
laid bonds upon me to fpeak no more. I fpeak not this becaufe
the Lord is unco* to me, but becaufe beholders, that ftand on dry
land, fee not my fea-ftorm. The witneffes of my fad crofs are but
ftrangers to my fad days and nights. Oh that Chrift would let me
alone, and fpeak love to me, and come home to me, and bring
fummer with Him! Oh that I might preach His beauty and glory,
as once I did, before my clay-tent be removed to darknefs! and
that I might lift Chrift off the ground! and my branches might be
watered with the dew of God, and my joy in His work might
grow green again, and bud, and fend out a flower! But I am but
a fhort-fighted creature, and my candle cafteth not light afar off.
He knoweth all that is done to me; how that when I had but one
joy, and no more, and one green flower that I efteemed to be my
garland, He came in one hour and dried up my flower at the root,
and took away mine only eye, and my one only crown and
garland. What can I fay? Surely my guiltinefs hath been remembered before Him, and He was feeking to take down my fails,
and to land the flower of my delights, and to let it lie on the coaft,
like an old broken fhip, that is no more for the fea. But I
praife Him for this waled† ftroke. I welcome this furnace, God's
wifdom made choice of it for me, and it muft be beft, becaufe it
was His choice. Oh that I may wait for Him till the morning of
this benighted Kirk break out! This poor, afflicted Kirk had a fair
morning, but Her night came upon her before her noon-day, and
fhe was like a traveller, forced to take houfe in the morning of his
journey. And now her adverfaries are the chief men in the land;
her ways mourn; her gates languifh; her children figh for bread;
and there is none to be inftant with the Lord, that He would come
again to His houfe, and dry the face of His weeping fpoufe, and
comfort Zion's mourners, who are waiting for Him. I know that
He will make corn to grow upon the top of His withered Mount
Zion again.

---

* Strange.　　　　　† Selected.

Remember my bonds, and forget me not. Oh that my Lord would bring me again amongſt you with abundance of the goſpel of Chriſt! But, oh, that I may ſet down my deſires where my Lord biddeth me! Remember my love in the Lord to your huſband; God make him faithful to Chriſt! and my bleſſing to your three children. Faint not in prayer for this Kirk. Deſire my people not to receive a ſtranger and intruder upon my miniſtry. Let me ſtand in that right and ſtation that my Lord Jeſus gave me.

Grace, grace be with you.

Yours, in his ſweet Lord and Maſter,

S. R.

ABERDEEN, 1637.

---◆---

CLXXXVI.—*To* ROBERT STUART.

[This ROBERT STUART was probably the ſon of Provoſt Stuart of Ayr, to whom ſeveral letters are addreſſed. Alluſion is made to his early converſion.]

(CHRIST CHOOSES HIS OWN IN THE FURNACE—NEED OF A DEEP WORK—THE GOD-MAN, A WORLD'S WONDER.)

Y VERY DEAR BROTHER,—Grace, mercy, and peace be to you. Ye are heartily welcome to my world of ſuffering, and heartily welcome to my Maſter's houſe. God give you much joy of your new Maſter. If I have been in the houſe before you, I were not faithful to give the houſe an ill name, or to ſpeak evil of the Lord of the family; I rather wiſh God's Holy Spirit (O Lord, breathe upon me with that Spirit!), to tell you the faſhions of the houſe.* One thing I can ſay, by on-waiting ye will grow a great man with the Lord of the houſe. Hang on till ye get ſome good from Chriſt. Lay

* Ezek. xliii. 11.

all your loads and your weights by faith upon Chrift ; take eafe
to yourfelf, and let Him bear all. He can, He dow,* He will
bear you, howbeit hell were upon your back. I rejoice that He is
come, and hath chofen you in the furnace ; it was even there where
ye and He fet tryft.† That is an old gate‡ of Chrift's : He keepeth
the good old fafhion with you, that was in Hofea's days : " Therefore, behold, I will allure her, and bring her into the wildernefs, and
fpeak to her heart."§ There was no talking to her heart, while
He and fhe were in the fair and flourifhing city, and at eafe ; but
out in the cold, hungry, wafte wildernefs, He allureth her, He
whifpered news into her ear there, and faid, " Thou art Mine."
What would ye think of fuch a bode ?‖ Ye may foon do worfe
than fay, " Lord, hold all ; Lord Jefus, a bargain be it, it fhall not
go back on my fide."

Ye have gotten a great advantage in the way of heaven, that ye
have ftarted to the gate ¶ in the morning. Like a fool, as I was, I
fuffered my fun to be high in the heaven, and near afternoon, before
ever I took the gate by the end. I pray you now keep the advantage ye have. My heart, be not lazy ; fet quickly up the brae** on
hands and feet, as if the laft pickle†† of fand were running out of
your glafs, and death were coming to turn the glafs. And be very
careful to take heed to your feet, in that flippery and dangerous way
of youth that ye are walking in. The devil and temptations now
have the advantage of the brae** of you, and are upon your wand-
hand,‡‡ and your working-hand.‡‡ Dry timber will foon take fire.
Be covetous and greedy of the grace of God, and beware that it be
not a holinefs which cometh only from the crofs ; for too many are
that way difpofed. " When He flew them, then they fought Him,

---

* Probably inferted from fome explanatory margin, "dow" being the
fame as " can." Should we not read, " *doth?*"

† Made appointment.   ‡ Way.

§ Hos. ii. 14 ; *margin.*   ‖ Offer made in order to a bargain.

¶ Set out on the road.   ** The hill's flope.   †† Small grain.

‡‡ The hand that holds the rod or wand in driving, and the hand that
guides the horfe.

and they returned and inquired early after God." "Neverthelefs, they did flatter Him with their mouth, and they lied unto Him with their tongues."* It is part of our hypocrify, to give God fair, white, words,† when He hath us in His grips‡ (if I may fpeak fo), and to flatter Him till He win to the fair fields again. Try well green godlinefs, and examine what it is that ye love in Chrift. If ye love but Chrift's funny fide, and would have only fummer weather and a land-gate, § not a fea-way, to heaven, your profeffion will play you a flip, and the winter-well will go dry again in fummer.

Make no fports nor bairn's play of Chrift; but labour for a found and lively fight of fin, that ye may judge yourfelf an undone man, a damned flave of hell and of fin, one dying in your own blood, except Chrift come and rue upon‖ you, and take you up; and therefore, make fure and faft work of converfion. Caft the earth deep; and down, down with the old work, the building of confufion, that was there before; and let Chrift lay new work, and make a new creation within you. Look if Chrift's rain goeth down to the root of your withered plants, and if His love wound your heart whill¶ it bleed with forrow for fin, and if ye can pant and fall afwoon,** and be like to die for that lovely one, Jefus. I know that Chrift will not be hid where He is; grace will ever fpeak for itfelf, and be fruitful in well-doing. The fanctified crofs is a fruitful tree; it bringeth forth many apples.

If I fhould tell you by fome weak experience, what I have found in Chrift, ye or others could hardly believe me. I thought not the hundredth part of Chrift, long fince, that I do now, though, alas! my thoughts are ftill infinitely below His worth. I have a dwining,†† fickly, and pained life, for a real poffeffion of Him; and am troubled with love-brafhes‡‡ and love-fevers; but it is a fweet pain. I would refufe no conditions, not hell excepted (referving always God's hatred), to buy poffeffion of Jefus. But, alas! I am not a merchant,

---

* Ps. lxxviii. 34, 36.　† Plaufible fpeeches.　‡ A hold of us.
§ Way by land.　‖ Take pity.　¶ Till.　** Into a faint.
†† Pining.　‡‡ Fits, or attacks, of love-ficknefs.

who have any money to give for Him : I muſt either come to a good-cheap* market, where wares are had for nothing, elſe I go home empty. But I have caſten this work upon Chriſt to get me Himſelf. I have His faith, and truth, and promiſe, as a pawn of His, all engaged that I ſhall obtain that which my hungry deſires would be at; and I eſteem that the choice of my happineſs. And for Chriſt's croſs, eſpecially the garland and flower of all croſſes, to ſuffer for His name, I eſteem it more than I can write or ſpeak to you. And I write it under mine own hand to you, that it is one of the ſteps of the ladder up to our country; and Chriſt (whoever be one) is ſtill at the heavy end of this black tree, and ſo it is but as a feather to me. I need not run at leiſure,† becauſe of a burden on my back; my back never bare the like of it; the more heavily croſſed for Chriſt, the ſoul is ſtill the lighter for the journey.

Now, would to God that all cold-blooded, faint-hearted ſoldiers of Chriſt would look again to Jeſus, and to His love; and when they look, I would have them to look again and again, and fill themſelves with beholding of Chriſt's beauty; and I dare ſay then that Chriſt would come into great court‡ and requeſt with many. The virgins would flock faſt about the Bridegroom; they would embrace and take hold of Him, and not let Him go. But when I have ſpoken of Him, till my head rive, I have ſaid juſt nothing. I may begin again. A Godhead, a Godhead is a world's wonder. Set ten thouſand thouſand new-made worlds of angels and eleɛt men, and double them in number, ten thouſand, thouſand, thouſand times; let their heart and tongues be ten thouſand thouſand times more agile and large, than the heart and tongues of the ſeraphim that ſtand with ſix wings before Him,§ when they have ſaid all for the glorifying and praiſing of the Lord Jeſus, they have but ſpoken little or nothing; His love will abide all poſſible creatures to praiſe. Oh, if I could wear this tongue to the ſtump, in extolling His high-neſs! But it is my daily-growing ſorrow, that I am confounded

---

* Very cheap.   † I am not obliged to run ſlowly.
‡ Favour, influence.   § Iſa. vi. 2.

with His incomparable love, and that He doeth fo great things for my foul, and hath got never yet anything of me worth the fpeaking of. Sir, I charge you, help me to praife Him; it is a fhame to fpeak of what He hath done for me, and what I do to Him again. I am fure that Chrift hath many drowned dyvours* in heaven befide Him; and when we are convened, man and angel, at the great day, in that fair laft meeting, we are all but His drowned dyvours: it is hard to fay who oweth Him moft. If men could do no more, I would have them to wonder: if ye cannot be filled with Chrift's love, we may be filled with wondering.

Sir, I would that I could perfuade you to grow fick for Chrift, and to long after Him, and be pained with love for Himfelf. But His tongue is in heaven who can do it. To Him and His rich grace I recommend you.

I pray you, pray for me, and forget not to praife.

Yours, in his fweet Lord Jefus,

S. R.

ABERDEEN, *June* 17, 1637.

* * *

CLXXXVII.—*To the* LADY GAITGIRTH.

[LADY GAITGIRTH, or ISABEL BLAIR, daughter to John Blair of that ilk, by Grizel his wife, daughter to Robert, Lord Semple, was the wife of James Chalmers of Gaitgirth. To him fhe had five fons and five daughters. Mr Fergufhill of Ochiltree refided in the vicinity; fee Let. 112. Her hufband, to whom Rutherford expreffes his obligations in the clofe of this letter, was a man of worth. He was made Sheriff-principal of Ayrfhire in 1632; and in 1633, he and Sir William Cunningham of Cunninghamhead reprefented Ayrfhire in Parliament. Embracing the caufe of the Covenant, he zealoufly promoted the meafures adopted for its fuccefs. In 1641, he, with Caffilis and Caprington, were fent as commiffioners from the Scottifh Parliament to Newcaftle; in 1646 he was in the Committee of War, and in 1649 he had a troop in Colonel Robert Montgomery's Horfe. (*Robertfon's Ayrfhire Families.*) His

---

* Debtors, drowned over head and ears in His debt.

great-grandfather, James Chalmers of Gaitgirth, who lived at the time of the Reformation, was a very zealous reformer, and is defcribed by Knox, Calderwood, and Spottifwood, as one of the boldeft and moft daring men of any who took part in that important revolution.

The name is often written Gathgirth and Gadgirth. It is in the parifh of Coylton, about four miles from Monkton. The modern manfion occupies the fine fite of the old, on a wooded knoll that overhangs the river Ayr, and at one point commanding a view of Arran and Goatfell. It is a fmall eftate.]

(CHRIST UNCHANGEABLE, THOUGH NOT ALWAYS ENJOYED—HIS LOVE NEVER YET FULLY POURED OUT—HIMSELF HIS PEOPLE'S CAUTIONER.)

MISTRESS,—Grace, mercy, and peace be to you. I long to know how matters ftand betwixt Chrift and your foul. I know that ye find Him ftill the longer the better ; time cannot change Him in His love. Ye may yourfelf ebb and flow, rife and fall, wax and wane ; but your Lord is this day as He was yefterday. And it is your comfort that your falvation is not rolled upon wheels of your own making, neither have ye to do with a Chrift of your own fhaping. God hath fingled out a Mediator,* ftrong and mighty : if ye and your burdens were as heavy as ten hills or hells, He is able to bear you, and fave you to the uttermoft. Your often feeking to Him cannot make you a burden to Him. I know that Chrift compaffionateth you, and maketh a moan for you, in all your dumps, and under your downcaftings ; but it is good for you that He hideth Himfelf fometimes. It is not nicenefs, drynefs, nor coldnefs of love, that caufeth Chrift to withdraw, and flip in under a curtain and a vail, that ye cannot fee Him ; but He knoweth that ye could not bear with upfails, a fair gale, a full moon, and a high fpring-tide of His felt love, and always a fair fummer-day and a fummer-fun of a felt and poffeffed and embracing Lord Jefus. His kiffes and His vifits to His deareft ones are thin-fown. He could not let out His rivers of love upon His own, but thefe rivers would be in hazard of loofening a young plant

---

* Pfa. lxxxix. 19.

at the root ; * and He knoweth this of you.   Ye fhould, therefore,
friſt† Chriſt's kindnefs, as to its fenfible and full manifeſtations, till
ye and He be above fun and moon.   That is the country where ye
will be enlarged for that love which ye dow‡ not now contain.

Caſt the burden of your fweet babes upon Chriſt, and lighten
your heart, by laying your all upon Him : He will be their God.
I hope to fee you up the mountain yet, and glad in the falvation of
God.   Frame§ yourſelf for Chriſt, and gloom ‖ not upon His crofs.
I find Him fo fweet, that my love, fuppofe I would charge it to
remove from Chriſt, would not obey me : His love hath ſtronger
fingers than to let go its grips¶ of us bairns, who cannot go, but
by fuch a hold as Chriſt.   It is good that we want legs of our
own, fince we may borrow from Chriſt ; and it is our happinefs
that Chriſt is under an act of cautionary ** for heaven, and that
Chriſt is booked in heaven as the principal debtor for such poor
bodies as we are.

I requeſt you to give the laird, your hufband, thanks for his
care of me, in that he hath appeared in public for a prifoner of Chriſt.
I pray and write mercy, and peace, and bleffings to him and his.

Grace, grace be with you for ever.

Yours, in his fweet Lord Jefus,

S. R.

ABERDEEN, 1637.

---

* The river Ayr flows clofe to Gaitgirth ; fo that, in time of flood, Lady
Gaitgirth would often fee an exemplification of what is alluded to,—the water
loofening the tree's roots.

† Defer till another time.   ‡ Ye are not able to.

§ Set yourſelf in a fit attitude, as Hos. v. 4.   See Let. 32.

‖ Frown, be fulky.   ¶ Firm hold.   ** Suretyfhip.

(DESPONDING VIEWS OF HIS OWN STATE—MINISTERIAL DILI-GENCE—CHRIST'S WORTH—SELF-SEEKING.)

REVEREND AND DEAR BROTHER,—Grace, mercy, and peace be to you. My longings and defires for a fight of the new-builded tabernacle of Chrift again in Scotland, that tabernacle that came down from heaven, hath now taken fome life again, when I fee Chrift making a mint* to fow vengeance among His enemies. I care not, if this land be ripe for fuch a great, wonderful mercy; but I know He muft do it, whenever it is done, without hire. I find the grief of my filence, and my fear to be holden at the door of Chrift's houfe, fwelling upon me; and the truth is, were it not that I am dawted† now and then with pieces of Chrift's fweet love and comforts, I fear I fhould have made an ill browft‡ of this honourable crofs, that I know fuch a foft and filly-minded body as I am is not worthy of. For I have little in me but foftnefs, and fuperlative and exceffive apprehenfions of fear, and fadnefs, and forrow; and often God's terrors do furround me, becaufe Chrift looketh not fo favourably upon me as a poor witnefs would have Him. And I wonder how I have paft a year and a quarter's imprifonment without fhaming my fweet Lord, to whom I defire to be faithful; and I think I fhall die but§ even minting* and aiming to ferve and honour my Lord Jefus. Few know how toom‖ and empty I am at home; but it is a part of marriage-love and hufband-love, that my Lord Jefus goeth not to the ftreets with His chiding againft me. It is but ftolen and concealed anger that I find and feel, and His glooms¶ to me are kept

---

* An effort made; a putting forth of what is in one's power.
† Treated as a fondled child.
‡ An ill-brewed quantity of malt, an ill-managed matter.
§ Only; not attaining further than the attempt.   ‖ Empty.   ¶ Frowns.

under roof, that He will not have mine enemies hear what is betwixt
me and Him.   And, believe me, I fay the truth in Chrift, that the
only gall and wormwood in my cup, and that which hath filled me
with fear, hath been, left my fins, that fun and moon and the Lord's
children were never witnefs to, fhould have moved my Lord to
ftrike me with dumb Sabbaths.   Lord, pardon my foft and weak
jealoufies,* if I be here in an error.

My very dear brother, I would have looked for larger and more
particular letters from you, for my comfort in this ; for your words
before have ftrengthened me.   I pray you to mend this ; and be
thankful and painful,† while ye have a piece or corner of the Lord's
vineyard to drefs.   Oh, would to God that I could have leave to
follow you, to break the clods !   But I wifh I could command my
foul to be filent, and to wait upon the Lord.   I am fure that while
Chrift lives, I am well enough friend-ftead.‡   I hope that He will
extend His kindnefs and power for me ; but God be thanked it is
not worfe with me than a crofs for Chrift and His truth.   I know
that He might have pitched upon many more choice and worthy
witneffes, if He had pleafed ; but I feek no more (be what timber
I will, fuppofe I were made of a piece of hell) than that my Lord,
in His infinite art, hew glory to His name, and enlargement to
Chrift's kingdom, out of me.   Oh that I could attain to this, to
defire that my part of Chrift might be laid in pledge for the height-
ening of Chrift's throne in Britain !   Let my Lord redeem the
pledge ; or, if He pleafe, let it fink and drown unredeemed.   But
what can I add to Him ? or what way can a fmothered and borne-
down prifoner fet out Chrift in open market, as a lovely and defirable Lord to many fouls ?   I know that He feeth to His own
glory better than my ebb§ thoughts can dream of ; and that the
wheels and paces‖ of this poor diftempered Kirk are in His hands ;

---

* Sufpicions.   † Pains-taking.   ‡ Befriended.   § Shallow.

‖ The weights of a clock.   In a fermon at Anwoth, we find him ufing the
fame figure when preaching on Song vi. 1.   The word is from the French,
" pefer," to weigh.

and that things fhall roll as Chrift will have them :—only, Lord, tryft* the matter fo, as Chrift may be made a houfeholder and lord again in Scotland, and wet faces for His departure may be dried at His fweet and much-defired welcome-home! I fee that, in all our trials, our Lord will not mix our wares and His grace overhead through other ;† but He will have each man to know his own, that the like of me may fay in my fufferings, "This is Chrift's grace, and this is but my coarfe ftuff: this is free grace, and this is but nature and reafon." We know what our legs would play us, if they fhould carry us through all our waters. And the leaft thing our Lord can have of us, is to know we are grace's dyvours,‡ and that nature is of a bafe houfe and blood, and grace is better born, and of kin and blood to Chrift, and of§ a better houfe. Oh that I were free of that idol which they call *myfelf;* and that Chrift were for *myfelf;* and myfelf a decourted ‖ cypher, and a denied and forfworn thing! But that proud thing, *myfelf,* will not play, except it ride up fide for fide with Chrift, or rather have place before Him. O *myfelf* (another devil, as evil as the prince of devils!), if thou couldft give Chrift the way, and take thine own room, which is to fit as low as nothing or corruption! Oh, but we have much need to be ranfomed and redeemed by Chrift from that mafter-tyrant, that cruel and lawlefs lord, ourfelf. Nay, when I am feeking Chrift, and am out of myfelf, I have the third part of a fquint eye upon that vain, vain thing, *myfelf, myfelf,* and fomething of mine own. But I muft hold here.

I defire you to contribute your help, to fee if I can be reftored to my wafted and loft flock. I fee not how it can be, except the lords would procure me a liberty to preach; and they have reafon. 1. Becaufe the oppofers and my adverfaries have practifed their new canons upon me, whereof one is, that no deprived minifter preach, under the pain of excommunication. 2. Becaufe my oppofing of thefe canons was a fpecial thing that incenfed Sydferff againft

---

* Appoint.   † One with the other, promifcuoufly.
‡ Debtors.   § Defcended from.   ‖ Difcarded, out of court.

me.   3. Becaufe I was judicially accufed for my book againft the Arminians, and commanded by the **Chancellor** to acknowledge that I had done a fault in writing againft Dr Jackfon, a wicked Arminian.†   Pray for a room in the houfe to me.

Grace, grace be (as it is) your portion.

Yours, in his fweet Lord Jefus,

S. R.

ABERDEEN, 1637.

---

* Thomas Sydferff, now Bifhop of Galloway, was the chief inftrument in procuring Rutherford's banifhment to Aberdeen.   He was firft minifter of the College Church, Edinburgh; and afterwards fucceflively Bifhop of Brechin, Galloway, and Orkney.   He had early imbibed Arminian principles, and promoted the meafures of Archbifhop Laud.   He was fuppofed to lean to Popery; and it was generally believed that he wore under his coat, upon his breaft, a crucifix of gold, which rendered him fo unpopular, that, on appearing in the ftreets of Edinburgh in 1637, when great excitement exifted on account of the Service Book, he was attacked by the matrons of the city.   He had equal reafon to "cry to the gentlemen for help" under fimilar attacks in other places.   At the Reftoration of Charles II., he was the only furviving bifhop in Scotland.   He was then nominated to the fee of Orkney, but furvived his promotion little more than a year.

† Dr Thomas Jackfon, Dean of Peterborough, firft held Calviniftic fentiments, but afterwards became an Arminian,—a change which recommended him to the favour and patronage of Archbifhop Laud.   He was a man of talent, and the author of various theological works, of which his " Commentary on the Apoftles' Creed" is the moft important.   Rutherford's book againft the Arminians, here referred to, in which he treated Jackfon with little ceremony, and which was one caufe of his banifhment by the High Commiffion Court, is entitled, " *Exercitationes Apologeticæ pro Divina Gratia.*"   It was publifhed at Amfterdam in the beginning of the year 1636, and gained the author no fmall reputation abroad.   Baillie, in giving an account of Rutherford's trial before the High Commiffion Court, fays; " They were animate alfo againft him for taxing Cameron in his book, and moft for his indifcreet railing at Jackfon."—(*Letters and Journals.*)

END OF VOL. I.

Murray & Gibb, Printers, Edinburgh.